1 MONTH OF
FREE
READING

at

www.ForgottenBooks.com

By purchasing this book you are eligible for one month membership to ForgottenBooks.com, giving you unlimited access to our entire collection of over 1,000,000 titles via our web site and mobile apps.

To claim your free month visit:
www.forgottenbooks.com/free776666

ISBN 978-0-483-13741-7
PIBN 10776666

The Overland Monthly

Vol. LXXIV—Second Series

July-December 1919

OVERLAND MONTHLY CO., Publishers

259 MINNA STREET   SAN FRANCISCO, CAL.

INDEX

148835

INDEX

INDEX

Monthly

JULY 1919   PRICE

Opportunity's One Knock

When *Opportunity* knocks, will we hear her?

Or will our ears be so deafened with debts and our minds so filled with money worries that we do not hear her happy message?

W. S. S. and Thrift Stamps help Opportunity knock loudly—one knock enough.

W. S. S.—
Everybody's Opportunity

Savings' Division
War Loan Organization
Treasury Department

AN ILLUSTRATED MAGAZINE OF THE WEST

CONTENTS FOR JULY, 1919

NOTICE.—Contributions to the Overland Monthly should be typewritten, accompanied by return postage, and with the author's name and address plainly written in upper corner of page. Manuscripts should never be rolled.

The Publisher of the Overland Monthly will not be responsible for the preservation or miscarriage of unsolicited contributions and photographs.

Issued Monthly. $1.20 per year in advance. Ten cents per copy. Back numbers 3 mc or over 25c; six months or over 50c; nine months or over 75c; 1 year or over $1.00. Postage Canada, 3 cts.; Foreign, 5 cts.

259 MINNA STR

Raven Wing, Photographic Study by Emma B. Freeman to Illustrate the
Blanket of Fate, See Page 15

In the Lobby of the Y. M. C. A. Building

OVERLAND  MONTHLY

Founded 1868

BRET HARTE

| VOL. LXXVI | San Francisco, July, 1919 | No. 1 |

What more than an Emergency Agency Is the Y. M. C. A.?

By Lyman L. Pierce

I WANT to illustrate what I mean by an emergency agency and then point out what the progressive Association man aspires to make of the Y. M. C. A. The world has called on the Association in many an emergency. It was in the Civil War as the "Christian Commission." It was with the Japanese Army all through the war with Russia. It was in every camp and naval station in the war with Spain. Since then, it has been in every camp and naval station of the regular army

The Swimming Pool

The Gymnasium

and navy as a permanent agency. It has been one of the greatest factors of Democracy in the far East, where it is the clearing house of inter-denominational activities. It is today working wonders in the new-born nation of Europe.

In the last war it was drafted to meet the greatest emergency in the lives of men that the world has yet known. The men needed entertainment. The answer of the Association has been 56,724,000 feet of movie film overseas in a single month; 10,743 miles of it— enough each month to reach from New York to Sydney, Australia — enough for 9,354 movie shows, which would have cost the boys $1,000,000 over here, but which was free over there. This is in addition to thoussands of vaudeville shows by the best artists. It is only an incident in the big program.

These men in the army and navy were the best instruments to maintain morale at home. .The "Y" kept them constantly reminded of the home letters. The "Y" shipped enough letter paper to Europe to reach three times around the earth. 305,290,631 sheets of letter paper have been supplied to the A. E. F. alone.

The men wanted a chance to play. The "Y" supplied the A. E. F. with 152,776 baseball bats. The "Y" supplied them with 640,420 baseballs, all free; enough to supply the National and American leagues, using five balls per game, for 103 years. The "Y" supplied them with 74,474 footballs, 96,890 playground balls, 20,405 basketballs, and 15,171 pairs of boxing gloves, all at a cost of $1,630,000 and all free. Association trained athletic directors went over to stimulate programs and help in directing sports.

The men needed a warm place for recreation, writing, reading and entertainment. The "Y" provided 3,356 such places for the A. E. F. and Al-

The Recreation Room

lied Armies. Sometimes for a single brigade it was necessary to have several such places in a month because of the movements of the brigade. Seven portable sawmills helped turn out the lumber needed. The coal used cost from $70 to $100 per ton.

The "Y" from the first has planned to meet the emergency needs of men in transit. The importance to morale of the first journey to the camps was apparent; so a "Y" secretary was put on every troop train. There is at least one "Y" man with every troop train now, for the men who are coming home. Since July, 1917, the "Y" has manned 6,662 troop trains carrying a total of 3,906,000 soldiers covering 6,600,000 miles. Every troop train has been supplied with stationery, reading material, music and games, always free.

Since March 4, 1918, 1,381 "Y" secretaries have sailed on 971 sailings of troop ships. They have supplied to these transports $630,574 worth of complete equipment for free use in transit. 2,750,000 men have been served on ocean transports. Until the signing of the Armistice, November 11th, the "Y" was the only organization to have representatives permanently assigned to army transports. This does not take into consideration the great huts at Chicago, St. Louis, Pittsburg, and other transfer centers. At Hoboken, the great port of embarkation and debarkation, six buildings are used by the "Y," five rented, and one the largest "Y" hut in America. In April, alone, these huts at Hoboken served 276,100 men. This and work like this, shows how the Young Men's Christian Association meets the emergency calls.

The Association movement was established by a young draper's clerk in London to meet the social and spiritual emergency in the lives of a small group of his fellow clerks, who were

The Writing Room

strangers in the great city. They met in a now historical room in the draper's shop. A group of young men with kindred needs joined them. It was in the American cities that the Association first recognized that one of the greatest needs was in the physical lives of men. Many men were below par, physically; many were down and out. This is strikingly illustrated by Major Orr, a medical officer of the army, who tells us that formerly two or three out of every four applicants for the regular army were rejected as being physically unfit. The examinations of the Life Extension Institute show only one man in a hundred wholly free from disease. Heart disease kills three times as many as it did forty years ago.

The Association created a great new profession in its physical directorship. At first these directors of physical education were possibly professional athletes, circus performers, or stunt artists of a similar nature. They de-

veloped big muscles and freak stunts rather than all around physical efficiency. Today the Y. M. C. A. physical director is a community leader. The Association has supplied seventy per cent of the male directors of physical education in schools and colleges of North America.

From the outset in meeting the emergency physical needs of younger men, it has been the practice in the Y. M. C. A. that before admission into a gymnasium class a man should receive a careful physical examination by the director in order that exercise may be prescribed to meet his needs and to correct his defects. He has, also, been given a medical examination by a doctor to discover what degree of exercise the system would permit. During this examination in the private room of the physical director, far-sighted men in this profession have traced back to their causes the physical limitations of the man. Therefore, the physical director has

A Group About the Fireplace in the Lobby of the Y. M. C. A.

become more than an emergency man. He has thought in terms of causes and prevention.

It is a good thing to square the shoulders, fill out the chest and stimulate the physical life of a gymnasium of, say, fifty men, but it is a greater thing to insure that every child in the schools know the significance of diet and exercise. The professional leaders of the Y. M. C. A. have aspired to multiply the Association's usefulness by laying the foundation for vigorous physical manhood through the home, the school, and other community avenues and to decrease by wholesale the need for correction of physical defects.

The gymnasium class justifies itself a hundred fold, but that is a matter of addition. The community propaganda for health is a matter of multiplication. It is a great thing to minister as the Association does to thousands of groups of men and boys, who can

never live their maximum lives unless they shake off depression and inertia and sleeplessness and other symptoms. But unless community life at its inception, in its children, has a chance to develop a normal physical existence, then only has our obligation been discharged.

It is said that in the process of determining the sanity of patients in a sanitorium the test was made of turning on the faucet, giving the patient a dipper, and telling him to dip the water out of the basin. The insane patient dipped and dipped, while the sane patient turned off the faucet. A sane community will determine that the child must not only be able to analyze a Shakesperean play correctly, but that he shall be an instrument in the home for sanitation, diet, and health.

The Association early took note of the fact that less than two per cent of the boys of America ever attend col-

The Automobile School In Session

lege. It is now calling attention to the fact that in our population of more than 100,000,000, there are only 600,000 boys who enter high school. Sixteen out of every hundred boys reach high school. Five out of the hundred graduate. One goes to college. One in 1000 of our boys learns a trade. Yet, there are six boys who work to every one in high school. Nine out of ten who work have no idea of investing their lives for the benefit of society. To meet the emergency the Association provided for the great multitude of young men in the twenties, and younger, who awaken to the fact that they are forever handicapped unless their education be increased.

The Y. M. C. A. pioneered the greatest system of night education for men who needed just a little help in getting started toward the goal of their ambitions, that the world has known. But, in this case, as in others where the Y. M. C. A. has met an emerg-

ency, it has realized the necessity of striking at the cause of the emergency need. Back of the physical bankruptcy of many a man was a youth of ignorance with reference to the laws of the physical life. Back of a condition which limits the college education to virtually one per cent of the male population, there is a serious condition in community life.

So the Association educational program has developed beyond the reading room, which was formerly such a big feature, and beyond even the night school, which justifies itself a hundred fold every year, it has become an organized propaganda agency *for education*. It has traced the causes leading boys to leave school. It has found that sometimes the cause is traceable to home needs which could have been overcome; oftener it is to parental indifference.

Then it went into shops and factories and homes where tens and hundreds

A Glimpse of the Stairway, Y. M. C. A. Building

of thousands of fathers have heard through the Association extension program of the value of education and of the family calamity that it is to have a boy, or girl impoverish their life by neglect of this instrument of developing education. Sometimes boys leave because of dissatisfaction with their teachers; often, because of a preference to go to work. Then the Association shows that every day spent in school is worth $10. By experiment this has been demonstrated. Other causes for leaving school are too much and undirected play; dislike for study; slowness in learning, and lack of encouragement. Many lagging boys have been stimulated by the fact that ninety-two per cent of all the Presidents have been college men, eighty-four per cent of all Congressmen, while in the list of 12,000 names in

Y. M. C. A. Building, San Francisco, California

"Who's Who in America," 10,391 of them are college trained.

The Association started to get jobs for men. They developed a wonderful system of securing employment. Then they discovered that a man is only happy in the job for which he is fitted by temperament and training and where he has a chance for self-expression. The Association employment department then became the Association Vocational Employment Department with the object of not merely getting a man a job, but with the purpose of fitting men who were unhappy and working at disadvantage, into the places where they could have the largest expression and joy as well as elevated standards of living through increased earning ability. The Employment and Educational Departments have entered into partnership to this end. The Association is now promoting vocational guidance in school and community. It is seeking to fit round pegs into round holes.

At one time, the social program of the Y. M. C. A. consisted in creating a social atmosphere in the building and supplying wholesome entertainment and recreation. This part of the social program has not decreased, but, rather, is being multiplied many fold. However, the Association has awakened to the fact that it is not sociability alone, but society that is involved in its social program. One Association expressed this idea by conducting a summer non-equipment type of Association work in twenty different industrial centers, giving athletic, social and moral emphasis, but more than that, calling into its program every agency which was interested in phases of community life.

The Legal Aid Society taught industrial people, and foreigners in particular, what they ought to know about American laws and customs. The Pure Milk and Ice Association gave lectures to mothers of children, and supplied life-saving materials. The Associated Charities sent visiting nurses with helpful propaganda. The Playground Association used vacant lots which had been cleared by the boys of the community. The Y. M. C. A. conducted twilight games, gave moving picture and stereopticon lectures in the evenings with attendance running into hundreds of thousands.

They covered in the range of this program, disease prevention, health promotion, thrift, patriotism, child welfare, higher standards of home life, and the great fundamental virtues which are, after all, their own reward. At the noon hour in shops and factories in scores of large cities tens of thousands of men get their first real revelation of what play means. In the City of San Francisco groups like this can be seen playing volleyball, indoor baseball, and other games during the half hour of the noon luncheon period, thus creating an appetite for wholesome recreation.

In other words this wider vision finds exercise while the Young Men's Christian Association with its investment of $125,000,000 in great buildings in the United States, is reaching countless thousands of men at a time when they need it most. At the San Francisco Association, for instance, every fourteen seconds of each ten-hour day a young man or boy *with a purpose* enters the doors of its Golden Gate Avenue building. This is only what happens in practically every city of any consequence in America. Many of these men come to meet an emergency in their own lives. The Association seeks to meet the emergency in the wisest possible manner, through educational classes, recreational activities, social environment, entertainments and moral and spiritual stimulus. It goes further than this and seeks to place within the purview of the people of the community the great need of preventive measures, through instruction given to the adolescent, through parent training, and by a vision of the revolutionary need of child welfare.

The "Y" has taken the far view in its boys work program. Gladstone said: "As go the colleges, so goes the nation.' The Y. M. C. A. has said: "As go the high schools, so go the colleges." The "Hy Y" movement of the Young Men's Christian Association and the American Standard Program for Boys are being recognized as the most constructive programs for physical, social, moral, and spiritual development that the country has ever seen. Many high schools have been transformed by the "Hy Y" movement which is made up of self-governing groups of high school boys with high purposes and ambitions for themselves and their associates.

In like fashion the student movement in the colleges and universities takes into consideration the multiplied influence of the college graduate. It also takes into consideration that intellectual development alone may make of a man only a clever devil. For many years the student movement of the Y. M. C. A. has been guiding tens of thousands of future statesmen and world leaders into the best investment for their lives and in getting men to think soberly about unselfish service in life work. Former President Patton of Princeton once said that the Young Men's Christian Association had well nigh a monopoly of the programs of this kind in the American colleges and universities.

transportation systems of America. This began with meeting an emergency in a man's life.

In former days the train man must, perforce, spend his leisure time in a saloon or low social resort. Many terminal points offered no other social center. So, often, trainmen went out on their daily runs unfit for service, with unsteady hand and bleary eye.

Main Entrance Y. M. C. A. Building

Who shall say that by the acceptance of the Young Men's Christian Association by the American Railroads as their welfare agency they have not taken the biggest possible step for a better balanced personnel and for mutual understanding? Great railroad presidents have stated that the Y. M. C. A. is one of the major factors both in safety in travel and in the unparalleled advance of the great

With higher social aspirations came better understandings and better wages and better living conditions and less discord, fewer strikes, and more satisfaction in all respects. The history of the Y. M. C. A. is full of illustrations like this of the emergency type of work leading out into something much more significant. Those which I have mentioned are meant to be merely illustrative.

The House Delightful

By Ida Ghent Stanford

Would you know the kind host in the house of delight?
Do not picture a mansion with columns of might,
   With a garden, where amethyst moss fringes beds
   And where millions of blossoms lift proudly their heads.
There are mansions, yes many, as herein portrayed
With gardens and columns which money has made.
   But the house of delight among these is not found.
   Search you well for a sprinkling of meal o'er the ground.

Now this brings to your mind little knowledge, I trow,
So the curtain I'll lift, that this house you may know.
   Come with me to the plains of the west, wild and free,
   Where the blue and the gold of the sky dance in glee.
Arizona, the house of delight's blessed home;
The fair "City Eternal," past whose gates we roam
   Away out to the desert. Such rude huts, you say,
   And these wild, heathen Indians, with faces of clay,

Are the hosts? Is the house of delights but a hut?
O, my friend, of what joke have you made me the butt?"
   Sit you down, I'll explain; see that Navajo there?
   His hut rude? It is founded on song and on prayer.
He a heathen? God grant that a heathen I be,

If this home is a heathen abode which we see.
There was never house builded, with incense as sweet
As is found in yon hut, kissed by brown, unshod feet.

From the felling of log, to the kindling of fire,
Are these huts sacred kept. They are free from all ire.
Should a post slip its place and a cross word be spoke
Soon the whole is a ruin of ashes and smoke.
All these homes that you see stretched over the plain
Are houses delightful, built for love and not gain.
Where the Medicine Man sprinkles meal from a bowl
While he chants from the deeps of his innermost soul.

"To the East, to the North, to the South, to the West,
I now scatter this meal that peace here may find rest.
That this house be delightful, the four posts are blest
With meal from my bowl, that true love fill each guest
Who seeks here a shelter from sun or from storm.
May this house be delightful for children unborn.
May all who here enter, as friend or as foe,
Be filled with the Presence of God ere they go."

Every figure on basket or blanket speaks rare
All of duty and love. Every weave is a prayer.
O, brave Navajo Indian, come build me a home
And pray bless with your meal, that Love's peace shall not
        roam.
And O, Navajo Chieftain, come teach me the art
Of just building for love; that each arrow and dart
Shall be sent forth all white and all quivering with peace;
That my house be delightful; that love may increase.

Forgive me for treading where daring fools tread.
Here the angels step softly, their white wings outspread,
In rich blessings unnumbered, though known to so few,
In most humble contrition I bow before you.
Arizona, no marvel thy skys are so blue,
No wonder thy atmosphere's fresh as the dew.
Let us pray that our country, so favored and blest,
Shall be filled with the Navajo's peace and his rest.

The Indian Camp

The Blanket of Fate

By Lucien M. Lewis

E came upon it unexpectedly— that ranger's cabin in the heart of the Oregon Sierras. Riding back to camp after a morning's hunt my Indian guide and I were making our way down a heavily-wooded hill, when suddenly the timber gave way and before us was a level meadow, eight or ten acres in extent, on the edge of which was the cabin.

Smoke was coming from the chimney and even at that distance I had a feeling that a woman lived there. I guessed it by the flower-bordered walk, by the dainty window curtains tied with ribbon, and, more than all else, by an indefinable home-like air about the place that only the delicate touches of a woman's hand may give.

We were about to ride by, for it was nearly noon, when the cabin door opened and a man stepped out and hailed us. He was about thirty, dressed in the regulation uniform of a ranger, his lean face bronzed and hardened by wind and sun.

"Light and look at your saddle," he called, holding open the gate.

As he stood there, I read hunger in the man's eyes—the hunger of one long denied comradeship with his kind.

"Get down, both of you," he insisted. "It's about dinner time. And, say," he went on eagerly, detecting my momentary hesitation, "how would fresh venison and gravy, muffins and home-made jam and coffee with real cream strike you?"

"It strikes me below the belt," I answered. And I signed the Indian to put up the horses.

The ranger led the way to the house, opened the door, a boyish grin on his face and shouted inside, "Dinner for three!"

For reply there came the merry ripple of a woman's laugh within.

It was a pleasant autumn forenoon, with a soft breath from the hills, so the ranger gave me a rocker in the rustic porch and took one opposite. He lighted his pipe, stuck his feet up on the railing and dreamily watched the wisps of smoke lose themselves in the hazy atmosphere.

"You wouldn't think," he said between puffs, nodding toward the Indian sprawled on his blankets in the shade of a pine, "that I came near being a member of his tribe—he's a 'Warmspring,' isn't he? Yes, I came within a blanket's length of it."

"That so?" I inquired. "Taken prisoner, were you?"

"Yes, a prisoner—and captured by a girl," he grinned at me. "I might as well unburden myself while we are waiting for dinner. It would cause domestic complications if told at the table."

"It happened ten years ago, when I was reckless and irresponsible as an unbridled cayuse. I had finished my first year's work as ranger and had been granted thirty days' vacation. With my pockets full of money, where should I put in those thirty days? That was my problem.

"And then I thought of the Warmspring Indians who lived just over the mountains, of their wild, carefree existence, whose lives were a continuous round of dancing, roundups, hop and berry picking, fishing and hunting. With a few of them I had become acquainted, and with one young buck, 'White Feather,' he called himself, had struck up a real friendship, having once saved him from arrest by a game warden. To show his appreciation 'White Feather' had invited me to visit his tribesmen at their annual roundup and hee-hee, which came off around the first of July.

"I knew Indians well enough to appreciate their love of pomp and show. In fact I had a little weakness in the same direction and liked much to make the grand impression. I fairly swelled as I pictured the show I would make riding down upon them mounted on 'Jimmy Britt,' my black stallion, my saddle set off by the gaudiest of 'Navajo' saddle blankets, bridle studded with silver stars, with a huge silver bit and reins of handwoven horse hair. A buckskin suit I had bought especially for the occasion, tan-colored boots with tinkling spurs, and a big sombrero encircled by a band of rattler's hide. Ah, life came to me in big gulps in those days.

"It was well along in the afternoon when I struck the reservation. From a passing Indian I learned that the 'Warmsprings' were encamped about six miles away in Beaver Creek valley; and were in the midst of a big roundup. Thither I proceeded full speed.

"It had never occurred to me that I might not be given a cordial welcome. And if such a thought had struck me, what did it matter? I had my horse and sleeping blankets, so, like 'Sancho Panze,' could ride on seeking further adventures.

"So I rode boldly up to the Indian encampment, my horse's head as high as my own, for he, too, seemed to have sensed the coming of a new adventure. On all sides were strange sights and unfamiliar smells, so warily he pranced and sniffed and snorted.

"And what a picture! In a little green valley, with the hills aflame with flowers for a background, were the tents and tepees of the 'Warmsprings.' Through the middle of that granite-walled valley, Beaver Creek sang and purred; while from the top of those granite walls, the green-timbered hills rose grandly, fading gradually into mountains of silver. All my life I had spent out of doors, but never had I seen anything so wildly picturesque.

"With an air of studied indifference I rode slowly round the encampment. Outside, in the shade of their tents and tepees, the Indians were lounging, the men playing cards, the women working with beads and bas-

Indian Dancers

kets, while half-naked children scudded back and forth.

"When I figured that I had all the redskins sitting up and taking notice, I dismounted and walked over to a corral where a bunch of trapped cayuses were vainly circling and fighting for freedom. While I stood watching, a hand was laid upon my shoulder. I turned—and there stood my old friend, 'White Feather.'

"'Hello,' he greeted me in good English. 'You didnt forget my invitation, did you?' You see, 'White Feather' had been away to school. Perhaps that is how he got his name.

"'Come with me over to 'Chief Queahpama's' tepee,' he said, when we had talked for some moments.

"He led the way over to the center of the encampment, pulled back the flap and signed me to follow. Lounging on a huge blanket in the middle of the tepee were four old Indians playing cards. 'White Feather' spoke in his own tongue, and immediately one of the men arose and came toward us.

"I knew at once that the man be-fore me was 'Chief Queahpama.' Tall, erect, broad-shouldered and heavily muscled, though sinewy, he looked every inch a chief. His square face was stern and immobile as though cast in bronze, his long black hair hung loose over his shoulders, his black eyes keen as steel light; and when he spoke his voice rumbled like falling water.

"'My son,' he said, speaking in Indian, with 'White Feather' interpreting, 'White Feather tells me that you have been a friend to my people. Therefore I bid you welcome. Go where you will, and at eating time come back to my tepee.'

"When I had thanked him, he dismissed me with a wave of his hand and resumed his card game, while I followed 'White Feather' outside.

"As 'White Feather' and I strolled about, we chanced to pass a tepee somewhat apart from the main encampment. Squatting near the entrance, mending a bridle, was an old man, his flowing hair sprinkled with gray. Nearby, beading a pair of moccasins, slouched his squaw, fat, thick-waisted, and strangely resembling a feather tick with a string tied around the middle.

"'That is Running Deer,' said 'White Feather', nodding toward the old man. 'He was a famous runner in his day.'

"I was just on the point of passing him when I glanced inside the tepee. And the picture there set my heart to pounding like a trip hammer. An Indian girl was preparing a meal over a camp fire—a mere slip of a girl— but what a beauty.

"She wore a dress of fancy colors, made in loose Indian fashion that fell away from her neck and arms, showing a gaudy necklace and bracelets of heavy silver. Her eyes were the softest brown my own ever had looked into, her dark face touched with a delicate shade of pink, and her blue-black hair fell over her shoulders in two braids, tied with ribbon.

"'That is Raven Wing, Running Deer's daughter,' White Feather announced.

"I had to say something or else be whisked away by 'White Feather,' so I asked in Chinook, 'Is supper ready?'

"And then she laughed—a little rippling laugh like that of a mountain stream. I knew then, that she spoke English, and was laughing at my miserable jargon.

"'It will be ready in a leetle while,' she answered, with just a shade of native accent, and again she laughed merrily.

"Just then old Running Deer's squaw said something to him in Indian, which I, of course, didn't understand. But from the look she gave me I guessed it was something like this: 'That strange buck is getting altogether too gay with our girl. Isn't it about time you were butting in?'

"Anyway Running Deer came up, his crafty old face concealing his native curiosity, and looked me over from hat to spurs. 'You got heap money? he asked.

"'Oh, a little,' I answered indifferently.

"'You heap fine boy. We be hyu

tillicums (good friends),' he confided, patting my shoulder.

"And then, through 'White Feather' he had me understand that next day the Indians were sending out for a load of supplies. He didn't ask me outright for a donation, but so cunningly did he maneuver that I was lighter by the weight of a ten dollar gold piece before I left him.

"I was loath to leave 'Running Deer's' tepee without again seeing 'Raven Wing,' but the clanging of a gong at 'Queahpama's' tepee warned us that supper was waiting. That 'Chief Queahpama' maintained the ancient traditions of royal hospitality was attested by the number who partook of his bounty; for when 'White Feather' and I entered his tepee we found a half hundred men and women sitting around in a circle, scooping up food from off blankets spread out on the floor.

"As the Indians finished their meal I noticed that they stole away in groups. I turned to White Feather for enlightenment.

"'They are going to the dance,' he explained. 'Tonight we have what you whites call a courting dance. The Indian girls of marriageable age start dancing alone, then the young fellows dance out to meet them, each choosing a partner by placing his hand upon the shoulder of the girl he prefers. If this girl favors his suit, she allows his hand to remain and finishes the dance with him. And this is not merely a choice for one dance, but is a public announcement of his intention to marry her.'

"'We will go,' he said, seeing my interest.

"The dance took place in a leveled space alongside Beaver Creek. Blankets spread out beneath them, the Indians sat around in little groups, their dusky faces lighted up by a blazing camp fire in the middle of the dancing space.

"Pretty soon the ceremonies began. Spooms, an old medicine man, whose sightless eyes, wrinkled face and white locks made him strangely resemble a

Chief Queahpama

grizzled wolf, arose and sounded a tom-tom. Out around the fire danced the girls, casting shy glances toward their expectant partners. Immediately the gallant braves danced out to meet them, each choosing a partner as 'White Feather' had intimated. If the hand was allowed to remain, away they would whirl; otherwise the disconsolate suitor would slink away to his corner, looking much as one of our lads when his lassie refuses to walk home from church with him.

"And then a wave of jealousy overwhelmed me. I had glimpsed Raven Wing and her people off to themselves. Would the girl take part in the dance And if so, would any of those bucks presume to put a hand upon her shoulder?

"Just then my questions were answered, for out sailed Raven Wing as light and graceful as a swallow. Her head was proudly erect, her lithe body swayed rhythmically to the beat of the tom-tom, and her eyes shone like stars. And immediately a young buck danced out to meet her. A giant of an Indian he was, over six feet, with the fine bronze and classic features of the artist's Indian. He wore a suit of buckskin with vest and moccasins beaded in fancy designs and patterns.

" 'Ah, Red Wolf! Red Wolf!' whispered White Feather, as the brave danced up to Raven Wing and laid his hand upon her shoulder.

"I would have given worlds just then to have seen Raven Wing fling off that red hand. But no, she smiled up at Red Wolf, and away they whirled.

"I didn't remain to see that dance through, for such an unreasoning anger and jealousy seized me that I strode outside under the starlight to reason myself into sanity. 'Look here,' I said to myself, 'you are a fool to fall head over heels in love with an Indian girl. What would sweet little Helen think (and here my conscience smote me) to see you with a painted buck for a rival; she who kissed you good-bye and bade you God speed on your journey?'

"But Lord bless you! it was no good. My main trouble, I think now, was that I had too much imagination. For whenever I would think of those great brown eyes, that exquisite body, from which seemed to pour a flame of superabundant vitality, all else was forgotten.

"When I got back inside, the Indians were in the midst of a worship dance — a sort of religious ceremony in which they joined hands and danced around a camp-fire. When this dance was ended, I waited patiently, hoping that the girls might again dance singly, and if so, firmly I had resolved to dance with Raven Wing. But no opportunity offered, so, in desperation, I had to resort to a subterfuge which I had fixed upon outside.

"Calling White Feather to one side, I explained that I had a gold watch and chain which I wished to give to the best girl dancer. However, they must first dance before me that I might render an impartial verdict.

"White Feather arose and explained my proposal to the Indians, betraying in his face, I thought, a shade of misgiving as to the outcome. There were grunts and whispers and heated arguments, then a long delay. But finally the tom-tom sounded, and out danced the girls, looking wistfully at the prize I held before them.

"At once I danced out toward Raven Wing, intending to put my hand on her shoulder and fasten the chain around her neck. But Red Wolf, evidently anticipating any move, beat me to her. He was just on the point of sailing away with her when I came up, seeing red in more ways than one. Beside myself at Red Wolf's insolence, I struck his hand from Raven Wing's shoulder and placed my own thereon.

"The tom-tom stopped. There were grunts and shouts of disapproval, and Mrs. Running Deer came running up, jabbering and making faces at me, as she pulled Raven Wing away. I shot a glance at Red Wolf, standing proudly by the fire, and returning me such a look as no words may express.

"Just then Chief Queahpama relieved the tenseness of the situation by announcing that hardtack and canned salmon would be served; so our little affair of the heart was lost sight of in the louder call of the stomach. And while the Indians feasted, Running Deer and White Feather came over to where I stood gloomily aloof, still nettled over my encounter with Red Wolf.

"White Feather began: 'Running Deer says that he wants to speak to you straight from his heart.'

"'Go ahead,' I snapped.

"'He wants to know if you really wish to marry Raven Wing.'

"That certainly was a stunner, but I came back at him. 'Tell Running Deer that I have thought it all over and that I want Raven Wing more than anything else on earth.'

"When White Feather interpreted my answer, Running Deer mumbled something, then White Feather continued: 'Running Deer says to tell you that what you say is good—very good. But he says that it is the Indian custom for the suitor to give the girl's father ponies or money. How much will you give him for Raven Wing?'

"'Tell Running Deer,' I retorted hotly, 'that I don't believe in buying a wife, just as one would a horse or

Red Wolf the Indian Lover

cow. Ask him if Raven Wing shouldn't have some choice in the matter.'

"There was more mumbling, then White Feather turned to me: 'Running Deer says tell you that you whites have your laws and customs and that we have ours; that your laws and customs are made for whites, but are no good for Indians. He also says tell you that his woman wants Raven Wing to marry Red Wolf, but that he leans toward you. What do you say about the pony and money proposition?'

"Inwardly I was raging at so monstrous a proposal, but holding my temper in leash, I replied, 'Tell Running Deer that for every pony or dollar Red Wolf offers I will make it two. How does that strike him?'

"'Ugh! heap good,' the crafty Running Deer grunted, not waiting for White Feather to interpret.

"Next morning after breakfast, I detected a new tenseness in the men-

tal atmosphere. The Indians were moving about excitedly and barking gutturally. Pretty soon I caught sight of Raven Wing, and she, too, seemed to have caught the infection, judging from the way she flashed and danced about. 'What's up, anyway?' I asked myself.

"Then White Feather and Running Deer came over to me and the former began: 'Running Deer says tell you that he and Chief Queahpama talked it all over last night and decided that there's only one way to decide who shall marry Raven Wing. You have a race horse, and so has Red Wolf; you are to race those horses, with Raven Wing as the stake. What do you say?'

"I was thunderstruck, but realizing that Running Deer held the whip hand, I prepared to meet him on his own grounds. Of the outcome of such a race I had no misgivings, for Jimmy Britt, true to his thoroughbred sire and Arabian dam, had never been beaten, and I felt positive that an Indian cayuse had not the ghost of a show against him.

"'Tell Running Deer that proposition suits me,' I made answer. 'When shall the race take place?'

"White Feather went over and conferred with the Indians, then came back and announced: 'Red Wolf says that now is as good a time as any. Does that suit you?'

"'Yes,' I snapped. 'Tell Red Wolf to trot out his racer;' and I strode off after Jimmy Britt.

"When I got back, Red Wolf was mounted and waiting for me, riding slowly up and down. His mount was a trim buck-skin mare, lean and long-bodied, with arched neck and silken mane and the flaring eyes of the nervous racer. I knew at first glance that she could run like a deer and that no common horse could beat her.

"White Feather, standing in the arched gateway with tom-tom in hand, surrounded by that motley throng of jabbering Indians, motioned us to ride up alongside. As we swung around neck and neck, I proudly noted that

Jimmy Britt loomed a full hand over the buckskin. Snorting and eager and ready for battle he was, his mighty heart pounding rhythmically and his eyes flashing defiantly.

"'Its a standing start,' explained White Feather, 'and off at the first tap. You are to race through the meadow to where the stream crosses it, then back. The horse first through the corral gate is winner.'

"I could hear the quick breathing of that dark circle about me, broken occasionally by sharp grunts; but above all, the shrill protest-voice of Mrs. Running Deer. I must confess that my heart beat a wee bit faster as I again caught sight of Raven Wing, this time standing on the fence, the center of all eyes. And would you believe it? Nearby stood old Running Deer waging his saddle against another Indian's blankets on the outcome; and from their maneuvers, I felt sure that the crafty old renegade was betting on Red Wolf.

"'Are you both ready?' White Feather called.

"Boom! sounded the tom-tom, and we shot out together like two arrows from the same bow.

"Level as a floor lay the clean-cropped meadow, with not a rock or mound in our course. Straight ahead, one-half mile away, the timber began, and just on the edge of it was the stream where we were to make the turn for the home-stretch.

"The first few leaps, the nimbler and quicker buckskin took the lead, and this brought a wild shout from Red Wolf's followers. The Indian was leaning forward in easy fashion, riding with free rein and holding his quirt in reserve.

"Then I spoke to Jimmy Britt. With an eager snort, he gathered himself together and shot forward in great leaps that fairly ate up the space between me and the flying Indian. Half way down the course, and Jimmy Britt's nose was at his rival's flank; then neck and neck we raced, Red Wolf now urging with quirt and spur. But the gallant little buckskin

had shot her bolt, and in a few more leaps I could hear the pounding of her hoofs safely in the rear.

"Then, for the first time, my danger flashed upon me. Could I make the turn? For my horse was running like a thing possessed, senseless of the bit or the sound of my voice, heeding naught but the puffing of his oncoming rival.

"Pulling with all my weight and strength, I spoke to him and attempted to quiet him. But with a leap, he cleared the stream, broke into the timber, and when finally I wheeled him in a wide circle into the course, I caught a glimpse of a yellow streak far in the lead.

"Then I drew my quirt and lashed Jimmy as he never had been lashed before. 'Run!' I called to him. 'Run! run!'

"I have always wished that someone might have been there and held a watch on Jimmy coming down that home-stretch. I feel sure that he came close to a world's record for that half-mile run. For not only did he run, but bounded and flew until his nose was at the buckskin's flank, then a few more leaps and we were safely in the lead. Wildly the Indians were yelling at Red Wolf, but the little mare had been run off her feet and her spirit broken.

"I was pulling Jimmy Britt in for the gate, sure of an easy victory, when a momentous thing happened. Fate stepped out — yes, Fate in the shape of Mrs. Running Deer. As I pulled in for the home-stretch, I caught a glimpse of her standing in front of the gate, madly jumping up and down and waving an enormous red blanket; and before I divined her purpose, she threw that blanket squarely in Jimmy Britt's face.

"With a startled snort, he swerved and ran down alongside the fence. When I finally brought him in check and looked back, it was to see Red Wolf dismounted inside the corral, and Raven Wing at his side, looking up at him with shining eyes, her hand on his shoulder.

" 'Red Wolf wins!' White Feather shouted. 'He was first through the gate.'

"Just what happened the next few moments I have no distinct recollection. I can only recall casting one more look at Red Wolf, his head up, his beaded vest glinting in the sunlight, and Raven Wing looking proudly up at him. Then I turned my horse squarely around, and, amid the derisive shouts of the Indians, rode madly down the valley into the timber and on till I had cleared that reservation.

"No sooner was I off that reservation than a wave of revulsion swept over me. Those last few days seemed to have been a hideous dream and only the timely fluttering of Mrs. Running Deer's blanket had prevented it from becoming a reality.

"And say——"

Just then the door opened and in the doorway stood a sweet-faced little woman, a wreath of wildflowers in her hair, and looking much like one herself. She smiled shyly from one to the other of us, then at a nod and a word of introduction from her husband, took my hand.

"Dinner ready, Helen?" the ranger asked, smiling up at her, his voice soft as a love-note; and as we followed the little woman inside, the ranger winked at me over his offshoulder, grinned and whispered, "Remember, that blanket story is my one state secret."

SWEETHEART MINE

(Song)

The happy birds are singing, the skies above are fair;
I hear the bluebells ringing, the day is free from care;
I stand below thy lattice, beneath the clustering vine,
Oh, whisper that thou lovest me, Oh, sweetheart mine!

The swallow swiftly winging in merry month of June,
The nightingale soft singing beneath the silver moon,
The moth at even flitting where scarlet blossoms twine,
All answer to the call of love, Oh, sweetheart mine!

The fading sunset flushes and tints the waving corn;
The rose with beauty blushes, the stars await the morn,
And I am waiting, waiting, Vouchsafe me but a sign
To show me that thou lovest me, Oh, sweetheart mine!

JOHN RAVENOR BULLEN.

Jack London and Mrs. London Aboard the U. S. S. Kilpatrick

Jack London's Women

By Grace V. Silver

THROUGH his writings Jack London has shown us but two kinds of women. He knew life as no other writer of our time ever knew it; he knew science and history and philosophy as well. In the creation of his characters he brought into play all his varied knowledge, and this knowledge and experience taught him that there were but two kinds of women in this world. He had intimate knowledge of both, therefore he knew them too well to attempt to classify either as "good" or "bad." He never created a woman wholly bad, for none knew better than he the effects of environment on the human character. His "bad" women are infinitely better than the good ones of other and less observing writers.

One might say, almost, that London had drawn the portraits of but two women; that he has taken two women whom he himself knew, placed them in all possible situations, analyzed them mercilessly, yet unobtrusively, scientifically examined and recorded their development under different and varied environment, and given us the result of his observations in the most wonderful series of pen portraits of modern women ever drawn.

He realized that womenkind are divided into two classes. There is the class who live to get all they can out of their menfolk and who give as little as they need, or as much as they are compelled to give in return for the economic support and love which they require. Then there is the other class of women — mate-women, London called them—who go through the battle of life side by side with their men; women who are comrades and friends as well as lovers; women whose love for their menfolk is maternal as well as sexual; women who mother the men they have mated; women whose desire is to give rather than to receive; women who, giving all that woman can give to man, are yet rewarded by all that man can give to woman.

One woman is a parasite and the other a co-worker; one is a housewife, the other a homemaker; one is a courtesan, and the other a comrade; one is only a wife, and the other is greater than a friend; one is a sex-grafter and the other a mate-woman. Some of London's critics say that his women are stilted, women. Some of them are, and in their very artificiality they are true to life.

If some of those critics could get far enough away from their own class to get the proper perspective they would realize that their womenfolk are stilted, wooden, and that London has merely held up the mirror to their class. The other type of woman is so foreign to them that quite possibly they cannot understand her at all.

Take, for example, the case of Saxon, the laundry girl whom he made the heroine of the "Valley of the Moon." And, in passing let us remark that no one but Jack London could have written a successful novel with a laundry worker for a heroine and a burly teamster for a hero. Preeminently a mate-woman, all the instincts of the primitive woman who toiled for — and with — her man, are Saxon's. She knows love when it

comes to her, and fearlessly and honestly, without shame or coquetry she welcomes it. There is not lacking the element of parasitism in her make-up. It is the same kind of parasitism that every woman who is kept — or supported, if you wish to be polite—by any man must have. Her husband, after the manner of his kind, cultivates this trait in her. He will support her; he will furnish the home, supply the food, pay for her clothes, place her in a position of absolute economic dependence on himself. When economic necessity compels them to rent a room, his pride is outraged—she must not work.

Saxon, relieved from the grind of the laundry and the necessity of earning a living for herself, devotes her time to making herself pleasing in the sight of her man. From him come all her wants, all her needs; therefore in all her life there is nothing so necessary as the art of making and keeping herself attractive in his eyes. She is a parasite; but such a wise, intelligent parasite! Her mental viewpoint is that of the favorite sultana of a harem, but so wise is she that we scarcely realize her deficiencies. Advised by her friend, Mary, that she is spoiling her husband by waiting on him so much, she says in reply:

"He's the bread-winner. He works harder than I do, and I've got more time than I know what to do with— time to burn. Besides, I want to wait on him because I want to, and because —well, anyway, I want to."

But Saxon does not remain forever a parasite; she has too much intelligence to be satisfied in that role. When Billy, her husband, went out on strike, Saxon stood bravely by till the last bit of food was gone. Then, one night, Billy came home to tell her that he had been offered a foreman's place and one hundred dollars a month to go back to work. Saxon said:

"You can't do that Billy; you can't throw the fellows down."

She was rewarded by Billy's handclasp.

"If all the other fellow's wives were

. like you we'd win any strike we tackled," he replied.

"What would you have done if you hadn't been married?"

"Seen 'em in hell first," was his reply. And Saxon answered:

"Then it doesn't make any difference being married. I've got to stand by you in everything you stand for. I'd be a nice wife if I didn't."

There was rioting, and Saxon's baby was born dead. They lost their furniture, could buy no more food, and Billy was jailed. Still Saxon stood by. All the parasite in her, handed down through the ages when woman's best if not only means of support was her sex, cultivated by custom as something to be cherished, slipped away from her. She become the mate-woman, mother, as well as wife, of her man; and, when Billy was released from jail, homeless and penniless they tramped over California till, together, they earned a home for themselves in the "Valley of the Moon."

There might be a considerable amount of human folly prevented and human misery saved if every girl, and every woman could read with open mind the "Valley of the Moon."

Dede Mason, heroine of "Burning Daylight," is another of London's mate-women. Co-worker in all things, all heart and all brain, she will not marry the man she loves—because he is wealthy; because she would cease to be a fellow worker of his in the office, and become the kept plaything of his leisure hours. To become the wife —and therefore the kept woman—of the man she has loved for years is to her unthinkable. She is very wise, and she knows that to place a woman in a position where in order to live she must calculate, "How much will my husband give me?" is to begin to destroy that woman's love for her man. She is wise enough to know that a real woman loves a man more for what she gives to him than for what he gives to her. When he is financially ruined she comes to him freely and gladly.

The Little Lady of the big house, and Labiskwee who starved herself on the long trail by the Yukon, that Smoke Bellew might eat and live, are both mate-women— very much alike for all the difference in race and environment. They are wonder-women, and like Lizzie Connolly in "Martin Eden," they take no thought for themselves. Their business is to battle side by side with their men for bread, for life, if need be; to give rest and content, joy and happiness; to bind up the wounds which civilization has inflicted on her children.

To one who knew the Londons, these women of his books seem to be vivid incarnations of Charmian Kittredge. Mate-woman was one of the names by which he called his wife, and well did she deserve it. Always, everywhere, she was his companion and co-worker; always all that man could expect of woman. No one can read his "Cruise of the Snark" without realizing that the portraits he has drawn of these other women are based on his life with Charmian. When their boat leaked and all were sick; when they were becalmed for weeks on end and they had no longer strength to steer their frail craft and the boat floated for days an inert mass; when the tropic sun caused Jack's white skin to peel off in silvery scales, ultimately sending him to an Australian hospital—then he realized to the full the meaning of the word mate-woman. Charmian came back and wrote the cheerful, optimistic "Log of the Snark;" Jack wrote the "Cruise of the Snark," laying bare the tale of their struggles and privations, and dedicated it to the woman who wept when the voyage had to be given up.

As for London's other women characters, most of them seem to bear a close resemblance to a lady who came intimately into his life soon after he began to write. To the discerning reader, his Ruth of "Martin Eden," is a shining example of the purely parasitic woman. Martin interests her; she imagines she loves him; but she thinks he can't make money enough to keep her properly and throws him over. Her psychology is identical with that of the dance hall girl who picks as a partner a man who will spend much money on her before the night is past in preference to a better man who has less means. Ruth is very good, very refined and very virtuous; but she must marry a man abundantly able to keep her. Her father and mother have trained her to look on her sex as the most valuable, most marketable, commodity she possesses. Her mother is a real lady; she knows nothing of vice, and the ways of the underworld. But all the same, she has an attractive daughter for sale, and intends to get the best possible price—or husband—for the girl. Martin is successful; he makes money, and they wish to resume acquaintance with him; he now has the means of buying Ruth.

And what about Maud, that most artificial lady of the "Sea Wolf?" Alone on an uninhabited island with a man who has saved both her honor and her life, with a man she loves and who loves her, she does not dream of giving him a caress, or sign of love till they are rescued, months later, by a passing ship. Love is of no consequence to her unless it can be publicly advertised amongst strangers as well as friends, with suitable clerical ceremonies. She was looking to see what she could get out of marriage — not trying to see of how much comfort she might be to the man she loved. And there was nothing to be gotten from such a connection on a lonely island.

Some of his parasite women wear the cloak of respectability and some do not. London realized the truth of Kipling's line about the Colonel's lady and Judy O'Grady; they are both the same as far as morals are concerned. Training, economic circumstances, environment, personal taste, cause the seeming differences to appear. He found parasite women in the Klondike and in the London slums, and he found them amongst the working class and the cultured homes of Berkeley. At times he idealized them,

endowed them with attributes they did not possess, imagined them to be nest builders, mate-women, when they were not. Such a composite type is Margaret in "The Mutiny of the Elsinore." More convincing, but still a composite type growing out of his own longing, is Avis, in the "Iron Heel."

He had always an ideal, as most men have, of what a woman ought to be; but in the first few years of his writing he could only describe the ideal; he had not intimately known the reality. Consequently the woman characters of his earlier writings seem and are, more or less artificial. But they are no whit more artificial than their prototypes in real life. He drew them better than he knew; the world is full of women of their kind—artificial products of an artificial social system, crippled daughters of a soul destroying civilization. He drew their portraits without bitterness; none knew better than he that society had made them what they were, commercialized in body and in mind. They were good, too, but Jack London realized that no woman can be quite as bad as a thoroughly good woman; that none can rise to the heights so well as those who have plumbed the depths.

London is often spoken of as a "man's author," because apparently more men that women admire his writings. Some women understand and admire; many realize subconsciously, that the parasite type is a portrayal of themselves, and are resentful; many more have been so overcultured by civilization and have been weighted down by the forces of custom and petty superstition and mentally and morally stunted by economic pressure that the race instincts which all women once had in common are either dormant or dead. Artificial themselves, London's mate-women seem to them artificial.

His popularity among men is not altogether due to the fact that he writes of the mine and the trail, of the open road and the sea, of labor and ranch. It is due as much to the fact that most men have searched for their mate-women, and searched in vain, and have married without finding them, as to the virile character of his stories. Contrary though the idea may be to popular opinion, which is usually wrong, most men have more sentiment and less commercialism, as far as love is concerned, than have most women. Far more so than wo-men, they have retained the healthy normal mating instincts. London's mate-woman—his ideal—is the ideal woman consciously or unconsciously in the minds of millions of men. That such a woman, such an ideal relation-ship, is for most men unattainable, and remains forever an ideal, causes London's women to possess a lasting attraction for the men who read his works.

Queer Korean Superstitions

By Matt Smith

WHILE sojourning as a mission-ary in far-off Korea during the first four years of the present century, the most difficult part of my task was to eradicate from the minds of my pupils the many strange super-stitions and ideas which prevailed among all classes of the natives.

Like their Chinese cousins, the Ko-reans prefer to follow the moon rather than the sun in their division of the year, and the most important moon in the year is the silver sickle that they see suspended by an invisible cord, the first night of the first month in the year. All the natives made a new beginning, with the advent of the new moon, and it is celebrated as a time for restitution. Debts are paid, old scores are adjusted, and, most im-portant of all, a complete suit of new clothes is donned.

The Korean holiday season begins on the first day of the first moon and ends on the fifteenth, at which time the natives keep busy, and none but the most indifferent and inexcusably careless will neglect to attend to the various little matters whereby the spirit of disease, trouble and famine must be appeased or bribed.

Their special dread and greatest imaginary foe is one old fellow whom they call "Au Wangi," since on the fifteenth day of the first moon in the year this malicious spirit descends from ether space to earth and goes the rounds of all villages, trying on the straw shoes before each door. Ko-reans, like all other dwellers of the Orient, who wear sandals, slip them off before the door, never entering the house with their shoes on. Those whose shoes he finds are sure to re-ceive from "Au Wangi" some gift not desired nor longed for, but objection-able and dreadful, for this evil spirit's gifts come in the form of malignant, hideous disease, famine and pesti-lence. To avoid his gifts and puzzle the old fellow, the shoes are usually taken within and a light kept burning through the night. But those who fear even that this precaution is insufficient seek to attract his attention by plac-ing a common wire seive on the straw thatched roof of the little home, with the hope that he has such a mania for counting little holes he will be kept occupied that he will fail to note the flight of time. When midnight comes; his power to scatter pestilential gifts passes away, and he is compelled to depart and leave that house in peace.

Poor ignorant Koreans, from year to year they live in constant dread of the approach of the fifteenth day of the first moon of the year, when they ex-pect "Au Wangi" to promptly return to earth, accompanied by countless myriads of other evil spirits which they believe fill ethereal space.

Sacajaweah

By Frank M. Vancil

ON leaving their winter camp, April, 1805, among the Mandan Indians on the upper Missouri River, Lewis and Clark, the great Western explorers, employed a Canadian Frenchman, named Chaboneau, for a guide. His Indian wife and baby went with them. The woman whose name was Sacajaweah or "Bird Woman," was of the Snake or Shoshone tribe beyond the mountains. She had been captured in battle and taken more than a thousand miles down the river, where she became one of the three wives of the French trapper.

The early home of Sacajaweah was near the mountains, and her return with the party to the land of her birth and kindred was an event of great rejoicing. Through her influence, her brother being a chief of the tribe, the good will of the Indians was secured. She returned from the Pacific Coast with the explorers to her native land in the vicinity of Three Forks, Montana, where a suitable monument has been erected to her memory.

Much has been written about this "Bird Woman," but all that we know of her is given in the journal of Lewis and Clark who describe her as an ordinary and obedient Indian squaw. She was, however, of superior birth, the great chief, her brother, says Clark, "is a man of influence, sense, easy and reserved manners, and appears to possess a great deal of sincerity." Lewis gives this account: "Sah-car-gar-we-ah, our Indian woman,

was one of the female prisoners taken at that time, though I cannot discover that she shows any emotion of sorrow in recollecting this event, or joy in being restored to her native country. If she has enough to eat and a few trinkets to wear, I believe she would be perfectly contented anywhere."

Rev. John Roberts, a Missionary among the Indians for many years, remembered Sacajaweah and officiated at her burial at the Shoshone Agency in April, 1884.

It appears that when Toussant Chaboneau, her French husband, became old and feeble, Sacajawea returned to her own people, the Shoshones, roaming from Idaho to Wyoming. Young Chaboneau was a well known guide to Bonneville and Fremont, and is often mentioned.

While Sacajawea was known as the "Bird Woman," in Dakota, in Wyoming she was "The Boat-Pus her." She was also called "Wadzewip," the Lost Woman. Those who knew her, describe her as short and small, lively and spry to the last, dying when she was 94 years old.

At the grave of Sacajawea on Wind River in Wyoming, the Daughters of the American Revolution have recently erected a concrete monument with a brass plate bearing the inscription: "Sacajaweah, died April 9, 1884. A guide with the Lewis and Clark Expedition, 1804-1806. Identified by Rev. J. Roberts, who officiated at her burial."

A Page of Sonnets

FAITH

I who have watched the opal in the
    west
The while it faded to the palest gray,
Have seen the crimson on the linnet's
    breast,
And listened to the lark's inspiring
    lay:
Have seen the vineyard purple in the
    sun,
And watched the orange turn from
    green to gold—
I know, I know that there is only One
Who could have wrought these won-
    ders manifold.

          CAROLINE CHRISTIE.

BY THE RIVER

The light is miraculous — golden and
    rare;
    The stream is a silken and shim-
        mering flood.
Swallows and orioles sport in the air,
    Ecstasy lives in their blood.

The trees rear their branches; leafage,
    sun-bright,
    Waves a *bon voyage* to the boats on
      the river.
The gifts of the season are hearts
    brave and light,
    And strong as the hands of the
      Giver!

          ARTHUR POWELL.

REMEMBRANCE

Evening—a room with shaded light,
A rose whose perfume haunts the air,
Her song—a fairy viol at night,
Her mystic presence everywhere.

          R. R. GREENWOOD.

THE CALL OF THE WILD

The blue of the mystic mountains,
The call of the rushing stream,
The luring whine of the wind-swept
    pine
Awaken again the dream—
Dream of the old-time freedom,
Dream of the old-time thrills
And I hear once more as in years
    before
The call to return to the hills.

The sleeping spirits have wakened
And the heart of me is aglow.
A vision calls from the canon walls
And the soul of me says "Go!"
The trails stretch out before
Straight to the mountain's span,
Like a beckoning hand from some
    fairy land,
And I'm off to the hills again.

          FORD C. FRICK.

HOPE

How glorious yonder in the eastern
    skies
Over the edge of night dawn's foun-
    tains rise!
Pure as the gold of youth and fair
    to see,
Even as hope is fair, diurnally.

        HERBERT EDWARD MIEROW.

QUATRAIN

The winter hills, snow-softened,
    through the pane,
The leafless boughs in sober, quaker
    guise,
Within, the music of the leaping
    flame,
Her lyric laughter and *her* azure eyes.

          R. R. GREENWOOD.

One Result of Repeated Ground Fires

Our Forests in July

By Charles H. Shinn

IF one could overlook the whole of California in these midsummer days, he would note that thousands of tired men, women and children were climbing towards the snow-peaks, or returning to the valleys, were resting in camps by mountain streams, lakes and meadows, were sitting around camp fires and telling tales of romance and adventure. He would see other armies of toilers, not pleasure-seekers, looking after sheep and cattle, building roads, felling timber, running sawmills, hauling out the forest products. From San Diego to Siskiyou, the whole mountain land would be throbbing with magnificent life.

Then, coming down to details, this state-wide on-looker would begin to observe what political text books call "the system of checks and balances" which one somehow finds everywhere —system, supervision, slowly developing order, knowledge growing from less to more, expert scalers estimating the board feet in logs, keen-eyed rangers counting in the sheep and cattle, fire outlooks on lonely peaks far above the forests, aviators, perhaps, flying overhead to report the first upcurling ribbons of smoke from new-starting fires.

Not in the least a pipe-dream, this last, for the experiment of using aircraft over our forests has been initiated over large areas in California, New Mexico, Arizona and elsewhere. Army airplanes are beginning to fly while these lines are being written; doubtless by the time you, dear reader, scan this page, the newspapers will be telling how some young American who won his fame over the war front is reporting fires and saving American forests. While on this subject, it is also worth saying that the vast possibilities in the use of air ma-

3

chines were seen from the first by many in the Forest Service, and also by many mountain men and lovers of the great out-doors, so that suggestions about using overhead scouts have come from all over California.

Seeing these things, you if in a National Forest on a camp this July, will perhaps remember some of the beginnings—the rude home-made fire-rakes of the late Nineties which forest guards used; the total lack of telephones, the three or four days spent by hungry sleepless men in the gulches and on the high divides, corralling a big fire. You will remember dozens of hero tales of pioneer forest

stations alone and done it quite as well as any man could.

The past twenty years' history of fire-fighting experiments in California deserves a book to itself, so full is the period with thrilling incidents and steadily evolving experience. At one time, for instance, a number of fire-break lines were cut through thick brush at high cost, so as to protect valuable bodies of timber. But they grew up again very fast indeed, and it was soon found that except under special conditions fire lines are not altogether a success, but that the lookout towers, telephones, the ability to rush a lot of fully-equipped fire fight-

Echo Lake, Eldorado National Forest

work that have become splendid traditions helping to create still greater loyalties to the growing spirit of American forestry.

You will have watched the building of those first rude fire-outlook cabins on hill tops near the western fronts of the National Forests, back in the first ten years of this century, to be rapidly followed by much more useful fire stations on higher peaks, miles away from neighbors, where men lived and worked in isolation for months; where brave women sometimes lived sharing their husbands' vigils. In a few cases women have kept these fire outlook

ers to the spot quickly (in these days largely by machines) are the things that count.

Now we shall have aircraft besides. But the really important matter, as everyone knows, is the growing unity of effort and spirit of fellowship among all the people who believe in forests. Anybody who spends a little time in one of the eighteen National Forests of California and Nevada soon discovers all this. "Some thing brings us together," a newcomer said one July: "It's partly the wild life, the outdoorness; it's still more the forests and their primeval solitude. When we go home again we are better and more useful people for our summer days up here."

But all this health-giving beauty and potential wood-product resources over thousands of square miles are at the mercy of a careless match, a forgotten camp fire, an ignorant, foolish or criminal person who starts a blaze in our dry season, and perhaps destroys thousands of acres of timber, lessens the water-storage capacity of our mountains, and injures the American people.

The statistics sent out by lumbermen's associations and the Forest Ser-

fornia, burning over some 12,000 acres.

Now, when everyone, young and old, settlers, tourists, hunters, fishermen, prospectors, cattlemen and all the rest of us, realize the vast issues involved in the fight to save our forests from any fire loss whatever, fires in California can be reduced to merely those started by lightning, perhaps fifty a year, and the total acreage to less than a thousand, the losses to "next to nothing."

In order to reach this much-desired result public education must be constant, beginning in the primary grades

A Summer Home on the McCloud River

vice prove that fires on our timber lands in 1918 cost the Pacific Coast $6,500,000 in the destruction of merchantable timber, besides, of course, the losses to livestock, the killing of small trees, the destruction of soil fertility and lessening of water supplies. We had 6249 separate fires, and 321,827 acres were burned over. More than two million dollars was spent by the Government and by private individuals in checking and finally putting out these forest fires. It may be added that 1030 of these fires were on the National Forests of Cali-

of the schools, extending throughout all social groups of men, women and children. Here is an immense field for the best work of boy scouts, campfire girls, normal schools, outing clubs, and all sorts of associations, but especially for every force that has to do with agriculture and horticulture.

Another book might be written upon the sad, silly, and yet often amusing-performances of careless people who go to the mountains. Once, not twenty miles from Truckee, a couple of men camped on the sawdust pile of an old, abandoned mill, built their fire, sprang

A Result of Carelessness With Camp Fires

from their blankets a few hours later, and ran for their precious lives! Their camp, horses and wagon were wiped out; the fire burned for a week or so, destroying much timber. The men went into Truckee and asked a lawyer if there was any prospect that they could recover damages from the owner of the old mill site!

The late B. B. Redding, of the Southern Pacific, "one of Nature's noblemen," and a man whose love for wild life and the forests was beyond expression, once found some campers on the McCloud river who were setting fire to dead pitch-pine stumps, and also making huge piles of logs against the face of a granite cliff, so that when set afire the rock would split, explode, and fly off in huge masses. He reasoned unavailingly with them. "Came up to have a good time," they said. From that incident dated Mr. Redding's desire for fire patrols, more stringent laws, and a broader public education. It was a long time ago—about 1878, I think, but John Muir, John Sweet, Sam Williams of the "Bulletin," Prof. Joseph LeConte, Dr.

Hilgard, and old John Rock, the nurseryman, were among the men who talked Forest Protection with men like B. B. Redding, in those times.

Dr. Hilgard of the State University, used to say: "Start school gardens; show the infants how a seed grows, and becomes at last a tree. Take them to the mountains; show them the best way to camp, how to live, how to find their way around, what to do in case of accidents. Make them, in brief, children of the great outdoors. Then, when we have Government forests" (this was about 1880) "every Californian will know how to stand up for them."

But more than thirty years of time —and the world-war lies between— more than forty years, if one goes back to B. B. Redding's experiences, have elapsed. Where are we now? There has been a far-reaching system of fire-protection created so as to discover, reach, and rapidly conquer every fire. There has been much written and said towards the education of the public. Best of all, a policy has been developed which aims at interesting every owner of a piece of land upon which forest trees grow, whether just a wood

Fire Lookout Tower, Tahoe National Forest

Forest Hill Fire, Tahoe National Forest

lot or whole square miles of virgin timber. Colonel Henry S. Graves, Chief of the Forest Service, in a recent address before the Lumbermen's Congress at Chicago, discussed this policy in the most thoughtful and practical manner. He outlined the vital importance of forest renewal private lands, in other words the restoration of timber growth on cut-over lands. This involves changes in the present methods of taxing forest lands, and many other things, but it rests upon the full recognition by the American people of the necessity of saving, utilizing, restoring and forever continuing our forest resources. First of all, this means cutting out the fires. Let us all help to enforce the State and Federal fire laws. Let us forever get rid of the notion that "light summer burning" is ever a good thing in our forests. That long-discredited theory is of the Piute Indian order; it clears off great areas; it destroys the reproduction as well as much larger growth; it changes forests in brush-covered and worthless areas. Systematic fire protection is the only scientific method known to foresters.

Now for the practical turn — the "what to do this very year: First keep posted on Forest Service, and University literature; get acquainted with forests and forest people; use safety matches, and pinch out the stubs. Secondly, consider the immense place which forests and wild life occupy in our civilization, and how empires that wasted these resources have gone down in pain and in darkness. Then, once for all, say to yourself 'We can put an end to fire-losses in the California forests, excepting of course, the few that come from summer lightning strokes.' "

The Phantom Engine

By F. H. Sidney

Have You Ever Thought of the Harrowing Happenings and Lonely Vigils of the Tower Signalmen, Who Guard the Passing Trains and Human Lives. These Two Narratives, "The Phantom Engine" and "The Celestial Wireless," Will Glimpse for You the Inner Life of These Men, in the Still Watches of the Night. The Author, a Railroad Man, Writes Out of His Own Experience.—The Editor.

IN the old days before there were any Federal nine-hour laws, Interstate Commerce Commissions and relief men," said Signalman Jones to his friend, Bill the locomotive engineer, "we signalmen often worked twenty-four, thirty-six, and seventy-two hours at a stretch."

"Yes, I know," replied Bill. "I have often stayed at the throttle fifty hours myself."

"Those were the times," said Jones, "that after being on duty long hours without rest, that we often 'saw things.' I remember working a seventy-two hour stretch at 'WG' Tower fifteen years ago. The last eight hours were the hardest I ever put in. I was so tired and nervous I couldn't have slept if I had had the opportunity.

"About three o'clock in the morning on the last lap of that long 'trick,' something rang in on the track circuit. It was a short ring, and I concluded it must be an engine running light, but what engine? I had listened to the 'OS,' and knew just what was moving on the division at the time, and there was no 'light engine' among the extras that were being reported. Furthermore the nearest thing to me at that time was an extra freight at Berkshire, forty miles away.

"It might have been something that I did not happen to hear reported, I thought, so I set the route for main line. In a few minutes an engine came in sight, and whistled as it passed the distant signal. The whistle had the strangest and most beautiful sound I ever heard. I leaned far out the window as the engine approached the tower. I wanted to be sure and catch the number of the engine that had such a beautiful, musical whistle. As the engine approached the tower the bell rang, and what a wonderful bell it was; it sounded as though it was made of silver, and it was tinkling clearly and musically as the engine drew near the tower. I tried to catch the number, but it was obliterated. In the dull morning light I saw 'she' was one of the small old style engines, and just about fit for the scrap heap. The paint had worn off, and the top of 'her' diamond stack had rusted away. Her exhaust sounded as though all the packing had been blown out of the valves, 'she' was moving slow and working 'one side.' This is funny, I thought. Are they sending that old scrap heap to the shop to be made over into a shifter?

"Just then I caught a glimpse of the engineer, his hand was on the throttle, and he was looking out of the side cab window facing the tower. I could see he was an old white-haired man. His head was bare, and his face was deadly pale, the coat he wore was as white as snow. He waved a white gloved hand at me, then the engine disappeared. 'She' disappeared as though swallowed by the earth. The engine was moving slowly as 'she' passed the tower, and it is straight track for a mile to the west, as you well know."

Bill nodded his assent, and Jones continued:

"I can swear that engine disappeared less than fifty feet from the tower. I did not dare to report that strange engine to the train dispatcher, he might think I had been asleep and dreaming. I was as wide awake then as I am now. I thought, perhaps, if it was a real engine, and I didn't 'OS' it, the dispatcher would call for a report of it, and I would be safe to give it to him then. Consequently I made a note of the time, in this old diary. See there it is now. 'Phantom Engine departed west, 3:02, A. M.'"

"That," said Bill, "was old Uncle Eddie Eastman, who went over the bank in a washout near 'WG' about forty years ago. The engine and twelve freight cars rolled down the bank, and uncle Eddie, two brakemen and the firemen, were buried in the

mud under the engine, and suffocated, I presume, or they may have been killed outright. I came down here with the wrecker, and they were dead when we lifted the engine, and picked up their bodies. They say every little while the old man gets restless, and digs his old engine out of the scrap heap and takes a run over the road. His engine was the old Number One, and 'she' had the old style bell and whistle, that's why they sounded so strange and musical. They don't make any such bells and whistles these days," said Bill rather sadly.

"Now isn't that strange," exclaimed Jones. "I was reading an account of that wreck in an old newspaper clipping I found in the locker, the day before I had this strange experience."

"That accounts for it," said Bill. "It came out of your sub-conscious mind. The human mind is certainly a strange instrument."

THE CELESTIAL WIRELESS

SIGNALMAN JONES, like most telegraphers, was interested in wireless telegraphy. He built a receiving set, which he put up in the tower; and when not busy he amused himself by listening to messages that were being transmitted between ships at sea and the stations along the coast. One day Jones had a very strange experience; and after that time he never touched any part of a wireless set. He disconnected his plant and stored it away. Jones told the story of his experience to his friend Bill, the engineer, as follows:

"At the time I learned telegraphy, one of my school mates who was about my own age became interested. The consequence was he took up the profession and became a telegrapher. We worked together on the lower end of the road, until I was transferred to the tower service up here in the hills, while he remained down near the city;

working as a ticket agent and telegrapher at one of the suburban stations. We visited back and forth and corresponded regularly.

"Jack, (that's my friend's name), became interested in wireless. He studied at evening schools in the city and fitted himself for the position of constructor of wireless plants. After completing his studies he entered the employ of one of the wireless companies. Jack constructed wireless stations at points along the Atlantic coast. Finally the company sent him to the Far East to take charge of the construction of some very powerful stations. He wrote me some very interesting letters from the far-away places. I often thought as I read his letters: Suppose Jack should contract one of those Eastern fevers, what would become of him in those strange far-off lands? Then the thought came to me: Jack is a Mason, they are to be found everywhere, and he will be cared for in case he is sick or in distress. I felt more comfortable after that."

"You're right; they'll take care of him," replied Bill. "I've met Masons among the savage tribes in Africa, in Afghanistan, and other out-of-the-way places. I travelled some in my younger days."

"I remember feeling particularly blue one night," continued Jones, "and I thought I would listen to the wireless a while to see if it would cheer me up. I picked up all sorts of messages from ships within radius. It is five hundred miles from here to the coast, and I could easily pick up messages from that distance. I heard one of the new battleships communicating in code to the Boston Navy Yard. It was just before Germany declared war. I often wondered what that message meant. As I listened, this Biblical quotation came to my mind: 'There will be wars and rumors of wars.'

"After listening to the ships a while," said Jones, "I 'tuned' my instruments and picked up some nearby amateurs. While listening to their idle chatter I thought to myself, what poor senders they are; most of them sound as though they were using their foot to send with. Finally everything was quiet and I decided to close my station. When suddenly in clear, sharp Morse came the signal 'SY' (my personal sign). It came so suddenly I didn't have time to wonder

who might be signalling. And mentally I answered the signal. I say mentally because I did not have any sending apparatus connected to my station. It was only a receiving set. Then came this strange message, and sent by one whose 'sending' I recognized:

" 'Calcutta, India, Aug. 7, 1914.

" 'To 'SY,'

" 'WG' Tower:

" 'After several days of suffering with one of these terrible Eastern fevers, I passed away shortly after noon yesterday. The fever has left me and my sufferings are over. I am happy now. All messages from this Celestial World where I have been brought are transmitted by telepathy. There is no need of any mechanism here. Every one is happy and no one suffers. Here and only here, does the real Brotherhood of Man exist. Goodbye with love to you and everybody else on earth.

(Signed)   " 'JACK.'

"Many a night since then have I listened for a telepathic call or message from my friend Jack who has gone to that undiscovered country, from which no one returns. I know when the message does come that I shall recognize the 'sending.' "

"Yes, Jones," replied Bill slowly. "I too, have been waiting this many years for a message from my loved ones gone before. I know I shall recognize the 'sending' when it does come."

SIGNALMAN JONES' QUICK MOVE

I T was on the day of his fifth anniversary in the railroad service and on the day that the signalman at "WG" Tower began working eight-hour shifts instead of twelve. Jones had been assigned to the last "trick," which began at 11 P. M. and ended at 7 A. M.

It was a windy, snowy night, and at 11:05 P. M. Jones set the route for

Train No. 27, to cross from the Conway Branch to the outward main line. Number 27 made the customary stop at Bellville Station and approached the tower slowly. The rules of the road were that "trains crossing over at junction points should do so under full control." In obedience to this rule Bill Perry, the engineer of No. 27, had his train under control as the train approached the "home signal" of "WG" Tower. Just about that time an extra freight train on the main line reported to Jones.

On account of the route being set for No. 27 to "cross over," it was necessary for Jones to hold the extra freight at the main line signal until No. 27 had cleared, as these two routes conflicted. About the time the freight train approached the main line signal a sudden gust of wind blew the snow against the tower windows and Jones was unable to see what was going on outside. When the atmosphere cleared a few seconds later Jones noticed the extra freight was nearing the main line signal at a rather rapid rate.

"I wonder if they intend to stop?" he said half aloud. "If they slide by there's liable to be a smash-up." This was before the days of air brakes on freight trains, and the freight train crew were all out on top of the cars setting hand brakes to assist the engineer in stopping the train. Unfortunately it was down grade from the main line signal to the tower and the rails were wet and slippery from the snow.

The engineer of the freight train realized the brakes were not holding and the wheels were "skidding," and said, "She's getting away from us."

"What will we do?" yelled the fireman from the opposite side of the cab as he slid down from his seat and prepared to jump.

"Stick!" cried the engineer, as he gave a yank at the throttle, and reaching up for the whistle he blew two long blasts, the "off brakes" signal. The intention of the engineer was to increase the speed of his train and pass the tower before No. 27 "took the cross-overs." If he could do this it would save a wreck and the only damage would be a few broken switch points. Otherwise he would strike No. 27 "amidships" and probably kill and injure many of the passengers on that train. The freight

crew quickly realized what the engineer hoped to do, and they began running over the train letting off the brakes they had set to increase the speed of their train.

"There's only one chance in a thousand we can make it," yelled Fred Baker, the conductor as he flew over the train as fast as his short fat legs would carry him.

"If we 'cross their bow' and not hit them amidships even though they nose us behind the engine there won't be any one hurt," replied Frank Nelson, the middle brakeman, who had been a sailor, as he raced over the train, his long legs enabling him to cover the length of a box car in three strides.

Just about that time the water glass in the cab of No. 27's engine burst, and the cab was soon filled with steam, consequently neither Bill Perry nor his fireman could see the approaching freight train, or they would have stopped and allowed the freight to pass.

"Wide Awake Jones" heard the extra freight whistle "off brakes," and he realized it meant danger. Glancing at the position of both trains, and taking in the situation in an instant, he sprang for the levers and with a few mighty throws, he succeeded in diverting the route of No. 27 to the "long passing siding," just as the extra freight train rushed madly by.

In the meantime Bill Perry had succeeded in getting his water glass shut off, and when the cab was clear of steam, he found his train moving down the "long passing siding" instead of "across the road." "What in the devil are we doing here?" cried Bill to the fireman as he stopped the train.

Just then Jones signalled No. 27 to "back up" and with only a few moments delay they were on their way again. The passengers on that train never knew how near death they were on that cold winter's night.

Poison Jim Chinaman

By Owen Clarke Treleaven

TO a devotee of the Western yarn, the Old Timer is apt to prove disappointing; he has no beard nor top boots, and he figures the time of day by a · watch, instead of the number of drinks, and shades of Bret Harte, he doesn't drink.

In the old livery stables which once sheltered the four and Concord coach the print of which the S. P. used in advertising the newly established line, now stands at intervals the big ma-chines, that have succeeded the Old Timers first stage line from Sargent to Hollister.

There I met the Old Timer Leagan and he was pleased to meet me and yes—he'd be able to spare me some time and tell me something of the country.

"Well say," he said, "I was goin' down to see Jim, our famous old Chinaman down here, p'raps yuh'd like to go along, huh?

"I hafta go anyway and I can show yuh the old buildin's that was used as a retreat by the young fellers learnin' to be priests; they'd go down there durin' retreat when they couldn't talk yuh know and rest and pray; les crank the ole flivver and go." So we did, we cranked and went.

Arriving at the Chinaman's ranch and stopping at the familiar tin mail box, we went through a wooden turn-stile and up to the usual shack and lean-to that does duty on a ranch of that sort as home, harness shop, store room, and whatever else may be deemed essential in the Oriental con-ception of comfort.

Any pleasant thoughts I may have had concerning our prospective visit were quickly dispelled by our recep-tion. In answer to the Old Timer's loud "yuh home Jim?" the door was slowly opened wide, to be quickly closed again as Jim recognized in me, a stranger, that is nearly closed, for I became aware of a scrutiny that bid fair to be embarrassing, when he spoke in a cracked faded old voice: "H'lo Mist' Leagan."

"How're yuh today, Jim. I come down to see if yuh wanted anythin' over to Hollister. The boy's goin' with the stage and I thought might's well see if yuh wanted anythin'."

So he opened the door wider, never taking his eyes from me—the in-truder, and I saw a picturesquely typi-cal Chinaman of the old school daz-zling in contrast amid the squalor of the surroundings with the sheer rich-ness of his attire, his brocaded silk over jacket with the gilded buttons so necessary to the ensemble, and the un-der coats faintly in evidence in a fairy web of blue and white silk.

On a ranch, at that time encased in sticky mud by the rains, to see crease-less blue broadcloth trousers and white socks in the soft slippers of China, caused one to wonder anew at the Oriental vanity that makes for the poetry of the life of the unfathomable Chinese.

Back of him was a cook stove and several pots simmering and giving out the pungent smell of teas and herbs, that combine with the long stemmed little pipe and its choking odor in giv-ing one that lasting impression of the Chinese at home.

"Oh, sick, Mist' Leagan, too sick."

"What's the matter Jim, ketch cold I'll bet, huh?"

"Yeh, ketchum cold, Mist' Leagan, sick thlee, fouah day, hot, too hot you sabe, yeh ketchum cold."

"Well, that's too bad, Jim. Is there anythin' I can do fer yuh?"

"Oh, Mist' Leagan, you go Hollista' you gettee l'il China med'cine?"

"Well no, I'm not goin' but the boy is and he'll get yuh what yuh need."

"You no go, Mist' Leagan?"

"That's all right Jim, you tell me what yuh want and I'll see to it yuh get it."

"Aw li', me fixum li'l paper, you gettee med'cine, China med'cine."

So he shuffled around inside and presently appeared with a much folded bit of brown wrapping paper.

"Oh, Mist' Leagan, you sabe China boy med'cine man Hollista, you givum paper, you no losum?"

He showed plainly his reluctance to relinquish the paper until given additional assurance that the errand would be faithfully executed, and I appreciated the gentleness and understanding when the Old Timer patiently replied: "I sabe the feller, Jim, and 'course I won't lose it. Good bye Jim."

We started away, but before we had reached the stile Jim shouted: "Oh, Mist' Leagan come, you come."

We both went back and this time Jim came out of the shack. "Oh, Mist' Leagan me forglet China boy no home today. Gimmee paper, Fliday he home, you come Fliday Mist' Leagan?"

"All right, Jim, all right."

"Poor duffer," said the Old Timer, as we went out to the machine, "he was afraid I'd lose that note or the boy'd forget the medicine, and that's the only excuse he could think of to get it back. Oh, well, I'll come again Friday."

I thought and said as much, emphatically, that a quarrelous old heathen seemed to expect people to go to considerable trouble to dance attendance on one who would not be generally considered exactly in a position to command attention, and why did he propose returning Friday when he knew it was only anxiety over the note's safety that prompted Jim to call us back.

The Old Timer paused in the act of luxuriously rolling his much-chewed cigar to the opposite side of his mouth, removed it, spat calm and eloquent forbearance of my total lack of comprehension, and with ready candor admitted that p'raps it might do some good if he told me Jim's story and so began.

"Yuh see, Jim's alwa's lived here and alwa's been called 'Poison Jim,' and how come he got that name was like this:

"'Bout forty years back they was sheep in some parts of this country, cattle in others and all the valley land was in grain, solid stuff miles of it, pretty say to look out over thousands of acres of it on a mornin' when the sun was jes turnin' the heads, and the mountain breeze was makin' it wave like the little ripples yuh see on Monterey Bay when it's good fishin' yuh know, say it jes made yuh feel good.

"It was a happy place to live in them days, they was Spanish rancheros here and there, and they'd have barbecues and dances, fandangoes they called 'em, and I can remember on their fiesta days the ranch owners ridin' in to town on big black horses, their vaqueros on their ponies cuttin' didoes and shown' off before the women folks who'd be in the surreys and carryalls, and then the weddins' they'd have, days of feastin' and good times from one ranchero to another. Then in harvest time they all got in and helped each other 'stead of cuttin' throats like they do nowadays, and they'd make a fiesta out of the harvest.

"Then the Indians would come stragglin' back to town from the ranches where they worked; they had a reg'lar village down where Fourth Street is now, and they'd store the grain and stuff that served as wages, in the old Mission buildin' here and some of 'em worked 'round the Mission and so on.

"Oh, it used to be more like livin' them days.

"Now I was goin' to tell yuh how 'Poison Jim' got that name, wasn't I?

"Well, it seems he had more luck than anyone else 'round here mixin' poisoned grain to kill off ground squirrels. Them Chinese have more up their sleeves 'bout everythin' than we know anyway, so Jim earned a pretty good livin' poisin' squirrels. That is how he got the name of 'Poison Jim.'

"Then one spring came the mustard and it seemed to spring up over night all over the valley, and it began to look bad for the grain.

"These old Spaniards didn't use to be savin', they lived along in as much comfort as they could and generally without any thought for the morrow, 'manana,' as they called it, except as a time to do what they didn't want to do today.

"So this mustard had 'em worryin,' some called it a sort of a visitation and others argued 'bout a story they'd heard that the fathers goin' on foot from one Mission to another had scattered the mustard seed along the trails so they could find their way easier next year, and some of it had blowed over this way and got a start.

"Well, when it looked like this mustard was goin' to mean ruin to so many it was old 'Poison Jim' that stepped to the front, first off he seemed mildly surprised when the folks didn't do somethin' to rid the mustard off'n the land and then one day he learned that they didn't know how. Bright and early the next mornin' Jim climbs onto a pinto horse he'd got from an Indian here in town, and started makin' the rounds of the rancheros.

"By sometime the next day Jim had seen all the ranchers and got their consent to his cleanin' up their fields in his own way. He asked them all if he could have all the mustard seed. Well, the ranchers didn't know whether he was crazy or they was, when they heard that kind of talk, but they all says 'Go ahead, and pleese Jeem go queek.'

"The next day Jim had disappeared and the ranchers did some tall speculatin' on his whereabouts and prob'le plans, until a little over a week later the whole town turned out, Indians, dogs and all to witness what was prob'ly the queerest procession ever seen in San Juan.

"It was 'Poison Jim' leadin' ninety or a hundred Chinamen he'd corralled over near Monterey somewheres, they was crab fishin' or somethin'—I've forgot now what it was, and he'd brought 'em over here to clean up the mustard. Well Jim marches 'em out to the nearest ranchero, dumps all their stuff in an old corral and there they camped and rested that day.

"The next mornin' they went at it, and what d'ye think they was doin'?

"Cuttin' off the heads of the mustard and carryin' them to a sort of central place they'd cleared off in the field, and when they finished one field they'd take all the mustard to the corral they was campin' in and spread it out to dry, then on to the next field and so on.

"Well, they worked along like troopers, and when they got through there wasn't any mustard left in this whole valley, 'course the crop was gone for that year, but the mustard couldn't get a start next year 'cause the seed was gone, so the ranchers was all satisfied.

"Now I s'pose you'll wonder what Jim wanted with all that seed. Well, sir, them Chinamen turned in with hand flails and flailed the seed out of the pods, and sacked it up and stored it away and then one mornin' we woke up to find that we had only one Chinaman in town again, our 'Poison Jim.'

"Yuh know some people say all the Chinese race, now what d'ye call it, les see, syck or sickic, what do you call it now, huh? Oh, yes, phsycic, that's the word, well they say they know things ahead of time anyway—now I never did take much stock in that sort of thing, but jes the same I had a feelin' all along that Jim knew what he was doin' and he sure must have, for that fall, one day in October, I brought a man in in my stage, a Frenchman he was, who was in the condiment business in South Africa—made peppers and mustard and things into condiment. He had come all the way from Africa to California to look for mustard, because the crop had failed down there, mustard crop failed mind yuh, and landin' in San Francisco some one told him they'd heard about some mustard bein' threshed down here and here he was. Can yuh beat that, huh?

"Well, the long and short of it is, I took him to 'Poison Jim' and believe me, young man, Jim drove the all-firedest bargain I ever heard of. He got thirty-three thousand dollars from that poor misguided Frenchie, who started movin' the mustard right away. I met a man once who saw it on the docks at Panama. They must have packed it 'cross country down there.

"Jim bought the little ranch yuh saw jes now and started raisin' flax, all that money didn't seem to bother him any; he jes come and went 'bout his business like he alwa's done, but that deal was the talk of the whole country for a good long while.

"Things went along 'bout as usual for several years and then gradually things seemed to go 'topsy-turvy', first there were the two dry years and then the few things that did get above the ground burned up with the hot winds, and grain was a total loss.

"Then the sheep and cattle that were out in the hills on the thousands of acres of pasture were dyin' off in bunches—no grazin' for 'em yuh know, so the owners banded together and sent droves of cattle and sheep into the mountains in charge of some of the most trustworthy of the Indians.

"There were some of the old fellows who argued that all this hard luck came on account of the burning of the cross on the hill yuh see over yonder, yuh see they's another one there now, over there on that high hill to'ard ole Gabilan.

"Well, the fathers had put it up there as a sort of inspiring object for the Indians, and one stormy night a herder had burned it to keep warm, and then being scared, came in and confessed and had to put up another as a penance.

"Father Ubeck, he's the one described in 'Ramona' as the priest who married Ramona. Well sir, he had a use for that cross I bet yuh never heard of; yuh know he'd see Indians setten' 'round the Mission or somewheres, as all young folks will, yuh know, huh. Well he'd summon 'em before him and talk to 'em nice about the sacredness of love and the married state and all that, and then send 'em on a jaunt to this cross to sort of meditate, yuh know.

"Yuh see, they's a spring half way up, see that level space up there? Well, very few of 'em got clean to the top, they knew what to expect when they got back anyway, so they'd jes go back and Father Ubeck'd marry 'em, get the idear?

"So now things looked pretty blue and the ones that suffered the most were the poor whites and the Indians right here in town who had no work and no money and soon nothing to eat.

"Down in the Indian village conditions was awful, they was beginnin' to get sick and die off—God! I've seen little babies at the squaws breasts stiffen out and the squaws fall over with weakness—tryin' to dig the little graves.

"Yuh know the Indians never was treated very elegant as yuh might say, their lives didn't amount to much around here, 'specially with the early settlers, but we did what we could and that didn't go far, so then the state took a hand and built a sort of poorhouse and hospital for 'em.

"Now about fifteen years back there had been an epidemic of smallpox with the Indians, and one of 'em, a big buck, was bein' hauled out to be buried. However, he didn't happen to be dead, some sort of trance, I s'pose and he came to and clawin' his way out of the rags they wrap 'em in got his finger in his eye and lost the sight of it, so they called him 'One Eyed Jim.'

"And it so happened that this 'One

Eyed Jim' and an ole squaw they called 'Cross Eyed Mary' for a very good reason, were the first to be taken starvin' and sick to the new poor farm and they died within a week there.

"Well, sir, there wasn't another Indian would go there, they thought d'ye see, that it was a new scheme to get rid of the poor beggars and they'd hide out, to keep from bein' sent there and yuh can see that only added to their misery.

"Then came that day in October, a day I think I'll always remember— and I'd like to ferget it if I could.

"One of the inspectors out to the poor farm had come into town and gone down among the Indians to try and round up a few of the poor old feeble ones and one or two that had fever bad, and the Indians were scared of him, they were yellin' and dartin' in and out of their shacks, the squaws screamin' and dogs yelpin' so a lot of us went down to see the ructions.

"A little before this there had been a general row in one of the bigger shacks over a sheep one of the old fellers had swiped somewheres, and even then when I got there I could hear grunts and blows and see a buck come tearin' out with what was prob'ly a bigger piece of mutton than the owner thought was his share, and say it sure was pitiful to see them poor devils go for the feller that had the meat and try and tear a piece off while he was holdin' it up over his head and I never saw dogs go for anything like them poor beggars did, runnin' and tryin' to shove it all in their mouths to once.

" 'Poison Jim' had come to town that mornin' to see me about gettin' him some new harness on my next trip out and he follered me down to the rumpus and was standin' a little to one side, takin' it all in and his face was as calm and steady like as a wood statue. I remember thinkin' he didn't have much of a heart, because that scene was kinda—well, yuh know, ugly.

"I started over towards Jim when I see a rancher, a Spaniard he was—I never did have much use for that feller—who had been in town all night playin' and drinkin'. Well I see him comin' on a wabbly run 'hell bent for election' and roarin' drunk. We found out afterwards that a greaser, a hired man he was, on this rancher's place, had jes rode in to report that an old Indian had run off with a pet sheep that belonged to the Spaniard's little girl—so the rancher hearin' of the cause of the row in the Indian village, and his sheep, put two and two together and here he was comin' fightin' mad and follered by his man Friday.

"The inspector had gone into the back lane by this time lookin for the sick, and if he'd been out where we was, what came out of that mess might not have happened.

"The Spaniard came plowin' his way through the crowd that was there by this time, roarin' in Spanish for the son of a dog that dared to steal from him to come out, jes as the old Indian who stole the sheep succeeded in gettin' rid of the ones who was botherin' him, and shovin' the last one through the door with a shove that well nigh threw him — stood there in the doorway with the foreleg of a sheep in his hand.

" 'It is he Senor! he is the one that you seek' yells that little Mex to his employer, 'it is he.'

"We was all watchin' the Spaniard, we knew what was comin' all right, but yuh couldn't a'done anythin' 'specially for an Indian in those days, yuh know, well he didn't make any ado about it, — jes reached in under his coat they carried 'em under their arm pits, generally, and drew a long-barrelled army gun."

"Indian girl in the crowd screamed, every one else was holdin' in, somehow in the face of things like that people get so still it gives yuh the creeps and I recognized her as the old, Indian's daughter, — she was holdin' her baby in her arms—and straight as an arrow she went to that poor old feller standin' there, not quite understandin' the things that was goin' on —jes as that gun roared!"

"That heavy slug hit the girl first, turnin' her before she fell, and passed through to her father and tore a hole in his neck big as a dollar—they both jes crumpled up and sank where they stood, the baby rollin' to one side!"

"Then we saw what 'Poison Jim' was made of, the first sign of life in that crowd came from him. He very quietly walked up, lookin' straight ahead, and pickin' up the baby, went into the shack and closed the door."

"A few days later when that harness came for Jim, I took it down to that ranch of his but no one was home and nobody knew where he was, so I brought it up to the stable thinkin' he'd show up in a few days."

"Well, sir, he sure did show up! Four days later I seen somethin' on the road behind me comin' up from Sargent, but didn't see what it was 'till after I reached town and unhitched and I see it comin' up the road here."

"And then I saw 'Poison Jim'—a comin' along in a two-wheeled rig, and leadin' a string of twelve freight wagons each one with four hosses and a driver and in them wagons, Sir, was fifteen thousands dollars worth of provisions he'd bought in San Jose, 'bout cleaned the town out, I reckon, well old Jim went straight to that Indian village and stopped."

"Our old 'Poison Jim' was about the biggest thing in town that day, he'd drive up to a shack and say to the driver, 'you leavem sack bacon, sack floua, sack corn, and so on to the next shack, and all through, not only the Indian camp but the whole countryside, wherever help was needed."

"It was 'Poison Jim' and his money that kept those who couldn't help themselves, goin' till the rains came and the cattle and sheep come back and the whole country came back to itself, and since that time, it has alwa's been our old 'Poison Jim' the down and outs go to for help—and they get it!"

"D'ye see, young man why I'm goin' back there Friday?"

IN THE SUNSET'S GLOW

Let me watch the blushing river,
    In the Sunset's crimson hue,
Watch the waters gleam and quiver
    As I drift and dream with you.

With my oars both resting idly
    Let me feel the twilight's grace,
While its fading glory o'er me,
    Throws a halo on your face!

With that rosy light before me,
    Painting every cloud I view;
With that smile of heaven o'er me,
    Let me drift and dream with you.
                WASHINGTON VAN DUSEN.

Loleeta---An Indian Lyric

By Alice Phillips

NOTE.—The Klamath Indians Believed that they Descended from the Gray Wolf, and Many Beautiful Legends are told of this Animal. The Nighthawk, or Whip-poor-will, was said to Guard their Tobacco Patch. Loleeta was a Quarter Indian.

PRELUDE

Flow on, Oh River of my dream!
Where'er they silv'ry course may
   gleam,
Signs of a vanish'd race remain,
Tho, gone for'er their noble strain;

Their songs heard only in echoes
Chanted by thy stream, as it flows
Onward into the golden west,
The sunset harbor of thy rest!

Stories and songs manifold,
That ne'er in summer were told,
Repeat'd in accents drifting low,
By the winter fire's glow.

So, with a sad and solemn voice,
Spoken in words of her choice,
Repeat'd the legend of her race
With all its wondrous grace.

LOLEETA

In some sunlit forest grove,
Where the gentle south winds rove,
The first violet lifts its head,
Ere yet the April storms are fled.

Born of the sun and winter's rain,
It rears its modest head again,
And breathes upon the virgin air
Its fragrant offering of pray'r.

And thus, within the forest glade,
Loleeta, fair, the Indian maid
Dwelt, with heart untaint'd by love
And pure as the heavens above.

As fleet as the woodland fawn,
Often seen at early dawn
Bounding thro' the dewy vale,
She ran with the wild March gale.

But when the stars shone overhead,
Her white blood strove with the red,
And a longing, wild and sad,
Filled her soul where all was glad.

When a wolf, all gray and lean,
Crossed the starlight path between,

Loleeta in her olden tongue
Began with words half spok'n, half
   sung:

Listen, in the still cold moonlight,
Thro' the lone hours of winter's night!
Hear you his wild, defiant cry—
His song of Ages long gone by?

A time there was, when beasts alone
Liv'd here, before we came to own
Hunting grounds and fishing streams—
Alas, that time is come again, it
   seems!

Our race is fallen, we are gone,
Like Autumn's golden leaves are
   flown.
Yet unlike them, *we* come no more
When spring calls, laughing at our
   door.

When earth was void and with no
   light,
When o'er the deep reign'd blank
   night,
Ten moons rose in the western sky,
And as each tipt the Cade on high,

The wolf, with arrows and his bow,
Slew all of them, save one, from far
   below.
Thus you can see but one moon now
Rising above the mountain's brow!

A glowing orb, all cold and still,
It hangs above the distant hill,
Where the night-hawk, with coarse
   sound,
Guards the weed on coal-burnt ground.

And the cricket all night long
Is chirping its lonesome song:
"Chiteep-chiteep!" far and near,
A song it sings to charm the deer!

All day hiding its black head,
The cricket still mourns the dead;
But at night the hunter again
Hears the chirp of its magic strain!

The Volunteer

By Robert Wingate

OH, I don't see why you need to Tom! Ain't there plenty of others to go?" Mrs. Stirling pushed away her plate and gazed at her tall son through eyes suddenly afflicted with an unaccustomed dimness. Then turning swiftly to her husband—

"There ain't no call for it, is there Abner? Tom's got a plenty to do right at home without going off to that terrible war."

Mr. Stirling had not moved since his son's announcement. Now he drew a long breath and said slowly: "It don't seem's if he was needed right now for the army. But we can't tell, Sarah. These things ain't for us to decide. Maybe it looks to him like his duty."

"Oh, but when there's so many others I don't believe it's duty at all. Why should he go and let them stay?"

A grim smile now overspread Tom's homely and earnest countenance. "I guess if everyone said that, we wouldn't have much of an army to beat the Germans. They're not much afraid of the fellows that ought to go but don't."

"The President's called for volunteers," said his father, "but he's also said how important it is to keep up farmin' at the highest notch. Maybe you can do more good right here, Tom."

"Oh, I probably should be some good here, if I stayed," returned that square-jawed youth, "There's work enough between the farm and the lumber mill, but you know we haven't but forty acres anyway, and Buddy's gettin' to be about the same as a man. He's sixteen this spring, and he can drive the farm machinery just as well as anybody. You could get along pretty well."

"It ain't so bad as it would 'a be'n two or three years ago," said his father. "We've had two mighty good crops and good prices for 'em. The mortgage is lifted, and we've got quite a lot of things we needed."

"How 'bout Chet Thayer?" said Mrs. Stirling suddenly. "Has he got any idea of going?"

"I don't know, I'm sure," returned Tom, reddening, "He ain't said anything to me."

"He might git drafted," said his father, "they're talkin' of that in Congress, ain't they?"

"No, they wouldn't get him," replied Tom. "He's a skilled mechanic. He's buildin' him a pretty nice house in the village, and they say he's bought out Jim Wilson's garage."

"Oh, I'll warrant you he'll find some way out of it. He likes to drive that new, shiny car too well," cried Mrs. Stirling. Then turning suddenly to her son,—"Tom, why don't you go over this afternoon and talk this all over with Lily?"

Tom's face flushed yet more deeply under the tan, and his throat seemed badly obstructed when he answered —"Oh, I guess she wouldn't be at home. She's rather likely to be out on a Sunday afternoon."

"Yes," said Mr. Stirling, "I see her go by in the automobile with young Thayer, half an hour ago."

"Well, now!" exclaimed Tom's mother, "I think it's just a shame. I ain't never said anything before — I think young folks ought to manage these things themselves, if they show

4

any sense. But here you are going off to the war because Lily's taken a kind of a fancy that won't last six months for that young sprig with his pretty neckties and his shiny automobile. I s'pose he has got some money too, but nobody knows how long he will have. And you'll leave the field all clear for him; and he'll prob'ly marry her, and she'll be good and sorry ever after. She comes of good stock, Lily does, and really deserves better'n she's got sense enough to understand."

"Why! said Tom glumly. "I don't know as we've got any right to call Chet Thayer names just because he's a better looking fellow than I am, and has got more money, and the girls like him better."

"He ain't better lookin,' " returned Mrs. Stirling fiercely.

Tom laughed. "I guess you're just about the only one that'd say so, Mother, and you're a terribly prejudiced witness. Anyway, we don't know a thing against him except that he wears a white collar on week days and is the best dancer that ever comes to the Grange Hall. It don't seem's if a regular fellow could spare the time to learn to dance as well as he does—but maybe that's just a countryman's idea. Perhaps he'll volunteer too, and make a better soldier than I will."

"Oh, I know you, Tom Stirling,' cried his mother in a voice in which laughter and sorrow and pride were mingled. "Nobody'll ever know how much anything hurts you from anything you let on. You're just the same today as you was that time fifteen years ago when you and little Danny Smith got mad and got to throwin' stones. You've got the scar now on your forehead where one of 'em hit you. And you come home with your face all bloody, and said that you hit your head against a stone. And you never let on how it happened or that it hurt any, and when we found out from Danny, himself, a month afterward, you said you didn't tell about it because you warn't goin' to have him licked for somethin' that was just

as much your fault as his. Oh, that was just like you."

"Well," said Tom, "crying never gathered up any spilt milk. But that's neither here nor there. I'm going over to Morton tomorrow, and I shall probably *try*, anyway, to enlist. You might tell Buddy when he comes in." And, taking his hat from the nail, he went out by the back way and crossed the orchard into the woods.

The heart of any recruiting sergeant would be made glad by the sight of Tom Stirling. Tall and broad-shouldered and clear-eyed, moving with the nervous vigor that Europe has come to associate with American youth, he was the perfect type of the men of whom were to be formed the armies of the Republic. Labor on the farm and in the mill had hardened his muscles, and temperate and contented living had given him nerves fit for the endurance of hardship and peril. No shadow of doubt as to the righteousness of the cause had ever crossed his mind, and now the motive so quickly divined by his mother added its deciding weight. All questions of his duty to the country and all his personal problems should be solved by one act. For this he claimed no credit and desired no sympathy.

The shadows were cool under the pine trees. As he slowly paced the familiar path that led by the side of the brook and beyond to the chestnut woods, the pulses which had been pounding at his temples like the steam hammers of the forge shops gradually subsided. At the delicious call of a bluebird Tom stopped to locate the songster, as by long established habit, and forgot his intention of the previous moment of pulling off the starched Sunday collar which had seemed to be stifling him. From the half-formed leaves and buds came the medicinal odors of the forest; the familiar flowers of May made their offerings of beauty; the brook sank still the song he had always known and which had accompanied so many of his childish musings.

The pathway led down past the

Fort Rock, — scene of boyish campaigns of desperate attack and defense—through the birch thicket that had sheltered many an ambuscade, and up into the grove of giant chestnuts where, on frosty October mornings, Tom and his mates had so often gathered cherished stores in gay defiance of the squirrels' chattered protests.

As he walked on his heart grew lighter than it had been for weeks. All the arguments and uncertainties, all the self-questionings and condemnings, all the fiery, leaping hatred of his successful rival were gone or fast going. His country needed him, and he would go. Lily should have her happiness undisturbed by him, and he would live out the brief and lurid career of his boyhood dreams, — the camp, the voyage and the field,—battle, victory and defeat, glorious struggle — and the singing messenger of death.

For an hour he strode along half-overgrown forest ways. Through the interlacing branches the sky overhead was of an entrancing blue. From the lowlands at the right came the liquid notes of a thrush. Tom walked on with such a glow of happiness in his breast as he had thought never to know again. No longer the awkward lout he had called himself,—with no choice but a pretended indifference in the face of defeat,—no longer the helpless and ridiculous spectator of another's triumph—the guest-to-be at Lily's wedding, with smiling face and clumsily-expressed good wishes that would deceive no one—but a soldier of the Republic,—one of those whose names would appear in those ominous lists with the heading—Killed in Action—as in the old papers of Civil War times he had found long ago in the garret. Perhaps they would raise another Soldiers' Monument in the town square, and amongst the names to be read by every passer would be that of Thomas Stirling——

Would *she* read it sometimes, perhaps? Would she pause when crossing the square with her husband, or possibly her children — Here Tom's heart gave a most painful wrench, and his new-found happiness threatened to desert him utterly—and read that name, cut so clearly and evenly in the granite, and perhaps — wipe away a tear, as she passed on? He could see her now, before his eyes, hurrying along beneath a bleak December sky of low-hung clouds — a little shawl about her shoulders, her face lined and aged before its time and her dark hair streaked with grey—

Tom sat down on a fallen tree and began to call himself bitter names,— quite in the old manner of the days before his decision. The glory had gone from the day. The sun was hidden by a cloud, and one of the chill winds of inconstant May came sighing through the valley.

After a few minutes he rose and started briskly on. He had come a long way, but now he planned to return by a different and longer route. He told himself that the woods along the North Branch were fine at this time of year, and maybe he would get some of the haw blossoms that Mother liked so, in the Mansfield pasture. Anyway he had plenty of time today, and might not be going that way again for a long while. Already his willing feet were carrying him along a well-known path.

An hour later Tom was sitting on the Spring Rock under a clump of oaks, a quarter mile from the roadway. The setting sun was shining cheerily again, and the scattered trees of the pasture sheltered a full-throated choir of feathered songsters. Half visible through the orchard trees, was the abode of the one girl of any consequence in the world, and off to the left lay the path across the field that had often proved such a long shortcut on the way home from church or singing school.

Tom had just decided in the negative, for the third time, the question whether he should go to the Mansfield house to bid Lily good-bye. He would stop on his way to Morton in the morning. She would be in the kitchen with her mother; he would call her out to the gate, and tell her what little there was to be told. It would look queer for him to go away and never say a word. Folks would probably talk a whole lot anyway. There was no need of making any more of it.

She might ask him to write to her from over there. If she did, should he promise to do so? If he did write, would she reply? Wouldn't any such letters serve to keep his mind entangled with all the jealousy and misery that he meant to leave behind with his civilian clothes? No, he wouldn't write to her. He would have a reduction made from the photograph he still had hidden in his desk at home, and keep it in the back of his watch. That would have to suffice.

Still he made no homeward move, and the question of going to the Mansfield house was just coming up for a fourth decision, when suddenly a voice was heard at the pasture bars.

"Co-boss, Co-boss."

Shrill-voiced Jimmy Mansfield usually escorted old Dapple back and forth from barn to pasture, but though this call was surely of treble pitch, Tom never for a moment believed it proceeded from the throat of that young mischief-maker. Cautiously pulling a bough aside, he could see Lily standing by the bars, a dozen rods away, impatience plainly written on her face.

"Oh, plague take it!" she said, all unconscious of any auditor, "Where is that old cow? I s'pose she's way down in the swamp, and doesn't intend to come in till morning." And, noisily throwing down the bars, she came down the slope, straight toward Tom's hiding place—

"Hello, Lily!"

"Goodness! Tom Stirling, how you startled me! What are you doing there?"

"Oh, just resting a bit," said Tom as he came forward, "I've been over by the North Branch. Say Lily, I was just thinking of stopping to see you tomorrow. Maybe though I could tell you what I had in mind just as well now."

Lily's dark eyes twinkled maliciously. She had never looked so distractingly pretty.

"Oh, I've got to hurry and get that cow. It'll soon be dark."

"I'll get your cow for you all right," said Tom, "but for now I'd very much appreciate it if you'd sit down here for a minute. I've got a little piece of news for you."

"Now see here, Tom," said Lily, more seriously, "it really won't do any good to tell me your news. I know what it is anyway. And I've got to hurry back. I'm expecting company this evening."

"If you know what I was going to tell you," said Tom, considerably taken aback, "you must be a mind-reader —unless—unless Mother's been over to see you this afternoon."

"No, she hasn't been here, but I know just the same what a great man you're going to be. I'm glad as I can be for you. Father says you'll surely do well. But really its no use to go over again the things that we talked of when you were at my house the last time. You surely know me better than to think I'm going to change my mind on account of a thing like this."

"How does your father know what I was planning? And how do you know? If you'll please tell me," said Tom humbly.

"Oh, we knew before you did yourself. Mr. Ormsby was over yesterday to get Father's advice, and Father told him you were exactly the man for the place, that the only fault you had was being so young, and that you would probably outgrow that in time."

Tom's eyes opened wide with astonishment. "Mr. Ormsby!" he exclaimed. "Now I know you're talking about something altogether different from what I am. What is it that Mr. Ormsby is planning to put me into?"

"Oh, Tom Stirling! Don't you know really? I thought of course you were going to tell me about the new place at the lumber mill. Perhaps I ought not to tell you, but I've already told most of it, anyway. I think it's such a fine chance for you, and just what you've been wanting. You know you used to tell me last winter how you'd like to be manager of the lumber mill, and all the things you could do to make money for the company if you were. Well, it seems that Mr. Ormsby has bought a controlling interest in the mill. He's got some Government contracts, and he's going to run it the year 'round right along. Now it seems that he's taken notice of you working there in the mill the last three winters, and he's been making up his mind you're the man he wants for manager. He says the place will pay a good salary, and the use of that brick cottage near the big mill goes with it. He said he was going to send for you to come and see him last night."

Tom drew a long breath — "Maybe he did. We were all away at the War Issues Meeting at Morton. So that's what he had in mind when he was talking with me at the Town Hall last week. Well, I'm very much obliged to Mr. Ormsby for considering me for that place, and to your father for recommending me. If things were different, it would be exactly what I'd want, but, as it is, I can't take it. I'm going away."

"Oh Tom! Aren't you foolish to do that? Think what a good chance this is for you to get ahead. You won't find another like it right away."

Lily was now seated on the rock beside her once favored lover, and looking earnestly at his bronzed and manly countenance. The thought flashed through her mind that he certainly was growing better looking.

"I know I won't," said Tom. "If things were different, I'd take it in a minute. It's just the thing that I've been thinking I might get some time, —maybe ten years from now. As it is,——"

But Tom's further explanation was interrupted by a loud whinny which came from a clump of birches near the brook. A young mare emerged from the thicket and came trotting toward them. She was jet black from head to heel, and the perfect proportions of her lithe young body, with her arching neck and flowing mane and tail, made a picture well worth seeing.

"Oh, isn't she a beauty!" exclaimed Lily, as the mare halted a few feet away, "I only wish I had some sugar. That's what she wants, you know. We've made a regular pet of her. Come here, Susie."

Susie advanced slowly, snuffing eagerly for the coveted sugar, and allowed her neck to be encircled by the arm of her young mistress.

"She's just the darlingest horse," went on Lily, "just the prettiest in town! But Oh, Tom! I've got to send her back to you."

"Send her back? What for?"

"Why you know, Tom, — the way things are—it isn't right for me to accept valuable presents. And Father says she's worth two hundred dollars."

"Well, if she is, she wasn't worth half that when I gave her to you a year ago, and then you had a perfect right to accept her. She was only a yearling colt then, but now you've kept her for a year, and your father's had her broken this spring."

"Yes," said Lily with a sigh, "Father said I could drive her myself after a little while. She's such a dear! She never would hurt anything. But just the same, Tom, I don't believe it's the right thing to keep her. Do you, now?

"Sure, I do," returned Tom sturdily. "Giving's keepings in my family—always has been."

"Well, I'll talk to Mother about it," said Lily. "But I know well enough she'll say I ought to send her back. She hinted something about it the other day."

"I'll tell you what!" exclaimed Tom, struck by a bright thought, "We'll leave it that she's mine. But I haven't any use for her and couldn't take care of her now. You just keep her and treat her as yours until I send for her."

"Oh, I know what you're planning, Tom Stirling!" cried Lily, "I see just what you mean to do. You'll never call for her at all. That's just your scheme for getting your own way about it. You old stubborn, generous thing!"

Here Susie, finding herself no longer the center of attention, gave up her hopes of sugar and turned and trotted away. The young people resumed their seat on the rock. Old Dapple and her milking time were forgotten.

"Well," said Tom, "it's perfectly true that I wouldn't know what to do with her. I'm going away, and probably for quite a while. That was all the news I had. I just wanted to tell you good-bye."

"Oh, Tom! Are you really? Where are you going?"

"To France, I hope. I'm going to Morton and enlist."

"Oh, what for? There's no need of it, is there,—so soon?"

"The President seems to think so."

"Yes, but think of all the others who might just as well go."

"Perhaps they're thinking of me in the same way."

"Tom Stirling, you give up this idea. You're needed at home, and you've got good chances right here at home."

"So have lots of the others. It would be a poor army that was made up of fellows who were no good at home."

Minutes passed, and they sat in silence. Twice Lily drew a long breath and opened her lips to speak, but conflicting impulse choked back the words. At last she said in a smothered voice—

"I — never thought of your doing anything like that, Tom. What does your mother think?"

"The same as a million other mothers."

"Oh, Tom! That sounds as though you didn't care."

"I do though, but the fact is this war has got to be fought through, and

she hasn't any better right to have her sons kept at home than the others have."

During the next minute or two Tom could distinctly hear the ticking of the watch in his pocket. His lips were straightly set, and he gazed steadily at a maple tree in the hollow before him.

When Lily began speaking it was with a little catch in her voice that to a more subtle observer might have told volumes:

"Chet Thayer says he doesn't believe that there's any need of people getting excited and rushing into the army—that the war will be over before any American troops can get into it."

"Maybe he's right, but they don't seem to think so in Washington."

"Say," said Lily softly, "When Chet came over Friday night he brought oh—a beauty of a diamond ring. I'll bet it cost a hundred dollars. And he wanted me to wear it."

The hammers were pounding in Tom's temples again.

"Yes," he answered in a half-choked voice, "and what did you tell him?"

"I told him 'Not yet'."

After half a minute Lily whispered:

"Tom, are you going away to the war?"

"Yes, Lily, you know I've got to."

More minutes passed in silence. Then suddenly occurred the most amazing thing in all of Tom's twenty-four years of experience. Lily's arms were flung about his neck, and her tear-wet cheek was pressed against his own. He held her close in a wild embrace. The grass and streams of the pasture shimmered in a flood of purple and gold.

"Oh, Tom! Oh, Tom!" she sobbed, "If you go to Morton, I'm going with you. I've—I've used you terribly, but now you'll see. I'll marry you tomorrow, and then — when you're in the war you'll know you've *got* to come back to me."

Though Tom's response was poor in words its meaning was wholly beyond mistake, for to some situations the language of gesture is beautifully appropriate. The last rays of the setting sun gleamed on the pale green of the new leaves; the shadows fast lengthened on the greensward, and it was already night under the pine trees. On the two young faces seemed to glow the light of an unimagined happiness.

LITTLE DANDELION

Yellow little flower
  Nodding in the sun,
How much you would be wanted,
  Were you but two or one.

But blooming by the thousands,
  On lawn and garden path,
Where in spite of all our care
  You toss your head and laugh;

We hardly can be thinking
  There's heart as pure as gold,
Or in your growing
  Worth still left untold.

Nodding little flower
  Blooming in the sun,
I wish your wandering career
  Hadn't quite begun.

You keep me ever busy,
  With knife and pick and hoe;
I wish I knew a proper place,
  Where dandelions may grow.

ELIZABETH HUEBNER.

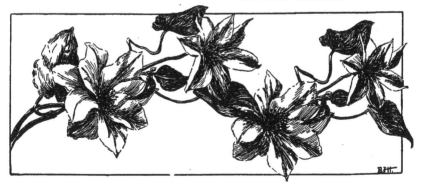

Jumping a Claim

By Frank M. Vancil

Bold, adventurous men were they,
  Pioneers of a hidden land;
Seeking in a devious way—
  A valiant, fearless band.

IN the early settlement of the Great Plains of Kansas and Nebraska there were often exciting contests over lands homesteaded by the immigrant. Attractive situations, containing timber and water, were limited, and were often the object of strife and litigation.

There was a kind of Freemasonry among the primeval inhabitants—a sort of brotherly love and interest, and a disposition to assist each other in toil and privation. Alike poor in worldly goods, the greatest hospitality prevailed, and nowhere is the trite saying more in evidence that "a fellow feeling makes one wondrous kind" than on the wild frontier.

Hence, it was but natural that any and all efforts of a new comer to appropriate the labor and home of a previous settler, however humble, were viewed by the neighbors with great disfavor. Owing to the poverty of most homesteaders, and the failure to secure employment near, many were forced to leave their claims for a few months, a privilege which the law allowed.

It often happened that during this enforced absence some avaricious "tenderfoot," spying the inviting location, would summarily take possession of the sod house or "dug out," the few etceteras within, and proceed to make himself at home, upon what he termed an abandoned claim. Of course, upon the return of the original occupant there was trouble and lots of

it, for be it known that those frontiersmen were a fearless lot, and were not out there to do missionary work.

While sojourning in this land of luxuriant zephyrs and periodical blizzards, an aggravated case of claim-jumping came under my observation. A horny-handed yeoman from the East had taken up a homestead on a beautiful stream in western Nebraska; built himself a sod house and stable, and with his wife, three children, two ponies, a cow and three dogs, solemnly wagered Uncle Sam the sum of sixteen dollars that he could stay a citizen there for five years, hot winds, blizzards and coyotes to the contrary notwithstanding.

Game was plentiful, and subsisting chiefly on a meat diet, the summer was passed in health and free abandon. But the winters in that treeless country are long and severe, and lucrative employment a negligible quantity. So, to escape its incident hardships and to accumulate a little capital by which to improve his ranch, this tenant by sufferance, along "when the frost in on the punkin," locked up the door of his shack, loaded in most of his earthly belongings, and, followed by old Brindle, Blanch, Tray and Sweetheart, hied himself and family back to his wife's relations beyond the Big Muddy, fully intending to return with the bluets in the spring and to pitch a crop.

Along in the early winter, when old Boreas was holding high carnival with the struggling willows and cottonwoods, an adventurous prospector spied the inviting situation and very unceremoniously took possession. He was kindly informed of a previous occupancy, and urged not to infringe upon the rights of another but it was of no avail. He stoutly affirmed that the claim was forfeited by removal, and that, knowing a good thing when he saw it, he was there to stay.

Being alone, the trespasser supported himself by trapping and hunting during the winter; and, being of a suspicious looking character, his acquaintance in the neighborhood was limited. He had all the earmarks of being a bad man, a fugitive from justice, and to dispossess him was calculated to prove a deal of trouble if not tragedy. The absent settler was a veteran soldier and had smelt powder upon more than one occasion, and was not to be intimidated.

About April 1st, when the balmy breath of spring was beginning to clothe the valley in freshened verdure, and daisies had begun to dot the hillsides, the absent settler drove back only to find within his home an incorrigible occupant. The condition was a serious one. Here was a man, intrenched and defiant, clearly in the wrong, but having the nine points of law in his favor, that of possession, desperate and unscrupulous by nature, on the one side, and a battle-scarred soldier at the head of a family on the other, each unyielding in demands.

A parley at the threshold ensued, and strong language and bitter threats were exchanged. The surly dweller asserted that he "was not born in a thicket to be scared by a cricket," and the old veteran retorted that he had faced many a musket, and proposed to regain possession of his home, peacefully if he could, forcibly if he must.

Universal sympathy was with the ousted settler, and it was but a short time until a company of a score or more of bronzed homesteaders had allied themselves with the dispossessed, and expressed a willingness to assist in ridding the neighborhood of such a doubtful character. To avoid a tragedy, it was decided to use strategy if possible. The shack, in which the trespasser was fortified, was not of a combustible material, hence to burn him out was impossible. To storm the inclosure would doubtless result in fatalities, therefore it was resolved to smoke him out.

The sod structure had but two small windows, one on each side, so the building could be safely approached from the gable unseen. The stovepipe extended above the roof near the center of the comb of the building. An old cook stove below was used in preparing meals and in warming the room, which was only some 20 by 30 feet in dimension. Around this stove, the claim-jumper sat with his rifle at his elbow, scarcely attempting to peep outward, for fear of being met by a volley of lead.

On a dark and stormy night, a short time after the return of the homesteader, a full dozen of strenuous and determined men surrounded the rustic abode, armed with a goodly supply of weapons, powder and sulphur. To creep cautiously up to the gable end of the building and to mount the low roof, guarded by a platoon of pointed rifles, was not a heroic task, and was accomplished without difficulty. Neither was it difficult to crawl along the comb of the roof to the stove-pipe and to pour down therein a pound of sulphur upon the smouldering coals

This clandestine act producted a commotion within—a hurrying to and fro and a gasping for fresh air; but which was not a circumstance to the scene following—the dropping of a pound of powder down the same avenue. There was a flash—a terrible explosion, amid a scattering of dirt and ironware. A breathless, coatless, blackened specimen of humanity was met near the door and the ultimatum prepounded to him in vigorous monosyllables. He was at first disposed to argue the question of exit, until seeing a lengthy lariat in the hands of one of the party, he quickly agreed to abdicate the realm instanter, and he did. He was assisted out beyond the limits of the neighborhood, and advised to hit only the high places in his journey west, and he kept on going.

Silver Peak Ranch

The Romance of Silver Peak

By Henry W. Mahan, Jr.

PART II.

N O, No, Miss. I said I'm to shoot him a signal when I get the names of the folks on this stage if there's a certain party aboard."

The girl seemed more interested and excitement had caused her to make more room than she realized was really there. "Well, what, what — name did he think would be in here?" She hesitated. The question sounded strangely to her.

The old man looked about and tried to get a good look at her.

"Miss Gladys Wallace! He's been a telling me for some time — Five Blasts if she's aboard — Five Blasts, now Ames, don't forget. And I ain't forgotten neither."

The girl said nothing. She was quivering with joy but her nerves were restraining her speech.

The stage was nearing its destination now and the rain was ceasing slightly. "That's the Hotel up there," the driver remarked. "We'll make it in just a few minutes now." They skidded around curve after curve and down the trail that surrounds the steam cave baths and up through the mesquite-lined trail, until the music and laughter of the guests had floated down to them. No sooner had the passengers planned their arrival than the stage had swung up before the Hotel and into the garage. The driver sounded his klaxon three times.

"What's the idea?" queried the old man.

"I'm to give Mr. Gleason three blasts when we hit the hotel safely."

"I thought you said 'five blasts.'

That guy up there'll get his signals twisted if you ain't careful."

"No. It's five if Miss Gladys Wallace is aboard. Now then let's see." He had climbed from behind the wheel and unfastened the curtains and commenced to remove the luggage.

The girl had already alighted and assembled her equipment. "Well, Mister Driver!" He looked at her wonderingly. "I'm Miss Gladys Wallace," and she extended her hand. He grasped it more than heartily.

"Well, well. Mighty, mighty, glad to know you, Miss. He's been a looking for you. And now here goes."

He stepped over to the wheel and placing his gauntlet on the klaxon sounded off five sharp blasts.

He looked around and laughed a real mountaineer's laugh. She was stooping and gazing sharply up the mountain side toward the row of lights while he sounded the call.

"He's a shaking hands with himself all right, Miss." And Ames completed unloading the luggage. The girl, with a tear or two rolling down her cheek followed the page into the lobby of the hotel.

When Gladys Wallace had completed her toilette and prepared herself for her evening meal, she descended into the lobby of the hotel and found her way to the dining room. It was a huge affair, with massive pillars that lent a dignified scenic appearance. The guests were many in number and there were notables whom she had read of and seen upon the screen and stage in the city. Here

and there a table with a well-known
screen star, and occasionally a call
for some person of note was sounded
by a page.

She was engaged in contemplation
over her journey. She had waited a
long time for this very event to take
place. Here she was now all ready
for the conclusion of the story she had
dreamed so about. She felt of her
bosom. They were there all right, a
package of his latest letters, and some
of them postmarked with this very
hotel. Her dreaming caused her to
search about for the box—there it was
right by the desk and he had mailed
them there. She had been abroad for
many months, had returned and now
was ready to complete her dreams of
the sweetest thing in life.

When she had finished her dinner
she retired to the main lobby where
there were folks engaged at bridge,
writing letters, and enjoying billiards.
There were conversations running
from tennis to golf, and back to hunting, and the chase above the springs
and the outdoors in general. And
there was regret for the rainstorm mingled with that indescribable sensation
that springs from an open fire in a
mountain inn.

She had fallen to thinking. One
more day and he would be there. An
Episcopalian clergyman passed her
chair and joined a group before the
fireplace.

She followed him with her witching
eyes. She concluded that this was the
gentleman that Carter Gleason had
told her of, and who would join them
in marriage. She wanted to speak to
him, but she enjoyed her visionary
dreaming and was contended to sit and
dream. She had retraced her steps
to this wonderful hotel and figured
over her enchanting future, when there
suddenly seemed to have arisen a
commotion near the front entrance
that distracted her attention.

"It's Mister Glenn," she heard murmured about her. "Graham Glenn —
he was found laying in the roadway
above the hotel a mile or two, possibly fallen from his horse."

The girl was startled. "Graham
Glenn here?" She was somewhat
dazed. She arose and hurried to the
scene of the entrance. She looked
through the crowd that had gathered
where two men had placed the injured
fellow upon an easy couch.

The Hot Springs Doctor had been
summoned upon learning of the young
man's injuries and was attending him.

"What is your name my lad?"

"Graham Glenn, Sir."

The girl could not mistake the voice.
She looked again and could see him
now. Sure enough it *was* Graham
Glenn. The one fellow in the world
whom she had devoted her time with
before she had become engaged to
Carter Gleason.

"Could it be possible that Graham
Glenn was here also?" She shook
herself. This was no time for questions. Graham Glenn lay there injured.

"It's all right, my lad," assured the
Doctor. "No bones broken. But a
bad shock. When were you going
down again?"

"I had contemplated returning tomorrow, Doctor. I don't like to wait.
Couldn't I make it tonight? I am
needed back in the city right away."

"Well, you're not suffering much.
It's more of a shock. You have your
car here, have you not?"

"Yes, my Roamer Limousine, in the
garage."

"Well, with a nurse you can do it.
What train do you want to get?"

"I want to catch the 3:30 limited
in the morning at San Bernardino. I
think I'm all right, Doctor."

"There are no nurses here at present. Let me see" — and the Doctor
was thinking.

The girl watched the two and listened to the conversation. She was
likewise thinking. He had saved her
brother's life at one time. He was in
need of help—a nurse, any assistance,
to catch the 3:30 train. She thought,
and as she thought she stepped
through the crowd of guests that had
gathered and touched the Doctor on
the shoulder.

He turned toward her. "Doctor, I know this young man. If you will let me, I should like to do him this service that he needs as nurse. I'm not a nurse but I can assist him to catch his train I'm sure."

The doctor looked at Glenn and as he did so Glenn caught sight of the girl. He was not as awkwardly surprised as he might have been she thought to herself, but of course he had been injured.

The two exchanged greetings, in a haze of excitement. The doctor assented. She had explained to Glenn that she was returning for the ceremony of which he had already heard the day following and he had volunteered to her his car for her return trip. With an expression of congratulation he took her hand.

"Thanks, Gladys. It's mighty good of you. You can make it in the Roamer if you're not afraid to try it."

She returned to her room and gathered such paraphernalia as she thought she would need. She surveyed the room to see that she had left nothing. Her wrist watch was laying on the dresser, and she returned to get it. She looked at it. "Just twelve o'clock," she said.

"Rather late to be trying an adventure of this sort, but if it's got to be, it's got to, that's all." She assured herself. As she flashed the lights out in the room a streak of lightning hit overhead. She stepped to the window. The room was dark, and she watched the light over the country below. She followed it back up the mountain side.

"Too bad, too bad," she mused. "Must have hit something up there. The top of that mountain burns a flaring red."

When she had found her way back to the lobby and onto the side veranda Glenn was waiting in his car. She was assisted by a page who helped her to the seat beside the wheel.

"Here boy, give this note to this gentleman when he calls. His name is on the envelope," and he slipped the boy a quarter.

"Yes, sir, I—"

The boy did not finish the sentence, whatever he would have said. A tremendous crash sounded up the mountain side as though the whole had collapsed.

Glenn shuddered, seemed faint, and finally spoke. "I guess that fall is on my nerves, Gladys, that thunder sure seemed to frighten me a great deal."

"Was that thunder, Graham? It sounded different from thunder. I noticed a red flaring light on the mountain top. Maybe something caused a landslide."

"Maybe, so." Glenn was clearly not himself. They were started on the downward journey. He looked back and seemed to recoil as he put his attention again on the soaking roadbed. "Probably a fire there," and he motioned in the direction of the flaring light.

"What is that up there, Graham?" She seemed interested in the light as she asked the question.

"That's Silver Peak."

"Oh yes," and she fell to thinking. Her words were muffled.

Graham Glenn and his girl assistant were hitting the road for the three-thirty west bound Santa Fe Limited.

When Carter Gleason had planted his red torch on the crest of Silver Peak he unbuttoned his heavy coat and stood before the light the brilliant torch afforded. It was burning a steady red, and over it he rubbed his chilled hands for it offered some warmth. He felt that he had accomplished a worthy errand—he reflected, as he stood gazing down below into the maze of sleet and fog. The valley was dim with its diamond like radiance now, and the chasm below him was as quiet as a graveyard in the early morn. It was dark as pitch save for the torch.

"They'll be getting the signal now," he ventured to himself. "And they'll all be glad the road is going through I guess. Ned's probably got the boys there now for the big blast. Great fellow, Ned—he'd help his enemy before himself."

Gleason still pondered as he watched the maze below him. He was clearly in a confused state of mind. Way up here in the end of nowhere almost, giving a signal to help his fellow ranchers, and preparing the way for his search that would follow him down there.

"They must be having a time to get the fuse laid right," he thought out loud. He went back to where he had hitched his horse. His knapsack was fastened to his saddle, and from it he took the flask of whiskey, and a generous gulp, for the night was testing his physique. He braced up and then reached for his revolver. There was no telling what he might meet before a blaze like this. He couldn't meet a prowler single handed, and his Colts Automatic was a steady friend. He raised it skyward to test it out, then pulled the trigger. A mightier sound than he had expected reached his ears from below the hazy mist.

"They're going through," he fairly shouted. Then turned and put his hand upon his horse's head. They've cut her through Pal. Didn't you hear it? We'll be passing that cut tomorrow, for the garden of my—"

Gleason was mumbling in contemplation. He strode forward before the torch. The fog had gradually lifted. Fumes of powder had reached his nostrils. He pierced the panorama with his vision, and it fell far below. He could imagine many things.

"Must have scared them out down there," he thought. "Maybe the 'Mark Twain' on a midnight run for supplies. Never knew her to hit the lower road this time of night before.' He was tracing a dim ray of light on the auto road below that was close by the hotel. It flickered from his vision. He looked about to see that he had left nothing, fixed the torch more firmly in the tree stump he had chosen, then remounted his horse, and set forward to retrace his steps to Silver Peak Ranch. His horse was weary from the steady climb, but faithful unto death. Now up, now down, curve after curve, and switchback, through mud and snow with an occasional branch hitting either of them, but the sure footsteps of the horse always gaining headway. Gleason was more lighthearted but at once uneasy in his return to the ranch. He argued with himself.

"That can't be! If they've got it through, why should I waste time over night here?" He seemed to be in a puzzled state of mind. The horse, with its burden, seemed to realize a journey of achievement. Its step would have signified an answer to his questions.

"Do you think you can do it, Pal? Do you want to push onto Ned's cabin tonight?" The horse was closer to the ranch house now. She seemed to know the path without any effort, and was jogging more easily. As she swung around a final turn they came upon the south gate, and she galloped like a happy boy onto the path that landed them presently at the front door. Gleason sat in his saddle for a moment. He was thinking. He reassured himself.

"I'll do it." He looked at his watch. "Just two-fifteen A. M.," he said. As he queried a figure approached him from the veranda. He reached for his Colts.

"Halt!" he shouted hoarsely, for the air had clouded his voice. "Who's there?"

"Pablo, Senor," and the answer was somewhat terrified.

"Pablo? Well, what are you doing up this time of night?"

"I fix Senor's stuff in package. I watch light from Silver Peak and hear the noise and think Senor go right on."

"What do you mean, Pablo? You think I'm going right on? Why?"

"Well, Manuel come here again tonight with message. I have 'em here, Senor," and he brought forth another scrap of paper which he tendered to Gleason. He read it.

"Tell Mr. Gleason he had better

come right on. Have a trace of his cattle thief. Ned (Ranger)."

"But I thought Ned wasn't letting me know about the herd, Pablo. Did Manuel say anything else?"

"Si, Senor, Manuel say 'Mister Gleason must go right down. You tell 'em, Pablo'."

Gleason hesitated a moment, tapped the note against the saddle, and looked down at Pablo who was obediently awaiting orders.

"You go, Senor?'

"Yes. I'm hitting the road tonight. Right now, Pablo. Let me have the stuff." And he reached down and pulled the package of clothing to the saddle. "Tell Nela, I'll be sending her a message when I'll be making the trail to return. She'll understand." And Gleason touched the reins to his horse.

"Adois! Senor. I fix 'em all right." He was on the veranda again.

As the lower gate closed some sparks fell over it. He puffed on his pipe in the drizzle that covered him.

"Stay with it, Pal. We've got to pass that cut pretty quickly. We'll call it quits at Ned's cabin and you'll have all the rest you ever want. It's not so long now."

They jolted on together. The snow had started to melt into a slidy slush but the horse found herself equal to the journey. Gleason looked at his watch by the light his dimly burning pipe afforded.

"Quarter to three!" They were swinging into the snow-bound section, and timber was strewn in shattered bits on either side of the trail. The path was open but uncertain. They wandered somewhat slowly, until voices reached them.

"We've made it, Pal. A bit more and we'll be under the roof at Ned's." No sooner had Gleason spoken than they were winding past driftwood and shattered trees that the blast had cast aside, and he heard the Mexican lingo floating across the cold air to him. He now began to recognize the way and before many minutes was on the homeward stretch into the Ranger's

land. Before him a light and a few more yards and they were standing in his yard in a pool of slush and rain.

"Who goes there?" It was the ranger himself.

"Carter Gleason!" He had not finished repeating his name when Ned approached him.

"Mean work, Mister Gleason. We had a devil of a time forcing her open but you've found us able, I guess."

"More than able, Ned. It's mighty fine of you, old man, but how about the herd. You're good to have kept me unawares. I'd a gone crazy if I'd a known it sooner. Nela told me just tonight. What about them?" Gleason had alighted and was nervously confused. He led his horse back to the stable, accompanied by the ranger, and having found it shelter for the night, they dropped back to the cabin. They entered and placed themselves on the couch before the open fire.

Gleason looked at his watch again. "Don't know what makes me watch my time all the while—I've been keeping my eye on that watch a dozen or more times tonight."

Ned glanced at the alarm clock in the corner, instinctively. 'Three A. M."

"You've got to work fast, Mister Gleason, can you do it?"

"Work fast, what do you mean, Ned?"

"I mean that we got a trace of that cattle thief up here tonight. I 'phoned Manuel to give you the word. Did you get it?"

"Sure I got the message, but what about it?" Gleason was plainly alarmed.

"Well, it's a fellow that's been hanging out down below at Arrowhead. A flashy fellow. He's been prowling around these parts pretending to buy a ranch and we traced him up to the second ranch today where that new rancher just came in, and he was making arrangements to unload your whole herd on him. He acted like he was your agent. I sent one of my boys to head him off, but he's a slick fellow. Not much of a mountaineer, for he had a hard time dodging us on his horse, but he slipped us up, I'm ashamed to admit. He told the rancher up there that he was returning on the three-thirty limited, that west-bound train this morning, and would take the money with him. Your cattle are up there, all corralled, safe and sound, but that scoundrel's somewhere down below. He didn't have time to get the money. We slipped in on him just as he was closing the deal. I wanted you to come on down tonight just for the reason that I want you to get him before he flys the coop. Will you do it?"

Gleason was sharply aroused and confused beyond discussion. "Who is he, Ned? Did you get his name?"

"Nope, don't know his name. But he told the rancher that there was a woman down at Arrowhead that was waiting for him—maybe his wife, we don't know—and that he'd have to close the deal up and hurry back 'cause she was waiting on him. They had to make that train."

They were talking fast now. Ned was up and starting for the door. Gleason after him. "You gotta travel fast, Mister Gleason. You've gotta get that fellow."

Gleason stopped short and put his hand on Ned's shoulder, looking him squarely in the eye. "Wait a minute, Ned! Before I go what about this woman? What was her name?"

"Dunno, Mister Gleason. What difference does that make? Come along."

Gleason stood still. He was reservedly determined in his answer and slower in his speech.

"It makes a lot of difference, Ned. I've got to know that."

"Well, he intimated something to the rancher about her coming up to meet some big rancher and that they were to be married shortly at the hotel below. He explained about some old romance that sprung up a long time ago, and ventured that he was here to beat the other man's time. He put on a lot of airs about being a prosperous cattle owner when he brought your herd in there."

Gleason had reeled back to the couch again, then across the room to the telephone. "So, that's his game, is it? The dirty thief. Take my cattle —then take my girl?" He hesitated, for he had composure under his manly self-control.

"What do you mean, Mister Gleason, do you know this fellow?"

Gleason was silent. He had rung a number on the automatic. He waited for response. "Know him? I couldn't miss him on that description."

The ranger watched him intently and pricked up his ears for the conversation.

"Hello—Hello!" Gleason was squirming. "Is this Arrowhead? Yes, yes. Well, this is Carter Gleason." He clicked the receiver. "He's gone, Ned. He's gone." Gleason was desperate. He listened furtively with his mouth against the telephone. He looked at his watch. "Three-thirteen A. M." Then he clutched the receiver as he heard the voice at the other end of the wire. "Yes, this is Car-t—" he did not finish. "A message for me —read it—yes read—quickly." It came over the wire to him.

"When you get this we'll be hitting the ties for the city. Be a sport and take the litle joke. I did you a good turn and moved your cattle farther up the range. She is going to be my wife.—Graham Glenn."

Gleason snapped the receiver against its rack. He was awkwardly dizzy, but he pulled himself together. His face was white as a sheet and his teeth were set against his pinched lips.

"He's double crossed me, Ned. That fellow's forcing my hand. It's three-fifteen. I've got to make that three-thirty at San Ber'do. We've got to, Ned, we've got to." Gleason was infuriated with his nervous tension.

Ned had already opened the door and motioned Gleason toward him. "Come along, Lad. He can't beat two sons of the low Sierras."

A minute later and they were tearing the tarpaulin from the powerful Curtis biplane that lay anxiously propped for the mission it was headed for.

Graham Glenn Abducting Gladys

"Climb in, Mister Gleason. Bundle up!" He had already climbed in. The ranger spun the engine. It hummed a powerful tune against the drizzle and breeze. He likewise found his place, and behind the wheel.

"Wait a second. Who's that prowling up back there?" And Gleason motioned toward the shanty.

"Oh, that's just old man Bell. He's the sheriff of these parts now. Came down to help us get this guy."

"Hey there! Old man Bell!" Gleason was calling his loudest.

Bell approached on a run. "What do you want of him, Mister Gleason?"

Gleason was on his feet, had the sheriff around the waist and hoisted him into the biplane.

"Let 'er go, Sheriff!" It was Gleason that hollered.

With a burst they shot off into the snapping air that caught them. Ned, Mister Gleason and Sheriff Bell were hitting the air for the three-thirty west-bound Limited.

When Graham Glenn and the girl had made their departure from the Arrowhead Hotel and rolled down the road a ways from the illuminated hostelry they fell to talking in a more detailed manner.

"How long did it take you to make the trip up on the stage this evening, Gladys?"

"About three hours, Graham. It was very wet on the grade and we had to take it easy in places."

"We can make it better than that. We've got to. Our train goes at three-thirty. We'll speed ahead." And he put his foot on the gas.

"Our train?" She laughed, for his expression seemed odd. She looked forward, as though frightened with the move.

"Why, of course, our train." She said nothing; now she was watching him closely for they were driving rather rapidly.

"Tell me something, Graham. How does it happen that you were not more surprised to see me, when I spoke to the doctor tonight?"

"Because I was looking for you."

"Looking for me? What do you mean?" She was curious.

"Yes. Looking for you. I knew you would come to me when you heard of my misfortune."

"But how did you know I was there?"

"I follow the papers. Three days ago I read of your return from abroad; your intended journey to Arrowhead, and then your—well, you know the rest. And then I got to thinking of our love affair some many moons ago. I figured it all out. He never liked me. I always hated him. He's not the right man for you. You want someone that's got an established way about them—not a slinking mountaineer—you—"

"Don't. That's enough, Graham. If you're going to talk that way, I shall get right out in this rain and travel every step of the way to the hotel."

"You can't do that. You promised the doctor you would help me catch my train. Now you're going to do it." He sat closer to her, guiding the car with his left hand. His arm stole about her and he hugged her tightly to him. She screamed.

"Graham Glenn, you'll stop that! I came along to help you—it doesn't look as though you were very helpless now does it?" She was truly frightened but with some composure.

"The doctor might have thought it. I never felt healthier in all my life. I could have made this journey a dozen times tonight, but I managed it so that we would make it together. You're going down with me. He'll find out soon enough when he hits the hotel tomorrow." He was sitting closer to her now and speaking his words emphatically.

"Find out what? What do you mean?"

"The note. I left that note with the page, addressed to him. He'll retrace his steps quick enough when he finds you've promised to be my wife." She swooned. Then realizing her situation, sat rigidly upright, turned slightly in the seat and shot a piercing look at him. She was dazed and terrified, but she was herself.

"He's out of luck. Snowed-in tighter than a trap, but he'll make the hotel by the time we make the city—and when he does, he'll have the one big surprise of his young life." Glenn laughed cynically.

She was losing ground. She felt herself reel, then regained her senses, and resolved to fight her way through. "How can you do that? You've no way to force me into this. I'll show you." Her teeth locked in defiance.

He laughed again. Then spoke more decidedly. "Oh, I guess I can. We'll see about that." A train whistle sounded from afar. "Do you hear that? That's the west-bound Limited now. It's crossing the Cajon Pass; perhaps on the down-grade from Summitt. It's a fast race but we'll make it." He talked with graceful confidence.

She was unstrung with words and thoughts. "You'll be sorry for this. You can't do this." Her expressions were clearly nerve wrought and shaky.

"Oh, yes, I can. He's on that train right now, and he'll do the little deed—you wait and see."

"Whose on that train? What do you mean?"

"The minister from Devore. He's an old friend of mine—we went to college together. I wired him the word and he's flagged the Limited—probably what she blew her whistle for a while ago."

The car rolled on; the grade was almost finished. It was still drizzling and the wind-shield was covered with dew. They swung down and out of the last canyon. He held his wrist-watch down against the light on the dash-board. "Three A. M. and twenty miles to go. That means work." He threw on more gas and the car slid and tossed over the bumpy gulches. She was frightened, although she said nothing. As they wheeled around a sharp corner that brought them out upon the highway he heaved a sigh of relief, and he chuckled lowly. It was lowly too, for she cast her weary eyes

at him, and her mouth twitched and she pushed herself to the far side of the seat. She wished she might jump out, but she was unwrought and powerless. He held the speedometer at forty and fairly slid down the splattered highway. The lights of the village were more discernible.

She spoke. "Who else knows this?"

"He does—perhaps. I dropped a word, unintentionally at a ranch house up above. But the snow-bound are out of luck up there. Maybe it was his house that slid the cliff—it was in that direction." His remarks were heartless. They had their desired effect, for she was coldly excited.

They wheeled around another curve. Far ahead the searchlight of the Limited lighted up the darkened roadbed. "That's the one—see it?" And he pointed exultantly toward the oncoming train. "We'll have to step to make it. She crosses the road a mile down here. We've gotta cross that grade first or we miss the train." He stepped with cowardly bravado on the throttle and the car jumped forward anew. She was thinking. They crawled closer and closer to the approaching train. The whistle sounded—clearer now, and the lights of the cars were visible. At right angles they were making even time. He was bent on crossing first—to make the switchback and reach the station on time. He placed his watch before the dash light again. She was watching him. The whistle blew more vibrantly. An idea struck her, as he pulled his arm back from the wheel. She was frenzied, the train but twenty yards away. Down went her hand to the dashboard and the lights of the machine flashed out.

"Look out—my God!" he screamed a terrified shriek, instinctively snapping his feet to the clutch and brakes. Her hand was on the limousine door. It opened, and she shut her eyes as she heard the crash. She had jumped—she knew not where. The car had met the oncoming engine on its own terms.

"What do you suppose that is down

there, Ned?" It was Gleason that spoke. He had been following the Limited from the time it left the down grade and rolled on down into the valley.

"She must have hit something. Probably a ranch wagon. Those old boys fall asleep and breathe their last on that crossing many a night." The propeller of the plane was grinding incessantly and their voices were muffled. "One time an auto was making that grade crossing at about forty an hour, a fellow and a girl were in it. It turned out later that he was trying to steal her from her parents. She had presence of mind enough to flash his lights out before they hit the tracks. She jumped, but it was good-night to him."

"I see the train has stopped. We can cut down our speed now—coast a while." Gleason kept his eyes upon the crossing. The moon had swung from behind a cloud, and the rainy valley was partially lighted up.

"Let's circle around a bit, Ned. We can wait till they pick up—it's a short run now." Ned wheeled on his control and accepted the suggestion. They spun above the scene.

The girl looked up, from where she had regained consciousness. Three people were by her side and she was watching the machine overhead.

"That's it all right—sure enough— the airplane," she was mumbling to herself, quite forgetting the crash that lay behind her.

"Why doesn't he come down?" She queried with herself. She wondered.

The train regained its steam. "All aboard!" Another blast of the whistle, three more to recall the flagman, and the Limited pounded off down the tracks for the village.

"Throw on your gas, Ned. We'll make our landing before she pulls in." And they threw it on, and they shot straightway above the rolling engine of the track below, ahead of it, and down across the village.

"The yard's clear. We can flop down there all right." Ned cut off the power, and set his mechanism for the drop. They volplaned gracefully and rolled forth on a wave of atmosphere that planted them presently before the platform of the depot.

The old brick depot was dark, except for the vigilance of the night telegraph clerk who was preparing his orders for the incoming flyer, and from the window there was a constant clicking of the key and a green light shown onto the wet brick walk. The green light of the semaphore dropped an arm, and the whistle of the Limited sounded as the headlight flashed around the curve.

"There she comes, Ned. Full power ahead for the village too. She's cutting off her steam now, for the platform, she's slowing up." When Gleason had finished speaking, the train had come to a standstill beside the walk. Ned and Sheriff Bell followed him to the only car that opened its vestibule. The Pullman conductor alighted and started for the telegraph office.

"Hey there!" The conductor wheeled about. "Got a couple of reservations aboard here for me?"

"What's the name?"

"Glenn—Graham Glenn."

A stranger had appeared in the vestibule door. He was in clergyman's attire. The conductor turned to him. "Give the operator in the office this paper, will you. It's got the names and data on the collision." The clergyman scrambled off.

"Your in car three, sir!" Gleason hesitated. "Collision?" He was puzzling to himself. "Where was Glenn? Sure enough he had reservations for the Limited. Where was he? Where was the car?" A cold shiver ran down his back. He stood stock still, Ned and the sheriff were likewise quietly pondering. The 'grade-crossing' scene flashed again through his mind. "No—that can't be!" Gleason had muffled a smothered shout of fright.

"Yes, sir; car three!" repeated the conductor. Gleason turned. He had quite forgotten the situation. The clergyman was returning on the run from the telegraph office.

"Board-d-d1 All aboard!" The conductor's voice was shrill.

"Hold it!" It was the clergyman. "Hold it!" The conductor paused. Gleason turned to Ned. He was shiveringly silent. The big ranger was quietly breathless and Sheriff Bell was hesitantly aside. The two supported Gleason as they headed for the telegraph office.

The clergyman was speaking again. "Hold it!" "They're making the time all right. He phoned the operator from Highlands — they're due here now." Gleason wheeled about. Subconsciously the words meant something to him. As he stood with bated breath a klaxon sounded from around the corner of the Station. Gleason was alert. He listened. The conductor twirled his lantern twice to signal a cut-off for the engineer — they would wait. The clergyman bent his attention in the direction of the klaxon.

It was he who spoke. "Sure thing! It's Mr. Glenn's car all right!"

Sheriff Bell's hand snapped to his revolver. The big ranger was aside Gleason. They held their ground. Gleason reassured himself. "Was it true?" A scream from the car. It was a girl's scream. Gleason was on his toes—he sprang forward. In an instant he was grappling before the car. His prey was in his muscular arms—it was easy work for a powerful mountaineer.

"There he is Sheriff! Take him away." Gleason had stepped to the other side of the car and *she* was there. She was coming out of a faint—it seemed visionary.

"Gladys!" and he threw his arms about her and helped her from the car.

"Carter!" she whispered drowsily —"you did come down, didn't you?"

Sheriff Bell held his prisoner resolutely. With him the clergyman was talking—an explanation ensued. "We didn't make the time," Glenn was speaking in jerks — the blow had stunned him. "She thought the train had hit us, when your engine caught that wagon." The clergyman seemed to comprehend. Gleason was engaged, when the former tapped him on the shoulder.

Gleason turned. The clergyman had a prayer-book in his hand. He nodded.

"All Aboard! Aboard-d-d!" Gleason lifted her from the Roamer, shouted a word of departure to his partners of the range, and with the clergyman hurried to the puffing train. They boarded.

When the West-bound Limited got up steam to leave the San Bernardino station the moon broke over the mountain top and down upon the platform. The biplane, Roamer, and the three men were beside the station telegraph office.

On the platform the clergyman stood with his back to the rising moon. He was reading. She had quite recovered her real self. Carter Gleason braced himself against the railing — it had been a fight worth while.

"Carter. What's that red light on the mountain top?"

"That's Silver Peak, my dear!"

(The End.)

Spell of the Rainbow Scarf

By Donna Reith Scott

S quiet, staid Mrs. Stanton tied her horse to the shed, she sighed with relief as she looked at the vast sweet space around her, at the big old-fashioned farm house and at the great pepper trees flopping in the cold mountain wind.

She had just come from Cedar Grove, four miles away, where all the country-side had assembled at the village school picnic. She came alone; her three children had coaxed to remain and come home with the Browns. As the unusually cool June afternoon waned, though she was energetically full of life, just on the brink of middle age, she left all the merriment with nothing more thrilling in her mind than to go home and get her elderly husband's supper and spend the evening with him.

Hurrying inside, through a labyrinth of petunias, hydrangeas and roses, she flung off her coat from about her rounded, slender form. While loosening the tie under the collar of her black silk dress, preparatory to removing it, she hesitated, glanced at the clock, retied it, and went into the kitchen.

The kitchen was large and high-ceilinged, with windows and doors ajar, through which flowed the cool breeze. As she put a handful of twigs in the range, she gazed out of a large window at the rolling fields of grain, flooded with the tender amber light of sunset, and the mountains shimmering blue-gray in the distance. Way over a low hill she discerned a reaper with a man on the seat. Satisfied she withdrew her eyes from the landscape, then entered the dining room. This room was cooler than the

kitchen. She shivered slightly as she went about setting the table.

The day previously her fifteen-year-old daughter had been graduated from school. Her presents were scattered around on chairs and on the window seat. One of them was a large, knitted silk shoulder throw in beautiful rainbow tints. Mrs. Stanton took this up and put it on. As she did so she hastily and half unconsciously viewed herself in the side-board mirror. Suddenly she stood tense and looked long and close, examining herself as if she were an astonishing stranger.

She found that her eyes and hair were of a soft night-like blackness and that from the beating wind and the pleasurable excitement of meeting her neighbors her cheeks had turned a warm deep cerise.

Although but thirty-seven, she had worn black or dull shades of blue or gray for years. Now the broad line of brilliant color cutting the duskiness of hair, eyes, and gown in twain had transformed her exquisitely from an ordinary-robed, commonplace woman to a beauty of Oriental fascination.

The vibrations of light and color from the rainbow scarf were reflected into her soul. Tumultous feelings of regret, for what, she did not know, swept her being. A throng of sensations surged through her, unrest, longing for gayety, distaste for her quiet home environment, an onrush of life such as she had not known in the eighteen years since her marriage.

She started from her reverie when the puff of an automobile and "Halloa" sounded outside on the driveway. Before answering the summons, which came from the front of the house, where the wind was sharpest, audibly swaying the vines and trees, she glanced once more in the mirror and arranged the scarf more gracefully across her bosom.

"Halloa," she heard again, and dreamily moved through the living room to the front door.

The door opened under the pergola, which was roofed and wreathed with a luxuriant vine ponderous with crimson blossoms. Mauve shadowed hills and hazy blue mountains were to the left of her; and to the right vineyards, orchards and grain fields slanted away toward the glittering village.

Before her, in his machine, under a great tossing pepper tree sat Mr. Troy a new neighbor, wealthy and a bachelor. He was a large, worldly appearing man, of the genial red-haired type, near her age, clad in an expensive suit of gray.

He had met her twice before, but had not noticed her particularly. Now he surveyed her with an appraising eye. She had suddenly become different, fascinating.

She smiled a trifle embarrassed, sensible of his admiration and waited for him to speak.

"Is Mr. Stanton around?" he called over the wind.

"He is reaping in one of the lower fields," she answered.

He leaned from the machine, shaded his eyes with his hand, and gazed far beyond in several directions. "I don't see him."

She came to the edge of the step, near to him. "Take the road," she explained, pointing, "winding back of the barn, then the road between the apple trees and—" She paused and laughed a little, showing a row of well kept teeth. "There's so many hills. I know each one. But I can't point out just where he is. He'll be up to supper soon."

"I only want to speak to him a minute about the pasture." He added after a moment's thoughtful silence, "Why not get in the machine and run

down and find him."

She climbed in, the wind blowing strands of her hair about unheeded. She directed the way as they twisted over the rough road. When at the top of an incline, his gray eyes on her face, he took a long breath. "This mountain air is great, healthful and a wonderful beautifier. People are good-looking here in these hills."

She knew it was a veiled compliment, and that she was worthy of it. She stirred uneasily, turned her head and kept silent.

They rode down a hardly distinguishable road, grown over with grass and pulled up near the reaping machine. Gray haired Mr. Stanton, tall, nearing sixty, but well preserved, saw them, got down stiffly from his seat and came toward them with tired steps.

"How are you, Troy?" he said. Then he scanned his wife, his eyes on the rainbow scarf, its fringed ends fluttering at her back. "I thought it was Dottie," he declared.

A shade of resentment came into her eyes, her lips parted to speak.

Mr. Troy glanced significantly, with a slight amusement, from husband to wife and spoke before she could. "Got any pasture to spare, Mr. Stanton?"

"Yes. Yours giving out?"

"It's about gone. I'd like to rent pasture for two of my horses for the rest of the season."

"Turn 'em in. There's plenty."

"All right," Mr. Troy replied. "That's what I wanted to see you about. Thanks."

He backed the machine and turned around.

The old man called after his wife, "I'm coming up directly."

"Yes," she answered absently. She had forgotten to tell him supper was ready.

Curving under the orchard branches Mr. Troy bent toward her. "Are you going to the dance at the grove tonight?"

"I was to the picnic this afternoon."

"I was there,' he asserted surprised, "I didn't see you."

"Nevertheless I was there," she smiled.

"But there was no dancing this afternoon."

"I never—" she began.

The breeze wafted the scarf against her face. It was delicately perfumed. She caught and held it down, twisting the fringe around her fingers. "I haven't been to a dance in years. In fact, scarcely anywhere in the evening."

"Well, that's too bad," he murmured sympathetically. "Your husband, of course, doesn't dance any more."

She shook her head and for the first time felt ashamed of her elderly husband.

"Everyone for miles around will be there," he added.

"Mr. Stanton never did care for dancing," she admitted slowly, turning her head away. "And he's always tired in the evening.

"I presume so," he said pleasantly affable. "Let him go to bed." His accent changed to one of cordial sympathy. "I am going to take my mother and two young lady nieces, who are visiting us, down shortly. If you care to go, I'll pick you up as I come by."

"Oh no," she began politely but broke off abruptly. A shadow of a big walnut tree wavered back of the wind shield making it like a mirror. Her striking appearance rushed over her anew.

"Oh, come for a short while."

To her surprise, she found herself saying, "It would be rather delightful to dance again. And I could come home with the children,' she concluded.

"I'll be along in an hour or so." He stopped, let her down under the crimsoned pergola, waved his hand genially and was gone.

A curious vexation with her easy going husband fretted her when he came in to supper. She hadn't noticed before how lined and sunburned was his face or how slow and old he had

grown or how hastily and noisily he ate. Until now she had not thought of him as old. The years she had lived with him had flowed by in connected contentment. Now she was discontented and restless.

"George can't you eat more quietly," she exclaimed with annoyance, standing beside him pouring his tea.

He looked up from his plate and chuckled, "I don't make half as much noise as that drapery you've got on."

She walked into her room, her eyes flashing in contempt at what she considered a very poor joke. She put her daughter's tight-fitting patent leather pumps on her feet, combed and rippled her hair and put a red rosebud in it. And then she pinned the scarf on to her left shoulder with a full blown rose and a horseshoe pin of garnets.

The evening glow was gray and the wind had diminished to a whisper when Mr. Troy's automobile swung into the yard. Mr. Stanton went out. His wife came from her room and fluttered close beside him. She wore no hat but was drawing on a pair of gloves.

While the machine was still a short distance away, coming slowly, the husband gazed mystified at her unwonted toilet.

In a very low voice, without looking at him, she explained, "I'm going to the dance at the grove awhile."

"Dance?" he questioned amazed, his wholesome round face losing a trifle of its ruddiness. "Dance, did you say Minnie?"

"Yes, I said dance!"

Now the machine stopped. Mr. Troy cried gayly, lifting his hat, "I'm going to carry your wife away."

"I see," the husband returned, pleasantly impassive, leaning against the veranda post. "I see," he repeated, lighting his pipe.

"He's a very bad boy," Mrs. Troy scolded adoringly. Then she introduced the two fair-haired, giggling girls beside her as, "Alice and May, my granddaughters."

"I'll come home early with the children," Mrs. Stanton said, turning toward her husband, her foot on the running board.

As she settled in the only vacant seat, that next to Mr. Troy, she caught his more or less conscious gaze of admiration and felt like a woman who had been denied her rights. Her husband waved good bye, but she wasn't looking that way.

Mr. Troy was in a jolly mood. Much to his nieces' enjoyment he let the machine out on the descending grade and in an incredible short time reached the entrance to the grounds.

The twilight was dim; night was hovering near. Lights isolated, in clusters and in rows, sparkled among the tall trees. The notes of a piano and a violin and numerous voices shouting and laughing floated out to them. Summer clad girls, civilian and uniformed boys and men were thickly scattered over the grounds.

Going in they were met by a group of young men. And soon Alice and May were being conducted toward the music. A party of hilarious old people sitting on a bench claimed Mrs. Troy. And then as though there was nothing else to do, Mr. Troy and Mrs. Stanton, bowing and smiling to acquaintances, strolled toward the open tree-embowered dancing platform.

For an interval they loitered under the row of globeless electric lights strung saggingly on the outer edges of the platform. The music pealed forth "Nights of Gladness." Mr. Troy's arm encircled her waist. Simultaneously a half-breathless murmur of amazement and incredulity ran through a group of neighbors, sitting below the platform, at her roses, the kaleidoscopic scarf and her dancing.

She did not hear it. Her buoyant vitality thrilled through every nerve and fibre as under Mr. Troy's skillful guidance, she quickly mastered the never-before attempted hesitation waltz.

They circled the crowded floor time and time again. Occasionally she had other acquaintances for partners, but Mr. Troy would invariably come to claim her for the following dance.

Later when she was the merriest of a gay party partaking of ices, her daughter, Dottie, came with a new, shy expression in her eyes, and half-whispered, "Mother the Browns are starting for home. Are you coming? Sonny and Willie have gone home already."

"No, dear," the mother replied, while Mr. Troy playfully stole her dish of ice cream and hid it under a paper on the table, "run along."

"But papa'll be waiting," the girl vouchsafed timidly, her arm around her mother's neck, her shining brown head pressing her cheek.

"Run along," the other commanded blithesomely, dismissing the subject, turning and laughing at the missing ice cream.

However Dottie's remark troubled her a little: " 'Papa'll be waiting.' " The joyousness was beginning to pall. To the rear she heard some one remark, "How handsome Mrs. Stanton looks tonight." "Yes," another voice assented, "and I never thought of her as handsome before."

Thereupon she banished the unpleasant thoughts and her spirits revived. The hours dashed swiftly by. Mr. Troy and Mrs. Stanton were more and more inseparable, mingling with the crowds around the ice cream and lemonade booths, when they were not dancing, or promenading with others along the starlit paths.

Then when it was near twelve o'clock and they were waltzing near the railing, Miss Larkin, the school principal, who was noted for being very outspoken, said sighing, "The ancient story of the husband old while the wife is still young, Mrs. Stanton." She walked dutifully, primly away with a straight held head.

Mrs. Stanton blushed furiously. A sharp retort surged in her throat. But her tongue was not trained to sharp retorts and Miss Larkin was a distance away before it was ready to be uttered.

"Ha, ha," Mr. Troy chuckled. "Funny old maid."

Self-consciousness arose. She bent her head to hide her burning face and torturing thoughts and down the length of herself she saw nothing but darkness, the black silk dress.

The rainbow throw was no longer draped over her shoulders. She felt alien here in the night among the whirling couples, the music and chatter. This evening of dancing, laughing and jesting seemed no longer a part of herself; it belonged to a picturesque stranger, with brilliant cheeks, roses in her hair and clothed in a rainbow. She became again the quiet, commonplace wife, the mother of three children.

She stepped aside from the mass of couples. "I've lost Dottie's scarf," she murmured distantly.

"Must have become unpinned," he said, not noticing her changed mood. "Fell on the floor probably."

He took a few paces to where he could get a better view of the entire floor. He shook his head. "Isn't here. Let's search along the paths."

So they hunted within the glare of the lights and without the glare of lights, but with no results.

Near the candy booth Mr. Troy put his hand on her arm, arresting her footsteps. "What's the use hunting?" he suggested. "I'll write a notice and put it up here offering twenty-five dollars reward for its return."

"I object to any such thing," she protested, drawing away. "It's of no consequence. I wonder if your mother's ready to go home?"

"Oh, mother," he grinned. "I let Bob Smith take the machine to run the others home. He hasn't returned yet." He took her arm again. "There's another hesitation. Let's not miss it."

"I don't wish to dance again."

"What's the matter," he coaxed familiarly in the unruffled tones of a man sure of his ground, and his eyes said more than his voice. "Life is just beginning for you. I have no ties that bind; and surely your husband under the circumstances can expect—"

He was interrupted by a boisterous friend who slapped him on the back and pulled him off the path. There the friend gleefully related something.

For a moment she had only a vague realization of the meaning of his unfinished sentence. And then as she knew, her heart flamed with regret and anger, anger not so much with the man as herself.

Unnoticed she disappeared among the thinning strollers. Without glancing to the right or the left she swiftly threaded her way out of the glimmer of the artificial lights and close air into the sheltering starlit highway.

In the small tight slippers she teetered painfully along the ruts of the road. As she trudged on in the dust she felt relieved as the music and the clatter of feet grew fainter. Then she heard Mr. Troy's voice coming nearer.

She slunk in the shadow of a tree and waited for him to pass. But he evidently returned to the park as nothing near her broke the silence but the hoot of an owl.

After she had gone a mile on the ascending road and made the first turn, her heart fluttered as she distinguished the pat of a horse's feet and the roll of a rubber-tired buggy.

In the darkness she waited. Shortly the moving carriage lamp threw a dim yellow flicker over her.

Her old husband pulled up and smiled out to her. "Is that you, Minnie?"

"Yes," she answered.

"I reckoned you'd be getting lonesome for home about now." His voice broke off trembling. "So—I so—I—"

He leaned over and handed out her great coat. "It's chilly. Fog's coming in through the cut. It'll soon be here."

Her lip quivered, and tears sprang to her eyes. He watched until she had put on the coat. Then he held out a scarf. As she took it she sensed it was silk. She brushed away her tears and held it close to her eyes. It was the rainbow scarf.

"Why—" she faltered, "how—"

"Dottie," he interrupted carefully

gentle, "didn't think you looked good in it. So she took it and the roses off of you just before she came home — when you were eating ice cream."

Her head dipped. Her forehead pressed against his arm.

"But, never mind—wear it, dearie, all you want to."

"Bowery Buck"

By Alan George

(Geo. J. Southwick and Alfred S. Burroughs)

Yes, pard, it's a rough lookin' fiddle an' not very useful, I know,
But there ain't enough gold in the diggin's to tempt me to part with it, though.
As long as I live I'll jest keep it right here in my cabin with me,
For to me its more precious than jewels, no matter how costly they'd be.
You're right, there's a story about it, an' one I don't mind to relate,
For it calls to my mind a true hero an' a noble an' brave cabin-mate.
To start at the first o' the chapter, I'll state what most people don't know
This camp isn't now what it was then—some forty-odd winters ago.
The mines they was new an' a-boomin', and I was the head foreman then,
But I didn't put on any airs, pard, though bossin' a hundred-odd men.

Well, one day a strappin' young feller came into the camp huntin' work,
An' said he was right from the Bow'ry—a city chap fresh from New York.
Good lookin'? Well, no, pard; his front teeth were big an' so far outward stuck
That the boys in the diggin's fixed on him the high-soundin' title o' Buck;
An' as he had come from the Bowery, the name "Bow'ry Buck" seemed to fit,
But the chap took it all in good natur' an' seemed not to mind it a bit.
In short, he was one o' them fellers that take the world jest as she goes,
An' makes friends o' everyone 'round 'em an' never are bothered with foes.
An' that's how the chap came among us, an' somehow it fell to my luck,
To have a stray bunk in my cabin that just seemed to fit "Bow-ry Buck."

Nights, after our day's work was over, down here to this cabin we'd go
An' Buck would take down this same fiddle an' rosinin' up this same bow,
He'd play what he said was a two-step—the finest tune ever was heard—
An' I would jest sit there an' listen for hours without speakin' a word.
There was somethin' about that sweet music that made my heart happy an' light,
An' tired as I was, an' rheumatic, I was achin' to dance' ev'ry night!
No matter how blue an' down-hearted, no matter how things would go wrong,
That "Bowery Buck Two-Step" would cheer me an' life would be all a glad song.
An' oft when the boys got to drinkin' an' started to wrangle and fight,
That soul-stirrin' tune from Buck's fiddle would settle all arguments right.

One night—I will never forget it—while we were both sittin' in here,
An' Bowery Buck was a-playin' the two-step I loved so to hear,
We heard a great yellin' an' shoutin' jest down at the foot o' the hill
Where some o' the tumbled-down cabins are ling'rin in evidence still.
We rushed to the door o' the cabin an' the first thing that greeted our sight
Was the glare of a roarin' big fire there that lit up the shadowy night.
"Come on," shouted Buck; " 'tis the hash-house, an' it's bein' burned up fit to kill,"
An' away we both sped like a whirlwind, zig-zag down the dark, rocky hill,
Where scores of the miners had gathered, a-yellin' like imps o' old Nick
An' shoutin' about a child lyin' upstairs in the buildin' an' sick.

Buck questioned the miners around him an' learned it was Widow Smith's child,
Who still was upstairs in the buildin', an' then his grief nigh drove him wild.
"She must not—she shall not—be burned, boys," he cried in most resolute tones,
"I'll rescue that sweet, tender flow'r, if I char up my own worthless bones!"
An' though the flames swept o'er the buildin' an' scorched ev'ry beam with their
    breath
Brave Bow'ry Buck dashed through the doorway—just actually courtin' his death!
Stout-hearted men there were a-plenty, who'd brave the old Nick in his lair,
But there wasn't another among 'em who'd dare to plunge into that glare;
And while their bronzed faces grew pallid an' hearts became icy with dread,
They raised a hoarse cheer for the hero, tho' feelin' they'd next see him dead.

An' higher the flames leaped an' crackled, with awful an' furious roar,
Till that weak, wooden shell of a buildin' from roof to the undermost floor,
Was simply a wild roarin' furnace whose heated an' torturin' breath
Was addin' new proof ev'ry second that Buck had but rushed to his death.
Widow Smith, the poor agonized mother, who kept the bedoomed boardin' house,
We'd carried, half dead, to the spring near, as helpless an' scared as a mouse;
Yet midst her bewailin' an' moanin' she oft murmured Bow'ry Buck's name
An' prayed that he'd bring back her darlin' unscathed by the death-dealin' flame.
An' mebbe 'twas this mother's prayin', o'erheard 'bove the din and the roar,
That kept his brave heart beatin' in him an' guided his feet to the door.

For while the poor mother was prayin' there 'rose all at once a great yell
An' Bow'ry Buck reeled from the buildin' a minute before the wreck fell.
He staggered, half dazed, from the doorway, his clothin' all spangled with flame,
An' with the child wrapped in his own coat, toward the glad mother he came.
He laid the child safe on her bosom, though speechless an' weak an' distressed,
Then tottered an' fell; an' we miners, when quickly around his form press'd,
Beheld that our hero had perished, that a little wee child he might save—
Had met the fate others have suffered who tried to be helpful an' brave.
Look, pardner, he lies where that pine tree stands there like a lone sentinel
To show us where sleeps a true hero and show us the spot where he fell.

There, now you have heard the whole story—a sad one, you'll call it, no doubt—
But its always to me kinder cheerin'—a deed good to tell men about;
An' though 'tis a mute, rusty fiddle, I feel that its melody lives
For the memories waked by its powers sweet solace an' comfort still gives.
The whispering pine bendin' o'er him seems often to whisper to me
An' bid me to guard my rare treasure with loyal an' true constancy.
With his pulseless old bow an' mute fiddle that here in my cabin are laid
I cherish the soul that inspired 'em with strains that no other have played.
An' long as I live I will tell it, that the richest vein ever was struck
Was when thro' this rough-lookin' fiddle breathed the soul o' brave Bow'ry Buck.

Betty---The Story of a Brave Heart

By Elizabeth Huebner

BIRCH CROFT lies near the head of the lake, just within the arm of the second point on the East Leland side. In steamboat and railroad guides it is listed under hotels, but upon nearer view and in its own setting it reminds one of a great cottage home. Its usual summer guests are, in the expression of the North, "Illinois People," but in this year of 19—— there were three people who had traveled greater distances in the hope of finding quiet and rest. One was a man from the far West, the other two, a woman and a girl from somewhere in the East.

Out under the trees on the north side of the cottage there is a small vine-covered arbor, which overlooks Lake Leelanau and stands only a few feet from its shore. It was here that "Auntie Fay" and the girl, Betty, spent their mornings, and at times the greater part of the day, for although they had come north to rest there were still proofs to be read and correspondence to be taken care of. They both loved the great out-of-doors and made the most of their retreat, which took them quite away from other people and still allowed them to feel their nearness.

Auntie Fay a great many of you undoubtedly know — if not personally, you at least know her through the books she has written. Betty was just a girl, like many another girl, without any particular distinction in the world. She was of medium height, but when not being measured against other people, her youthful slenderness gave one the impression that she was much taller. Her soft, light brown hair, which she wore low over her forehead and arranged in a soft coil at the back of her head, framed a face, which although of regular features, carried more of sweetness of expression than of beauty. She was eager and fully alive to the joys which came her way, though her young shoulders had been forced to carry burdens far too great for one of her years.

One day about two weeks after their arrival they were spending the morning as usual in the shady arbor. The lake lay a wide expanse of clear crystal, with not a ripple stirring its surface. It was one of those warm, humid days when it is simply impossible to concentrate one's thought upon work. Betty's thoughts in particular were wandering, following in the wake of each group of people as they strolled through the grove on their way to the dock or the tennis courts. Listlessly she followed them in thought, until finally her attention was attracted by a lone figure threading his way in and out among the green trees.

"Auntie Fay," the girl's tones were in keeping with the listlessness of her mood, "don't you think the 'Silent Man' may be brooding over some secret trouble?"

"Whom are you talking about, child?" Auntie Fay looked up from her book, and following the direction of the girl's gaze, saw the man from the West just entering the cottage door. "Do you mean Mr. Howard?"

"Yes, Auntie Fay, I have given him the name of 'Silent Man' because I think it suits him better. He impresses me as a person who is afraid to talk— afraid to laugh; his only happiness seems to be in wandering away from

every one and living entirely by himself."

Auntie Fay laughed a low, clear,
rippling laugh. Betty's seriousness
had always amused her. "What a
foolish thought, child. He impresses
me as being quite an average man,
very much engrossed in his work."
And Auntie Fay returned to her book,
leaving Betty to her own thoughts.

That evening out on the wide east
veranda, Mrs. Fay was struggling
with a large wicker chair which had
caught in the reed rug as she tried to
move it nearer the porch rail. In an
instant the Silent Man, who stood
near, came to her side. "May I help
you? It seems to be rather heavy."

Mrs. Fay's smile was one of welcome as she thanked him, and to the
man who towered so far above her
she confided that because of her want
of greater physical strength she did
sometimes mind her meager height.

"I assure you I would hardly think
of it as a grievance if I were you. It
has given me pleasure to be of help,"
and the Silent Man turning sank into
a chair near the one he had placed for
Auntie Fay's comfort.

When Betty came out later in the
evening, she paused in mild surprise
and would have turned back if Mrs.
Fay had not spoken to her. And this
was the beginning of a friendship
which slowly drew Betty into its
meshes and held her fast.

During the days which followed, the
Silent Man often joined them in the little arbor, or invited them to go for a
stroll along the lake shore in the early
evening. And sometimes after his
canoe had swung out into the lake and
rounded the pier, he would touch shore
again on the white sands before the
arbor and call a glad invitation to the
two people there. This invitation, however, Auntie Fay always declined, for
she had a fear of the water after the
shadows began to lengthen, though
she would urge Betty to go, for the
girl loved to be out on the water at
any time of the day and found keen
delight in skimming along over its
smooth surface.

July and August were fading into
the past and September was drawing
near, when one evening the Silent
Man's canoe again touched shore before the vine-covered arbor, and Betty
in keen anticipation of the pleasure
which lay before her, skipped lightly
down to the water's edge and took her
place among the cushions.

It was an unusually warm evening.
The sun still held its own in all its
sunset glory above the western hills,
so the Silent Man and Betty under the
mystical lure of the North—the lure
of the setting sun — ventured farther
up the lake than was their custom, and
when they found themselves beyond
the bend of the first ·point, with the
darkness of the coming night still
poised in unreality, they decided to go
ashore and stroll the short distance
through the wood to the little spring
which bubbled clear and cool under
the willows just beyond this point.

Following the trail which lay close
to the water's edge, they went on for
some distance until suddenly, to their
astonishment and surprise, the trail
ended in a tangle of vines and underbrush. They had taken little heed of
the oncoming darkness, and now when
they turned, confident that they could
still retrace their steps, they saw even
this part of the trail lost in the deepening shadows of the forest. But
Betty's mind held no thought of fear.
She knew the man who stood beside
her would be able to find a way out,
and take her safely back to Birch
Croft. Turning she spoke to him, but
the Silent Man did not seem to hear.
He stood looking out across the lake,
deep in thought.

Suddenly he took a step forward
and drew the girl into his arms, bringing her near, nearer his heart. "Betty
—Girl, do you know how much I love
you?" His voice though vibrant with
emotion held firm, and in a torrent of
words and caresses he poured forth
his love — a love which had grown
deep and still. The quick change in
his mood startled Betty, but soon his
words conveyed his meaning to her
and she felt a warmth and light filling

her life which she had never felt before. It was a dream. A beautiful dream. The dream of her life come true. And then, swiftly following his words of love came a plea in the intensity of a strong man's will: "Betty tell me it isn't too late. It isn't too late, Girl?"

As slowly as his words of love had awakened the warmth in her heart, so slowly, but surely, did these words fill her heart with an icy fear. "Too late, too late!" The words echoed and re-echoed through her mind. What weird spectre was this lurking in the foreground to rob her of her dream of happiness? Was all life coming to her, too late?

Gently but firmly, Betty drew away, the Silent Man offering no resistance, his arms falling slowly to his sides. The thought which had prompted the utterance of those fateful words evidently prompted him also, to hold in reserve any further expression of his love.

For a time they stood still in the silence of the night, each trying to unravel the invincible web of destiny. A light breeze blowing in from the lake, and a sense of the creeping darkness brought to them a realization of a present problem still unsolved. It was Betty who first broke the silence. "It is steadily growing darker. Don't you think we had better try to find our way out?"

"Yes," said the Silent Man, "let me think—to try to locate the canoe would be useless, it is quite safe where it is until tomorrow. The road which leads to the old lumber camp is only a short distance east from here. If we keep our bearings and push steadily on through this bit of brushwood, we will reach it in a short time. Come, we will at least try. If you will keep close behind me, I will lead the way and part the bushes."

As they expected, the old lumber camp road was soon reached, and after that they had no difficulty in finding their way, for although the overarching trees cast their shadows along the way, the ground was smooth and

the road led straight to the highway which passed the Birch Croft grove.

While they were forging their way through the brushwood neither had spoken except as they were concerned in each other's safety, and as they passed along the woodland road, the silence was broken only by the sound of their footfalls. But when they at last reached the highway, where the rising moon cast a white light over the dry grasses and the sands, Betty turned to the Silent Man with a plea for an understanding in her eyes. "Tell me—tell me about it," she said.

The Silent Man gave a slight start as if suddenly brought back into the present. "Must you know, Girl? Do you really want me to tell you?"

Betty's answer came without the least hesitation. "Yes, tell me in justice, since you have told me the rest." Surely the truth no matter what it might hold could only bring to her a keener pain than this doubt, this dread of an unknown certainty.

Slowly, falteringly the Silent Man told her the story of his early life. He pictured for her the home of his boyhood, with a fond mother and an indulgent father. He told her of his life at college and of the dark-eyed little girl he met in his senior year, and of the care-free love which had grown until it had ended in an early marriage, and then——

They had reached the place on the high road, beyond the brown shingled cottage, where the blackberry bushes brow by the road side. One of them had caught in Betty's sleeve and the Silent Man stooped to free her from its thorny hold.

"Go on," said the girl in a calm, low voice, as they resumed their walk, "tell me—all."

It was quite evident, from the man's hesitation, that the story was growing infinitely harder to tell. However, with an effort he continued. "The first two years were happy enough, and a son was born to us. I think it was he who brought the first differences into our lives. We didn't seem to agree where he was concerned, and after a while there was little else upon which we did agree. A little girl came to us later. I left shortly after that. There was an opening for me in Denver. When I first went out there, I meant to send for her, but I never did. All the warmth had gone out of my love for her."

"Were you long in the West?" asked Betty in even tones.

"Three years by the calendar," answered the Silent Man.

"And you have not been happy?" came the girl's second question.

"Happy?" echoed the man in a voice now grown harsh, "how can a man be happy with a dead thing like that hanging about him?"

"There were the children," ventured Betty.

"The children—They were only infants when I left. I hardly knew them."

During the latter part of their walk, the road lay flooded in light, the moon now sailing high in the eastern sky. The two travelers were again intent upon their own thoughts, but when they turned and entered the grove at Birch Croft, the Silent Man drew Betty nearer and in a voice intense with feeling, he asked her again, "Betty, tell me, Girl, if I came back free, would it be too late?"

For an instant, Betty stood as if hesitating, doubtful; the man beside her grew hopeful, but it was only for a fleeting moment. Her answer came low and clear. "Free! One cannot buy freedom through the pain one gives to others. Go back—go to the children who need you. They need a father's love and protection. You will find happiness there." Betty paused and then went bravely on. "Go back to the little woman you have deserted. She has learned her lesson by this time. If she ever loved you, she loves you now—a woman's heart does not forget."

"Betty, if you loved me, you would not tell me this."

The girl struggled to free herself, but the man's strength held firm.

"It is because I love you that I am trusting in your strength to do right, and if you truly love me, you will go back. A strong love can bridge the petty differences in life. Keep your love strong for her." Again the girl paused. "I shall not ask you to forget me. It would be folly to do that, but whenever you remember — be a little kinder to her, a little more thoughtful. It is only a mean nature which would fail to respond to such an appeal, and hers is not that."

"Betty—Girl!"

For an instant the girl's head drooped, but it was soon lifted and she looked bravely up into the strong face above her. That last kiss out under the dome of the Birches and the greater dome of the sky was not the breaking of a trust, but rather the sealing of a vow that each one would live in the greater faith which had grown in the hearts of both.

It was with a keen sense of relief that Auntie Fay welcomed Betty, for she had been gone longer than usual; but noting the pallor of her face and the tenseness of her manner, she refrained from asking any questions after Betty explained about the lost trail. Some time or other she knew Betty would tell her, tonight the girl needed rest; so after Betty assured her that she was quite well, she bade her goodnight, and the girl crossed the hall to her own room.

Slowly Betty sank to the floor before the window which overlooked the lake, and pillowing her head upon her arm, she rested her cheek against the cool sill. The first rays of the morning light found her still there, with a longing in her heart which only time could still.

Three days later a messenger was sent across the lake with an order for the steamer Leelanau to stop at the Birch Croft dock, on her downward course, as one of the guests was leaving.

Since the eventful evening when fate had played so important a part in the lives of two people, they had gone on, at least from all outward appearances, very much the same as before. Neither the Silent Man nor Betty had made any effort to avoid the other, although their meetings were always in the presence of Auntie Fay. But on the morning of the third day Betty did not see him, and Auntie Fay who saw that the girl was living under a nervous strain suggested a walk to a neighboring farm house in search of harvest apples. Betty welcomed the invitation and rambled along in her conversation, dwelling only upon light, trivial things. Not until their return did she speak the thought which was uppermost in her mind.

"Auntie Fay," the girl stooped to pick a bunch of wild asters, "when the Silent Man comes to say goodbye, will you please ask him to write to you?"

"And you, child?" Auntie Fay's tones were full of loving solicitude.

"For me, he will always be just the Silent Man," said Betty as she rose and went on down the hill.

In the early afternoon the Silent Man paid his last visit to the little arbor. It was hard for him to bid farewell to the two friends who had come to mean so much to him; but under Auntie Fay's guidance that last hour which they spent together would always be a pleasant one to remember. And he did not see them again, for Auntie Fay and Betty were not among the people who thronged the pier, later in the day, in the excitement of seeing the steamer dock.

For Betty the North had lost its charm, but she was reluctant to leave before Auntie Fay heard from the Silent Man. Just a few days before their departure, the long looked for letter arrived. It told of a pleasant trip to the East, of his meeting with his own people, and of meeting old friends; and then he told of the little woman and the children. He had found them with her parents. The closing words of his letter were:

"We made quite a happy family party. Mrs. Howard had been looking forward to my return for some time, and it is quite evident that she has been weaving tales about me for the entertainment of the children. They take me quite for granted, and have set me up as rather a hero in their small lives, a delusion which I will at least have to try to live up to, or fall in their high esteem. My stay in the East will be short as I am returning to my work in Denver about the first of October. And this time I am taking my family with me. We are all looking forward to the new life in the West."

And that was all, not one word for Betty. She did not want it; had not expected it. He would not have been strong in the strength she wished him to have if he had failed her. But with the finality came the breaking of the tension, and burying her face in her hands she gave way to broken sobs, "Oh, I am glad; I am so glad."

"Yes," said Auntie Fay as she tried to comfort the girl, "and in the years to come you will find a greater happiness than the one which could have been yours at such a price."

The following evening Birch Croft was giving its annual party, the rooms were decked in festive gaiety, and out in the grove lanterns were hung. All girlhood bloomed in dainty summer frocks; and young manhood came correct, debonair, clothed in light sport suits, their jovial natures leaping in happy anticipation of a pleasant evening spent under the Birches.

Betty was at her best in a rose-colored voile, excitement lending color to her cheeks and a sparkle to her eyes. Without any apparent effort her spirits soared at will to the sound of the drifting music. Her program was well filled before the evening fairly began, and young Thomas Turner wishing to detain her after a dance, tried to lure her out into the night and the moonlight.

"I say, Betty, lets get away from this music for a while." His boyish voice held a note of anxiety. "I say we go down by the lake and talk about something serious. This light stuff tires me."

6

Although Betty followed him down the steps she had no intention of going much further. The moonlight held memories for her—the music and rhythm of the dance forgetfulness.

The orchestra began to play another number and Betty turned to retrace her steps. "Oh, listen," she said, "they are playing 'Smiles.' We must not miss that dance."

Young Thomas was peeved. "Oh, I say, come on. Why do you want to go back?" And as Betty continued to lead the way, he added, "One can easily see you have never taken life very seriously."

"Taken life seriously!" repeated Betty. "Why need one unless necessity demands it? And now I want to dance, to dance with a wind's will."

Salem's Fleet of Pepper Ships

By Frederic Mariner

The following narrative of merchant marine accomplishment in the past presents a striking contrast of our present lack in this direction. The historic incidents told in this story have a direct bearing on the plan to upbuild a strong merchant marine to safeguard our interest in the future.—The Editor.

THE quaint old city of Salem, Mass., has felt more keenly, perhaps, than any other port in the United States the decay of the American shipping industry that prevailed previous to the declaration of war. At that time only ten per cent of our shipping was carried in American bottoms, while in 1810, 91 per cent of American commerce was handled by our own merchant marine.

In 1807 Salem boasted of a fleet of 252 ships engaged in deep sea commerce; the largest fleet owned by any community of its size in the world. By the year 1900 Salem's famous merchant fleet had dwindled to nothing.

The story of the pepper trade is an interesting one. Ever since the year 1509 Portuguese vessels had brought pepper from Sumatra, on their return trips from searching for the fabulous island of d'Oura, where it was said cargoes of gold bars and nuggets could be picked up along the beach. Later on the Dutch and English joined in the quest; and in 1621 the French became aware of the importance of the pepper trade. They sent a fleet to Sumatra carrying magnificent presents for the Sultan of Acheen.

In 1793 Capt. Jonathan Carnes sailed in a schooner from Salem, Mass., to the East Indies. While in the harbor of Bencoolen, Sumatra, he heard of the pepper trade, which was at that time confined principally to Padang. Capt. Carnes sailed for Padang without any knowledge of the course, although the route was uncharted and dangerous to navigation. On arriving there he found very little pepper was raised in Padang but that it was brought there by the natives in their proas, from points farther north. He finally succeeded in obtaining a cargo and sailed for Salem. Unfortunately he was wrecked in the West Indies, losing his vessel and cargo. Finding his way back to Salem he told his employers what he had discovered. They immediately began to secretly construct the brig "Rajah" for the pepper trade.

In 1795 Capt. Carnes sailed in the brig for Sumatra and a cargo of pepper. On this trip Capt. Carnes visited the northerly ports of the island without charts or guide of any kind, making his way through coral reefs which even today are a dread to navigators. There was great excitement in Salem when Capt. Carnes arrived with his cargo of pepper. This lot of pepper cost eighteen thousand dollars, and sold for one hundred and forty-four thousand; a profit of seven hundred per cent.

The place where the cargo was obtained was kept secret for some time. Finally vessels were fitted out in both Salem and Beverly for Bencoolen where it was supposed Capt. Carnes learned about the pepper trade. These efforts were fruitless for the European colonists of the pepper ports became extremely jealous. They feared the rivalry of the Yankees. No charts or sailing directions of the coast north of Padang could be found. All sorts of stories of the dangers of the coast were circulated to frighten the Yankee adventurers; nevertheless by the first of the nineteenth century many American ships sailed to Sumatra for a share of the pepper trade.

Capt. Joseph Ropes in the American ship Recovery finally located Padang in November, 1802, and sailed away from there with a cargo of pepper. Two years later the Putnam sailed from Salem, and also obtained a cargo of the precious spice at Padang. Boom towns sprang up all along the Sumatra coast, bearing such picturesque names as Analaboo, Soo-soo, Tanger and North Tally Pow. It was this same venturesome captain with the Salem ship Recovery that entered the harbor of Mocha, the first American vessel to enter this port. This resulted in the establishment of the American coffee industry.

Salem ships were first to engage in commerce with Hindustan, Java, Japan, Fiji Islands, Madagascar, New Holland and New Zealand. They were among the first to sail the west coast of Africa and South America. A Salem ship was the first to round the Cape of Good Hope, and the first to carry the American flag through the Straits of Magellan. The Salem ship Atlantic, in command of Capt. Elias Hasket Derby Jr., was the first to fly the Stars and Stripes in the harbors of Bombay and Calcutta. The Peggy, another Salem ship brought the first cargo of Bombay cotton to New England. It was the Astrea under Capt. Henry Prince of Salem that began our trade with the Philippines in 1796.

These voyages were not pleasure trips, neither were the captains of these ships adventurers. They were merchants, soldiers and ambassadors. They faced many dangers, from pirates, the ships of hostile nations, treacherous natives, coral reefs and the fierce typhoons of the tropics.

This service developed a splendid type of manhood; and no city in the early days of the nation could boast of prouder names than the Derbys, Crowninsheilds, Forresters, Thorndykes, Peabodys, Pickmans, Wests and Silsbees of Salem. The very nature of these voyages gave a peculiar character to the people. The length of time spent on the oceans by these captains gave them a splendid opportunity to improve their minds. From among the masters, supercargoes, and other officers of these Indiamen, there have been many members of the Massachusetts legislature, three members of Congress, two secretaries of the navy, a United States senator and a great mathematician, second to none in ancient or modern times, one who corrected the works of Newton and enlarged the heavens of La Place.

It was the merchants of Salem, Marblehead and Beverly, who were the first to take out letter of marque and reprisal and formed that fleet of privateers whose services turned the fortunes of war in our favor both in the Revolution and in 1812. The privateersmen of New England won more victories, and captured more prizes in both these wars than the entire fleets of our navy.

In 1798 the citizens of Salem voted to build and equip a thirty-two gun frigate, and present her to the U. S. Navy to suppress the French ravages on our West India trade.

This ship was called the Essex, and she was launched in 1709. After protecting our West Indian trade for several months she was sent to the Barbary Coast, where she took part in the defeat of the pirates that preyed on our commerce. Her name was made illustrious during the war of 1812, when she won a heroic battle from a superior British ship. At that time Midshipman Farragut, who afterwards became Admiral, was a member of the crew.

These incidents prove the value of a merchant marine to the prosperity and security of the nation. A country whose sons are trained in the hard school of the sea; and which has as a nucleus for national defense its own native born sailors, need not fear the ships of any enemy that may attempt to invade its shores.

We must regain our old prestige on the seas; to open to our young men the channels of a trade closed to them for a generation, and in this way develop for national defense that sturdy manhood which comes from those whose life and love are for the sea.

The patriotic citizens of this country, backed by that patriotic organization, The Home Market Club, have been and are now urging upon Congress to adopt a vigorous American policy for the upbuilding of an American Merchant Marine.

The Cave Man's Wooing

By Eleanor Valentine

I HEARD her voice on the mountain, as I walked the trail, and back again to the cave, now so desolate. Like the evening shades' mantling charm, my heart seemed to darken with the loneliness of the life I had led.

Reluctantly I approached the dwelling I had loved, where I lived in such quiet seclusion. Now, the grey of the cavern chilled me. The shadows of the moonlit trees lengthened into grotesque shapes. Their weirdness enthralled me. My eyes moved along with their slowly shifting forms, the while her voice, dominating every chord of my memory, changed with them, blending within me into shapes of things yet unborn.

I dragged the sheep-skin nearer to the play of light and shadow, that nothing might escape my eager outlook. All night, and into the break of day, I lay in the opening. Sleep would not close my eyes. The same enduring, tender voice, had brought new life. My blood rioted mad. Oh, woman! I, the rough-clad and scraggly male of human-kind, craved the companionship of a woman. A woman, delicate in tracing and expression, the one, the only one, whose soul is linked unto mine. Even so far apart! Yet must I ever seek you. I must leave the cot in the mountain, and seek afield for my mate. Oh, woman, to denude my Paradise of its peace! The blood of my ancestors, and yours, calls for you, yearns for your presence.

The dawn budded pink o'er the mountain. The dew-kissed grass in freshness allured me. I waded through grassy depths to the woods, for morn's baptism. Within the many crevices of rock and bank, ferns grew, and as I passed by, I touched one fragile maiden-hair fern, and it quivered its dainty leaves in response to my caress.

I thought how soon the woodland would miss me, and would she care for each beloved woodland flower as I have cared? Then came to me denial. I needed no companion in this wilderness. Morn strengthened me, subdued the night longings, and blotted out the shadows. Dawn's awakening recalled me to mother nature. What mortal soul of man or woman can bring to this place a greater thought of harmony? Nature! I but forsook you, to be more ravished by your charm. Loveliest of all, again am I your adorer, and the worshipper at your shrine.

Lightly and happily, I walked back to my cave, the cavern in the mountain, this my home and shelter. The morning light brightened its grey walls. Even the dew-sprinkled rock ferns freshened their shade, and I loved and revered my home.

The sun-ripened hazelnuts lay beside the woodland path, the burst husks covering the ground, I gathered and ate their rich kernels. The sparkling brook's cool waters quenched my thirst. Oh, man of the city's mold, you might envy my paradise. The rich garnet of May apples, the harmonizing ebon shades of huckle and blackberries, mingling with the deep orange of the mulberry, all such as these, are mine, mine in the sacred precincts of the forest. I am monarch of all this domain, crowned with the laurel leaf, my Court the courting of woodland flowers; a king who in himself has found the inner crown purpling his royal hours.

The sun is warming the paths. The trail to the mountain beckons me. Before the noonday's pulsing heat, I shall have walked to the summit of the mount. It stands, a monument to Time's patience. Indeed, it is nature's great king. I raise my eyes to you in reverence, Oh, king, my homage is justly yours. Ah! Upon your slopes, what splendors do you grace. Your sparkling lake, your forest deep, and my own cavern above your cliffs.

The beasts of the forest have learned their ways, and appreciate their worth. I am not the ruthless male of mankind, destroying for selfish ends the children of the wilderness, nor do I feed upon their flesh. The gentle deer, from dark, velvety eyes, look on me as their protector and friend.

I have been to the mountain top, through depths of russet-brown woodland path, through to the lake, to carry home the water-cress which thrives among the stagnant pools, my salad for my meal at eventide. I found a nesting of wild duck eggs among the rushes, and three became provision for another meal. I could not abuse your trust, Oh, mother-fowl, and left remaining four. Other duck lives, and your little brood amid the myriad colony, will quite suffice to populate the lake's wide edge. I promise to refrain from taking your nest again.

As dusk came over the woodland, I slowly loitered home. The fading light softened the tones of my rock walls. After my meal of abundance, my ravenous appetite stayed, I read, in the fading glow, my books, my Masters, portraying destiny. I am rich in the knowledge of the world, and satisfied with my Masters, but even the student may add to their reasonings, the wisdom bred in his soul, and life has much to teach. Clearness of mind, such as mine, can improve the thought of the world, and on the day it needs me most I shall be ready to point out the truth.

Young and old can appreciate the works of a master soul, which would but propagate the wisdom gained by truth. Oh, could you worldlings but share my knowledge, but understand the law, God's law, and live as nature meant! How unnecessary that thing called ill-health would be, that destroys what nature lavished upon you.

In the flickering light of the candle's glow, I read far into the night. Book reading quells many desires, I have found, but I am restless tonight. The tramp through the forest has made me energetic, perhaps. I need the solace of sleep, so kind to us mortals.

As I lay on my sheep-skin, I heard the cooing notes of birds. The moonlight fascinated me. Each tree seemed a part of me, and I searched, by the moon's light, to discover the mated birds, who my peace so disturbed, cooing, softly cooing, each tone coaxing me from my rest.

Again her voice, touching memory within! I ever hear her calling me. The maze of thoughts o'erwhelms me. Is she a part of the universal plan? Does she ever seek, in the city, the throbbing heart of the world, as I have sought, in the woodland? I live in the expectation that she has the understanding of my ways.

I carried my mat outside; the cavern is sultry. Outside, the stars gleamed quietly, peacefully down; the vale and the mountain's summit were silver in the moonlight. To fathom the thought-builder, erecting a dream palace unto the skies, to sense the substance of its ground-work, and its texture, I searched within. Will she accept the building of my dreams? Or when I find her, shall the world have sheathed her form in its desires?

Impatiently I sought the woodland glade, drank of the brook, cooling the riot of flaming thoughts and wonderments. At last, I lay beside its edge, listening to its monotone, in the cool damp. The dews gathered over me and soon sleep's cooling draught lulled me, while yet I heard her voice calling, calling, ever so far away.

This morning, I despised my weakness. Night had overwhelmed me. I needed her cover to hide my shame. Oh, woman, so to lead me on! In the freshly beaming morn, I exult, I am free in the woodland, teeming with the ardor of nature.

Yet shall I find you, woman of my thoughts' realm. High have I placed thee, clothed in purity's veil.

I returned to the cave, happy, confident, and in peace. Nature would have mocked me, but now I know the time has come to leave the woodland, and go far from the mountains, into earth's heaving mass of humanity, and for your sake, sweet woman of tender dreams, you who called that night on the mountain, you who still cling to me in thought.

Down the trail leading from the cavern, the hermit steadily wended his way toward the distant city. A tall, slender man, tanned, and with a beard bronzed from the sun's rays. Even the hair that fell in long locks over his neck, was sun-bleached and streaked with gold, nature's markings.

Timidly he approached the city. The noise appalled him. Hesitating, he turned backward to the great highway, but immediately again toward the city's gate. The populace stared at his approach, amazed. Heedless, and with strong step, he walked along their main street, followed by curious crowds, and the careless jests of men, while the women sneeringly gazed at his comeliness, and children hooted and laughed.

Bravely he wended his way down the streets, up narrow alleys, till, with just a few of the most curious followers behind him, near the edge of the town, he spied a house standing alone, seemingly unoccupied. And all weary and dust-stained, he knocked at the door of the house, while the curious watched from without the gate.

A kind-faced woman opened the door and gazed at him, shocked, but pityingly, when, in calm, dignified manner he asked for shelter. Her pity turned to mild surprise as she invited him to enter.

In all sincerity, he told her of his life on the mountain. Out in the world, somewhere, her own son was a wanderer, perhaps another mother sheltered him. And when this lonely son of some mother, asked the privilege of living in the old barn, she tearfully asked him to make her humble dwelling his home for the time being. He refused, and asked again for the barn. "For I have always lived with nature," he said, and thus again, nature gave her beloved a resting place, and peace even within the city's thrall.

The barn, with honeysuckle vines entwined around it, stood beneath the shade of an old, spreading cherry tree, studded with shining red cherries, while pink and white roses clambered everywhere. And he sat himself upon the grass, and spread before him the forest nuts, and ate in thankful mood, while blessing the kindness of the one soul who sheltered him. As dusk came darkening the day, he silently watched and waited for night. His recollections of the cavern, and his longings to be there, saddened the hours. Away from home, away from the mountain, all his domain stood pictured clearly before him.

As for her, the excitement of the day had abated his insistent thoughts. Not woman, but dark gloom of the cavern, beckoned him for quiet and rest. He but wished the seclusion of his rock in the mountain, away from his fellowmen.

Far into the night, he tremblingly waited, afraid to approach the highway. And, even as the hours passed, he hesitated to leave this shelter.

At last, when bravery had conquered his timidity, out through the gate he went into the unknown. Along the pavements, his bare feet softly trod upon the city's walks. Some lone gardens stood forth in the clear moonlight, a touch of their green wildness reminding him of the wood flowers, his garden spot. The sweet odors soothed the tumult in his breast, and promised him his night's rest.

At early morn, he started toward the misty hills. Of a sudden, he heard a voice, coming from a latticed window, singing:

"Holy nature, ever free,
Let me ever follow thee;
Guide me with a hand so mild,
As thou wouldst a little child."

The voice! Her voice! "My Father in Heaven," he cried, "I thank Thee for Thy guidance. I have obeyed the call, and reap the reward Thou hast provided."

The voice ceased. He recalled each sweet sound, burying it in his heart. Lightly were his steps now homeward bound, across the streets, across the park, back to the honeysuckle bower. That night, in light slumber, he dreamed of the one he sought.

With daylight, he arose, freshened from his long rest. The brook was not here for him, but he used the means at hand, and bathed in the clear water of the trough, which for years had provided refreshment for man's most faithful friend. Even the city is kind to nature's lover, he thought.

A vegetable garden thrived back of the house, and with his benefactor's consent, he lived upon Earth's product, and in return, helped her as the wandering son might have done, and she appreciated his worth. Peacefully he lived in his shelter among the roses and honeysuckle vines. Even the curious ones were admirers of his industrious habits.

Evenings, he passed the door of his beloved, and one night, in early twilight, a tall, slender girl, with braids of dusky hair twined round her head, was softly singing while plucking her flowers. He gazed, enraptured by her beauty, while she looked up from her flowers, and from the depths of dark brown eyes, gazed inquiringly at him.

"Pardon, dear lady," he said, "Often I look on your flower garden; its flowers bring to me memories of the wild flowers in the hills."

"Oh, nature man," said she, "if you desire these flowers I have plucked, you are welcome to them."

He walked through the gate, and took from her outstretched hand the bunch of flowers, then stood and gazed upon her loveliness, clad simply and becomingly in the whiteness of snow. He looked upon her little feet, encased in sandals. She is mine, he thought, and I have the right to wonder over her charms.

Blushingly, she acknowledged his scrutiny, and modestly turned toward the house, while he gently said "Good Night," and moved away, back to the home he was now accustomed to. "I have seen her," he cried, when within its safe shelter, "Mine, mine, and only mine!"

And soon, he thought, as he gazed on the moon's last quarter, when the waning nights pass, I shall take her to the cavern on the mount. And she will come, I know. Did she not call me from its depths? And now the time has come for her to brighten its dark walls. I yearn for the wilderness. I long for its peace and shelter. How must the mists, that wrap their cloak round the mountain appear tonight! Would that we were there! But the new moon will see us in that haven of peace.

The new moon came, pale in its crescent shape, and lo! the city's gate brings forth two souls from its enclosure. A strong, bronzed, bare-headed man, leading a delicate and timid woman along the broad highway. A heavy cloak envelops her slender form, as he tenderly guides her steps. Happily they walk along their way, their hearts too full to speak the needless endearments that mankind lavishes upon its loved ones. Only the stones in the roadway retard their pace along the highway.

In the distance, the mountain loomed against the sky. The mists were absent this night, and the silvery moonlight enhanced the clearness of its slopes. Past miles of fences, and dusky ways, through silent woods, again upon the moon-lighted road, they followed the trail to the mountain. And as they climbed the rocky paths, she clung closer to him. The rustling of the leaves frightened her. His soft voice, "Quiet, 'tis but the birdlings amongst the leaves," soothed her endless fears.

The sparkling lake shimmered before their eyes, and he gazed lovingly upon it. She, too, seemed enthralled by its beauty, and time passed as the watchers stood by its edge. Then down the trail, past steep cliffs, to the cavern, outstanding against the mountain's side, with the shadows of the moonlit trees before it.

He led her to the opening, and tenderly embraced her. "Our home," he whispered, "Come, the new moon will soon be passed over, and morn will claim its day." Then, through the mouth of the cavern, they passed into the depths of its shadows.

In the Realm of Bookland

"Blue Grass and Broadway."

There are many books being written and while we recognize the truth, the tragedy or the passion of these creations, few have the individual charm, the imaginative vision of Maria Thompson Davies' romances. Was it not Pindar who said of himself "There is many an arrow in my quiver, full of speech to the wise, but for the many, they need interpreters?" It is not so with Miss Davies' drama-stories. They are so human-hearted that they ring true. She knows Broadway and she knows the player-folk that frequent it, for it is there that her own plays are produced. Her latest story, "Blue Grass and Broadway," is the tale of a sweet, spirited, Kentucky girl, who comes to New York, to see about a venture of her own in the dramatic world. She is plunged into the mad, merry and the tragic theatrical life that environs her. Her happiness, her hope and all that she loves is at stake. It is a great game that is played there. You will want to read it for you cannot take it for granted.

"Blue Grass and Broadway."—The Century Co., New York; cloth, ornamental, 12 mo. 373 pp.; $1.50.

"Uncle Sam's Boys With Pershing."

The "Altemus Boys of the Army Series" has been still further strengthened by the addition of another volume "Uncle Sam's Boys With Pershing," by H. Irving Hancock. This story is fully up in thrill and dash to those that have gone before it in the boys series by Mr. Hancock. The young readers will follow the fortunes of Captain Dick Prescott at grips with the Boche with absorbed interest. They will rejoice with him and sorrow with him and live right with him and his friend, Tom Reade, the daring aviator, from cover to finish. These boy heroes are strong and vital and they have the zeal and push that are inherent in the real American wherever he may be at home or "Over There."

"Uncle Sam's Boys With Pershing." —Henry Altemus Co., Philadelphia; cloth, ornamental, 12 mo. 255 pp.; 50c.

"Twelfth U. S. Infantry."

There are a number of regimental books, in the course of preparation, but at the time when the men of the Twelfth Infantry began their book, last December, the idea was a new one. Their book is also the first one that is off the press. It is therefore a pioneer, as it were. California dearly loves a pioneer, especially when they are "native sons," and the men who have written this history story are largely Californians.

The book is made up of unsigned sketches of army and camp life, charming little bits of fiction, poetry and regimental life and history. It is bright, witty and reaches the spirit of comradeship, the universal spirit of brotherly love, which is illuminating of this epoch-making time, when as Carlyle voices it, "A small Poet every Worker is." The Photographic work was done, for the most part, by two moving picture directors from Los Angeles; Edward R. Watkins of Berkeley, has his name on a number of clever sketches. Then there are also the drawings of Timothy Brereton, a resident of Los Angeles, whose work the critics of New York thought so promising. That is a pathetic phase of the work as he was accidentally shot and killed before he saw the completed book. The business and publicity end of the book was upheld by men from San Jose, Bakersfield and Mill Valley. Former President William Howard Taft wrote the Foreword from which I append a part, "The spirit of the men at the front was felt by the men training at home —nor should these typically American boys and their commanders allow themselves to feel that they did not take part in winning this war. The Germans showed a yellow streak in not fighting this war through to the end. They surrendered in anticipation of the just punishment they and their country would have suffered by being subjected to the devastation of war, had they further resisted. They did not further resist because they knew that the United States had two million men on French soil and two million men at home, who were being hastened to the front and that with these reinforcements defeat was as certain for them as if they accepted it by immediate surrender. The army of the United States was a unit. Those who were in front were strengthened, protected and given weight, by those who were back of the front. Every man in khaki was part of the forces that won the war. The Twelfth Regular Infantry was a unit in the Army of the Republic and carries the laurels of the victory. This book is its history. May it have a wide circulation."— "Twelfth U. S. Infantry," from the press of G. P. Putnam Sons, New York; cloth, illustrated, 8 vol.; 425 pp.; $2.50. On sale at Paul Elder's, San Francisco.

"How to Live."

This carefully prepared book comes to us enlarged and rewritten so that the subject of hygiene both personal and general is right up to date. Its sponsors, Irving Fisher, Professor of Political Economy, Yale; and Eugene Lyman Fisk, M. D. Medical Director of Life Extension Institute, are eminently qualified to place this health saving volume before the people. Former President William H. Taft writes the foreword. In it he quotes from Disraeli, the great statesman and writer, who alert to the influences affecting national prosperity stated: "Public health is the foundation on which reposes the happiness of the people and the power of a country." Without individual and family care there can be no public health. This book is a guide and a moving factor in bringing about an improved physical condition and an extension of life among our people.

A chapter on "air," which embraces, housing, clothing, outdoor sleeping and deep breathing, is among the many subjects treated. Food, activity, alcohol, tobacco, as well as all the necessary factors for the making of health and the toning up of the system are exhaustively gone into. Tables, guides and charts are supplied, as well as illustrations. If you will study this book faithfully with an open mind you may be like unto— "Olympian Bards who sung
Divine ideas below,
Which always find us young
And always keep us so."
"How to Live."—Funk & Wagnalls Co., New York and London; cloth, illustrated, 12 mo., 460 pp.; $1.00.

Overla
Mon

August   1919

Opportunity's One Knock

When *Opportunity* knocks, will we hear her?

Or will our ears be so deafened with debts and our minds so filled with money worries that we do not hear her happy message?

W. S. S. and Thrift Stamps help Opportunity knock loudly—one knock enough.

W. S. S.—
Everybody's Opportunity

Savings' Division
War Loan Organization
Treasury Department

Vol. LXXIV   No. 2

Overland Monthly

AN ILLUSTRATED MAGAZINE OF THE WEST

CONTENTS FOR AUGUST, 1919

NOTICE.—Contributions to the Overland Monthly should be typewritten, accompanied by full return postage, and with the author's name and address plainly written in upper corner of first page. Manuscripts should never be rolled.

The Publisher of the Overland Monthly will not be responsible for the preservation or mail miscarriage of unsolicited contributions and photographs.

Issued Monthly. $1.20 per year in advance. Ten cents per copy. Back numbers 3 months or over 25c; six months or over 50c; nine months or over 75c; 1 year or over $1.00. Postage: To Canada, 3 cts.; Foreign, 5 cts.

Published by the OVERLAND MONTHLY COMPANY, San Francisco, California.

259 MINNA STREET.

Yellowstone Brown Bear

At Rest in Yellowstone

Mountain Lion Killed by Government Scouts in Yellowstone

OVERLAND  MONTHLY

Founded 1868

BRET HARTE

| VOL. LXXVI | San Francisco, August, 1919 | No. 2 |

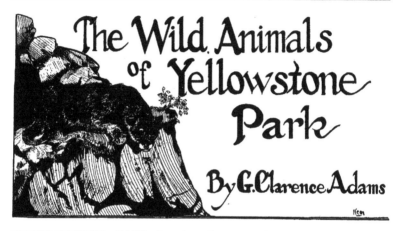

The Wild Animals of Yellowstone Park

By G. Clarence Adams

YELLOWSTONE PARK is the natural home of wild animal life. It is the largest and most successful preserve in the world. It covers 3,300 square miles of mountains and valleys and is nearly as nature made it. The 200 miles of roads, the five enormous hotels, with a big Wylie Camp near each, the two lunch stations, all this is as nothing in this vast wilderness. No tree has been cut, save for road, trail or camp. No firearms are allowed, excepting for the official destroyer of some predatory beast. Visitors keep so closely to the beaten track that the animals have learned in all these years, that the strangers mean them no harm.

People filling the long trains of stages from point to point during the season, seldom see any of the animals, but the quiet watcher on the trails may see deer, bear, elk and antelope to his heart's content, and he may see sheep, moose and bison by journeying on foot or horseback into their retreats. The deer, especially, gather in large numbers around the hotels almost as soon as the season is closed and the noisy life is over.

One interesting lesson is taught, i. e.— Wild animals are fearful and dangerous only when men treat them as game or enemies. Even the grizzlies will make every effort to get away; if this fails, he becomes very dangerous, indeed.

This wild animal farm, using the figures authorized by Uncle Sam, contains 30,000 elk, several thousand moose, innumerable deer, many antelope and a large and increasing herd of buffalo.

It is also a wonderful bird preserve. More than 150 species, living natural and undisturbed lives. Eagles are numerous among the crags. Wild geese and ducks are plentiful. Many thousands of large white pelicans help to create a scene of picturesqueness in the Yellowstone Lake.

My first acquaintance with this wild life began when we came out into the valley through which the Yellowstone River winds and flows, seeing what at

A Mule Train on the Last Swing Into Yellowstone Park

that distance looked like droves of cattle feeding. On getting closer we found they were large herds of. elk, deer and mountain sheep feeding on the abundance of rich pasturage on the slopes and widening out valleys. Their number were hard to estimate with any degree of accuracy, as some were so far away on the sloping hillsides that they were only specks, but there were many close enough to get a good look at. There were hundreds upon hundreds of them. None of our party estimated them at less than a thousand and some at two, while no one could even conjesture how many were back behind the lines of the travel. They did not court close inspection, but our driver assured us that later in the season much of their shyness dis-

appeared. However, we were close enough to many to see, judge and voice our sincere admiration of them.

From now on animal life spread out before us along the valley and banks of the blue winding Yellowstone River, all the way to the big lake at its head. It was here that we saw elk and deer in abundance. The huge horns of the male elk and deer made them look not unlike a herd of the old time Texas steers, although the elk were much larger. The deer were in small groups of seven to twelve. Calves and fawns were numerous. The fawns, full of grace and beauty, capered around as if they enjoyed every minute of life and were glad of a chance to show that they did. During the season, which lasted three months, I rode

Buffalo Grazing in Yellowstone

A. Yellowstone Grizzly Bear

repeatedly over this same part of the park and never had the faintest glimpse of those herds or any part of them again, and only an occasional deer.

For two weeks during the first part of the season, at about the same hour in the early morning, 5:30 A. M., a herd of deer came along under the front windows of the hotel—but sometimes not so close. All were fully grown and with head up and coat looking like they had been manicured that very morning. One morning the second porter came rushing around the hotel corner with a kodak; for a snapshot, scaring them so badly that they came no more. I was disappointed, as I always enjoyed seeing, and looking over their symmetrical graceful lines, and their wild pretty brown eyes and shy ways appealed to me.

There was another visitor that regularly for more than a month came each morning to the back door of the Hash Emporium where the drivers and stable men were fed. It was only a short distance from the hotel. This was a fine full grown female elk. No one seemed to know much about her, but there was rumor to the effect that she had been disabled in some way when very young and had been nursed and fed by one of the caretakers who stay at each of the hotels during the nine months of the year when there is nothing but snow, ice and water in the park. She was supposed to have a calf somewhere out in the wilds, but no one had the temerity or sense to go out and look for it. She was fully grown and a superb specimen. She never came closer than thirty feet from the back door, that seeming to be her limit. Someone was always on hand with a plate of biscuit, of which she was very fond. I have gone over a number of

Great Falls of the Yellowstone

times and tried my hardest to even touch some part of that elk besides her tongue, lips or nose. But it was all in vain, for try as I would I could never succeed in touching any other part. All of these members were freely proffered for the tempting biscuits. I never got my hand on her, so I could know what her coat of hair felt like. She would dodge like a flash. Just so far and no farther, was her motto. And I succeeded just as well the first as the last time. She would follow that biscuit closely with her nose, long tongue and big eyes, but would stand for no liberties anywhere else. I finally gave it up and when I fed her

lows. These were shortly followed by three Silver Tips. They were all fully grown. Cubs seemed scarce that day.

As I sat there all my long ago boyish ideals about bears came back to me— stories of all that bears had done, their great strength, what they could do, all came staring me in the face and daring me to try not to realize that these were bears in their natural haunts. I could see a lot more snouts barely showing back of the others, afraid to come out. I was on a bench a little back in the woods, but could see out all right. The bears kept coming my way, turning over everything and getting a little closer all

A Bunch of Yellowstone Elk

after that I did it the easiest way. She was a noble beast; fat and smooth-haired but lacking the pretty, soft brown eye of her relative, the deer.

I took a book one day and went out to what is called the Bear Dump, about a quarter of a mile from the hotel. This is a clearing with woods on all sides, where the garbage from the hotel tables is thrown out free for all comers, but is mostly patronized by the bears. I timed it so that it was their usual visiting time and did not have to wait long. First came two black bears. Pretty soon a little further on came three big brown fel-

the time. One of them, especially, seemed fond of my location. I at once gave him my undivided attention. But just as I was about to go away from there something happened. Every bear was rigid, on his hind feet, with every snout pointed in the same direction. While I was still staring, here came two lumbering monstrous Grizzlies. Neither showed any signs of friendliness and they were not pleasant to look at. The effect of their entrance upon this peaceful scene was galvanic. Away went every bear at top speed. That long, awkward gallop of theirs gets them over the

Yellowstone Lake, Yellowstone Park

ground surprisingly fast and soon lost them in the woods.

I can now understand why the bear hunters say it takes a good horse to keep a bear in sight. I also believe it to be true when they claim a bear can run faster up hill than down or on a level. Part of the retreating force climbed trees and the rest were swallowed up in the woods. A Grizzly cannot climb a tree—at least he never does. I never realized before what a terror a Grizzly is to the rest of the bear family. The new arrivals did not tarry long, just nosed around a little and with a sweet consciousness of a duty well performed, vanished. The bears that had advanced backward in such haste soon returned, bringing a number of their intimate friends with them.

When I saw those bears for the first time, while everything was new to me, come sauntering from different directions into the dump, with their sniffy, suspicious snouts in the air, it made me think of what I used to read when I was a boy, and the blood-curdling bear hunting stories until my hair stood straight up and the ends split.

I went out to the dump one day and found a big steel cage almost as large as the cages that confine the bears under the big circus tent. It was really a trap and I became fully convinced before many days that it was strong and big enough to hold any size bear that the big door thudded behind. All hope abandons any bear that entered there. On going back to the hotel I learned that the Smithsonian Institute, Washington, D. C., had sent out for as good a specimen of the Cinnamon bear as could be procured and that trap was the first step towards the filling of the order.

On the afternoon of the second day I went out to the dump and seeing a group of bears very much excited about something, I ventured a closer investigation. The bears all left at my approach and I found that big cage filled by a Cinnamon bear. The men in charge had evidently been trying to get him changed into something that they could haul him away

in, but for the time being had given it up as a bad job. How that rascal did make things hum, soon raised the hum to a full whistle. He shook that cage like it was thistledown and told me in a very ugly way what he thought of me. He seemed to have the whole thing studied out and wanted to get rid of it. He was one mass of white lather.

I tried to push a flat basin of fresh water nearer the cage, using a pole a little less than forty feet long, but he let loose such a bunch of snarls and had such a paroxysm of rage while his long, ugly claws came outside so much farther than I ever thought they could, that I really wanted him taken out of the park. I dropped my pole, backed out, turned around and went away.

It must have been at this dump that the bears got the tin cans on their feet that the late Theodore Roosevelt, while President, wrote to John Burroughs about and which is published in Natural History, a journal published by the Museum of Natural History, New York. I give that part of it relating to the bears here in insert letter:

White House, Washington,
August 12, 1904.

Dear Old John—

I think that nothing is more amusing and interesting than the development of the changes made in wild beast character by the wholly unprecedented course of things in the Yellowstone Park. I have just had a letter from Buffalo Jones, describing his experiences in trying to get tin cans off the feet of the bears in the Yellowstone Park. There are lots of tin cans in the garbage heaps which the bears muss over, and it has now become fairly common for a bear to get his paw so caught in a tin can that he cannot get it off and of course great pain and injury follow. Buffalo Jones was sent with another scout to capture, tie up and cure these bears. He roped two and got the can off of one, but the other tore himself loose, can and all, and escaped.

Think of the Grizzly bear of the early Rocky Mountain hunters and explorers,

A Bit of Wild Life, Yellowstone

and then think of the fact that part of the recognized duties of the scouts in the Yellowstone Park at this moment is to catch this same Grizzly bear and remove tin cans from the bear's paws in the bear's interest!

Always yours,

(Signed)   Theodore Roosevelt.

A Monarch of the Yellowstone

There were two grown bears that came up to the hotel sometimes and were so tame that with a little coaxing with sugar, could be snapped while on their hind legs reaching for the tempting morsel. I had some fun with one on a number of early mornings, back of the hotel. He was one of the largest I have seen. But I quit it—I was afraid I might be mistaken in the bear, and if a bear of that size was to hit me I wouldn't want anything on this earth but a doctor, and wouldn't want him much.

There was one bear about two-thirds grown, that was the prettiest and, if I may use the expression, the daintiest bear I have ever seen—always so clean and glossy looking and the only shiny blue black one that I saw during the summer. I could always tell him readily enough, as he outclassed anything in the park. I enjoyed feeding him, but he never came near the hotel.

I also passed some pleasant times with the squirrels there, they were often amusing. They were mostly the grey variety, but smaller than our California grey timber squirrels. The season being too short for nut growing, there are not many squirrels except around the hotels. They would run all over you and would shell a nut very quickly while you held it in your hand, but if you let go, they would go off with it. As long as you would furnish the nuts they would do the hulling and proceed to fill their pouches with the kernels. No sooner were their pouches filled than away they would go to their dens, empty them and come back for more.

We called one of them John D. Rockefeller because he wanted all you had for him, and also all you had or were trying to give to any other squirrel. The minute John had filled his pouches he ran at his topmost speed to his domicile, emptied his pouch and came back just as fast, and woe to any squirrel that interfered with his real or prospective lunch. He had to run for his life or take a threshing. He always ran, and ran well.

THE WONDERLAND OF THE PACIFIC

By THOS. J. McMAHON

APAU (or British New Guinea), is a land of great commercial prospects, of magnificent scenery, home of the Bird of Paradise, and of wild peoples with weird customs. Next to Australia, New Guinea, as it was once called before it was shared out to three nations, is the largest island in the Southern Pacific. It will probably be one day the most wonderful, for it teems with great, useful, varied and necessary tropical products. This immense island is now subdivided into Papua, or British New Guinea, Kaiser Wilhelm Land, or German New Guinea, and the whole of the northwestern portion known as Dutch Territory.

The island is remarkable for its great rivers, deep, swift, and navigable for hundreds of miles to very large steamers, its interesting and savage tribes of natives and especially so for its noble, towering mountains. Like a backbone these great mountains run through the center of the island, with Papua to the south, German New Guinea to the north. Hid away in the depths of these mountain fastnesses the wonderland of the Pacific exists.

Running up to 12 and 13 thousands of feet in altitude, the central mountains of the Papuan side are overpowering and inspiring in their grandeur; to their highest summits they are verdure-clad and with the slanting rays of the tropical sunshine upon them and due to atmospheric conditions, they assume mammoth figure-heads, or land-marks of burnished gold, dazzling in the extreme, filling the mind with awe, and creating in fancy a land of ethereal peoples, cities and ideal climatic conditions.

It was to this wonderland that an adventurous band of white men—four in number, including the author—with 120 native carriers, 72 well-armed native constabulary, and a hundred or more of body servants led by the Governor of

2

The Home of a Papua Writer

Papua, His Excellency Judge Murray, sallied forth from Yule Island to the southeast, to attain the secrets of nature, of the pure Papuans, a pigmy people, and to explore the prospects of those central mountains to at least seven thousand feet high.

This journey had to be accomplished on foot and took six weeks of constant traveling, climbing steadily day after day, triumphing over one series of ranges to be confronted by the abrupt inclines or walls of others, and the misty outlines of others again away in the mighty distance. It was a journey of exertion, but it brought exultation to the mind and heart, and as the glories of the magnificent scenery unfolded to the astonished eyes, it grew in romance and increased in beauty.

Down from the mountain sides came mountain torrents pouring themselves over and over in their haste, tearing their courses out by a daring, headlong rush, roaring foam-flecked, mighty, sparkling like rivers of gold, dashing past hugh black boulders, to fall away into gentle meandering streams, and thence through deep, dark, tropical jungles to swell into broad-bosomed rivers as they progress to the distant sea. These rivers flash in the midst of the jungles like great silver ribbons. Or again looking upward a mass of silver waters drops down from some towering height, a waterfall of surpassing loveliness in its setting of foliage.

There are literally thousands of such waterfalls on every side to be seen in a day's march. One day the tourist world will awaken to the Wonderland of Papua and countless numbers will throng there to witness how magnificently grand nature can, under tropic skies, bloom forth.

There are many features of those mountains that are uncommon, but none of them are more entrancing than the effects of the mists that play about the mountain tops. These changing mists now pure snowy white and now a kaleidoscope of colors stolen from vivid rainbows, coming up in great billows,

Port Moresby, Capital of Papua

sweeping against the mountainsides, like waves of the sea, now rising and now falling and again dissolving, laying bare the sharp outlines of pinnacles, the glistening dew-washed verdure. Here and there tremendous patches of bright red soil, and gaps seen along mountain peaks the result of vast landslides. Yes the mists of the Papuan mountains are beyond compare.

In these mountains there is everlasting sunshine and gladness, for though even at mid-day every day precisely on time, great storms come up, with thunder rumbling and lightning flashing and rain falling in torrents, there continues a brightness that is marvelous and sometimes unearthly. To the north, the south, the east, the west, on every summit, on every crag, on every spur, and away in the dark valleys below are native villages, brown splashes of color against the strong green of the trees, the shrubs, and the endless native gardens that dot the landscape.

The natives are pigmy people, very small in size, but perfect in limb and proportion, handsome of feature while young, but hideously ugly when old. These little beings, both men and women, (stark naked, save for rows of necklaces made of dog's teeth, a nose pencil of bone, and a few ear ornaments of shell), are shy when first approached, friendly when satisfied that there is a return of friendship, but treacherous and cruel if offended. They roam about in little groups armed with large bows and poison pointed arrows, and are dexterous marksmen with these weapons.

The young men not married and of marriageable age wear as a sign of this, and a hint to the ladies, needless to say, a tightly fitting wide belt of finely plaited grass. This signifies that the wearer hopes to charm some sweet maid and to assure her that whatever faults he may have, and of course he really has none under the circumstances of love-making, he is not a big eater. The reason for this is that the women are the suppliers of food. They are the workers in the gardens and as it too often happens, divorce and domestic troubles arise out of

Native Carriers in the Mountains of Papua

the healthy appetites of their lords and masters. The women, not unlike women of every land and color, pretend a great deal, and while still single and in irresponsible girlhood romantically lay stress upon the ideal that the men they each one and all may marry must be normal in their consumption of food.

Alas! if man were only constant, he were perfect, but in this case he is not and no sooner does he win his bride than he throws off the belt and displays an appetite that well nigh appalls the lady, and ever afterwards she is his slave— the slave of a perpetual gormandizer, for if there is one striking thing about those pigmy men it is they never—after marriage cease to eat, they chew and chew, and sugarcane, or betel nuts are always in their dilly bags ready to help stay an unending hunger.

One reason for the visit of Judge Murray and the small army of native constabulary with us was to try and put down the continual tribal warfare in which these people are persistently engaged. They commit the most dreadful murders, and massacres, wiping out whole villages, burning and slaying as they go along and this becomes so serious every little while that the Government has to take drastic steps to bring about a cessation of hostilities. Magistrates are sent out with armed police, not to shoot down the natives, for this is sternly forbidden, but if possible to capture unruly chiefs and bring them to justice, which means getting a few years' imprisonment and this is effectual, inasmuch, that the banishment into a strange, new world affrights their savage natures. When they are carefully and humanely restored to their own tribes and districts by the Government, they spread the story of the power of the white man, of what the white man thinks is wrong and the wonderful weapons the white man uses when he fights, the magical and unseen bullet from guns, which the white man puts to his shoulder, so! pulls a trigger, so! and bang! and the enemy drops dead. Thus by humane and persuasive means these mountain savages are coming to

A Natural Bridge in the Mountains

know that tribal strife will one day have to cease, for the white man will come along and win from the rich soil of the mountain-sides all the fruits and favors of nature, to put them to use for the benefit of the greater, wider world.

But it will be many years before this desirable end is attained; the mountains are thickly populated and nature in her bounteousness supplies every want. Still nearer the coast they are gradually coming under the influence of a wonderful Roman Catholic Mission, conducted by the Fathers, Brothers and Sisters of the Order of the Sacred Heart. These brave people, men and women are eagerly penetrating the wilds of the mountains and setting up numerous mission stations. By kindness, by the power of healing and by commendable patience they have already subdued many thousands of the natives. This is manifest in the decline of cannibal feasts, which were common, and in the gross immoral dances, and rites that always led to war which were the sparks that set their fiendish natures alight and began slaughters of friends and foes alike, just for the mere delight and lust of killing; they were German pure and simple in their Kultur!

Once civilized they become charming and interesting, but strange to say they rapidly decline in numbers, due it is thought to giving up their wild customs and a loss of spirit, the spice of life, goes with the ending of their savage instincts. In their village life they are fearfully careless and dirty, their huts raised, six or seven feet on thin stilts are smoke begrimed, smelly, and dark, while underneath the native pig, an ugly long-snouted creature wallows in a mire of oozing black mud. Under such circumstances it is little wonder that there is a big percentage of the people suffering from a skin disease that is a form of leprosy and which is incurable after childhood. Here the missionaries are doing a splendid work in rescuing children and bringing them into or near the mission stations, where they are tended until healed, when they invariably stay about the mission and become useful.

On our march we met, 90 miles away from this station, one of the good Fathers carrying a native child that he had found in a village and the poor little thing was repulsive from the result of this leprosy. At a village we saw a tiny

Wild Blacks Ready for a War Dance

infant but a few days' old, its little body, from head to sole, so thickly clustered with what looked like warts, but really was the first signs of the leprosy, that it was impossible to find an opening for a pin's point.

At the mission stations on a Sunday the natives crowd in to attend mass, and it is rather a whimsical and amusing scene to see the men on one side, the women on the other, all quite naked, lined up to receive Loin-cloths for the men and Kate Greenaway-dresses for the women. These are to be put on to go into the church, and taken off and returned immediately after service is over.

The mountains of Papua are the rendezvous of that gorgeous creature, the Bird of Paradise, the only place or land in the whole world where this bird is found. It is now protected by law and very severe penalties are inflicted for shooting the bird, or for even the possession of a Paradise plume. Beautiful as this bird is, it still belongs to a low family, to wit, the common crow, and with all its dazzling plumage its call is an un-musical caw. The natives do not regard it in any way as a supernatural being and with their arrows shoot it for feathers for adornment at their native dances.

Another remarkable and weird feature is an insect very like a common cricket and of that family. It is weird and uncanny, that for the tiny size of its body it sends forth a flood of sound that is absolutely deafening. It is called the Six-o'clock Beetle, and no time-piece could be more precise in keeping time. Exactly every night, by comparison with our watches this little giant of sound would at six o'clock pour out a noise similar to a very loud electric gong at a railway station announcing the departure of a train. We could set our watches by its preciseness. For a quarter of an hour myriads of these insects would fill our world with an ear-splitting noise. The hills around us echoing back the sound until we were likely to go distracted. In contrast to this noisy creature with a most pleasing musical sound was a little green-grey frog, called by us the Bell Frog, for it tinkled for all the

The Pigmy People of the Mountains and the Stalwart Men of the Coast

world like a distant bell. It was a cheerful companion; night and day it welcomed us along our march.

Our progress did not permit of more than 12 to 16 miles a day, and that was hard walking, for ascending is tedious and tiresome. When by two o'clock each day we put into camp, having left at perhaps four in the morning, our limbs were often, indeed, very weary. Our native servants did everything for us, pulling off our heavy boots, bringing dry clothing, serving refreshments, having baths ready, and while we lay on our camp stretches they would bring along our dinner, we being sometimes so fatigued that to sit up was impossible.

It was while in the cool of the evening, in the hour of twilight, that the natives from the villages around apprised of our approach would come up and gaze and make offers of friendship. They were generally preceded by native women, the tiny creatures carrying immense loads of yams or bananas. They would present these taking as a reward what they liked best and treasure most

usually a handful of coarse salt. In fact salt was the coinage we used all the way to buy food, or for the services of guides. A peculiar custom of these mountain peoples is, that as a sign of mourning, the women with faces already a deep black, paint them a deeper black, from a mixture made out of charcoal and a plant juice. As to face painting the warriors streaked and touched up their faces in marvelous designs of red and white earthy pigments, having astounding and fear-inspiring results.

Many years ago a body of scientists sent by the late Baron Rothschild into the jungles at the foot of those central mountains came back with wonderful stories of how a kind of wireless communication was used by the natives, and that news by this means was carried hundreds of miles away right into the remote mountain gorges in very short time. The power of this wireless was found later to be greatly exaggerated, though the natives had a very simple, yet effectual means of carrying news, and this we came to understand. As we approached a village a man with a deep, resonant voice, the village crier, would stand on the jetting spur of a hill, and from there give out long regular deep-chested calls. Instantly the echoes would awake, and then criers from the hundreds of villages would take up the calls in turn so that in a space of half an hour the news of our coming would travel many miles.

No matter where we arrived the natives knew for days before that we were coming. This led to friendly relations on the one hand, and on the other gave quarreling tribes time to get out of the way.

We eventually, however, got right into the heart of the zone of tribal warfare, and our native constabulary in a very short time did good work in gathering in oppressive chiefs. Fierce little men were they when brought in, declining food, and ever on the alert to escape. By the sensible methods of Governor Murray, all the tribes were soon separated or dispersed. When we left on our return journey we had the satisfaction of knowing the visit had produced good all-round results and war would or could not break out again for considerable time. Besides, the chiefs captured meant that while they languished in prison there could be no more fighting, their followers were too scared.

Papua has already attracted many Americans and much American capital. There is not the slightest doubt that now the war is over, there is going to set in a tide of wonderful prosperity and progress for this rich country. It is a territory that, though in the tropics, has a variety of climates from the scorching coastal heat to the mild and salubrious temperatures of the mountains we had traversed. It is capable of producing not only every tropical plant, fruit and vegetable, but in the mountains the missionaries have proved that cereals of temperate climate and fruits can grow luxuriantly.

Papua even now is bounding ahead in progress through British and American energy, capital and enterprise, and the day is soon coming when Papua will be known as the WONDERLAND OF THE SOUTH PACIFIC.

Noon

(Written in Washington Square, the Park in San Francisco's "Little Italy," 1918.)

By "The Stevensons"

A shaft of granite glitters grayly in the noon sun. At its base, clean blue water drips in cooling rivulets from a white fountain. Half hidden in the shade of drooping peppers, a jaded workman sleeps. His brown sleeve rubs companionably against the yellow smock of a little art student whole pallette glows with daubs of blue and emerald, white and rose.

A tawny skinned Italian with work-bent shoulders, but a marigold in his jaunty hat; a soft cheeked girl with bold black eyes; old women in shawls tinted like crushed flowers; a wizened Neopolitan, gold hoops in his shrunken ears; a slender, fawn-like boy from far Palermo; two white-cuffed laundresses, chattering in French; a tall Athenian with pale gold hair; these stroll idly by.

A green fly drones indolently about a mass of purple bloom. The grass is soft and summer-scented.

I sleep.

Camel Caravan, Peking

Peking Dust

By Ellen N. La Mottie

Just now when China is so much in the public eye it is of interest to note what Ellen N. La Mottie has to tell us of how China is parceled out and made subservient to the Greater European Powers. We append below from her recent book "Peking Dust," published by The Century Co., New York.—The Editor.

HERE we are in Peking the beautiful Barbaric Capital of China. For Peking is the capital of Asia, of the whole Orient, the center of the stormy politics of the far East.

Peking is not a commercial city, not a business center; it is not filled with drummers or traveling men or small fry of that kind, such as you find in Shanghai and lesser places. It is the diplomatic and political center of the Orient, and here are the people who are at the top of things, no matter how shady the things. At least it is the top man in the concern who is here to promote its interests.

Here are the big concession-hunters of all nationalities, with headquarters in the hotel, ready to sit tight for a period of weeks or months or as long as it may take to wheedle or bribe or threaten the Chinese Government into granting them what they wish—a railroad, a bank, a mine, a treaty port.

The Western nations are in accord, and the Orient—China—belongs to them.

The Way Chinese Farmers Plow

But with Japan it is different. So in future, when you hear that Japan has her eye on China, is attempting to gobble up China, remember that, compared with Europe's total, Japan's holdings are very small, indeed. The loudest outcries against Japanese encroachments come from those nations that possess the widest spheres of influence. The nation that claims forty-two per cent of China, and the nation that claims twenty-seven per cent of China are loudest in their denunciations of the nation that possesses (plus the former German holdings), less than six.

Our first actual contact with a sphere

Driveway in Peking

of influence at work came about in this wise: After we had spent two or three weeks in Korea, we took the train from Seoul to Peking, a two days' journey. In these exciting days it is hard to do without newspapers, and at Mukden, where we had a five-hour wait, we came across a funny little sheet called "The Manchuria Daily News." It was a nice little paper; that is, if you are sufficiently cosmopolitan to be emancipated from American standards. It was ten by fifteen inches in size, comfortable to hold, at any

China on the ground that the Sino-American railway loan agreement recently concluded, infringes upon their acquired rights. The Russian contention is that the construction of the railway from Fengchen to Ninghshia conflicts with the 1899 Russo-Chinese Secret Treaty. The British point out that the Hangchow-Wenchow railway under scheme is a violation of the Anglo-Chinese Treaty re Human and Kwanghsi, and that the proposed railway constitutes a trespass on the British preferential right to build

A Chinese Wall

rate—with three pages of news and advertisements, and one blank page for which nothing was forthcoming. Tucked in among advertisements of mineral waters, European groceries, foreign banking houses, and railway announcements was an item. But for our young man on the boat, I couldn't have known what it meant. We read:

ALLIES PROTEST TO CHINA

Great Britain, France and Russia have lodged their respective protests with

railways. The French Government, on behalf of Belgium, argues that the Lanchow-Ninghsia line encroaches upon the Sino-Belgian Treaty re the Haichow-Lanchow Railway, and that the railway connecting Hanchow with Nanning intrudes upon the French sphere of influence.

There you have it! China needing a railway, an American firm willing to build a railway, and Russia, England, France, and even poor little Belgium blocking the scheme. All of them busy with a tremendous war on their hands, draining all their resources of both time and money, yet able to keep a sharp eye on China to see that she doesn't get any improvements that are not of their making. And after the war how many years will it be before they are sufficiently recovered financially to undertake such an expenditure? China will just have to wait patiently.

On each side of the rocking railway with the immense interior provinces of China — these sunken roads and the rivers.

Just then we passed a procession of camels, and for a moment I forgot all about the article in "The Manchuria Daily News." Who wouldn't seeing camels on the landscape! A whole long caravan of them, several hundred, all heavily laden, and moving in slow, majestic dignity at the rate of two miles an hour!

Chinese Temple

carriage stretched vast arid plains, sprinkled with innumerable villages consisting of mud houses. The fields were cut across in every direction by dirt roads, unpaved, full of deep ruts and holes. At times these roads were sunk far below the level of the fields, worn deep into the earth by the traffic of centuries; so deep in places that the tops of the blue-hooded carts were also below the level of the fields. Yet these roads afford the only means of communication Coming in from some unknown region of the great Mongolian plains, the method of transportation employed for thousands of years! Yes, undoubtedly, China needs railways; but she can't have any more at present, for she has no money to construct them herself, and the great nations who claim seventy-nine per cent of her soil haven't time at present to build them for her. And they object to letting America do it. A sphere of influence is a dog in the manger.

War's Gifts of Words

By Warwick James Price

In this thoughtful and painstaking compilation, Warwick James Price shows how our vocabulary has been enlarged and our language, in many instances, enriched by the new words coined during the war. These word-makers in seeking to express themselves, have realized that henceforth and to all time heroic deeds are now our Epic.—The Editor.

SPEAK plain English. Putting up a barrage like that all 'round what you mean! Camouflage gets across to deceive Boches, but don't dig in when it's only me."

Nothing extenuate nor aught set down imagined, this veritable behind-the-counter comment proclaims one result of the great war. New ways and policies the world over have brought new words and phrases. If it has always been so with a single invention, how much more with twenty-five nations wrapped in a struggle threatening civilization itself?

And not new words only; new content has been read into old ones, till old has become new. The nomenclature of geography itself can never be the same again. France, once held by a much speaking minority to be suggestive of not less than decadence, is now a synonym at once for unyielding steadiness and uplifting inspiration. The vivacity we knew has been found no stronger in the people than a miraculous cheeriness; if we were not surprised at their elan, we have been amazed by their calm endurance. And Belgium? Aside from the mental picture which the name calls up, a picture of horhors long drawn out and heroism beyond measure, the word promises to give us a verb as eloquent as awkward. We may never come to say "to Belgiumize," but we were saying "Venetia was near being made another Belgium," and none mistook the meaning.

Rheims and Louvain, which once connoted the arts and treasures of mind and spirit, now stand types to all men for those arts and treasures desecrated by gross materialism. The Marne is no longer just a peaceful river but a rallying cry like Thermopylae. Who now thinks of Gallipoli as a peninsula, scarce known save to Levantine travelers? It is a glorious blunder, a magnificent mistake, a forlorn hope failing of brilliant success only by the narrowest of margins—yet not so narrow as to leave no room for heroes' graves. That Jutland, which once told of faint, forgotten, far-off Alfred and Canute, has been written down the heading for yet another chapter in the naval annals that shall stir man's blood through years to come. Even Enden shall no longer be index merely to an East Friesland port of gabled houses and frequent fairs, but takes its place along with **Bon Homme Richard** and **Alabama** in the chronicle of privateering gallantry—a gallantry so genuine as to show the traditional exception by which one proves the rule of German maritime beastliness.

There is, too, a whole verbal phalanx of words yesterday quite specific in meaning but now so general as to approach the generic. A "push" or a "drive" takes on a military background of disciplined effort. A "Prussian," for generations now unborn, will imply a human as utterly untrustworthy and as consistently dangerous as some wild thing, even as a "Bolshevik" will suggest a silly, selfish ultra-socialist (whatever the name may originally have meant), a term, moreover, as redolent of reproach if not of scorn as "a Brest treaty," which can never mean aught but lie and cheat. Kultur, materialism's reductio ad absurdum, evermore must equal "atrocity;" as will Lusitania — its syllables embodying no more the thought of that sun-bathed province of luscious grapes but a bitter realization of the acme of all that is cruelest and pre-planned.

The words are legion which show how the new wine of current happenings has been poured into the old bottles of more prosaic events. "Heatless" and "wheatless," and "meatless," and all the rest of that galley, speak now as always in semi-humorous tone and are fast slipping back into the limbo of similar purely transitory counters of speech, and yet today they are as understandable in a specialized sense as "U-boat,"—and what name, in itself so wholly harmless, can ever take on a color so dark as has this adder of the seas! "U-boat behavour!"—what more utterly sweeping condemnation could be passed? "Propaganda" has followed fast down the same steep hill. The worthy Webster read into it no more than an academic "organization for spreading a system of principles," but the man in the street envisions with it such hitherto unthinkable trickery and low deceit that mere self-respect long will shun it. "Hun" was ever an ill-sounding noun, but Attila was rather ancient after all, and its reproach was distant and not overwhelming till the Bernhardi methods, put into red execution by Ludendorf and Bissing, et id omne genus, showed a horrified world that, as "German" was become synonymous for destruction afield and good faith ignored, so Hun was to indicate all the worst and basest in the German make-up. By the same token, never again will "made in Germany" be the cold commercial labeling it has been; it takes on a note lacking all economics and embracing all that is vile.

"Sector" and "unit," somewhat to turn the penny, have moved across from mathematical to militaristic parlance, thence are progressing to not less than a slangy use, general and vague, by no means the clean-cut words that once they were.

The war has given us no one word of such immediate and sharply specialized use (unless it be Hun or Prussian) as camouflage. Not long ago an American writer found it necessary to explain its content to the gentle reader before employing it as title to his short story. To-day it is as much a fixture in our popular speech as "bluff"—often enough used as its equivalent, by the way, which it assuredly is not. Barrage is a second word on the lengthy list which we have been taking over from our French allies. If it meant a "curtain of fire" in the first place, it now means anything that protects and covers. "Drum fire," too, originally exactly technical, has broadened out to betoken any continuous and heavy attack.

"Slacker," of English parentage, is permanently acclimated on this side of the Atlantic. Normally formed and for long years set to dictionary pages, it jumped into general use with this mighty struggle, telling its own story, and is here for as definitely long a stay as human nature, itself, whose less admirable traits it labels. "Profiteer" was half a joke, albeit the man so called was more than half a criminal. Begotten quite as was "copperhead" in the sixties, it has as ominous a sound and will last and spread.

"Dug-out," the noun, and "dig-in," the verb, are further instances of late enrichments of our language. Each, of essentially technical meaning primarily, has budded and burgeoned till to dig in is to conceal oneself, while the place dug (to drop into the stiffer phrasing of the rhetorics) is any place of refuge. And a propos dug-out, how pleasantly truthful was the returned soldier who, telling of the intricacies of the Teuton trench caves along the Somme and interrupted by a query as to how the English built theirs, replied: "They don't build 'em, they take 'em."

Another three of these technical words,

now become as general as they are popular, are "ace" and "low visibility" and "gas mask." How the "ace" came to be transferred from a deck of playing cards to the deck of a working plane will be interesting to hear some of these days; how it came to be transferred from the man who has accounted for at least one of the enemy machines to a man who excells whatever his task is as plain as has been Franco-Anglo-American air supremacy. Where once on a time we said "He is a King," when we wanted highly to commend, so now we'll say "He is an Ace,"—and the ace takes the king, anyhow. When the Jutland news first came to us, "low visibility" was a little puzzling, though not too hard at least to guess it. Now everyone understands not only its strictly naval content but also its implication of something hard to see. So, too, gas mask was a thing undreamed till kultur tried the conquest of the world; unknown till after second Ypres, it is forever set in the language.

The list could run far of wholly new words used more or less accurately, and with no metaphorical or suggestive broadening. Poilu and "tank" and "lorries" are cases of such recent arrivals in our tongue; albeit present-day enthusiasm for the "hairy" Frenchman makes his nickname nearly the same as "hero," and tank may imaginably be broadened later to indicate any freak engine of destruction. It is a welcome relief from the overworked "steam roller." Lorries※ came to us as a Kiplinesque noun not long ago; it is now as usual to our speech as truck.

War has been, again, a ready teacher of words distinctly technical, yet understood by the veriest laymen. The British War Office immediately adopted the French communiqué for its daily statement of military events, and the American command followed suit, though the purists were for proving that "statement" or "report" would be preferable, both as English and as shorter. We say escadrilla, not squadron, of air craft; and we refer to "75s" and "Taubes" and "periscopes" and "depth charges" and "liason officers" and "listening posts" and "shell shock."

More than a few of the words here proposed are at least a shade slangy in their usages, and there are more than a few to be added to the list, which are entirely slangy. Boche, for instance. Perhaps it meant "block-head" at the first (there is a debate as to its genesis), but today it means as nearly "beast" as anything else, and is no more fit to be set toe to toe with poilu than the man it labels is worthy of standing beside his French foe. "Blighty" is another new word destined to grow old in service. A phonetic spelling of the Hindustani "bhilati," meaning home—it means home today as surely as though it was spelt with its same four letters—and a "blighty" wound was, therefore, one serious enough to mean a home journey, even as a "cushy" injury could mean only a short lay-off in a hospital behind the lines, in the land whose coucher begot the word from Mr. Thomas Atkins. "Fag" and "Busy Berthas" and "pillbox" are other verbal inventions of Atkins, word which our "Sammees" may bring back to us, but which have not yet arrived. We have "rookie" though.

If that same "Sammees" is a handle not to last, despite the unusually pleasant little fable which told of its birth, "Anzacs" has as positively come to stay as any single word in all the roster. To weave a euphonious name from legitimately official initials is as out of the ordinary as was the magnificent courage of these same Australian and New Zealand Army Corps heroes in the day when the Gallipoli fighting yet held first page and top column. Then, those "Ladies from Hell!" Not even the long and picturesque history of the Scotch has held a phrase more eloquently typical of all that a combination of kilt and courage can give. The Highlanders will carry the sobriquet as long as they cling to their broad vowels and narrow thrift.

The whole history of this war might be vividly summarized in a brief half-dozen phrases, unknown yesterday, everywhere accepted today, destined to last through many a tomorrow.

"Scrap of paper" began it (unless one go back to the ultra-frank Bismarckian "Blood and iron"), and somewhere in the

※ An old word – A lorry in civil life

list might be set "No annexation and no indemnities" and the spurlos versenkt of Count Luxburg, but the direct line of argument has run to some purpose as this: "Do your bit," "Over there," "Carry on" and "Over the top."

It is not only the map of Europe that needs revising now that the conflict is over; a new dictionary is called for. Not wholly in fun did "Evoe," in London's Punch, send his lady-love verses cast in the new mould; there's a deal of sober truth, in such excellent fooling:

"If no artillery of vows
 Nor creeping barrages of prayer
Compassion in your breast may rouse,
 But I am still a stranger there—
On bended knees with outstretched hand
 In No Man's Land;

"If labouring this I may but win,
 Prepared by batteries of art,
A temporary footing in
 The outpost trenches of your heart,
That is not good enough for me,
 Hermione.

"For somehow I must surely seize
 The full objective I desire;
The buds have raided all the trees
 And Spring has burst the Winter's
  wire;
A strong offensive round us thrills
 Of daffodils.   a

"Then plague on all cajolings sweet
 And drumfire of continued woe,
I'll rush you, lady, off your feet
 And take you prisoner ere you know;
Triumphant, forcible and frank,
 I'll play the Tank."

Land o' Dreams

By Ford C. Fick

Where the azure rim of the sky dips down
Till it touches the earth at the horizon;
Where the giant tips of the rugged peaks
Lure out the man who forever seeks—
Seeks for the joy of a lost romance,
Seeks for the thrill of the West that's gone;
Spirits that revel in luck and chance,
Hearts that are tuned to the break of dawn—
This is the land of dreams.

Out where the wide, wild mesa turns
And stretches away in the sun that burns
Its purple mirage in the hot, dry air
Awakening the spirits that linger there;
Out where each trail o'er the broad expanse
Stretching away from the things that are
Whispers its tale of a lost romance
Luring you on like a guiding star—
This is the land o' dreams.

Here where the heavens and earth are one;
Here where the glow of the western sun,
Bathing the range with its ruddy light
Welcomes the stars of a perfect night
Here where the ghost of the days now gone
Waken your soul to the spirit that thrills
You anew with its power, and beckons you on
In the spell of the West and the lure of the hills—
This is the land o' dreams.

The Strike in Funeral Range
By Milton Barth

THE hot August breeze, like a fiery blast, swept the barren hills and desert sand. A plump, round moon gazed lazily down on two prospectors who, with their burros, were slowly and silently wending their way through the desolate waste. Silas and Hardy were not tender-feet. The wilderness was their home and they loved it, but of late a change had taken place in the hearts of each unknown to the other. As they trudged wearily along behind the heavily laden burros, each thought of the scenes of his youth, of long forgotten sweethearts and of other lands and places. Together they had roamed the frozen North; together they had quartered; together braved four hard Alaskan winters, yet they grumbled not.

Now and then they passed large cactii amid a meagre sprinkling of sagebrush, while here and there huge boulders rose like deserted monuments. A hearty laugh from the older man broke the prolonged silence and in a gruff tone he sang to his pard and the desert:

"Old Slickery Sy, the Cap't'lst Guy, now lives in a Fifth Avenue flat
While his time he abides agoing joy rides and his wife is so dear—but so fat."

As he finished, he pulled forth his bandana and mopped the dripping sweat from his brow.

"Going in fer literature, Eh!—poety perhaps," sneered Silas ironically. "Mighty kind of you, old chap, this here taking such a fatherly interest in me."

"Well," replied Hardy with a drawl, as he drew from his mouth his odorous corn-cob attachment and hit it a sharp rap over his knuckles scattering the ashes in the wind. "You know I didn't mean nothin'. Just sort a wishin'—a——that somethin' nice like that might happen to me. Been a'hikin' these legs o' mine over these bakin' sands 'bout long enough. If it isn't an oven it's an iceberg. Sy, I call it quits—this is my last trip. What business, anyhow, has a fellow past fifty walkin' and workin' himself to death lookin' fer a fortune he never can find? I say, pard, we got to strike it this trip! You heard what I sayed, pard, this is my last."

As he finished, he suddenly pulled something from his watch-pocket and as quickly replaced it. Silas noticed this, while at the same time his keen eyes perceived that an occasional tear found its way down the man's cheek. He understood but said nothing.

By midnight, they had entered the hilly regions to the west. Behind them the Amargosa Waste lay veiled in silver glory; silent and desolate, while to the north, buried in the gloom beyond, Tonopah and Divide swarmed with restless humanity and sent forth their trailers into the night.

Dawn found them upon the western slope of Funeral Range. Here they made camp beside a large boulder. Below them the parched and billowed sands of Death Valley stretched and yawned in the

3

early morning like a huge demon awakening from his slumber.

Hardy, after a brief exploration, discovered a spring in a nearby canyon. Here he quenched his thirst and that of the ever faithful burros. On his return he brought several well-filled pails of the crystal liquid for "family use," as he termed it.

Leaving Silas to complete the cooking Hardy slung his pick over his shoulder and walked over the edge of the promontory to survey some rocks which by chance had caught his attention. No sooner had he struck his pick into the rocky soil than he upturned several chunks of the long-looked for gold.

He grabbed them eagerly and examined them weighing them first in one hand and then in the other. His heart beat fast, again he felt the joy of living —it was great!

"At last, we've struck it Sy," he called wildly in his excitement. It's the real stuff—high grade—it'll go two hundred to the ton—grass roots down." He waved frantically holding the gold in his hand.

"Slickery Sy" jumped with a sudden start as he realized that the opportune time had arrived. The gold fever seized him as it never had before. Instantly, he dropped the half-opened can of beans and jumping up with a loud shout followed by a still louder, "hurrah," he started pell-mell for the ledge, upsetting in his haste the steaming pot of coffee.

So great was his excitement that he did not realize how fast he was going nor where he was stepping. When he did, it was too late. As he rushed madly to examine the ore which Hardy held in his hands, he tripped on a rock, falling heavily against his partner, knocking him backward over the precipice into the ravine, hundreds of feet below.

For a moment, Silas lay dazed upon the brink. Upward from the ravine below came the sickening chud-chud of a human mass as it struck the cruel rocks. A dull thud; then all was silent, save now and then the crunching of a tiny avalanche as it rushed downward toward the corpse. Silas staggered to his feet, wringing his hands in despair.

"My God! My God! I've done it!" he

shrieked. Then uttering a piteous wail, he skirted the cliff for some distance and dashed madly down the slope, running, jumping, rolling and falling. When he reached the bottom of the ravine, he beheld his late companion half-buried beneath a small avalanche of loose earth and rock, while from a gory mass of flesh, cold glassy eyes, bulging in their sockets, stared fixedly into space. The jaw was set, the muscles rigid, the fists clenched and in them lay the price of his adventure—gold.

"Hardy, Hardy!" he cried aloud in his anguish, but no answer came. Stooping down, with one hand, he lifted his friend's shoulders from the ground and placed the other to his partner's heart; it was still. Then, he concluded that his friend was dead. Overhead at a safe distance, swooping and circling a saucy vulture, scavenger that he was, waited patiently for his prey.

Sy lifted his head with a start. Nearby lay his chum's old silver watch. Through the broken crystal, the picture of a woman with accusing eyes stared at him mockingly and almost cruelly. "You've robbed me—you—you killed him," they seemed to say.

"Did I?—Me?" he sobbed aloud, and his eyes filled with tears. "The poor thing," he muttered, "She loved him— and so did I."

Blood-red, the sun rose in the east, casting on the nearby cliffs a reddish glow and painting with deep vermillion the peaks beyond. No longer the little brown birds sang in the bushes nor the gray squirrel barked in his hole. All was quiet save for the wail of a mourning dove in a nearby thicket. All nature seemed sorrowful.

"I'll go to Tonopah and tell it all," he said to himself. Then his gaze fell upon the picture. Again those accusing eyes pierced him and again they seemed to cry out: "You've robbed me—you— Sy Benson—you killed him!"

"To Tonopah — never!" he cried. "They'll never believe me; I must flee; the sooner the better."

"Good-bye, old boy," he called as he scrambled up the steep cliff.

Wild-eyed and delirious, he reached the

In the Funeral Range Country

top. How he got there, he never knew. Grabbing Hardy's pick, he up-turned a number of chunks of high-grade ' ore. These, he thrust into his pockets. He started to go, then paused. Pulling the ore from his pockets he threw it to the ground. "Hardy's gold! Hardy's gold!" he wailed. "I can't; I won't take it."

He went to the camp, slapped a pack-saddle on his burro, threw on some provisions and located several flasks of whisky without much difficulty. At the usual signal—a terrific kick in the ribs— the animal started; Silas following close behind.

Among the scorching sand-dunes, he wandered, day after day and night after night, sleeping but little now and then in some secluded spot. Many times, he searched for water. Several times he succeeded in finding it. It was warm and stagnant, but he drank it eagerly; it was the best there was. It quenched his thirst, moistened his parched lips and brought relief to his swollen tongue. What more could he ask? Then, he would fill his flasks and the several canteens, give the donkey a drink and press on—on he knew not where.

One night the burro disappeared carrying with him on his back the meagre stock of provisions. All the morning Silas sought the beast, but failed to find him. About noon, he stumbled upon the remains of a prospector's camp. A small heap of live coals and several half-charred sticks marked the spot where, a few hours before, some hungry gold-seekers had prepared their breakfast.

Thirsty and exhausted, he sank to the ground beside the embers. Two weeks had passed; his hat was gone; his shoes were almost soleless; his clothing hung in shreds upon his body.

For two hours, he lay unconscious. When he again opened his eyes, a newspaper, which had partially escaped the flames, held his attention. He grabbed it. In blaring headlines, he read:

MURDERED FOR GOLD

Great Stampede: Richer Than Divide: Fabulus Wealth Exposed in Funeral Range

Prospector Meets Death at Hands of Friend. Sheriff and Posse Hot on Trail of Murderer

Then in smaller type:

Several prospectors arrived here late last night with the news of a horrible murder in connection with a fabulous strike in the Funeral Range. Prompted by the lust for gold, Silas Benson, alias George Dickhaut, commonly known in these parts as "Slickery Sy," murdered his partner, James Hardy, by pushing him over a cliff.

The sheriff and posse are in hot pursuit of the murderer and it is only a matter of time before he is taken. Orders have been given to "shoot on sight." A reward of One Thousand Dollars ($1000), is offered for his capture, dead or alive.

That was enough for Silas.

"This was the Sheriff's camp?" he queried. Something seemed to tell him that it was. Instinctively, he reached for his pistol—it was gone. He tried to rise but fell backward to the ground. He wanted to run but could not. Again he tried, but without success. At last, grimly determined, he drew himself together, collected his energy and with a mighty effort staggered to his feet.

Out into the burning sands, he tottered beneath a blazing sun. Many times, he fell, struggled up and stumbled on. At last he fell upon the ground and could not rise. No longer, he saw the cooling shades of night; to him all was day. In a simmering sea of sand, he swam. For three long days, he crawled and edged himself along. One large blister covered his unshaven face, his body was terribly contorted, while his tongue, swollen twice its natural size protruded from his mouth.

Dying of thirst and hunger, he crawled blindly on. Suddenly, his hand struck something hard. A large boulder cracked in half and shifted by the elements confronted him. Into the crevice, he crawled. It was cool and restful. Thirsty, hungry and exhausted, he fell asleep.

For many hours he slept. When he woke, his vision was better. Dimly he saw two walls of rock towering above him. Near by a rattler wound himself into a coil, waving his venomous head from side to side, rattling and hissing, while in and out of the reptile's mouth

darted a fiery tongue with lightning rapidity.

"Ha, Ha," Silas chuckled, his reasoning completely gone. "Now, I've got you — good food you are," and he tried to smack his swollen lips. Desperately, he grabbed at the reptile. With a quick spring, the demon sank his fangs into Silas' right arm. Out from the rocks Silas crawled clawing his way through the sand. His arm began to swell. Larger and larger it became. Soon it was turning black. Inch by inch, he pulled himself along. Now, he appeared to be going downward; he made more headway. The pain in his arm had become almost unbearable.

Ready to give up in despair, he found himself at a small spring. It came from beneath a rock. Beside the water lay some scattered bones, bleached and brittle, while in the edge lay a human skull. He cared not for this. Water, he must have. He lay with his face in the pool. When he was satisfied, he dragged his head from the pool and turned over on his back—the water was poison.

For a moment, he beheld the face of his friend, ghastly and horrible. It vanished and in its place appeared the face of the beautiful woman with accusing eyes that stared at him mockingly and almost cruelly. "You've robbed me—you killed him!" resounded in his ears. He was silent. Darker and darker grew his face as the poison surged through his veins. His features contorted terribly. His muscles grew rigid. Up at the blue sky he gazed with that same uncanny stare that he had last witnessed on the face of his late companion.

For some minutes he lay motionless. Then, he turned his head to one side and tried to force his body upward and away from the pool. At first, he did not succeed; he was too weak. Again, he tried. This time, he forced himself to his knees and staggered to his feet. Once, twice, thrice, he fell, but the fourth time he rose and slowly tottered toward Funeral Range. The poison spring water had counteracted the vemon of the snake. The swelling was rapidly subsiding in his arm.

"I will go to Tonopah and give myself

up," he muttered.

He had journeyed about a mile across the burning sand and alkali when he perceived a cloud of dust ascending from the sparsely covered hills ahead. As the cloud advanced, his blurred vision made out three horsemen. Nearer and nearer they came, headed straight in his direction. They now aproached so close that he could see the glint of their rifles and spurs. Silas threw his hands into the air and tottered toward them.

At two hundred yards, they leveled their rifles at him and rode three abreast. "Surrender! Surrender!" they cried in unison.

Silas did not answer. He fell upon his trembling knees; his swollen tongue filling his parched mouth.

The sheriff dismounted and sprang forward. He laid his rifle on the sand. Taking a flask of whisky from his pocket, he poured the contents down the blistered throat of the outlaw—emergency whisky.—Nevada is dry.

"Snake," mumbled Silas.

The men then noticed Sy's black, swollen arm. The sheriff pulled the lead from a rifle shell and rubbed the dry powder into the wound.

In the distance, a lone horseman, traveling in great haste, swept toward them over the barren hills of Funeral Range. As he bore down upon them, he waved his hat wildly in the air.

The sheriff's posse awaited his arrival with eager expectancy.

"Hay! he shouted, when within hailing distance. "Hardy's not dead—he came too, soon after you fellows left, and I've chased all over the devil trying to find you. Hardy says it was an accident."

"Thank God!" exclaimed Silas. Then he sank into unconsciousness.

The return journey to Tonopah began. Silas sat astride the sheriff's horse, before the officer, unhandcuffed his limp body, held securely by the officer of the law.

Late in the night, the four horsemen rode into Tonopah. In front of the Golden Bull they brought their horses to a halt. The hour was late; the streets were surging with people. Five months before, Tonopah counted her population

"Slickery Sy."

by the hundreds, now she counted by thousands. Divide City and Tonopah were booming.

Silas opened his eyes as the sheriff lifted him from the saddle. "Where are we?" he asked.

"Tonopah," answered the sheriff. "We're going in to get a bite to eat. Can you walk now?"

"I think so," replied Silas.

The five men entered the Golden Bull. Silas leaned upon the arm of the sheriff. The house was full to overflowing. People rose and nodded as the sheriff passed. They walked toward the rear of the building. Suddenly Silas spied Hardy. He moved toward him with outstretched hands. "Raised from the dead —put her here, old pal! How in Hell did you do it? You rich old devil; you come near stretching my neck, didn't you?"

"Never mind, pard, we're rich. We've started something bigger than Tonopah Divide. Our claim is just lousy with gold."

"By Hicks! shake on it, old boy," cried Silas. "But who is this pretty dame you've got here?" Silas nodded at the girlish looking woman who sat opposite Hardy. "I've seen that face and those eyes before," he said.

"My wife!" exclaimed Hardy. "When I came too and realized how rich we were, I telegraphed her at San Francisco. She sure came and the knot's tied."

"H—m," grunted Sy.

"You and me's rich, boy. I bought this joint yesterday. It's a blamed good cafe and a money-grabber. Sit up and order what you want and all you want. Don't mind the expense. Your gold's helping pay for it. We kin buy out the whole town of Tonopah, Divide City and Wall Street if we want to and have money left to buy Christmas presents for the kids."

The Shepherd's Conversion

By Pearl La Force Mayer

Deep in the heart of the désert it is almost morn.
Tense is the hush and the silence waiting for day to be born.
The mesquite trembles in the clear cold air.
The cholla bows at the call of prayer.
Long, low, gray hills kneel at the desert's rim—
Waiting forms of power, still and faintly dim.
The yucca bells ring where the trails lead on
And wake the birds to the praise of coming dawn.
Devout and reverent the sweeping space as with day it fills:
The faint gray light grows brighter on the hills,
And they lift their breasts bare and clean to God—and wait!
Joy grows in my heart with that growing light:
Gone is its night!
Forgot are my sins in the haunts of man
As I stand in that far flung desert space—
Clean washed by its infinite ages of storm
Purified in the fire of its glorious sun.
Free rises my soul from earthly stain,
Washed in the sun of its sorrows,
Purified in the fire of its pain.
In adoration sweet and still
It lifts its white forgiven breast to God,
Bare and clean as a desert hill.
From my heart leaps the age old cry:
"Praise, Praise to Thee, oh my God!"
A pink flood of light has conquered the night
And bursts o'er the hills—
With my soul and the desert 'tis dawn!

The Lost Lizzie Wilde

BY WILLIAM — WALLACE — FAIRBANKS

The Lost Lizzie Wilde was launched in the early fifties. She sailed away from San Francisco with a full cargo and crew on her maiden trip and was seen no more. William Wallace Fairbanks writes an interesting story of what befell her.—The Editor.

 WARM day in the early fall with the soft blue haze of Indian Summer hanging low over the mountains to the East and along the rough and rugged shore line, into which is set the little harbor, with the surf swashing convulsively upon its pebbly beach.

The harbor itself stirred gently now and then, as a long undulating swell came in from the open sea; and the great mass of sea weed, growing upward from the reefs some fathoms deep, rose and fell with its gentle motion. Inland to the East the foot hills of the Coast Range, heavily timbered with forests of redwood, pine and fir, crept down towards the sea; for it was in the fifties and the advance guard of the new civilization had but just begun upon the work of their destruction.

At the little harbor on this quiet day of Indian Summer, all was activity and excitement; for the restless energy of man, regardless of the example set by nature, was every where in evidence. Upon the timbered ways, leading from above high water mark out into the deep, was the hull of a beautiful schooner, all ready this day for the launching.

For, it must be remembered, these were the days of sailing craft; and in the early fifties, no steamer's prow cut the waters along the coast, or entered the harbors in their quest of freight—the early products of the country. Schooners — two-masted sailing vessels, were the common carriers of the day; and these were frequently built at different points where timber for construction was plentiful and easy of access.

And so the long summer's work was drawing to a close; and this little craft, more beautiful and shapely in her lines than any that had yet been built, was being made ready for the plunge into the element for which she was designed. And naturally it was a busy and an exciting day. Busy for those who so far had carried along the work of construction; and full of excitement for those who had come from various points along the coast, or the pioneer settlements back in the woods, that they might be present at the launching. For these it was a gala day. Lunches were brought and little picnic parties formed—gathering in groups upon the rocks along the shore; or far above at the top of the bluffs overlooking the harbor. And when at last all was in readiness, and

"All around them and below
The sound of hammers, blow on blow
Knocking away the shores and spurs
And see she stirs—
She starts, she moves."

The little vessel took her first plunge into the blue waters of the Pacific. That night when the sun like a disk of burnished copper, had sunk below the ocean's rim, away off somewhere in the West, the little schooner rested like a bird upon the water.

She was named the Lizzie Wilde, and she sailed first to San Francisco, where she received her final equipment, including officers and crew, and finally a cargo of freight for northern ports along the coast.

It was another day of warm sunshine, with the blue haze of the Indian Summer hanging low along the Marin shore, when the Lizzie Wilde sailed out through the Golden Gate with her white sails and clear bright spars glinting in the sunlight of a California Autumn day. And when months had passed, and then years, and no tiding came of her—her name went down on the list along with the names of many others that had sailed away and had never returned.

For a time there was much speculation among those who had known of this craft as to just what her fate might have been. Among sea-faring men it was said that her spars were too lofty—that she was too slenderly built for the rough coast weather. Others said other things; and a few intimated on the quiet, that the schooner and valuable cargo might have been to captain and crew a temptation not to be resisted; and in those days it might not have been so difficult to just sail away to some destination suitable to their purpose, and there dispose of schooner and freight.

I was of the younger generation of pioneers just growing up, and a deep impression had been made upon my youthful mind by the tale of the lost schooner. My own memory could not reach so far back, and it had been told to me as one of the not very remote legends of the coast.

PART TWO

A row of scraggly cocoanut palms fringed the small bay that opened out at the mouth of Haiku Gulch, on the Island of Moui. Kukui trees grew here and there, and under the wide spreading branches of one of these there sat three of us one day, awaiting the coming of the little island boat on which we expected, or hoped at least, to take passage to Honolulu.

It was noon time now and the boat might make her appearance around the point at any moment; or it might be full sundown before she came; one could never tell. Anyway, all we could do was to remain in the shade and wait. The soft breeze that came in from the open sea was just cool enough to be pleasant, and there was no reason whatever why we should not possess our souls with patience and abstain from worry.

There was the engineer, Mac Graw— whom one might safely suspect of being Scotch. A hardy, grizzled man, whose age, judging from looks, might be placed at almost any point between fifty and one hundred. A silent man usually and one not given to light talk. And yet with the air of one who had had many experiences in many parts of the world. Young Fisher was an Oakland boy who had been knocking about the islands seeking adventure, which having found, he was now heading homeward.

I, myself, had in early youth found the Pacific Coast much too tame and was gaining a knowledge of the outside world from actual and sometimes violent contact with certain portions of it.

And with a probability of a long afternoon ahead, we reclined in the shade of the Kukui tree and talked as men will who are thus for a brief period thrown together.

On the point of the island, some miles distant, was what seemed to us the remains of an ancient wreck; and it was this that directed our conversation naturally in that direction. The engineer had pulled away at his pipe for some time in silence, his small blue eyes looking out from under shaggy brows and off towards the ancient wreck.

"When I see the remnant of what was once a ship," he said, "there comes to me the memory of something that happened many years ago; and I have often wondered if I might not be the one, and probably the only one, who could throw some light upon what must have been at

Marin Shore, North of San Francisco Bay.

The Island of Moui.

that time another mystery of the sea. And though I have read much, I have never seen any mention made of any thing relating to what I have to tell.

"It was upon the California coast that this happened—upon the northern coast where there are rocky cliffs and bold headlands reaching far out into the sea. And it was long ago, too, that it happened—before you were born, perhaps, or not long after; and at that time the place of which I speak, was a wild and isolated region and for a long stretch of coast line there were but few whites. I was there awaiting the building of a saw mill that was to tap a belt of timber, and having idle time, my attention was directed a bit towards an Indian settlement not far away. From where we were the ocean lay a day's journey distant on foot, and it was over a rough mountain range, too, with no roads—just the old Indian trails. It was the custom of the Indians to make visits now and then to the sea coast, which furnished them much in the way of food, such as fish and various kinds of shell fish. It was the Fall of the year, I remember,

and the Winter would soon come with storms and driving rain, when trips to the coast would be made impossible; and so their visits there were now more frequent, that a stock of food might be laid in for the Winter.

"When a small body of them returned from such a trip one day, I noticed that they had provisions—flour and sugar and other stuff, and they seemed to be greatly excited over some unusual event. They gathered around in groups and made much talk—something unusual for Indians; and then early on the following day half the camp was gone—nearly all the able-bodied, who two days later returned laden as before. And all the information they would give me was that they had found some wreckage on the beach.

"I knew that coasting schooners would sometimes, in a heavy sea, loose their deck load; but there had been no storms as yet, and when I noticed one of the Indians with a piece of sail, resembling in size and shape a schooner's jib, my curiosity and suspicions even were aroused.

"Thinking the matter over that night, I decided to make a visit to the coast myself. It wasn't so easy either, I soon found, for it must have been twenty miles or more through the wildest kind of a country and over an old Indian trail by no means easy to follow. Then, besides, I had to move with more or less caution, for I didn't care that the Indians should see me and think that I was spying on their movements. They were not over scrupulous as to taking the life of a white man should his actions displease them. When near the coast I found a new trail branching off from the old and following this I soon came out on a high and rocky cliff, and though I have seen some wild country in my day, nothing that I have seen anywhere equaled this. The cliffs to both the north and south, as far as one could see, rose sheer above the ocean several hundreds of feet, with here and there a bit of sandy beach at their base that would be uncovered when the tide was low. And reaching far out were jagged reefs—sharp ledges of rock over which the surf broke constantly.

"Down the face of one of these cliffs was a zig-zag trail, cut or worn in the soft rock, with stair-like steps in the steepest places, which enabled one to climb up and down with more or less difficulty.

"Making my way down to the narrow strip of beach below, I found a few fragments of broken boxes, but that was all. Looking closely, however, I noticed signs of travel going towards a point or rock; but against this point the waves dashed so wildly that no one could pass; and from the cliff above nothing could be seen but the boiling, seething water below.

"It was now afternoon and the tide was falling. I resolved to wait till low water, thinking that then I might find a passage around the point, and a couple of hours later, with some difficulty, I succeeded. It was a strange sight I saw and one that caused me to sit down upon a ledge and look upon it with wonder. I saw a semicircular cove between the point I had passed and another directly opposite, about a hundred yards away. The little cove swung inland in the form of a half circle with cliffs rising all around to a height of several hundred feet.

In the right of this circle, and facing me from where I stood, was the entrance to a cave—a vast, large opening in the face of the cliff.

"It was nearly a hundred feet high and about the same in width. Because of the falling tide the water had receded from the floor of the cave and by making my way carefully along a ledge of rock, I finally reached the entrance, from which point I could easily walk back into the cave itself.

"The depth of this cave must have been a hundred feet or more, and as I moved forward my eyes became accustomed to the dimness of the light so that I could see plainly all about me.

"Only the highest tide reached back apparently to the end of the cave, and here thrown close against the wall of rock by heavy seas lay a beautiful schooner. Her top masts had been shattered from contact with the roof of the cave; but her lower masts and spars. clean and new, and the whiteness of her sails, which still hung to the booms, proved that she was a craft but recently built. From a projecting ledge I climbed onto her deck, where I found much freight scattered about in great disorder —evidently by the Indians; but no trace could I find of any of her crew. Washed overboard by the heavy swells, the strong undertow would probably carry them far out to sea. Looking out through the cave's entrance, I plainly saw a channel reaching well out, with low rocky ledges on either side, barely coming to the surface of the water.

"With the tide rushing shoreward at the full of the moon, the current through this channel and into the cave beyond, would be irresistible to any vessel coming within its reach, and it seemed plain enough that this new and trim little craft, becalmed outside, felt the suction and was gradually drawn in shore until the inrush of water seized her and threw her fiercely against the farther wall of the cave. And in this mad inrush of water, no human being could live.

"And so the Indians, in their search for food along the coast, found her here, and from her stores laid in big supplies.

"Returning to our camp the next day, I related to several what I had discovered, and we planned an early visit to the wreck. But a violent storm arose and the rising waters in the streams made traveling impossible for a week or more. And then arriving on the spot, we found that no trace of the wreck had been left by the storm, except a few spars and timbers scattered along the beach."

The story was told, and it was well, for just at this time there came creeping around the distant point, the black hull of the little island boat, and we began getting our belongings together in readiness for the small boat that would soon come ashore for us.

But the Scotchman suddenly paused, "I almost forgot," said he, removing his pipe, "that when I left the schooner's deck, I walked around under her stern, and looking up for the first time I saw her name in bright, new gilt letters— THE LIZZIE WILDE—San Francisco."

Camping

By John Ravenor Bullen

Camping! it's life....out in the woods!
   Start the wild echoes shrieking with mirth,
Down with conventional primness and pride
   Bred in the populous portions of earth.

Out in the woods....oceans of sun
   Flooding the green rimmed by the shade.
Borne on the breeze, medley of tune
   Poured from the tree-tops circling the glade.

Into the lake liquidly cool,
   Opaline, hyaline, brisk as champagne,....
Dive to the depths, float on the crest,
   Cleave through the shallow, bubbles a-train.

Camping! the untrammelled life of the wild,
   Boast not of city, of London, of Rome,
Sing of the bosky green pine-scented dell
   Bathed in a sunset of crimson and chrome.

Drink to the depths, long lasting draughts
   Drawn from lethean coolness of dusk,
Nectar of Flora, her vintage of winged
   Ottars of roses and odours of musk.

Camping! it's life....out in the woods!
   Start the wild echoes shrieking with mirth.
Down with conventional primness and pride
   Bred in the populous portions of earth.

Training A Spirit to Telegraph

By F. H. Sydney

These two stories by F. H. Sidney reveal thrilling experiences in a railroad tower signalman's life, one being the narrative of training a two hundred-year-old Indian chief how to telegraph his message from Spiritland, and the other dealing with a despised hobo, who turned out to be a hero in misfortune's disguise.—The Editor.

"SAY Bill," said Signalman Jones to his friend, Bill Perry, who had run down to "WG" tower one night to pay Jones a little visit, "did I ever tell you the story of how I taught telegraphy to the spirit of Pon Jore Jok, the Indian Chief that had been dead two hundred years?"

"No," answered Bill, "I'm going to stop with you till Number 17 comes along, a good two hours, let's have the story."

"All right, as soon as I set the routes for the next two trains due," replied Jones as he deftly manipulated the levers.

"Having worked as a substitute operator and signalman on the 'lower end' in the summer vacations during my high school days, the chief dispatcher was always on the lookout for me as soon as school closed. A few days after I graduated, I was assigned to the night trick at 'NB Tower' to fill a temporary vacancy caused by the sickness of the regular signalman. I worked the night trick there about six months and that is where I had the strange experience of teaching telegraphy to the wandering spirit of Chief Pon Jore Jok.

"There was in use at 'NB Tower' at that time a sounder invented and patented by John Delaney one of the oldest telegraphers on the system; like most inventors, Delaney died poor, and he never realized a cent from the sounder I speak of. He was offered two thousand dollars for it, but refused to sell for that amount, and as he had no funds the sounder was never placed on the market. It was the loudest and clearest instrument I ever heard. There was something strange about this sounder, however, for whenever the weather was clear and frosty it would work with the key closed. After midnight when all the keys were closed and the wires quiet, I could hear somebody or something trying to work the wire which this sounder happened to be connected on. It sounded like a person drawing a jagged piece of iron across the wire. At the same time there would come from just outside the building a long drawn, quavering cry, which had a human sound and yet was unearthly and shrill; at other times it would be a low guttural wail, like the moan of a lost spirit. I've seen strong men turn pale and tremble at this sound, and they often remarked that they would not stay in that tower alone at night for any amount of money. But I never was troubled or worried by these sounds. It dawned upon me one night that somebody or something was trying to communicate with me through the medium of 'Delaney's sounder.' I began to adjust the

wire hoping to 'pick up' this strange operator, but it was a long time before I
was able to do so. I was positive that
someone heard me and was trying to
answer me; and I soon realized that this
person did not understand Morse Signals, but would instantly reply to my signals whenever I made a long string of
dots and dashes, and invariably answer
me by making exactly the same number
of dots and dashes that I did, and with
the same touch.

"After thinking the matter over I decided to try to teach this person the
Morse alphabet; then perhaps in time
we could engage in conversation and
clear up a mystery which had interested
me very much. I began by teaching my
strange pupil the letter A, and when he
was able to make that letter to perfection I went on to the next and so through
the whole alphabet and numerals. My
pupil was a long time learning to make
the letters J (—.—.) and K (—.—). The
work was intensely interesting, and by
degrees the spirit telegrapher became a
good 'sender' and a fair reader of Morse.

"One night in February, 1882, and five
months after I began teaching the spirit
I asked, 'Who are you?' This startling
answer came back slowly and clearly.

" 'I am the wandering spirit of Chief
Pon Jore Jok, of the Wamesit Tribe,
whose principal villages were located in
this place by the Sweet Waters.'

" 'How long have you been in the
Spirit Land, Chief?' I asked.

" 'Two hundred years,' he replied. 'I
was murdered by one of your tribe,
whom I had broken bread with and treated as a brother. I came to him with outstretched hands to greet him as a friend
whom I had not seen for many moons.
He deliberately aimed his musket at me,
and said. 'Die you Indian dog,' as he
fired; the bullet passing through my
body near the heart. While I lay dying
he picked up my body and threw it into
a hole made by an upturned tree which
the wind had blown down. My false
friend did not even wait for my spirit to
leave my torn and suffering body, but by
a great effort tipped the tree back on top
of me, and went his way, leaving me to

smother. I had been taught by the good
Dr. Eliot to love and trust the white
men, and to know their God; and I and
my people were always the white man's
friends as a result of his teachings. Well
do I remember when he came up the
river in a large canoe with a white chief
called Danforth, who traveled over our
lands with long chains driving stakes
here and there.

" 'At that time many of our people were
sorrowful and sick at heart for those
who had been taken by the Great Spirit
many moons before. The terrible sickness had been brought to our village by
a wandering Passamaquoddy, whose village was many sleeps towards the rising
sun. Our tribe had been a powerful one,
but when the sickness came our squaws
and children fell like ripe acorns, and
hundreds of our best warriors took the
long trail to the happy hunting grounds
of the Red Men. Those that were spared
were mourning when the good Dr. Eliot
came among us, he comforted and cheered our sad hearts by telling us of the
white man's God, who loved all, even
the red child of the forest. The Wame-
sits always remained true to the promise they gave him, never to turn upon
and slay the white man or his children.

" 'We were urged by the chiefs of the
five nations to join with them in driving the white man from our lands; but
we never even attended their great coun-
cils. On this account our brother redmen despised and annoyed us, and at
the same time the members of the great
white tribe seemed to mistrust and fear
us. Whenever the warriors of the five
nations went on the war path, we were
made to feel the wrath of our white
neighbors. As last all the able-bodied
members of our tribe met in council. It
was decided at this council to abandon
our old hunting grounds and go farther
north, two sleeps away, where a branch
of our tribe lived on the big river at a
place we called Penacook.

" 'The older members of the tribe were
too weak to travel and hated to leave
the hunting grounds and villages of their
fathers. These we left behind in one
big tepee. After we had gone some of

our white neighbors piled firewood about the lodge in the darkness of the young moon, and burned our old people to death, while they looked on with fiendish glee, a matter of record in the town history of Billerica, Mass. I was told this many moons later by the big hunter with the long yellow hair, executioner of Charles I, who fled to America after the restoration. He was my friend, though he was hated and feared by my white brothers, because they whispered in the white man's country, across the sea, he had cut off the king's head with a large tomahawk. The new king, a son of the be-headed king, had put a price on my friend's head, but none dared to try to take him because he was so powerful and so terrible in his wrath.

" 'The next Green Corn Moon a powerful war part of Mohawks under Chief Wampanoag went to avenge this. Wampanoag was a son of Chief Leaping Deer, a memer of the Penobscott Tribe, who took Singing Bird, a daughter of Chief White Fox, for his squaw. White Fox was a chief of our tribe, but only half blood Wamesit, as his mother, was an Algonquin squaw. The father and mother of Wampanoag died with the terrible sickness and the old Chief White Fox gave Wampanoag to his friend, Chief Tall Pine of the Mohawks, whose village was by the big mountain, five sleeps towards the setting sun. Wampanoag grew up a hater of the white man and his children, he was a cruel and crafty chief, who planned many raids, and killed and burned the hated white man and his homes. As I said, this half-blood Wamesit who had become a Mohawk Chief, lived in our principal village as a papoose, and there he learned to hate all white men. Wampanoag hated the 'old knitter' who used to sit by the well under the big tupelo tree and knit stockings all day long, because once when Wampanoag was a small boy, the 'old knitter' found him milking his cow, and he kicked Wampanoag hard. Always on his raids Wampanoag looked for the 'old knitter' in order that he might be revenged, but the old man was never found out side the blockhouse until this last

raid. Then the war party came so quietly and so quickly that the whites had no time to get to the blockhouse.

" 'Just as the sun was half way down on its journey, Wampanoag crept up to the 'old knitter,' who sat knitting by the well, and killed him with his tomahawk, then threw his body into the well. Many others were killed that day, and some were carried away never to return, for when they became tired, and could no longer keep up with the warriors, Wampanoag had them killed. Among those killed were the six papooses of the white squaw who was hung on Gallows' Hill, as a witch because she had been charged with having the evil eye. The 'old knitter' was the father of the white brother who shot me.'

"It took Chief Pon Jore Jok a long time to tell me all this, as it was hard sometimes to understand his poor spelling of English words, and at times he must have forgotten and used his native tongue, which of course I could not understand. But after a month's patient work I got the story as I am telling it to you, Bill."

Bill nodded his head as a signal for Jones to proceed with the narrative.

Jones continued the story by saying: "I asked the Chief why his spirit was restless and he replied as follows":

" 'My spirit is restless because I had been taught to believe in the white man's God, and had turned my back upon the Great Spirit of the Red Men, and when I was murdered by my white brother who believed in his God, I felt I had done wrong to desert the God of my fathers for a God whose children committed murder without cause, and against his commands. Consequently before my spirit left the body, I expressed a desire as I lay choking under the tree roots to return to the Great Spirit of my fathers and live in their happy hunting grounds. This was denied me, as I had not been buried with tribal rites in the ground made sacred by our ancient medicine men. I have made all this known to you 'pale face,' because I wish you to take up my bones from where they have rested for over two hundred years, and re-bury them at a spot, I will show you, and with the rites of which I will inform you, as soon as you have located my remains. Put down these directions and follow exactly. March 29th, when the sun is two hours high, walk north on the path of the 'iron horse' until you come to the seventh pole of your talking machine, and follow the shadow of the pole to the end; drive a stake there, walk thirty paces towards the river, and dig.'

"The Chief then gave me explicit directions what to do with the remains after I found them. They were to be reburied just east of the ancient fordway, not far from the abutment of the present fordway bridge. I was given certain directions regarding certain rites. I never carried these out for several reasons. In the first place the Chief requested me to do this alone, taking no one into my confidence; but I had a friend who was interested in Indian lore, and who had made a very fine collection of Indian relics. Foolishly, perhaps, I took him into my confidence. He became very much interested and took another friend into his confidence. Consequently on March 29th, these two gentlemen and myself made an early start in search of the remains of Chief Pon Jore Jok.

We followed the Chief's directions and commenced to dig. One of the men soon gave it up because there was frost in the ground and made the digging hard. Myself and the other man, whom I will call Charles were convinced and in earnest, and we kept on digging. After a while we came across some small bits of well rotted wood, and then some dark red loam, and at last about four feet down, I discovered a piece of a thigh bone, then a skull in fair condition, after these legs, and shin bones in perfect preservation, and finally on the ground before us lay the remains of Chief Pon Jore Jok, as I firmly believe to this day. My friend, Charles, was delighted with the proof of what he termed 'Jones' dream;' he took the bones to his office where they rested on his desk for years. I often urged him to allow me to carry out Pon Jore Jok's

wishes to the letter, but he laughed at me.

"I never heard from the Chief but once after. He called me on the wire one night and asked me when I intended to carry out his wishes, and I promised to do so, fully intending to keep my word, but I never did. The Chief warned me not to break my promise. I neglected it because of Charles' smile when I referred to the matter. Later, as I firmly believe, I received my punishment in a strange and uncanny manner.

"Several weeks after I had promised the Chief I would carry out his wishes, a tall person with folded arms would stand outside the tower, just beyond the circle of the large hanging lamp, that was suspended over the interlocking machine, the light from this lamp extended twenty or thirty feet beyond the tower. At first this strange presence did not worry me, but after a while it got on my nerves, as good as they were. When this shadow began to follow me around at night, whenever I had occasion to go out of the tower, I became fretful and impatient, not afraid—but sort of out of balance.

"One night this shadow was so persistent in its unwelcome attentions that another person who happened to be in the tower with me called my attention to it. I looked and it seemed to me that it was nearer and plainer than ever before. Then I completely lost my head. Grabbing a heavy flag staff in my right hand, I rushed down the stairs, threw the door wide open, and sprang towards the shadow, landing on the frozen ground, and breaking my left leg at the knee."

"I looked for this person that had annoyed me but saw nothing. There came a sighing noise in the air, then a low guttural laugh, and all was quiet again.

"The friend who was in the tower ran down when he heard me fall, and carried me into the tower, after this he summoned the doctor and the day man, because he knew I would be unable to continue my duties as a signalman.

"I was 'laid up for repairs' three months. When I recovered and reported for duty, I was assigned to another position, the regular man having returned to service. Since then 'NB Tower' has been discontinued as a Junction point and torn down. I've never seen or heard from the Chief from that day to this," said Jones as he concluded his story.

"I noticed your left knee was a little stiff and often wondered how it happened," answered Bill. "It's a mighty interesting story, Jones, and I thank you for telling it to me. Well there's Number 17 whistling in, and guess I'll go home to Berkshire; Good night Jones."

"Good night, Bill."

The Hobo-Hero

WHEW, what a storm," said Signalman Jones as he walked into the tower at eleven o'clock one stormy night to relieve Sam Smith the second trick man.

"I hate the thought of going out into it," replied Smith. Every train on the road is running late, and the wires are working so bad it is almost impossible to get a line on what's coming over the road."

"If we get through the night without a wreck I won't complain," answered Jones. "I'm always afraid of washouts in a heavy rain like this."

"Well, Jones, I guess I'll start towards home," said Smith.

"Better take a lantern with you for its pitch dark outside."

"Don't know but that's a good idea," answered Smith and he picked up one of the lighted lanterns that stood in a row behind the interlocking signal machine. "Good night," he said as he opened the door and went out into the storm.

"Good night, Sam," and then Jones threw off his rubber coat and rubber boots, and put on a pair of slippers with heavy soles, that he kept especially to wear in the tower. After this he tried all of the levers in the interlocking machine to see if everything pertaining to the switching and signalling apparatus was working all right. Finding every-

thing to his satisfaction, Jones then peered out of the windows to see if the signal lamps were all burning.

"Thank God, I won't have to go out and climb a sixty foot pole to light any signal lamps tonight," he said. "If they have burned up to this time the chances are that they will burn the rest of the night."

After this he walked about the tower nervously, he seemed possessed with an uncanny feeling that something was going to happen, he couldn't tell what. Railroad men who have been long in the service acquire a sort of sixth sense. This accomplishment has helped to save unnumbered lives.

The next thing Jones did was to adjust the springs and pull back the magnets of the relays, to see if he could get them to work in order that he might get a line on the trains. "This is the worst of wet weather," Jones cried aloud. "You have to keep adjusting in order to hear what is going on over the wires, and if it continues to storm for any length of time the wires stop working altogether. To be without wires in case of a wreck or any other emergency is like being cast away in an open boat without oars or any other means of propulsion."

Finally he managed to get one wire adjusted so that he heard some "os" which gave him an idea where the trains were. He then peered out of the windows and tried to look down the track; it was as black as pitch, and the wind howled and the rain fell as before. "Gee whiz, I wish this wind would let up," he said to himself. "It sounds like the wail of lost souls." Then all at once that feeling of uncanniness came over him again, and at the same time some one knocked loudly at the door of the tower.

"I wonder who can be wandering around on a night like this?" As a precautionary measure Jones took his pistol from the desk drawer placed it in his pocket, and went down to unlock the door.

A shabbily dressed man about thirty-five stood shivering on the threshold.

"Can't I come in and get warm Mister?" he said. "I've walked thirty

4

miles today without a bite to eat. I'm so weak I can hardly stand."

"Come up stairs where its warm," replied Jones. "I have a basketful of lunch that you can have."

"Thank you Mister," answered the man as he preceded Jones up the stairs.

The wanderer sat by the stove, and attacked Jones' lunch with an appetite that showed he had been a long time without food. After eating he pulled off his shoes, socks and outer garments, and placed them by the stove where they would dry. He sat by the fire evidently in deep thought, then suddenly he asked Jones when the next train would be along. Jones told him the next train was the fast "Overland Express," which would be there within half an hour. Jones then asked him jokingly if he wished to have the "Overland" stopped in order to board "her."

"No," answered the wanderer. "There's a big tree on the track about half a mile west of here. It was too heavy for me to lift off. I thought perhaps some one should go there and get it out of the way."

"Great God!" cried Jones. "Why in hell didn't you tell me about this before? and he sprang for the telegraph key.

"I was too cold and numb to think of it," replied the outcast.

"Just my luck!" exclaimed Jones. "The wires are down. What shall I do?" Just then he happened to think of the track-man's velocipede, which was lying beside the tower. Quickly getting into his rubber coat and boots, and gathering up a red and white lantern, he rushed down the stairs. As he ran the velocipede on to the track, he heard the puffing of the "Overland's" big Pacific type engine, as the train began the ten-mile climb up Shelburne Grade.

"I'm afraid its too late," he panted as he pumped the machine as fast as his arms would allow. "If I don't get near enough to signal them before they tip the grade, the jig is up. All hell won't stop them if they come down that hill at full speed; and if they hit that tree the chances are that the whole train will roll down the bank. What a stupid fool

that hobo must be," thought Jones as he sped down the track pumping the little car till his body ached with the strain. The "Overland" whistled for a crossing about two-thirds of the way up the grade. Jones had still several hundred yards to go before he would be in a position where the engineer of the express could see his danger signal. Jones gritted his teeth, and savagely pumped the handles of the velocipede, the little car fairly flew ahead. Reeking with perspiration and gasping for breath Jones reached the spot where the tree lay across the track, just as the "Overland's" headlight flashed into sight at the top of the hill.

Jones frantically swung his light across the track, and as two long blasts from the locomotive whistle told him that Bill Perry, the alert engineer of the "Overland," had seen his signal, Jones collapsed in the middle of the track, and the red light dropped from his hand.

Bill Perry dropped his train down the hill slowly, and came to a stop about fifty feet from where Jones lay unconscious. "By jove," Bill called across the cab to his fireman, as the glare of the huge gas headlight flashed on the unconscious man lying in the track, and also the huge tree that completely blocked their passage.

"Hello, there, with the red light," called the engineer. "He must be sick or injured," said the fireman, as he jumped off the engine and ran toward the inert figure in the track. The engineer lighted his torch, then signalled several sharp short blasts with the whistle to call the crew up ahead, then he climbed down off the engine and started towards the place where his fireman was bending over the unconscious Jones.

"It's Jones from 'WG' tower," said the fireman. "He must have come down on that velocipede, he's probably all fagged out from pumping that car at top speed against this heavy wind; it's lucky for us he got here, though. If we'd ever hit that tree, at the speed we come down this hill, it would have been good bye."

"Let me try his pulse," said the engineer, who was a first aid to the injured enthusiast. "It's beating like a trip hammer," he exclaimed. "He probably nearly pumped his heart out to get here. It's pretty strenuous work for an old veteran on a night like this," and the engineer lifted Jones in his arms and carried him into the baggage car and laid him on the floor, then he went out and helped remove the obstruction. The messenger in the car got out the 'first aid kit,' applied restoratives, and in a few moments Jones regained consciousness. By the time the crew returned from removing the tree, Jones was able to talk.

"Hello, Bill," he said weakly as the engineer came toward him. "I'm glad you saw me swing you up when you did, for I was about gone, and couldn't have swung that lantern again if I wanted to."

"How did you find out the tree was there, Jones?" asked the engineer.

"A hobo came to the tower and told me about it, he's up at the tower now. Please load on the velocipede and stop at the tower and let me off. I'll be all right to work again by the time we get there."

"Just as you say."

By this time the passengers had gathered around, and when they learned what had happened, a big breezy drummer suggested "passing the hat," for Jones.

"No," said Jones firmly. "If you're going to pass the hat, pass it for the poor hobo up at the tower."

"Right'o," some one cried. "Pass the hat for the "Bo." The hat was passed and the collection amounted to one hundred and three dollars. This was handed to Jones for the poor wanderer.

When Jones returned to the tower he found the man sound asleep on the floor. After he waked up next morning Jones asked him if he had enjoyed a good nights' rest.

"I never slept better in a bed than I did on this floor last night," he replied. "I am more than grateful to you for the food and shelter you gave me, I hope some day to be able to repay you. By the way did I tell you about a big tree in the track a mile or so back there, or was it a dream I had last night?"

"You told me about the tree, my friend." Before I forget it, may I ask what your name is?"

"Henry Jackson," answered the man, "and a descendent of the famous Andrew Jackson. I'm ashamed to be in this condition. I'm a machinist by trade. The shop I worked in shut down six months ago."

"My wife and child were taken sick and died shortly after that. The doctor's bills and funeral expenses used up all my savings. There was no work to be had in Belmont, where I had lived for years, so I struck out through the country working at odd jobs. As you no doubt know, general business conditions have been so poor there's not much work to be had. I earned barely enough to keep alive. Then when my clothes began to look seedy no one would hire me and I was reduced to the level of a tramp. If I could only earn money enough to get a decent looking suit of clothes, I think I could get work in Greenville. I saw in a newspaper I picked up on the track, that the big shop there was advertising for machinists. Have you any idea where I could get something to do?" he asked wistfully.

"On behalf of the passengers of the 'Overland Express,' whose lives you were instrumental in saving, I am pleased to hand you the snug sum of one hundred and three dollars, to it I will add this two-dollar bill, to make it even money. You will come to my house and breakfast with me. Then we can go to a clothing store where you can buy some clothes; then if you wish, you can take the noon train to Greenville. I have a son, foreman in the machine shop there. I will give you a letter to him, and in all probability he will put you to work. I have also wired the division superintendent of this road of what you did; and he informs me he will bring the matter before the board of directors, who will no doubt suitably reward you. He wants me to keep informed of your whereabouts, so that you can be reached when they decide what to do."

"Great God," cried the poor fellow, "this is too much," and he broke down and wept.

"Brace up Jackson," said Jones. "I can see my relief coming, and we want to be already to skip out as soon as he comes. Go down stairs and 'wash up.'"

"All right," replied the wanderer as he descended the stairs.

Wallace, the first trick man who relieved Jones, looked at Jackson rather suspiciously; it made the poor fellow feel embarrassed.

"Shake hands with Mr. Jackson, Mr. Wallace," said Jones. "Jackson is the man who saved the 'Overland' from being wrecked last night."

"There's an account of it in the morning paper," said Wallace as he grasped Jackson's hand. "I hope the railroad company will reward you."

"I think they will," replied Jones.

"Come on Jackson, we'll go over and get some of mother's hot buckwheat cakes and honey. So long Wallace."

"So long," answered Wallace. "Good luck to you Mr. Jackson."

"I thank you, the same to you," answered Jackson.

Steamship Humboldt

By Arthur Lawrence Bolton

> The Humboldt is one of the last of the great fleet that operated between San Francisco and Skagway during the days of the great Klondike rush.

You come to us from Ketchikan,
From Juneau and Skagway;
You come to us from the Northern Sea,
Where you plied for many a day;
And with you come the wraiths of those
Whom you bore through the Golden Gate;
The wraiths of those, and the broken hearts,
From "The Trail of Ninety-Eight."

I see again your laden decks,
The dogs, the sleds and the gear;
I hear the parting shouts of the throng
That you shipped that fateful year;
Stout were the hearts that you bore away
To The Gate of The Unknown Land,
Strong to answer adventure's call,
And the lure of the golden sand.

*   *   *   *   *   *   *   *   *   *   *   *

Well have you earned an easy berth,
For the ships that lay by your side,
Are wraiths like the wraiths of the men you bore,
In their graves beneath the tide.

The Fiddle Creek Range

Halbert H. Sauber

OBE FIELDS was deliberate of speech, deliberate of thought and deliberate of purpose. Like most men who preface action with reflection he was to be reckoned with in affairs of moment. Jim Botts was energetic, restless and eager for personal gain and was unhampered by scruples.

These two had struck the High Plains of the upper Sacramento Valley in the same year—1880—and had squatted upon adjoining claims. Wool was high, mutton in demand, and summer range free, so the herds of Fields and Botts brought easy money to their respective owners. Botts kept a sleepless eye upon the markets, and bought and sold with amazing frequency. Fields held loyally to his original herd and improved the strain by importing rams from Vermont and Ohio. At the end of five years Botts was rated the wealthiest sheepman on the High Plains. Fields was known to have the best herd in Tehama County.

During the formative period following the Civil War California opened her doors to an inrush of hungry settlers. Lands she had in abundance and these she bestowed with lavish hand. Rich bottoms sold at the rate of two and a half dollars per acre. Range was as free as the air. It was not until the eighties that the stockman awoke to the fact that free range would soon be a thing of the past. Obe Fields, in his deliberate way, sensed the coming change more slowly than some of his neighbors. As a consequence he had two sections of railroad land bought from under his nose. It was at first reported that the purchaser was a stranger from Texas, but inside of a week Jim Botts smilingly informed Fields that the land was his. Botts' winter range lay along Fiddle Creek, two miles north of Fields' camp.

Obe's range was gutted. He studied the situation through one dull, miserable evening and the next day, rode to Mayo to file a pre-emption claim upon the quarter-section where his lambing camp lay, but once more his habit of deliberating had cost him dearly. A nephew of Jim Botts had filed upon the tract the preceding day. So matters stood on the first of May, when the drive to the summer range began.

Obe summered on White Rock meadows, a verdant valley in the heart of the Sierras, Botts on Outlaw Creek, thirty miles further north. The two did not meet until August, then Botts rode up to Fields' log cabin, in a late twilight, on his way to the Sacramento Valley. The two squandered no time in wasted civilities.

"You ain't figuring on elbowing me off my homestead, are you?" asked Fields bluntly of the man on horseback.

Botts spat prodically, and bit off a fresh chew of tobacco, his teeth showing to the molars.

"Not by a damn sight," was his laughing reply, "but I'm going to fasten my fangs on Section Twenty-one, if you want to know."

Obe's gray eyes dropped. Section Twenty-one lay south of his winter cabin, while Fiddle Creek broke out of the hills three miles to the north. It had not occurred to him that Jim would think of buying a section so distant from his winter quarters. Obe had fully made up mind to buy Twenty-one himself as his best chance of making his range good after losing the two sections in the spring. Eagerness to get an early start across the mountain in order that his herd might pick the cream of the trail feed, had prevented him from visiting the land office at that time. He fully intended to make that his first business in the fall. Now, he was too late.

"Going out now for that purpose?" he asked, lifting his eyes.

"I'm on my way," was the triumphant retort. "See this old sorrel?" Botts slapped the raw-boned beast on the rump, "He'll carry me to Mayo before sundown tomorrow. The land office is open for business till seven o'clock. Say, want me to put in a bid for you?" and the pushing man of business laughed again with brutal frankness.

Obe's glance traveled out across the meadow, which lay flat and fertile in the twilight.

"I can't get away now," he began hesitatingly, "I've got a Spanish boy who don't know much about the range, and I can't leave him alone."

"Who's expecting you to get away?" laughed Botts with offensive gayety, "I ask, do you want me to put in a bid for you? You know the railroad company is itching to sell its land."

"Of course I was a damn fool to think you would let up on me once you'd got your hooks on the best part of my range," said Obe bitterly. He threw a look at Botts full of cold contempt. "Wouldn't trust you, Jim to put in a bid for a blind orphan, if you want to know; but since you've got the screws on me I'm willing to pay the doctor. I'll give you a dollar an acre if you'll turn back and leave Twenty-one to me."

The laughter of Botts rang out in the twilight.

"A dollar an acre," he mocked.. "Six hundred and forty iron washers for a pleasant day's ride. Well, that wouldn't be so bad now, would it? But all the same I don't see it that way. Foothill range is going to double in value in the next two years. A dollar an acre! No, Obe, you're cheap. Twenty-one is mine, as sure as this old red wolf can carry me to Mayo by sundown tomorrow." He slapped the sorrel again. "And by ——, if he caves in on me I'll buy another rack of bones, and toddle right along. Horses was made for man to kill, anyway."

"You've got the name of being the one who can kill them," was Fields' cold retort.

Botts accepted the charge as a compliment.

"You bet your sweet life," he cried, "and I make the killing pay, don't never forget that."

Fields' gray eyes no longer sought the ground. They shot level glances into Bott's restless face.

"What if I should happen to beat you to the land office?" he demanded with a peculiar drawl.

Once more Blotts' laugh rang across the meadow.

"On the old gray mare?" he shouted derisively," I'll pitch camp, and take a good night's sleep, and then will dust you from Hell to breakfast, if that's your game. You're said to be good at legging it, Obe, but you'd surely look sick after trying a break with me at the saddle game. I was raised on a horse."

The rider jerked himself stiff in his saddle, and shoved his hat to the back of his bullet head with a swagger. Baring his teeth he went on boldly: "I suppose yon won't set the hounds on me if I pitch camp down by the lake? I expect to hit the dust early."

Obe was absently scratching his chin. "Pitch your camp where you like," he replied thoughtfully, and, after a moment added: "You may turn your horse loose in the pasture if you want to. The sheep have left poor picking outside that fence."

Botts accepted the offer of his rival both as to pitching camp and to using the fenced enclosure. Fields returned to his cabin under the tamaracks, gravely turning over in his mind the problem presented by Botts' appearance.

It was nearly nine o'clock. Obe had heard Jim boast of being able to do with six hours' sleep. On an occasion deemed urgent he could probably do with five. He ought to be in his blankets and asleep by nine-thirty. Allowing him half an hour in the morning to eat a bite of breakfast, and saddle his horse would leave him pounding the road to the valley by three o'clock.

By way of the Carson freight road Mayo lay seventy miles from White

Rock. The Morrow Trail was a longer course by ten miles. The former course was deep-rutted with travel at this season, the latter an unused forest path. Botts would follow the road, so Obe decided to take the trail. Eighty miles was the figure, reduced to its lowest terms, which lay between him and the loss of his winter range. Jim had credited him with being good at legging it. A queer smile seamed Obe's sunburnt face at the recollection.

By the time the night shadows had enveloped the lake and the fertile meadows Botts was in deep, untroubled sleep. Fields, on the other hand, was very much awake. His reflections had brought him certain definite conclusions. Jim would be up and away by three o'clock. He would have seventy miles of mountain road ahead of him including one summit of seven thousand feet and another of five thousand. A king of saddle horses could not be forced over that course under twelve hours. The boney sorrel would probably die on his feet before hitting the lower foothills, but Jim had announced his purpose under such a contingency. Twelve hours, or thirteen, or fourteen would take Jim into Mayo before the land office closed its doors. Cut out all probabilities in the way of delays, and call it twelve hours. That would mean the valley town by three o'clock. Thus was the problem simplified.

Obe had but to reach Mayo before three o'clock to win the race. Afoot, could he do it? He believed that he could. He would enjoy two advantages over his four-legged competitor—intelligent co-ordination of mind and body, and unrestrained freedom of action. If Obe should find his endurance failing him he could rest. There would be no rest for the sorrel short of death.

The lank, and sinewy sheepman had stepped every inch of the Morrow Trail a dozen times in the wake of his shambling herds. He knew every cut-off and blind side trail. His advance would not be interrupted by his meeting or passing other travelers. He would leave the gray mare in the pasture to disarm Jim's suspicions.

The Mayhew buck camp lay on Black-water Meadows, twelve miles east of White Rock. Beyond was not a single inhabited hut until one reached Fanshaw's cabin at the edge of the High Plains. Mountain going it was every inch of the way, heavily timbered, and solitary.

It was ten o'clock when Obe set out from White Rock. At midnight he was passing the sleeping buck camp. From this point onward, straight into the black forest to the west, there was an easy ascend for twenty miles, culminating in a crest six thousand feet above the sea. Obe took that stretch at greatly reduced speed. He reached the summit at half past three. There had been a moon to light his way thus far through the solemn aisles of the forest. The moon had drooped so low, now that the woods were left in impenetrable gloom.

Scraping together a bed of pine needles the mountain man stretched out on his face and slept heavily for two hours. He awoke in a dull, cold dawn a trifle stiff, slightly chilled, but in nowise depressed. The waste places of the mountains brought a benediction to his pioneer soul. The brooding silence of the deep forest might have fallen pall-like on one unfamiliar with its blessings. To Obe's spirit it brought encouragement. He loved to conquer difficulties as some men love ease.

The longest leg of his journey was still before him, but he had calculated his course deliberately before turning his back on the cabin under the tamaracks. The Carson road was an up and down passage from the big summit to the edge of the pinery; the Morrow Trail was steadily downward to the last lap of the foothills.

Refreshing himself with pinches of sugar from a bag tucked under his belt, Obe leaned forward once more in the race. He proceeded at a swinging walk for several miles, sucking lipfulls of sugar as he traveled. His hunger was satisfied by the time he reached Lone Camp, so he turned off the trail and cooled his tongue with a deep drink at the spring under the hill. Back once more in the trail, he broke into an easy trot and for mile upon mile, padded at tremendous speed along the forest floor.

Finding his breath growing labored in the region of the Hog Back, he slackened his pace and took it easy for half an hour. Feeling his lungs and legs in perfect tune at the end of that period, he broke again into his easy, soft-footed trot. He did not find it necessary to consult his big silver watch. An occasional glance at the mounting sun kept him apprized of the passage of time. He knew that he was eating miles at a rate that would kill the best saddle horse in California.

It was nine o'clock when he reached the western rim of the pinery. Twenty miles of parched foothills lay between him and the great, hazy valley. The heat, here, was excessive, but the long-legged wayfarer had still a vast amount of endurance conserved under his craggy ribs. He had been wearing a flannel shirt against the chill of mountain heights. He pulled it off, now, and cast it into the chaparral.

The trail forked at the edge of the pinery. Obe took the left-hand branch which followed the bony ridge above the sounding backwater. Half way across the foothills he met Gabe Quibley, the trapper, slowly mounting the long ascent. The two exchanged foothill greetings, and stood for a few minutes in talk on the rim of the big canyon. Obe did not mention the errand that was taking him to the valley at this season; Quibley asked no questions.

Half an hour before noon Obe greeted Fanshaw in the door of his sun-bleached cabin at the mouth of Blackwater canyon.

"Can I have your horse to drive to Mayo?" asked the sheepman, as the squatter responded to his greeting.

Fanshaw, mean, close-fisted, and curious unloaded a mouthful of eager questions, which Obe answered by drawing a long buckskin purse from his pocket. No other argument was necessary. A clumsy old plug of a horse was dragged out of a shed, harnessed and hitched to a wobbly cart. Obe climbed into the cart seat, hammered a cloud of dust out of the old plug's back and was off. It was called eighteen miles from Fanshaw's place to Mayo, but the road lay along the level floor of the Sacramento Valley.

Jim Botts carried the sunken-eyed sorrel into Mayo on bloody spurs. That ruthless rider threw the horse loose at the door of Fleck's stable and swore a gay greeting to a friend as he started stiffly along the plank sidewalk toward the land office. In front of the entrance of that dull-looking edifice he staggered back with a startled, indrawn imprecation. Obe Fields, gaunt, grim, but smiling, leveled a look at him from the doorway.

"Good God!" gasped Botts, rolling his tobacco dryly in his mouth," Good God! The old gray mare?"

Obe slapped his lean thigh, much as Jim had slapped the sorrel the evening before.

"Old shanks!" he retorted harshly.

Jim, his tobacco-stained lips hanging apart, looked particularly ugly, but not at all truculent. The gleam of conquest had faded from his countenance, swept away in a flood of astonishment. After a moment, Obe went on ironically:

"You know more about horses Jim, than the man who invented them, but what you don't know about men would fill a damn sight bigger book."

Botts sagged back against an awning post and fumbled weakly at his hat rim. "You can't tell me you legged it from White Rock," he blustered feebly.

"Anyhow, I'm here, ain't I?"

Jim's glance traveled waveringly toward the dusty window of the land office.

"And you've nailed your number on Section Twenty-one?" he murmured in tones half of awe, half of respect.

Obe indulged in a harsh, scornful laugh.

"Twenty-one," he mocked, "I've hit on bigger game than Twenty-one."

Jim tried to hook his shoulder about the awning post for better support. He was feeling unaccountably tired. After a moment he muttered dully:

"I don't get you."

"Why, I've torn a leaf out of your book, Jim, and much obliged for the suggestion. I've coppered the best three sections of your range on Fiddle Creek, if you want to know."

A Distinguished Westerner

By Rebecca J. Gradwohl.

DAVID LUBIN, who recently died in Rome, was in every sense of the term, a self-made man. No accident of birth, no chance nor combination of fortuitous circumstances contributed to his success. A poor Jewish lad, thrown upon his own resources at an early age, he was an example of a man who, by his industry, indomitable will, superior mind and ambition sky-aspiring, raised himself from obscurity to a position not only of wealth and prominence, but of world-wide usefulness.

Although born in Poland, Lubin was distinctly of the west. He came to America when a child. He was but a youth when he found his way to San Francisco where, without education or business training, he earned a livelihood in a small way. It was not long, however, before he realized that California was the land of opportunity for those who earnestly seek it, and, in consequence, in 1874 we find him in Sacramento, that Mecca for pioneers, whence have come many of the most prominent men of the west. In that city he and his brother launched the mercantile firm of Weinstock, Lubin & Co. Thus was laid the foundation stone of what was to be a marvelous and interesting career.

The history of this business venture need not be told here. Suffice to say that it was a success and brought material prosperity to David Lubin. What is of importance in this connection is the fact that Lubin was not content with the title of rich man; this was not his ambition. The intellectual bread he had hungered for in his struggling youth, and which had been denied him, he now resolutely determined to have. In spite of business cares and family responsibil-

ities, for he had married young, he set about obtaining this knowledge.

Fortunately, he understood his educational deficiencies. Hence, with that breadth of vision that later distinguished him, he knew that to rear an edifice on an unsound foundation would be like building on sand, so he decided to begin where, if circumstances had favored him in his early years he would have started —that is at the lowest rung of the ladder of knowledge. He secured teachers and studied with them the rudiments of learning.— spelling, reading, arithmetic and grammar. As time went on, he proceeded to the higher branches of education.

At night after business hours which, in those days were long and arduous, when the house was wrapped in slumber, he plodded on, and often the early hour of the morning found him poring over his books. His mind responded to learning as a seed to soil and water, and in time it became a tree of abundant knowledge and put forth blossoms of thought and wisdom. He pursued certain philosophical problems the result of which was his book, "Let there be Light." He was also interested in science and several small inventions, all of which were patented.

Thus, in a decade, David Lubin by industry and business sagacity became a man of wealth, and by tireless study a broadly educated individual whose mind was richly stored with the lore of past ages and the wisdom of his own time. Business had been his vocation, study his avocation. The combination of the two made him the remarkable character he finally became.

Another of Mr. Lubin's vocations was

farming at which he experimented for a brief period on a farm near Sacramento. Though he did no actual labor on it, the experience served to give him an insight into the life of the farmer and awakened his sympathetic interest in a class whose labors early and late might, because of an untimely frost or a year of drought, yield but a pitiful harvest. And, moreover, a harvest that might become still less through an unscrupulous middleman or clever speculator. Thus, years, before the great idea of an agricultural institute took form, the germ of it was born, but Mr. Lubin thrust it back into one of the cells of his brain to await the time then, the trammels of business set aside, he could bring it forth.

The time came when he decided that the knowledge he had gained at so great an effort must not be selfishly kept for himself; that the torch he had lighted should illuminate others. He turned it, therefore, toward the lifting of the burden of that class that had aroused his sympathies in his own agricultural experiment—that is the farmers.

Having carefully formulated his plans, he gave up active participation in business, and about fifteen years ago, he went east and presented those ideas to Congress. But Congress turned a deaf ear to his plans. Nothing daunted, he crossed the ocean, and at his own expense traveled from country to country urging the necessity of a scheme whereby an exact knowledge of the crop outputs of the world might be formulated. But again he met with no response. Finally on Italian soil he gained the recognition for which he pleaded. King Victor Emmanuel saw the wonderful possibilities of Mr. Lubin's ideas, became their ardent advocate and gave them material support. He built a palace for the use of the proposed institute and endowed it with an annuity of sixty thousand dollars. In this way, the International Agricultural Institute at Rome was founded, and the United States, which at last recognized its value, made Lubin its delegate.

During the last eight years, with the exception of occasional visits to America, Mr. Lubin resided in Rome where he carried on the crowning work of his life. He lived to see the full fruition of his labors, and to know that the Institute was of incalculable value during the war when exact knowledge of crop out-puts was essential for the establishment of prices which were on wheat and other cereals.

In appearance Mr. Lubin was strong and rugged looking, with the broad, high brow of the scholar, the kindly eyes of the humanitarian, and the firm mouth of the man of determined purpose. He was once described as resembling in appearance the pictures of the prophet Isaiah. In spirit he was not unlike the great seer who hated shams and despised rewards.

In every sense of the term he was a true American. His life typified the spirit of the land that puts no shackles on the poor, or obscure of any creed, but permits them to rise to whatever heights their genius beckons them. Its one requirement is work, and work was David Lubin's creed. "Seeist thou a man diligent in his business? He shall stand before Kings." Throughout all the years of his life, David Lubin had been diligent in whatever had been the business of the moment, and he stood before a king whose broad vision made possible the beautiful dream the outward symbol of which is a palace that stands on an eminence in the "Villa Borghese."

A Romance of the Mountain

By Belle Young

OULD we never reach the bottom of this canyon? Surely if there were such a place in existence as the "bottomless pit," we had found it.

We had been hunting in the Santa Cruz Mountains. It had been cloudy all day and we were anxious to get home before it began raining. But we had lost the trail. It was fast growing dark and the wind was beginning to blow furiously.

Just as I was beginning to think we were never going to get anywhere, we came out on a little level place containing a few acres of ground and covered with trees and bushes. In the midst stood an old house almost hidden from view in a tangle of giant ferns and vines. Large drops of rain were beginning to fall and we hastened to find shelter.

The door in the front was nailed fast on the inside, but on going around to the side we found a door which we opened and entered just in time to escape the storm. We picked up some old wood and soon had a roaring fire in the old fire-place.

The room was perfectly empty, yet we could see by the fire light that it was also very clean. The house, as seen from the outside, had the appearance of having been deserted for years, yet on the inside it was clean enough to have been occupied the day before.

My two companions were amazed on seeing it. They had hunted on the mountains for years and had never come upon it before. We ate the rest of our lunch, then made pillows of our coats and stretched ourselves out in front of the fire, only too thankful we had found this shelter for the night.

The storm was raging outside. I think I never heard more desolate or uncanny sounds than the wind made as it rushed through the canyon. Wild shrieks that seemed almost human, then low, wailing sounds as of some creature in despair. The rain came down in torrents and beat against the old house in a fury.

We told ghost stories and mysterious experiences we had had and at last we began a discussion as to the former inmates of the old house. Strange characters we had it peopled with, but not even in our wildest conjectures did we come near the real story of the ones who had lived here long years before.

The fire had gone down and it seemed to me I had just fallen asleep when I was suddenly awakened by the sound of a hand on the latch outside. The storm had ceased and after the loud noise of the wind and rain, which we had heard just before going to sleep, the silence seemed almost supernatural.

I aroused my companions, and in another instant the door was opened by a priest bearing a lantern, followed by a Mexican carrying a large bundle. He came directly to us, and speaking in a pleasant voice, though with authority, he said: "I do not know your business here nor have I time now to explain mine, but I ask you to take your things and sit over there in the darkest corner of the room, and remain perfectly silent until we are through and I will explain later."

We obeyed the order and he and the Mexican proceeded to stretch a dark curtain across the corner of the room near the fire-place. They had just finished when a young lady and gentleman entered. They did not see us in our dark corner, but we looked in amazement at the two, who on removing their long cloaks took their places in front of the curtain.

The young man, who was a Spanish officer of high rank, as we could see by his uniform, was resplendent in gold lace and medals, and the young lady, elegant in her court dress.

Hardly had they taken their places, before the door again opened and there entered four young men carrying a cot, on which lay on old Mexican woman. As they placed the cot before the fire, we could see her distinctly. Old and feeble, with a wrinkled brown face.

When she caught sight of the two, she cried out, "My blessed senor, my beautiful lady, I knew you would come." They smiled lovingly at her and she went on, "They told me you would never come, that you were drowned in the dreadful sea."

They bowed their heads sadly before her. She looked at them in wonder and then seemed to realize what they meant, as once more she cried out, "Yes, yes, it is true, for you are young and I am old, and we were all the same age, but you have come back from the dead to tell me that you know old Juanita has kept her word. She promised to take care of your home until you returned and she has kept her promise."

Once more they bowed lovingly before her.

"And tonight, tonight," she cried, "I will go with you, my work is done."

Looking upward they made the sign of the cross, and as they did so, the priest knelt before the old woman and began a prayer. Before he had finished the two had stepped behind the curtain, and when she looked to see them once more, she saw only the dark curtain, which to her dim eyes seemed only one of the darker shadows of the room. But she was happy and satisfied. Her work was done. Tenderly and carefully they carried her out of the room.

The two young people then came from behind the curtain, once more in their long dark cloaks. They knelt before the priest, who blessed them for their great kindness to a poor, desolate old woman. They kissed his hand and followed by the Mexican went out into the night.

The old priest threw some more wood on the fire, and as we gathered around, he told us the story of the old house. "Years ago, before California became a part of the United States, a young Spanish officer was ordered to take command of the Spanish troops at Monterey. He was betrothed to a young lady of high rank, with the consent of both her family and his own. But when the young officer was orederd to America, her father absolutely refused to let the marriage take place. He would never give his consent for his daughter to be taken so far away. Tears and prayers were all in vain, so escaping from the house, she met her lover and together they boarded the ship in time to sail for America.

"The first six months they lived happily in Monterey, and then came the request that he resign from the army. Her father, having great influence in the affairs of the nation, had not rested until he had had revenge in the way that he knew would prove the greatest disgrace to him. The young officer would not tell his wife, but told her that he had not been feeling very well, so had consulted a physician, who had ordered him to resign from the army and live as simple a life as he could in the mountains and, in so doing he might hope to entirely recover his health. She very willingly consented to go, never dreaming there was any other reason. He had this house built and a smaller one in the rear for Juanita, her servant, then a young girl.

"He confided in this young Mexican girl, so that she would help him to keep the truth from her young mistress, whom she almost worshiped. Two years they lived here. He was quite an artist and painted many pictures, which we still have in the monastery at the foot of the mountain.

"Juanita carried their food and whatever else they cared to buy from Monterey. He had an income from his estates in Spain and with Juanita's help all knowledge of the real state of affairs was kept from the young wife. At the end of two years came a letter from her father begging them to come home. He was dying and longed for their forgiveness. He had used his powers to rein-

state the young man in his former position in the army.

"He only read that part of the letter
referring to her father's sickness to her
and told her as he had entirely recovered
there was no reason why they could not
go at once. They were to go on a small
sailing boat from Monterey Bay to Santa
Barbara and from there on an ocean
vessel to Spain.

"They left their home, just as it was, in
the care of Juanita, promising her that
they would soon return. He felt that
he could never live in Spain where he
had been treated so unjustly and she,
thinking it was the only place where he
could have perfect health, was quite
willing to return.

"The small boat on which they sailed
from Monterey was never heard from
again. Whether it burned or how it
went down no one ever knew. No other
ship had seen it and no one of the crew
or passengers lived to tell the story of
its loss.

"For weeks and months after everyone
else had given up hope, Juanita still
watched and waited for news of the
missing boat. Until at last her mind gave
way and she forgot all about the loss of
the boat and now only asked for news
of ships from Spain, expecting her loved
ones on each one. She lived alone in the
little house she had occupied when they
were here and kept this house in perfect

order for years. When she became so
old and feeble, that she was no longer
able to take care of it, we persuaded her
to let us remove everything of value to
the monastery. But we still have to
come up once a week at least and clean
this house thoroughly to satisfy her.

"A Mexican and his wife stay with
her at night now, as she is perfectly helpless. Every night they have to lift her
to the window to see if there is any
light here. She expects them to come at
any time. Tonight the light from your
fire could be seen so plainly from the
window and she insisted on coming over
at once. She was sure they were here.
So we promised to bring her as soon as
the storm was over.

"The young couple you saw had come
to the monastery to be married and were
detained by the storm, so we persuaded
them to put on some of the clothes left
by Juanita in our care, trusting to her
failing eye-sight to carry out the deception, with what success you have seen."

We thanked him for telling us the
story and, as it was near daylight, we
very gratefully accepted his invitation to
breakfast. We followed him down the
rocky canyon to the monastery, where
we were very kindly served.

We felt, as we went on our way back
to the present-day world, that we had
had a real glimpse of the old Spanish
California.

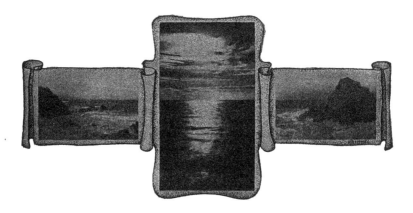

The Wreck at Clay Hill

By Harold E. Somerville

WITH expert fingers, Dr. Harrell knotted the split end of the bandage and adjusted the sling.

"There," said he, to the young man sitting on the sofa, "that'll serve you till I come again. And I'm sure this young lady and her parents will continue to give you the best of care." A very pretty girl, wearing a diamond solitaire, who occupied the other half of the seat, smiled and lowered her eyes.

"Yes," agreed Roger Stanley, "Marie certainly makes a great nurse. And this house is any amount better than a hospital. With all due respect to the New England Northern Railroad, and much as I miss my engine, I'd rather be laid up here a while than be sound and back on the job. What do you think—will I get out of the shops with a good side-rod?"

"Your arm," replied the medical man, "worried me a bit when I first saw it. The break was an awkward one—nearer the elbow than I like—but it's in very good shape now, and I believe I can pull you through without a stiff joint."

"Glad to hear that, Doc, but I can't kick if you don't—I'm lucky to be alive."

"Very lucky indeed," confirmed the physician. "It was little short of a miracle, the way you slowed up your train—on that down-grade, too. And the wreck occurred just where the curve winds through the big cut in the ledges —how did you ever see that freight in time?"

"I didn't see it."

"Then how the deuce did you happen to have your brakes on?"

The railroad man hesitated. The very pretty girl took his big left hand between her two small ones and spoke with gentle persuasiveness.

"Tell him your story, Roger—the doctor won't laugh at you."

"You tell him, Marie," said Stanley.

"No," insisted the girl. "Let's go fifty-fifty—I'll tell my part, and then you'll tell yours." To Dr. Harrell, she added: "Roger, you know, is afraid you'll think his strange experience affected his head——"

"Come, come!" laughed the physician. "I'm growing curious—what's the mystery?"

"We'll tell you about it," replied Marie, "and then perhaps you can explain it, being a wise man. It's the queerest adventure I ever had, and Roger says the same thing for himself. It's positively uncanny."

"But for the love o' Mike, Doc," put in Stanley, "keep it dark!"

"As you know," began the girl, "while father was ill I ran the station here at Montague Junction—working the night trick, part of the time."

"No place for a woman," remarked the doctor.

"Of course, it is a lonely spot," admitted Marie. "Sometimes when it was pitch dark, and raining, and the wind was moaning in the telegraph wires, along toward two o'clock in the morning, I would feel the creeps coming on, and I'd begin to imagine I saw and heard all sorts of weird things. But then I would think of Roger, in his cab, climbing up through the mountains on the single track, and facing real danger, and I'd just laugh at myself for being nervous in my dry, cosy little office."

"Oh, you're safe enough there," said Harrell. "I was merely thinking that the work is a man's job."

"Last Monday night was one of those dismal times," resumed the girl. "After the Boston Express went through the Junction I didn't see a soul for hours, nor heard a sound except the rain driving against the windows and the gale howling around the station. And Roger's train was turned over to him an hour late at White Springs, so that he didn't pull into the Junction until three o'clock. His orders, which I had taken myself, were to run as usual without stop to Waterville, where he was to meet southbound freight No. 395."

"Engine 395 is a hoodoo,' obsĕrved Stanley. "Wish I had finished her for the scrap heap."

"But the operator at Waterville," continued Marie, "forgot to set his board against the freight, and it got by him— all that's been in the papers. As soon as he realized his oversight he reported it to the despatcher, who called me, just as Roger's train was pulling out, and told me to hold it here until 395 made the Junction. The despatcher started to explain the trouble, but I didn't wait to hear him—I just grabbed a red lantern from the floor and ran out. But I was too late—the tail lights of the express were away down at the end of the long platform, and I knew I hadn't one chance in a thousand of stopping it then. However, I ran after the train, and screamed. Some passengers had got off the express —only to find that the branch train doesn't make the night connections except in Summer—and they shouted. I ran out into the railroad yard, and then —it was silly of me, I know, but I was simply frantic—I threw the lantern toward the express. But nobody on the train heard or saw anything. Then I tripped over a switch frog and fell, and everything went dark."

Marie shuddered.

"The passengers carried me into the station, and I came to. The despatcher was calling me, and he read me the articles of war for leaving my wire—but apologized when I told him what had happened. Then he said he said he had ordered out the wreck crew, and told me to telephone to Montague for doctors. After I attended to that I had nothing to do but wait. I put my coat on over my wet dress, turned down my lights, and looked out of the window toward Waterville—into that awful blackness."

Her voice lowered, and she slipped her arm into the elbow of her engineer.

"I could see that heavy express tearing along through the rain and darkness, flying past the station at Middleton, which is closed at night, and then dropping down the five-mile grade toward Waterville, around the sharp curves above the river, and through the rock cuts below Clay Hill. And I could see the freight, puffing, puffing up the grade, coming nearer, nearer, nearer——"

"And all those hundreds of passengers, asleep in their berths," suggested the doctor.

"They never entered my mind," said Marie. "I thought only of Roger. I knew he would have his throttle wide open, instead of coasting down, as he does when he is running on time. And I saw him sitting there in his cab, with no thought of danger, but planning how he could make up a part of that lost hour in the hundred miles of his run this side of Montreal. He had waved his hand and smiled at me as he pulled into the Junction—and when I thought that was the last time I should ever see him I almost went crazy. Oh, how I wished I could be there in the cab with him, to warn him of his peril! There was just one thing left for me to do, and I did it—I prayed."

She turned to Stanley, and he took up the story.

"I was certainly trying to make up time, all right. I had the general superintendent's private car at the tail of my train and three directors of the road with him. In one of the Pullmans there was the Governor of some big Western State and the president of an insurance company, as I learned afterwards. We also had a car full of theatrcial people going from Boston to Montreal, and there were some famous actresses in that party. We were making around seventy miles an hour when we passed the Middleton station—our wind almost sucked it along after us. Then we hit the down grade—you know the spot—on one side of us was Clay Hill, which slides down on the right of way in carload lots of real estate every Spring, and on the other side, a hundred feet below us, was the river. Beyond Clay Hill is the long reverse curve through the ledges."

"Worst place on the road," commented Dr. Harrell.

"You've said it. Well, just as my engine was tearing along above the river, and I was sitting, thinking of nothing in particular—guess maybe I might have been sort of dreaming about Marie, at that—it seemed, all of a sudden, as if she stood right there beside me, kind of gentle-like and sympathetic. As if she were all of a flutter, like a breath of air —it's hard to describe the feeling I had. I was startled and I must have turned to the left a little—like you do when you think somebody has spoken to you, or is looking at you from behind your back, though, of course, I didn't see anyone there. And as I turned I pulled the throttle back, without meaning to. But —will you believe me, Doc?—it seemed almost as if somebody put a hand on mine and MADE me close that throttle. There was no hand there—any fool could see there wasn't—but just the same, I had a queer hunch that there had been one."

"I credit your story," said Dr. Harrell. "I consider it entirely possible—stranger occurrences are on record in books on mental phenomena, as I can prove to you if you will drop in at my office. And then what happened?"

"The exhaust of my engine stopped, of course, when I shut her off. She'd been using a lot of steam and her safety-valve didn't pop, so the only noise was the roar of the train. I was about to open her up again, when I thought I heard a locomotive whistle—but the sound was so faint I couldn't be sure. I looked across the cab at my fireman—he was staring at me, his mouth open, and his face a dirty gray. It must have been as white, under the soot, as this bandage.

I held back the throttle and then I heard the sound again, as plain as you hear me now—some engine whistling for a crossing."

Marie tightened her grip on Stanley's arm as she listened.

"Maybe the sound," said he, "was magnified or reflected, somehow, in coming through the cut. Or perhaps the damp air carried the blast better than in dry weather. But I knew there was another engine not very far away, and I knew it must be ahead of us—nothing on wheels could have caught up with me from behind. And we were due to hit anything ahead, whether it was going or coming. Believe me, Doc, I jammed those brakes on to the tires if ever a man did!"

"And then?"

"We had just taken the curve into the long cut through the ledges. I couldn't see the iron three hundred feet ahead— nothing but walls of rock in the glare of my headlight, and not much of that, in the driving rain. All I could do was to sit there, tickling the air to get the most of the shoes, expecting every second to see the enemy's headlight poke around that curve, and wondering whether I was going to be instantly killed, slowly boiled to death, or just merely crippled for life."

"And your train crashed into the freight, head-on."

"No, sir, it didn't—we kept on going and going, slower and slower, until, just when we had almost stopped, the freight came thundering up and bumped into us and I fell down in front of the fire-box and got this broken wing. You can believe me or not, Doc, as you see fit, but what I've told you is true as a piston rod. I don't know whether it was a sort of vision I had, or just a fool fancy, but I do know that if I hadn't shut her off when I did I wouldn't have heard the freight engine whistle—and I wouldn't be here. And there'd have been a lot of other jobs for the undertaker. But it's no credit to me that I had a little wreck instead of a big one—I was doing my best to pile up rolling stock in a heap when I got wise to that hoodoo, 395."

"You are right, my boy," seconded Harrell. "The credit belongs, not to you, but to this young lady."

"You mean——?" said Marie, mystified.

"I mean," replied the doctor, "that, while I give Stanley full credit for his presence of mind, and for his nerve in sticking to his engine and for his skill in practically stopping his train, you are the one who averted the disaster."

"But doctor, I don't understand."

"Mental telepathy. Scientific men to-day, in many instances, admit the possibility that the mind of one person, when it is in a state of intense agitation, may create a vivid impression in the mind of another person, many miles away, if that other mind happens to be in a vacant or receptive condition and the two persons are in close sympathy. Soldiers, at the moment of danger or of death, seem to be able, in many cases, to appear in visionary form before near friends or dear relatives at home. It is a sort of wireless telegraphy between mind and mind."

"And you think," said Marie, "that I—

did that?"

"You were in the greatest distress as you sat in the window, following Stanley's train, in your imagination, to its destruction. And he says that he was not thinking of anything in particular — his mind was in a receptive state at the very time when your thoughts were centered upon his peril. The conditions appear to have been wholly favorable for telepathic communication—just as a perfect electric circuit makes possible the sending of a telegram. I leave it for you and Stanley to decide whether or not a mental message was transmitted."

Dr. Harrell took his hat and medicine case and rose to go. But at the door he paused and looked thoughtfully at the couple seated close together on the sofa.

"I might add," he said, with a twinkle in his eye, "that you people seem to answer exactly to the description of persons in close sympathy—near, very near, friends. Yes, I diagnose this as a case of mental telepathy."

DOORS

The grey small stream, a wayfarer,
Winds down between sad shores,
Like one who carries dying hopes
To ever closing doors.

And dying hopes to closing doors
Are borne by you and me.
I wonder; will the doors stay shut
Throughout eternity?

—Nelson Antrim Crawford.

5

The Winds of Retribution

By Ethyl Hayes Sehorn

A NUT brown sea of dusty, dry rushes lay motionless under a shimmering noon-day sun. Out in the heart of it a vein of pale smoke curled heavenward, spiraling the hazy atmosphere of the warm autumnal morning and finally floating away to lose itself in higher zephyrs. Suddenly without herald, an arrogant north wind whipped down through the basin. Immediately, as though birthed by a savage combustion, dense banks of thunderous clouds —voluminous and irascible, writhed and fought and tossed and tumbled like a maddened tide of inky billows twisting toward the sky.

A man and a maid, pattering along on an old, hard beaten path, did not see the threatening coils of the smoky consternation. Possibly it was because they were traveling southward, but far more likely because they were eloping sweethearts and had eyes for little else save one another.

"Te amo, si, te amo de veras—tra lala ——," sang the lover. Then laughingly switching to the first two lines of the second stanza, he sang in English the words:

"No longer now silence that oppresses, No longer silence that destroys, tra la la—,"

"I don' understan' all dose wor's en that song," his sweetheart poutingly complained.

"I seng et for you all en thee Engleesh, den," responded her accommodating cavelier.

"I love you, yes, I love you truly—" he began when the Indian girl reached over and tickled the end of his nose with a long downy cat-tail; then jubilantly she exclaimed:

"I know one, too. Yes, I know a Spanish song that es good for today. Lissen!" and she swayingly began to sing, translating as her lover had done to English,

"Vamos, arriba, muchachos—
Up an' away, my jooly boys all;
Fasten your boots ver' tight to your feet;
Up an' away to gay Monterey,
Sweetest an' choicest of acorns to eat."

Her lover laughed, "That es good— that song. That es where we ar' goin' an' what we ar' goin' for, but you, leetle glorondria—my leetle swallow, I am 'fraid your feet weel git ver' tired . for we get to ole Monterey."

"Oooh, I bet no! What you wan' to bet me?" his lady challenged.

"Bravo! You ween!" shouted her admirer, "I weel not bet with such a fair lady. You ween, cara paloma!"

"No, no, no," the girl shook her head laughingly, "Today et es Carlos that weens everything, for today he weens me! Joe Raven he tink you ween, for today you tak' me away from heem for ever!"

Carlos frowned. Even as victor decamping with the spoils, he could not bear the mere mention of his hated rival's name to enter Paradise.

At Mrs. Bissett's ranchero this Joe Raven had suddenly risen to be a commanding figure among the work-a-day people on the wide-spreading ranch. A few weeks ago, a month perhaps, and little or naught was known of him—save that he belonged to the tribe of the Tehamas to the northward and had wandered in, and aimlessly enough at that, to Mrs. Bissett's and applied for work. Today he was on par with the foreman, in fact, he took no orders from anyone, save Mrs. Bissett, or Master Philip, themselves.

None could ride a horse as Joe Raven. None could quiet and curb the untrained colts as he. In the branding of cattle, the Tehaman showed a skill and dexterity that astonished the oldest of branders. He could cock more windrows of wheat in a day than three ordinary men in the same given time. His toiling with the harvesters was inexorable. Unsufferable heat, blizzards of flying chaff, and clouds of strangling red dust failed to deter him a minute in his labors on the thrasher.

He was possessed with the swiftness of the deer, the cunning of the fox, the endurance of the bear, the trickiness of the bob-cat and the ferocity of the wolf —so the Indians said—and they, one and all, disliked him. Philip Bisset said it was because they, themselves, were lazy, and Joe Raven as an Indian was exceptional. But old Charlie Mountain-Trout shook his gray-black head and muttered an intelligible something about Joe Raven to which all the other Indians stolidly nodded their heads in a silent but well-approved agreement.

One day Joe Raven discovered Nakoma in the 'kitchen. That for him was the beginning of a new day. On the spot he wanted the maid, and when Joe Raven wanted, his desires were insatiable, implacable, until gained and satisfied. So he wooed accordingly. But the Washoe maiden's affections were shuttling. Some days she favored the bold buck from Tehama, but more often she smiled upon gentle Carlos, the Mexican half-bred, part Mayo from a far away Sinaloa, but veined more with Spanish blood from yet more distant Spain.

Carlos was not a very good worker. In Mexico, the land of his birth, the day of hard work was always "manana." But Carlos, be he indolent, was always kind and sweet-tempered and ever in high favor. He played low slumberous ballads on his guitar, that filled the warm summer nights with soft, twanging melody. And sometimes he sang—sang in a voice as clear and vibrative as the liquid tones of a meadow lark carroling in sheer joy

for the first green grasses and flowers of the early spring. Yes, Carlos in his way, was a great favorite, even with the Bissetts.

As the days passed Joe Raven became bolder in his love making. His attacks of courting became inflexible, commanding, unrelenting. At the same time the soft calling of Carlos' sweet love plaits were making themselves irresistible to the Indian girl's heart.

At last she could deny her choice no longer, and on this same delectable morning, had consented to run away with Carlos and escape from the grip of the persistent Tehaman.

Now out on the trail, Nakoma threw a handful of tule down at her lover and inquired archly:

"You don' lak to talk 'bout Joe Raven, Carlos?"

Carlos was on the verge of making an acidulous retort in reference to one Joe Raven, when a darkening mist like a blue-black fog shadowed the sun. The man looked up, then turned and looked back.

As out from a mammoth funnel, black swirling clouds wreathed through the air with vivid, frightened contortions. At first it flared as from a central nucleus, but seemingly on the instant, became volant — took wings and ·blew from hither to thither, from this place to that with such surprising rapidity, that even before Carlos could exclaim, the whole sky was obscured and the plains enveloped in duskiness.

"Madre de Dios!" he cried in bewilderment, "the tule grass! The tule grass es on fire, my angel!"

Nakoma stood dumbfounded; but Indian-like she remained immovable.

"We mus' hurry an' git out of thee grass—ef we don'—why we git burned up, eh?" she said calmly.

Carlos coughed. The smoke was already becoming stifling.

"Come," he said, "come quickly. We mus' make to thee river."

"Thee Sacramento, Carlos?"

"No, Los Plumas. See thee wend, my darlin'. We may 'ope to beat the fire, but we can' beat the wend."

"But ef we run to thee east——"

"We ar' runnin' from the fire weth thee wend at our backs."

"I understan' now," cried the wary Indian, "I understan', but always I stop to mak sure of thee bes' way. First I thenk of thee swamp lands of thee Sacramento. We ar' nearer them, I thenk."

"No, no, thes a-way. That would lead us ento thee fire."

"I see——I see——"

"Quickly Nakoma, quickly, we don' wan' to be burned up!"

A' gust of wind screamed by with a merciless, torrid breath that brittled and burned and blistered.

Nakoma cringed.

"Le's run," she cried, "et weel catch us on thes trail, sure. Oh, see Carlos, dere es a new plac' blazin' over dere—and over dere—and dere and dere!"

"We must take a cattle path. Here thes one Nakoma! Now run!"

"But we can' see where et es leadin' us—in thes tall tule. We can' see where we ar' goin' en here!"

"Mak thee haste, Nakoma—thee fire! —you see—et comes! an' thee smoke! Dios! soon we can not breathe!"

"We mus' not burn," declared the girl, "we mus' not burn, for that would please Joe Raven. How he would laugh ef he knew we were out here weth thee grass on fire!"

"Ef et was not for thee Raven we would not be here. I would hav' waited till I could buy a horse for you to ride. But I know by that tim' he would keel me or I would 'ave to keel heem, so I thenk best to go today, but I was wrong, mia beloved, to git you out here en thes fire. But how was poor Carlos to know that thee tules would burn today?"

"We weel git out, Carlos. Hey! thes way—thes way! Oh, that smoke—I choke, Carlos——I choke——"

"Come on, Nakoma! 'ow I wesh you were back at thee ranchero! but et es too late to thenk about that now. Hurry! you mus' run faster, Nakoma, you mus' run faster!"

"Mis' Bissett weel be angry—good Mis' Bissett!" gasped Nakoma. "I run away an' lef her wethout no help en hee ketchen."

"Vamos! Vamos! my love——thee flames! thee smoke, et es gainin'! et es gainin'! Thes path, my golondrina, see, see, here where thee cows hav' run!"

"No, no, my Carlos, thes way—thes way!" his sweetheart pleaded, "that trail goes back to thee north and but leads us back to thee flames!"

"I can' see—thee tules ar' so high!" the man panted, "ef only I had left you back en Mis' Bissett's ketchen!"

"But—Joe Raven, Carlos?"

"Joe Raven could not harm you en jest one more day, Nakoma."

Nakoma shrugged her fat shoulders dubiously. Perhaps he could, and perhaps he couldn't, but Nakoma had no faith in this parvenu—Joe Raven.

On a little farther and the girl complained:

"Oh, my Carlos, thes trail es so crooked, I'm sure I don' know where we are runnin'!"

"We weel turn back, mia paloma, for et es easy to see we ar' runnin ento thee fire—thee wend now beats en our faces an' et grows hotter every minute."

They turned to stumble back over the steps they had just trodden. Black seas of smoke curled down over the pair in dark tantrums of blinding fury. Cinders scorched them and stung them and flying whisps of blazing grass set their clothes afire.

On the next instant the smoke lifted and the blaze roared before them. In a flash Nakoma's face was blistered, her eyes seared, her long hair singed and crinkled.

Carlos staggered along in a paroxysm of coughing, the acrid vapors punished his throat and teased his lungs.

"Back Nakoma, back! We hav' agin come wrong!"

"Thes trail—no, thes one! Thes one! That es thee one we hav' jest come over, my Carlos!"

On for a moment, then a wail from the woman.

"We ar' lost, my lover, we ar' lost!"

"No, Nakoma, no, le's try thes trail. Ah, Dios!"

"Your shirt es on fire, Carlos!"

The river, through the tule, which the lovers struggled to reach.

"Run, Nakoma, we can' stop for burnin' shirts!" urged Carlos.

Nakoma turned to the right and down through another track of dusty, parched tules the couple fled. On—on through the tangled lobryinth of crackling reeds they fought their way feverously, desperately—obsessed with the madness of terror.

On they struggled, stubbing their toes in the dry, rutty hoof holes of the cattle. Staggering and coughing, they helped one another to keep to their feet as the blinding sheets of smoke passed over them.

"My Carlos! My Carlos!" the girl at length managed to gasp, "we are but runnin' round in a circle. See, dere es that leetle dried up arm of the Butte Slough! Tree times we hav' crossed et —an' see agin we approach et!"

"Ay! Ay! These paths ar' lak the spider web——" a furious fit of coughing finished Carlos' sentence.

Confused, bewildered and on the verge of insanity with fear, the man and the woman scuttled down another opening while streamers of sparks eddied and hissed at their backs.

Down the vast plain the fire swept, leaping, dancing, spreading in impish maliciousness. Stealthily it came, yet eagerly, greedily, hissing and spitting an aspish undertone to the waxing roar of its temulent overhead flames.

Turgid masses of dense purple smoke circled and twisted and spewed their nightish folds into the very heavens. The sun was obscured and the whole Sutter Basin shrouded in impenetrable dinginess.

On the heels of the Mexican and his sweetheart the snapping and sizzling increased. The heat grew unbearable, the smoke life-defying.

Once more Carlos stopped.

"Agin' we ar' but runnin' a circle. There es no gittin' out of thes grass— we ar' lost, mia paloma, we ar' lost!"

But the girl was yet undaunted. Snatching his hand, she again dived through an opening in the mesh of the heat-shriveled tules.

"Oh, Carlos," she gasped, where es

that ole wellow clump? Le's try to make for the wellow clump!"

"I thought et was out here," said Carlos, "but you see that et es not!"

"But thee ground es damp," the girl panted, "may be et es a leetle way over dere."

"No, I am of thee certain that thee weelows ar' not out here."

"Ef we could fin' a hole of wet mud— a cow wallow—thee ground es wet, dere mus' be one out near here somewhere. May be over dere!" the girl pointed.

But when the spot was reached no cow wallow marked its identity. The little hollow was drier, if possible, than the ground surrounding it.

"We are indeed lost!" the girl admitted, "I don' know where in the worl' we are!"

Lost in the maze of matted marsh weed, blinded in a maelstrom of smothering smoke, the helpless creatures watched the lapping phalanx of fire approach them.

Carlos lamented bitterly in Spanish:

"To think that it was I who brought you out into this!"

"But I say, Carlos, dere mus' be a mud hole about here close. I feel weth my feet that the ground es oozy," the woman insisted, as she saw her lover on the edge of collapse. "A few steps thes way an' may be yet we can fin' et!"

Up and out of the old dry hole and over and back a few hundred feet brought Nakoma to her mud hole. But when she saw it—so small, so shallow, and oh, so dry for a mud hole, the girl threw up her hands and lamented hopelessly in the tongue of her lover:

"Ya no hay comedia!"

"The game es up!" Carlos repeated her cry in English.

Unreconciled, fearful, horrified, Carlos gazed out before him, while Nakoma reeled toward the mud.

"Come on Carlos, come on—we weel bury ourselves the bes' we can," she cried, pulling him down with her into the little depression. "Try to cup your face en thee mud, Carlos!"

A few minutes later she grieved:

"Ay! Ay! et es wirse than I thought.

Nuthin' but a puddle of watery slime—not enough even to hide our faces en. Oh, Carlos, here es where we die, you an' me!"

Carlos, too exhausted to answer, tripped and with a groan fell sprawling in the mud. Nakoma sank wearily beside him and watched the flaming fringe of the coppery hued flames rusing toward them in running, vaulting, ever-consuming waves.

Her face was scorched, her body in blisters, but so filled with fear was she that she had been insensible to all physical pains. Now in the throes of hopeless despair, Nakoma felt the cruelty of their torture.

But she sat in the mud and clung to Carlos, crazed, awe-stricken, dreading, yet silent, uncomplaining, frozen in inperturbable horror.

Carlos, by reason of his Latin blood, was inclined to be far more excitable, but the smoke had almost stifled the life out of him, so he lay in the mud, depleted and panting, while the flames withered his skin and singed his black hair.

Suddenly Nakoma lifted her ear. With the cat-like quickness of the Indian, she instinctively sensed the clatter of horses' hoofs over a nearby cow path in the flaming rushes.

"Lis'sen! Lis'sen!" she gasped. "Lis'sen, Carlos!" and she shook him impetuously. "I hear the runnin' of horses! Some one es comin' for us! Lis'sen! Don' you hear someone callin'? He-ey! He-ey!—He answers! He answers, Carlos!"

"You haf gone mad," the man told her. "There es no one callin'."

"Hey! He-ey! Here! Here! Here! —There es some one, Carlos. He answers!"

Carlos lifted his head.

"Et mus' be Joe Raven," he ventured "None but Joe Raven could ride like that —none but thee Raven would be bold enough to ride out here. He'ey;—Here! —Here! Call agin, my Nakoma, call loud. The voice haf been scorched out of me."

Nakoma called again—as long and as loud as the remaining strength in her would vouch for an atom of energy.

"That es good of thee Raven to com' fin' us. We weel never forget et! Blessed Joe Raven!" Carlos was wheezing, when a voice close at hand answered Nakoma's last call.

Both Carlos and Nakoma looked up startled.

"That es not thee Raven's voice!" the girl cried excitedly. "That es Master Phelep's!"

"Si, si!" declared the Mexican, "et es Master Philipe! Master Philipe Bissett!"

"Carlos! Nakoma!—Oh, Carlos!" the horseman called and swooped down on them.

"Here! Here! Here!" cried the runaways rising to their knees and sobbing aloud with thankfulness.

The rancher sat astride a charging iron gray colt and led in the rear, a beautiful high strung bay. Both horses were covered with foam, manes and tails charred ragged and glossy coats scorched deep in many places to anguished hides.

Philip Bissett with his eyes on the fringent tongues of the baneful flames, hurriedly dismounted and helped the unfortunate pair to their feet, then gave orders quickly.

"Mount the bay, Carlos. Hurry!—and Nakoma, get on behind him. What's the matter, Carlos? Here, you can't take time to faint now! Why, his leg is broken! That's what has played him out so! Nakoma, you take the bay, and I'll swing Carlos on in front of me, where I can hold on to him. He's sure done up! Hurry up, Nakoma, can't you see the fire has eaten the rope on the halter while we have been standing here! Come on, follow us now, Nakoma!"

And then like a whirlwind, the horses turned and dashed down a trail through the blazing tule.

"But——" pleaded Carlos, "how do you know where to go——en what direction? We weel but get lost agin en thes burnin' grass forest!"

"No," answered Philip, "I know all the trails well. If we can keep out of the fire, I can find the way."

"Gracias a Dios!" Carlos fervently gave thanks.

On dashed the horses, wild and snorting with fright and atremble with fear of the terrifying flames on all sides of them. Philip Bissett talked to them, patted them and assured them as he lead them bounding like streaks of lightening from the wake of the fire and up toward the levee of the river.

"Safe! Safe at las'!" panted Nakoma.

Then, as by some perverse whim, a gale of east wind shrieked down the basin with the viciousness of a thousand unleeched hell-cats. The fire turned, and with renewed bitterness swept back to leap at the yet untouched bulrushes on the western side of the valley.

"Thank God, indeed, that we made for the east side instead of the west! If there is anybody out there now—they are gone! Ah! she turns to the south! That catches the northwestern side of the sink. Listen to that wind, will you —whistling like a herd of banshees!"

"How good that we come thes way— how good!" breathed from Nakoma.

"Gracias a Dios! Gracias a Dios!" piously chanted Carlos.

At the ranchero Mrs. Bissett, the pioneer woman, was awaiting them. At sight of her son, she ran and flung herself upon him.

Lathered with horse sweat and covered with the muck and moil from the mud hole, the rescuer and rescued descended from their horses.

"Thank God you got back!" exclaimed Mrs. Bissett.

"Yes, we've all been thanking Him, particularly Carlos," her son told her.

"Carlos," his mistress scolded. "Why did you run away before you were married? Shame on you, Nakoma!"

Carlos and Nakoma hung their heads.

"There es no dominie at thee ranchero," Nakoma ventured.

"Well, we'll have one here by next boat day, if you two promise not to run away in the meanwhile. Come on into the house now and let me tend to your burns," said the practical woman.

Supper time came and passed. The men came in from the fields, washed and ate the evening repast, demanding vivid accounts of the fire and the harrowing experiences of Carlos and Nakoma and the brave rescue by the young master.

Twilight came and nightfall, yet Joe Raven did not come. The men in the heat of the excitement did not notice his absence until quite late, and then came the query: "Where is the Raven?" No one knew. Who had seen him last? No one remembered having seen him since noon, until at length a very sleepy little Indian boy woke up enough to recall that he had seen Joe Raven going out toward the northwest.

Could he have been trapped by the trick of the winds? Everyone looked solemn. Then the drowsy lad added that the Raven was carrying fire brands, the boy guessed he had gone out to brand cattle.

Charlie Mountain Trout grunted, and each and every Indian in the circle, without so much as a movement of the head, looked cunningly into the eye of his neighbor—but said nothing.

Quietly, without undue ostentation, the east wind died down and hushed its dolorous whimperings. As a boomerang of just exaction, it had played its part this day.

Out on the gaunt, naked burned plains myriads of nebulous embers fleered with sullen glows of decisive winkings. A soft west wind sprang up and played wistfully over the dismal bed of smoldering ashes. Down by the river came the lonesome cry of the loon. And above it all, an unforgiving sky fought with the filmy wrack of now fast fading smoke.

Treasure Trove

By Ronald A. Davidson

OME on old timer, one more drag and we're up and then you can blow awhile." The leading rider of the little cavalcade encouraged his weary mount with a friendly slap on the shoulder and once more commenced the grinding ascent. The rest of the horses raised their heads and again started plodding methodically up the trail. The party which slowly made its way up the slope of the brown Californian foothills was composed of three riders and a pack mule, well loaded with miscellaneous bundles and encouraged by the last of the horsemen.

Since ten o'clock that morning they had been progressing slowly into the rugged brown hills. The first part of the trip had been along a canyon bottom which, though the stream in it had dried up several months before, offered partial shade and protection from the September heat. But for the last three hours, through the hottest part of the day, they had been struggling up the sheer bare face of the first range of foothills. The trail they followed was only a cattle path which wound in endless switchbacks up the almost perpendicular slope. Except for clumps of wild walnut trees which studded the landscape in irregular patches and a few scrub oaks in the ravines there were no trees. The ground was covered for the most part with a short growth of wild oats, now dried to a brittle brown crisp which even the sheep would not touch. The wind ran down in long waves of furnace like blasts which raised the dust of the trail in choking clouds.

Steve Haines, or "the boss" as he was usually called, who lead the troup was the manager of the Copa d'Oro Land Company's modern stock ranch which occupied one of the green squares that appeared like checker-boards over the floor of the valley below. He was a young man of more than average height, his dark hair and thick eye brows over clear grey eyes gave a hint of a serious, almost sullen, nature. However he mixed with his strict "attention to business" traits, enough love of fun and good-fellowship to have made him a well-liked man in his undergraduate days, and one of the best managers of men who had ever registered on the company's payroll.

The youngest member of the party was a short, well set-up chap of twenty, with a bearing which announced to all who saw him that Stanley Holmes was ready to take things as they came, and make the best of them. He was new to this life, being city bred, but was putting in the summer on the big stock ranch as an adjunct to a college course in agriculture. Now that the bulk of the summer's work was over the boss was taking him on that long promised trip to the upper ranch, which consisted of a cabin just over the first range of foothills and three thousand acres of hill land which furnished good grazing ground in the winter and early spring.

The third member of the party was one of the typical leftovers of the former cattle ranch days. His tall angular figure was clothed in the regulation overalls and blue shirt and a much battered felt hat, with a woven horsehair band, was pushed far back on his head. With his drooping grey mustache and the tobacco stained stubble on his face, he might have posed in any scenario as "Alkali Ike" or "Mojave Mike," but his real name was Henry Roscoe Peters and he was universally known as "Pete."

The trail had now become more level and following along the bottom of a shallow ravine came out finally at the top of the range. The scene was a jumble of more or less rolling hills forming a sort of sloping table land, leading up to the snow-tipped peaks in the distance. Here the leaders halted, slacked their bridles and gratefully took in the green, tree-dotted, upper hills.

"Well, Buddy, how do you like your trip to the peaceful hills," grinned Pete, as a profane and perspiring Stanley drew up, urging the stumbling pack mule to a last effort.

"Some party," was the gasping reply. "Say boss, the next time I have my choice between dragging galvanized iron irrigating pipes around an alfalfa field and shoving a mule up this God-forsaken desert on end, there won't be much hesitation on my part. Gosh! I almost wish I'd stayed in Monty's place even if I would have had to milk those blamed cows. Monty seemed to want to make this trip."

"Don't worry, Stan, the worst's over now. No more up hill and it gets cooler; in half an hour you wouldn't trade places with Monty for a whole cafe full of iced drinks. He wanted to come alright, but I thought he'd better stay home with his wife; that's what he gets for being married." Steve knew his friend too well to take this grumbling seriously.

"Yeh," agreed Pete, "by tonight you'll be moseying around under the pines, potting squirrels and maybe getting a bead on some old buck and you'll forget you ever had any troubles. And when you get around the old camp fire tonight with your belly full of mulligan, say boss! remember that last stew I doped up when we were here before! Got a bunch of garlic and——"

"Yes," interrupted Steve, who knew too well Pete's fondness for recollections of his culinary achievements, "and speaking of hunting I'm going to drift around the upper trail and see if there are any signs of anyone trespassing. There are always a bunch of would-be nimrods around this time of year. You fellows go on down the canyon with that mule and I'll meet you at the cabin."

"What's the idea?" demanded Stanley, "Got a kind of royal preserve around here, where you can hog all the game yourself?"

"Well, it's our land, so why not? And then some pinhead sport is always set-ting the brush on fire or shooting up some stock so we have to be careful. Well," Steve gathered up his reins and turned his mount up the slope, "See you later. Try to pot something and have a good mess cooked up when I get there."

"Say drawled Pete, meditatively as he gazed after the disappearing rider, "what the hell's the matter with that gent anyway?"

"What d'ye mean, matter with him?"

"Well," Pete pursued, awkwardly, "it's none of my business and I ain't the kind of a cuss to go prying into other folk's troubles, but I can't dope it out the way that kid feels about the women. You heard what he said about Monty being married, en he's always making some remark along that same line, knocking the holy bonds of wedlock and the female race in general. You'd think a good looking kid like that would be in town when he gets a chance, chasing around with the skirts, but when he gets a day off he piles on his horse and migrates to the hills. He's got a bunch of swell look-ing pictures stuck around his room of different dames, but well doggone it, it's none of my affair, but I just figures somebody must have handed him an awful jolt sometime."

"Oh, that's no dark secret! Steve used to run a lot with women around college. Always spotting some soul mate, pulling all kinds of strings to meet her, and making a pale green ass out of himself in general, and then finding out she wasn't as lovable as she looked. But he finally got it fixed up with a little girl in his home town, she was O. K. too, had a lot on the ball for looks, style and disposition, but when Steve got home after his graduation he found she'd been married a month. All the time though, she had been keeping up the sweet correspondence, her idea of let-ting him down easy, I suppose."

"It hit the old boy pretty hard, espe-cially her not telling about it. He didn't make any fuss, he's not that kind, just kind of took it to himself, but it has knocked a lot of the jazz out of him. But that was three years ago, he ought to get over it pretty soon, though when

Steve takes something seriously he sure takes it. Gee, ain't it the bunk though? There he is with a swell job and lots of good prospects. If I was fixed like that believe me I wouldn't have to have that heathen Chink around to fry the eggs!"

In the meantime Haines had crossed the ridge and dropped down into the wide wooded valley which formed the eastern section of the range. It was here he expected to find interlopers because it was a good game country and also lay nearest the little mountain settlement of Walnut. Nor was he disappointed for just before he reached the timbered bottom he caught sight of a figure plodding along the trail which led along the opposite side of the valley to the old abandoned limestone quarries just north of the ranch. The distance was too great to distinguish anything except that the trespasser was clad in the conventional blue overalls and shirt and slung a long barreled rifle in his right hand.

Steve pushed forward swiftly through the scattered trees and on reaching the trail put his tired horse into a trot. At least the poacher's clothing marked him as a ruralite, probably one of the worthy citizens of Walnut, out to nab a morsel for the family larder, and not one of the khaki-clad, leather-puttied sports from the city. Nevertheless, Steve was determined to put a stop to all infringements on his property and was busy rehearsing in his mind a suitable reprimand, when he came suddenly upon his quarry.

Right there Steve Haines got the premier surprise of his more or less eventful life. For there, seated on a boulder, almost under his horse's feet, sat a woman, no! she was only a girl, and an extraordinary pretty girl at that. True, she was clad in blue overalls and shirt, and was undoubtedly the figure he had been following. She was perched rather precariously on the edge of a rock, one booted foot drawn awkwardly to one side to allow his horse to pass. She had taken off a boy's cap, which she held in her lap, and her hands were busy braiding up the flood of rich blond hair which was

pulled over one shoulder. This was all Steve noticed at the first glance, and, tearing his hat from his head he began a stammering explanation.

"I beg your pardon, I didn't know it was you. I——that is, I mean I thought it, I mean you were a man, a poacher you know and I was just going to kick you off. Excuse me, I'm awfully sorry——"

"Oh that's alright," she replied easily, returning his agonized glance with a frank half smile, "you really didn't startle me so much, I heard your horse."

By this time Steve had taken cognizance of the rest of the scene. He saw a young woman in the early twenties, the loose hair had given the first impression of girlishness. She was of about medium size and build, with a rather round clear complexioned face and round blue eyes under exceptionally heavy lashes. Her feet, which were now more comfortably crossed on the edge of the trail, were clad in hiking boots, which had originally encased the legs of the overalls, but these had worked out until they hung almost to her ankles, like baggy Dutch Boy trousers. At this point Steve received his second shock. Lying at her feet was the object which he had taken for a gun, but which now proved to be an iron crow bar about six feet long, with one end broadened into a blade. It was of the type used for churn drilling in soft material and had been newly drawn and ground.

"Well," said Steve, having by this time somewhat collected his senses, "I guess of the two I was the most surprised. One doesn't expect to find women (he almost said pretty women) wandering these woods, especially in overalls and toting crow bars."

The smile faded from her face, at this last, and Steve knew he had started on the wrong line.

"I'm sorry if I have been trespassing, I didn't know this was private property."

"Oh, no, that's O. K. We only don't allow any shooting here. But really, I don't mean to be inquisitive, but what under the sun are you doing with that crow bar?"

"Why," she replied, after a moment's pause, "I was just over at Walnut having it sharpened."

And, as Steve still looked puzzled, she continued, "You see father is studying, that is experimenting or examining——I mean the limestone quarries over the hill. I just took the bar over for him, as he only has one man to help him and he was very busy."

"Oh! I understand," lied Steve, for this puzzled him still further. "I thought you might have been out looking for treasure."

"Treasure?" She seemed to give an involuntary start and regarded him with more interest.

"Yes, indeed," he laughed, "that's the standard occupation around here. You see there was a train robbery over at Hermit last Spring and the robbers were captured not far from here. Rumor has it that they hid the loot under a large rock somewhere in this vicinity, and it has been quite a common sight around here to see someone roving around turning over boulders, so that was the first thing I thought of when I saw you with that bar."

"Oh, I see, but really I wasn't looking for it."

She paused, giving Steve a sudden searching glance and the corners of her mouth twitched into a mischievous smile. Steve had an agonized moment wondering what could be so radically wrong with his appearance, but she sobered again and continued, "No, really, I had never heard that myth." Another embarassed pause. "You don't happen to know how much there was of the hidden fortune do you, I mean how much there was supposed to be?"

"Oh Heaven only knows, the amount grows every week. In a few years it will reach a fabulous sum that the population of Walnut will spend all their spare time rolling rocks. The future generation will surely develop some strong backs. But seriously the whole thing is only an entirely unconfirmed rumor, which is improved upon at each telling."

"Well, what do you think about it?"

"Of course it's all bunk, but," he ad-

mitted sheepishly, "I do sometimes look twice at favorable looking rocks, though I've never lost any sleep over it."

He was just trying to decide whether to ask her more about her strange position and what her father was doing experimenting in a quarry which had been abandoned years ago because of its inaccessibility, or to move on about his business, when his horse solved the question for him by starting wearily off. However he felt it was at least only courtesy to ask to help her with her burden, but she declined hurriedly.

"It isn't heavy and I've come most of the way already and, well, I can get along alone very nicely thank you."

This left no grounds for further conversation, so he made no effort to stop his mount, but with a mumbled apology for having bothered her, continued on his way.

"Please don't let that worry you," she called after him, in smiling contrast to her last remark, "I'm glad I won't be trespassing because I'll probably be making this trip quite often."

Steve puzzled over the encounter all the way down to the cabin without arriving at any explanation of the affair. She had acted normal enough until he had chanced to mention that treasure yarn and then her conversation had appeared to be as muddled as his had been at first. To dismiss him with an almost rude remark and then call after him what was practically an invitation to see her there again, well it was beyond him. Women were queer creatures and he ought to have sense enough by now not to worry about them. Nevertheless there had been something more attractive about her than any woman he had met for a long time and he could not dismiss her from his mind.

He had always a failing for taking a sudden interest in a woman at first sight, although, as Stanley had remarked, a good many times, "the affairs never panned out according to the proper rules of romance." However, his engagement with a girl he had known for years had been far from a happy affair and he had told himself savagely at the time that if he ever did marry it would be a woman he met one day and married the next. During his almost hermit life of the last three years he had practically convinced himself that he was a confirmed woman hater, but now, on thinking it over, he had to admit it was probably only lack of opportunities. At least he would arrange to see her again, he'd be a fool to pass up a chance like that.

Dusk had fallen over the jumble of foot hills and the evening air that settled down brought with it a breath of the snow from the sentinel peaks above, which came almost as a chill after the inferno of the daylight hours. The pulse of new life was reflected in the trio around the little fire behind the cabin and their conversation was bubbling with cheerfulness and contentment.

Stanley and Pete especially kept up a continual flow of words, the youth enthusiastically recalling jokes and parties of college days, and Pete reminiscencing in a tedious monotonous tone the joys of the good old days. Steve supplemented Stanley's anecdotes with some of his own experiences and questions about old friends at the university. But during Pete's monologues, most of which he had heard over and over again, he remained inattentive studying the glowing tip of his cigarette or gouging furrows in the soft soil with a roweled spur. Finally, during a moment's silence which followed one of Pete's egotistical yarns, he mentioned his afternoon's adventure.

"Say, what would you boys say if I told you I ran into a pretty woman over on the quarry trail this afternoon, dolled up in overalls and boots and packing a six-foot crow bar?"

"Well, I'd say right away that you'd been visiting our friend the sheep herder, sampling too much of his home-brewed Tiger Soup and sleeping off the effects in the sun," ventured Pete.

"I could almost think so myself, there was something darn queer about——"

"Toting a crow bar did you say?" interrupted Pete with sudden interest. "I'll bet she was out looking for that swag!"

"Well, that's the first thing that oc-cured to me, but when I mentioned it, she stammered around and said she was taking it over to her father, who is working in the quarry."

"The quarry!" protested Pete, "why they ain't worked that quarry for years. I remember well when they give it up, back in '99 it was, the creek washed their road out every Winter and the haul was too long anyway. She was kiddin' you, that's all. What did she act like when you let on about the treasure?"

Steve recounted the meeting in detail and Pete listened with rapt interest.

"Well, doggone my bones, if I don't bet she was on the trail of that loot," he declared when the boss had finished.

"Well, if she was I don't see anything to get wildly wrought up about," interposed Stanley, "she isn't the first one that's spent good time pursuing that pipe dream."

"No, a lot of the country hicks have fell for it, but when some high-class society jane, like the boss here, doped her out to be, starts out for it, looks like it might amount to something. For all you know she's got a tip about it. It might have been that she was in with the crooks that hid it or perhaps she might have a drag with one of the deputies that has some dope on it or——"

Now Pete always had more than a passing interest in the treasure rumor. He had prospected in the early days and the lure of fortune hunting was still strong within him. He was always ready to hear the latest rumor, no matter how wild it was and was always developing new ideas and plausible theories.

"You bet! Pete," encouraged Stanley, who liked to get the old man started, "you've got the plot for a fine yarn there, though I can't quite picture any of the society buds I know out in dungarees mucking around with a crow bar."

"Of course," Steve broke in, "I don't put any stock in that part of it, although it's perfectly possible she might have an imaginative old man who got the gold fever from some wild Sunday supplement account. However, I was more interested in——"

(To Be Continued Next Month.)

The Wolleson Experiment

By Charles H. Shinn

HERE was a time in the forest work when strange and amusing events occurred on old San Joaquin," said Ranger Maine as he sat by one of the Sierra Club campfires, in the King River canyon.

"Tell us about it," said several charming school teachers, who had returned from a tramp to the top of the divide. "Tell us the very worst of those events."

"You see," said the grizzled pioneer ranger, looking far up to the snow peaks which he had known for forty years, "you see if I tell you about our Wolleson experiment back in 1906, you must not lay it up as too hard a bang at the service. It isn't at all that, but it sure illustrates how not to do a thing."

"I infer," said one of the listeners, "that this is to be 'a tale out of school.'"

"That's about it," the ranger replied. "It's just a glimpse of the curious difficulties of early days. You see when the service began to develop the reserves —as they were called before 1905—everything had to be put into shape as hard and as fast as possible. There was not a minute to lose."

"Why not?" someone asked.

"Because some people wanted to smash it up; because some folks thought that the War Department ought to have the reserves; because millions of plain Americans were watching, thinking, making up their minds about forestry, and at times were just a little inclined to go against it.

"For these reasons," the ranger went on, "we had to rush things. Every man took on enough out-door work for three fellows, and had to struggle with all sorts of new form-blanks, reports and office work, in addition.

"Ranger Stout used to say that the best fellow was 'the one who needed least sleep.'"

"I don't see why you did it," said one of the campers.

"Because we loved the work, and further, because there was a Big Chief in Washington who blazed the trail for us. The work was hard, of course, but it seems to me that the main thing which kept the service going in those times was the fact that everyone was completely devoted to it. We rangers drove ahead day and night, and those over us worked just as hard. Then, too, there was everywhere a wonderful spirit of hope, of courage, and of high fellowship. Our wives and children helped us to build cabins and fight fires.

"I used to see a light in Supervisor Black's office till midnight and past; he was working over his accounts and reports, after a full day in the field. His wife went out and helped him just as soon as the dishes were washed."

"You give us a charming picture of those pioneer days," said a young teacher "I suppose it was like the rose of dawn for American forestry. You were creating something new. You believed in everyone; you were brothers and sisters in the forest work."

"That's it," said Ranger Maine, with a look on his face which no one had seen there for years. "We had absolute confidence in the men over us, and they deserved it, too."

He went on describing the beginnings of an office system. "We had no clerks," he said, "and so we had to learn lots of things. New forms and regulations were being tried out, and so incessantly that we couldn't seem to get a breathing-space ahead. When it rained, all of the older rangers would come in to the office, battering a typewriter almost to pieces and trying to help the over-worked supervisors.

"In these days when I'm telephoned for and ride into the main office of the forest I like to look at the cheerful women clerks, making music on their typewriters, filling out all sorts of forms and taking letters from dictation. The place is both home-like and business-like —as it ought to be.

"When I think of the way that our first clerk Wolleson used to swagger in, loud and grumpy, looking at us rangers as if we were mere dirt under his feet, it seems to me that it would be fun to tell the office girls of today all they would stand for about their notorious predecessor. I never tried it, though, for they wouldn't believe one word of what I told them; I should spoil my reputation, all for nothing.

"Well, after we had mulled along by ourselves that Winter of 1905-6, there came a welcome telegram, and the Washington office sent Wolleson along with the finest kind of letters. They said he knew all the inside ropes, so we were told to turn him loose, and see him create a model office for old San Joaquin.

"About that time the supervisor had a new barn—you all know what that means in these hills! He gave a dance one Saturday night; the little Irish fiddler came from Hildreth; tables were spread in tents; the ranger women prepared supper.

"On the top of it in comes Alexander Wolleson, chipper and very well dressed. He made a good impression all around; we thought he was the best thing that ever happened for San Joaquin.

"He was so popular at first, with his little jokes and pleasant smiles, that when the stage-driver called him a 'gay bird,' and hinted that we would have 'plenty doin' later,' we told him to chase himself down the road.

"The supervisor heaved a sigh of heart-felt relief.

"'Push this office work right ahead,' he told Wolleson; then he saddled his horse and rode out to see about trails and bridges, to meet people, and to fight fires with us, as he had been doing in earlier years.

"Ranger Ramsden was the first man to remark that Wolleson was somewhat different from everyday people—'queer inside,' as he put it. 'Think he is the sort that has had a past, and is liable to slide off again.'—Ramsden used to work in mines, and he went on, 'it's only a knife-blade vein; it's likely to pinch out—this new start of his.'

"The rest of us couldn't see it that way, for the new clerk was buckling right down to business, and the office showed results. Everything was ship-shape. When the mail came in the supervisor dictated answers; Wolleson took them, handled all the routine, and found time now and then to give pointers to all of us.

"The village was quite a distance from headquarters, so a nice young forest guard and Wolleson lived in a ranger cabin. Wolleson couldn't cook, but the guard didn't mind doing all the work.

"One Sunday Wolleson — 'Alexander Wolleson of Washington, D. C.'—as he wrote it once on a girl's dance card, hired a horse and rode over to our camp, where a lot of us had gathered to do a little rifle shooting. He couldn't shoot, so we quit, and sat down under the oaks listening to him. We hardly opened our heads for two hours; the deal so surprised us.

"There he was, young, handsome, well-educated and filling a mighty important place—and he was suddenly breaking out all over as if he had varioloid.

"First, he told us of his distinguished parentage, the millionaires and politicians in his family, the United States Senators who were his bosom friends, the unbreakable pull that he possessed, the high places that were waiting for him elsewhere. 'I only wanted to take a look at the wild and woolly West, you know.'

"'You rangers mean well,' he added. 'You are warm-hearted, rough chaps; but you haven't seen life.'

"We listened so easy-like that he began to run down our boss and his, saying things that all of us knew were crazy. We didn't say anything, though it riled us inside, but the boss was one of those men that such things fell off from like water off a duck's back. If he had been there himself, he would have listened awhile, and then would have said, just as likely as not: 'O! I am much worse than that, Wolleson!' Then he would have laughed right out, as free as the wind is blowing. Suddenly he would have jumped up and taken Wolleson by the elbow, to lead him off into the woods, and there dressed him down with a few unforgettable sentences, cutting clear to the bone. Then he would never have mentioned it again.

"But we rangers did not know how to say such things to Wolleson, nor was it up to us to report it. We sat still and listened. In the main what he said was just a special bad brand of 'great big me.' We wondered why someone hadn't knocked it out of him. We had several reasonably effective ways of curing ordinary cases of big-head, but they seemed useless for such an attack as his.

"Then Wolleson invited us to spend an evening at his cabin. Some wanted to get out of it, but there was the forest guard to consider, and in the end we went.

"We never forgot that night. Wolleson made himself the whole thing. He brought out a fiddle, and hit off some pretty fair coon songs. Then he showed a lot of low-down pictures. Then he trotted up and down the floor, acting out things, and telling silly, coarse yarns.

"There we sat in his cabin, and the nice forest guard kept looking at us as if he said to himself, 'Now you fellows know why I'm all run down, and off on my grub!'

"Rangers are short of speech sometimes, yes, and rough, too; but we remember that we had mothers, and we respect good women clear through. That fellow seemed to think that every man and every woman was just his own, low-down sort.

"Wolleson saw we were looking at him in a dazed kind of a way; he thought it a compliment, and he bowed all around.

" 'That's just a glimpse of the kind of a man of the world I am,' he said, mop-

ping his forehead, and laughing.

"We all jumped up together. We needed fresh air. 'Must you go, boys?' he said. 'Come up again!'

"We trotted off down the trail, and the forest guard told us that after we left he said, 'What ignorant brutes all these rangers are!'

"The youngest of the bunch spoke up after awhile, mad as blazes. 'A healthy lot of men we are,' he said, 'to listen to all that kind of stuff when we hated it. I suppose it was his cabin, but now we can send him to Coventry! Drop him hard—ker-plunk!' he cried. 'Don't speak to him social while he stays here.'

"It suited us, and we said so. After that we cut him dead. We spoke of him among ourselves as the End Man, or Nigger Minstrel.

"A hard punishment, you say? None too hard. Every man had to draw his line somewhere. That was ours. Nor were we alone in this matter, for after each dance down in the village—and the End Man was easy on the floor—a few more of our mountain women dropped Wolleson. They did it very quietly, indeed, but so thoroughly that before long he was shut out of everything first-class.

"Of course his office work fell off, and it was plain to us that he was taking stimulants. The supervisor began to tackle the office at night again, and he went after Wolleson good and hard. The forest guard had quit, and so the clerk boarded in the village, but he slept in the little old cabin. It looked fearful inside, and it smelt queer, not of whisky, but of something worse.

"Old Weston, the stage driver, joked us those days about 'Alexander Gaybird,' as he called him. Told us the reputation of the forest service was not helped by such clerks.

"One morning I had a letter that my brother was very low, and I took the stage out. When I looked at the bunch going down I thought, 'Now I'll hear all there is—and some more!' One tin-horn gambler from the lumber camps; several lazy hangers-on of the Indian rancherias.

"After awhile one says to another:

'My friend Wolleson of the forest service remarks to me last night, when we was drinkin' at Nigger Pete's cabin—he says that none of them fat rangers earns their pay.'

"Of course I made no rise at such a thing as that; but as they went on it seemed that every no account cuss knew him well.

"The tin-horner turns to me: 'You blasted old ranger; why don't you get some fun out of life, same as Wolleson does?'

"'It's against regulations,' I said, shortly.

"'Wolleson can fix it up,' he answered. 'He showed us how. Puts some dope into the whisky he drinks every day. It knocks the smell; it fools you fellows every time."

"This riled me up, but before I could say a word, another one broke in: 'Ain't he bully when he does his song and dance up at Nigger Pete's, and tells all them stories!'

"Of course I kept still after that. No one could mend it; the pitcher was busted. But I advised myself to break a good old rule when I got back to the forest and tell the supervisor about Wolleson.

"A week later I returned, hopped into my saddle, meeting Ramsden on the bridge.

"'What's news?' I asked.

"'Main thing is that the End Man has ended out at last.'

"'That suits,' I told him. 'How did it happen?'

"'Supervisor was on for some time. He went into End Man's cabin one midnight, found him drunk on his bed; clothes all on, and a burning candle close to the bed-clothes. He took the candle, threw away the dope, and rode down to my cabin.

"'So, about four o'clock in the morning, the supervisor and I harnessed to a buckboard, and druv down to Wolleson's cabin. He was in bad shape, but we worked over him. We loaded him in with his trunks, and truck; we carried him to the village, him a-cussin' all the time. We took him to the hotel for breakfast.

"'The supervisor paid for his breakfast, paid the stage fare, and gave the poor heathen five dollars besides, for he had been cleaned out the night before at Nigger Pete's.

"'I shall not require your services any longer, Mr. Wolleson,' the supervisor remarked, as kind as a Summer morning.'

"'Gracious!' I said to Ramsden, 'I never supposed it could be done that way.'

"Neither did Wolleson, but it was. Nobody minded what he said, but it appeared that he was going to telegraph to the President of the United States.

"'The supervisor reported it, I suppose, but we heard nothing more about the matter,' said Ramsden. 'However, we cleaned up that dirty cabin of his, burned the trash, and so closed accounts with our clerical experiment.'

"'Ramsden,' I said, 'it beats me how the Government picks up such specimens. Let's ask the supervisor.' And so we did, one night when it came handy.

"'Boys,' he told us, 'the forest service always does the very best it can for us who are in the field. This man passed a high examination somewhere; and the other facts were not known.

"'When he first came here, he started very well; he 'braced' and took hold of the job. Then he slumped on a sudden. He was a poor, foolish, impudent wretch, but at least he tried for a while. You boys sent him to Coventry one evening, and he had the cold shoulder everywhere. Really he found no company, no appreciation, except at Nigger Pete's roadside house.'

"Our youngest ranger always had nerve; he leaned forward and said, 'I can tell you why he was sent to Coventry, sir. It was because we never had anything like him in these clean old mountains. We ought to have ducked him in the river, and washed his mouth out with harness soap. But we knew that you needed a clerk, so we kept still about it.'

"That same young ranger cut the epitaph on Wolleson's old cabin. It ran this way:

Sic Transit Gloria Mundi
In memory of
the
GREAT PURE ELOQUENT
and
Universally Respected
ALEXANDER WOLLESON
End Man; Man of the World
and
PRIDE OF NIGGER PETE'S
Requiescat in Pace

A Sierra Club camper wondered whether rangers were ever guilty of Latin and epitaphs.

The ranger answered sweetly and seriously across the fire: "Last year," he said, "we had five graduates of five universities doing plain ranger work on San Joaquin forest. We had lots of such fellows in the days of Wolleson. One of them carved the tailpiece."

"What was that?" one of the school teachers asked.

"Only the mask of a clown, and two whisky bottles crossed."

Where the Spanish Dagger Keeps Silent Vigil

By Sarah Ingham Spencer

H! A grave, Pedro! Is it the grave of some noble warrior, or only the resting place of a desert nomad?" When dad suggested that I take Pedro along as guide and protector, I laughed at his carefulness.

"Why, dad, I supposed the West had long ago been tamed. I supposed I would be quite as safe here as on the old school campus!" I told him banteringly.

"But you are not, my dear," he answered me, "even though you are not afraid of rattlers it will be nice to have some one along to kill them—and rattlers are not the only enemies of woman found in the brush, you will no doubt learn before you are here many weeks. You must take Pedro along, he will be company; your rides will be pleasanter and there are many interesting things he can point out to you."

So there was nothing for me to do but let Pedro trail along after me. And I was really glad after getting out of sight of the old ranch house; everything seemed so still, only now and then a rabbit—frightened by our approach—scampered across the road before us, or a gaudy road runner raced us for some piece, only to desert the track for the safety of the brush.

Pedro named all the birds and animals along the roadside, the calls we heard in the brush; told me, tales, weird and laughable, of the coyote stricken with madness.

I looked at Pedro as I asked the question about the grave, his wrinkled face, so worn and sallow, seemed to have changed greatly; instead of the light, jovial expression, there was a quite graveness. I was sure that I surprised tears in his faded eyes as I looked up at him quickly.

"It is not the grave of a kinsman?" I asked him after some moments of silence, as I looked again at the rather short mound, with its rude cross formed of two, none too straight, mesquite limbs.

"No, Senorita," he answered me with the least little choke in his voice.

"Not a kinsman, Senorita, but one very dear to old Pedro. That mound is the resting place of a very beautiful American Senorita, no older, perhaps, than yourself, and no larger."

"But why was she buried away off here, Pedro?" I shuddered, as I looked around; just one over-grown mesquite, everywhere was there, hot, sandy soil, dotted here and there with cactus, mesquite and other desert shrubs. The only green grass in sight was the little that grew over the lonely little grave, perhaps because it was protected from the hot sun by the shade of the squat bush; one puny little rosebush at the head of the mound seemed to be fighting a losing battle with the hot wind and scorching sun. It was more than desolate, as I thought of the American Senorita who lay beneath the blistering sand, I felt hot tears burning my eyes.

For some time Pedro sat on his horse, straight and silent, apparently too choked by old memories, phantoms of the past, appearing before his weary eyes, obliterating my own presence; stealing a look at him, I caught him looking at me through misty eyes.

"That is a long story, Senorita," he answered my question in a voice that neither quivered nor faltered.

"Well," I said getting off my pony, "I don't care if it is a long story we have plenty of time, and I am very anxious to learn why any girl should be buried so far from civilization!"

"But Senorita," he remonstrated, "it is much too depressing a story for your childish ears. I fear the good Senor would behead me in his anger, were I to tell you the story of this lone little grave!"

"I am sure I am not half as childish as you think me, my good Pedro, and besides, dad won't care. I know he won't he never cares so long as I am amused. And then, too, he will know nothing of it!" I told him slyly.

"Of course Senorita, if you insist! I was given strict orders to obey you, but I am sure you ought not to hear such stories!" He threw out his hands in an unmistable gesture.

"That's a good boy, Pedro, let's hear it!" I called as he climbed down slowly because of his stiff legs. I slung my quirt around to scare away any rattler or tarantula, that might be hiding in the cool shade, and flung myself down on the scarce grass in the refreshing shade of the old mesquite. Old Pedro came hobbling over and squatted down at my side; for a space he was silent; when he commenced his voice was drawling, very much like the American way of speaking; gazing off at the horizon, I could easily imagine it the voice of an American, had it not been for his softly spoken 'Senorita,' slow and caressingly as only a Mexican can make it.

"It was a long time ago; I was years younger then, my hair was black and my eyes were bright; I was big and strong. You have not yet seen the site of the old 'Mesquite Inn.' I will take you there some time; there's not much of it left.

"It is here my story must begin. I was working for Senor Herman who kept the Inn; there were few travelers those days, but when the cowboys came into town, which was rather often, the Senor got a full pocket. The between times were dull and long; now and then a traveler sightseer came along. It was not the place to encourage sightseeing, less then than now.

"One day during one of our few rains, a couple horsemen came up. They were coated and hooded and we did not know until they took off their cloaks before the fire, that one was a woman. A slender, frail little thing. She complained of being tired—she looked it, too—so Senor Herman had me show her to her room, and it looked so old and shabby beside her white lovely face, I crimsoned as I opened the door for her to pass in. She did not protest, perhaps she was too tired to notice the shabbiness.

"Her companion was big, tall, straight and hard-muscled, with his black hair rippling up from his high, white forehead, his brown eyes sparkling behind thick, black lashes, one did not wonder

that the little Senorita could love him.
For in his big, frank way he was almost
as handsome as she was lovely in her
sunshiny sweetness.

"Neither seemed to have much knowledge of Spanish, but at least enough to
get along comfortably. He, Senor Hamilton, told Senor Herman that he was a
natural scientist (I am sure Senor Herman knew no more what that meant
than I did), and was after some specimens that could only be found here.

"He had me buy a couple of good saddle horses and they rode a great deal;
they were always so happy together;
much like two children enjoying a long
anticipated holiday.

"After her night's rest she had seemed
as peart as a kitten. Smiling — Ah!
When she smiled! Her grey eyes danced,
her pink cheeks dimpled! There is
nothing with which one could compare
her beauty; even at her more sober
moods she was entrancing, but when she
was mirthful she was so distractingly
lovely I often had to turn from her to
keep her from seeing the sparks of pure
worship that leapt into my eyes against
my will.

"Very often I was taken along to guide
them to some place, and then, too, sometimes Senor Hamilton would go off and
be gone two or three days—sometimes
even longer — and then Senorita Murrel,
as she was better known in the settlement, would get me to accompany her
on her rides.

"I can see her even now, the red lips
parted in a smile, her milky teeth gleaming like tiny pearls! Even her hair, beautiful in any way dressed, but as she wore
it, smoothed back from her white brow
and caught at the back with a ribbon,
allowing it to hang nearly to her slim
waist, a glittering mass of curls.

"With all her joviality and seeming
childishness, she had a mighty soft little heart. On one of our rides, just she
and I, the Senor having gone on one of
his frequent trips, her horse stumbled
and broke his leg. We think nothing of
shooting a horse when one breaks his
leg, or any other accident which causes

an inability to get about or be cured.
Of course it is the only thing one can
do, I told her, and that I would have to
shoot the animal and she could ride my
pony back and I would walk. She was
patting the poor brute's neck and talking all sorts of nonsense. She looked at
me in that frightened, half pleading way,
and the little puckers that always came
between her eyes when she was dis-
pleased were now quite prominent, as
she caressed the injured animal.

" 'You are only teasing me, Pedro.
I know you can't possibly mean to shoot
this poor creature!' "I could see the tears
in her eyes, that had grown dark at the
horror of my suggestion. My hand, in
which I held the gun, trembled. I would
far rather have killed myself than cause
her one moment of pain, but what was
one to do, so I undertook to show her
the reason for my seeming heartless-
ness; show her that it was kinder to
shoot the brute than leave him there to
suffer days of agony. When I finally convinced her, she did not try to hide from
me the fact that she was weeping, and
looking at me with humid eyes, begged
my pardon for having spoken crossly
to me. I had not even realized that she
spoke crossly, so concerned was I over
her distress."

For a long time Pedro sat silent gazing out towards the distant horizon, and
I wondered if he had not been quite a
handsome fellow in his youth and capable of winning the love, even of a very
beautiful American Senorita.

"Somehow she seemed to have a peculiar liking for this lonely spot," Pedro
went on in his drawling, soft speech.
"Often she would come out here with
books and candy. It was she who taught
me to speak, read and write English.
Hour after hour she would sit here trying so hard to drive something into my
thick head. I had a splendid education
in Spanish and I suppose it was easier,
even then it took lots of patience to
teach poor stupid me. I still have her
books, all of them, and know them by
heart.

"She seemed to love the loneliness of

the place, and she always referred to it as, 'Old Lonely,' and it was her special wish that this be her last resting place. But I am getting ahead of my story.

"They had been here more than two months; it was one of those between times when there were few customers. Senorita Murrel always rode before breakfast. She had just come in from her usual ride, still with her riding 'togs' on and sat down to breakfast. Senor Hamilton had gone away the day before. She sat with her back to the door, munching her breakfast. She did not turn when some one called loudly to the chore boy without, nor when he came stamping into the room. I looked up and beheld a man very much below the medium height, rather pudgy, with a face so ugly, it appeared comical. Long and thin, much too large for his small body, with a ridiculous little black mus-tache. Apparently he was trying to hide his small stature by a big noise, for he walked heavily up to the bar and called loudly for service.

"A pitiful, choked little cry drew my attention from the rude stranger to the Senorita in the corner; she was stand-ing with her back against the wall, her slim fingers clasping the napkin; her face ghastly white, her large eyes dilated so they seemed two pools of fire in her small face.

"Grabbing a bottle of wine I ran to her, making no connection between her illness and the stranger's presence. His atten-tion too, had been drawn to her, for he strode in before me, and catching her white arm, he slung her around from the wall. I saw red! Senorita! I think it is not in the heart of woman to feel the hot anger—or madness, one might better call it—as a man when he sees a loved one abused. I flew at the man, my hands found his throat, I begun tightening my grip; I saw his small eyes bulge, his sallow face took on a ghastlier shade; I threw him from me. I was in-sane! I did not want to kill him, I only wanted to torture him. With only my hands I could have broken him in two, but I did not want to, I only wanted to torture him.

"Senor Herman came to me and shook me. 'You fool,' he said, 'What are you trying to do, commit murder?'

"My jaws were clamped like a vise, and I dared not loosen them because I had such little control of myself.

"Senor Herman carried water and bathed his dirty face, and I stood off waiting for him to regain consciousness, so if necessary, I might do again what I had already done.

"'Go sit down, Pedro! I think you are crazy, you don't know but he had a right to address Mrs. Hamilton as he did.'

"'Your pardon, Senor, but I know he did not! No one may abuse her while I am around. I am her servant and it is my place to protect her from such black-guards during the Senor's absence.' Any reply that he meant to make was inter-rupted by the report of a revolver in-side the room.

"I don't know why I felt so, unless it was because of the earlier row, but some-thing seemed to snap within me. I felt wild, I knew in my heart that all was not right with Senorita Murrel; I all but tore the entrance door down trying to get through quickly. I rushed to her room. I have seen some mighty ugly, sickening things in my time, Senorita. I am not the kind of fellow to turn dizzy at the sight of blood, but I came so near fainting at the sight I beheld, that every-thing turned black before me; I stag-gered to the bed. Senorita Murrel lay across it, with a small revolver still smoking, grasped tightly with her pretty fingers. For ages, it seemed, I stood there unable to move, and finally bent down over her, and I knew at once that no life remained in the limp little body, but I put my clumsy hand over her heart and it came away red! Red, with her precious blood! I tried to call Senor Herman, but my voice was only a croak. I raised from over her body, the hot tears unchecked, falling on her white calm face, my eyes were attracted by a white slip pinned to the pillow.

"With shaking fingers I got the pin out and seeing that it was directed to me, I slipped it hastily in my pocket.

For a moment I bent down close to her face, and before I realized the meaning of my own action, my lips had brushed the fair brow that had not yet grown cold. Others might criticize but I don't think she—could she have known—would resent that kiss of reverence which I bestowed upon her.

"Softly I stole from the room, in the hall where I met Senor Herman; his look was a question; I only motioned him into the room I had vacated. I stole to the back and opened the note; enclosed within mine was one for Senor Hamilton."

As I sat looking at Pedro with his set jaws making a hard line from chin to temple, his face so gray it almost was white, I knew that he was living over again those moments of tragedy. My throat was dry, my eyes hot; I dared not meet the eyes of the old Mexican lest the tears I was having such difficulty to restrain might rush forth; not daring to speak lest my voice sound hoarse, breaking the silence too abruptly. So I sat and waited until he should go on with this tale of tragedy.

He changed his posture and opening his riding coat, brought forth a bright metal box, which was attached to a black tape.

"Your eyes will be the first to see the letter she wrote me, Senorita. Always I have carried it next to my heart; reading it again and again; at first I did not fully understand all, knowing only the little bit she had taught me, but since then I have studied a great deal. It is badly worn, but you, perhaps, can make it out."

He handed me the letter; his gnarled hand trembling visibly; from the corner of my eye I saw the tears stealing down his withered cheeks. The little scrap was worn nearly bare in some places; the writing was small and dainty. By putting it on my knee and holding the worn places together I made out the words:

"Dear Pedro:

"It is to you that I must look in time of trouble. First I must say that I cannot find words to tell you of my appreciation for your gallantry of a few moments ago. But you should not have made trouble for yourself to protect one so worthless as I.

"I am not going to thank you for all the kindness you have shown me during my short stay here; there are many pleasures and comforts I would not have known had it not been for your thoughtfulness, anything I can say will seem so inadequate, it is better left unsaid. Aside from poor Frank you are the only person who has ever gone to any trouble to show me any kindness; I tell you this to help you understand my appreciation. I am not trying to make excuses for my sin; I suppose that even you, my faithful friend, will loathe and despise me when you know me for what I really am.

"If you have not already learned it from him, I will tell you that the man from whom you protected me, was, or rather, is, my husband! I suppose as usual I was partly to blame—but no one will ever know his cruelty as I have known it. And when Frank came, with his kind attentions and sincere sympathy and his promise of happiness, it was too much for one as weak-willed as I.

"I shudder to think of poor Frank's grief! You must do what you can, Pedro boy, to make it as light as possible; he really loved me, and his big heart will be filled with grief.

"I am going to rely on you to do as I did, dear friend, knowing well that my wish is your law. My last wishes are few and simple.

"You will remember 'Old Lonely,' the old mesquite, as we know it; I want this to be my last resting place. In life I have always been crowded out of everything, and in this spot I am sure I shall never be crowded, so it is here you are to put me, where the tall Spanish Dagger keeps his silent vigil and the coyotes send their weird calls to the stars.

"The riding suit I have on is to be my shroud, I should not like to be put in white; white means innocence; it is in this suit that I have experienced the few joys my lonely life has known. I have no right to any name; when I forfeited the right to my husband's name,

I placed myself among the nameless, so I want only a cross of mesquite limbs to mark my grave.

"Don't delay because of Frank; he is to be gone several days and it is better to have it over with before he returns; I should like to know that he saw me last, smiling and happy as when I gave him his good-bye kiss.

"That is all; don't grieve, Pedro. If the knowledge of my sin has not sickened you of me, remember that it is better so, it was to come sooner or later; when I swapped my claim in heaven for a few short years of happiness with my love, I little knew it would be so short; but it is well, perhaps Frank may yet find happiness.

"Good-bye, friend Pedro! Do all you can to console dear Frank. And with my last thought of anything rational, I thank God that I have no mother to grieve over the wreck of what once was,

"MURREL."

I felt I would choke. I lifted my canteen hastily to my dry lips; the tears came unchecked down my hot cheeks. For a moment I sat trying to control my emotion. I looked at Pedro as he sat, his shoulders stooped low, his head bent, his bony hands clenching the grass blades.

I arose hastily and went to him, with my hot hand I smoothed back his greying hair; I could not speak, but the simple attention seemed to soothe him as nothing else probably could; his shoulders gradually straightened and he looked at me with humid eyes, a sad smile hovering over his thin lips.

"Life seems hard sometimes, Senorita, but God knows best. His will be done! I am very glad you insisted on my telling you, I feel much better after letting you share my secret!"

He arose and walked silently to the grave, in his queer hobbling way, I followed.

"The little rose bush is one I planted years ago. It seems not to have done well, I know little of such plants.

"Ah! Senorita, the nights I have spent over this grave! You perhaps, think it presuming in one of my position; I worshipped her silently while she lived and so have I gone on worshipping her silently these many years, worshipping her memory. No one—unless it be the Senor Hamilton — knew of my love for her; no one has ever heard her name on my lips, until you just heard my story. With the laying of the sod upon her rude coffin, a weight was laid upon my heart, never to be lifted until the sod is thrown upon my own coffin; my only hope in life is that I meet her in heaven!"

"But, what," I asked him, "ever became of her Senor Hamilton?" I was sorry before the words were scarcely out of my mouth, thinking it might bring his sad mood again upon him, but he answered with an even voice.

"Ah! Senorita, I did not finish my story. There is little more to tell. After she was buried I spent nearly the whole of each night at this silent spot, grieving and praying at once that her sin— if what she had done be regarded as such —might be forgiven, and I believe if there ever were any black marks against her they have surely been wiped out now, because of the many prayers I have sent.

"It was on the third night that Senor came, he had been to the Inn, I knew by the way he dismounted and staggered toward the tree; the moon shone brightly and gave his haggard face a ghastlier shade; I knew by the heaviness of my own heart something of what he must feel. I did not want to witness this strong man's grief, so I arose hastily and crept away, but not soon enough not to see him throw himself across the mound and with heavy sobs breaking the silent night. It was not the weak weeping of a woman, Senorita, when a strong man weeps; it is terrible; you who have never known love, can not understand the depth of a man's heart.

"It was dawn when he appeared before the Inn; all night I sat out awaiting his return that I might give him the letter. He opened it slowly and I saw that his hands shook like a man with an ague; he looked like an old man; the face that before had been smooth and handsome, was now drawn, his eyes were red and swollen; I turned my back while he read the note.

"For some time he stood with the paper in his hand, then folding carefully he placed it in a pocket. He put his big hand on my shoulder as he might have done any comrade.

" 'Good faithful Pedro!' " he said in a husky voice. 'Where did he go, Pedro? That hound!'

"I don't know, Senor. The last I saw of him was as he lay on the floor, perhaps Senor Herman may know.

" 'Herman told me of your action, and I can't thank you, Pedro. I know of no word that would suit. I am going after the hound, and if God lets me live long enough I am going to kill him! KILL him, Pedro! And when I.have found him and made good my vow, I will come back and tell you of it and I will spend the rest of my days here. Take good care of the grave, boy. She loved roses, sometimes you may find some. I am going now, good-bye!'

"His hand shake was so hearty I all but winced. He went into the Inn and presently came out with his canteen and food, throwing them onto the horse that had been made ready for him, he threw me a final farewell.

"That is the last I have seen of him. I don't know that he has ever made good his vow. At every sunset I send a prayer to my maker that the hound who caused the death of the Senora may cross the path of Senor Hamilton and thereby receive his just desserts." '

Pedro, with his shabby hat in hand, bowed his head over the little mound, and I knew that it was this prayer that was moving his colorless lips; and I felt in my heart that it would not be hard for one to feel so bitterly who had loved so devotedly.

* * * * * * *

A month since Pedro's tragic tale; the lonely little mound is a mass of blossoms. With Pedro's help I have planted the sweetest and prettiest flowers I could find in our own garden; with careful watering, even the sickly little rosebush has grown wonderfully.

How Hermit's Peak Gained Its Name

By R. M. Whistler

Not many miles from the picturesque city of Las Vegas, New Mexico, stands a giant mountain whose peak towers 4,000 feet above that city, an altitude of 10,000 feet in all. This rugged old sentinel of nature is described as having perpendicular synite cliffs, a thousand feet in height. Venturesome tourists and mountain climbers have made the strenuous trip to the summit and are loud in their praises of the magnificent view. On a clear day—and most every day is clear in New Mexico—the distance from the city of sixteen miles, looks to be less than five.

For centuries this great mountain stood solitary and unknown, save to an occasional party of daring pedestrians. Its natural beauty claimed the interest of few until a mysterious person took up his adobe in one of the cliffs and after years of secluded life disappeared as suddenly as he came. Without any design on his part, this cliff dweller of modern times gave a name to this majestic peak, which has attracted the curiosity of the public and added a new interest to a journey well worth taking.

The story of the hermit was fast becoming a myth when from an authentic source the truth was made known in print a few years ago. The hermit came to Las Vegas in 1864. He claimed to belong to the celebrated Antonio family of Venice. At first he spent his time visiting the people, teaching and preaching. He was without means and solicited charity, which the people generously bestowed. Afterwards he withdrew to the retirement of the mountain, which bears his name, and devoted his time to prayer and meditation. About once a month he came down to visit the people of the villages and towns, talking religion and begging supplies for his subsistence, to which the people always responded most generously.

After a year or two the people began to visit him in his retreat and thereafter these occasions became a sort of religious festival at which the hermit conducted services. His followers in return brought him supplies and made him more comfortable in his dwelling place, also adding stones to the monument where the open air worship was conducted.

The followers of the old man came from Las Vegas and the smaller villages along the Sappelo and Gallinas Rivers. As these pilgrimages became a fixed custom, the hermit's visits to the villages became less frequent.

One summer evening in 1874 his friends found a note written in charcoal on a piece of cardboard, telling them of his departure to other fields of usefulness. Some months later word came from Las Cruces that the hermit was there teaching and preaching as he had done at Las Vegas.

A year passed and it was rumored that the old man had secluded himself in the mountains east of Las Cruces and had been killed by savage Indians or bandits.

Each year since, in the dusk of late summer, may be seen from Las Vegas a light at Hermit's Peak. These are the fires that rise heavenward on the lonely rocky ledge of the mountain made by a remnant of the followers of the man who left behind him the imprint of his religious fervor and devotion.

Not much survives to mark the former habitation of the hermit, but the years of his life spent in the shelter and seclusion of the cliffs were sufficient to give to this lofty old mountain the name it now bears, "Hermit's Peak."

In the Realm of Bookland

"Civilization."

Of all the books that the late war has caused to be written there is none to my thinking so tragic, so strong, so imbued with the great spirit of understanding as Dr. Georges Duhamel's "Civilization," the book that won the 1918 Goncorest Prize. The volume consists of a series of short stories of wounded French soldiers, Dr. Duhamel was a surgeon for four years on an automobile ambulance at the front. Heart stories, they are, so vividly drawn that they lay bare the very souls of these martyr heroes. Seldom if ever have life stories been recounted with such skill, such dramatic art. Stoical though you may be you will grow teary round the lashes as you ponder them. Their moving pathos will discover to you new lights. Your vision will expand and you will know the heights and sublimity of soul to which these men who went through the fiery crucible of war's hell, arose. This body guard of the Freedom of Man, who wounded, maimed and stricken yet kept their faith in the infinite goodness of God. The book, "Civilization," is an Epic for it is active heroism.

"Civilization," The Century Company, New York; cloth, 12 mo., 288 pp. $1.50.

"Aristokia."

This is a fanciful story of the light comedy order. To read it is to laugh and yet underneath the mirth is a serious motive. You will find wise reader, for the book that remains with us and makes a lasting impression is more than a mere entertainer. This story is the imaginative conception of a community of kings composed of the German left-overs ten years after the war. There are startling scenes and specular happenings in this land of Aristokia and the high cost of living and the labor unions are very cleverly satired. An ardent love story runs through it and—can you imagine the hero of a love story being named Smith? He was not like the man who said "his name might be Smith but it wasn't." His was really Smith, Smith the hero of love's young dream. Is not that enough to pique your curiosity?

"Aristokia," The Century Company, New York; cloth, illustrated, 12 mo., 214 pp., $1.50.

"Seneca Fiction, Legends and Myths."

The "Handbook of American Indians" states that The Senecas,—(a place of stone)—are a noted and influential tribe of the Iroquois, or the so-called Five Nations of New York. It is the traditions, the folk lore and the mythology of these peoples that is embodied in the present volume edited by J. N. B. Hewitt from material collected by him and Jeremiah Curtin. "We have now in North America," says Mr. Curtin, "a number of groups of tales obtained from the Indians which when considered together, illustrate and supplement one another; they constitute, in fact, a whole system." These tales we may describe as collectively the creation myths of the new world. In substance these tales show the primitive Indian mind as it is, its fixed principles and its supreme devotion to its spiritual ideals. "Nothing that an Indian has is of human invention, all is divine." The following version of the Dipper gives an idea of the lore of this remarkable book:

"The Seven Stars of the Dipper."

Long ago six men went out hunting many days' journey from home. For a long time they found no game. One of their number said that he was sick (in fact he was very lazy), so they had to make a litter of two poles and a skin, by means of which four men carried him. Each man had his own load to bear besides. The sixth member of the party came behind, carrying the kettle.

At last, when they were getting very hungry, they came on the track of a bear, whereupon they dropped their sick companion and their burdens, each running on as fast as he could after the bear. At first the track was so old that they thought merely, "We shall overtake the bear at some future time anyway." Later they said, "The track can not be more than three days old," and as it grew fresher and fresher each day, they finally said, "Tomorrow, it seems, we shall overtake the bear." Now the man whom they had carried so long was not tired, and when they dropped him, knowing that he was to be left behind, he ran on after them. As he was fresher than they were, he soon passed them, and overtaking the bear, he killed it.

His companions never noticed in their hurry that they were going upward all the time. Many persons saw them in the air, always rising as they ran. When they overtook the bear they had reached the heaven, where they have remained to this day, and where they can be seen any starlit night near the Polar Star.

The man who carried the kettle is seen in the bend of the Great Dipper, the middle star of the handle, where the only small star near any other of the Dipper stars is the kettle. The bear may be seen as a star at the lower outside corner.

Every autumn when the first frost comes there may be seen on the leaves of the oak tree blood and drops of oil—not water, but oil—the oil and blood of the bear. On seeing this the Indians say, "The lazy man has killed the bear."

The book is published at Washington, D. C., under the title of Annual Report of the Bureau of American Enthnology of the Smithsonian Institution.

"The Diamond Pin."

Ever since Conan Doyle's detective stories became the vogue there have been innumerable writers of this class of mystery-fiction while none of them can approach Dr. Doyle in felicity of expression and character delineation there are yet many of these stories readable and likeable. None are more so than "The Diamond Pin" which goes to make an-

Pioneering Wireless Speech

On the morning of October 22, 1915, an engineer speaking at Arlington, Virginia, was heard at Eiffel Tower, Paris, and at Pearl Harbor, Hawaiian Islands. This was the first trans-Atlantic and trans-continental message ever sent by wireless telephone. It was an achievement of the Bell System.

During the Fifth Liberty Loan nearly a million people, in throngs of ten thousand, heard speeches and music by wire and wireless. The loud-speaking equipment was a main feature of "Victory Way", New York. Wireless messages came from aviators flying overhead and long distance speeches from Government official in Washington. Messages were ofte magnified several billion times. Thi demonstration was the first of its kin in the history of the world. It als was an achievement of the Bell System

Historic also were the war time use of wireless telephony, giving commu nication between airplanes and fro mother ships to submarine chasers.

All these accomplishments and use were made possible by the work o the research laboratories of the Bel System.

AMERICAN TELEPHONE AND TELEGRAPH COMPAN
AND ASSOCIATED COMPANIES

One Policy   *One System*   *Universal Servic*

other volume of Carolyn Wells' detective series. We have followed Fleming Stone, the great American detective, through all the plots and counter-plots that are a detective's portion in the web of fate and we like his skill in gathering up the threads, his cunning weaving of facts out of fancy and his lucidity of thought and expression. The story of "The Diamond Pin" shows him at his best. The mystery concerning the death of a wealthy widow who was found dead in a locked room with no means of egress and the search for her jewels puts him on his mettle. The dead woman's niece and her late husband's nephew are the leading actors in this many cornered drama and yes, too, the love that makes the world go round is there.

"The Diamond Pin," J. P. Lippincott Company, Philadelphia; cloth, ornamented, 12 mo., 300 pp., $1.35.

"Why Joan."

Eleanor Mercein Kelly, fashions her stories out of simple, wholesome Kentucky life, but there is a harmony of thought and a reverent strength in simplicity and she has caught it and woven it into the web of fate which she spins in "Why Joan," her new novel. The story is, in a way, unique as it has no particular heroine or hero either for that matter, but the characters all bear well sustained parts. We are inclined to think the woman with a past, the woman who came back, is the strongest figure of the story. Her little individualities and quaint cheer do much to liven things up and she has the enduring strength of the unfortunate. Joan, fascinating and fair, self-centered and selfish, serves the good purpose to bring out vividly the composite qualities of the others. There is a shifting of scenes and a touch of "Over There" which will please you.

"Why Joan," The Century Co., New York; cloth, ornamental, 12 mo., 406 pp.; $1.50.

"A Daughter of the Northwest."

This story, by Irene Welch Grissom, is of unusual freshness and charm. It is written in the first person from the heart of the great Northwest, "where rolls the Oregon and hears no sound but its own dashing." What a pity that noble river's name was ever changed from Oregon to Columbia. But Columbia it is and there, in the forest primeval, at a big red sawmill on the banks of this mighty river the tale unfolds. Then are shifting scenes that run across the continent and the story-folk are full of life and action and the old, old story, that anomaly of life which is ever new, plays the dominant part. You will want to read this Northwestern romance and see that fine large country from the viewpoint of a girl's eyes.

"A Daughter of the Northwest," The Cornhill Company, Boston, Mass.; cloth, 12 mo., 255 pp., $1.50.

EPTEMBER 1919

15 CENTS

Opportunity's One Knock

When *Opportunity* knocks, will we hear her?

Or will our ears be so deafened with debts and our minds so filled with money worries that we do not hear her happy message?

W. S. S. and Thrift Stamps help Opportunity knock loudly—one knock enough.

W. S. S.— Everybody's Opportunity

Savings' Division
War Loan Organization
Treasury Department

Vol. LXXIV

No. 3

Overland Monthly

AN ILLUSTRATED MAGAZINE OF THE WEST

CONTENTS FOR SEPTEMBER, 1919

NOTICE.—Contributions to the Overland Monthly should be typewritten, accompanied by full return postage, and with the author's name and address plainly written in upper corner of first page. Manuscripts should never be rolled.

The Publisher of the Overland Monthly will not be responsible for the preservation or mail miscarriage of unsolicited contributions and photographs.

Issued Monthly. $1.50 per year in advance. Fifteen cents per copy. Back numbers 3 months or over 25c; six months or over 50c; nine months or over 75c; 1 year or over $1.00. Postage: To Canada, 3 cents; Foreign, 5 cents.

Copyrighted, 1919, by the Overland Monthly Company.

Entered at the San Francisco, Cal., Post-office as second-class matter.

Published by the OVERLAND MONTHLY COMPANY, San Francisco, California.

259 MINNA STREET.

Will You Help Us — Get to "Sea Breeze?"

With the hot sun beating down on their frail underfed bodies—with no hope of relief in sight—the little children and tired mothers of the slums are facing another grim summer in their empty lives.

Help Us Give These Unfortunates A Chance for Health

Sea Breeze—the Association's fresh air home—gives the one chance for rest, nourishment and care for many of these families each year—but help is needed at once if we are to provide for the long waiting list.

Will you give—just a little? Allow 60 cents a day, or $4.00 a week for each one whom you will send as your guest.

The New York Association for Improving the Condition of the Poor

Room 250   105 East 22nd St., New York

Please

George Blagden, Treasurer
A. I. C. P.
105 East 22d Street
New York

Enclosed is $...................... with which you are to give fresh air relief to the most needy cases on your list.

Name..

Address..

Diana Greeting the Sunrise.   —Jesse T. Banfield.

The Spirit of the Wildwoods.

—Emma B. Freeman.

OVERLAND MONTHLY

Founded 1868

BRET HARTE

| VOL. LXXVI | San Francisco, September, 1919 | No. 3 |

The Nude in Art -- and Life

By Courtney Cowper

TO write of the nude in art is something like writing about the alphabet in literature. Historically, this is certainly true. The very first hunter of the stone age, who, with a bit of red clay pigment, drew upon the walls of that famous cave in Southern France, crude outlines of the forms of life with which he was familiar—bison, deer and human, started the fashion of treating as legitimate material for art, the undraped human figure.

All the early artists followed his lead. And it might almost be said the higher the value of the art of any early civilization, the more frequent the use by painter or sculptor of the absolute nude. Certainly such civilizations as those of Persia and Assyria, Egypt and Yucatan, where, according to our present valuations, art did not reach the degree of development reached in Greece, there was a tendency to depict costumed figures, conventualized after the national mode. But the Greeks, especially at their zenith of cultural glory, had always, even when they draped their figures, the feeling for the nude. The swift flowing garments of the Victory of Samothace might have been of the lightest chiffon—so do they reveal the beauty which they cover and enhance.

Aesthetically this is just as true. For an impersonal or "objective" attitude toward all life and phenomena, lies at the very beginning of art appreciation. The woman who can not view the Winged Mercury without a sneaking sense of shame, and the man who cannot gaze at the Venus de Medici without the subtlest tinge of lasciviousness coloring his thought, are both really incapable of ap-

preciating any form of art, for they could always read a personal, gross, literal, vulgar meaning into any representation —even of landscape.

Perhaps the real purpose of art is to give us a detached "outside" view of our own emotions, sensations, passions. Herein doubtless rests the source of that cooling and soothing effect which galleries have upon those who love to haunt them.

A belief that there is anything wrong or shameful in the contemplation of the beauties of the human form betokens a vicious attitude of mind in the person or community holding it. It is always attended with other vices and evils, of which the greatest is provincial ignorance.

Anatole France, in his allegorical and fantastic satire on human society, "Penguin Island" tells how the devil introduced lasciviousness into a primitive and uncorrupted society.

It will be remembered that the penguins are a comical sort of bird living near the South Pole, who are nearer akin to fishes and reptiles than any other bird not extinct. Those who saw the Peary South Pole Expedition movies will also remember that at a distance, with their erect attitude, characteristic movements and peculiar "coat and vest" markings, they somewhat resemble clothed diminutive human beings.

In France's book, a short-sighted medieval missionary, mistaking an assemblage of these birds for humans, preaches to them, becomes convinced by their movements that he has converted them, and straightway baptizes them for the remission of their sins.

He thereby caused the celestial authorities much embarrassment.

This embarrassment arose out of the theological problem of how it might be possible to remit the sins of a race which had never yet sinned—never, in fact, as yet been capable of sinning.

A sort of convention of the saints was called, and France's report of the alleged doings of that heavenly assemblage, with its bickerings, its suggestions, arguments and counter-arguments, is not altogether unlike an Examiner reporter's write-up of a stormy session of the Board of Supervisors, with Andy Gallagher and "Jemmet" in full swing.

The problem was finally solved by the suggestion of one of the saints—I forget which one—that the penguins be turned into men and given a chance to accumulate a few sins (in order that said heavenly authorities might have a chance of fulfilling their contract to remit the penguins' iniquities).

This was accordingly done, and for once the Prince of Darkness fell in with heavenly designs — by undertaking the promotion of sin among the penguins.

When the penguins were turned into men, they, of course, lost their feathers, and went about clad rather airily, considering the probable climate of their island, which France places near the pole.

Up to the time that Satan got busy, the female human penguin meant just as much to the male human penguin, as she had meant when they were both mere birds—just that much and no more.

Such a state of affairs did not suit Satanic purposes.

His very first activity on the island, according to France, was to catch a poor naked unsophisticated — and awkward — female penguin and teach her the art of dress,—that is to say, of covering her form in a manner to call attention to, and enhance (or create) its charms.

The point of all which is that the origin and everlasting source of all unhealthy sex mysticism and over-emphasis is in clothes. That lasciviousness and over-lust is based more upon a lack of knowledge and appreciation of the beauties of the human form than it is upon the presence of that knowledge.

This observation is not original with the writer — nor did it originate with France. It is an ancient, although sometimes imperfectly recognized truth.

To tell the truth, sex and sex allure is the most over advertised commodity on earth.

Sex, love, marriage, et cetera, have been press-agented by every poet from Homer and Omar to Amy Lowell and Witter Bynner—that is, of course, if it is admitted that all four are poets — by every dramatist from Euripides and Shakespeare to George Cohan and David Belasco — with the same provisionary condition, of course.

Sculptors, painters, novelists, musicians, newspaper reporters—in short, all the world's literature and all the world's art, good, bad and indifferent, have devoted their efforts to the creation of an illusion and emphasis which, to tell the truth, the subject doesn't merit.

Such people as Ellen Key and Havelock Ellis, who pretend to strip away the veil, don't do anything of the sort. They have merely found a new way of singing the song and telling the story. They draw the curtain well enough, but only to discover to us an artificial stage setting—perhaps new and original in design and plan, but unreality, nevertheless.

And of all the press-agents of sex, the priests and the purists, the preachers and moralists have been the most efficient.

If sin and sinful women, for instance, were only just one-half as alluring and charming in reality as the oldtime sunday school teacher used to make out, how much more joyful a place this old world would be! But the wild, wild women are so sadly tame after all!

One of the most baffling and confusing things in life is not only that love and marriage, but that sin, "sweet sin," itself, as experiences, never come up to anything like the reputation given them.

Not only is the bliss and joy that is claimed, missing from the actuality, but the very deep agony and torment of which the poets sing, exist mainly in their songs.

The queer thing is that although prac-

Woodside Nymph Visiting the Mirrored River at Noontide.
—Emma B. Freeman.

tically the whole of every generation finds this out before they die, it never gets through the thick heads of the next succeeding generation. You'd think they'd guess sometime—but they don't.

Of course it is a good thing they don't, conceding that the human race is worthy of perpetuation.

But there is a point, and here is the crux of the discussion, where all this razzle-dazzle about sex subjects ceases to be desirable of a matter of race utility, and becomes the source of anti-social evils that threaten the very life of the race. It is hard for the most subtle moralist to place and define this point in words, but instinct and common sense recognize the "limit."

In creating this age-old glamor, the dressmakers, modistes, and corsettieres, have been merely the tools and accomplices of the priests and the poets, but they have been such a help! They have carried the light into regions where the influence of neither priest nor poet existed, and they have helped wonderfully to tie up the tradition and literature of the subject to every day actuality. Their talent for making a drape of cloth tell a clever lie has covered what a multitude of sins of society against the health and beauty of the race! They have clothed generation after generation of defectives that the illusion might not die, and if their clothing tended to make each generation more defective, they grew still more skillful in covering the faults they helped to create, — and finally how often they succeeded perverting taste until these very defects could be emphasized for the same purpose,—that is just as points of beauty had once been emphasized.

Witness the recent rage for the "debutante slouch," whereby a rickety, anaemic female with a spine curved like the letter C was supposed to create pleasurable sensations in the breast of the tired business man, when the Venus de Milo could she become perfect flesh before his eyes, would have left him unmoved.

It is gladly admitted that dressmakers are necessary. Besides the need of protecting our ridiculous bodies from the heats and colds of the earth's unfriendly surface, there are few of us who are so beautiful that we would not welcome at times, at least, the comfort and protection of some clever modist's or tailor's lie. I can imagine there were times when Diana herself would have enjoyed "slumping down" under the protecting folds of some old worn "knock-about" mantle, safe from the strain of being beautiful. For even were we all blessed with the beauty of Venus and Apollo there would come times when we'd tire of posing.

And the wildest-eyed advocate of eugenics would not undertake to promise us, even if all his theories were adopted, that we could ever build up so perfect a race that a little occasional aid from an expert costumer would not be welcomed.

Turn back and read Mark Twain, when Mark becomes frank and tells the truth about the miserable, ignorant, bombastic, artificial and hypocritical '60's and '70's—those days when a woman's slippers were supposed to be mysteriously suspended from her hips, to fall just at the edge of her crinoline. That she might have legs was unimaginable, and along with the denial of the existence of these very useful limbs, went the denial of a number of other truths. Women were imagined, or said, in those days to be a number of things which women are not, never have been and never will be. Men, likewise, claimed certain qualities and attributes, which men never possessed and quite probably never had any real desire to possess. Upon such wrong hypotheses calculations were sure to go astray. So the generation abounded in all sorts of wasteful, grotesque, unjust and stupid customs.

It is not at all impossible that the Greeks reached such perfect heights of civilization simply because every Greek knew exactly just how a perfectly healthy, strong and excellent human body ought to be formed. And knowing this, he took an absolutely impersonal attitude toward the beauty of such a form.

This knowledge seems to be a sort of talisman, or a sort of corrective standard for thought, whereby any nation may

Nymphs Reposing 'Neath the Shadows of the Redwoods.
—Emma B. Freeman.

be kept to a certain sane manner of thought upon the vital truths of life.

At any rate, in decadent and corrupted stages of civilization, the popular conception of human beauty has been of something misformed, grotesque, and grotesquely costumed. Among the moderns we have only to refer to France in the period before the revolution, and among the ancients whether in India, in Egypt, in Asia Minor or in Greece and Rome, or in the far away civilizations of prehistoric America, periods of social decadence have always been accompanied by accentuation of ornate, grotesque and complicated costume, disfiguring and masking the human form in the age's art.

It is as though we humans conceived of truth in the form of a beautiful, perfect woman or youth, and once having forgotten the outlines of such a form, we seem to forget the nature and existence of truth.

So, if the moralists, by generations of vicious ancestry, have forgotten to take joy in the beautiful nude in art, they should awaken to its beneficent social effect.

Arthur Ruhl, in his charming book, describing a trip through Russia in the winter of 1915-1916, before the curse of war and its resulting political chaos had destroyed the normal ways of Russian life, tells of a characteristic adventure at Kiev—a swim in the Dneiper.

He says: "Kiev is on the bluffs of the west bank. The east shore of the river consists of low sand-flats, an ideal bathing place, and people rowed across from Kiev, walked up the sand a bit, and went into the river au naturel, like small boys in the old swimming hole."

Ruhl was at first somewhat disconcerted by the sight of heavy handsome men and women splashing in the water with their children "like happy walruses." But the impersonal attitude of these men and women and children to the others and to themselves soon penetrated and he found somewhat to his surprise, he tells us, that the human animal, once all men lay aside clothes, is no more naked or exposed than any other animal. Immodesty is a thing of custom. Yet it is immodest to do what

other people do not do. And did nine women out of ten go unclad every day and any day down Market street, the tenth woman who assumed a skirt and coat would be "lectured at" as an immodest vicious creature—as she no doubt would prove, and the idle men would turn to look after her, just as now they turn to look after the skirt that is shorter or tighter than the average.

So, again, we of today, the children and grandchildren of the silly '60's, and heirs to all their vices and miscalculations, have much deliverance to be thankful for.

For instance, there was the fad for barefoot dancing. It has freed us forever from a lascivious attitude toward all dancing. No one of our grandmothers could have stood up in a skirt to her ankles and have done any sort of a solo dance, with the slightest of kicks, without losing her character.

Queerly, in spite of all this false modesty, all the dancing of that period tended toward lasciviousness. Where now is the skirt dance with its one revealing kick to the ceiling that was supposed to be so exciting and wicked? Where now are the pink tights and the wasp waists of the Amazon chorus of old?

After all it was not what these poor ladies of the stage, who no doubt were only trying to earn an honest living, did that made them seem evil. It was the thought behind the eyes of the audience that watched them.

Nowadays, a dancer who is a real dancer, can come out clad in a piece of chiffon the size of a pocket handkerchief, and because she has no tights to mask and hamper, give us the opportunity of joy in beautiful movement which we can accept and appreciate to its full—because there is evil neither in what she does, nor in what we think.

But in the beginning our fathers thought much evil of the barefoot dancers—until the barefoot dancers shocked it out of their systems. Now there is such a dancer on every vaudeville program, and they can do little but bore us, unless they have real and exceptional art in their dancing.

To a certain extent the "curse" has

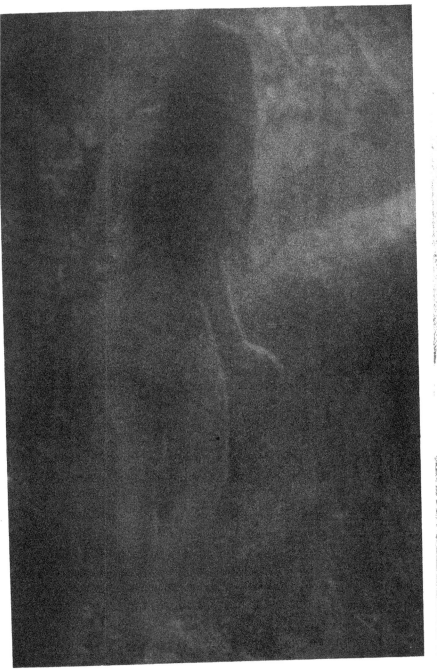

A Dryad in the Forest Primeval.

—Jessie T. Banfield.

"Autumn." The Figure Suggests the Sorrow Nature Feels for the Dying Year.
—Jesse T. Banfield.

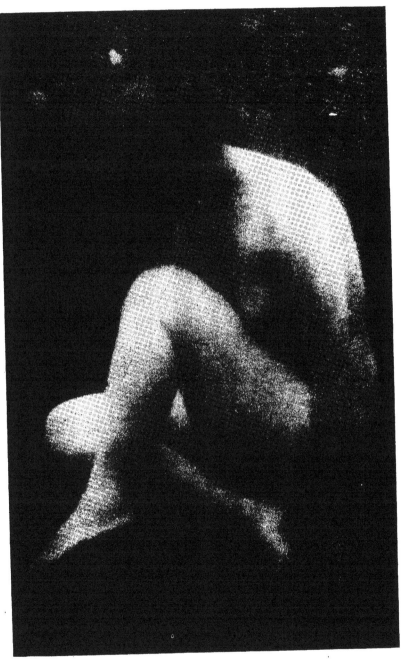

"Contemplation."   —Jesse T. Banfield.

been taken off the nude for us, because we are beginning to realize it was in our own eyes, — a sort of shadow of the clothes with which the form was wont to be covered.

When the grinning Chicago crowds blocked traffic to stare at "September Morn," it was not because the picture had any great value as a painting, nor merely because the lady therein was uncovered by any garment. Rather it was because of a certain feeling that the lady should have been dressed—that she had a regular modern costume back on the shore somewhere which she would soon run back and shiver into. The crowd had a sense of peering into a scene forbidden—and that is just what the artist intended, and the reason that "September Morn," as a painting, is not a work of art, but a vicious trick in the name of art, which every lover of the nude resents. Yet this picture in the end worked its good. It became famous and popular on penny postcards, and the ordinary public learned that they might look upon a nude picture without being stricken by a bolt from the blue. They finally got used to it, and there was the blessing—they immediately lost interest in it, and in any other nude that appealed merely because it was unclothed. After that a nude would have to be clothed in the artist's intellectuality and conception of beauty, before they could again be interested.

The first nude figure by an American artist to be exhibited in America, was the "Greek Slave," by Hiram Powers. A picturesque incident was the securing by Powers of a round-robin signed by several prominent Philadelphia ministers of the gospel, that the "Greek Slave" was "pure" and wouldn't hurt the public by being gazed at. There is no doubt about the figure being innocuous. Poor Powers in his determination to thoroughly sterilize his work from any bad associations had to destroy all trace of personality or beauty. It is a woodeny, stupid thing enough, that "Greek Slave." It missed being a real work of art by exactly the opposite method to that taken in case of the painting just mentioned, but we must, nevertheless, be grateful

to Powers. He did his best. The main desideratum was to get the American people to gaze at a nude, as a rightful and good thing to do. He accomplished that. He overcame the tabu, and started a movement to destroy a fetish.

But Powers' and most sculptors and painters reach only the "exclusive and cultured" stratas of our society. Their work in correcting and making sane our ideas of some of the most vital things in life, do not penetrate very far.

(Of course the sculptors and painters have no idea—at least, many of them have not, that they are doing anything of the sort. Very few artists are moralists. They create the beautiful as they see it, and their social use is incidental.)

But the art of photographing the nude has reached so high a point in America, and especially on the Pacific Coast, that it promises to do great "missionary work." These reproductions are as good as "originals" — they have the advantage, really of being originals, and the prices are not too high to place them out of reach of the general public.

The personalities and temperaments of the artists who have taken this art upon the coast have been most fortunate. Such artists as Emma B. Freeman and Jesse Banfield have succeeded in steering safely between the two evils that beset the path of every student or portrayer of the nude. Without making their studies so innocuous as to be meaningless and lacking in personality, they have nevertheless succeeded in avoiding any lewd suggestiveness in subject or treatment.

True enough, Banfield is a believer in glamourie. He invests his plates with an atmospheric softness and illusion. His figures seem almost shadows—spirits of the wood, that will fade into the background and disappear should we rub our eyes too briskly. He is a veritable poet of the place.

Miss Freeman's plates show a more realistic, and perhaps intellectual treatment of the relation of the human nude to nature in its primitive forms. She loves to catch her dryads in the deep woods, and she gives them a certain solidity, as of the warm brown earth.

In Yosemite

By Henry Meade Bland

Because there is a rosy memory
Of stream and flower and a face divine
Woven with high crag and lilied lea,
I, Inno, child of the Dawn and the White Sunshine
Write these soft rhymes and dare to call them mine.
Now in sweet fancy I am again a boy,
And lose myself among the ancient pine,
Climbing the highest cliff in silent joy,
Lone as lorn Paris driven by fate from song-built Troy.

How can I read the glacier chronicle,
Of heaped moraine, or rock-wall scarred and seamed:
Its story seems to fall sardonical
Upon the yearning soul that once has dreamed
On labyrinthine mind or once has deemed,
That he has found perfection in a face:
And all the magic of that face is reamed
Into his brain, woven in immortal lace,
Whose beauty only an eternal love can trace.

Too many memories ensnare the heart,
And seem to hold it from the days to be.
I shall forget the things of which I was a part:
I turn my gaze upon the flowered lea,
The joyous thrush is rhyming now for me,
The waterfall is singing hour by hour:
Make me, oh Crag, of thine eternity!
Give me, oh Vale, the glory of thy dower!
Touch me, I pray, with thy strong majesty and power!

Clear as a star reflected in the deep
Of silent Mirror Lake, that face to me!
No breath of air breaks in upon the sleep
Of jewelled water, shining radiantly:
Thus in that quiet lake of memory
(As in the silver pool) upon the star
I look with eager wondering eye and see
The meteor-flash of beauty from afar;
And fain would turn the key, the sacred past unbar.

I walk in silence by the mossed stream,
The ousel sings, the summer clouds are high;
My mind runs only to a single theme—
An eager face that ever flashes nigh.
I gaze the long prospect to the tender sky:
Lo, it is there, and ever seems to rise.
Then comes the gray dove's plaintive loving cry
Only to be broken by a sweet surprise;—
Through the dark oak leaves gleam those eager talking eyes.

And yet how often I linger on the trail,
Eager to catch the first night-melody of Pan
Floating afar from shadowy rock and dale!
How often do I hear the joyous clan
Of fairy and nymph, a merry caravan,
Hurry at eve from tree or leafy bower;
Or when the new moon leads the starry van
How often come deep voices, hour by hour,
Spoke by the thundrous fall in majesty and power.

Perhaps the Master-Mind has subtly given
This, the great glory of the primal world,
Scarred with old-time and with the thunder riven,
Where by His foot the stream of streams lies curled;
That, turning thence to where in power is whirled
The wheel by which He shapes the soul of man,
One may adore the flash divine unfurled
Upon the brow of smiling child, or span
The way unfolding life's inexplicable plan.

All the sweet harmonies of Eden-Time
Are here. The Winds in summer melody
The water-ousel song; the rippled rhyme
Of snowy waters, and the minstrelsy
Of immemorial pine. Such harmony
Greek Homer played; on such a steep he sang
When that he fashioned fair and joyously
The throne of Jove: And, as his music rang,
Straightway the temple of the gods in glory sprang.

Once on the trail I stood while sombre clouds
Loomed threat'ningly around the Valley rim,
Swaying in ominous, shadowy, eager, crowds—
Dark offspring of the summery seraphim,
Who sang a deep, titanic, snow-born, hymn;
Then came the thunder, not a single crash,
But like the shout of hosting cherubim:
The day was night, and fiercely lash on lash,
Wild dome and spire signaled many a fiery flash.

There gleams the rainbow over Vernal Fall.
There glows the great Nevada, haloed white,
And stubborn Half Dome lifts his granite wall
Where bold Tenaya flashes mystic light.
The clear Mercedes wings in gentle flight
Where the Great Fall is singing evermore!
The Bridal Maiden laughs, a radiant sprite.
There gleams El Capitan, and o'er and o'er
Recounts his thunder-scars. Be silent and adore!

A hundred thousand years of mountain bloom!—
The tall Oenotheras, the mimulus, the blue
Pentstamon, fabric woven in the loom
Of Juno; violets dipped in heathery dew,
Lilies and daisies and all the lightsome crew
Of rose or heartsease for which lovers yearn,
Each, in a wonder, spring by spring renew,—

Nepenthe, asphodel and quiet rue,
And all the fine embroidery of leaf and fern!

In such a vale beloved Endymion
Reclined when Adonais secret-dwelt
Within his bower deep-hidden from the sun;
Where twilight mysteries forever melt
Into the starlight, and through the night is felt
Strange presences unseen. In such a vale
The star-crowned Bard of shining Avon dealt
With Fate, creating ghost or phantom pale
Telling of love and war in many a sweet-sung tale.

The great Earth-Mother carved, long, long ago,
And fretted these high crags, and gently drew
Her finger in the sand. She taught the snow
The way of the stream. She hung the rose with dew.
She hollowed out the caves, and tuned anew
The hills to low Aeolian refrain:
She gave the sky its deep eternal blue:
She changed the snow to singing summer rain;
And trailed the hills, an endless golden chain.

Here fair Niam, the Oread of the Wind,
Waits on the shadowy river's flowerd stream,
Moaning and sighing because she cannot find
Her lover. She waits where gleam on gleam
The lightning flashes in a joy supreme,
Till longing sweet o'er-fills her eyes of blue,——
Waits the old tryst upon the hills of Dream,
He saw her spring fairer than poet's pen
And now she spreads her couch in many a sunlit hue.

And here star-eyed Idalean Venus rose,
Bewitching messenger from gods to men.
Greek Hermes, so the Attic story goes,
Said she was born of foam: clear to his ken
He saw her spring fairer than poet's pen
Ever set forth. He erred. The magic One,
Sweet Love, leapt from the glorious rainbow when
The great Fall is wed unto the noonday Sun,
Fairest of all beauty great Poesy has spun.

Here on a flowery day came John o' the Mountain,
And shaped he many a far and deep-hid trail.
He saw with loving eye each stream and fountain
And sought each secret of the rain-bowed vale;
Until the white-winged angel, Israefale,
Touched him and beckoned, and gently upward led
Him over the Range of Light; and now his tale
Is told in flower and stream and sunset red,
And every tree the wilding folk have tenanted.

And I, too, came and saw, and loved; and listened
To the divine song of cataract and air;
Gazed where the starry domes in wonder glistened,
Where the high towering pine and fir were ever fair;

2

Dreamed by the river, watched with tender care
The robin build, and happy, hour by hour,
Trailed through the meadow where the debonair
Sunshiny blossoms made a witching bower,
Fashioned of buttercups the happy children's dower.

All the long summer afternoons me-seemed
To have been carried away to Aidenn-Land,
Where sweet the smiling leaves of lotus dreamed.
The spiced pine soothed with many a fragrant hand
The happy brook laughed over the silver sand
Only by Pan's wild flutes was the silence broken
While rosy Iris arched her flashing band.
Love drank libations from his chalice oaken
And a new friendship smiled with many a happy token.

The rainbow fades upon the purple hill
But in the soul its glories never die
A smile may pass as ripples on a rill
But in true hearts its circles ever lie
The gold that passes from the morning sky,
Is gold forever in great Memory's reign:
Psyche is ever a tenant in love's sigh,
And gentle Baldur, by blind Hoder slain,
Is deathless in spring's never-ending flower-train.

Sun Cups

The Mate's Revenge

By Tom Devine

FIGHTING HANS BENSON, skipper of the schooner "Carrier Dove," stood on the poop deck with his lean legs far apart. One hand was holding the binoculars to his eyes and the other was savagely sawing circles in the air. He was looking aloft at the jigger top mast Slim Anderson was painting. His actions showed anger; his voice and words disgust.

"Hey aloft, there! Yes, you, you slab-sided, beach-coming swab, cover them there holidays. Where? Holy salt mackeral, can't yer see? On your port. Don yer port! Oh, limped-eyed saints above, can you see that corn-planter looking to his starboard? Yes, that's the spot, now paint, paint it! By the brimstone smells of Hell, he's dropped his brush! I never seen such an awkward potato pl—"

He got no farther in his tirade. Something rubbed against his leg. It was Davy Jones, his black tom cat. He picked the cat up, smuggled him in the hollow of his arm, and as he stroked its back with his tarry hand, he went below. Davy Jones was his only friend. Fighting Hans lavished all his rough affection on him; confided his joys to him; his sorrows, his misgivings, and if he ever spoke a civil word it was to his cat.

Yet, with all his cussedness, Fighting Hans was mis-named. He did not belong to that old school of skippers who argued with a belaying pin. He was a fault-finding, nagging old woman of the sea. Still, his bodily appearance was that of a fighter. He was built square from his hips up. Even his whiskers had square outlines and his head—Take another look at the name and judge for yourself.

He had sailed and hauled ropes since he was a boy. Consequently his arms were nearly as large, and long as his legs. But his eyes, when they could be seen amid his shaggy eyebrows and whiskers that grew well over his cheek bones, showed his weak nature. They were of a washed blue color, flecked with muddy specks, and, yet they held a repulsive gleam.

He was named about twenty years ago at Guymas, Mexico, by the wit of the ship's crew, to perpetuate the memory of a fight between Carlos Schuler, a second mate, and Fighting Hans. This Carlos was a cunning scoundrel, half Mexican and half German, who had gone ashore and drank some of the liquor courage the peons extract from cactus. A little of this juice inside the waistband of a Mexican forecasts a tempest of dark words, punctuated by the glint of daggers, and followed by a nice quiet funeral.

When he came aboard he was carrying quite a cargo in his hold, besides a deck load of one quart in his hip pocket. He was looking for trouble and Fighting Hans. He found both. They exchanged sarcastic greetings and some six-cylinder compliments, remarkable in themselves for length and strength. But this was salt in old wounds so they shut their mouths and hands and proceeded to settle their troubles.

Carlos, true to his Mexican blood, whipped out a dagger and made for that part of the skipper located behind the third button of his shirt. Fighting Hans avoided him with a nimble sidestep; reached out and snatched the bottle from his pocket. With a deft, backhand blow he broke the bottle on the mate's shoulder. He crumpled on the deck with a muffled clatter that ended in a slap as his face hit the hot deck.

Carlos staggered to his feet, still clutching the dagger. He made at Fighting Hans again, chattering like a monkey from maniacal rage. Fighting Hans had no other weapon but the broken, jagged, bottle-neck. In the cutting, cleaving, tom-cat scrimmage that followed, Fighting Hans ripped the mate's cheek from ear to mouth.

With a bellow of pain and rage, like a wounded beast, he grabbed his cheek, wheeled, leaped the rail and started down the gang-plank. Fighting Hans assisted him with a slush bucket between the shoulders. Carlos got well out on the dock, turned, struck a prophetic pose and shouted back, "You will pay me for this, but not in money. You will pay me, me, me!" Then he hurried up the dock to get some of the dark age medical witchery practiced in Guymas.

Any remorse that Fighting Hans ever felt over this fight was never shown. Yet, indirectly, it influenced his treatment of the seamen until the worst part of his nature was developed to the fullest extent. The different crews he shipped judged him by his name. They thought him to be a roaring, rough and tumble old demon of the sea. Holding this conception in mind, they treated him with mingled servile awe, and contempt that invited rough domineering treatment. This provoking attitude of the sailors soon changed his passive nature into a positive, savage barking old sea dog.

His name soon ceased to remind him of the fight and he quickly forgot it. No one had ever mentioned it to him save his shipper in Seattle just before he sailed on his present voyage. It was the last thing the shipper said as the ship was leaving the dock. He told Fighting Hans that he heard that Carlos had enlisted in the German Navy and had risen to the rank of submarine commander.

Then as the ship was drawing out in the stream he shouted to Fighting Hans, "I don't suppose you will find him cruising around in the South Pacific to collect the debt he promised you about twenty years ago. Well, hope you have a good voyage, Captain. So long."

The shipper did not tell Fighting Hans this hearsay as a warning, or to make him uneasy. Just a word about an old enemy, nothing more. Yet, curiously enough, it aroused a feeling of indefinable

dread that increased the further South he sailed, until now as he lay becalmed in about latitude 20, longtitude 120 of the South Pacific, it became a mental obsesion.

The motionless ship, the unbroken horizon and the damp, drugging tropic air made his body sluggish and his imagination a thing of torture.

Asleep or awake, his imagination invented scores of revengeful disasters perpetrated and executed by Carlos. Why these torturing visions came, he did not know. Why they stayed seemed an omen. He could not reason them away or banish them with a contemptuous grunt and a wave of the hand. He began to regret, for the first time, that the fight had occurred.

His mind, peopled with these phantoms, drove him to nagging the sailors, which in turn drove the sailors to a near mutiny. In fact, a mutiny was being planned by Slim Anderson. He wanted revenge for the useless scolding Fighting Hans had given him that day for dropping his paint brush.

The night following his one-sided clash with Fighting Hans, Slim Anderson was posted as an all night lookout. Instead of staying forward on the forecastle head, he felt his way aft. He sat down on the break of the poop deck and leaned against the rail.

The night was dark as only a tropic night can be. He could not see the misty outlines of the sails; not even his hand. To try to look at the sea was like peering into a motionless black pit. The sea was as placid as a mountain lake. There was not a smooth, heaving swell, or a catspaw, or the phosphorent glitter radiating in long lines from a shark's dorsal fin, to mar the glasslike surface of the sea.

Slim Anderson felt keenly his utter insignificance and helplessness in this vast watery waste. Just a microbe on a hallowed chip at the mercy of the elements. Such surroundings may well make the man with a clean record wish for daylight and company. But to Slim Anderson, who had shipped on the "Carrier Dove" to defeat justice, his wish was more like an unuttered prayer.

His memory opened the book of his past life to the blackest page. Then his imagination fed on the revolting details of a murder he had committed. He saw before him the lifeless body, ghastly beneath the lurid lights of the gambling hall. He could hear the blood dripping with a sickening spatter on the linoleum. That dripping of the blood, how realistic it sounded. It was only the drip of the dew from the booms.

The scurry and squeak of the rats in the lazerette worked into his imagination. First it slightly amused him. It sounded like the hurried march of an army. Then it changed to the footsteps and voices of pursuers. He caught himself listening with half consciousness for an officer's approach and slightly moving aside to escape hands that seemed to reach through the pitchy darkness to grab for him.

Suddenly on the port he thought he saw a light flash. His heart flew into his mouth and his breath came in burning gasps. "God," but it frightened him. It seemed that he must scream and break the awful silence.

Then from the starboard side, right beneath him, a metallic, terror-filled voice rang out, "For God's sake, pick me up. I've floated on this watery hell for seventeen days."

Slim Anderson collapsed on the deck nearly delirious with fear. Every nerve and fiber of his being was taut from fear of that nameless voice that died in the awful silence with a pitiful quaver. His ears strained, fairly yearned to hear that loathsome voice again, and banish the uncertainty that it had been nothing but a bad dream.

Then again that ghostly voice with its plea for aid broke the solitude like the cry of a tortured soul. "My God, Mates, you won't leave a castaway to die on this watery hell, will you?"

Slim Anderson leaped to his feet and started for the forecastle. He fell from the poop to the main deck. He regained his feet and stumbling over hatches, ropes and bumping masts and deckhouses, he finally reached the forecastle. He tumbled in a cowering heap on the floor.

A light was lit by the awakened seamen who asked what the row was about. Slim could barely control his quivering voice enough to whisper between gulps and sobs. "They's—a—ghost—on the—starboard stern."

This brought forth a roar of laughter that stopped as suddenly as it started. That voice, now cold and commanding rang out once more, "For God's sake, pick me up!"

There is courage in numbers, so they took the sea lantern and hurried aft with Slim Anderson among them. Fighting Hans had been awakened by the commotion and was on deck, as nervous and frightened as any of them. But when he saw them coming down the weather side of the ship, his sneering manner returned.

"All here, all here," he said. "Holy Saints, are you all here? Can't you speak? Answer me, answer me! I never shipped such a bunch of beach-combers before."

One by one, they reported present in hushed voices as they clustered about the lantern. Then silence fell. Something rubbed against the quivering leg of Slim Anderson. He jumped aside. There was a soft scurry on deck then a plaintive "M-e-o-w."

The sailors broke into a suppressed laugh. That angered him so much that he forgot his fear and launched a random kick in the general direction of the cat. It landed in Davy Jones' midriff. He sailed, yowling, through the air and splashed in the water, followed by the heavier splash of Slim Anderson's sea boot.

Fighting Hans instantly sensed what had happened and with an oath, sprang for him. He grabbed him by the throat and then a blinding glare came from an upward angle. He stood petrified. He let Slim Anderson slip from his fingers to the deck where he began to blubber a prayer.

Fighting Hans alone remained standing. A scraping and soft rasping noise was heard on the side of the boat. Then Fighting Hans cried out, "Save me, save me, Oh, God, I'm not ready! Good-bye, mates, an octopus has—" The rest of his speech was muffled incoherency.

When daylight came the sailors saw a life raft alongside with a barrel on it, that obscured all but the legs of a man. Davy Jones was howling and vainly trying to climb on the revolving boot.

There was nothing to the man but legs, and they were straw, and a pair of trousers. The barrel was a metal contraption, fitted up with wires and batteries. Some of it was stamped "International Wireless Telephone." The sailors saw no use for it. It had a mighty uncanny atmosphere about it anyway, so they sank it with scrap iron.

When the sailors got the ship into port, no two of them agreed as to how the skipper disappeared. Yet, they all agreed in pointing the finger of suspicion at Slim Anderson. He was tried for taking the skipper's life and heaving him overboard. He was found guilty and given a life sentence.

It is odd, but he is still there. Perhaps the hand of God, sometimes called fate, is what keeps him there. He is innocent of the crime he was found guilty of, but he is guilty of a crime he was never tried for.

When the German submarine base was captured in the South Pacific, Carlos Schuler was found in command of one. In a hospital ward was found Fighting Hans. He made his personality felt before he was seen by his words, "Say, you sauer-kraut-eating horse doctor, hustle me a drink, drink, drink!"

Fighting Hans was lying on his stomach, allowing a raw spot in his shoulder to heal where a patch of skin had been artistically removed. In the next ward was Carlos Schuler lying on his back, allowing the same parcel of skin to grow on his face and hide a livid scar inflicted nearly a quarter of a century ago.

When Carlos was asked how he got such a realistic note of terror in the voice he transmitted over the wireless telephone, he replied, "I had a passenger. I just held a knife to his throat and told him what to say."

When he was asked why he did not sink the "Carrier Dove," he meaningly replied, "She did not owe me anything."

The Sunbeam

By Felix Fluegel

Myriad colored sunbeams
Creep through the forest
And light the bows
Of the dismal colored trees.
Resplendent in unfathomable happiness
The violet nods its head,
Its velvet eyelids sparkling;
And the buzzing of the bee;
The wild lilac quivering,
Moist with the tears of the night!
And the brooklet singing,
As it dashes over silver colored rocks.
It is the sunbeam that gives life
To nature's untold wonders!

The Chameleon

By Evelyn Lowry

SEE what I have up my sleeve," Julian Bower casually remarked to his friend, Al Keef, as he nudged close to him on a crowded street corner just as the five o'clock crowds were pouring out of the sky-scrapers from all sides and surging restlessly toward the transportation centers which would start them on their way homeward.

"That's no friend to have up your sleeve. Ooh! You sometimes remind me of a creeping insect." And Al Keef shuddered.

Such were his impressions when he saw only outer appearances. If his eyes could have been focused so as to perceive the inner man he would have found in Julian Bower all of the chameleon and more.

"Well, how's business today?" Al Keef inquired.

"Booming. I sold over 100 bottles of 'Curo' today. Pretty good for a rounder like me don't you think?"

"I'll say it is," Al Keef replied. "But just how long can you keep this up?" he asked in an uneasy tone. "Have you no fear that your popularity might run out? Won't people get tired of buying?"

"What's this for?" Julian Bower counter questioned, confidently tapping his forehead. "Inside that brain of mine is unlimited cleverness. With it I can combat with any opposition; can defy it."

As he spoke he drew himself up to his full six-foot two, and squared his shoulders. He seemed indeed a dynamo of physical power while at the same time his decisive, positive attitude gave one the impression of mental power.

Al Keef looked at him doubtfully and then shrugged his shoulders.

"Perhaps you're righ Bower. But I'm glad it's you and not me."

Julian Bower folded his arms and took a deep breath. Then he replied in a calm, low tone:

"Thin ice isn't so bad; if you know how to skate on it."

Al Keef in the jostling crowd had to stand very near his friend. With his five feet four, his head came none above Julian Bower's shoulder. Bower's folded arm touched close to Al Keef's neck.

Keef suddenly felt a chilly sensation run up and down his spine as a cold, paralyzing object touched the back of his neck. He wheeled furiously and confronted his friend.

"Keep your arm away from me," he muttered. "You needn't think I want any snakes down my neck."

A sly, triumphant smile passed over Julian Bower's face.

"Afraid! Afraid of a rattle snake! And a harmless one at that."

But nevertheless Al Keef accompanied Julian Bower home that night to dinner.

"I hate to do this," Al Keef commented. He gazed out the window of the swift moving elevated and thought a moment. "It takes no fool to see that your wife dislikes me worse than I do that snake," he finished.

"Don't let that worry you," Bower replied nonchalantly. "You're not the only one Zara dislikes."

He reflected a moment on what he had said then chuckled gleefully to himself. And Al Keef was puzzled but not abashed.

As Zara Bower hung up the receiver of her telephone her face was contorted with wrath. After a moment's reflection she started out and began to pace, like a tiger in its cage, backward and forward then, forward and backward the entire length of her two-room, convertable sixty dollar a month apartment de luxe, located on the second floor of a many story building occupying half the block.

Stopping beside the glass door over-looking the court she stared intentedly out. Yet it was not the objects out there that she was seeing but in her mind's eye she was picturing Al Keef's face across the dinner table again this even-ing.

"It makes three times this week," she was mumbling to herself. "And how I do detest that man. If Julian Bower had the sense of his childhood he would stay away from him completely. But he never takes my advice; yet it always turns out in the end that I'm right."

As she reflected she heard steps in the stone corridor and presently a key turn in the entrance door across the room.

Now the history of Bower's life story if told in minute detail might fill a vol-ume. He had lived so fast and expe-rienced so much in his brief thirty-five years that details from the past were vague in his own mind. Consequently he often became muddled and confused when he tried to put fragments of events together.

And Al Keef, he noticed, seemed to enjoy his confusion as he took advantage of every opportunity to produce it.

To state it briefly, the parts most con-cerned here, Julian Bower first saw this world's light in a circus car somewhere in the mid-Western United States. His parents were stellar performers on a well known circus.

At a young age he, too, started his career on the saw-dust. Time brought him recognition, popularity, even fame. But he soon got a case of the almost in-evitable conceit, the usual aftermath of such honors and it went to his head.

As a relief he forsook the footlights and became a glob-trotter. His wander-ings carried him on an exploring tour through the wilds of the Andes. It was here that he learned from the native In-dians how to mix the herbs for his 'Curo' tonic which he guaranteed would cure all the ills that humanity was heir to.

Soon afterwards he found himself in Buenos Aires where he struck up a friendship with one Von Schroder which was proving to be the one most regret-table event of his life. For Von Schroder

was wiley and before Bower knew it he found himself in a clutching vise of in-trigue from which he had never been able to escape.

He finally drifted to San Francisco and there married Zara Winters, a former team-mate. Zara had also forsaken the footlights and had rented a suite of fur-nished rooms, out of the front window of which hung the sign:

MADAME ZARA,
The Honest Clairvoyant,
Readings 50c and up.

About that time there was a crusade against clairvoyants, in general, and un-scrupulous ones of Zara's type in par-ticular, so her professional sign was re-versed to a "To Let" sign and together she and Julian Bower departed for Chi-cago.

They conceived the idea of manufac-turing this "Curo" tonic and in due time obtained a factory and went to work on it. Guided by Zara's penetrating mind, for she did have occult talent and gov-erned by the uncanny ways of fate had adopted business methods of a queer, unusual sort, but which soon won him immediate and tremendous success.

Purchasing a motor truck and obtain-ing a chimpanzee monkey, a yak and a rattle snake, and the aid of a former cir-cus friend, he sat up for himself a mina-ture show. His troupe was made up of a dangerous combination and his per-formances were sometimes highly excit-ing; and they drew the crowds.

These shows he reeled off four times each day at four designated places in the slums of the big city. And after each show he went through a five-minute mon-ologue preparatory to selling "Curo." He had a good, clever, convincing line of talk and it was surprising to see how many denizens of the slums fell for it and paid the 50c for a bottle of the tonic. This day he had done unusually well and sold over a hundred bottles which brings us back to the evening in the apartment with Al Keef as his guest.

Al Keef took a deep puff at his after-dinner cigar then regarded it thought-fully for a moment.

"Bower, how did you ever come to get

into this business?" he asked.

"That's no business of yours," Mrs. Bower cut in uncermoniously.

"I've often wondered myself," Bower answered with disregard. "I've often tried to figure how I ever came to be in such a business as this."

"You forget to mention that it was I who put you there," Zara put in.

Al Keef cast a sharp, sidewise glance at her but said nothing. What he was thinking was that this Zara had one of the sharpest tongues of any woman he had ever encountered. And he had seen it evidenced only when it was well under restraint. He was trying to picture how it would be when under the pressure of her ungovernable temper, it would be turned loose completely. Though he little knew it then, there was destined to come a day when he was to hear Zara Bower's entire raving vocabulary, almost in one breath.

Al Keef had no sooner stepped outside the door that night when the following stormy session was heard to ensue:

"That man Keef is a government detective; mark my word for it J. B."

"What makes you think he is? Bower questioned.

"You can't fool me. I've seen enough types in my day to know. If he's not a detective he's a crook of some kind."

"You're not sure, then, that he is a detective?" Bower persisted.

"Not sure but I think he is. He's submarineing around here I can tell that."

"You're a great spiritualist, you are. I don't only think he's a detective. I know it."

"Why J. B. And you bringing him here to this house."

"Why not? I like this fellow, Keef. No matter what his business is he's a real man."

"But J. B. this is playing with fire!"

"You should worry. I'm doing nothing wrong; why need I fear him?"

"You are steering your ship on the rocks, J. B. You are moving fast toward your doom. Something tells me that very plainly." Zara said this in her slow, solemn, professional tone which in by-gone days had so often directed the destinies

of those who had come to seek her advice.

But it carried little weight with Julian Bower.

"I've got a good pilot?" he muttered. And that ominous characteristic of the chameleon, that same sly, sarcastic, triumphant smile was once again seen to cross his face.

If Zara had forseen Julian Bower's doom on the night before she did not long to wait for its first harbinger on the following morning.

Answering a ring of the buzzer she learned that some acquaintance from out of town was seeking Julian Bower.

Inviting him up she found that he announced himself as Von Schroder from New York and explained that he had known her husband in Buenos Aires.

Zara found Von Schroder to be a man after her own heart. They had the same standard of social ethics, both of the anarchist order, and they looked at life from the same angle. It did not take them long, therefore, to become warm friends and to find themselves sharing each other's plots and confidences just as though they had been life long acquaintances.

"I wish I had met you two years ago," Zara was saying, "we might have been millionaires by this time."

"How is that?" Von Schroder questioned.

"Why, through the manufacture of 'Curo' tonic. That's a wonderful thing. But J. B. hasn't got get-up enough to go ahead and do the way I want him to, about it. He's too blamed honest. He had ought to have been born a saint, that man had."

Von Schroder reflected a moment and his eyes narrowed.

"Yes? Bower is rather too honest. But he, too, has his other side. And he can change from one to the other so completely that he completely eradicates the first; a veritable chameleon he is. And he possesses the clearest brain of any one I have ever met," Von Schroder added.

Here Zara blurted out a disagreement. "Clever! J. B. clever? He's never showed it around me." And she scoffed at the idea. "I've always been the one to go ahead and do all the planning; blaze all the trails."

"Perhaps you've never got him started on the right track. You can't drive him you know. He's too sensitive for that. You just have to let him go along and pick his own way."

"Pick his own way! Ha, we'd soon be in the poor house if I waited for him to pick his way."

"You're not very good team-mates are you?"

"Not as life partners, no. Before the footlights, in the world of make-believe, we made a go of it. Then, too, that was when J. B. was attractive and a somebody. Now he's nothing but a plain peddier," she finished with contempt.

"You know," Von Schroder remarked thoughtfully, "I believe you are just the person I've been looking for for a long time."

Zara seemed to comprehend but did not reply for the door had silently opened and Julian Bower stood on its threshold.

Down at the headquarters of the Intelligence Service Al Keef leaned back in his easy chair and thoughtfully puffed at his cigar. The latest "extra" lay folded in his lap as yet unread. A fellow detective came up and tapping him on the shoulder casually remarked:

"I hear Von Schroder, alias Fritz Herman, has arrived in our city."

"Yes, he's in our midst," Al Keef laconically replied.

"He's your man. Don't let him slip out of your noose," he was cautioned.

"Don't be concerned. I know just where I can put my hands on him. But I want to let him go for a few days. I'm waiting for further developments."

But a week went by without any "developments" materializing; that is, so that Al Keef might see them. But deeper things were happening right along in the Bower factory which he knew nothing about. And this Bower factory was the source of trouble which the whole Intelligence force were keenly on the alert to find. But they didn't know that either.

It all started one morning some few days after Von Schroder's arrival. It was Zara who first outlined to her husband a proposition whereby he could not only sell his tonic, but could make worlds of money on the side.

Bower listened in silence till she had finished, then calmly gave her a piece of his mind; told her what he thought of her crookedness and plotting and said he would have none of it.

Seeing that she was losing ground Von Schroder stepped up.

"You refuse?" he asked with a tone of menace in his voice.

"I most certainly do," Bower replied without flinching.

Then Von Schroder retorted to his mighty and effective weapon which never failed him. He knew he had Bower in his clutches and he let him know the fact.

Bower had come to a parting of the ways and he didn't know just which road to travel. If he turned and opposed Von Schroder, as here in his own country he felt he dared, the best he could hope for would not make for him a very rosy future. He could probably escape from Von Schroder's clutches but would doubtless be hounded the rest of his life.

But he had just about decided to take a chance at it when Zara in some subtle manner changed his mind. He would also have to oppose her, he reasoned, and oh, well, if she could travel down hill to the bottom of life's strata he, too, could go along.

So that afternoon Von Schroder presented him with a doped bottle of tonic to take along with him on his journey to the slums.

"You see, it's wrapped differently," Von Schroder advised. "Now do be careful and don't get it mixed up with the others or we'll all have the fiddler to pay."

"I don't see why you can't come along down and pass out this abominable bottle yourself," Bower said peevishly.

"You fool! Don't you realize I'm watched? Haven't I said I don't dare go out in your company or meet your companions, especially your friend Keef? I'm shadowed. You're not; and it would be an easy thing for you to do as I ask. You are running no risk at all."

"I don't like the idea of it," he muttered as he went out the door.

Julian Bower had fully made up his mind to take that bottle to Intelligence Headquarters and show it to Al Keef. He could explain himself out of the situation he was sure for he had not as yet committed any overt act of wrong-doing.

But on his arrival he learned that Keef was not there. Julian Bower was silent a moment; he was trying to think what to do. His hand was on the bottle in his pocket. In two minutes he could produce it and explain the whole thing. But the sleuth who happened to be destined to act as the pivot force in this turn of Julian Bower's career was a stranger to him and did not encourage the confidence, so he turned and left the room with the bottle still in his pocket.

Outside the door he stopped and hesitated; he too took the bottle out and looked at it. Soon that sly, triumphant smile of the chameleon crept over his face and he hastened on to his work.

At the appointed hour the short, well-dressed man with the black hair and black mustache came up to a conspicuous place in the crowd and twirled his cane three successive times — the signal for the bottle.

Then the stranger went on his way; but the next morning the exciting headlines on the front pages of the newspapers told the grim story of how a powder mill a short distance away had been blown up and of the fearful loss of life as the result. Next time it was a munition factory; another time, a bridge. And still no clue could be obtained by the officials in charge of the work of tracing it down. But chance and science often go hand in hand, and sometimes chance proves its practicability over science.

It happened so on this day when Karnes, one of the heads of the Intelligence Service, found himself enjoying an aimless stroll through the slums. He happened upon Julian Bower and his side-show. He stopped and listened:

"This 'Curo' tonic," Bower was saying, "contains all of the curative elements in existence. I don't care whether you have sciatica, neuralgia, rheumatism, or just an ordinary tooth-ache, take a bottle

home with you and be well in the morning. It's only fifty cents. You spent that much for a patent medicine at the druggists and it does you no good. You know that's true. Come now, how many of you are going to show that you believe in miracles and buy a bottle of 'Curo' for 'Curo' works miracles."

This all, somehow, sifted through Karnes' crusty indifference and he listened with interest, which was unusual for him. It made its appeal chiefly because Karnes was suffering from a bothersome tooth-ache at the time and any means of curing it appealed to him.

"Guess I'm a fool to buy the stuff," he thought to himself, "but here goes."

Obtaining the bottle he put it in his pocket and started on homeward.

Julian Bower had gone ahead and finished that show on schedule and incidentally handed out the special bottle at the given signal; had gone up to his next place and was about half through with his show there when a messenger rushed up in haste, with a message to return home immediately with the utmost speed.

Bower read the message through twice, the sly smile crossed his face, and he went on with his show. It was another parting of the ways and the route he took hastened him on toward his destiny.

Karnes back at headquarters sat chatting with Al Keef and incidentally produced the bottle of tonic.

"Where did that come from?" Al Keef inquired.

"I bought it for this pesky tooth-ache. Think it will cure it?"

Al Keef laughed heartily.

"I doubt it. I am familiar with the inside facts about that stuff. I know the man who makes it."

"You do," exclaimed the miffed Karnes trying to open the bottle. It seemed to be glued to the carton so he started tearing it off. As he did so a little square of paper fluttered to the floor.

"That must be the inside directions you speak of," Karnes said sarcastically, as he reached for the paper.

But as he started to read it the utter amazement registered on his face showed that it was not the directions concerning the tonic. It was written some in code, some in English, some in a foreign language; and on the reverse side was a detailed map of the ground floor of the post office, with direction for placing a bomb.

Needless to say, it did not take Al Keef and Karnes long to get back to Julian Bower's corner. And this last side-show of his was given a touch that was highly dramatic. It was a brief affair but proved highly exciting during the three or four minutes that it lasted. Julian Bower offered no resistance nor did he explain matters. He knew what Al Keef had come there for and he realized that the game was up. So they took Bower minus his motor and paraphernalia, but plus his rattlesnake, along with them.

But over in the Bower factory much consternation was going on. Von Schroder fidgeted restlessly, going from one desk to the other, and from one end of the office to the other, keeping constantly on the move. He looked at his watch about every two minutes, then unseeingly compared it with the office clock. The short man with the black mustache followed around after him, submissive, obedient.

Finally Von Schroder turned his tense, set face toward him:

"Here, take this," he said, handing him a roll of bills. "Now beat it; you know where to. That is if you can make it; if you can't . . . . do the other way."

The little dark complected man hesitated a moment, then slowly started toward the door.

"Good-bye, and may luck be with you," called Von Schroder.

"The blundering idiot," Von Schroder remarked to Zara as she came up. "It looks as though he hasn't even sense enough to come home."

"I'd give a whole lot to know whether he sold that bottle or not. There's still a chance that it might be among those left over—but there goes the phone. Maybe it will enlighten us."

It was calling Von Schroder and it must have enlightened him for he scooted like lightening out of the office to be gone for all time.

Zara was left standing in amazement

and the next thing she knew Al Keef walked into the room. She noticed a certain positiveness in his manner and a deliberateness in his stride she had never seen before. A moment later a strange thrill of fear seized her as she felt a cold steel revolver pressed against her side.

But her fighting instinct soon arose to the surface and Al Keef found before he got through with her that he was encountering a veritable tiger in petticoats and then some. As it happened there was no one else in the office to give aid to Zara should they have been inclined to do so. But she was equal to the occasion herself, and when Al Keef walked out of that office he was minus his collar, a few handfulls of hair, a button or so, on his waist-coat, and his dignity. It needn't be added that Zara got away.

After Bower's military trial, Keef called to see him. It was more of a friendly call than anything else camouflaged under the guise of professionalism.

"Tomorrow, Keef, they say I face the firing squad. They tell me it was you mostly who convicted me, but in my heart I find no room to blame you. I've had time to think it over these last few days and life doesn't mean to me what it used to. But deep in my inner consciousness burns the deepest resentment against those who have dragged me down. To my last hour I'll pray for their doom. And when I die I intend to go the limit toward securing their undoing; haunt them, too, if I can."

And in his life's final scene Julian Bower proved that he was equal to his destiny for his demeanor was still that of a conqueror and not the conquered and on his face lingered the same sly, tranquil, triumphant smile of the chameleon.

The next day the sirens blew and bells rang, heralds of the dawn of peace on earth once more and which the populace joyously and noisily celebrated. Al Keef's thoughts somehow went back to his late friend Bower.

"If he could have kept above that tide of intrigue for another week it might not have engulfed him," he mused, half aloud. "He was technically false to his country though in his heart I am convinced he was loyal. He seemed to be condemned through no fault of his own . . . . well, a traitor deserves a traitor's death." And Al Keef's jaws squared while he resumed his silent smoking.

Never Again

By Frank M. Vancil

Never again, how sad the thought
How bitter with remembrance fraught;
To know and feel we can regain
Life's parted pleasures, never again.

Never again will youth's gay morn
The pleasing spring of life adorn;
Never backward our steps we'll tread;
Never again the day that's sped.

Never again can we recall
The woeful wrongs, that like a pall
Obscure the light with shadowy tears
Along our path in earlier years.

Never again will time extend
A beck'ning hand our paths to mend;
Over again no more, alas—
We may review, but not repass.

Never again will the forms we meet
In crowded hall or busy street,
Appear to us as met before,
Or as they were in days of yore.

Never again will a loved one's voice
Bid our hearts anew rejoice;
A presence dear we shall retain
Never again. Never again.

After Twenty Years

By Theodore Pratt

PRETTY Delores Van Nest tossed her well-shaped brown head with a jerk of impatience. She and Ralph Thompson had gone for a day's outing on the Ramasee and were now spending the hot afternoon on the cool grass of the river bank watching the boats travel and toot their way up and down.

"Why don't you give up this writing idea, dear?" she asked a trifle impatiently, "we've been engaged three years and yet you can't make enough for us to get married." She looked at him half-wistfully, half-angrily, as if waiting for him to concede.

"I know, I know, Delores," he said a bit dreamily, "and as God knows I am sure it will come—soon. My stuff is better; I know it is — within another year . . . ." Ralph was twenty-two, dark, not extremely handsome but good to look upon, and her elder by a year.

"But another year is too long, Ralph," she frowned, "you've been writing for seven now, and where have you gotten yourself? It can't hang on like this. Your stories are good; I know enough about writing to say that; but that is your whole trouble, they are only good. They must be distinctive. Now—"

Delores, please," he broke in, "my stories—"

"Don't sell."

"Give me time, dear," he pleaded, "one more year and the editors will be glad to buy my work; I know, I have faith in myself. I could succeed now if I lowered myself to dribble, but I can't do that, I must make literature." His proud, rather young face had a look of eagerness as if the matter were already a fact.

"I know all that," she cried, "you've told me—so many times. Just the same the editors won't buy your work — you know—you've tried them all. Why can't you get a position?"

"My temperament wouldn't stand it, Delores, and I would fail worse than ever."

"Yet we could get married," she argued.

"Yes, we could get married," he said, "but neither of us would be happy. It would be a sad life for us both to know that I gave up my life work for a position. I don't believe I could live, yet make it happy for you."

"Then you persist in this writing idea that will ruin both our lives?"

"I can do nothing else, Delores, dear."

"Then I—I can no longer keep our engagement, Ralph."

"Delores." He spoke her name softly and then repeated, "Delores, dear. Yes, oh, God, I see how you look at it. Yet you love me?

"I love you, Ralph! I do love you!"

"I am glad, Delores, glad, and yet I will free you. Some day one of us will be sorry. It may be you or it may be I. We shall see."

The girl sobbing for a time and the man pensively moody, they drifted silently back to the dock and then said goodbye for the last time.

In the nine mortal months that followed they saw each other many times but did not once speak. There seemed to be a common agreement between them that each had cast the other out of their life forever. Delores went about with Sam Scott, a young man who worked diligently at nothing and lived on his father's rather corpulant income. Ralph's life was one long dreary tread of work. He labored or studied fourteen hours a day. He wrote, he typed, he revised, recast, rewrote, tore up, mailed, and once in a while sold. He was steeped in authorship, magazinedom, technique, style, plot, point of view, subject matter, titling and all the decalogues that go with it. The once in a while became oftener as the months slid by. Ralph was earning his place.

A year after their scene on the river bank Ralph was an accepted author. He was even becoming famous, and yet, he did not now care.

He had won out and Delores had deserted him. Life seemed empty and dead. He expected Delores to marry Sam Scott yet she never did.

Delores in the meantime had been having hard sledding. With no parents and the same amount of money she had taken up teaching. Her meagre income only but succeeded in making possible her existence. Her fresh, bright beauty was waning and Delores was becoming a white ethereal lily, devoid of animation and life.

One day, he did not know how it came about, Ralph found himself talking about Delores with Mrs. Burton, one of his few women acquaintances.

"It was unfortunate—more than unfortunate," he said, "and yet she really cannot be blamed. I loved her—"

"Do you still love her, Ralph?"

"In the great way, I do," he replied, "although sometimes I don't. If I ever saw her again I would know."

"Do you think—would you marry her now if she came back to you?"

He sat for a long time thinking deeply. At last he said slowly:

"If she came back to me of her own free will, with no knowledge that I would yet marry her—I would. But she will not—would not—cannot."

"And yet she might," commented Mrs. Burton, and she seemed to be thinking to herself.

"However, nevertheless — won't," he said.

But the day after Mrs. Burton's call he was astounded by a visit from Delores. They had not spoken to each other for a year. She was pale and nervous and he yearned to tell her how sorry he was, and help her if he could. He could see that she was weeping.

As Ralph took her hand and led her in she cried for a time and then said:

"Ralph, my eyes have been opened—I have seen that I was wrong; you have and could have succeeded."

He waved that aside but did not speak. She continued:

"And yet I have not come to ask your forgiveness, for you can never forgive me. I have come to tell you that—that I love you—cannot do without you—and I thought, you see, I kind of thought—"

"You would have me take you back?"

"I do not deserve it!"

He slumped in his chair and did not see. His inner-most instincts were for him to clasp her in his arms and press his lips to her hot bloodless ones a thousand times. Yet—Mrs. Burton had told her. She would not otherwise know. His pent emotion cooled and with the cooling he spoke.

"Once, Delores, I loved you. God, how I loved you! I would have died at your feet had you wanted it . . . . you deserted me because you thought I could not win—I have won now and you would come back. I still love you—I shall always love you; God knows that! Yet not of your own free will you would come back to me. My heart is still and dead. My very soul is shriveled and gone. Everything is crushed and beaten. And with it—you."

She rose, swaying and her cheeks were wet.

"I—I could not expect you to believe anything else. If you can, forgive me. Forever and ever—good-bye." She was gone.

For twenty long years Ralph did not write. In those years he spent his time in every part of the globe that was inhabitable by man. After twenty years, gray and aged beyond his time, he returned.

A little, tired looking woman got off the train at the time he also stepped to the platform. Once her drawn face must have been beautiful, but now it was old and tired. Her pure white hair was arranged all in too young a style for its color, and yet the style for its age. Delores too had grown old before her time.

He was not startled when he recognized her. When she saw him she gave a weak little cry and a bright new light lit in her eye.

"It—it is you, Ralph?" she questioned timidly.

"Yes, Delores, it is me, grown old and gray as have you."

"And you—you have not married?"

"No, Delores, there was no one for me to marry. And you?"

A watery mist covered her faded eyes that all too well answered his question. A deep silence followed and by common consent the two old young people walked up the deserted street.

"Delores," said the man, "you probably know that if you had come to me that day twenty years ago, of your own free will, we could have been happy. Now we are both old and gray—and neither of us married. Oh, if Mrs. Burton had never told you and you had come!"

"You mean—you told Mrs. Burton you could be reconciled if I came to you of my own free will?"

"Yes."

"And—and she told me?"

"Yes, Delores."

A strange light of mingled horror and amazement shone in her face. Then she thought of twenty long years of misery, toil and lonesomeness. She thought of what might have been and caught him tightly by the arm. "Ralph, Ralph— dear," she cried and moaned as she looked up into his worn face, "Mrs. Burton— Mrs. Burton never told me—I came that day—of my own free will! Twenty— long—years."

The Two Pathways

By Lovina M. Atwood

Two pathways stretched out there before
  me—
One broad, and so smooth, and so fair;
Fine trees to cast cool shadows o'er me—
  Sweet flowers lent their breath to the air.

The other was rough, and my going
  Would be much more tiresome, and slow;
But I sprang to that rough pathway, knowing
  That it led where I wanted to go.

And hopes blossomed out to fulfilling,
  Were the flowers that bestrewed that long
    way,
And kind deeds by hearts brave and willing,
  Made duty a pleasure each day.

The Race

By Charles Jeffries

THE sun was at his best; the dried leaves gathered in little windrows; the cracks in the ground gaped wider and wider — cotton-picking time had come.

The cotton was good, and some real feats in picking were being performed round about. It was mainly the local champion, Bud McCaslin, and the stray hand, Raz Farewell, who were breaking the old records. This naturally bred a desire in the neighborhood to see the two men pitted against one another. So, after a good deal of talking and some little purse opening, a race was matched.

The contestants were to begin picking at sun-up, rest an hour at noon and pick till sundown; which, at that season, meant about twelve hours of many-trying work. Two of their backers, Radford and Smith, were to carry the cotton to the scales, bring them water and render any other legitimate assistance. An umpire would weigh the cotton, see that it was picked clean and settle any difference that might arise.

At the word, the men began picking at a smooth, steady "lick." At first, they did not pick much faster than the other hands, crawled on their knees and reserved their backs for the later strain. They were not working side by side, but when they came close enough, they carried on a sporadic conversation — the weather, the coming dance, anything but the business in hand. Under their light talk and careless air, they were probing and prying, each other, trying to learn just how formidable his opponent was, especially if he had something up his sleeve.

Toward the middle of the morning, somebody brought a jug of cold water from the well. They drank and Raz stopped long enough to roll a cigarette.

Bud, accepting the truce, sat down, removed a pebble from his knee and cut off a chew of Star Navy. It was not theirs, however, to enjoy fully the old weed. After a few hurried puffs Raz threw away his cigarette and Bud, twenty minutes later, spat out his chew of Star nearly as full of juice as when he cut it off.

Their scraps of conversation grew wider and wider apart, finally ceasing altogether. They increased their speed till by ten o'clock they had worked up to a real championship gait. A fine breeze fanned them and their splendid muscles flexed almost without friction. It was worth while to watch them. Raz was the stronger man. He had a powerful chest and a well-shaped hand. But was built slender after the Southwestern model. His hair was red and his forehead narrow. Raz attacked a stalk in a series of little, jerky movements that removed the cotton astonishingly. Bud always began at the top of a stalk and worked downward, using a kind of slippery "lick" that was hard to understand.

At a little after eleven, it happened that both their sacks were weighed at the same time. Bud was three pounds ahead. Radford came back from the scales and told Raz. Raz, for the first time that morning, got up on his feet and went to picking cotton. The movements of his hands became too swift to follow. With the quickness of a cat, he would catch a ball and with the artistry of a violinist, his fingers would seek the intricacies of the burr. Each hand worked independently of the other and almost without the aid of eyesight. When a burr pulled off, he caught it between his teeth or drew it across his pants leg and did it without a break in the work. That was the beauty of the work—the ma-

3

chine-like regularity. It was from one boll to another, and on to the next, ever on to the next.

Bud, when he saw his opponent speeding up, turned himself loose too. His movements were slower, but he got the cotton all the same. His long arms wound and reached through the stalks, cleaning up the bolls as they went. He sank his fingers deep in the burrs and rarely failed to pull out all the cotton at the first grab. He was a little more light and careful in his movements and pulled off fewer burrs than Raz.

These peculiarities of work were too fine and too swiftly performed to be detected; about all that a casual observer could make out was that Bud, with less exertion, appeared to be picking as much as Raz. But he wasn't. Very, very slowly Raz crept ahead and at noon he weighed up ten pounds the most.

No extensive preparations had been made for the event. Dinner was brought to the field. The only protection from the sun was the meager shade cast by the wagon. Chairs and table there were none, but what cared these men of the rough? All hands sluiced their heads and arms with cool water, then did what any bunch of hungry men would do. Bud and Raz left to the others the good things in the basket and stuck rather to the bacon and cornbread and beans. As soon as the meal was over, Raz pulled off his jumper, slung it on a cottonstalk, spread his sack under the wagon and in one minute was sound asleep.

Bud did not relax so readily. He leaned against the wagon-wheel, took a chew of tobacco and talked a little. But when the drowsiness did come over him, it gripped him strong and stretching out on the hard ground, he too, slept like a child. At two minutes before one o'clock the umpire awoke them. Bud arose at once, put on a clean jumper, took a drink of water and at the word "go" began picking at a good, swift gait.

Raz was hard to wake. He rubbed his eyes a good deal, gaped, rubbed his bare arms and worked the joints. When Radford reminded him that it was nearly time to go to work he said, "ughhuh," drew a long breath and arose heavily.

It was only by a mighty effort that he took his place at the end of the row. The sleep lay heavily in his bones and, to save his life, he couldn't speed up. Bud picked off from him and at the first weighing, gained back the ten pounds.

The real race had just begun. The morning's work was more a wearing off of the wire edge, more of scheming and conserving strength for the final dash. This evening they would go through at full speed. Their staying qualities would be tested, doubly tested, for the August sun now looked down with unpitying eye. The fine breeze had ceased to blow, great yellow clouds slowly piled in the northeast and the heat was sickening. Not a buzzard sailed in the sky, not a red-ant stirred, not a wasp moved. Of all created things only these men worked. The wilted leaves of the cotton hung straight downward. Across the fields, in a million winking eyes, the lazy-lawrence shimmered and danced. The heat seemed a thing real, a tangible something of spirit and life that gripped and pervaded and absorbed. It was more noticeable than any thing else on earth, ay, more noticeable than the earth itself or the sky above the earth. Its effect, together with that of the glare and stillness, was more weird than any moonlight or snowstorm.

More trying on the men than the heat or the back-breaking work was the lack of water. The last jugfull had been drunk and the man who had gone after more, for some reason had not come back. But Bud and Raz were accustomed to such inconveniences and though the sun dried them out like rags before a fire, they didn't mind it greatly. They were not thinking about the heat and thirst; they were not thinking about anything—they were picking cotton. With faces contorted by ugly sun-grins and the grime thickening on their necks, they sought the elusive "lick." Unreasonable as it might appear, their clothes were dry, the fierce sun-rays evaporating the perspiration as rapidly as it pumped it from their bodies. This was evidenced by the grimy salt-circles that spread to their jumper tails. Especially stiff were their sleeves where they wiped their faces. Even their shoes showed the white, saline incrustations.

Though the ground burned their feet and the white glare hurt their eyes and the dry air parched their throats, they sacked the cotton. They enjoyed it. In complete abandon, they were doing their best; and in doing one's best the pleasure is always greater than the pain. At long intervals, a wisp of wind fanned by and though it was like a draught from a furnace to the two racers it was breath from heaven. It helped them beyond words, cooling their roasting bodies and filling their lungs with good live air.

After a time the water arrived. Bud tilting up a jug, with one eye shut, emptied it without breathing. Raz threw away the dipper and drank from the rim of the bucket, drank all he wanted. And during the remainder of the evening, contrary to all hygienic law, they, every thirty or forty minutes, drank water in unbelievable quantities and, what is more, drank it without the slightest ill effect. They stood such drinking because they were fit. They stood it because their ancestors before them had picked cotton and drunk water.

Suddenly, without ceremony, Raz straightened up and announced: "If I'm to pick with that gink, I want to get by his warm side." And, crossing the intervening ten or twelve rows, he dropped in behind Bud.

This closer proximity had a marked effect on the racers. They, somehow, got yet more out of themselves. From then on, neither one again picked on his knees. They gradually lost, or rather shelved their mentality. They became oblivious to their surroundings. What little intelligence they retained was centered on the work before them—the getting the cotton out of the burr. They had no idea how much they had picked during the day. They had no idea how long they had been picking. They never thought to ask for water or to change sacks. Smith and Radford looked after these things. And Smith and Radford, who understood the psychology of cotton picking, were very particular about stopping them when in full swing. The umpire, realizing their danger, took it upon

himself to stop them at regular intervals to drink and rest.

As they metamorphised themselves into machines, their movements became super-accurate and almost magical. To all appearance they but passed their hands around a stalk and the cotton jumped into their grasp. Smith and Bradford and the umpire stood in the sun and watched them. The other workers, men born and raised in a cotton patch, stopped work to watch them. All agreed that Bud and Raz were picking "some" cotton.

Now that they worked side by side, the race, to them, changed in character. Like race horses, they looked on it more as a matter of keeping ahead rather than picking the greater number of pounds. If from some natural advantage, a skip in the row, say, one of them slipped momentarily ahead, the other would work like a slave under the lash to catch up. The terrible work was telling. The clashing against thousands and thousands of sharp burrs had worn their fingers to the raw, broken and torn loose the nails. Their wrists were swelling. Their breasts and shoulders where the strap worked were rubbed raw. Their faces, from the constant wiping of perspiration were rubbed raw. The perspiration, running in their eyes, together with the glare of the white cotton, half blinded them. And their backs were so stiff they could hardly straighten up.

Indeed their plight was such that the umpire suggested that the bet be called off and the race stopped. Smith and Radford agreed willingly but Bud and Raz would not hear to it. They had gone too far to stop. Forgotten was any pecuniary reward that might be theirs. The spirit of contest animated them. They wanted to win, soul and body, they wanted to win.

It had long been evident that their staying qualities rather than speed, would decide the race, and as to which would first flag, opinion was divided. Raz had the muscle and lung power; but he needed them to offset Bud's economy of motion. Again, Raz did not change sacks nearly so often as Bud, and consequently did not lose the lick nearly so often, but

the heavier load he pulled was more ex-
hausting.

When the sun was about a half hour
high, it happened that for the first time
since dinner, both men's sacks were
weighed at the same time. When the figures were added up, it was found that
Bud had picked a thousand and five
pounds, while Raz's totaled a thousand
and twenty. Radford, highly elated, came
back and said to Raz: "You've got him,
old hoss. He'll never get by that fifteen
pounds." And to Smith he couldn't refrain from bragging: "You are going to
lose your bet; the time's too short for
him to ever catch up."

Smith paid no attention to Radford,
but watched Raz. He came quite near
Raz and studied his hands absorbedly.
Finally as if coming out of a trance he
turned to Radford and said: "I'll bet you
a hundred dollars more that Bud beats
him."

For answer, Radford filled out a check
and handed it to the umpire. Smith wrote
one for a like amount, but before turning
it over to the stakeholder, stipulating: "I
am doing this with the understanding
that the men will not be interfered with.
Their sacks will not need emptying any
more and there is no danger of sunstroke
this late. Is that agreeable?" Radford
nodded and the umpire gave his assent.

To Raz, who was picking some yards
in advance of Bud, Radford said: "Beat
him and that hundred is yours. All
you've got to do is stay ahead of him—
don't let him pass you."

Exhausted as they were, the way the
men responded to the inspiration was a
marvel. Raz said he would make it fifteen pounds better, and the way he
sprang to the work showed that he meant
it. The unswerving confidence that
Smith put in Bud must have stirred that
young man profoundly. He picked cotton as he had never done. Inch by inch,
he gained on Raz. Still it was clear to
the spectators that his slightly superior
speed would not gain back the fifteen
pounds; eight, or ten, they figured, was
all he could possibly recover. But, as if
sure of success, Bud bent to it. Powers
over which he had little control drove
him on.

Radford saw Bud's slow advance; and
while he knew there was little danger he
sought to encourage Raz, telling him to
keep steady and not let Bud pass him.
Raz must have divined something; anyhow he looked back. He saw Bud creeping up on him and while it caused him
no uneasiness, he tried to screw up his
speed a little. He got very close to the
cotton and his fingers left red stains in
the burrs.

Five or six minutes later, though he
tried not to, he looked back again. Bud
was considerably nearer. This inexorable creeping bothered Raz. He had
thought all along that in a burst of speed
he was the faster. From time to time, he
lost several precious half seconds in
looking back. It was not long till he
could see Bud without turning his head.
Like a machine, Bud was coming on. The
"shrish," "shrash," "shrow" of his salt-
stiffened jumper grated on Raz's ears in
his overstrained effort to stay ahead, he
fumbled the bolls and pulled off burrs.
In spite of all he could do, Bud continued to gain on him. Bud reached his
side—passed him. Raz made a frantic effort to recover the lost ground, scrambled
badly for a minute, then suddenly quit
and sank back on his sack.

Radford, fearing sunstroke, was at his
side in an instant. Raz would not answer
his anxious questions, but, in stubborn
silence, sat pecking at the ground with a
little stick. In great solicitude, Radford
continued to ask him what was the matter and if he wanted to be carried to the
wagon. Finally Raz, rather defiantly, replied that he wasn't going to kill himself
picking cotton for nobody, and, without
more ado, he straightened up, shouldered
his sack and walked off toward the
wagon. In a towering rage, Radford
started after him. Smith interceded, saying: "I wouldn't bother him; he's done
all he can do."

"All he can do, the devil! He's not half
as tired as Bud McCaslin, there."

"Probably not but Bud could, and
would, die a-picking; Raz couldn't. It's a
matter of will. I am surprised that he
held out as long as he did."

"Why? I like to know."

"Look at his thumb nails."

"Huh! They ain't in half as bad shape as Bud's" nails are, replied Radford cynically.

"Oh, not that. Look at the half moons. See if they are not blue instead of white."

"You mean he's part nigger?"

Smith nodded. "The high pressure brought it out."

"Well, I'll be dogged. Say, there, Bud, there ain't no use in you workin' your crazy self to death; pull off that sack and quit. You win."

Beyond the End the Trail

By Charles J. North

Out where the spirit listens
  To the rustle of unseen wings,
Out where the ear bends low to hear
  The voices of hidden things.
Out where the vision wanders,
  While a Presence uplifts the veil,
When days soft light fades into night—
  Beyond the end of the trail.

Out where the mem'ry glistens
  Through the rings of the blessed tears;
And souls of men grow strong again,
  To vanquish the waiting fears.
Out where the faith sees clearer
  Through the purple and thinning veil,
And far away into that day—
  Beyond the end of the trail.

Out where the wild vines clamber,
  And the shadows of green trees fall;
And ferns grow sweet where wild paths
      meet,
  And wild things are under all.
Out where the streams are flowing
  From a source that will never fail;
Where all that's best blends into rest—
  Beyond the end of the trail.

The Queen of the Silver-Sheet

By Milton Barth

JOHN BARCLAY hated women — hated them from the bottom of his heart. If he had been a woman, probably, he would have despised them. Just why he hated them was not known to his few but curious neighbors. They believed that he had a reason for this hatred and that that reason was a good one.

He seldom spoke of women and when he did, he referred to them as "skirts."

"Leave the 'skirts' alone,' he would say. "They only bring trouble. They do just as sure as a cloud brings rain."

I chanced upon his cabin at the Honeywell Mine over near the famous Yellow Horn Ridge some miles out of Jackson. It was situated in a lonely God-forsaken gulch. He met me at the door and invited me in. He would ask any man or dog into his hut but a woman — a woman couldn't get in if he were dying.

During the month that I stayed at his cabin, he worked incessantly at his pocket mine. I never heard him utter an oath. He had only one bad habit; he smoked continuously. At night, he would lean back in his chair or lay sprawled upon the bed and puff, puff, puff at his big pipe. A cloud of blue fantastic ill-smelling smoke always hung under the cabin roof.

I had not shaved for several weeks, having come to the Sierras for a period of rest made necessary by overwork, and I appeared very rough and unkept in the broken mirror nailed on the cabin door.

One night after a hard day's toil, Barclay and I were sitting before the open fireplace.

As the evening wore on, we told stories by the flickering light of the pitchy logs; first he and then I, his pipe glowing red in the semi-darkness, the blue smoke rising in crowning halos over his head.

I had just finished telling about a girl I knew and loved, but because of her pledge to another man, I had lost.

He drew a sigh when I finished. "Don't tell me, Wilson, that there are any "skirts" that are virtuous. Man——! Hell is paved with preacher's daughters; I ought to know. I will prove it to you! He choked, and cleared his throat. I never have told this to a soul before. Maybe I shouldn't tell it to you. Perhaps you wonder why a soft-featured man like I should be roughing it up here; why I choose this sort of an existence; why I chose to live apart from my fellowmen — to bury myself as it were out in these God-forsaken hills. For gold — yes — and no! I came here to get away from a face; a face that haunts me; a vision that is driving me mad.

"I wandered from town to town. Wherever I went, she followed me — I mean her picture. I could not go to the theatre but her face would flash across the screen — across the silver-sheet. She was always there, before my eyes to damn me. I dreamed of her every night. Ah, man, she was pretty, and that pretty face proved my undoing.

"I had been married about a year; our honey-moon was over. She became restless and without my consent secured a position on the stage in Los Angeles. She was a beautiful thing to look upon, so sweet and innocent, with big dark eyes and rosy cheeks, and lips that tempted a kiss.

"One night a screen manager spied her. Then, she went to Hollywood to make pictures. She pleaded with me to come to the little town, but I was raised in a strict faith and could neither tolerate nor compromise with her. She said it was a choice between the pictures and me and that art meant more to her than love.

"So I kissed her good-bye and she went to Hollywood to live. I took the train for San Francisco. Before long, I read of her in the papers—scandalous things about Billy Barclay and Raymond Hart.

"One evening, I attended a theatre on Market Street and that devil, Hart, was hugging my wife. He made love to her beneath the trees; she smiled at him and he kissed her. My head swam; I saw red! Grabbing my pistol and rising in my seat, I shot the villainous cur, Raymond Hart."

Barclay had risen in his chair and stood leveling his finger at the wall.

"I shot him!" he cried, "I did! The people scattered; two policemen caught hold of me and rushed me to the station. I got sixty days—served under the name of Peter Roe.

"I never heard from my wife again, though I saw her picture in every city I visited. Her fame and picture was broadcast. It was painted on every billboard. Strange men laughed and jested about her when she appeared in half-garments exposing her beautiful, shapely body to their wicked gaze. Oh, it was Hell!—and to see her smile—the same old smile that she used to smile at me.

It got on my nerves. Wherever I went, from Frisco to New York, from Chicago to New Orleans, she peered at me and made love to this blackguard, Hart; her picture was always there to damn me. I sought refuge up in God's great out-of-doors where the pines sing and the sweet zephyrs blow. I have tried to forget her —I do not know why I have told you this," he hesitated: "There is something about you that I like."

I shuddered lest he might recognize me.

"Let me tell you," said he, drawing his revolver and beading it at the low blazing log, "If I ever meet that dog face to face, I'll fill him so full of hot lead that he'll never smile again on my Billy girl."

"I have met Hart," I said, shifting uneasily in my chair.

"What manner of a hound is he?" asked Barclay.

"I thought him a pretty decent sort of a chap but you sure have shown him up in a bad light. He is a friend of mine and in love with a girl named Lily Downs, an actress in the Jesse MacKay Company."

"Are you sure?"

"Yes."

"But those scandalous motor rides, etc."

"Oh, that was newspaper talk— done for publicity—to draw the crowd— for the almighty dollar."

"You think so?"

"Yes—I know Billy Barclay, well, She told me she had searched for you for years; employed a detective at a big salary but could find no trace of you. At rehearsal, I have often watched her wipe the tears from her eyes as she leaned on my shoulder."

Tears swelled in Barclay's eyes, yet he said nothing; he was dumbfounded.

"Many a time I have seen her brush away the hot tears and go before the camera forcing a smile. Those tears were for you, old boy—I am Raymond Hart. If you want to shoot Raymond Hart, now is your chance."

Barclay choked hard; the black handled colt revolver struck the floor with a thud. He held out his trembling hand. "Shake, and forgive me!" he cried.

I took his outstretched hand and gripped it warmly. "Your wife will be here tomorrow," I said. "The director promised to pass these diggings on the thirtieth and this is the twenty-ninth. I have recovered my health and am dying to get to work in the big mining picture to be staged in these hills. We'll work you in, somehow, and you and Billy can take another honey-moon and at the expense of the company. Shake again, old boy."

My Peril

By Marion Evans Herald

I T had been a wet, dreary day, that twenty-first anniversary of my birth, and Clarice and I had been sitting so long over our fancy work in the old oak room, that we had exhausted every topic of conversation, save one—that one, ever nearest my heart, and too sacred to be spoken of to my ex-governess.

After a few minutes silence, she laid down her work, gave a deep yawn, and remarked:

"What a fine contrast you and I make, Barbara. No man would admire both of us; we are so totally different."

She had made a true remark. We were totally different. She was short and plump, and I was tall and slender; she. was dark as night, with handsome black eyes; I was blue-eyed and fair-haired.

As she sat there, with her dainty laces and furbelows, she looked every inch a French woman. If I had one single point of beauty it was my hair. I delighted in the heavy golden waves which fell unconfined below my waist, and persisted in wearing it that fashion, in spite of Clarice's "You will never get a lover while you look so babyish."

At her request I had looked in the glass and was turning away with a smile; but she caught my hand and detained me.

"Now which is cousin Ned's taste?" she said, with a laugh that had a mocking ring in it. In spite of myself, my face flushed with annoyance, for this was the one subject which I could not talk or jest of with Clarice. I had never loved or respected her; but the light hand with which she had held the reins of government had reconciled me to her companionship. At that moment I felt that I positively disliked her. With a touch of her own sarcasm I replied:

"It is absurd to compare a girl of twenty-one with a woman of thirty odd."

It was an ugly, spiteful speech, and the next moment I was heartily ashamed of it. "Forgive me, mademoiselle," I pleaded, laying my hand in hers, but I might have known that I had committed an unpardonable offense. An impertinence she would forgive, but no mortification of her personal vanity, and on the tender subject of her age she was particularly sensitive. She pushed me angrily aside and left the room. I walked to the window and gazed through the rain-dimmed panes, and began to think. What could have induced me to be so rude and unladylike?

Could it be a feeling of jealousy, that poor Clarice D'Arcy should have a share of good looks which might possibly attract the attention of the man who was to be my husband? "Oh, Barbara Blake," I thought, "what a contemptible being you are for, such a noble man as Ned Mayo to dream of calling wife."

He was my ideal of the noble and chivalrous. My love for my soldier-cousin had been intense, beyond my years, and the tears I shed at his departure had been among the bitterest that my life had known. I was an orphan. My mother's gentle life had ended when mine began, and my dear father now had not been dead quite a year. How lonely and desolate I should have felt, but for one sweet hope.

It had been my father's wish that Ned and I should marry. But, did he love me with any thing more than cousinly or brotherly love? That was the question that tormented me day after day. For me to be his wife would be happiness supreme—but for him? After an absence of two years, he was to return and that very night, the question upon which my future happiness depended, would be answered. Twilight came, and I was still keeping watch at the window. At last I heard the sound of wheels coming up the avenue and among the shadows in the dim distance, I saw my hero once again.

As he approached he looked eagerly at the windows. But I had hidden behind the curtains, for a sudden fit of shyness had come over me. I longed to run down and greet him, but decided to wait until I was sent for. In a few moments the summons came.

"Miss Barbara, the Major has arrived and is asking for you." Slowly and demurely I walked down the broad stair case, though my heart was dancing with delight. I could hear his voice in the library and supposed him to be talking to my aunt. The door was ajar, and before I entered, I thought I would take a peep at him to see whether he was much altered. He was standing near the window, and his tall figure and handsome face stood out clearly against the light; but to my great astonishment it was not my aunt to whom he was talking in that low familiar tone. It was Clarice. She whom I had supposed a total stranger to my cousin, was standing close to him, her hand upon his arm, her face raised to his with an expression of earnest entreaty. I heard her last words: "I have never ceased to love you."

For a moment I was bewildered and the thought rushed to my mind, it cannot be real. I am certainly dreaming and shall wake in a moment. But my aunt's hand placed upon my shoulder roused me to the reality. In another moment Clarice came forward, smiling, and said:

"Barbara, my dear, the Major and I have met before, in Paris. Is not this a pleasant coincidence?"

He held out his hand to me with much seeming warmth and eagerness, but when he would have drawn me to him and kissed me I drew back coldly. I could not be satisfied with Ned's cousinly love, so in the future he must treat me as a woman, not as a child. He smiled in an amused manner, and turning to my aunt, began to converse with her. Beyond him I could see Clarice's dark eyes, with a laughing triumph in them. No doubt she was thinking how favorably her wel-

come contrasted with mine.

My heart seemed bursting with grief, and I could not remain another moment in their presence, so I went quietly from the library and up into the old oak room, where such a little time before, I had been watching for him, with so much joy and pride, and there wept long and bitterly.

I did not notice how dark it was growing until a light streamed into the room and Clarice entered with a lamp in her hand. She started in astonishment and said:

"Why, Barbara; alone and crying! What is the matter?"

I raised my eyes, red with weeping, indignantly to her face.

"Clarice, you are a bad, deceitful woman; I have found out your secret. You knew and loved Ned before you knew me; but, why have you deceived me all this time? Why did you let me go on hoping?"

"Heaven!" screamed Clarice, her eyes flashing, and her voice shrill with passion. "How did you know it? You have broken open my desk, and read my letters."

"Nothing of the sort," I replied, "but I saw the interview between you and the Major and heard you confess that you loved him."

"Well, and what then?" she asked, with an evident relief, which I could not understand. "Major Mayo is free to love where he chooses, I suppose. Am I to be blamed because he follows the feelings of his own heart, rather than carry out the mercenary plan of a deceased relative?"

With this cruel taunt she left me. And so my golden dream vanished. Oh, if he had only loved some one nobler and worthier than myself, I could have borne it. But Clarice, whom I knew to be vain, mean and untruthful. In my bitter disappointment I was becoming uncharitable again; yet in my heart, I believed that I did not judge her unjustly.

One thing I determined upon—they should not see that I was unhappy, so I sang gayly as I went about the house, became pert and flippant to Ned, and altogether assumed a character as different from my own as possible. It was evident that they did not know what to make of the change. Clarice would open her great eyes at each of my wild moods, but Ned's face looked distressed. He did not approve of this new Barbara, apparently. I steadily avoided being alone with him, and contrived that Clarice should sit next to him at the dining table. To my surprise he took no advantage of the situation, but treated her with cold politeness, while to me he was as he had ever been; gentle, kind and tender as a brother.

"It is a new deception," I thought. He wishes to hide his love for her. One morning Ned found me alone. I had arisen early, taken a book, and gone to my favorite arbor, intending to read until the breakfast bell rang. Major Mayo was a great smoker and had taken his cigar there thinking he would be undisturbed. I could not turn back without being positively rude, so I quietly took the seat he offered me. No sooner was I seated than he placed his arm around me, and said: "There, now we are comfortable. The early bird is proverbially a fortunate one. Do you know, Barbara, this is the first tete-a-tete we have had since my return? I have not had an opportunity to tell you how much I find you altered."

"For the better, I hope."

"Well," he returned, "from a girl you have grown to be a woman—and a very charming one, too. Two years ago I felt sure of little Barbara's love. But now what am I to say?"

"I do not love you any less, cousin Ned—and, as a cousin, I shall always love you."

He spoke very gently in reply:

"But it is not cousinly love that I want, Barbara. Why are you so changed? You scarcely suffer my arm around you at this moment; you have not kissed me once since I came. Two years ago you would have done so without the asking."

His words bewildered me. Starting to my feet, I exclaimed: "Major Mayo, you must remember I am no longer a child. Would it be right for me to make those advances you mention before the woman who loves you, and whom you love?"

Suddenly he seemed to understand, and holding out his arms to me, he cried:

"Come back to me, Barbara, come, dear, oh, how you have been deceived."

I hesitated a moment, and lost my chance. A rustling in the bushes near the arbor startled me, and immediately Clarice appeared in the doorway. She was flushed and panting, and a smile which she endeavored to make agreeable, parted her lips.

"I am sorry to disturb you, Major, but a parcel has come for you; and the bearer is waiting to deliver it into your own hands."

Ned hesitated, looking from her to me, then quietly placed my arm in his.

"No, no," said Clarice, taking my hand as if to draw me away. "It is so hot; Barbara and I will follow slowly."

"Excuse my rudeness, Mademoiselle D'Arcy," he said, "but I am anxious to resume the conversation you were compelled to interrupt. My cousin and I will come after you in a few minutes. The messenger may wait."

Clarice looked baffled. "In turn, excuse me, Major Mayo. Barbara a few words to you."

As I bent toward her, she whispered: "Little stupid, he wants your money, not you.." Then she hurried out of sight.

The long winding path to the house seemed to me the road to Paradise, as I walked along slowly, Ned's strong arm about me, while his beloved voice, in low earnest tones, was telling me of his love—how he had known Clarice in Paris some years ago, while I was a child, and he too young to know what real love was; how he had been fascinated with her for a time; till he had found how unworthy she was—till he had felt that his love for his girl cousin had grown to be the hope and aim of his life. As we halted in the path, I reached up and took his dear brown head in my hands and kissed him, as I had done two years ago. How proud I was at that moment of my noble, handsome lover.

Ned was compelled to be absent all that day, but I was happy. Even Clarice's spiteful speeches fell harmless. If she had truly loved Ned, I could only feel the deepest pity for her. She had slept in the same room with me. I had no inclination for her company that night, but could not easily invent an excuse for departing from the usual custom; so having undressed in silence, I laid my happy head upon the pillow and fell to dreaming of my beloved. Suddenly I woke with a scream to find Clarice standing at my bedside. The room was filled with a singular rosy light. I could not hear distinctly what she was saying, but her face and lips were ashy white, and her eyes starting from their sockets. In another instant her voice pierced my ear:

"Barbara! Awake! Awake! The house is on fire!"

I raised myself upon my elbow, still stupified with sleep. I saw her rush wildly about the room, seizing her jewel case, her desk, all that she could grasp that was valuable.

Presently she turned and looked at me, it was a singular look, and I have never forgotten it. I can recall it now as plainly as upon that dreadful night. She moved half way toward me, then halted, and a fixed determination and earnestness settled upon her features. Again she turned, grasped her treasures, and rushed from the room, closing the door behind her. That seemed to break the spell that was upon me. I jumped from the bed and flew to the window. It was a frightful scene. To the right of my bed room all was in flames. A balcony which extended along in front of the windows had already caught. I sprang to the door. Oh! Heaven! It was locked— on the outside. I shrieked; I raved; I battered the door till my hands bled.

"Oh, Clarice, you must have been mad with terror—you could not have doomed me to such an awful death."

Once more I ran to the window. Nearer and nearer were creeping those awful tongues of fire while below looked up horror stricken, ghastly faces. I could distinguish my lover, carrying in his arms a senseless figure. It was Clarice. Then her words were true. She was the love of his heart, and he had flown to her in the first moments of danger. Be it so; but life was so sweet—so sweet— and I was so young to die. I stretched out my hands imploringly toward him.

"Ned, Ned, save me too! Oh, save me! Do not let me die!"

My voice reached his ears. He turned toward me with a great cry and rushed into the house. A strange calm came over me. I no longer shrieked, but stood near the window with my eyes fixed upon the door, for I knew he would save me or die. Only a few moments, though to me it seemed an age, then I felt Ned's beloved arms carrying me over the hot floor, and down the stifling stairs, while he murmured:

"Thank God that I have saved you, Barbara."

Then all became dark. I was insensible for many days, and regained consciousness in a strange room and house, for my dear old home had burned to the ground. Clarice disappeared on the night of the fire, but some months later I received a note from her. It contained a few brief words:

"You will never see me again, but I write to tell you, though I hate you, I am glad you were saved. It was the madness of a moment which prompted me to lock your door. Had I not fainted from the smoke, I should have returned at the risk of my life, to set you free."

Scarcely a hair of my head was singed by the fire. But, alas, my poor Ned. Even now there are scars on his dear face and hands which I lament—over which he glories in as the price of his wife's life.

A Glorious Fourth

By F. F. Smith

TOMORROW was to be my wedding day and as I looked out of my window onto the St. Francis Woods, through the dark green trees, over the outlying bay, I could see one of the planes from my father's works. In front of me, sporting in and out of the wistaria, were two yellow butterflies. Tomorrow! what a glorious Fourth it would be, the first since the world war, and Dad—he's a wonderful Dad— had given orders for Heath Court, our home, to be opened to the whole staff of men from the Aviation factory and school, to celebrate. Everything was ready and the whole grounds running down to the beach had been in the hands of the decorators for hours.

My wedding was to be at six o'clock. Jimmy and I had planned it a year ago, just before he left for France, and Dad and I thought it would be a suitable ending for a novel Fourth—for had I not stood side by side with the boys at the works the last year? Dad had said, "We'll open Heath Court, Ruth, and give the boys a jolly Fourth," and then I told him of our plans.

"And Jimmy will be here, Dad," I added, "for he said , 'I'll come back for that even if I have to sink Germany.'"

So Dad took out his check-book and said, "Here's the starter," and gave me a check in four figures.

Turning away from the window, I opened my cedar chest and buried my face in its misty lace. "Jimmy dear, what a splendid Jimmy you are!" and lifting up the folds of my wedding veil, I took out the picture of James Littlefield Grey, my own Jimmy. He stood by his machine, in his overseas suit, six feet, one—dark wavy hair and clear blue eyes. Sometimes just before he started on one of his air trips, they would turn dark purple, the color of violets, and he would take my hand in his firm clasp and say, "It's all right, little pal—watch for our signal," and then, way up there in the air, he would send back to me our love signal with his great airship.

And now he would be here in my arms tomorrow—a real live Jimmy. I closed the chest and ran over in my mind some of the plans for the day. The first thing the men would parade after an old-fashioned custom which I had seen in New England, while I was there at school. "Horribles!" they were to have every kind of ridiculous costume and conveyance one could think of. They would parade at seven. Then breakfast, gipsy style, at the beach in tents. Then games, dinner, speeches, flying, then—the wedding and afterwards dancing, while Jimmy and I were on our way in our machine (Dad's present) to "Knarled Oaks," his place in the Santa Cruz mountains.

How I loved to be up there, winding in and out of the snowy clouds or darting down into the air-pockets by his side. What wonderful trips we had had after we had coaxed Dad to let me go! Jimmy had come from New York as instructor, a son of an old college chum of Dad's, and he had been at the works a year when the war broke out. After the first month he had made Heath Court his home, for Dad said he needed him. There was so much room for, besides Dad and myself, our family included only Dad's brother, Uncle Ned, a bachelor, who was having quite a time deciding between two comely matrons. One he wanted, and the other was determined to have him. Jimmy used to play chess with Dad, checkers with Uncle Ned, to quiet the nerves of the later after his encounters with the matrons, and spent the rest of the time with me.

I had been home six months when Jimmy came. I had been studying aviation in Boston when the war broke out. I took up the practical side of things, going to the works with Dad at six-thirty a. m., and working at all times or overtime, as the whole staff did. I had learned to fly—after Jimmy came—and could do a twist, turn and a few other things, which he taught me, when Dad was not around. It was my intense desire to perfect myself in these things that made me stay after Dad had gone home one night, a week before Jimmy left. I knew he was going and was determined to learn from him this particular trick of steering —a protection against sudden currents and air squalls. "Time to go, Ruth," Dad had called and, after giving him a good hug, I said, "Coming later tonight." He looked rather suspicious but. Uncle Ned, driving up with the "determined one," took him away. "Not later than seven," he called back, and I waved him a good-bye and hurried out to meet Jimmy.

Passing one of the big sheds I had heard voices. "The head bookkeeper," I whispered, and a shudder went over me as I remembered the noon when he came into the head office, the day after Jimmy came, and tried to force his attentions on me by kissing me. Jimmy stood in the door and in a twinkle of time threw him to the floor.

I peeped through a crack and listened. "Those machines over there in the west sheds. Do you hear?" he was saying, holding up a paper to five of the men. "They must be fixed. Look at this diagram. Here, do you see under the steering gear? Cut this connection. You'll get hell from headquarters if any more of these sailing devils go over there perfect. Do you understand? Here's your extra" — and he gave them a roll of money.

What was to be done? Quick as a flash I turned to find Jimmy. Into the main office I flew. No one but old Davis was there.

"Where are the night watchmen?" I gasped. "Where's Mr. Grey? Where ——?" What was I to do? "Davis, break open that drawer. Do you hear me?"

"I will, Miss," and he started to pound at Dad's private desk drawer with the handle of his broom. "Fool!" I muttered. "Here," and picking up a chair, I smashed away. What was that lying on the mat—a key? Yes, Dad's key. Would it fit the drawer? It had to, for I knew what Dad kept in that drawer—a couple of good six-shooters. I must get to those sheds before those men did and stand guard until the night watchmen or someone else came.

Where was Jimmy? Never before had he failed me. Thank God! the key fitted and grabbing the six-shooters I said, "Davis you come with me and don't open your mouth or I'll fix you."

"Yes, Miss," and out of that office we fled down the long row of outer buildings. Coming to an open place I just caught sight of a black speck up in the air. "It's Jimmy," I whispered. "Come round here, Davis. Here, follow me!" and I flattened out and crawled across the open space to the door of the western shed, which held fifty machines ready for shipment. One was missing— yes, it was the one. Jimmy was up in the air there, trying it out. He had to come down and yes, the door of No. 49 was open.

"Here, Davis, get in here and keep still," and Davis, his face a perfect blank, climbed into machine No. 1 and I in after him.

"If they come in at the other end of the sheds, near No. 49, I'm in a fix and—"

Hearing footsteps, I turned and pointed a six-shooter under Davis' nose as the door near us swung open and a rough voice growled, "I'm tired of this. We'll get hell at this end, if we're not mighty careful."

"You like the bull, just the same," said a second voice.

I could hear the chugging of No. 49 coming nearer and nearer, but voice number one was saying, "Hold that candle closer. Here, you——"

"Hold up your hands, you scum of Germany!" I called out and standing up in No. 1, I covered them with the revolvers.

"Davis, you go back to the office and call Douglas 20. Be quick!" He climbed out and hurried for the police. Nearer and nearer came No. 49. In a few moments I heard the great whirring propellers and a clear voice whistling, "We don't want the bacon!" A swift look of fear ran from face to face of the five men and I quickly lifted my right hand and fired two shots—in the air—as the door of No. 49 closed. They had heard the incoming machine and the clear whistle and had not counted on this.

"Don't you move, Batch, or you, Steiner. I know you, you German left-overs. And every man of you back up in that corner!"

Hurrying up came Jimmy, surprise, consternation and wonder filling his face.

"Ruth!" and turning he followed the direction of my outstretched hands. "My God! what is the meaning of this?" and he walked up and took Batch by the collar.

"Just this, Jimmy. Make him give you the paper in his left pocket and tell you his plan—but here come Dad and the police."

And so we had saved the shipment.

Fourth of July broke with a high fog. Grey and restful clouds hung over the city. At five I awoke thinking, "The boys will be here at seven." Taking Jimmy's last letter from under my pillow, I read over and over the closing lines: We fly at ten tomorrow. Last trip before leaving for home.

The exact time, allowing for all setbacks, would bring him at six o'clock, just one hour! Jumping up I caught up my curls—they were auburn—into a cap and my mirror showed a dimpled, happy face, with hazel eyes. "No, I won't call Susan. I will steal down to the garage and see if Jimmy's machine is trimmed."

Betty, the parlor maid, opened the door for me, with her sunny smile, and I walked out into the gray misty morning and down through the pine trees and shrubs. Flowers everywhere—beautiful rose trees, groups of woody ferns. San Francisco, in the distance, was awakening, and its busy hum came to my ears.

Carl, one of the gardeners, was walking away from the garage so I opened a side door and went in. The great white wings of the machine were edged with

red, white and blue and out in the front was Old Glory. Everything was perfect, It was our machine and in the afterglow at the end of this glorious Fourth, we would sail away into the clouds and love! I gave a start as I heard the noise of a machine. "Jimmy must not catch me like this!" and I sped out of the garage straight into a motorcycle.

"A special letter," said a voice and an official leter was put into my hands, addressed Miss Ruth Dayton. Then the lad was gone. I tore open the letter. It would tell me he had arrived in New York—was leaving for California — had received mine telling him about the celebration. Why, Jimmy, himself would be here in a short time. Then I read four words: James Littlefield Grey—dead.

My Jimmy dead! and turning, I flew back into the garage. It could never be, not after the year we had had together. During this last year I had studied and followed to the minutest detail Lawson's book on "How to Protect Our Boys, or the Secret of Divine Protection." I threw my arms over the great white sails. "No, Jimmy, it cannot be. This is our own bird and we will fly away tonight together." Just then six o'clock rang out from a nearby chapel. What should I do? "Oh, Jimmy, what shall I do?" Then a calm still voice said "Miss Ruth, your bath is ready," and I turned and lay my head on the soft brown neck of my Susan.

"Susan, read!" I sobbed and I handed her the letter.

"Yes, Miss Ruth, but it reads: "It was supposed to be the body of Mr. James Littlefield Grey!" and her calm tones read: "Aviator killed. June 1. Supposed James Littlefield Grey dead."

"Thank God, Susan, supposed! Come let us hurry. Not a word to Dad or Uncle Ned. Not a word to the boys — this must still be a glorious Fourth."

After breakfast I caught Dad's eye watching me. I tossed him a kiss and, going around to his chair, whispered, "Remember what Jimmy said—that if he had to sink Germany he would be here," and fled to Susan. Susan was my treasure. Five years before, when Dad came back from Honolulu, I was at school, but, when on my return I bounded into his library, after hugs and hugs, I saw something moving in a big leather chair. "Here's a live doll for you, Ruth," and Dad led me over to a soft bunch of sunshine, with eyes like two stars.

Bishop Lane of Honolulu had promised Susan's father to look after her. "Take her to Ruth," he had told Dad. "Tell her it's a live doll." Susan was then twelve years old.

It was a tough fight, but all day I threw myself into the lives of the boys, who spared nothing to make it the Fourth of Fourths. And now at five o'clock came the flying. There were to be all kinds of maneuvers. There were six of the machines out there in the field east of the garage and tears filled my eyes as I turned into my room thinking of the seventh.

"Susan, I will dress. Yes,"—as a strange look filled her eyes—"there is nothing but God. Susan, let's get ready for Jimmy."

A soft knock sent Susan to the door. "Yes, Mr. Dayton, she is dressing." Down by the cedar chest I dropped and, closing my eyes, I prayed and knew.

At five forty-five I went to the low French window opening on to my sun porch. There were the six machines maneuvering over our grounds. How high they were. "And look, Susan, look, there is another, a government service one. Quick! Bring my glasses. Yes, Susan, it's giving the Love signal. Look! It's one dip—that is the 'I'; a dip and loop is the 'love'; and two backward forward turns and loop is 'you.' 'I love you!' It's my Jimmy! It's my Jimmy."

That night as we stepped into our machine amid the cheers and cheers while the afterglow lit up the whole country, forming a veil over Susan's face as she stood up on my porch waving her good-by, I looked back at Dad surrounded by the boys on the lawns and knew we had had a Glorious Fourth!

Violet

By Warwick James Price

When April's warm rain kisses old earth awake,
And the bluebirds hymn praises for grim Winter's death,
And the buds from their overcoats bourgeon and break,
Then the hillsides grow fragrant with Violet's breath.

Little daughter of Springtime, as timid as sweet,
Why hide yourself there in your snug bed of leaves?
Why challenge the tread of the world's careless feet?
Why shrink from the homage true beauty receives?

Is it modesty moves you to dwell so obscure?
The chum of some pixy, the love of some elf?
Nay, the cause I can guess; it is this, I am sure:
You fear to eclipse the proud Queen Rose herself.

Treasure Trove

By Ronald A. Davidson

CHAPTER II.

THE woman," supplied Stanley. "Well you old rounder, so you're going again, are you? Better find out her sorority and get one of the sisters to introduce you, same old line you used to work."

Steve took this jibe in silence, but Pete was fairly started now and launched himself into a long speculation on this new angle of the mystery. He had fully convinced himself that this young adventuress held the key to the secret and he waxed so eloquent on the subject that Stanley finally admitted grudgingly that there might possibly be something in it.

"Why worry," yawned Steve, rising, "enough of this for one day. I'm turning in. I'll admit though I'm liable to see her again some time."

The next day it could hardly have been called accidental when Steve, walking his horse slowly up the ridge, just after noon, again saw the blue-clad figure plodding up the canyon. In fact he had had that trail pretty well under observation all the morning and it was only after quite an argument that he had persuaded his comrades from doing likewise. Spurring up his mount he skirted the edge of the canyon and crossed over at the top to the spot where the trail passed through the boundary fence. He timed his arrival to coincide with hers and his formal "Good morning," was acknowledged with a cheerful smile.

"I'm on my way to Walnut," he explained. "If there's anything I could get for you and save you the walk—it's a good two miles and pretty steep going." He felt the awkwardness of this remark and had a moment of misgiving as to how she would take it. But she seemed to see nothing over familiar in his offer and after a moment's consideration: "Really, that's very considerate of you, if you're sure it wouldn't be too much trouble—it is a tiresome walk."

"Not at all. I was going over anyway, and if it's something I can carry on the horse—"

"Oh, yes; father only wanted a new bridle. His horse stepped on the reins yesterday and tore the old one all to pieces."

"Certainly, that's easy. I'm sure I'll be able to get one at the store."

"You have a horse then," he continued, seeking to prolong the meeting. "I should think you'd prefer to ride up here when you make the trip."

"Not me," she laughed, "I suppose it sounds foolish to a man but I'm scared to death of horses and when it comes to going off alone over a trail like this—well, I don't mind walking anyway."

"Why," said Steve, seeing his opportunity, "next time you want to come up it wouldn't be any trouble for me to—"

"Thanks," she interrupted curtly, "but we're going tomorrow, early."

This was somewhat of a crusher both in manner and purport but Steve wasn't ready to give up.

"Oh, I see. You'll be going down the old wagon road by way of Caliente canyon I suppose?"

"Yes. That is the way we came in."

"It's the shortest way if you want to get to a railroad, as I judge you do."

Steve was making a determined effort to draw her into saying something about herself, but as this last effort met with only a curt nod he dismounted, opened the gate and led his horse through.

"I'll try to make it back in an hour or so," he stated briefly, and trotted off.

When he returned she was seated against the foot of a tree, her hair again free from the tight fitting cap and hanging over her shoulders. As he negotiated the gate she wound it into a coil and deftly arranging it on her head once more jammed the cap on and settled the visor well over her eyes.

"Please don't think I always have my hair running wild," she smiled as he approached, still leading his horse, "but it's such a relief to let it out from under that stifling cap.

That was the first real feminine remark she had made and Steve took it for a good omen.

"Yes, you ought to have a hat. I got your bridle O. K. It isn't much to look at, but I guess it will serve." He untied the bridle from his saddle, but made no move to give it to her.

"Thanks very much. How much was it?"

"Two dollars," which was all it was worth but not all he had paid for it at the rural store.

She produced the money from the overall pocket and handed it to him and, since she still held her hand extended she had no choice but to surrender the bridle.

"Thanks again," she said, tucking it under her arm. "I had a fine quiet time here all by myself. It certainly is wonderful up in these hills."

"Yes, you bet it is. I spend most of my time down in that blazing valley but when I get a few days off this is the only place for me."

They managed quite a friendly conversation for the next few minutes, but only on general topics. Steve made several attempts to get some light on her identity, but, although she continued more than gracious, it was easily evident that she had no intention of continuing the acquaintance.

"Well, I must be going," she said finally, "thanks again for your trouble."

But Steve wasn't going to give in without a struggle.

"Wouldn't you care to ride my horse a little way. I can go back your way just as well as not."

"Please don't bother. I'm rested now,

thanks, and I don't mind walking alone."

That "alone" was unnecessarily cruel he thought, but it steeled him to make a final plunge.

"Don't think I'm trying to pry into your business, but wouldn't you please explain to me a little more about yourself, that is what you're doing here. Not that I think you were stringing me yesterday but some of the things you said were, well, sort of queer you know."

Steve was avoiding her eyes a little shamefacedly but she looked fairly at him and suddenly burst out laughing.

"And you didn't guess after all?"

"Huh!" gasped Steve, staring at her in surprise.

"I was sure I'd given myself away. I acted so silly when you mentioned it, asking you if you knew the amount like that."

"You don't mean you really were—"

"Guilty. But really," she sobered suddenly, "it wasn't such a rainbow chase, at least it didn't seem to be. I might as well tell you the whole dark secret. Maybe you can profit by it more than we did. You see father was attorney for one of the robbers and even though he didn't save him from a conviction the man was grateful enough to repay his efforts. He told father that they had hidden the loot, they didn't have time to figure it up, a lot of it being bonds and securities, by the side of a big rock about fifteen feet high. The top of the rock tapered to almost a point and then widened out a little into a sort of mushroom top. He described the location as the upper Caliente canyon, saying that they had buried the loot in a box on the north side of the rock and then rolled another boulder over it.

"Of course, as soon as father could get off, he hired a man and came up here. He let me tag along because I was wild about the romance of it and I just love to roam around the woods in this kind of an outfit. But I guess after all it's only a myth because they have scoured the whole upper canyon without any luck and daddy has to get back to work tomorrow."

She paused a moment, but as Steve could only stare at her, speechless, she continued:

4

"So now you possess the key to the secret and perhaps with your knowledge of the country you can make better use of it."

"Why, yes, thanks awfully," but Steve's mind was off on another tack. "Won't you let me know where I can reach you, for if I should find it, I would owe at least a part of it to you."

"Oh, that's very considerate of you, but I'll relinquish all claims. Thanks again for your kindness. Good-bye."

Steve was at the end of his rope by now, and his mind was so absorbed in searching for some excuse to stay her further that he forgot even a good-bye. When he did realize his omission she was some yards down the trail and it looked so awkward to shout a farewell after her retreating figure that he simply stood there and stared until she had disappeared around a bend in the trail.

Steve never had a chance to get back to camp with his story. Just over the ridge he was met by the others, Stanley with his rifle was making at least a pretense of hunting, but Pete had spent the last two hours in waiting for the news and made no attempt to conceal his impatience. However, his face fell when he saw the boss' dejected attitude.

"What's the dope?" he shouted, spurring up the trail, "didn't she tell you anything; has she already found it, or what the hell is the matter?"

Steve regarded his interrogators sadly. "She told me where it was supposed to be alright but they couldn't find it so I wouldn't give much for our chances. It's probably the bunk anyway."

"So she really was looking for it?" laughed Stanley. He had never wasted much worry on the matter anyway and from Steve's attitude he dismissed the prospect without further interest. But not so with the old prospector. He had taken it too much to heart to give up hope without more explanation.

"Where did she say it was. I know every rock this side of Mentone. For God's sake don't quit so easy, what's the rest of the dope?"

The old fellow was so in earnest and looked so tragically expectant that Steve laughed in spite of himself.

"Why, she seemed to have had a tip about some rocks about fifteen feet high with a kind of a mushroom top on—"

"Not the mushroom rock in Pine canyon?" gasped Pete.

"No, she said this one was in the Caliente canyon near the quarry."

"But Pine canyon runs into Caliente right above the quarry. I've knowed that place for years, used to be one of the curiosities to show the tenderfeet that visited the quarry, come on I can take you there in half—"

"Don't go off from the hip there," snapped Steve seizing his bridle as he tried to crowd ahead on the narrow trail. "Wait until you have heard the rest of it."

"Oh, come on," encouraged Stanley, his enthusiasm returning with a surge, "it won't hurt anything to go and look, you can give us the details on the way down."

"Yeah, for the love of Mike let's get there before they stumble on it themselves."

"No you don't. They're camped down there somewhere and we'd run right into them. They're pulling out tomorrow and if your enthusiasm lasts over night we can go down then."

A wild argument ensued in which Steve remained taciturnly firm.

"Oh, well," admitted Stanley finally, for he knew better than to try to sway Steve, "I guess it's a good hunch. It wouldn't do to find it and have them around to try to horn in on the loot."

Pete was far from satisfied but he gave in grumbling. The ride back to camp was an animated series of conjectures, mostly by Pete; Stanley getting an opportune remark in, now and then, but Steve keeping a morose silence. Arrived at the cabin. Steve gave details of his encounter, although he laid more stress on his informant's personal appearance and actions than his comrades thought interesting or necessary. Speculation waxed so hot that even Steve felt a little interest returning and by evening Pete was wild. It was only after a definite and forceful order from his employer that he quieted down enough to prepare the evening meal and even then he forgot to put the garlic in the beans, an oversight which he would ordinarily never have forgiven himself, but which now passed unnoticed.

No one slept much that night, though Steve tried to assign his wakefulness to an over-interest in the blond adventuress, his mind was not free from conjectures on the treasure hunt. It would certainly seem that such a prominent thing as a large mushroom rock could hardly have escaped the notice of the other party if it was so near their camp, but Pete had pointed out that they would have been searching the main canyon and the rock in the side ravine might easily have escaped their notice. At least it was worth a trip down to the canyon. But he was determined not to arrive before the other party had left, for he was more than a little piqued at the way the girl had treated him, stopping his efforts at familiarity, and his obstinate pride prevented him from making any appearance of forcing himself upon her.

Holding back the expedition next morning was no easy task for Pete was up long before daylight, preparing breakfast and getting the horses and tools ready. However, Steve remained firm and would not permit the start until eight o'clock though everything had been in readiness two hours before. From the limited ranch equipment they managed to procure a pick and shovel and a short crow bar, and armed with these articles they set out.

It was a good five miles to the quarry and the trail down into the canyon was in no condition for fast travel, but they made the trip in less than an hour. A few rods above the spot where the trail struck the canyon bottom, were the remains of some of the old quarry buildings, one of which showed signs of being only recently vacated. Steve would have stopped to investigate the camp but the others were pushing ahead toward the side canyon so he reluctantly followed.

He was just entering the mouth of Pine gulch which was a narrow rock strewn ravine, when he heard an exultant cry from around the bend where his companions had just disappeared. He spurred his horse up the empty water

course and rounding the bend came upon the object of their search. There, sure enough, was a large mushroom rock at one side of the ravine and rolled against the base of it on the north side was another large roundish boulder. Steve lost no time in joining the others who were already excitedly examining their find.

"That's her as sure as the Lord made green apples," shouted Pete triumphantly, "you can see where they have rolled down that other rock from the side hill, the marks are still there."

This was evident enough, for a raw gash showed plainly a few yards up the hill where the rock had been and a gouge in the soil marked the path down which it had been rolled to it's present position.

"I knew it," gloried Pete, fairly dancing around the discovery, "I just had a hunch I was due to pick up that swag ever since the first time I heard the yarn."

"Gosh!". gasped Stanley, "it sure looks like the réal dope, doesn't it? But what worries me is how they never stumbled on it themselves when it was so near."

There followed a few moments of awe-struck silence, even Pete being unable to find words to express his sentiments, but this time it was Steve who took the initiative.

"Come on," he said tersely, "let's get going. That rock won't move itself."

They fell to work immediately but the obstacle was far from light and their short crow bar gave them little advantage with which to move it from it's wedged position. Finally after some minutes of sweat and profanity, Steve saw the futility of further efforts in that line and adopted another method. He sent Pete back to the quarry for a timber which would give them more of a purchase, while he and Stanley set to work to dig out under the side of the bounder. The soil was hard and rocky and progress difficult but they worked like beavers and by the time Pete returned with a long four-by-four, they had made quite a cavity under one corner. By forcing the end of the beam under the opposite side as a lever the combined efforts of all three finally toppled the boulder to one side, revealing a loose mass of rocks and gravel.

Pete's face fell a little at this sight but Steve seized the shovel and began digging furiously.

"Stay with it," he commanded, "she said distinctly that they buried it first and then rolled the rock on top. This stuff is all loose, it's just been dug out and refilled."

For the next quarter of an hour all toiled furiously, taking turns with the pick and shovel and the odd man lifting out the larger rocks with his hands. In fact such was their enthusiasm that they hindered each other, for the pit, which was now beginning to take form was only about five feet square. Though the material had evidently been dug over recently it had been filled in tightly and packed and a number of rocks wedged together made digging difficult. When they had cleared out about three feet the workers were forced to call a halt for breath.

"Gee," gasped Stanley, "they sure put her deep enough." His excitement found vent in speech and he had been carrying on a line of rambling chatter all through the work. However, the nervous tension had reacted strangely on Pete and though his hands trembled and his eyes shone as though from the effects of too much liquor, he had been working in silence. Steve also was quiet, and doing his best to disguise his nervousness, but when he tried to roll a cigarette during their rest his hands trembled so that he had to give it up.

They had scarcely been at work again five minutes when the pick which Pete was feverishly wielding, struck something with a hollow "tunk." For a moment the diggers gazed at each other spellbound, and then all fell to work, pell mell. A few minutes of feverish effort, in which life and limb were endangered in their wild scramble and the top of a heavy packing box was uncovered. The work of extracting it from the rocks, which were wedged around it defied their disorganized efforts for some time but finally Steve and Pete managed to get hand holds on it and flung it up on the bank. It was not heavy and had no lock, the top being nailed securely.

They spent no time in contemplation or speculation over their prize, they were too sure of it now, but Steve deftly inserted the end of the pick under the top board and ripped it off. The box was level full, the contents being neatly covered with folded newspapers. Steve dropped to his knees and lifted the papers, while the others were almost falling over him for the first glimpse of the contents. In the middle of the box was a medium sized rock, the remainder of the space being jammed with crumpled paper and rags. Steve could only stare in dumbfounded bewilderment but Pete plunged his hands into the box, and began hurling out the rubbish. He soon reached the bottom of the worthless cache and seized a folded sheet of paper which lay there. It was addressed in a neat feminine hand, "To the Discoverer." Steve snatched it from Pete's trembling hand and unfolded it.

"What is it, what does it say?" shrieked the old man, climbing over the empty box in an effort to scan the written page. Steve dropped back to a sitting posture and after a brief glance over the epistle read:

"Dear Discoverer:—I can hardly expect that you will really find this but if you have been to so much trouble and disappointment I can at least give you an explanation. As far as the treasure goes the first I heard of the story was when you mentioned it and except for what you told me, I have no knowledge of it whatever. My presence here may be explained by the fact that my father is a geologist and made this trip to study the limestone formations in this section. This will also account for this excavation which he made to get at some lower strata, and then filled in for me, when I had explained my idea of a good joke. I trust you will be able to see some humor in the situation, also, although I fear it may be rather difficult after this disappointment. It really was a mean trick I suppose, but when you seemed so curious about what I was doing and then gave me such a beautiful opportunity, I could not resist the temptation, although afterward you were so nice and considerate that I almost changed my mind. Hoping you will not be altogether disgusted with me, for I only mean this as a joke, I remain, yours mysteriously,

"MISS OVERALLS."

"P. S.—If you still have any interest in this adventure, you might find something by digging further."

Steve read the note slowly in an expressionless tone and for some time the group remained in dumbfounded silence.

"Well, she sure gypped us," admitted Stanley, who was the first to recover, "that was some frame-up."

He surveyed the sum of their labors, the scattered debris of rock and the empty box and grinned cheerfully. He had been the victim and perpetrator of too many practical jokes to take this affair seriously.

But the humor of the situation did not appeal to Pete.

"If that's your idea of a joke, it ain't mine," he roared. "Three men putting a whole day's work on a damn wildcat chase to amuse a feather-brained flapper. God! I'd like to have a chance to tell that dame what I think of her playing a damn kid trick on me. I bet I could sure make her—"

"Well, you might as well cool off," interrupted Steve, quietly, still scanning the letter, "nobody dragged you down here, in fact, if I remember rightly you were about as anxious as anyone to come." But this was far fram calming the irate prospector.

"By the Almightly, I'll show her," he shrieked, turning toward his horse. "I can catch them before they get to the train and I'll sure make her wish—"

"Stop!" Steve sprang up and grasped his arm. "You start after them, and it will be the last ride you ever take. If you don't like the way things are going around here, beat it and beat it pronto!"

Pete was wild, but he recognized the dangerous glint in his employer's eye and realized that in spite of Steve's seemingly calm demeanor, he was in no mood to be crossed. He jerked his arm free and with a final glance at the others stumbled hastily over the rocks to his horse, and seizing the reins, swung into

the saddle, turned his mount on its heels, spurred savagely off down the gulch.

"Gee, that sure was a horse on Peter," grinned Stanley as they watched him out of sight. "I'll admit it kind of gave me a jolt at first but we might as well laugh too. It's a shame she didn't leave her address so you could let her know it worked."

"Yes," admitted Steve absently. He was gazing thoughtfully at the excavation they had made and for some time both remained silent.

"Well," said Stanley finally, "I guess the party is over, we might as well pack up our stuff and dangle home. I'm getting hungry."

"You go ahead," acquiesced Steve. "I'm going to see this through now."

"What do you mean? Haven't you had enough digging yet?"

Steve made no reply, but dropping to the bottom of the pit started removing the debris of rocks and loose earth. He soon had the bottom clean and since the formation was a relatively hard lime stone the floor was even and level. In the middle of it was a circle of loose dirt about four inches in diameter, evidently the top of a hole which had been drilled into the rock.

"Well, that's evidently what she meant by 'dig further,' but it will be some job getting that loose stuff out of so narrow a hole."

"Sure, and why fool with that?" protested Stanley. "The old man probably bored it down about a mile to see how deep the strata was and anyway what could there be there?"

"It can't be very deep," replied Steve, starting to loosen the dirt with the point of the bar, "because it must have been drilled with that bar I saw her with and that was only about six feet long. This stuff isn't very hard and I can widen the hole."

"Well, what of it? What do you expect to find when you do get to the bottom?"

"Oh, I don't know," replied Steve absently, "I just somehow got a hunch maybe there might be something there. I hate to leave things in this state after we've gone this far."

"Well, I wish you luck. I'm going to beat it."

Stanley busied himself picking up as much of the equipment as he could carry, meanwhile keeping up a one-sided and somewhat sarcastic conversation.

"So long," he called cheerfully as he started off down the canyon. "You can have my share of the treasure."

Steve found it no easy task to excavate the narrow opening and his difficulties increased as the hole sank deeper. His only means of procedure was to loosen the dirt with the bar and then scoop it out with his hand, and when it got too deep to reach the bottom he had to widen the opening sufficiently to get at the loose dirt with a shovel. He did this by breaking down the sides and although the rock was of a rather loose variety, the work was slow.

However, he was determined to see the adventure through to the end and after almost an hour's work he found his reward. He brought the object up and found it to be an old tobacco can, from it's weight apparently empty. But on opening it he found a small card, one side of which contained an alluring description of a brand of tobacco, and the other the following legend written in pencil:

MISS IONE HILTON
2518 W. 13th St.
Los Angeles

It was a week later when Steve, carefully dressed and more than a little excited, stopped his car before the Hilton residence. He painstakingly set the brakes, turned down the lights and locked in the robe while summoning up his courage for the encounter. Finally, with one last deep draw at his cigarette he mounted the steps and rang the bell.

He had rehearsed the meeting many times in his mind. He would probably be met at the door by a maid, ushered into the parlor and presently "She" would come in. He would stand silently in the middle of the room and gaze at her accusingly. She would stop, register wild surprise and gaze at him dumbfounded. He would then remark, casually, "Well, I'm here," and fix her with a stony stare

while she stammered apologies and explanations, and would finally unbend and grant her forgiveness and then they would spend the rest of the evening in a friendly discussion of the joke and perhaps, if she attracted him as much as before, a little spin in the machine later.

He was giving a final adjusting twist to his collar which was irksomely stiff after his accustomed garb, and wondering if his tan was deep enough to hide the burning he felt in his cheeks, when the light over his head snapped on and the door opened. It was no maid but Miss Hilton herself who stood in the doorway, now clad in a modish sport spirt and a white waist with the rebellious hair arranged securely in a neat coiffure. Nor did she stand and stare at him in amazement but instead her face lit with a surprised laugh and she extended her hand in welcome.

"Why Mr. Haines," she exclaimed as Steve mechanically accepted the outstretched hand, "I'd almost given up hope of seeing you. I was beginning to feel all my trouble had been wasted. Do come in, won't you, that is if you have come for a visit and not just to tell me what you think of my sense of humor."

"Oh, not at all," stammered Steve, dumbfounded by this sudden turn of events, "I couldn't get here any sooner, work on the ranch, you know—couldn't possibly get away any sooner."

"I'm so glad you didn't get angry about it. Here, let me take your hat and we'll go in and see father. He's anxious to see you again."

Steve surrendered his hat in silence and followed her across the hall. His tongue refused to work under this new shock. She evidently knew him, knew his name and father was anxious to see him "again." A dozen wild conjectures ran through his mind, now that he saw her in ordinary clothes he did seem to have a dim recollection of having seen her before, but where or when—

The mystery was suddenly solved when, upon entering the next room a tall bearded man with a kindly smile rose to greet him and a genial voice boomed out:

"Well, well, Mr. Haines, I'm certainly

glad to see you here. I feel we owe you an apology for that practical joke of my daughter's."

A sudden memory flashed through Steve's mind of the man before him, standing behind a lecture table and speaking in that booming voice of, why, yes, geology, Professor Hilton! What a fool he had been not to see the connection before.

"Why Professor Hilton," he exclaimed, "I never suspected it was you and Miss Hilton. I've been wildly trying to figure how she knew my name."

"Oh, Heavans!" broke in Miss Hilton, "what do you think of me for greeting you like that! Don't you remember when you met me at that Glee Club dance? I supposed of course you'd recognize father's name if you didn't remember me?"

"I'm afraid, my dear," laughed the professor, "that we professors may not make such a lasting impression on the students as we would like to believe."

"Oh, no, it isn't that," protested Steve. "I don't see how I failed to see the connection before. I do remember Miss Hilton now, although I didn't recognize her in her overalls."

"Of course not," she smiled. "I couldn't expect a big campus hero to remember a poor little freshman. I remember I was quite flattered at having met you and I recognized you at once when we met on the trail that day. I'll admit that my idea of putting up that joke on you came from a desire to get even with you for having treated me so patronizingly. But I did hope you would be interested enough this time to find my address."

This successfully broke the ice and a lively conversation followed in which Steve gave the details of the treasure hunt, and discussed his ranch and old college acquaintances. Finally Professor Hilton excused himself and Steve having definitely decided by this time that this was an acquaintanceship which would be worth while furthering, suggested a ride in the machine.

It was several hours later when the machine again drew up before the Hilton home. The time had passed pleasantly enough with conversation on general topics and mutual friends but so far he had made no effort to bring the talk into personal channels. However, he saw his opportunity when, in concluding the narration of a college chum's romance she mentioned it as a case of "love at first sight."

"Do you believe in that?" he asked her sharply.

"What?" she queried, somewhat surprised at his sudden change of manner, "love at first sight?"

"Yes."

"Oh, dear, no. It's very pretty sentiment and certainly gets overworked in the popular novels, but its pretty impractical."

"No, it isn't, not if it's the right kind. I've had, or at least thought I had, several cases of it but my friends always sprung this 'practical' stuff on me, and talked me out of it. So I went ahead and got a nice little engagement in the orthodox manner and, well, maybe you heard about it?"

She nodded without looking up.

"After that," he continued after a moment's pause, "I swore if I ever married a girl it would be one I met one day and married the next."

His arm had strayed over the back of the seat and his finger nails were nervously gouging holes in the upholstery above her shoulder.

"So this may sound awfully sudden," he went on, his voice becoming suddenly very low and hoarse, "but I'm terribly stubborn and when I make a resolution I can't bear to fall down on it. Won't you help me, let me, make good?"

His arm had dropped onto her shoulder and he drew her slowly to him until the crown of blond hair rested against his shoulder. She made no resistance or response but continued gazing fixedly at the pattern of the lights on the road ahead. Finally she looked up, her face set and serious but with an unconcealable flash in her eyes.

"I absolutely could never fall in love at first sight," she said slowly, "but even though you do seem to consider that you have just met me I feel that I've really known you for a long time. Long enough, anyway, dear."

Pacific Coast Defense

By Prank W. Harris

(Late Captain of Engineers, U. S. Army)

IN considering the defense of the Pacific Coast time will not be spent criticizing the present order of things, for today the Pacific Coast is defenseless, and nothing is to be gained by elaborating on that point. The defense of the Coast rests on the United States, so that it is of primary importance to investigate the ability of this country to perform the task. The military policy of the Pacific is very badly complicated by the large number of unknown factors. We know fairly well what to expect on the Atlantic seaboard —this cannot be said for the Pacific.

Wars are now battles of nations so that we must study every branch of our own, and foreign governments. There are two delusions which characterize the average man. In peace he believes that it will never be necessary for him to go to war, and in war, he believes that it is the other man who will be killed. Hence the country that bases its military policy on the average man's opinion, is defenseless.

The prizes of conquest are far more alluring than any pacifist dreams of. The world is growing smaller every day, and daily it becomes more evident that eternal viligance is the price of liberty.

Wars of nations are so vast as to be almost unconscious urgings. None, perhaps, deliberately plan them in all their minutiae, circumstances hurl them into the maelstrom. Our vision would have to be much keener than it is to say the last word about war, for we are in the vast domain of the forces of evil. The problem of evil has baffled the wisest of all ages, and if it is possible to legis-late by leagues of nations, this great scourge from the earth; then, indeed, is the day long looked for drawing nigh.

Norman Angell wrote a book called "The Great Illusion"—it tried to prove that war does not pay. Does the announcing of a long list of penalties stop crime? In all wars one side must lose, but this fact will not deter the future conqueror from faring forth, and at least making the attempt to realize his ambitions.

What man has done, man can do, and the future Ghengis Kahn will nourish his soul and mind with the achievements of Alexander and Napoleon. The whole danger in this situation is this: that the conqueror dreams, plans and works toward a certain well defined end. Everything must fit into the plan. On the other hand, the pacifist pursues the even tenor of his way, and when the storm breaks must improvise a defense. Is that a prudent policy?

Civilization pampers us until we lose all sense of national self preservation. The effect and lessons of war are soon forgotten in a democracy, as a democracy is organized for peace, and not for war. A democracy organized solely for war, would be an intolerable tyranny. The country would be governed by the most loathsome of all things; military arrogance and incompetence. There is, however, a happy medium: It is possible for a republic to have an intelligent military policy, which will insure to a reasonable degree peace, stability and contentment. We must admit that all nations will continue the struggle for a "place in the sun," and adjust our national behavior to conform to that fact.

It must be observed where necessity is driving a nation, in order to pursue a certain policy. In a world-wide struggle of readjustments, we must anticipate where our interests will clash in a vital manner. Our interests will be affected more or less in all national reorganizations; safety depends on clearly seeing to what limits we may safely make concessions. In war it is fast mobilization that counts, and a country should be organized with that end in view. To achieve this end, the United States should be divided into four governmental and administrative divisions, to be known as the Atlantic, Southern, Central, and Pacific Divisions.

The Atlantic Division: Maine, New Hampshire, Vermont, New York, Massachusetts, Rhode Island, Connecticut, Pennsylvania, New Jersey, Delaware, Maryland, West Virginia, Virginia.

The Southern Division: South Carolina, Georgia, Florida, Tennessee, Mississippi, Alabama, Arkansas, Louisiana, Oklahoma, Texas.

The Central Division: Ohio, Kentucky, Indiana, Michigan, Wisconsin, Illinois, Minnesota, Iowa, Missouri, North Dakota, South Dakota, Nebraska, Kansas.

The Pacific Division: Washington, Oregon, Idaho, Montana, California, Nevada, Wyoming, Utah, Colorado, Arizona, New Mexico.

St. Louis is the strategic center of the United States, and the Capitol of the country should be located close to this city. The weak point in the defense of the Pacific Coast is the fact that the Capitol is three thousand miles away. To get the full benefit of the Panama Canal, the Capitol should be in the center of the country. During the last war the Capitol cost us a loss of one billion dollars in inefficiency. All departments were swamped.

The need for these divisions is emphasized, for it is the only way by which we can work out a sound plan of rapid mobilization. The secret connected with modern national warwfare is the time necessary to mobilize. The surprises of

war must be perfected and worked out in peace. This is the coming field of strategy. Peace is a battle of brains. War is a battle of brute force. The struggle for foreign markets and trade will always produce war. The regular army will be sure of a job as long as we have so many different grades of civilization. The regular army must be divided into two hard and fast divisions, the line, and the services of communications and supplies; or combatant and non-combatant troops.

The line, will embrace all the fighting officers, and these men should never serve in the services of communications and supplies. Five per cent of the line officers should always be on foreign service, and foreign travel. This stipulation should be absolutely iron clad.

There should be a permanent advisory board consisting of leading railroad, steamship manufacturers, professions, and labor men to advise the army and navy on all questions of communications and supplies. The board should have a membership of one hundred men; the term of service to be four years, and members to be appointed by the President, on the recommendation of the secretaries of the various departments.

When the regular army abolished the National Guard in the war, they swept into the waste basket all of the glorious traditions of the Civil and Spanish-American wars. The 1st California Regiment of Infantry means something. Who knows about the 1026th Infantry? This destructive action seems to have bred nothing but a desire for revenge on the part of the National Guard. However, the advocates of the National Guard do not seem to be aware of their limitations. The state is a good tactical unit, but it has little strategic value; on the other hand the United States as a whole is too large. The National Guard will not have an opportunity for any real service until the country is divided into divisions. The Pacific Division, as outlined, is a military unit of real value.

The states must confine their efforts solely to the line, and allow the Regular

Army the control of the staff work, and all the Services of Communications and Supplies. The National Guard can furnish the Infantry, and a portion of the Artillery, and also a part of the Engineers, for combat service. The Regular Army will undoubtedly organize an Army Service Corps, which will handle most of the work carried on by Engineer and Quartermaster Corps in the late war. The defense of the United States naturally divides itself into two parts. The defense of the Atlantic and Gulf seaboards and the defense of the Pacific seaboard. The defense of the Pacific seaboard rests primarily on the navy—that of the Atlantic, with the army.

The controlling point in the interoceanic strategy is the Panama Canal. The Capitol of the United States must be moved to the strategic center of the country for adequate defense, and until the Capitol is located somewhere near St. Louis, all military plans for the defense of the Pacific are under a very heavy handicap.

The Pacific Coast must own the following territory for its own vital protection: The Galapagos Islands, the Revillagigedo Islands and Lower California.

The Galapagos Islands are situated on the equator off the coast of Ecquador. We need these islands as a hydroplane, airplane and submarine base for the protection of the Panama Canal.

The Revillagigedo Islands are situated about two hundred miles south of Cape San Lucas and would be used as hydroplane and submarine base. These islands would be solely under the control of the Navy Department and would form the outer line of defense for the Panama Canal.

Lower California is absolutely necessary for the safety of the Pacific Coast. Without this we are nothing. Mexico has no vital use for this territory, but is conducting a dog in the manger policy in the hope that it may some day prove to be "the Achille's heel" in our system of Pacific Coast defense. Nothing would please the Mexicans more than to be instrumental in the downfall of the colossus of the north. Magdalena Bay is the best anchorage that commands the protection of the Panama Canal. It is worth millions to us, and not ten cents to Mexico.

In a war involving the Pacific Coast our supplies must come from the East, and they must come by boat, that is absolutely certain. We would run a fleet of protecting ships for the convoys between La Paz and Panama. Our supplies would be landed at the mouth of the Colorado River. At this point would be the big supply base to be used for the defense of California.

Knowing that this must be in the case of war, it is absolutely imperative that Lower California belong to the United States. Any plan of Pacific Coast defense made, until we own Lower California, will be merely improvised; and at improvisation an enemy will have an equal chance with us.

Everything rests on the Panama Canal. Consequently it must be well protected both on the Atlantic and Pacific sides. We could exchange all of Northern Maine, north of the 45 deg. and 20 min. of Parallel of Latitude for British Honduras. The possession of British Honduras would enable us to command the Gulf of Mexico and the Caribbean entrance to the canal.

In planning the defense of the Pacific Coast, one of the most important points to consider is the supply of officers. We must have army officers, who know every road, hill, valley, swamp on the coast. We must have naval officers who know every island, shoal and tide rip in the Pacific. We can only get that class of men by educating them here. On Puget Sound should be a naval academy, the equivalent of Annapolis. In California should be located a military academy, the equivalent of West Point. The best site for purposes of strategy and training for the military academy in California would be at Monterey. The people of the Pacific states must fight to secure these academies with all their energies; for this is the only way that the

Pacific Coast can depend on properly trained officers in war.

From every angle it is seen that the weakest point in the defense of the Pacific Coast is the location of the Capitol at Washington, D. C., as it breeds ignorance of all Western conditions. If the Government was enlightened, these military academies would be on the coast today. The mere fact that they are not shows the indifference pervading a remote bureaucracy.

It is not necessary in making a plan of defense to pick out a particular enemy, or attribute certain motives. Certain assumptions must be made, but with great care and wisdom. In the Pacific Northwest the line of attack would be the Columbia River. The enemy would endeavor to capture Portland and push through and capture Spokane. Seattle would thus fall automatically. It would be wasting time to make a direct attack on Seattle. At Spokane, Washington; Lewiston, Idaho; and La Grande, Oregon; the enemy would stop and there build his defensive works. A railroad should be built from Natron to Vale, across Central Oregon, as this would be a great factor in the defense of the Columbia. The two railroads project that the defense of the coast demands are as follows:

First—The double tracking of the Southern Pacific between Sacramento and Portland. This is the weakest link in the whole system of the Pacific Coast railways. Second—The construction of the Natron to Vale railway. The need for this is so urgent that the Government should subsidize this construction by a grant of 100,000 acres of forest reserve lands in Eastern Oregon. The attack in California offers many more combinations than attacks in Washington and Oregon. The first move would be to establish a base in Lower California, as the Mexicans would offer no opposition. From this base an attack would be made on the rail line and an effort would be made to control San Bernardino and Tejon Pass. In Northern California the object of attack would be Sacramento and Stockton. No direct attack from the sea would be made on San Francisco.

Owing to the topography of the country, military roads have a vital importance. The roads parallel the coast with mountain ranges dividing and protecting them. The following description of these roads is from a measure now before Congress. Nothing has been accomplished, as only one or two organizations are doing any work to further the cause of these roads.

This legislation is largely the result of the work of the Pacific States Defense League and Mr. W. G. Scott of Bishop, California, who has made the military highway situation in California a close study. The following is a synopsis of the bill that has been introduced by Senator Miles Poindexter of Washington, while Hon. John E. Raker of California has looked after the interests of this road in the House.

1—The Balboa Highway, extending from Port Townsend, Wash., southerly along the Pacific Coast to Tia Juana, Mexico.

2—The Pacific Highway, extending from Blaine, Wash., and passing through Olympia, Wash.; Salem, Ore., and Sacramento, Cal., to Calexico, Mexico.

3—El Camino Sierra (the mountain road). Beginning at Oroville, Wash., thence extending in a general southerly direction along the east base of the Cascade and Sierra Nevada Mountains, connecting with all the mountain passes, intersecting the Pacific Highway at Mojave and terminating at Los Angeles, Cal.

The construction of the Balboa Highway from Port Townsend, Wash., to San Diego is of primary importance. This would be our most important military road. The defense of the Pacific Coast rests fundamentally on the navy. This road would connect with every beach and landing place on the Pacific Coast, enabling submarines, submarine chasers, torpedo boats and hydroplanes to take on supplies without going into the naval bases at Puget Sound, Columbia River, San Francisco Bay and San Diego.

The wealth of Washington, Oregon and Northern California is in its timber. This must be protected by a coast road. Landing and enemy raiding parties would make every effort to set fire to the timber all along the coast. This effort would not be made to merely destroy timber, but to furnish a pall of smoke to screen their operations. We must protect the coast forests at all hazards. Smoke from forest fires would render our scouting airplanes useless. The Pacific Highway is well protected by the Coast Range and would be the base on which all troops would be manoeuvered.

The El Camino Sierra, or Mountain Road, situated back of the Cascade and Sierra Nevada Mountains, would be a general supply base. These three roads would be the basis of all strategy for Pacific Coast defense.

The Balboa Highway would be used by the army and navy and the maneouvers would be carried out simultaneously. The navy would attempt to land men from the transports, and it would be the army's task to defeat the landing. The navy in attempting to land men would get a view of the difficulties that would enable them to defeat an enemy. This knowledge that the navy would gain by this maneouver would be of great benefit to the army, because it is presumed that when transports would be off the coast, that the enemy would control the sea. It is at this point that the experience of the navy would be invaluable to the army. When transports are off the coast naval officers must be on the army staff as advisers. This coast cannot be defended by army officers alone, in the event that our navy has been destroyed. The army and navy must lose that sense of separateness and work hand in hand, otherwise our forces will be divided and we will be defeated. Naval officers must thoroughly know the capacity of our three great roads and railroads. Army officers must know all about landing problems.

All of this adds to the necessity of having military academies on the Pacific Coast, for the proper time to obtain this army and navy knowledge is during the school years. The naval academy should try to land and the military academy should try to defeat them. This would do the country a lot more good than an inter-collegiate football game. To win a game on the field of strategy would be an honor. These sham battles should be annual events. They could take place in the month of August and consume the entire month.

The Redwood

By G. A. Lyons

Straight as an arrow from the bow,
    Aimed at a star in the silent night;
Shooting up in the air you go,
    Majestic and steadfast in your might.

Faithful sentinel of the hill,
    First in the morn by the sunlight kist;
Basking serene in its ray until,
    Wrapped in the cloud of the evening mist.

Sometimes capped with a crown of snow,
    Sometimes lashed by the driven rain;
What care you for the winds that blow?
    Fury of tempest is all in vain.

What care you for the world's mad race
    Swaying slow, to your anchor's fast?
Present and Future calmly face,
    Singing your song of the dim years past.

A Glimpse of the Salon in the Abode of the Artist, Showing Mr. Sumbardo and His Artist Wife. The Large Pain ing in the Foreground is "The Birth of St. John," a Masterpiece by Beato Angelico, Copied from the Original in Florence, by Mrs. Sumbardo.

The Abode of An Artist

By Agnes Lockhart Hughes

ACROSS the bay from Seattle, reached by motor, ferry or trolley, perched on a slightly eminence in West Seattle, is the imposing home of Mrs. C. L. Sumbardo, an artist who has brought the charm of Italian art with her and evidences it throughout her stately home and grounds. Mrs. Sumbardo is the wife of an American gentleman, an art connoisseur, who in his travels among foreign galleries, met this artist whom he married and brought to America—building a home in an ideal location, and housing the magnificent canvases painted by Mrs. Sumbardo from the old masters. To these Mrs. Sumbardo has since added the inspirations gained for her art on this side, and many exquisite bits of landscape, marine views, tapestries and portraits line the walls of her studio—a studio that has no peer on the Coast.

From the west wall, Andrea Del Sarto's "Madonna" looks down, while a Murillo "Madonna,"—"Aretino," a portrait, by Titian, "The Duke of Norfolk," a Titian also, "Madonna Detto Del Grand Duka" by Raphael, "An Old Rabbi" by Rembrandt, and a Rembrandt portrait of himself, decorate the north wall. Boltrafis' "Portrait of a Young Man," Boticellis' "Birth of Venus" hang on the east wall, and the south is gemmed with Susterman's "A Prince of Denmark," "Bassano and His Family" by Bassano, Beato Angelico's "Birth of St. John," a magnificent canvas, and Tintorreto's "Leda and the Swan." Then there are miniatures, and many beautiful moods of nature that Mrs. Sumbardo's facile brush have conveyed to canvas, that leave a pleasant and lasting impression on the beholder.

Of German birth, the daughter of a well known sculptor, Mrs. Sumbardo at an early age went to Italy, where she studied art, and practised it in the presence of the works of the great masters, in the galleries of Italy.

The Sumbardo home is idealistic in its situation; on a high elevation its sloping terraces face Puget Sound and the Olympic mountains. The garden is a riot of beautiful blooms, and bird houses in sheltered spots attract the feathered beauties who are privileged to eat their fill from berry bushes planted especially for them. A summer house where the family dine on pleasant days, leans against the sloping terrace its pagoda roof covered with climbing rose vines, and sweet scented honeysuckle. A plot beside the house has been given over to the two Sumbardo lads to manipulate as a farm, and they have done marvels with it, supplying not only the home table, but scores of patrons as well, from its plentiful yield of garden truck, and it has made sturdy lads of the little fair haired boys who landed in America only a decade of years ago, not knowing a word of English, nor anything about the soil.

Entering the Sumbardo home, from any window of which a magnificent view is obtainable, one passes down a wide hall, pausing instinctively on the threshold of the dining room, the ceiling and wall of which have been exquisitely frescoed by the young artist hostess, Mrs. Sumbardo. The scene depicted is the "Feast of Ceros"—carried out on the one side, with the Goddess enthroned amidst spring blossoms, while cherubs scatter myriads of blooms about her throne from overflowing cornucopias—and on the opposite side, Autumn in gorgeous portrayal of warm autumnal coloring, where cherubs spill fruits of the vine, and golden yield of the harvest from their horns of plenty, before the goddess. The work is splendidly executed, and has attracted much attention from art connoisseurs.

Crossing under this frescoed ceiling, the studio is entered—it is a long salon —the entire width of the house, and has a lofty crystal dome. The walls of this salon, are a veritable revelation—a bit of Italy transplanted to America, for Mrs. Sumbardo, imported most of the marvelous canvases from Italy. And the pleasure of the visit is enhanced by meeting the host, and hostess. This room is very sacred to Mr. Sumbardo—it is Mrs. Sumbardo's shrine—and she is never idle, as her inspirations find expression in art that gives keen pleasure to all privileged to view it, and the privilege is generously extended to all who care to visit the Sumbardo studio, on one day in the week set apart for the artist to receive—which she does graciously, never overlooking the hospitality of a cup of tea—and delectable sweets.

Across the hall which extends from front to back of the house, with a staircase to the left, is the library, and beyond that a morning room and private study —a sort of withdrawing suite, for rest and solitude. The wide, polished staircase, with its flying Mercury pedestaled at the bottom, leads to several roomy chambers with dressing rooms above, and ascending another staircase, from this floor, two view rooms are reached, from which a gorgeous picture unfolds, of gleaming waters, snow capped mountains and wooded hills.

The practical adjuncts of the house have not been overlooked, and the kitchen, scullery, pantry, laundry, and other features have all been supervised with the idea of convenience and comfort. In fact, the whole house, a choice structure of Colonial art, while large and roomy, exhales comfort and hospitality from its very threshold.

Added to her wonderful ability as an artist, Mrs. Sumbardo is a charming hostess, a devoted wife, the mother of two sturdy lads, and a beautiful daughter. These children, all foreign born, who were wholly ignorant of the English language, when they arrived in Seattle, now lead their classes in school, and are all talented musicians. And the abode of this artist—spells HOME.

Overtime

By Ralph Beals

A string of burros plodded slowly out of the desert wash, over the crest of the ridge, and then paused before descending into the next arroyo. Paused because the two men behind them with their ever-urging clubs had paused. The burros stood head down, a picture of weariness.

"Sure you know where we're at, Pete?" inquired the younger one anxiously. "It sure seems to me we've come thirty miles—more like fifty."

"Course. I just wanted to stop a second to get the lay o' the land here. It's jus' behind that little hill over there, four or five miles." In spite of his attempt to speak casually, suppressed anxiety sounded in every note of his voice. "It sure seems a long way," he confessed, "Must be the heat. 'S hottest day I ever seen in these parts, 'n that's goin' somethin'."

"How long did you say it was since you made this trip?" questioned the young man accusingly.

"Oh, 'bout three-four year, I guess," replied Pete, with attempted unconcern.

An inarticulate grunt from Smithy was the only reply.

The two men stood gazing over the valley—and nowhere did they see life, save for a kite wheeling—a mere pin-point in the blue. To the east towered dark and majestic the barren cone of black mountain. Somewhere at its base lay Pendleton's well, where the pair this morning had packed their score of burros for the long stretch to the New Hope mine and wells before even the faint light of the false dawn had dimmed the lustre of the stars. Pete "thought" it was "'bout" thirty mile, and so they had started with a single canteen of water apiece, for every ounce becomes pounds under the blaze of the desert sun. All day long they had toiled toward the out-swinging arm of the range that sheltered the New Hope—all day under the blistering sun—and now, as it dipped toward the western hills—even as the water in their canteens became lower and lower—the two partners stood on the rock ridge and searched the still distant hills for some promising sign of life, and gazed upon — nothing — nothing but the desert, silent, grim and forbidding. Down where the straight line of the railroad and the red roofs of Wenden now gleam, stretched unbroken the parched growth of the desert. And nearly twenty miles to the north, at the pass to the big blue river, where now is faintly to be seen the buildings of numerous mines, were nothing but the deep gathering shadows of late afternoon. Dry, desolate — desolate beyond the power of tongue or pen to express, "worse than Death Valley." "The hell-hole of the world," claim the venturesome souls who have defied it threatening solitude. And the two men stood gazing at the dancing dust-devils, wandering like lost souls, aimlessly hither and yon; gazing at the shimmering heat-waves and the tawny sands of the desert; gazing at the half-seen half-guessed blue of distant ranges; and gazing, were silent, enthralled by the spell of the desert. The sun sank imperceptibly lower, a burro stamped impatiently, and the spell was broken. The grim realities of life—or death—roused them once more.

"Guess we'd better go down the arroyo a ways," said Pete, briskly. "Gettin' too cut up here, close to the hills."

"Right," came the short reply. Fourteen hours of steady travel had not made Smithy over-talkative.

Laboriously, the line of burros descended into the arroyo, and plodded down the sandy bottom. The sun was sinking, a ball of glowing fire, beyond the outflung rampart of the hills, though still gleaming on the sands of the valley below—and still the heat intolerable, blinding, suffocating. The procession left the arroyo, wending westward once more. The last ray of sun left the valley almost at the moment that they drained their canteens of the last drop of their long-hoarded water. Gullies and more gullies, a barely discernible dividing ridge, more gullies, and then a steep drop into another arroyo. Half way across a burro stopped, threw up his head questioningly, and then started up the arroyo at a sharp trot. Too tired to pursue, the men stood and watched.

"Must smell water," said Smithy. "We'd better follow him up and camp there. We can get to New Hope tomorrow."

"Water," ejaculated Pete. "Water? There? They been lookin' fer water twixt Pendleton's an' the New Hope fer near thirty year, an' they ain't even found a dry spot. Let the fool Jack go. I know where I'm at now. Just an hour or so more."

"You've said that before," grumbled Smithy.

"Well go after your crazy burro, then. I'm goin' ahead," and Pete began urging the animals up the steep bank. "Wisht' we'd brought more water," he muttered to himself.

Smithy, after hesitating, joined him. In silence they toiled on. Already throats were drying. The country grew rough, the water courses more frequent. They seemed sufficient to carry the flood of a vast river; yet each ran into another scarce longer than itself, forming together a sort of a maze, or perhaps a Chinese puzzle.

The dark velvet mantle of the desert night drew itself over the earth softly, caressingly. The stars winked forth mellow and luminous and close to earth. A lone coyote, in a subdued sort of way, voiced its sorrow, the desolation of its hopeless quest for food and kind. And all this vast expanse of desert, these stretches of sage, of mesquite, of scorched sand, gave back no answering cry or sign of life. Only a faint breath

of air stole through the path, lent brief motion to the shrubbery and slipped away. But Smithy stopped short at the message he thought it brought, and listened to hear it again; but the air did not move again.

" 'Smatter," grunted Pete.

"Thought I heard a stamp mill up that way."

"Good Lord! y' ain't a goin' off yer head a'ready are you? Th' ain't a mill in seventy-five mile."

"I heard a stamp mill," snapped Smithy in reply.

"Humph. Purty soon you'll be hearin' a train whistle, an' the railroad's only a couple o' hundred mile from here. Come on." And Pete heaved a rock at a laggard burro. The outfit plodded wearily forward once more.

Silence, but for the sounds of their own movement. Stars dropped behind the Western hills and others rose in the East to take their places. The heavens moved closer to earth. The soft starlight flowed over the desert, bringing something it had lacked—still lonely, still desolate—but filled with an awful, a majestic, a more than earthly beauty. And those two atoms of human kind, pressing on they knew not whither, but driven by the gripping fear of death, they saw it not. The awfulness alone weighed upon them, not as a thing to be seen, but as a crushing burden to be felt.

The character of the land changed. The abrupt dry water courses ceased and gave way to rocky, rough ground, supporting still scantier vegetation. Some stretches of sand between rocky ledges, offered shelter for crawling things—an ideal place for one of those colonies of desert rattlesnakes where the reptiles gather to make their residence, rather than live alone in less unfavorable spots. And such a colony they encountered. Wildly the burros scattered. The two men ran after, striving desperately to keep them together and drive them forward. Writhing forms leaped at them through the shadows, to be beaten back by swinging clubs, or to strike futilely against heavy trousers or cow-hide boots. Sweat poured down their faces and saturated their clothes. Their breath came short, sharp, and forced. They spoke but little, for their dry throats forbade. But when they spoke, more parched than ever by this exertion, their few words flashed vivid as the heat-lightning that rippled and flashed and glowed along the peaks. Eventually, they passed the infested region and resumed their normal progress.

Perhaps an hour passed. They were making little progress now. Weariness was taking its toll, and the rough country held them back. Pete broke the monotony.

"I'm goin' up top o' that ridge, Smithy. You go on an' I'll catch you."

"Go on, ——?" remarked Smithy, "I'm goin' to lie down and rest till you come back."

"Right. Back in a minute," and Pete was gone.

Smithy stretched out upon the ground, and gave himself over to the joy of the tiny breeze that once more stole through the pass in the hills. It seemed once more that he heard the faint rumble of mine machinery. Faint, a mere suggestion, which would awaken no answering train of thought in the mind of other than Smithy. But Smithy had worked in the mines and with mine machinery, and was moreover blessed with imagination enough to consider all possibilities. Now his imagination merely turned to the possibility of his head ringing from his long hours of toil and thirst, and he arrived at no conclusion. And then Pete returned.

"Smithy, I—I—" he faltered, and then confessed, "I'm lost, Smithy. Don't know where I am."

"Well, what's next?" queried the younger, much more calmly than he felt.

"Why, I reckon' we better lay here till its light, so's I can see the country better. Maybe I'll recognize where I am.

"Well, not for me," snapped Smithy, "We'll last half hour after sunrise. Not time enough to get anywhere less'n we're right on top of it. I'm goin' to follow the noise o' that stamp mill. Can't make us any worse off'n we are now—Are you comin'?

"Well, I ain't much hankerin' "——

"Comin', yes or no, quick," interrupted Smithy.

"Ye——"

"Ye—es," hesitatingly.

"Come on then," Smithy struck the nearest burro with his club, resoundingly.

The outfit plodded southward and upward toward the gap in the close dark hills. They returned to the region of the water-courses, and plodded up and down in silence forced by their parched throats and swelling tongues. At last, they found what Smithy sought, the main arroyo. Here was a smooth path through most of the pass. Smithy slipped ahead and after a close scrutiny of the sands made out burro tracks going in the same direction. His cracked lips contorted themselves into what was intended for a smile. He felt sure he heard the sounds of industry louder, and looked at Pete to see if he also heard. But Pete dragged along with the hopeless expression of one going knowingly to his death, but unable to save himself. This troubled Smithy and stirred up in his mind weird fancies and told tales of men being led to their death by visions and seemingly natural happenings; until his imaginative mind became influenced and inflamed to such an extent that all semblance of rational thought disappeared.

The enfolding sides of the pass now rose dark and forbidding. The shapes of huge rocks, cactus plants, and shrubs now loomed thrice large in the dark, great monsters threatening and dangerous. Smithy's fancy went back to the days when he had studied and read. And he sought to give definition and explanation to his surroundings from the pictures of long-forgotten lore. "What is this place?" the question flung itself at him persistently. "The valley of the shadow," perhaps. Or, a suggestion from Dante, "The gateway to Hell." At last his mind settled on his being in "The Valley of the Shadow." If he could avoid the pitfalls and these threatening horrible creatures on either side of the path, he felt that he would survive the test. "But what if it be the gateway?" came the clamoring response to this. "Perhaps you should turn back. Who is leading you here?" It seemed as if some insistent voice from the outside were speaking. "Look at Pete. He is the one. He, your partner is guilty. He is betraying you." The voice seemed to become lower and nearer — confidential. "Perhaps if you should be rid of him, you would be all right. You are justified. You are betrayed. You would do but right if you should kill——."

At that word Smithy thought that he cried out, but never a sound passed his lips.

"One quick stroke with the knife in your belt, and you are free," persisted the voice. Smithy considered. The voice became more urgent, more insistent, more mandatory. His bleary eyes began to brighten. Unconsciously, his hand sought the wicked blade, sheathed at his belt. Unconsciously, he drew closer to the unsuspecting Pete.

By some fortunate turning of chance— or destiny, Pete stumbled and fell, plunging headlong in the sand. Another voice now spoke. "This is the valley— 'The Valley of the Shadow,' and this is one caught in a pitfall. Help him." Smithy leaned over and helped his partner up. The effort cleared away the foul imaginings of his brain, and left him free to plod on as before—unthinking, unfeeling, for he was numb from weariness that he no longer sensed. Only two sensations was he aware of—thirst, great burning thirst, and the half-realized thought that he must go on—on——

. The burros no longer needed urging, yet neither man noticed it. Half consciously they climbed out of the arroyo; half consciously felt the ground begin to slope downward. Smithy had occasional moments of conscious thought. Once he noted the black void of another great valley; noted the stars seemed dimmer, and endeavored to quicken his pace. Another time he saw the great arm of the hills, saw they were heading toward the abrupt end of this, and noted how rapidly the stars were dimming, and realized that in two or three short hours they would be stricken down by the hot rays of the sun—and then once more his mind became a blank. The last star faded away as they neared the end of the arm of the hill.

Painfully they picked their way through the jumble of rocks at the point of the spur, and unconsciously following the burros, swung back along the ridge. Ahead, nestling in a pocket formed by the hills, showed the bright paint of new buildings, and the scar of great dumps. The two men walked on unseeing, heads bowed, footsteps uncertain.

. The cook of the Balwin mine rubbed his eyes sleepily and yawned, magnificently, unabashed, a great cavernous yawn, revealing a vast cave, boarded by yellow teeth—permitted himself a final stretch, then stepped outside to cast "a look around," before turning to the day's work. Suddenly he stiffened, all traces of sleepiness vanished. He disappeared inside for a minute, and then was back bearing a canteen and running swiftly down the slope.

. Some thirty-six hours later, rested and refreshed, busily engaged in taking three meals at one time, Smithy paused and grinned at Pete, a grin that was somewhat marred by the arrival of a prodigious mouthful of potato.

The cook was filling up their plates for the fourth time. He addressed the awestruck assemblage of miners watching the wholesale destruction being performed by Smithy and Pete. "I guess it's mighty lucky for these fellows the mill was workin' overtime tother night."

Smithy paused again. "I guess," he said, "I guess the old desert thought we'd worked long enough and had our time checks all made out, but there's some power stronger'n the desert that puts it hand into things sometimes. I reckon it's you an' me that's doin' overtime now, Pete.

And Pete, who never in his life read a book, managed to say, "Lord , Smithy, but its hard to understand you sometimes."

Mother and the Peril

By Elizabeth Vore

SHE sat very often at one of the windows in her quiet little home on a side street of the Southern city where she had lived for years. She, herself, was Southern, and back in the dim years of her childhood, her father had been a slave-holder. One faithful old retainer, a white-headed old black man, had come with her to the town where she now lived, but years ago she had been forced by circumstances to let him go, since she could no longer afford a servant, and had for many years performed the greater part of the simple duties of her home herself. Her faithful old servant lived near, and although he made his living choring about town, he found time to give many a lift to his adored "Mis'" Rachael. For, notwithstanding the fact that she had been Mrs. Rachael Ladly for half a century, she was still "Mis'" Rachael to his loyal old heart. The Southern negroes never say "Mrs." Married or unmarried a woman is always "Miss" to them. They very seldom speak the last name of white people of either sex.

Mrs. Ladly—Mother Ladly, the neighborhood called her—was more often than otherwise sitting by the window where stood year in and year out the plain old-fashioned stand which held the large family Bible.

Sometimes she was writing, sometimes reading, her collar and apron spotless, her unpretentious dress in perfect order and irreproachable taste. At seventy, Mother Ladly's hair was beginning to whiten; it had kept its glossy darkness late in life, but the record of years was silvering it.

When passers-by saw her writing at the window it was suddenly remembered that she, to quote their words, "Had once been a great writer," and was reputed to have written for real magazines and newspapers in the big cities in the East. Some people guessed it was a fish story about the big magazines and newspapers —why, Mother Ladly lived in one of the most unpretentious houses in the town, and did her own work, excepting when old Uncle Ike came once a week and got her dinner for her and served her as he had done in past years when she could afford a servant. She had no children near her to do those things for her for love's sake, back in the dim years mother had laid one of them—her baby—to rest in a quiet churchyard, the others were far from her in distant cities.

One day the boy of the Searchlight— the Searchlight was the weekly paper— told a great secret. The poems that occasionally appeared in the Searchlight were written by Mrs. Ladly. Her neighbors had mostly forgotten that her first name was Rachael, and they guessed that Mrs. Rachael Ladly, the Searchlight author, was some other Mrs. Ladly and not old Mother Ladly.

But the office boy, Ted, knew better. He had taxed the editor who was also the owner with a searching question and the editor had told him the truth. Rachael Ladly was henceforth a heroine enthroned in his boyish heart.

"Why sure!" the editor had said with a softening in his big voice. "Dear soul! she used to be a great writer and I wouldn't turn her verses and stories down for the world."

Big, good-hearted Jim Walton, the editor of the Searchlight, was almost the idol of Mother Ladly's dear old heart. The Searchlight was the only paper published in the small city. It had held its own for eleven years and had run every other paper out of the business. It was the pride of the Searchlight staff, that the Searchlight was as sure of being published as the sun was of coming up in the East. The staff consisted of the editor and proprietor, Samuel J. Walton, and the office boy, Ted Cartright, who was printer-devil and compositor, the editor himself taking a hand at the case when an emergency called for his services in that direction.

Every Saturday night the Searchlight, smelling alluringly of printer's ink, came to Mother fresh from the press, brought by old Uncle Ike's trembling black hands, and an eager-faced old woman sat at the window where the stand which held her Bible stood, and with a faint flush on her sweet old face, read the paper from the first page to the last. If there were verses of her own in the paper signed by her own name, the flush in her face deepened and the light in her eyes grew stronger until she looked almost young again.

Saturday being a gala day for Mother, Uncle Ike always stayed and got her dinner for her, and served her as he had done in years gone by. Tip-toeing in and out softly, laying the spotless cloth, and getting out the old, rare China, the best silver and lighting the big shade lamp; and in the kitchen he would dash the tears from his faithful old black face muttering in mingled pride and wrath:

"God bless her! she's a great writer yet! an' they's sech fools they ain't one of 'em knows it, but old Uncle Ike!— 'ceptin' mebby it's that little gen'men what prints the paper—little Marsa Ted!"

And Mother, dear heart, would sit and dream before the fire after dinner, with her beloved paper in her lap, a paper to which she had been a subscriber since the first copy was issued eleven years ago, and which was one of the few connecting links in her life that kept her in touch with the past when she had written for the big magazines and newspapers in the East and West and had been editor

of several departments of the newspapers and magazines.

At one time in her life she had been associate editor of a society journal on which her brother had been foreman of the printing office, and in odd moments she had learned to set type, to help her brother and lessen the expense—for they had both owned an interest in the paper. She had even made up the forms on several occasions—there wasn't a step from printer to the editorial chair that she did not know perfectly; that dear brother's face came before her now in memory's sacred halls and dimmed her eyes with tears.

And now—Jim Walton, editor of the Searchlight, the office boy, Ted, and old Uncle Ike were her only friends in her immediate surroundings that connected her with the past, in which she had. been recognized as a distinguished woman, and she would still be recognized by people who knew her and her work in literature and journalism.

Occasionally from the Far East came a package of new magazines or newspapers from her children or friends of years past whom distance could not change in their fidelity. They were hailed with great delight for she could not afford to subscribe for many for her income had dwindled to a very small patrimony with the advancing years.

When such rare treats came a note would go by the faithful hands of Uncle Ike to the editor of the Searchlight, in a delicate old-fashioned hand writing: "Would the highly respected editor of the Searchlight care to look over some new publications which had been sent to Rachael Ladly from the East? Possibly they might contain interesting news which had not happened to come under his notice."

A reply in big, school-boyish hand would come back to Mother Ladly to the efffect that:

"We would esteem it a great favor to the Searlight if our valued contributor, Rachael Ladly, would send the periodicals mentioned, which would be returned when read." Signed with much state and dignity. "Samuel J. Walton, Editor of the Searchlight."

Samuel J. Walton was more often called Jim than by his first name. He was one of the big men of the town, but it hadn't spoiled him.

And then—into the flower-laden atmosphere, into the peace and quiet of the town, forcing its way into countless happy homes—came an unbidden guest, and the dreaded flag was raised at innumerable doors, with its legend of danger and death. And a great cry of terror went up from helpless stricken humanity:

"The yellow fever! The yellow fever!"

From lip to lip went the anguished cry, and those who could, fled—and those who could not, stayed to make the fight for life, for themselves and others and face their doom whatever that might be.

An aged woman with the tears running down her face sat in her chair by the window, her open Bible in her lap. Now and then she paused to listen for footsteps faltering with age. The dead-wagon passed by, and repassed, and passed again. The footsteps were an endless time in coming. Uncle Ike had gone to the Searchlight for the daily news of good cheer: "All is well. Searchlight staff is still here, and trust our esteemed contributor, Rachael Ladly, is O. K."

That was the daily bulletin from the Searchlight office, hoped for, prayed for, by trembling old lips. The footsteps came at last, but at the sound of them, Mother stood up trembling and white. They were running—Uncle Ike running at past eighty years, and crippled with rheumatism.

He burst into the room, his eyes rolling with terror and his black face a sickly, ashen hue.

"Gord Almighty!" he cried—Uncle Ike was apt to get an "r" in where it did not belong, when deeply moved—"Gord Almighty, Mis' Rachael be ca'm, honey! An' Lawd help us all! Dey is down— bofe of dem! de yaller debbel done knock

dem out! Dey ain't any Searchlight any moah—dey is bofe got de yaller fevah, dey drop wive it in de office, an' am took to de hospital—de Searchlight won't be published!"

Mother stood for a moment stricken dumb. Then her slender figure straightened erect and tense. Her head was lifted, her delicate nostrils dilated like an old war-horse that has scented battle. The Searchlight not be published? Such a thing was incredible! Jim Walton's paper break its record and fail to appear? Such a thing was impossible!

"The Searchlight will be published!" she cried in a ringing voice. "I will publish the Searchlight, myself, until further notice!"

Old Uncle Ike went down on his knees and caught hold of her garments whimpering in the hem of her dress.

"Oh Mis' Rachael—honey—chile! For Gord's sake don't go near de Searchlight's office! I done tole you dey is bofe drop in dey's tracks, in dat office wif de yallah pahal! de office am chuck full of de fevah infection! Don't go—I deploah yo', honey—chile!"

"Uncle Isaac, get up!" said Mother sternly, yet with a tender hand on his head. "I am ashamed of you. I shall take charge of the Searchlight for Jim Walton—I am the staff now—until I drop in my tracks! Did you ever know me to say what I did not mean, or fail to keep my word?"

No, Uncle Ike never had—and he got up trembling on his rheumatic old limbs and went out of sight and cried like a baby.

Mother put on a clean collar and smoothed her hair, and did up a kitchen apron in a newspaper and putting on her bonnet went immediately to the Searchlight office. Once inside the door of that sacred sanctum she stood for an instant in the silence, and her sturdy old heart almost failed her, but only for an instant. She was like a soldier suddenly drafted into service—to fail, would be to betray a trust to her highest conceptions of professional loyalty and friendship. She would have done anything within the power of a woman to have avoided the present catastrophe—she was the first to step to the front and offer herself and her life when the need came.

She stepped into editorial harness as naturally as if she had never left the work of years gone by. Going over to the telephone with an unspoken blessing in her heart for the man who invented telephones, she took down the receiver and called up the principal hospital— there was many improvised for the emergency—and asked if the Searchlight people were there.

"Yes," came the reply, "the owner and editor and the kid are both here. The editor very ill and unconscious. I understand that the Searchlight is not to be published."

"It·is a mistake," replied Mother's clear voice over the telephone. Her lips quivered for a second, but she steadied her voice and said decidedly:

"Tell Mr. Walton, please, as soon as he is conscious, that competent persons have taken charge of the Searchlight until the staff have recovered, and the paper will be published at the usual time."

If any one had seen the light of faith in her grand old eyes they would not have doubted the recovery of the Searchlight staff.

"Who in thunder could——?" it was the voice from the hospital, even in the midst of pestilence and death the amazed question was involuntary. There was a sudden click in reply—the telephone receiver had been hung up at the Searchlight·office, and "Little Mother," as she was sometimes called, turned away with an odd smile that no pen or pencil could describe.

"I don't think the Lord will consider that a falsehood, for He is back of me, and I guess he is a competent person, and if I didn't think I was—for a human woman—I should be ashamed to call myself an editor."

Mother did a good deal of telephoning during the time she was getting things started. "This is the Searchlight office," her clear voice came over the telephone, reaching every quarter of the town. "We want the news at the Searchlight—but we want facts. The Searchlight isn't afraid to face the worst, but it hopes for the best. Give us the straight news in this crisis. The Searchlight believes in the future of this city; and the news will be better tomorrow, and the day following."

"Yes, this is the Searchlight," Mother's dear old voice would say, if the paper was rung up. "All is well at the Searchlight. Our townspeople are making a brave fight, the Searchlight is proud of them! Of· course the situation will be better tomorrow. The yellow peril is passing away. The Searchlight has confidence in the city and its people. Cheer up! be courageous! God is greater than the destroyer."

Into the fever-stricken city where death stalked in its most horrible phases, that true voice vibrant with undaunted courage and faith winged its way carrying courage and hope to the despairing people and catching that life-giving infection, the panic subsided and they had strength to throw off the fear that had weakened them, the pittiless disease abated and day by day the situation improved. The minister and his heroic wife worked side by side in the stricken city and sent messages of good cheer to Mother every day.

Mother would put a newspaper up at the door of the composing room, for no one but trusty old Uncle Ike must find out, that the only one in evidence of the "competent staff" was a frail old woman —and donning her kitchen apron—which she carefully took home with her every night—she would set her stuff up in type.

At first it had been slow work at the case, her aged fingers trembled and dropped the letters in the wrong boxes, which would make her proof reading difficult, slowly at first, but with increasing speed as the old skill came back to her, she placed them in the stick line at a time, until the stick was filled. It was a triumphant moment when her fingers, strong with determination, emptied the first stick. She had not forgotten!— from the printer's case to the editorial chair she knew every round of journalism.

She sat sedately and with dignity by the dingy window of the Searchlight's editorial office and wrote her editorials in full view of the passer-by in the street below. They thought she was writing news, for every day at four o'clock she locked up the office, and donning her best black coat and her Sunday hat she started out with note book and pencil, going to every part of the fever-stricken town to get the news she could not get by telephone. Side by side with the yellow peril—into the very jaws of death—her erect old figure in its unobstrusive costume was seen.

"The Searchlight has got old lady Ladly to report for them," said some of the people. "Reckon they were glad to get anyone; it don't make much difference who they have, the old staff are not likely to live to come back. She's a game old lady though, as game as the people who are running the paper while the editor and kid are bowled out. No one knows who they are; door's marked 'no admittance'; wouldn't think that was necessary—not many people are likely to hanker after visiting the Searchlight office since the staff toppled over with the yellow peril in the office. The dead-wagon is a heap more likely to visit it."

But the dead-wagon did not call at the Searchlight office. It rattled past through the almost deserted streets many times a day, and Mother sat at the window calm and resolute and wrote her editorials and cheering messages for the townspeople with a steady hand. She learned to know the sound of those dreaded wheels and knew when the wagon passed without looking up, writing with a prayer in her heart and an unwavering trust.

Day by day the situation grew better; hope was growing in the hearts of the people. The day of publication of the Searchlight arrived. Mother had the biggest battle yet, for a woman, to fight and win. She had never made up the forms, but a few times in her life, and that had been in her brother's printing office many

years ago. But by the faith of a life time she knew that the Almighty was not going to desert her. After two hours' of painstaking work, the forms were locked up, and for an instant Mother stood nonpulsed. How was she ever to get them on the press? Her frail arms could never lift them! At that moment shuffling steps were heard on the stairs. The door was thrown open and Uncle Ike stood on the threshhold, crossed it, and came to her with the tears running down his wrinkled face.

"I come, Mis' Rachael, honey, old Uncle Ike ain't never disobeyed you before, but I ain't gwine let my little Mis' carry no such burden. I ain't gwine let my little Mis' what wrote and read the valadictator speech at the big college where she graduated, run no printing press! It would have broke yo' husband—Massa Hal's heart, an' it would have broke yo' bruddah, Massa Fenton's heart—my little Mis' Rachael what give de valadictator speech at de big college an' all dem grand folks scatterin' flowers for her little feet to walk on. Yo' ain't nebbah gwine run no printing press while Uncle Ike lives!"

With gentle force he put her aside, and taking up the forms he carried them across the room and placed them on the press.

"I 'clar foh a fact, I des plumb discumfuddled how I is gwine run dis heah consarn machine!" he said, eyeing the printing press ruefully. In a few words Mother explained to him how to run it and soon the big heavy press began to swing back and forth sent by old Uncle Ike's rheumatic hands. He turned his face away that she might not see the pain it caused his stiff joints.

"My little Mis' ain't gwine run no printing press—not foah de Angel Gabriel hisself," he said emphatically.

"You absurd old man!" said Mother smiling, "you can't remember that your 'little Mis'' is seventy years old, and has been Mrs. Ladly for many years!"

"No, Mis' Rachael, honey, I ain't nebbah gwine 'member no sech thing," said Uncle Ike solemnly. "I held you in my arms when you was old Massa an' old

Mis's new-born baby. Old Massa say to me: 'You am five years old pickaninny, an' now you hab done got a little Mis' to puhtect', an' you am my little Mis' as long as you live, what· give de valadictator speech at de big college."

Mother let him ramble on to the content of his affectionate old heart. She sat down white and tired, but with an inexpressible happiness on her face and looked over the first copy of the Searchlight as it came from the press, and thanked God for her faithful old black knight.

Back and forth went the big press, and downstairs in the street the passers-by heard it and stopped to listen.

"By Jiminy!" they said, "those Searchlight people are actually printing the paper! They have lived and won through —and the Searchlight will come out at the usual time!"

Well! I should rather say it would! The Searchlight was run by people who did not recognize such a word as failure, in what they believed duty and righteous undertakings.

Uncle Ike was running off the last papers, and Mother, who was too tired to take off her kitchen apron, sat holding her first precious copy, every line of which was written and set up in printer's type by herself, as well as all the news gathered by herself from every part of the pestilence stricken town, when again slow steps were heard on the stairs, as if someone coming up, paused often to rest on the upward journey.

A moment later the door opened, and Ted Cartright stood in the doorway, pale and thin, but eager-faced. He stood in silence for an instant regarding Mother Ladly and Uncle Ike with amazement too great for words. Suddenly it came to him like an inspiration—in a flash he knew that it was their valued contributor who had done this wonderful thing! There was no one else in the town who could have done it—this grand old woman so small in physique, so great in soul! All they had heard of her was true, a thousand times intensified, every particle of the boy in his hero-worshipping young soul swelled up and burst all bounds. He gave one delighted whoop of triumph—his poet had done this alone and unaided — for he knew Uncle Ike could not do aught but run the printing press. Catching off his cap he put it under his arm and came forward with wonder filled eyes!

"It has just come to me all at once, that it was you, Mrs. Ladly—who was the 'competent staff,' " he said chokingly. "If the boss was here he'd know what to say to you—I'm just a printer's devil, but I can say this much for him—we appreciate it!"

The memory of that little grave through all the dim years kept green in memory's most sacred halls, arose vividly before Mother's eyes just then and filled them with tears.

"Ted Cartright," she said, "I want that you should come here this minute! I want to shake hands with you! Printer devil! Printer angel rather! You come to your place on the paper you represent so weak that you had to crawl up the stairs! You're made of the stuff that great men and women are made of! Half of our most famous authors and journalists were printers and began at the case and were called printer's devils in the beginning!—it never hurt them any that I ever heard of! Horace Greeley was one of them, Benjamin Franklin was one of them, Bayard Taylor was one of them! and I want to say that there isn't a warmer corner in my home than the one I am keeping for you whenever you want to come and occupy it!"

In the entire vocabulary of the English language there seemed to be no words at that moment in which Ted Cartright could express his thanks, and not being able to express himself in any other way, he kent down and kissed the slender skillful hand of his aged heroine, leaving a great, boyish tear upon it.

Uncle Ike stood nodding his head and saying delightedly:

"Uh-huh! Uh-huh! Dat am talkin'! dat suttinly am talkin' right to de p'int!"

· Ted went and showed Uncle Ike how to fold the papers while he addressed the wrappers ready for mailing.

Mother, tired, but very happy sat in the editorial office to rest, before going home. She had not realized how weary she was, until the reaction came. Ted, passing the door of the sanctum, saw that she had fallen asleep, her glasses in her hand, a smile almost child-like upon her courageous old face. He and Uncle Ike walked on tiptoes and talked in whispers lest they might waken her, while they were going in and out mailing the papers. When the last papers had been taken to the post office it was very late.

Mother slept the sleep of sheer exhaustion, and when she awakened it was almost dark, there was a soft drizzle of rain beating against the office window, and Uncle Ike stood beside her, his shabby old overcoat buttoned up to the chin, his umbrella in his hand.

"It is rainin', honey, an' de city am saved," he said. "I done see de new doctah by de street doah, as I come up, an' he say de fevah wave am broke an' de city am saved."

"Thank God!" said Mother fervently. She arose and donned her hat and coat and leaning on the arm of her faithful old black servant went home in the gathering dusk.

But Oh, it was Christmas day when Jim Walton came back from the borders of death and sent a message to a number of his friends to meet him and his staff at the Searchlight office. They came and outnumbered the invited guests, for they knew Jim would be glad to see them. They filled the stairway and crowded around the street door, everyone of them loved big-hearted, jolly Jim. Mother had gone home to put on an elaborate bit of old filmy lace, which she pinned about her neck with an old-fashioned, oval brooch which was set with a single pearl in the center—an heirloom in her family for generations. She wore neither hat nor bonnet, but went with her dear old head uncovered to meet Jim whom the good Lord had given back from the jaws of death. And the Christmas bells were ringing in this glad land of blooms and sunshine, while the city lifted up its voice in thanksgiving.

People nodded and smiled, and made way for her as she went up the stairs, walking with the unconscious pride of her ancestors, which the well-born never lose.

"Howdy! Mother Ladly, howdy!" they said. "It was downright brave of you to report for the Searchlight through all the yellow peril."

"Thank you," said Mother very gently, "I did my duty."

The minister and his wife joined her at the head of the stairs. The large room in the Searchlight office leading to the editorial room was crowded, Mother had scarcely entered the office when a big, gaunt figure pushed its way through the crowd which gave a shout of welcome. The big fellow who was followed by the new doctor went straight past everyone in the crowded room, over to where a dignified old lady stood straight and composed, with a wonderful joy in her eyes. He took both her hands in his, the tears were running down his cheeks.

"Mother Ladly!" he cried, "Mother Ladly! Ted told me about it! there is not another person in the town could have done it!"

"Why, Jimmy, you are crying!" said Mother in wonder. "I wouldn't cry, if I were you," she added remonstratingly.

"Crying! I'm bawling!" cried Jim chokingly, "and I don't care if I am— and I don't care if the whole town sees me, or the whole United States! there are times when it is an honor to a man to cry!"

"Mrs. Ladly has been game alright. She has done your paper good service reporting for it through all this terrible siege, and we have been told that she used to be a great writer," said some of the townspeople.

"Used to be a great writer!" cried Jim explosively. "She is a great writer yet! When a man or woman has achieved greatness in literature or journalism once they never lose it! They are great always. No one can rob a man or a woman of what they have achieved by their own brains, and their own intellectual industry! Little Mother is the greatest writer that ever came to this state!" Jim's voice broke suddenly. "Such a fragile — delicate little woman — whom the years have not treated well. With a soul more loyal and a courage more indomitable than a man's—not one of us have appreciated her, although she has been an honor to our town every day she has blessed it with her presence!"

"Reported for the Searchlight? Yes, in the most dangerous portions of our pestilence stricken city, in the very jaws of death and peril—but what is more she has written every line that went into the paper, out of her own brain and her own experience and knowledge. She has set up every line she wrote in type, read the proof. The Searchlight was published by her and written by her and edited by her alone. She can accomplish anything that can be accomplished! Friends and neighbors I want to say right here, to all of you, that I never had a mother since mine died when I was a little chap, but from this day the Searchlight adopts Mother Ladly—I adopt her—as my own mother." The tears in Jim's eyes and the big sob in his throat robbed his words of the ludicrousness of adopting a mother. "After this Mother's name will appear on the Searchlight as managing editor. Mother and I and the boy, will run the Searchlight."

That was a proud moment for a shining-eyed boy encircled by Jim Walton's left arm, while his right hand held Mother's in a grasp that meant eternal affection and honor. There was a moment's silence and then the crowd burst into applause. The people kindly hearted and impulsive had not realized their lack of appreciation and with the true courtesy and generosity of all Southern people they made quick amends by cheer after cheer of good will and appreciation and a torrent of words of praise and wonder of apology and regret.

As for little Mother—she stood there —with the soft color coming and going in her dear old face, a great light of joy and surprise in her clear eyes. In that moment the years seemed to roll back and vanish. If there were wrinkles in that radiant face they no longer saw them, if she were aged in reality they no longer remembered it—they saw only a sweet, flushed face and tender, tear-wet eyes flashing with triumphant joy,— a woman crowned with eternal youth which time is powerless to touch.

Back of them just inside the threshold, stood an old, bent figure mopping the tears off his wrinkled face as he kept repeating between his sobs:

"Bress Gord, its Christmas day — an' dey hab done come back to rememorate it! Bress Gord A'mighty! Bress Gord A'mighty!"

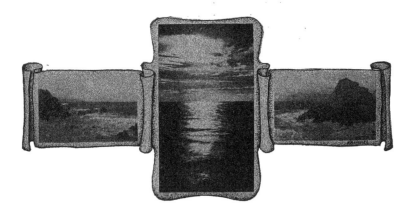

Spot

By F. H. Sidney

SPOT was a brindle, bow-legged, English bulldog, the property of "Big Jim" Keegan, who was more or less of a "drifter," wandering about from place to place working at numerous occupations. Sometimes he hunted for gold in the mountains, and then again he drove mule teams hauling supplies across the desert to mining camps. Jim was a bachelor and Spot had been with him ever since he was a puppy.

Whenever Jim had saved money enough to enable him to live without working for a while, he would quit his job, and he and Spot would go off into the woods, or hills and enjoy themselves on a camping trip. Many of these trips were spent among the mountains and streams of Northern California. How they did love to camp in the Shastas during the hot summer weather. Jim had taught Spot to stalk game, for a bulldog, if taken when young, can learn stalking very readily.

It had always been "Big Jim's" ambition to make a "stake" large enough to enable him to buy a little ranch in the mountains where he could live in comfort the rest of his days. Whenever Jim was in the mountains, he was always "prospecting" in hopes of sometime striking par ore in sufficient quantities to allow him to realize his ambition.

At the time of the Klondike gold excitement "Big Jim" had been working as a rock miner at good wages for a long while, and he had saved over a thousand dollars. Jim decided this would "grub stake" them to the 'new diggings," and there he might make his "stake." He always told his plans to Spot who wagged his stub tail as though he understood.

Jim gave up work, drew his money from the bank, and started for the north country. The steamer they sailed for Alaska on was crowded with men and dogs of all descriptions. It had been re-ported that sledge dogs would be scarce in Alaska, consequently many men were taking with them whatever dogs they could buy, beg or steal. There were dogs of all kinds on board, from the sad-eyed St. Bernard to the frisky collie. Jim was taking chances of buying what sledge dogs he needed when cold weather came on. Many men asked him why he carried Spot, for the thin-haired bulldog was not suited to the cold northern climate, and as he only weighed fifty pounds was hardly suited for sledge work. "Big Jim" smiled and said nothing; he and Spot were too good friends to be parted, even though the dog was not suited to the harness.

They arrived in Alaska at last, and Spot was glad to be on dry land once more. The weather was fine and warm, and everything seemed to be blooming the same as it was when they left California.

Jim engaged passage for himself, Spot and their outfit on a river steamer. They landed at Rampart City, and camped on the bank a few days before going back into the "diggings." Their claim was staked and located, and "Big Jim" went immediately to work.

Jim was lucky from the beginning, striking pay dirt very early. Not in very great amounts, but enough to pay him to hold the claim. Spot had a splendid time, the country was new and he explored all sorts of odd places. There were rabbits and foxes to hunt, once he followed a moose track through the forest, and suddenly came upon a gigantic bull moose standing at bay waiting for him. The bull charged, and Spot dodged into a thicket and made tracks for home.

Before cold weather had set in Jim built them a nice warm cabin to winter in. He expected to take several hunting trips into the wilderness in order to secure fresh meat; "perhaps we'll get a moose Spot," he said. Jim was unaware

that Spot had already tracked a moose
and the giant had driven the dog home.
Of course with Jim's support Spot would
take chances with a grizzly. Spot wagged
his tail in approval when his master told
him about the proposed hunting trips.

One day after the snow had come, Jim
put on his snowshoes and started for
Rampart City. It was his intention to
buy a sledge and some dogs. Spot was
delighted with the idea of going for a
run, and he ran ahead of Jim barking joyfully. The dog started several rabbits
and foxes and chased them a short distance, but Jim called him back. This
was not a hunting trip, there was business of greater importance to be transacted. Spot had no idea Jim was on his
way to buy a team of dogs, or he wouldn't
have been so joyful. He hated the treacherous wolf dogs.

On several occasions he had tried to
be friendly with them and had been
badly bitten.

Imagine Spot's surprise, when his master bought a team of six "huskies" and
a sledge. What ugly snapping creatures
they were. Spot was wise enough to
keep out of reach of their treacherous
jaws.

Jim harnessed the dogs to the sledge
and they started to "mush" back to camp.
Spot slunk along behind, he was not the
least bit pleased. Jim tried to cheer him
up but without any success. It was
plain to be seen that Spot was jealous.
He did not want any other dogs win a
place in his master's affections.

When they reached home Jim unhitched the "Huskies" and picketed them
outside, and he and Spot went into the
cabin to prepare supper. Spot and Jim
enjoyed a meal of bacon, beans and hot
bread. Each of the "huskies" were fed
a single dry salmon, which they swallowed with a gulp.

"Well, Spot," said Jim, "don't be jealous I need those dogs this winter, and
in the spring I'll get rid of them."

Poor Spot could not get over his feeling of dejection, he did feel so bad. It
didn't seem as though it could ever be
the same between he and Jim again.

Jim packed the sledge with supplies
one day, hitched in the dogs and started

for the woods. They were off to hunt
the moose. Spot didn't seem to care
whether he went along or not, but Jim
called him rather sharply, and he knew
it was best to obey. Jim ran ahead and
broke trail for the "huskies" while Spot
followed behind the sledge.

They stopped at midday, Jim built a
fire and cooked dinner, and after a short
rest they moved on. The third day out
they ran across moose tracks. Jim picketed the "huskies," while he and Spot
stalked the moose.

The snow was deep, which made hard
traveling for the big creature they were
following. Finally the moose turned on
them, but before he could charge a shot
from Jim's rifle brought him down. Jim
immediately dressed, and quartered the
moose, and tying the meat in a bundle
in the hide, he suspended it from a tree
out of the way of wolves, and went for
the team to haul it back home.

The moose meat kept them supplied
for a long time, this was occasionally
varied with rabbits and other small
game. Spot seemed to brighten up towards spring, and Jim concluded the
dog was getting over his jealousy.

Spring came in all its beauty, and Spot
spent a great deal of time in the woods.
In the meantime Jim disposed of his
"huskies," for he intended to leave for
California before cold weather came
again. Spot happened to be running in
the woods one day; when he suddenly
came upon a wolf. It was too late for
him to get out of the way, consequently
he made a stand. Spot braced back and
showed his teeth; but to his surprise,
the wolf seemed friendly. She was a big
grey timber wolf, beautiful as any dog
he had ever seen. After she had made
several playful advances Spot decided
to accept her friendship. She whispered
wonderful stories in his ear of beautiful
places in other parts of the north country, and begged Spot to accompany her
to the country she described. Spot did
not like the idea of leaving Jim, but the
call of nature was too strong, and he
trotted along beside her.

Jim was broken-hearted when Spot
failed to return. He hunted for the dog
all summer, but when autumn came with-

out finding him, Jim packed his goods and took passage on the last river steamer of the season. This brought him to the coast in time to catch a steamer for San Francisco. He hardly knew what to do when he arrived there, his hopes of saving money enough to retire to a ranch had been fulfilled; but he hated to go back into the hills without Spot. There were other dogs, of course, but Jim seemed to have no interest in them. The consequence was that Jim went to work in order to keep busy and try and forget the loss of the dog he loved so well.

In the meantime Spot in his new environment soon forgot all about Jim. He raised several families before he died; and his progeny in turn also raised families. After a while rumors were afloat of a new and unknown breed of wolves that had been seen in Alaska.

These were described as being peculiarly marked, bow-legged and with undershot jaws. They were almost human in their cleverness, always eluding capture and escaping being shot.

Jim happened to read an account of this new species of wolves in a San Francisco newspaper several years after he lost Spot. The very next day he took passage for Alaska. He traveled hundreds of miles in the north country with no other companions save his sledge dogs; he was looking for the new species of wolves, which he knew were the descendents of Spot. Jim would stand in the forest hours at a time listening to the howls of wolves, then again he would stalk them as he had game. But he failed to realize the object of his search.

The fiercest, coldest storm of the season caught Jim and his team on the trail. Their provisions had given out. The dogs became exhausted and laid down when they could pull no longer. Jim mercifully shot them, threw his blankets over his shoulders, and plodded on alone. He walked until his strength gave out, then laid down in the snow to die. Covering up his face with his blanket, he was soon fast asleep; a sleep from which he would probably never awake.

As the snow drifted over him, Jim felt the warmth coming back into his chilled body, and he dreamed that he was lying beside a comfortable fire in a cabin, and that Spot was lying beside him.

Jim slept under the snow for thirty-six hours, then the storm subsided. And after the storm along came a brindle, bow-legged wolf dog, with huge "undershot" jaws. He found Jim's sledge where it had been abandoned; and he dug out the bodies of Jim's dogs. Apparently this wolf was not hungry for he failed to make a meal off the bodies of the dead dogs. The wolf dog sniffed, and then whined. There seemed a strange and not unfamiliar scent about the sledge and outfit. Where had he run across such a scent before? He was only a year old, but it seemed as if in the distant past he had belonged to a man who bore such a scent. The wolf dog dug into the snow, picked up Jim's trail, followed it, and in a short time he was pawing the snow away from the place where Jim slept.

The dog soon had Jim uncovered, he pawed and sniffed at the blanketed face, and waked Jim up. Jim straightened out his body, and rolled over exposing his face to full view; the puppy saw the great undershot jaw and barked for joy, he recognized his master; even though he had been born several generations after the original Spot had mated with a wolf, and changed the breed of wolves in that section of the north country.

It took Jim several minutes to realize what had happened; then it came to him, and he said: "Hello Spot! "Where have you been all these years?" Jim got up onto his feet, and the wolf dog barked joyfully.

They retraced their steps and found Jim's sledge. Jim felt stronger after his sleep, and he drew the sledge, while the wolf dog followed along behind.

After three hours' walk they came to a mining camp. Here Jim found shelter for Spot, the wolf dog, and himself. As soon as he had recovered from the effects of his exposure, he started for the coast, arriving there safely, they took passage for San Francisco. As soon as they reached Frisco they took the first train for the Shastas, where Jim bought a little ranch, and he and Spot spent many happy years together.

The Great Stone Table

By Carleton W. Kendall

HE man staggered onward. His tongue hung out of his mouth. His eyes were bloodshot. His feet moved like leaden slugs across the fleshless desert.

He took three steps more—stumbled and fell in the sand.

"The Table — The Table — The Great Stone Table," he shrieked hoarsely and staggering to his feet again, stumbled toward the mountains — naked, vipered, desolate.

Before him, on one of these mountains —a bare rock dome—was a great boulder carved by erosion into the shape of a massive stone table. It stood out on the naked crest like the feasting-board of some Gargantua—a huge, bare rock.

Gordon Kingsburry had determined that there he would die.

He was an anthropologist by profession. Months before he had come into the desert to search for the ruins of an Egyptian Colony, said to have been founded upon the shores of North America. And for months he had searched. At last deserted by his companion, a Mexican, he had tramped across the sands alone. Now starving and without water he staggered on to die.

He was a young man, barely thirty— a devoted scientist and a lover of the great outdoors. He was too young to die.

The scorching heat of the sun absorbed the remaining moisture in his body. With leaden feet he staggered onward. The massive stone slowly grew nearer. He was now at the foot of the mountain. Painfully he began the ascent. He stumbled again. This time he lay still for a few minutes before climbing to his feet. He was half way now. He fell once more. He tried to rise but could not. It was all up with him. He got to his knees and crawled. If he could only make the

rock, he could die in peace.

The sun smote him. He divided the distance again. The great rock began to loom over him. He looked up at it and laughed—a hollow, brittle laugh,

"It wasn't a rock after all. It was a great umbrella—a great, green umbrella with water pouring off it. Funny, he thought it was a rock."

Summoning all his strength, he staggered to his feet and reached out his hands to catch the moisture. They grasped only dust laden air. "It was so funny." He laughed and shrieked aloud.

"He didn't spring high enough, that was the trouble."

He made an attempt to spring into the air. He seemed to spring out of his body and float in a vast, dismal void. In reality he crumpled up on the rocks to die.

Three days later, he awakened to find himself staring at the carved ceiling of a stone-lined room. In bewilderment he looked about him. He found he was in a square stone chamber whose high carved ceiling reminded him of a frosted cake. The only means of illumination was a hole in the ceiling, from which projected a beam of golden sunlight. This beam fell upon a young girl, clad in a spotless white robe of soft cotton cloth. Her arms and shoulders were bare. Their graceful curves and slender charm were screened by a thick abundance of raven black hair, falling naturally over them. Her face was fresh and delicate in its delineation. So beautiful was she that he wandered if she were human.

But he did not have long to wonder. For seeing him awakened from his stupor, she came quickly to his bedside. Taking a bowl of hot steaming broth from a table nearby, she raised his head cidedly better. And two days later he was again himself.

During this interval, he had a chance to learn much about his surroundings. He found he was in a deep, narrow valley—sunken down in the very heart of the desert mountains like a beautiful garden in a sanddune. The walls of this valley were smooth perpendicular cliffs. Its only connection with the outside world was a narrow trail hewn out of the face of the cliff and disappearing in a hole in the wall midway from the top. Directly over this hole — perched on the very edge—was the great stone table. And directly below this freak of nature was a tiny lake of clear, blue water, fringed with tufted cabbage palms. Upon one side of this lake was the ruin of a once prosperous Egyptian city—consisting for the most part of the stone house in which he found himself, an ancient temple and a scattered assortment of adobe dwellings—all occupied. The inhabitants, he found were pure blood Egyptians; that is, all but the girl. She was part American and spoke English. The rest, all save the old man who was the head of the village, spoke the ancient tongue. Her father, a mining engineer, had wandered into the little valley years before. Captivated by its charm, he had remained until his death, four years previous.

These discoveries made Kingsburry fairly itch to get out and examine the surrounding buildings and wealth of ethnological material. He anticipated little trouble in gathering his data. The people were a simple home-loving race, ruled by the old man whom they called the Pharaoh and held in high esteem. This old man, Kingsburry learned was the grandfather of the girl, Sais by name. She promised to bring Kingsburry before him, for an audience, just as soon as he regained his strength. He knew that if he could win over the old man his work would be easy. So he was anxious to get the interview over as soon as possible.

It was the afternoon of the second day. He sat in the stone lined room examining the architectual features of the in-

watching him.

"How are you feeling this afternoon?" she asked, speaking the words slowly and distinctly and with an affectation Kingsburry liked to hear.

"Alright," he answered, "thanks to your careful nursing."

The faint pink of the Amaryllis stole into her cheeks.

"I have made arrangements for you to see my grandfather."

"Good" he ejaculated, rising, "The sooner the better."

"Come then." She led the way down the dark corridor and out into the garden.

This garden was surrounded by a low wall—broken on the side facing the little lake by an imposing Egyptian archway. In its exact center was a fountain surrounded by trees, shrubs, flowers, palms and green grass. In the daytime it was a riot of color and shade. Birds, bees and butterflies swarmed amongst the blossoms.

Beside the fountain was a huge umbrella tree. And beneath this tree, Kingsburry saw an old man with white hair and a vivid scarlet robe and sphinxhood. He was seated on a richly carved chair of massive proportions. Behind him stood two attendants — naked save for loin cloths—their arms crossed in front of them.

As they approached, the old man arose feebly and fastened upon Kingsburry a pair of piercing black eyes.

"Your name and nationality," he asked croakily.

"Gordon Kingsburry, an American."

He raised his hand in a benedictial manner. There was a primative calm and quiet about him.

"You are welcome. Stay as long as you want," he said, then proceeded to tell him how they had found him in the desert at the base of the great stone table.

Kingsburry bowed, and thanking him, withdrew. He was satisfied. The task before him was simple. All he had to do was to gather his data and then make his escape. The thought of what his discovery would mean to the world of science thrilled him. As the days went by the magnitude of it overpowered him. It would be the greatest discovery since the Rosetta Stone. And the more he learned about the history of the city, the more eager he was to present it to the world.

He worked with an anxious rapidity. What if anything should happen to him before he could turn the facts over to his colleagues. He examined inscriptions and copied them into his one notebook. He measured buildings and ruined foundations. He talked with all of the sixty-four who remained of the once mighty race, which for a time swayed the Mediterranean. He found the colony had been sent out from Egypt during the reign of Ramesses II, supposedly to Further India. That a mighty storm had seized the boats and driven them far out into the Pacific — with the result that they had landed on the shore of North America. This much he gleaned from inscriptions on the inside of the Temple.

Nothing could have gone better. In three short weeks, he had accumulated the major portion of his data. Never had he performed field work under such pleasant conditions. His health was splendid. The little valley — with its wealth of foliage set in the dry atmosphere of the desert—thoroughly agreed with him.

Days he spent making drawings and immersed in a bustle of careful and accurate work. During these times he saw little of the girl. But every evening, after the heat of the day had subsided, he always found her in the garden. There they would chat until dark or climb up the narrow trail to the great stone table to watch the sunset.

This trail, itself, was quite an engineering feat. It lead up the face of the cliff. Then for over two hundred yards consisted of a gallery through the solid rock. This gallery emerged at the foot of a flight of stone steps, which in turn led up to the top of the great table, itself —inside the center pedestal. From this point of vantage, it was possible to obtain a wonderful view of the quiet little valley below and the fleshless moun-

tains, dividing it from the bustle and hum of civilization.

But every fifth evening the high priest —whom Kingsbury found to be very much like all primitive sorcerers—went to the great stone table and prayed to the sun god. To this ceremony Kingsbury owed his life. And so he and Sais always went around to the other side of the lake up on a little rise—from where they could get a view of the valley and the stone table above—and watched him perform its rites.

This night was such a night. The sweltering heat of the day had gradually subsided. The little patches of gardens which covered that side of the valley were deserted. The silver stream leading from the lake—it had no inlet—rippled over the rocks, gurgling and plashing until it disappeared in a swirling pool beneath the overhanging cliff, as if swallowed up in the mystic cauldron of some Necromancer. A curl of blue smoke wafted upward from the primitive houses. The rippled babble of a child's laugh sounded from time to time. The great cliffs towered in silence. The peaceful little valley was gradually being immersed in shadow.

Kingsbury — more thoughtful than usual—looked at Sais. She was dressed in a fresh white robe made from raw cotton. Her beautiful arms and shoulders were covered with a thin shawl of the same material. She was watching the shadow creep across the valley. Her whole being radiated natural, unaffected beauty.

"How did the work come along today?" she asked suddenly.

She had taken a keen interest in his work.

"Fine," he replied, "I'm finished now."

"And then you will want to go back to your own people?"

It was a question and a statement rolled into one.

Kingsbury nodded. "Yes I would like to get away. You see I don't want to live off your grandfather for ever. I don't want him to be offended, so I think it would be better to go without telling him." He knew the old man would want him to stay and he did not

For a moment Sais said nothing, then she nodded.

"Tomorrow, at this time," she replied.

Her voice sounded husky as she said it. And through the gathering darkness Kingsburry thought he saw tears come into the black eyes, before she turned her head.

And as he looked out over the simple, little valley before him — hidden these long years from the world—it cast its spell upon him. He thought of the modern civilization with its jangling trolley cars, its klaxhorning automobiles, its smoky cities, its mad swirl and tear for wealth. And he asked himself "what is wealth?" For thousands of years men had striven for it, fought for it, builded for it. They had trampled one another in an attempt to reach it — to make it theirs. They had erected vast civilizations to conquer it; they had made laws to govern its distribution; they had made their wills to dispose of it when they were dead — when all the time it had come to each man without his even taking the trouble to ask for it. As Kingsburry looked out over the now dusky valley, he realized for the first time the unnaturalness of the life he had been leading. In the gathering gloom, he saw before him the true wealth of life—a happy, contented existence.

But as they returned to the stone house, he forgot all in the plans for his departure.

The next day he checked up his data. Sais watched him with a saddened expression upon her face. But Kingsburry was too enthusiastic at his great discovery to notice it. He was lost in dreams of glory, honor and fame—those triumphant three which have made emperors and destroyed empires. When he emerged the world would kneel at his feet. He would prove once for all his pet theory of ancient communication between the new and the old world. He sorted his papers, thinking as he gazed upon each one, of what an uproar it would create in a few days.

That night he met Sais in the garden. Together they climbed the trail in silence.

appeared fairly opalescent as its surface caught the last slanting rays.

When they emerged on the top of the great stone table, he was spellbound. The heavens had outdone themselves to produce a magnificent sunset on this evening of his departure. He looked at the little sunken garden at his feet. It was beginning to fade before his eyes. The surrounding desert was bare as ever, but the sunset had tinged it a vivid pink until it was like an enchanted fairyland. Up there on the colossal flat stone, he felt as if they were above the slime and vissitudes of the earth-life. He took one last look again down into the valley. The only evidence of life was the blue curl of smoke, which melted away before it rose above the surrounding cliffs.

His "escape" was ridiculously easy. If the old man had any suspicion, Sais had so cleverly managed it that they had not been aroused. It was nothing unusual for them to go up to the stone table to see the sunset and as they had gone empty-handed, there was nothing outwardly different from their trip that night than from those of the past weeks. Sais had very cunningly had the provisions and Kingsburry's roll of data hidden that afternoon at the base of the stone table. So all he had to do was to drop to the ground, gather them up and walk away.

He looked at the waning light. It was time he was off. He turned to the girl. She was back of him, gazing out onto the pink desert. Her white gown had been tinged pink as well as the sand below. Her raven black hair hung loosely down her back. Her bare shoulders peeped from beneath the tresses. She was like a spirit of the sunset—standing there on the mountain top. Kingsburry thought of the happy days they had spent together in the little valley at his feet and he felt a pang at having to leave it. He took a step toward her—hesitated. Then, without a word, he went to the edge of the table and prepared to drop to the ground below.

A thunderous roar sounded from the north. The stone beneath him gave a preliminary quiver. The air was filled with crashing, tumbling sound. With a mighty jerk, he pulled himself back onto the rock. Springing to the center of the great table he threw himself face downward on the stone, pulling the girl down beside him.

He wasn't a second too soon.

With an angry crash the earthquake struck. The great stone heaved and shook. He prayed that it wouldn't be thrown into the valley beneath.

At one moment they swayed far out over the abyss; at another he fancied he felt the rock crack beneath them. The whole mountain side seemed about to split asunder.

How many minutes it lasted, Kingsburry did not know. The girl clung to him silently. Together they awaited the death they felt was inevitable. Kingsburry could feel her warm breath on his cheek. He could see her bosom rise and fall. Yet she uttered not a word.

At last the first great shock was over. But before they could take a relieved breath, it was followed by a second—more violent than the first.

This second in turn was followed by a succession of smaller shocks recurring at intervals. It was already dusk. To attempt to return to the valley would have been death. For all they knew the gallery might have caved in. So they huddled together on the top step of the stone stairway to await for dawn.

That night was one which Kingsburry long remembered. Throughout succeeding intervals, smaller shocks occurred—some as heavy as a number eight, others of greatly lesser magnitude. It was a night of terror. The girl clung to him silently. There was no need for words. They were both busy with their own thoughts. And throughout the long hours, Kingsburry did a good deal of thinking—thinking he had never dreamed he was capable of.

At last the air grew colder, sharper. The stars grew brighter—then began to fade. In the east, a faint paleness was visible. It increased. The shocks stopped. The paleness grew. At last the sky was bathed in the scarlet aura of the sun. Then with a burst of golden glory, the great ball emerged above the mountains.

Kingsburry arose and went to the edge of the table. When he looked down, a cry of astonishment broke from his lips. At his feet swirled a great lake of dirty, yellow water. Beneath it somewhere was the city, the palms and the floor of the valley. His great discovery had been swept away in a single night. It was now, no more. But curiously enough, he did not care. His one thought was for Sais. Returning to her, he took her in his arms.

"Come," he said, "I'm going to take you with me across the desert."

Her brown eyes looked up into his and he knew she understood.

"It is the will of God," he said, and kissed her.

In the Realm of Bookland

BELGIUM—Brand Whitlock.

While it might as well be confessed that the American public is rather "fed-up" on war literature of every sort, and that concerning Belgium and the invasion particularly, here is a book, which, because of its peculiar origin, will still command no little interest from the great public, and rightly so. First, because the writer and historian, a trained observer and skillful writer, saw what he records at first hand, and had, moreover, a better opportunity to observe the "inside" of things than any other person, and second, because Brand Whitlock has a charm of style which adds value to anything he sees fit to write.

His chapters describing the life about him in Brussels, and near his summer home, in those now long lost and pleas-

ant days before the war, are by all means the most enjoyable to the reader, as they, no doubt were to the writer. Whitlock was the American representative to the Belgium court and government, in 1914, when the Germans threw down the gauntlet to the world. He had distinguished himself as a novelist, and had been selected for the post in accordance with President Wilson's policy of chosing men of intellectual attainments for foreign diplomatic berths.

Whether because of the strain of the multitudinous duties which fell upon him as head of the American Relief work in Belgium, or whether his patience and temper were worn thin by the exasperating and baffling evils he was forced to witness, a note of querulousness creeps into the last chapters which rather mars the book; and sometimes even creates a reluctant feeling of something approaching sympathy in the breast of the reader for those against whom Whitlock testifies. At least, he creates at times an impression of being no longer a dispassionate witness. Notwithstanding, this work of Whitlock's (in two volumes) is a very valuable document upon the history of the great world war, and should be possessed by every student of those troublous times who is able to afford the rather high price. D. Appleton & Company, publishers—$7.50.

Piffle's Book of Funny Animals.

Here's a playtime book for those little ones who are learning to recognize their letters. The drawings and the rhymes are really funny, and calculated to catch the fancy of a child. It is a small gift-book, and gotten out by Henry Altemus, publisher—50c.

The Long Years Ago Stories.

This dainty volume of stories by Alice Ross Colver sets about accounting for various peculiarities of animals familiar to every child. The "legends" are original, ingenious and amusing to grown-ups as well as to children. The Robin's Red Breast, the Cat's Purr, the Rooster's Crow are all accounted for in a manner that will surprise and delight the youthful reader. The book is quaintly illus-

trated and bound in colors, and is suitably a "little book for little people." Henry Altemus—50c.

Off Duty.

This is a collection of short story masterpieces by such well-known and beloved men as Bret Harte, O. Henry, Sheamus McManus, William Dean Howells, and Stewart Edward White, compiled by Miss Wilhelmina Harper for the delectation of the tedious hours off duty of Uncle Sam's soldiers and sailors. While the timeliness of such a book might seem to be passed with the demobilization effected on July 1st, this is not true. Miss Harper has utilized her knowledge of what soldiers and sailors like to read, and compiled a volume of yarns which former soldiers and sailors, even if now out of uniform, will enjoy reading, and by the same token, all former soldiers' and sailors' "homefolks" will, as well, enjoy these tales. Century Publishing Co.—$1.50.

The War Garden Victorious.

The war gardeners and amateur canners have, themselves, been "put up" in a book by Charles Lathrop Pack, president of the National War Garden Commission of Washington, who has written a record of the win the war activity of the city farmer.

The book is for libraries and private circulation and is not for sale. This is unfortunate, as many a man and woman who, through a patriotic, propaganda was led to put themselves in the way of gaining the inestimable benefits of soul and the lesser if more easily computed benefits of health and pocketbook, which come from sincere amateur gardening, would like to have just such a record of this wartime phenomenon.

And since the war garden will remain with us, let us hope as an asset in times of peace, there are in the back of the book incorporated two very good pamphlets, one of practical advice to beginners on such matters as garden tools, fertilizer, seeds and garden planning, and last, but not least, on how to fight the bugs, worms and blight. The other pamphlet gives the same sort of advice to the

housewife on the subject of how to preserve, can and pickle her vegetables and fruits, once they are harvested. These pamphlets can be had for the asking, of the National Victory Garden Commission, Washington, D. C. Dr. Pack's book is published by Lippincott.

A Sample Case of Humor.

If Strickland Gillilan's humor always runs according to the samples contained in this "case," we would like very much to have him fill an order for a carload lot of the same article. Gillilan pretends in the first of the book that he is going to let us in on the secret of the manufacture of his stock in trade. He does nothing of the sort. After reading the book from cover to cover—and even a book-weary reviewer does read it through once he nibbles, we didn't know any more about writing and thinking up humor than we did before. But we did know that Gillilan knows how. This is an unusually refreshing book. Forbes & Co.—$1.25.

The Man Who Discovered Himself.

This novel is probably founded upon some experience or observation of the writer's own life. The hero worships his wife and two daughters, and so sacrifices himself to their welfare that he becomes of no value to them. Effectually discarded by the superficial mate of his bosom, and seemingly a hopeless tubercular wreck, he goes into the desert in search of death and finds life. He learns to value himself at his own worth, through the love and admiration of a young rancher who rescues the poor "lunger" from death and gives him a material start in life. With a new name he reaps a new career, and how, after he has become governor of Arizona, he encounters the selfish, foolish wife, we will let the novelist, Willis George Emerson, tell you. Of course there is a love interest—between the one daughter who really loves her father and the young

rancher—but we leave that tale, too, to the novelist.—Forbes & Co.—$1.50.

"The Harvest Home," is a charming collection of verse by James B. Kenyon whose rank among American poets is a high one. This little volume proclaims Mr. Kenyon an artist, one who has profound appreciation of beauty and whose reactions to its manifestations no matter what their nature, are extremely sensitive. There are in particular some fine nature poems of great beauty. Such Poems as "The Prisoner and the Lark," "Two Lives," and "In Arcady," touch the soul with tender strains and inspire with sublime ideals. He is of the line of Whittier, with a love of nature as intense as Wordsworth's. James T. White & Company, New York.—$2.00.

"Flesh and Phantasy," by Newton A. Fuessle, is a collection of short stories refreshingly different. They are well written and startingly original, although his style and unexpected endings are reminiscent of O. Henry at his best. The Cornhill Company, publishers, Boston — $1.25.

"Little Mother America," by Helen Fitzgerald Sanders is a war story—but with a difference. The interest centers around a young Belgian girl who flees before the Germans and escapes to America. The shock, however, has destroyed her memory and she begins life again here adopting the name of her new country for her own. Her love for America and high spirit of patriotism puts to shame many American born. The love story is tender and original in that the hero is an American laboring man — a true type of America. This little book is particularly well written and holds the attention from the first word until the inspiring end when Little Mother America makes the supreme sacrifice for her new country. The Cornhill Co.—No price given.

Opportunity's One Knock

When *Opportunity* knocks, will we hear her?

Or will our ears be so deafened with debts and our minds so filled with money worries that we do not hear her happy message?

W. S. S. and Thrift Stamps help Opportunity knock loudly—one knock enough.

W. S. S.—
Everybody's Opportunity

Savings' Division
War Loan Organization
Treasury Department

Vol. LXXIV

No. 4

Overland Monthly

AN ILLUSTRATED MAGAZINE OF THE WEST

CONTENTS FOR OCTOBER, 1919

NOTICE.—Contributions to the Overland Monthly should be typewritten, accompanied by full return postage, and with the author's name and address plainly written in upper corner of first page. Manuscripts should never be rolled.

The Publisher of the Overland Monthly will not be responsible for the preservation or mail miscarriage of unsolicited contributions and photographs.

Issued Monthly. $1.50 per year in advance. Fifteen cents per copy. Back numbers 3 months or over 25c; six months or over 50c; nine months or over 75c; 1 year or over $1.00. Postage: To Canada, 3 cents; Foreign, 5 cents.

Copyrighted, 1919, by the Overland Monthly Company.

Entered at the San Francisco, Cal., Post-office as second-class matter.

Published by the OVERLAND MONTHLY COMPANY, San Francisco, California.
259 MINNA STREET.

Subscribe for the LIVING AGE

IF YOU WANT every aspect of the great European War presented every week, in articles by the ablest English writers.

IF YOU WANT the leading English reviews, magazines and journals sifted for you and their most important articles reproduced in convenient form without abridgment.

IF YOU WANT the *Best Fiction*, the *Best Essays* and the *Best Poetry* to be found in contemporary periodical literature.

IF YOU WANT more than three thousand pages of fresh and illuminating material during the year, reaching you in weekly instalments, at the cost of a single subscription.

IF YOU WANT to find out for yourself the secret of the hold which THE LIVING AGE has kept upon a highly intelligent constituency for more than seventy years.

Subscription---$6 a Year.   **Specimen Copies Free**

The Living Age Co.

6 BEACON STREET, BOSTON

Scientific Dry Farming

Are you a dry farmer? Are you interested in the development of a dry farm? Are you thinking of securing a homestead or of buying land in the semi-arid West? In any case you should look before you leap. You should learn the principles that are necessary to success in the new agriculture of the west. You should

Learn the Campbell System

Learn the Campbell System of Soil Culture and you will not fail. Subscribe for Campbell's Scientific Farmer, the only authority published on the subject of scientific soil tillage, then take a course in the Campbell Correspondence School of Soil Culture, and you need not worry about crop failure. Send four cents for a catalog and a sample copy of the Scientific Farmer. Address,

Scientific Soil Culture Co.
BILLINGS, MONTANA

Giant Grizzly in the Golden Gate Park Collection.

Beautiful Statue for Francis Scott Key, Author of "The Star Spangled Banner."

An Eloquent Divine's Statue, Golden Gate Park.

Quaint Dutch Windmill, Golden Gate Park.

OVERLAND  MONTHLY

Founded 1868   BRET HARTE

| VOL. LXXVI | San Francisco, October, 1919 | No. 4 |

Finest of All Parks

San Francisco's Magnificent Public Playground, where Nature and Art Have Found Delightful Expression

By Henrietta Sevilla Christiansen

THERE is no question that in many respects, Golden Gate Park in San Francisco is incomparable, and in all respects admirable, both in its many picturesque features and efficient management.

It is almost impossible to realize that forty years ago the area of Golden Gate Park was a monotonous waste of sand dunes. What the landscape artist who transformed the dunes saw in his mind's eye, was not visible to the ordinary observer, and hardly in the range of the enthusiast's imagination. Men to whom the management of famous parks is confided, dwell with especial force on their triumphs in this regard, but it is doubtful whether in the annals of achievement anything can be found to match the measure of success attained by the founders and builders of Golden Gate Park.

The land lying between Stanyan street on the east and the Pacific Ocean on the west was selected as a park site because such selection tended to make easier the adjustment of Outside Land titles. The eastern boundary of the Park would have extended to Divisadero street had it not been for greedy land owners who resisted the extension by their influence on the Common Council and the Legislature.

Public sentiment in favor of a popular pleasure ground in San Francisco impressed many of the large holders of Outside Lands, and as early as 1864 the agitation for Golden Gate Park begun. It appears that the squatters and claimants all along the line from the ocean beach to Divisadero street were asked to designate what they would give for a park reservation. Under this arrangement about $800,000 was raised and 1013 acres of land purchased for Golden Gate Park.

As the Park grows in beauty and enchantment the men and women who are lured by its woodland charms and vistas of verdure, insistently ask the question: "To whom shall we accord the credit for this noble creation?"

The question is often asked by visitors to San Francisco, and also by many of its citizens of the present generation. Undoubtedly it was an outgrowth of a public sentiment, but the person who of all others had most to do in the crystallization of the idea was Frank McCoppin. He served in several positions of prominence including that of Mayor of San Francisco, State Senator and United States postmaster at San Francisco. He also served as United States Commissioner to Australia when that country held its great world's exposition.

As Mr McCoppin was a man of broad vision and foresaw the greatness of San Francisco as the metropolis of the

Golden Gate Park Lodge Home and Office of Supt. John McLaren.

Happy Children in Their Playground, Golden Gate Park.

Pacific Coast. He was associated in politics and in business with men of the same high type as himself, and Golden Gate Park was one of their best achievements. United States Supreme Justice Stephen J. Field was also instrumental in clearing all the obstacles to the realization of the people's park project.

In efforts to reclaim the original sand wastes of Golden Gate Park from Strawberry Hill to the Pacific Ocean, the Park Commissioners found that lupin and barley would not hold the sand. Grass seed imported from France proved its efficiency at once. The sea bent grass, a native of the European coast, was also used with gratifying success. This grass requires little moisture and no manure, but it is a wonderful catcher and holder of the sand. The grass performs the initial work of holding back the drifting sands until the Monterey cypress and other branches of the pine family can assist in the work of reclamation. In due time the meadows are sown with Kentucky blue grass, and on the hillsides madrone, manzanita, laurel and other native trees take hold. |, :

The first work of considerable magnitude in the creation of Golden Gate Park was the reclamation and cultivation of the Panhandle. This strip of land one block in width extends from Baker street west to Stanyan, a distance of eight blocks. The Panhandle was really the beginning of Golden Gate Park, from a constructive point of view. The original cypress and eucalyptus trees planted in the Panhandle have attained the size of trees that are commonly found in native forests.

The early Park Commissioners were hampered in a great degree by the lack of funds to procure loam aid fertilizing material. The inadequate supply of water was an obstacle that impeded the progress of reclamation. They labored assiduously and left a work which repays all their effort.

The park or garden in its modern aspect and under the sway of progressive humanity, has come to be regarded as a place where the weary, whether weary of head work or hand work, may be refreshed by breathing pure air, gladdened by the sight of flowers and trees, and solaced by the sound of running waters.

Its loveliness is satisfactory. There is no jarring note in its ensemble; its winding drives, bordered with noble trees; its forests of pine; its graceful and undulating slopes mantled in the richest verdure; its glistening lakes; its romantic waterfall.

Away to the west is the grand old Pacific Ocean, with the fine sweep of coast line. Quite distinctly can be heard the muffled roar of the waves as they roll upon the long stretch of sandy beach. In the distance at sea, faintly outlined against the horizon are the Farallone Islands, twenty-one miles away. Northward an enchanting view of the bay and the Golden Gate, so famed in song and story, is obtained; and looking beyond, the light houses on Points Arena and Bonita are plainly discernible. Nearer is seen Sausalito, nestling 'neath the purple hills of Marin; while to the right is Mount Tamalpais, whose aspect on a fine day is truly a brilliant one, especially when the sun's rays fall upon it, showing beautiful effects of light and shade.

Golden Gate Park fulfills the modern idea as a park at the door of the people, where the children may go for air and play—a park accessible to men and women who cannot go to the country for rest and recreation. Whatever policies may be adopted by inland towns or cities of ordinary size, the fact is now obvious that San Francisco, one of the leading cities of the world, and destined to become densely populated, has made ample provision for the workers in every avenue of industrial life.

The lakes, comprising a chain across Golden Gate Park from northeast to southwest, between Avenues Forty and Forty-two, add in a marvelous degree to the natural charm of the landscape in the western section of the grounds. The designer of the lake group has so cleverly applied the advantages of the site that one is impressed with the idea that nature in one of her happiest moods bestowed the shore curves, the inlets and the isles for the delight of artists in the field of landscapes beautiful. To create the lake effect desired required an im-

Main Drive in Golden Gate Park.

Feeding—Wild Fowl, Stow Lake, Golden Gate Park.

Feeding Wild Fowl, Stow Lake, Golden Gate Park.

Another Glimpse of Stow Lake.

mense labor and cost a good deal of money. It was well spent.

The great center of popular interest in Golden Gate Park is the umbrageous spot where stands the Temple of Music, a magnificent gift of the late Claus Spreckels, the sugar king. The design is in the Italian Renaissance. It has a frontage of fifty-five feet and a height of seventy feet, flanked by Corinthian columns. Extending from the Corinthian columns on each side are colonnades, fifty-two feet six inches by fifteen feet wide, each supported by sixteen Ionic columns. The temple is a thing of beauty in its pure simplicity.

In front of this Temple of Music thousands of people sit on Sundays and holidays to listen to the band and special solo artists. The scene is Grecian in its golden sunshine and has no counterpart anywhere in America.

In the vicinity of the Temple of Music is the splendid Memorial Museum erected by M. H. deYoung of the San Francisco Chronicle. This museum promises to be the nucleus of one of the most famous in the world and is already a source of delight and wonder to thousands. When completed and fully arranged by the public spirited citizen, who has presented it to the people of San Francisco it will be a monument of which any benefactor should feel proud.

Not far from the Temple of Music is another fine but smaller museum in which can be found many a most admirable zoological exhibit arranged by the Academy of Sciences.

The Stadium at which horse races and other athletic events take place is one of the features of Golden Gate Park that excites much admiration and reflects great credit on its designers, Park Commissioner A. B. Spreckels and Park Superintendent John McLaren.

The Stadium presents features which command the attention of park managers in many cities of the world.

Its area is thirty acres and it is oval in form. It is encircled by a trotting track, sixty feet wide. Sloping toward the center of the field is a grassy terrace ten feet high and thirty feet wide. At the base of the terrace slope is a foot path, twelve feet wide. Inside of the footpath is a bicycle track twenty-five feet wide. Near the easterly end and inside the bicycle track is a quarter of a mile cinder track. Paralleling the straight-away of the bicycle path, is a 220-yard straight-away cinder track. Inside of the oval formed by the quarter of a mile cinder track there are spaces for hammer throwing, pole vaulting, jumping, etc. Space is also given for one basket-ball court and six football fields.

The buffalo paddock is one of the sights of Golden Gate Park. Buffalo Bill remarked that the herd of buffalo was one of the best he ever saw. Early in 1890 the Park Commissioners purchased five buffalo in Montana. Three of the animals, surviving the journey by rail to San Francisco, were placed in the Park. The herd now numbers thirty-five and could be doubled or even increased to 100 if a larger number were desirable. It is noted that the animals born in Golden Gate Park attain normal size and are not deficient in vigor or health.

The Elk Park is another delight for sight-seers in Golden Gate Park. California is the natural home of the elk. Alvinza Hayward gave the Commissioners one pair of elk, and the band is now large. Parks in Los Angeles, Fresno and other cities have been supplied from the collection in Golden Gate Park. Several deaths resulting from fights have occurred in the drove. The elk born in Golden Gate Park attain great size.

The Deer Paddock attracts multitudes of people. In 1888 Alex Duncan, of Duncan's Mills, Sonoma county, gave the first black-tailed deer to Golden Gate Park. Later on, Korbel Brothers and L. L. Robinson donated deer. The deer paddock now contains twenty-five bucks, does and fawns. Spotted deer from Hawaii, donated by Mr. Bishop, were subsequently brought to the Park, and they thrive as well as the native California deer.

Kangaroo from Australia mingle with the deer, twelve in number and thrive in a most satisfactory manner.

In 1909 four moose from Alaska were given to the Park by Henry Fortmann of San Francisco. They were caught young and brought to San Francisco at the ex-

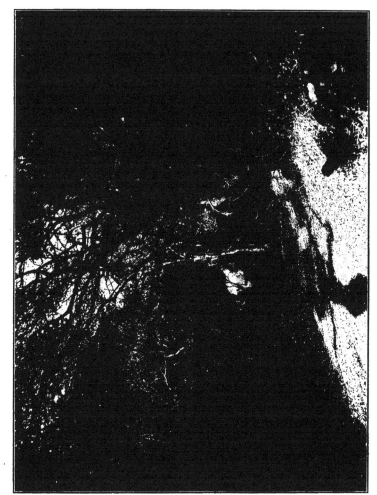

Pathway in the Woods, Golden Gate Park.

pense of the donor. They were given quarters near the deer and kangaroo, but have not done as well as the deer, elk and buffalo.

The Bear Pits in Golden Gate Park are a never-ending source of interest to old and young visitors. The Park Commissioners have difficulty in accommodating the numerous increases to their bear collection which includes the grizzly and many varied other huge varieties.

Stow Lake, where is situated the Golden Gate Park boathouse and where one can often see a great gathering of wild fowl, including all the migratory species of ducks, is one of the most picturesque artificial lakes in the world. In September the wild ducks from the Arctic, including the lordly canvas-back, begin to arrive at Stow Lake. One of the prettiest sights imaginable is that of children feeding the wild fowl, which become so tame during their sojourn that they almost take the food out of the children's hands. Swans, black and white, are numerous on the lake, and there are also pelicans and brant.

Huntington Falls which are part of Stow Lake are Park features of wonderful beauty.

The Lake itself is a marvel of the engineer's skill, art and nature being so subtly blended that one scarcely perceives the blending. The body of water is serpentine in form around the base of Strawberry Hill, leaving its banks and winding around many verdently fringed islands.

The drive around the Lake is famed for enchanting vistas which meet the eye at many of the curves of the roadway. The Lake is also a practical reservoir, having a capacity of 25,000,000 gallons of water. It is the central source of the park's irrigation system.

One of the most attractive resorts in Golden Gate Park is the Children's Playground. Here are swings, merry-go-rounds, May-poles, donkey rides, goat carts, restaurants and candy stands. The popularity or success of this enterprise is an object lesson to park governing bodies. This most admirable feature would require a long article in itself to do it justice.

The Commissioners in 1890 authorized the building of a Bird House. The Aviary with its many birds of goreous plumage, is one of the interesting features of the Park and is constantly improving.

An article on Golden Gate Park would be incomplete without eulogistical reference to the Conservatories, which were begun in 1877, at which time an appropriation of $40,000 for them was authorized. The Conservatories buildings were subsequently destroyed by fire, but through the generosity of Charles Crocker, the Railroad King, means were provided for their restoration. Since then nothing has occurred to prevent the horticultural development of Golden Gate Park. In no other part of the world is there such a wealth of rare flowers and plants, for perhaps no other public park, under the direction of a municipal board, is so fortunate in its selection of a park superintendent. In many respects Superintendent John McLaren of Golden Gate Park, is unique among botanists, for he not only possesses a perfect knowledge of the requirements of all forms of gardening, but is also a practical man in the fullest sense of the terms. Without Mr. McLaren's knowledge, energy, and honesty the Golden Gate Park of today would not have been possible of achievement. He nursed it in its infancy and guards it in its matured beauty.

In his long term of office as superintendent of Golden Gate Park, Mr. McLaren is being loyally supported by the various boards of Park Commissioners that have been appointed by Mayors of San Francisco. Under no board has there been any question of partisan unfairness, or misuses of the public money. The character of the citizens selected as Park Commissioners by the Mayors of San Francisco, has been such that suspicions of anything savoring of graft would be preposterous.

Park Commissioners have been chosen because they are men who had distinguished themselves in professional lines of commercial activity. Usually they have been men of large fortune, and always men of public spirit. They receive no salaries. Several of them have been liberal contributors out of their own for-

Chain of Lakes, in Golden Gate Park.

t
r
n
r-
.e
is
d
k,
d,
rk
lu-
en
ts,
ect
all
eal
ms.
en-
ark
e of
ncy

grin-
Mc-
the
mers
ts of
there
ness,
The
Park
San
inions
uld be

chosen
distin-
l lines
- they
and al-
receive
re been
wr for-

Another of the Picturesque Chain of Lakes.

tunes, to the beautification of Golden Gate Park.

A recent and notable case of such generosity was furnished by the late Banker Steinhart, whose principal gift will provide Golden Gate Park with a costly aquarium.

The donations of generous citizens have made the park museums treasure houses of art and historical mememtoes. The statuary of Golden Gate Park, which is far above the grade of monuments usually seen in such public places, also represents the contributions of patriotic citizens.

One might epitomize the attractions and advantages of Golden Gate Park, by saying that nothing is omitted from the list which should belong to a great popular playground, where hundreds of thousands of the citizens, annually, find rest, recreation and enjoyment.

Golden Gate Park, large, important as it is, forms but one link in the chain of public breathing places, which come under the supervision of the unsalaried park commissioners.

The list of parks maintained by the City of San Francisco include: Mission Park, Lincoln Park, Buena Vista Park, Union Square, Portsmouth Square, Franklin Square, Bernal Park, Duboce Park, Alta Plaza, Pioneer Park or Telegraph Hill, Holly Park, Alamo Square, Washington Square, Sunnyside Park, South Park, Garfield Square, Columbia Square, Hamilton Square, Lafayette Square, Lobos Square, Fairmont Park, McKinley Square, Jackson Square and several smaller and less important parks.

The Ground Squirrels of Old Grizzly

By R. A. Sell

T HE 'watch' of the mountain slopes, sly and inquisitive, but recklessly bold—this animated bunch of dead grass."

There are two well marked trails that lead from Berkeley to the top of Old Grizzly. Whichever trail you take, you will have at least two steeps from two hundred to four hundred feet in length with an elevation of fifty-fifty.

On entering the trail, there is a surprising suddenness of transition from populous city streets and suburban avenues to the quiet desolated hillside. The upper vales are peaceful and unfrequented. Beyond the foothills three populous cities appear as chess boards with houses for counters and the still bay stretches to the Golden Gate where it is framed in by a fringe of purple hills.

But there are cities above the clouds. Even above the campanile and the famous eucalyptus grove, the California ground squirrels have erected their sentry mounds and constructed their underground passage ways. According to Dr. Joseph Grinnell and Joseph Dixon who have made an exhaustive study of the ground squirrels of California, there are no less than three thousand individuals in the ground squirrel villages that are spread out along the sides of Old Grizzly. These villages have well-marked streets or paths that connect the open spots or sentry mounds and while an entrance to a burrow is usually found near the center of a bare spot, there are many entrances that are hidden by a bunch of grass, a few weed stems or a friendly stone.

This chubby ground squirrel is a looser animal than the swift striped "picket pin" of the prairie country, but there is something audacious about this half-skulking shadowy sentinel of the mountain side.

The air is notably cool and bracing on these open hillsides and there seems to be some kind of aromatic perfume born of these upper regions which tempts you to throw your shoulders back and inhale deep draughts; thus you may feel weary from the climb when your senses are alert making the conditions very favorable for observing these squirrels.

No one climbs Old Grizzly without seeing several of these cheerful little rodents but it takes two or three hours time and much patience to get on familiar terms with them. On one of those perfect afternoons when the buoyancy of the mountain air seemed to stimulate all forms of life, the squirrels seemed to be more numerous than usual and their ordinary round of play, which consists of running at one another and stopping in a crouching position, was enlarged upon by a series of circling around as though they were playing a sort of loop game of "tag."

Two youngsters dashed into the game. They seemed to be all animation; they were so reckless in making their jumps over the rocks that they often tumbled over and over. They would scramble over the old ones with as little concern as they would climb over a good sized rock. For a time the old ones continued their play without paying any particular attention to the youngsters, then a large well collared old fellow who was crouching in a well beaten runway, watched for a youngster and as it came up he deliberately rooted it over backwards. But instead of falling the little one swung around on its right hind foot and landed feet under like a cat. Then an old one followed a little one and thay had something of a game of "leap frog" over a line of grown-ups that happened to be posted along the path. For a time there was a general scamper, every one going in a semi-circle after taking a few jumps along the path.

The two youngsters seemed to be getting more attention than the others; even among squirrels, it seems that the play of the young furnishes entertainment for their elders. Soon after the game had assumed such proportions, there was an occasional whistle which was different from the ordinary call. It was the whistle of the young but it was so different from that of the adults that it was not immediately associated with those bits of animated fur that were flying around something like feathers in a whirlwind.

Soon after the young ones began to whistle, another youngster was in the game. This one was older and larger than the other young ones; it was a little more than half grown but it was just as wild and care-free. Then there were several more youngsters and they seemed to be increasing while they were being counted. Like the proverbial chicken that ran around the old hen so fast that it could not be counted, this flashing, running and jumping pageant of intermingling fluffy tails and glistening eyes was difficult to enumerate. The adults could be more easily counted; while the game began with eleven there were fourteen just after the third young one joined the party.

More of the young were joining in the game and their little squeaks and whistles were increasing. They came unnoticed and joined so easily into the game that about the only thing that the observer could be sure of was that there were more squarrels—more little ones than big ones. An actual count was impossible, but it seemed fair to estimate that there were twice as many young ones as there were old ones.

The play continued until there was almost a continuous squeak of the young, punctuated very frequently by a playful whistle of the old ones. These whistles were answered and repeated by others from more distant parts of the hillside but no more adults came to the party.

For about twenty minutes the spirit and animation of these youngsters increased and not infrequently one of them would miss its calculations and roll over. Sometimes these tumbles resulted in complete somersaults. The old ones seldom missed an opportunity to root over the young ones.

There came a shrill warning whistle from a distance and this was repeated almost among the players. A cloud of dust rose as the last three scampered into a large hole. The warning whistle continued as a large red-tailed hawk sailed overhead.

The Yellow Jacket

By Alvah E. Kellogg

WELL?" Frank Jinks grinned scornfully. "What're we going to do about it, Sam? Ol' Bill Shakespeare was right when he said, that 'there's a tide in the affairs of every man, what if taken at the flood, lead on to fortune but omitted lost,' you know. Shall we cash in?"

The sun flickered softly through a small cobweb covered window, upon a roll top oak desk in a dingy little office, in the little mining town of Gold Hill, Oregon. An assortment of ore was scattered broadcast over a large, dust covered table, standing in the middle of the room. The samples were from the Yellow Jacket group of claims. The mine was three miles out from the lazy little settlement, on the turbulent Rogue.

Sam McCall laid a paper on the desk. His hand trembled with emotion.

"If you are sure the assay is correct, and that the ore does not contain gold—then, Jesse Hunter, our lessor is broke—poor old dad is stung, for that money we borrowed at the bank to carry on the work—and, I would say that the Yellow Jacket is no mine," said the slightly built young man whom he addressed.

"Sam," said Jinks, "you amuse me—you sure do. You're the most unresourceful cuss. As my ol' dad'y would say, 'you're a damn fool.' After playing the game for twenty years, don't you think for a moment I'm quitting the Yellow Jacket. Forget it, guess again."

"But—how—can we continue?" asked Sam, as he gazed listlessly around the room.

"I'll tell you the game," said the old veteran of many a wild cat promotion scheme in the mining regions of the West, as he reared back in his swivel chair, hoisting his feet upon the desk. Then, beginning to stroke his heavy black mustache with a groggy hand, "while you're on your feet, Sam, hand over that bottle of Hunter's rye, and them glasses, will you? Yank that chair over here and sit down."

"Now," he continued, as the alcohol fumes from his breath and the well-filled glasses met pervading the musty quarters, "here's the proposition; none but you'n Hunter, me'n that ol' Doc Hig'ns at Los Angles shall profit from this deal. That ol' doc has made good on all his mining investments; and, several, on my recommend, too. His boob friends in the city are dying to get a hunch from ol' Doc to plunk their spare change into a mine. A word from the ol' doc will stampede the small fish. He'll be our financial agent."

"I have not the least idea," declared Sam, "what you are talking about."

Jinks suddenly dropped his feet to the floor with a thud, which startled Sam, and aroused him from his reverie. Then, with his black foxy eyes peering through narrow slits, Jink placed his trembling hand on Sam's knee, and in a low, firm tone said:

"Ol' pal, we'll salt her. I'll have ol' Doc come up from the city. When he returns—he'll pass the word around among his friends that Yellow Jacket is a trump card, and can be landed for a hundred thousand plunks; us four we'll split the melon."

"Excuse me if I am interrupting you but, what part, Jinks, am I to take in this—"

"Don't get excited! Keep cool, you cracked-brain creeter," said Jinks as he passed a glass of the Hunter's stuff to Sam, then gulping one down his own throat, "just let me explain, them victims of ol' Doc will incorporate a company down in Californey, but they'll have to have three directors in Oregon to do business. The three of us will be given a few shares each in the company, and they'll elect us directors. My influence with ol' Doc will place me as general manager; you'n Hunter will be elected secretary and treas'r, two important positions for us. I'll have the appointing of the super-tendant too—great technical knowledge—his'n my salary will be fat and juicy. The Doc will instruct his boobs to vote fifty thousand to equip the dig'ins. We'll get a commission on all the machinery and supplies purchased for the mine — we'll run the boarding house, too."

"Stop! Say, Jinks, do we get the hundred thousand, and all those fat jobs, too?" Sam's voice was growing husky.

"You poor imbecile; I'll tell you mining is a risky and very uncertain business. I never did care for mining. The only safe plan is, risk other people's money, other people's money, my boy," counselled Jinks, emphasizing his statement by bringing his fist down on the desk with a thud. Then filling the two glasses to the brim, again he passed one to Sam, and quickly disposed of the other himself.

"Swim or sink—I—" gurgled Sam strangled by the strong spirits. "I'm with you, Jinks—go on and tell me how you are going to do it. I am sure I don't see."

"Sam, Rube is our man. We'll use him —he's been there before. I just about own him—I can put him on the blink any ol' time, and he's onto it, too. He'll help us to do the job. Rube has made us a good foreman out at the dig'in's, he's a good, 'onest and capable fellow—we'll make him super-tendant, when we get organized, for assisting us. Ol' Bob Fitch, who found that bunch of gold nug'ets and rich ore that some ol' prospector buried years ago, and cashed in before he had a chance to call again, has got the dope we're needing to salt the dig'ins. The quartz compares favorable with that of the Yellow Jacket's. I've got a bunch of it stored away, right now—I'm putting it on the market for Bob. He can't afford to squeal on us, for he's bein' hounded right now by the claimants of the cache."

"Excuse me if I am interrupting you

again; but why do you take me into—"

"Mostly, because I'm needing you'n Hunter to keep up the organization at this here end. You're born and raised here—your ol' dad, with his fields and houses, he's 'onest. Hunter, he's in the mining game on the square, with his mill and mines—you two'll keep suspicions down until I can get the dig'ins equipped. Now you watch me," chuckled Jinks.

"Watch you! I will surely keep an eye on you, all right. A man that will skin his backers like this, will do most anything," said Sam loudly with a grin, as he arose from his seat and stood limply up before Jinks, his knees growing weaker and his voice stronger.

"But say, Jinks," continued Sam, "what will happen when the suckers find that the mine has been salted—do we go to prison?"

"Hell, no! That's easy, they'll never find it out," said Jinks, with a broad-flushing smile. "After the money is spent for the equipment—we'll freeze them out —nothing but assessments. One disaster after another will follow and all that sort of thing. We'll do bum timbering—the miners will refuse to work in her— they'll strike. A few convenient blasts put in by Rube, will cause the works to cave in—she'll fill with water. It'll cost thousands to reopen her. After a few heavy assessments the stockholders will refuse to come through. Then we'll run the mine in debt—the lien holders will foreclose—the machinery will be sold to satisfy the creditors. After that, we'll be at liberty to relocate the dig'ins, and go out and grab another bunch of suckers."

"Excuse me for the interruption, but say, Jinks, when does this thing start?" inquired the old man's victim, with a grinny smile, bowing his knees, and drawing up closer to the desk.

"You poor boob, she's started now," roared Jinks in rage, "you get a rig at the livery stable, go out to the dig'ins and get Rube. Don't you come back to the office with him, you keep away from here. There's no use of our mixing up in this affair right in broad daylight. You can't always tell how these things are going to come out—we may get into mighty serious trouble. I'll lay the plans well, and give Rube his instructions."

Big Gold Strike

So read the headlines in one of the leading coast journals. The article stated that the well known mine promoter, Frank Jinks, had uncovered fabulous wealth in the Yellow Jacket gold mine near Gold Hill, Oregon. A single blast in the mine had opened a pay-shoot, which displayed pure gold nuggets; the vein was lined with rich specimen ore. Using the term of the old-timer miner, "there are millions in sight." That Jinks and his associates had been operating the mine but a short time under a lease.

"Dr. Higgins, the successful mine operator of Los Angeles, was at the mine when the strike was made. He had just arrived to inspect the property with a view of purchasing it for people in his city and closed the deal for the mine, paying immediately $100,000 in cash. The doctor informed the Leader's correspondent that his people would organize a company and equip the property at once, and that Jinks would be made general manager," the article concluded.

One summer day a smooth-shaven young man of the blonde persuasion alighted from an early morning train passing through the town of Gold Hill. Around his tall gaunt frame a corduroy suit of tan hung loosely; his feet were encased in a pair of high-laced boots of the same shade. He wore a pair of rimless eye glasses; strapped over his shoulder hung a well-filled canvas bag, dangling at his side. In one hand he carried a gold pan, and a pick hammer. His general get-up was that of the typical tenderfoot of the region.

Doffing his corduroy cap, he accosted an old man standing at the edge of the depot crowd. "Say mister, where is the nearest quartz mine?"

"Just two blocks over there," replied the old stage driver, pointing up the street, leading past the depot.

"Well, I do declare, so near," queried the new arrival, "how long has it been in operation? Twenty years, did you say?"

Removing a pocket map from his side pocket the stranger opened it hurriedly and gazed on its outlines. Then he continued by asking the old veteran:

"Which way points north?"

Being shown, he strode over across the street and entered the leading hostelry in the little town.

The next day, after his morning meal, the tenderfoot with the pick and gold pan could have been seen wending his way out of town, headed toward a neighboring foothill, covered with a growth of pine and madrone trees, where several abandoned quartz mines were located. He continued these trips daily for nearly a fortnight.

One morning the town attorney, Joe Skinner, on arriving at his office, found a new arrival awaiting him at the door.

"Say, Judge, what will be your charges for drawing up a mining contract?" asked the tenderfoot of the attorney as he drew near.

"Five dollars, sir. If it should be an extraordinary document it will cost you more," abruptly spoke the student of Blackstone.

"Well! There is the lessor, and us three lessees. I will go and get my men and return at once," said the lessee, quickly disappearing down the street.

"Say, judge," began the new arrival, as the four parties to the lease filed into the attorney's office, "you make this instrument good and strong—and, I want three carbon copies to post on the mine. I will pay you ten dollars for your services. I just come from Coeur d' Alene—I had a lease on a mine up there—the blooming thing was showing up fine. Some fellows came along and told me that my lease was no good. They offered me five thousand dollars for all my right, title and interest in and to the said premises. They told me that the property never would amount to anything—that they wanted to run a railroad across the premises. I said, 'all right.' And, say, judge, what do you think? Well, sir, those fellows sold that mine the next day for five hundred thousand dollars. Never again—I want one of those leases, that I won't have to sell."

The lessor was Jim Dunn, an old time miner of the district. The other two lessees were a couple of tenderfeet, who had arrived in town, on mining bent.

"What is your name, and the name of the mine you are buying?" asked the attorney of the new mine operator, after he had completed the preliminaries of the lease on the typewriter.

"Robert Chamberline. Why, the Yellow Jacket."

Instantly the eyes of the attorney gazed over at Jim Dunn. Both he and Dunn were residents of the district in the palmy days of the Yellow Jacket.

"Well, Jim," said the attorney, with a broad smile, the next day, on meeting Dunn on the street, "how did you become possessed with the Yellow Jacket? Really isn't it a joke?"

"Why, hell, no!" replied Dunn flushing up. "Those Los Angeles people deserted the Yellow Jacket long ago. It has been five years since I located a mining claim over the old works. I am acquiring a mining title to the property for the timber that is on it. I don't expect the boob to ever buy it—I am just giving him the privilege of doing my annual assessment work for nothing."

Several weeks later the new mine operator and Jim Dunn entered the attorney's office.

"Well, judge," began Chamberline, "my two partners have deserted me. I want you to make out a new lease for Mr. Dunn to sign. We fellows milled ten tons of that ore taken from the Yellow Jacket and it did not produce a color. I am going to instal pumping machinery and commence at the bottom of the works. The consideration is two thousand dollars for the property in case I buy, just make the lease effective for six months from date, will you?"

One day several months after Chamber-

line had procured the new lease from Dunn, Attorney Skinner received a wire from a brother attorney at Los Angeles, asking for a report on Yellow Jacket stock issued fourteen years before. It also stated 'that the shares were the assets of a very needy widow woman.'

With a copy of the reply to the message, the attorney was in the act of visiting the nearby telegraph office, when in strode Chamberline flushed with excitement. He wildly rushed across the room with a small sack of ore, which he deposited on the office table with a thud, and was turning to address Skinner, when the attorney bluntly began:

"What the devil is the matter with you, Chamberline? For God's sake, when are you going to get wise to your surroundings? Look here! Read that!" he said, flashing the prepared message in front of Chamberline's face.

Chamberline read: "Yellow Jacket mine was salted; investors buncoed; they abandoned it; now being worked by a tenderfoot." With a smile on his face, Chamberline crushed the paper in the palm of his hand then cast it scornfully on the floor at the feet of the bewildered attorney.

"What are you doing?" snapped the excited Skinner, as he was in the act of picking the crumpled message from the floor.

"Look!" said Chamberline calmly, with beaming eyes, as he reached for the untied glittering gold nuggets and specimen ore in a string across the table.

"Great Heavens!" shrieked the amazed attorney, as he staggered toward the treasure, "where did you get it?"

"The Yellow Jacket."

"How?"

"Struck it in a new drift."

One Night in Bohemia

By Sophie Garwood Williams

IT was spring in San Francisco. You could tell that by the glow of the daffodils, and the wealth of flowers on every street carner and the salty smell of the early fog that brought with it a memory of the tropics. Yes, it was spring and it was San Francisco.

Frances Minchin leaned far out of the second story of her bed room window and gazed with gloomy eyes on the crowd below—a surging busy evening crowd. Ferry whistles sounded from the Bay, groups of soldiers and sailors passed by, shop girls laughing and happy on their way home from work. Altogether, it was a typical Saturday night crowd.

Frances was a young woman and she was lonely. If you had pressed her for the reason of this despondency she would have told you it was loneliness, sheer, desperate loneliness.

Four years of endless grind as a newspaper reporter had not destroyed her dream of romance; the laughter of the world was still in her eyes. She wanted to forget for a time that the morrow would dawn for her as other morrows had done, dull, monotonous and gray.

She had never been quite so lonely or depressed in the entire course of her life. She flung up her head and rose suddenly from her chair, decided and resolute. "Adventure and romance never dies, why should I not find it as others have done before me?"

Very dainty and charming she appeared as she made ready for the street, dressed in her little tailor-made suit of gray, the close-fitting turban that revealed the mass of dark brown hair beneath, and fell in soft abandon of tiny curls about her neck. It was late evening in Market street as she made her way slowly to Kearny street, the lights of the cafes blinked invitingly—she was not hungry, it was not food she craved, but the companionship of the care-free Bohemians.

She paused uncertainly a moment before the "Bologna," a Bohemian cafe familiar to all San Francisco dwellers. Entering the brilliantly lighted door way she made her way to a table in one corner of the room, where she could watch unseen the merry antics of the crowd about her.

A waiter came up and hurriedly cleared away the remains of the last feast. Frances gave the order listlessly and looked about her. Approaching her table was a young wounded soldier recently discharged, she thought, from Letterman Hospital.

An impulse seized her to speak as he paused at her table. "Won't you sit down and join me?" she asked with a kindly smile. He hesitated for a fraction of a second. "Thank you, I will with pleasure," he answered and sat down beside her.

They talked not of the war at first, but of those about them.

"Do you come here often?" he inquired.

"No, not often. Only when I am tired and despondent and rather than sit and mope at home in my room I come and watch these funny people enjoy themselves. It is really amusing to watch them from the side lines, the women, many of them smoking not because they really like it or enjoy it, but rather because it stamps them as Bohemians."

A crowd of diners at a near-by table attracted their attention. The girl had thrown her arm about the neck of her escort; he in turn drew her down to his lap.

A disgusted smile appeared upon Frances' face. "I suppose you wonder why I am here alone, and I do not blame you for thinking it odd, but tonight I started out for adventure. It has been the one dream of my life to find it."

"And do you expect to find it here?" he questioned.

"Why not?" she asked, "don't you really believe that life is an adventure and that romance never dies."

He looked at her closely and saw that she was entirely out of keeping with her surroundings; fearless and unafraid, she could make her way into the world of men, her very fearlessness proving her protection. Her eyes were large, grayish blue eyes; eyes that seemed to see and understand many things that others cannot. He understood her better and was sorry for the first half-formed opinion.

"You are—" she began, "one of our heroes. Won't you tell me something about it?"

"I would rather not talk of it," he answered, "I am just a lonely soldier tonight and would rather help you in your quest of adventure if you will allow me."

"Very well," she replied, "we will go and find it, and I will wager some adventure happens to us tonight."

"What do you call adventure?" he questioned.

"Why everything is adventure," she answered. "Just think that little flower girl over there might be a little Russian princess in disguise, and the man standing by the door a Robin Hood."

He smiled indulgently. "Suppose we go in search of it, then," answered he.

They made their way out slowly to Market street, amid the busy, surging crowd of men and women.

"Why not here?" she asked, "don't you think we could find the coveted adventure here in this place?" as they paused before a curio shop.

"If you say so," he answered.

They entered the shop and became ab-
sorbed in the Oriental carvings of ivory and teak wood displayed.

He begged to buy her a little gift, and she laughingly choose the little lucky idol, "but you must have one too," she declared, "and I must buy it from my purse."

They walked slowly out of the shop to the crowded street again, but nothing really happened to them they could call adventure.

The man looked down in the face of his companon and felt that romance might not be so difficult to find, indeed, he felt its nearness, as the girl walked beside him.

"But it is time to go home," she declared, consulting wrist watch, and drawing her fur about her shoulders preparatory to going.

He asked if he might see her home.

She hesitated and said "yes."

He hailed a street car. They entered, laughing and gay, then a surprised and startled expression came over his face as he reached for his fare and found his pocket empty of change. The girl saw his embarrassment. "Wait, I have it," and she turned to the vanity case she always carried with her, but the vanity case has disappeared also, and her look of concern turned to consternation. "Mine has been stolen, also," she exclaimed.

"Shall we get off?" he asked. "I suppose there is nothing else to do."

Laughingly they left the car and walked slowly homeward.

"Admit," said Frances, "that some adventure did happen to us tonight."

"Yes," he replied, "I don't regret my loss of money, though it was a month's salary, if I may only see my little friend soon again, may I?"

"Yes," she answered, and the man thought in the up-turned face he read Romance, rose-hued and charming.

Lonesome Bill and the Phonograph Girl

By Ellen M. Ramsay

"AWK-BURR-RR" went the phonograph. Lonesome Bill reached over mechanically and wound the crank, thereby restoring tempo and dash to Sousa's band as rendered by his only companion at the Solitaire Mine. People who live much alone acquire sooner or later the habit of talking to themselves, or to the inanimate objects around them. Bill now addressed the phonograph.

"Can't you give us a new tune, pal? I'm sure tired of the old ones. No? Well, let's have the good one."

He adjusted a new record as he spoke. There was a wheezy prelude and then the soft chords of a stringed orchestra. Bill sighed and leaned back in his chair contentedly, as a girl's fresh, clear voice began to sing "Silver Threads Among the Gold." He knew that the singer was a girl, for youth throbbed in every tone—warm, passionate youth, pledging itself to love that should live as long as life. The voice had that elusive, rich quality, known as color. Hard must be the heart that could hear it unmoved.

A rugged life of adventure had left Bill little time for sentiment, but he found himself responding to this song in some half defined way. He never tired of the song, although when he listened to it, he became possessed of a vague and wistful longing for something that he missed but could not define to himself.

The song ceased and Bill carefully removed the record. Thoughtfully, he tried to decipher the name in the center. "Sung by Vesta Carroll," he read.

"Carroll!" That was an appropriate name for such a singer. A sudden thought struck the miner. "Wonder what she's like? Is she pretty? and her hair—is it gold like the song?" Bill decided that it probably was—red gold, and she was surely pretty.

The more he thought of the matter, the more Bill became possessed of a desire to know just what Vesta Carroll looked like—in fact, just what she was like. A wild idea came to him. He had read of such things. Why not write to the girl and tell her how much her song had done to brighten his lonely existence? Perhaps she would answer and tell him a little bit about herself. At all events it was no more than courtesy to send her his thanks.

But Bill was bashful as he was big. Calling himself a fool, he sought his bunk and dreamed all night of a girl with red gold hair, who stood in the mouth of a monstrous phonograph horn and sang "Silver Threads Among the Gold." He remembered the dream next day, though he could not recall the girl's features.

Again he thought of writing Vesta Carroll a letter and he continued to think of it for many days, the idea finally becoming an obsession in his lonely life. Then one day, to his own surprise he acted on the thought and wrote a letter to Miss Vesta Carroll, care of the American Talking Machine Company, New York City. It meant a twenty mile ride to mail the letter, but Bill went, pretending to himself rather sheepishly that he was tired of canned beans and wanted to buy pink frijoles to cook himself, from the little store which also served as post-office for Broncho Springs.

II

Miss Molly O'Reilly, better known to the vaudeville stage as Vesta Carroll, was down on her luck. From a successful vaudeville star, she found herself reduced to the life of a poorly paid clerk in a New York department store, barely able to keep soul and body together.

An attack of grippe the previous fall had been the chief agent in her downfall. Molly had lost her booking, and worse still, when she finally recovered, it was with a weakened throat that would need much rest and care before she could again sing. Her small savings had been spent for doctors and drugs and she faced the problem of supporting herself in a new occupation.

The new work was hard on the weakened girl, and one cold followed another, until Molly sought the doctor again, to be told that there was a threatened spot on her lungs, and that she must seek a better climate and an outdoor life, if she expected to regain her health.

To Molly then, on the bluest day of her life, came a letter, addressed to Miss Vesta Carroll, care of the American Talking Machine Company, New York. Ordinarily such a superscription would have stirred the girl's curiosity, but today she was too tired to be anything but apathetic. She noted idly that the letter had followed her through three changes of address, marking the downward trend of her finances.

Then she opened the envelope and read the letter that held the result of hours of wrestling on Lonesome Bill's part with the English language, as he sought to express himself on the written page. It read:

"Dear Phonograph Girl:

Somehow I know you too well to call you "Miss Carroll," and you'll think I'm fresh if I say "Vesta," so I am calling you the name I think of you by to myself. You will think I am pretty fresh anyhow, writing this way without any introduction or anything; but I just had to tell you about that song of yours, "Silver Threads Among the Gold" on the phonograph record. I live up here all by myself in a little shack on a mining claim and it gets pretty lonesome at times. I bought the phonograph for company but the tunes got worn out. Only yours has always been a winner. I can't get tired of it and it has cheered me up a hundred times, when I was so blue I pretty nearly wanted to give up the whole claim, just to get back to a town and real people.

Lately I have been thinking about the girl who has such a lovely voice, and it seemed just naturally polite to write and thank you for the happiness you have given me. Of course, I don't expect you will answer this letter, but if you do, won't you tell me a bit about yourself? It would make the song even better, to know about the girl who sings it, and think of her as a friend.

If you ever come West, let me know where to buy tickets for your show. Best regards to yourself, and asking your pardon for butting in this way, I am, your respectful and humble servant,

WILLIAM (Lonesome Bill) BUTLER,

P. S.—A letter would always reach me care of Broncho Springs, New Mexico."

Molly had received not a few mash notes in her life, but this letter was so evidently genuine and sent with good intent, that she found herself thinking of the writer as a friend worth keeping. Of course she would answer and thank the miner for his appreciation. Then the address struck her—"New Mexico!" The doctor had said something about New Mexico. A breath of hope came to Molly. Perhaps—

III

Old Joe Perkins, store-keeper and postmaster at Broncho Springs, paused to scan the letter a second time. "Letter for Lonesome Bill," he murmured. "First one I ever seen him get . Looks like he had a girl. Hi, there, Slim! Take this with you and drop it at the Solitaire."

Thus it was that Slim Green stopped at the shack on the Solitaire Mine. only to find the door closed and Lonesome Bill away, presumably on a hunting expedition. Slim threw the letter through a half opened window and it fell squarely on the cabin table.

Bill saw the little square of white as he opened the door and reaching for it eagerly sent the phonograph on the edge of the table crashing to the floor. He had not dared hope for a reply to his letter but now that he had it, a strangely happy feeling flooded his being. He neglected even to pick up the faithful phonograph as he took the little missive to the light and tore open the envelope flap.

A picture fell out, and Bill beheld the smiling and autographed countenance of Vesta Carroll, in the days of her triumph. "Well, now," he mused, "her hair?—it's neither light nor dark. It must be medium—that is, red or red gold just like I thought." Then he turned to the letter that had enclosed the picture.

He read and a tender look crept over his face. The real girl was even lovelier than the imagined one if her letter were a guide. Molly had answered in his own friendly spirit. She had told of herself but touched lightly on her troubles. The brave spirit of her, however, and something of her need came out toward the last of the letter, as Bill read:

"So you see I may not be able to sing again, except through the phonograph records. You speak of my coming West. I wonder—do you know of any jobs out there? I can clerk or wait on table or wash dishes—any honest work, in fact, that will support me until I get my voice and health. The doctor says I must not spend another winter here. If you can help me in this, I shall always call you 'friend'."

Then there was a formal but friendly little ending. Bill read the letter and then reread it. He began to think more deeply and rapidly than he had ever done before in his life. One wild idea it seemed could lead to an idea even more wild, but Bill was bolder now.

"Wants a job in the West," said Bill. "We'll fix that. Anyway that little old stack of dust is getting too big to keep, and I've always had a hankering to view the sights in New York."

He turned to the cupboard and stumbled over the phonograph. He picked the instrument up only to find that it's wheezy voice was silenced forever. What would have been a tragedy a day before failed to touch him now, however, as he whistled "Silver Threads Among the Gold" in a very flat key and the best of spirits.

IV.

It was really too soon to expect a letter from the West, but Molly was looking at the mail rack in her shabby lodging house, when a man's voice arrested her attention.

"Miss Carroll?" it said.

"Why, yes," said Molly, surprised to hear the stage name, which none of her fellow roomers knew. Turning she looked into the honest, gray eyes of a very big man.

"Guess you don't recognize me," he said, "but I know you from your picture, though you are rather more peaked looking than a friend would like to see you. Red gold, too," he added.

The allusion to her hair was, of course, lost on Molly, but it did not take her Irish wit long to recognize her caller.

"Are you—you can't be Lonesome Bill, the phonograph man," she cried.

"You've said it," the big man replied enthusiastically, "and you're the little phonograph girl."

It did not take much persuasion on Bill's part to get Molly's consent to a dinner together. Her thin face and pale color hurt him somehow and gave him the feeling that he must see her eat and eat well. Instinctively, he knew that she was undernourished and needed good food as much as a change of climate. However, Bill was tactful in his invitation, claiming that he was "scared" of French waiters and needed a guide with him when he ate, or else he would starve to death in New York.

Seated at a table in a modest restaurant (Molly had declared her clothes not presentable at the more fashionable places), the couple soon found themselves talking like old friends. Bill had many original impressions of New York, and Molly was laughng, as she had not laughed for months. She ate well, too, as Bill noted keenly.

"If beefsteak could be divine, that teabone certainly was," she told him, finishing her portion with a sigh of content.

Lonesome Bill laughed.

"When you go West, you'll see a good deal of beefsteak," he said. "It's one of the natural products."

"Oh! have you a job for me?" asked Molly. She had been longing to question him but had waited for him to speak first.

"Why yes," said her companion, "I know of two jobs you might consider. Old Joe Perkins at Broncho Springs is getting pretty old-like and wants a clerk in his store. I showed him your picture and he fell for it at once. Said the boys would come in from forty miles around to buy goods from such a pretty saleslady. The hours would be easy, and you could have a little tent house to yourself to live in. You'd get well in no time."

"That sounds good to me," said Molly. "The other job will have to go some to beat it."

Big Bill blushed and Molly, looking up, saw it. . Then almost desperately, Bill plunged on.

"Well, you see, Molly (she had told him her real name), this other job is— You're lonesome and I'm lonesome, and I thought we might fix up a life partnership maybe. I know it's sudden, but I've been loving you since the first time I heard you sing that song. I've made the old mine pay and we'll be rich when I finish her; but half of its yours, anyhow, for I never could have stuck out all the lonesomeness without the phonograph and your song."

He stopped and fixed pleading eyes on Molly's face. Molly's own eyes were downcast and her expression non-com-mittal. Indeed she was thinking that partnership with Bill would always be a safe and solid proposition, but it was all so sudden. How could she?

"Molly," said Bill again, "when your letter came, the very same day, I broke the phonograph. I would have felt awful about it the day before, but somehow, when I knew you had to come West, I thought maybe it was a sign that —well, that the singer, when she knew about it, would take pity on me, especially as she was lonesome like herself."

Then Molly laughed and raised her eyes to Bill. They told him something that made his heart leap and thrill, but what she said was:

"Perhaps I'll never sing again. What then?"

"You're my girl and I love you," said Big Bill.

Again Molly looked at him and mischief filled her eyes.

"I've heard of a man marrying a wife to get a housekeeper, or a cook, or a teacher," she said, "but I never heard of one marrying a wife for a phonograph."

"If you never did," said Bill, and the thrill in his heart made him daringly bold, "you are going to, in just about sixty minutes more. I'm from the West where we believe in rapid action. Come along with me, ma'am, we're going to buy a marriage license."

California

By Annie E. Caldwell

Roses great and roses small
Rose leaves trembling to the fall
Overflow the crystal bowl

While sweet clouds of incense roll.
Roses white and roses red
Border all the garden bed
With a beauty none may tell
Beaming from each bud and bell

Water For Two

By Raymond S. Bartlett

HE man parted the bushes back, ever so slightly, to let the warm air blow upon his face. Below, ragged shoulders of the land ran down into the sage country like uncouth arrows aimed at the desert's heart. Around him little growths of juniper, rank with strange overgrowth, afforded shelter but nothing else. But for these stray patches and the continuous fragments of spiral rock, the slope of the whole mountain side was bare.

It was high noon by the August sun. Nothing betokened life, save occasional lizards that scurried from rock to rock, great brooding birds that basked in the boiling heat, and the man, himself, under the juniper. It was a land of shades, of lonesome distances. As far as the eye could reach the bitter summits ran up to a swooning sky. Noontide burned and sickened, twilight waned and smouldered. It was the country without a name in the great Southwest, the bad land of the desert.

Some of the birds rose in the eddying heat, flapping their dusty wings across the air, then circled two by two in aimless guise.

"Buzzards," the man ejaculated. He eyed them with a sombre interest for a time, then spat into the air.

"Damn you, you won't get me," he cried suddenly, venomously. Then he got up from his place, seizing some pieces of the rock and threw them wildly and with promiscuous aim at the circling birds.

The effect of throwing told on him. Back he sank, exhausted, into the juniper patch and feebly reached for his water bag.

"It won't last forever," he muttered, measuring it. "A little more than a quart." Whereupon he commenced to finger his holster as if, in some way, here was an answer to the whole business.

* * * -

Sheriff Ragan's horse was nearly spent. Her right foreleg was bleeding and the mare's pace was little more than a dejected limp. Ragan was leading her among the broken rocks and once, twice, stumbled himself, drunkenly.

"It's no use, Dolly," he said at length. "This here party ain't for us. No, sir. You're plumb through and I'm as bad, I guess. Damn this sheriff business anyhow."

With this he halted. It was none too soon for the mare's flanks trembled viciously, bloody foam was beginning to fleck her mouth and a sound came from her red, distended nostrils like a breathing bellows.

"Well, old lady, they's no use for YOU to suffer," rubbing her nose. "I reckon your trail ends here."

Letting go the bridle he watched while she stumbled to the ground. Then he took the water bag and haversack away, loosened the girth and pulled the saddle off. He hid this in a little pile of brush.

"Good-bye, old gal," he said affectionately, then pulled the trigger. A shot shattered the air and Ragan, bag and haversack slung across his shoulder, was on his way. Not once did he pause in his path across the rocks nor did he look back the way that he had come.

For an hour he stumbled on, halting only when obliged to. Now to shift the haversack and again to gulp a mouthful of the tepid water from the bag.

"Jim Anderson's a foxy bird alright," he found himself ruminating. "But then again, he ain't. He's got a pretty hidin' spot up here, but Gawd, the country ain't fit to cross over in an airship, let alone

3

live in. Rocks and rattlers, that's all it is."

* * - -

The man saw him coming when he was no bigger than a moving speck among the rocks. From his nest in the juniper he felt secure enough but he drew the gun from his holster, fondled it for a second and then rubbed away some moisture that was dropping into his eyes from his forehead.

"That's him alright," smiling grimly. "Now at five hundred yards there ain't nothin walkin' I can't plug. Partic'ly these two-legged rattlers. As for this sheriff cuss, he's smellin' his end of daylight sure enough."

With that he raised his hand, his forearm tauting with the earnest aim. His finger felt for the trigger but, as it pulled back, the arm fell like a dead weight in front of him and the ball rocochetted harmlessly down the rocky slope below.

"That's Jim, alright." The sheriff was peering out from his refuge down the slope." He's in that juniper. I saw the smoke when he was done with shootin'. Mebbe he's finished now."

The man moved with a start. The juniper was waving above him and splotches of sunlight were trickling through onto the ground. He felt for his gun but that was gone. His hat lay in the dust beside him, the water bag was still there and a little canvas sack in which he carried grub.

He raised himself, painfully, upon an elbow and peered out through the bushes. The sheriff saw him.

"Well, Jim, so you've woke up." Ragan smiled at him. "You've had a pretty nap. It's the heat I guess that done it. Otherwise, sonny, I wouldn't be standin' here. That was a mighty close shave for Mister Ragan though. Mighty careless way you've got of greetin' strangers. Oh, yes, I've got your toy. Able to travel?"

The man was silent.

"Forty hard miles to Benson," the sheriff went on." It's goin' to be a pinch for water at that. Mine's almost gone and I guess you haven't much to spare by the looks of things. If Dolly hadn't

stumbled we'd be there sometime tomorrow, mebbe. I missed the trail, as it is, that's when the others had scattered out, and here I am with you."

Then Jim Anderson remembered. Yes, here was the sheriff ready to take him back to the State known as law and order. He pictured the gang at Benson waiting for him. Crowley, the Wells Fargo agent, in particular. Ten thousand in currency. It seemed a pitiful, small amount, now, to risk one's freedom for. "Twenty to forty years in the big house," he found himself ruminating, then eyed the blazing rocks about him. Anything better than this though, a thousand fold, he thought.

"Well," he said at length and found his words were dry like the heat around him. "I expect they'll be SOME reception committee waiting. Crowley was sore, I'll bet."

"Oh, they're a happy gang at Benson. It's only been six days since you skipped out and, boy, you don't know how they've learned to love you in that time. That's why they sent me and the boys out. Feared you might get lonesome here alone. You've got the loot, of course?"

"Every bill. I didn't reckon to spend much of it up here. I guess, Billy, I took the wrong old trail this time. Where's the rest of your gang?"

"Oh, they've scattered out around the range. I wish I had their water, though. Mine's nearly gone."

Anderson shaded his eyes with his hand.

"Ever notice them birds, Billy?" he said.

"Notice 'em? Why damn their stinkin' skins they make me sick. Waitin' for somethin' to happen, I guess. Hope it ain't goin' to be us to happen for them."

"Well, I hope so, likewise. I ain't got much to go back for, unless you reckon a long term in the old pen somethin', but I don't reckon to sit here and sizzle up to suit THEIR taste. If this here drink holds out we'll cheat 'em. They's just one chance of water before we get to Benson. It's the Great Black river. I've been down there fishin' and huntin'. If we hit that we'll fill the bags only its a mean trail down to it. A thousand feet or more. But I know the way like a book. Dreamed of it last night, in fact."

Billy Ragan nodded.

"If you don't mind," he offered, "we'll get goin'. I don't expect no trouble from you, Jim, so we'll trot along like men together. It's past three o'clock and we can walk most of the night. The wife and kids are home and worryin' I'll bet. I've been out, now, for five days and nights."

Anderson rose to his feet wearily. He took an uncertain step or so and looked off ruefully at the rocks beyond him.

"I've got a game leg," he said, a slight limp showing in his gait when they struck out. "You won't get no trouble from me, young feller. Guess I'll have to take it easy at first."

That night a dry, high moon arose above the vast. There was no relief in its white light from the dusty heat of the day. When it was time for eating the men munched some hard bread from the grub sack and tasted the contents of the water bag gingerly.

"I guess we'd better stop." It was Ragan talking. "I'm clean played out. Damn this sheriff business anyhow. How's your water, Jim?"

"I guess I've got a pint or so. You'd better take a swig of it. I had a lot this mornin', and besides I reckon the Great Black ain't far off now. We'd oughta hit it sometime tomorrow mornin'. How far'd we come today?"

"I couldn't tell you. No more'n eight miles, I guess. If it wasn't for that game leg of yours we'd make it faster. How does it feel tonight?"

"Oh, not so bad Billy. But in the mornin' it'll limber up again."

The next day it was worse. The way grew rockier and sandier it seemed, the sun hotter, more piercing. The men fell into a stumbling kind of gait and at noon they paused, exhausted.

"We'd better halt," Ragan said, "and try the shade of these here junipers. Jim I've gotta have a drink. My throat is burnin' dry."

There was little left between them.

"Have some," the sheriff said, when he had done, and motioned Jim to drink.

"I ain't so thirsty, Billy. It's this damn leg that bothers. I'm a camel out here in this country. By the way, Jim, if you don't mind, how many kids was it you said you've got?"

"They's three. Little Bill and Marjorie and Mary. Marjorie's the youngest. She's got her mother's eyes. But Lord, that boy. He's after his daddy sure enough. His birthday's next week. I wonder what the little shaver's doin' now."

There followed a long silence.

"We'll hit the water this afternoon, sure." Anderson seemed to draw a mighty source of comfort from his words. "Then, Billy, we'll drink some, a whole bagful, mind you. That river's a wonder. There it goes splashin' down from the Big Bend country, it's water cold as ice. And the fish that's in it. Little speckled beauts they are. Gawd, but I can see it pilin' up in little sheets of spray along the rocks."

In the afternoon the pair pushed on. The water was all gone now. Once Ragan broke out in a little snatch of song.

"Stop that junk, Bill Ragan." The other's words were curt. "This sun has got you. This ain't no time for singin'. That river can't be much further along now."

And then night came. The sky burned from a dull red into shades of a cooler purple, streaked with fire. Then the yellow rim of the moon commenced to show over the mountains.

"Look, Billy, I told you so." It was Anderson talking. "There's the trail goin' down to the canyon. There, off there, by them little cedars. I know the place of old. You can't fool me."

He pointed to the ridge of rocks in the distance and beyond to where heaps of painted precipice shot up and met the sky. For a long time they stood there, like people of a dream, straining their eyes in the half light, while a sharp thirst racked their throats and little streaks of fire blazed in their brains.

"Tomorrow," Anderson muttered and then they camped for the night.

In the morning their eyes were streaked with blood, their lips were swollen, broken. But out they struck, Anderson in the lead, limping, while the sheriff followed dazedly a sort of dry cackle of song breaking at times from his lips. ·

"There's a spot in old Carlin where the cotton blossoms blow." His words quavered crazily and as he walked the juniper seemed dancing to the music.

"It's damn funny how these here bushes keeps jigglin' and rushin' past," he babbled. "Every time I look up they's some of it dancin' and dancin' right here in the trail alongside me. I don't like it, Jim, one bit. First thing I know the rocks will join in."

"You keep still, damn you," Anderson croaked, turning a pair of burning eyes on him. "It's this thirst has got you. We're nearly to the water now. Keep up your lip, sonny, and stop that daffy talk. You've got the kids you know."

Now the juniper commenced to grow in thicker patches, it seemed, and a short descent of the land began. Beyond them clear across, a mile or so it seemed, nothing but blazing space and purple heights. Below, for they were at the edge of the canyon now, the river crawled like a flushed serpent.

"I told you, Billy," Anderson was like a child in his delight. "That's it down there. The Great Black, they call it. See the rocks along the shore. You know the place. Water Billy, water, water, water, oceans of it.

The sheriff tittered.

"Water?" he rubbed his hand across his eyes. "I don't see no water. Now there's an old song that goes, 'She was bred in old Kentucky, get her boy you're mighty lucky, she's an ember girl but plucky, she's my Sue.'"

"Listen here, Billy Ragan." Anderson's words were sharp, insistent. "You sit down. Quick." He took the haversack from his back, laid it out in the shape of a head rest on the rocks under some stunted cedars. Then he slung both of the water bags over his shoulders and motioned the sheriff to lie down.

"Wait for me here," he said. "It's a damn bad trail down to the water, as I remember, and it may take a long time. I may slip besides, and then there won't be no water. But it's my place to go, of course. You've got your kids you know and I—why I've got no one in particular but Jeff Crowley, I guess."

"Goin' for water?" The sheriff tittered once more. "What water's that, Jim?"

Heedless, the other parted back some bushes at the canyon's edge and took one step forward to the narrow ledge-like trail. Down it he went, zig-zagging hideously. He took one look at the sheriff and then disappeared, some rocks tumbling down after him as he went.

It was a long, weary way and the bushes that grew in the limestone wall cut out at him wickedly, humanly. Sometimes he slipped and nearly lost his balance. Below, the water gleamed, and above, the birds flew, circling two by two. Once he thought he heard the sheriff calling after him and again there came on the air the words of the sheriff's crazy song.

"It's the thirst as does it," he muttered, keeping close to the wall and eyes always to the front.

At length he was there. Right at the river's edge. The water was limpid, flashing. Cool curves of shadows were falling over and into it and a few willows were letting their long, lush fingers sway idly in the swimming tide.

He knelt at the very edge.

"Water," he cried, rapturously, and bathed his face in it.

* * * *

"Gawd, look at that." It was Jack Barry talking on the afternoon of the same day. He pointed to some little clumps of dwarfed cedars.

The men leaned in their saddles and followed his gaze.

"Billy Ragan, sure as hell," someone offered. "And look, he's gone clean loco. The fool is singin'."

Horses were urged forward and they drew up before a strange figure that was the sheriff.

"Ragan," Jack Barry shouted. "Don't look at me like THAT. What in hell's the matter?"

"The trees is dancin'," the man before them croaked. And then he giggled. "Have you see Jim?" he whined.

"Anderson, you mean?" Barry was down from his saddle now, his water bag in hand. "You've seen him?"

"Seen him?" The sheriff tittered. "I've seen him sure enough. He's gone down to the river for some water. You know, the big river." He pointed toward the desert with a laugh.

"She was bred in old Kentucky——"

"Stop that song." The words of Barry bristled. "Water, the river? Where? He's got 'em, boys, this time." Then he looked out over the flat, rocky waste and his eye caught something that the buzzards had seen before.

They all walked over with him to a little patch of brush. And here they found him lying, the pair of water bags over his shoulder.

"It's Jim, alright." Barry was positive. "He's done his bit, Jim has. Water, Gawd." Then someone whistled.

"Well," it was Jeff Crowley talking. "If we stick it out on these damn plugs all night it's likely we'll hit the Great Black by mornin'. Damn this sheriff business anyhow."

Mount Hood

By Ella M. McLoney

A sturdy sentinel you stand,
    With rugged sides that tell of power,
A faithful watchman o'er the land
    To which your smile is richest dower.

Life's storms are shown by riven peak;
    The fires with which your heart once
        flamed,
Have cooled to ashes, and now speak
    Of ancient passions years have tamed.

Spirit serene and grandeur true,
    With matchless beauties, new each
        day,
These are the gifts time brought to you;
    These gifts are yours to hold alway.

From snowy crown, in magic dressed
    By sunrise glory, evening's glow,
A message comes to hearts oppressed,
    Which brings a joy that all may know.

It speaks of thought that fashioned all;
    Of love supreme that all enfolds;
Of care that answers human call,
    And time that every good gift holds.

It tells of peace that follows strife;
    Of purpose high that shall inspire
The daily round of common life,
    With radiant trust and pure desire.

On mountain top the vision clears;
    Life's beauties show their fullest
        flower;
'Tis fruitage of the hard fought years—
    Courage that dares, and love that's
        power.

Marionettes of "Success"

By Del Frazier

A DULL yet very distinct explosion attracted the attention of Policeman O'Brady. It was two o'clock in the morning and Van Ness Avenue was deserted. A nail in a number 10½ shoe had been troubling O'Brady all evening. He was sitting on the steps of the Scottish Rite Auditorium bending the disturber of the law over with a knife. He put the shoe on and started in quest of the scene of the explosion. He had no more than started when a Ford with the top up rounded the corner of Bush Street and Van Ness Avenue, and lizzied past O'Brady. He noticed that there was no license plate on the machine, otherwise he would have taken the number as a precaution. He proceeded up Van Ness Avenue one block and turned the corner onto Bush Street. Twenty feet back from the corner a large piece of plate glass had been cut out of the display window of an automobile concern. O'Brady climbed through the aperture, thus made, into the store. Here he found the cause of the explosion. The store safe had been dynamited. O'Brady commandeered the office phone and reported the crime to headquarters. In the course of the next week the police traced out the few clues they had. The criminals made good their escape because they understood San Francisco Police methods, and had carefully removed the license plate from their Ford.

In a little town twenty or thirty miles out of Oakland where automobiles turn to the left to go to a certain well known roadhouse or to take a detour to Sacramento, Speed Cop Wells was tightening a bolt on the clutch of his Twin Indian. A dull, yet very distinct, explosion caused him to pause in his work for a moment. Speeders don't make a noise like that, so he resumed the tightening of the bolt. What did concern him, however was that five minutes later a Ford with top up, and without a license plate rattled past him and took the detour to Sacramento. No license plate! Wells stepped on the starter, and caught up with the Ford before it had gone five hundred yards. The occupants, two tough looking men, acted rather suspicious, so he took them to the city jail. The next morning the proprietor of a local jewelry store called the police on the phone and reported that burglars had cut a piece out of his display window, had entered the store, blown the safe, and stolen nine thousand five hundred dollars' worth of jewelry and two hundred dollars in cash.

A search of the Ford disclosed the jewelry — a search of the prisoners brought forth the two hundred dollars. The criminals were captured because they did not understand rural police methods, and had removed the license plate from their Ford.

This story does not concern itself with those two robberies. I read about them in the paper. I have related the details here because they demonstrate a theory Bill Givens propounded the other day. Plod on two hundred and fifty words, gentle reader, and in its place you'll come to the theory.

First meet my friend Bill. Bill Givens is one of those Birds who takes the floor as soon as you've told him you're feeling better, and that your wife was elected president of the "Orphan's Welfare Society." There are people to whom you would rather talk than listen, but Bill isn't that kind of a talker. If you meet him in the hotel lobby he has a new joke. If you are riding across the continent with him, you don't need a Pullman, because he has a young book full to elucidate. Bill's calling is anything from treasurer of "The Florida House Boat

Land Co." to the Dr. Givens of "Givens' Light Lavender Lozenges for Lazy Loafers," guaranteed to cure Tonsilitis, Appendicitis, Paritenitis, Elephantiasis, Gout, Rheumatism, Corns, Hangnails, Dandruff, Black Eyes, and Cancer, all spelled with capitals. His latest is the North American Monopoly on Pink Lemonade.

The last time I saw Bill I was on my way to Frisco from the Santa Monica Road Race. Bill was on the same train putting miles between himself and the peanut peddlers he had sold the Pink Lemonade concession to.

· After the race I paid my bet, and when we were a few hours out of Los I went into the smoker to try the cigar my friend gave me when I paid him the fifty. Bill was in there smoking a cigar that he had bought with part of the fifteen hundred dollars lemonade concession proceeds.

"How are you?" said Bill.

"Oh, I'm feeling better," I said, lighting the cigar.

"And your wife?" he asked.

I started the old story, "She's been elected president of the—"

"Is this her third term, or just the third time you've told me about the same one?" and then without waiting for an answer "A very capable woman, but its the same old story anybody can make good if you put him in the right place. In fresh water a trout is about the most lively member of the Family Pisces there is, but put him in salt water, and as far as swimming is concerned he might as well be a hen.

"Did I ever tell you about my friend J. Sterling Bradford? No! Well the first time I met him was in a telephone directory. I was selling stock in the Rain Cloud Improvement Co. Just about that time the Blue Sky Law went into effect. As a consequence I was looking under 'A' in the pink section of the telephone book for an attorney. The most likely name I saw was J. Sterling Bradford so I called at his office. Ten minutes later he was my attorney.

"Brad's knowledge of the finer points of law compared favorably with Samoan's erudition of President Wilson's Four-

teen Points. But put him up before a jury, and with every movement of the tongue twelve judicial tears would drop. I don't know about music charming beasts, but Brad's chin music sure charmed the jurors. He could talk five minutes to a potato and then boil it in the tears which would well from its eyes. We will avoid unpleasant details of my own difficulty. All that need to be said about it is that a legal friend of Brad's furnished the knowledge of law, and Brad talked the Grand Jury out of a lot of tears and incidentally out of indicting me. Then he advised me to take up some other business, and remarked that a man will make money if you put him in the right place, but if he heads into the wrong pew the best he can do is make money for the lawyers. Then poor Brad unwittingly proved his assertion. It happened like this:

"It seems that a certain Chinaman named Gee Kwong was standing on the corner of Grant Ave. and Jackson Sts. one afternoon, when another slant eyed gentleman named Hong Lee Wo stepped up to him and pumped a couple of bullets into the back of his head. The shots were heard down at the Hall of Justice, a block away, and the Police thinking another Tong War had broken out rushed two patrol wagons and twelve stalwart enforcers of the law to the scene of the outrage.

"Hong Lee was surrounded, captured, and dragged before the Police Court. He said, 'No Sabee' and a plea of not guilty was entered for him. The following day young Bradford was retained by the court as Hong Lee Wo's attorney, and as soon as Brad got an interpreter and found out that the Chinaman had an oversized roll, he took a great deal of interest in the case.

"Before Hong had his preliminary hearing Brad relieved him of part of the roll, and armed with the filthy lucre, a list of Hong's friends, and an interpreter, J. Sterling dashed forth on a calling tour. Now if there's anything like a policeman in sight, its pretty hard to get a Chinaman to remember anything at the best, and if he has been persuaded with good American dollars that he has never known a certain friend who is in 'Dutch' —well I could listen without a quiver to Mrs. Sphinx herself say, 'My, Oh My, here I have been for three thousand years with a bunch of bunk secrets and haven't told a soul—now friends just step up and I'll holler'—But if said Chinaman under those circumstances said anything but, 'No Sabee' I'd die on the spot from surprise.

"The District Attorney had a couple of witnesses who saw the shooting, and all he needed to make a complete case was a motive; but here he got a jar. He hunted through Chinatown from one end to the other for someone who knew Hong Lee, but the best he could get out of any of the brother Orientals was a sweet 'No Sabee.' They even tried putting Hong through the Third Degree. They met with about as much success as a Rabbi would running for High Mogul of the K. of C. He even said, 'No Sabee' to the interpreter's questions. Then they figured, 'what's the use of a motive anyway. We have two witnesses who saw the shooting. It was in broad day light and certainly it was done in a very cold-blooded manner'. Also they knew J. Sterling Bradford's legal propensities. He didn't know enough about law to juggle it over to his side under better conditions than these. And who could make a jury weep over a Chinaman?

"That's how things stood when Brad called me up one evening and told me that the case was called for the following day. The defense of Hong Lee Wo would be his masterpiece. Not only was he to make the plea, but he was handling the legal side of the case as well. If I cared to see my friend the District Attorney suffer a humiliating defeat, I should be on hand tomorrow morning.

"There wasn't much of a crowd there that first morning of the trial. The case hadn't received much publicity because the prosecution had such a cinch. The jury had been sworn in and everything was set for a quiet walkaway for the State. I was in the court room a few minutes early, and from what I could learn of the case from the people around me I couldn't see where Brad got all that stuff about the humiliating defeat

of the District Attorney.

"The preliminaries were soon over and the prosecution called its first witness. He was an elderly man named Brown. He was out here from the East, and had been in China Town buying souvenirs on the afternoon of the crime. He had just come out of Sing Fat's Mercantile Store, and was looking right at the two China-men when the shooting took place. There was apparently no provocation. No fight of any kind. A very deliberate murder he would say. He didn't know enough about Tong Wars to duck and so he had watch-ed the affair until the police had arrived and arrested the defendant. Yes, he could identify Hong Lee Wo as the man who did the shooting. The defense did not wish to question the witness and he was dismissed.

"The next witness called was a China Town guide who was with Mr. Brown when the shooting took place. There was no quarrel between the two China-men and the whole affair was very cold-blooded. He had had more experience with Tong Wars than had Mr. Brown, so he ducked back into Sing Fat's as soon as the shots were fired. He could iden-tify Hong Lee Wo as the man who did the shooting. Again the defense did not wish to question the witness, and he was dismissed. The prosecution rested with the assertion that the apparent lack of motive for the crime proved its audacity and premeditation. A lawyer would have entered an objection to this, but Brad wasn't a lawyer. He was a wind-jammer.

"The first witness called for the de-fense was a Chinaman named Hi Lung. He was a friend of the deceased, Gee Kwong and also of the defendant, Hong Lee Wo. Hong Lee Wo had a wife who was very pretty and young. Gee Kwong saw her and decided to take unto himself a wife altho it be somebody else's wife. His attentions had been resented by Mrs. Wo and finally when she turned him down he had stabbed her in the back. The following day Hong Lee Wo shot Gee Kwong.

"Hong Lee took the stand next in his own behalf. Thru an interpreter he told the same story, adding that before he shot Gee Kwong he had gone to the police station and tried to get the police to help him. The police could not understand him and had kicked him out. Thereupon he became possessed of an evil devil and shot the said Gee Kwong.

"A sergeant of the police testified that a Chinaman had entered the police station the morning of the shooting, very much agitated about something. They couldn't find out what he was talking about and so they had told him it was all right and to beat it. He couldn't recognize the defendant as the man but then all Chinks looked alike to him anyway so perhaps Hong Lee was the one. The defense rested, and the first day of the trial ended.

"That night and the next morning that little old case got some· publicity. The papers called it the "Chinese Triangle" and the "Oriental Love Murder." Things were beginning to even up a little. The defense had more than a chance, and what was better here was thunder for the guns of J. Sterling Bradford.

"So it happened that the next morning the court room was packed with scandal mongers—and myself. Never before had such a sensational trial sprung up over night. Never had such a one come to so rapid a conclusion. All that remained were the arguments to the jury. The judge entered — the buzz of excitement was quieted. The court was seated, and the District Attorney began his plea.

"It was short but to the point, demanding the stamping out of these Oriental outrages. Suppose the defendant had shot a white man in his mad rage? The situation should be dealt with none less severely because his victim was an Oriental. More than likely the murdered man had a large family which was dependant upon him for support. In the interests of humanity and civilization, the jury should bring back a verdict of 'Guilty'.

"And then the great J. Sterling Bradford arose! He pictured a fair flower of the Orient, married and living happily with her husband, when the blaster of homes appeared. But what's the use of me trying to tell it. Just let me say that according to Brad's description that Chinese girl was a bird. As Pekin Ducks go, she

was some chicken. When help had been refused her bereaved husband by the police, he had in a fury of rage, shot the Breaker of Hearts and Wrecker of Homes. 'And gentlemen of the jury, what one among you would not do the same?' Thus it went. When Brad had finished, I noticed thru my tear dimmed eyes that twelve handkerchiefs in the jury box were wiping twenty-four eyes. Even the judge in his instructions to the jury added as an afterthought that perhaps justice should be tempered with mercy. Brad had evidently won his case; there was not a dry eye in the house.

"The jury filed out. Before their tears had time to dry they filed back in, and they looked with smiles toward Hong Lee Wo. The foreman of the jury stepped forward to read the verdict. He was interrupted by a commotion at the door. All eyes were turned in wrath to see who had the audacity to delay J..Sterling Bradford's moment of victory. Every eye in the room then followed a Chinese girl down the aisle. She stopped when she stood before the judge. When I looked at that girl I wished that I was a Chinaman.

"In any other court that young Pekin pullet would have been marched right back out the door she came in, but nobody could get their breath before she began to talk, and then they didn't want to stop her. She said she was the wife of the deceased Gee Kwong. After he had been killed she spent the best part of two weeks throwing spit balls at Old Man Buddha, asking him to keep the devil away from her Sweet Cookie. It was just that morning that she had read an account of the trial in a newspaper. It was all a lie! Hong Lee Wo wasn't married at all. He had made quite a roll in this country and was going to China. He asked her to go with him. She had always wanted to see China, you see she was born in San Francisco, but she couldn't as long as her husband Gee Kwong was hanging around. Hong Lee evidently took this as an invitation to bump poor Kwong off. She hadn't meant it that way at all, and now she hated Hong Lee Wo. Imagine that line from a Chinese girl! The judge asked her how she happened to care for a man who couldn't even speak English. Did he refer to Hong Lee? Oh, she never really cared for him, she just wanted to go to China with him. And besides he could talk English as well as she could. They went to the University together. He was born in San Francisco too. Nobody could figure out just why she went back on Hong Lee so abruptly, but that's one of the secrets Mrs. Sphinx hasn't divulged as yet.

"Well the District Attorney had her put on the stand and her testimony was entered in the records. Poor Brad didn't even have sense enough to object. This time the jury reached a decision without leaving the box, and along with the verdict they made the recommendation that the said Hong Lee Wo be given a death sentence."

Bill stopped. I waited a moment for him to go on. When he didn't, I began to get sore. "What's all that got to do with this, 'right man in the right place' stuff," I asked.

"Oh," said Bill "Brad had sense enough to see that he wasn't a Lawyer, and he quit. I saw him in Los Angeles yesterday. He's making more money in a day than I ever hope to make in a month."

I thought of the fifteen hundred lemonade money. "What's he doing?" I ventured.

Bill unfolded a San Francisco newspaper he had in his hand and pointed out an announcement in the Trans Bay News. It read:

"The distinguished scientist and lecturer, Mr. John S. Bradford, will give the first series of lectures to be given under the auspices of the Alameda County Poultry Raisers Association at the Oakland Municipal Auditorium tomorrow night. The first lecture by Mr. Bradford will be on 'The Domestication of Pekin Ducks.' "

Lake Tahoe

By Henrietta C. Penny

The snow-capped mountains meet the bending sky
  Around thy shores oh! Tahoe; their green feet,
  Tree-draped with fir and pine, thy waters meet,
And the pines are singing as the wind goes by.
Thy blueness shames the summer sky today,
  Thy rippling waves blend with the pine-trees song,
  Thy clear depths call me as I drift along
Round wooded point, or into rock-bound bay.
But now a storm-cloud on yon distant height
  Shows us the lightning's gleam, and then a sound
  Of rolling thunder; every peak around
Answers with echoes, and a flash of light,
  Showing thy sterner aspect; but e'en so
  I love thee, Queen of Lakes, oh! blue Tahoe.

A Vacation on the Yukon River

By Agnes Rush Burr

THE Indians who have an apt way of expressing the essence of an object in its name called the Yukon River, "Yukonna." The fine flavor of a name thus given is almost impossible to translate and to say that "Yukonna" means **"The River"** but expresses baldly what the Indians felt. The word was spoken by them almost with reverence, as if all other streams sank into insignificance beside this great river of the North, to them, majestic in beauty, terrible in strength, flowing on apparently without end.

But though they knew little of the other great rivers of the world, the spirit of the Yukon spoke to them truly. This river has a wild, primeval beauty few great streams today retain. It has a romance in the strange, fantastic fleet of the argonauts that sailed upon it in the wild rush of '98 which no other river of untrodden solitudes knows. And in the picturesque boats of the fur traders of early days with their loads of blankets, guns, tea and tobacco for barter with the Indians, and in the steamers of today with their mammoth barges piled high with the merchandise of the world is a fleet of commerce as interesting as that of any of the great rivers of the modern, busy world.

A summer holiday on it is therefore full of rare and varied interest. One reaches the point of river embarkation on comfortable steamers through the Inside Passage and by modern observation cars over the White Pass, the trip even thus far being through some of the finest scenery in the world. One ends his journey at a primitive, historic settlement on an island in Bering Sea. The beginning and the ending are typical of the linking of modern comfort and methods with the beauty and charm of the wilderness that

is the traveler's experience during the journey.

The boats for the trip down the river are taken at White Horse, a pleasant little town with wide, clean streets, numerous outfitting stores and several hotels. The barracks of the Northwest Mounted Police are here and if a wait for a boat is necessary, as is often the case, a visit to the quarters of this famous constabulary force is interesting. A trip can also be made by foot or by motor to the White Horse Rapids which are not far from the town and which in the gold rush days took such toll of life and property.

The steamers of the Yukon are flat-bottomed, light draught boats but modern and comfortable. An observation room is built forward on many of them so that one can sit in easy chairs before large plate glass windows and enjoy the scenery in comfort protected from wind and sun. Although far from the base of supplies, the menu includes fresh fruits, salads and such delicacies, and often moose and caribou steaks and other game in season. One is by no means out of the world, so far as creature comforts are concerned, though he is touching the edge of the Arctic.

The boat slips out of the dock at White Horse with an almost imperceptible motion and with scarcely a sound. In fact the absence of noise and the smooth movement of the boat make an impression by their very unusualness. The vessel first pokes its nose up stream much to the amazement of the traveler. But this is merely to reach a basin in which the boat turns round and heads down stream and the voyage of more than two thousand miles is begun.

At the very outset there is a wild, distinctive beauty about the Yukon that enchants. The river runs between high cut banks, straight as palisades, a clear, soft putty color in tone, the tops fringed with slender, spear-tipped spruce that are reflected in delicate wavering lines in the water. Sometimes these palisades stretch for miles, the fronts at times worn into rounded, bastionlike effect and here and there carved by wind and weather into strange faces and forms and hieroglyphics suggestive of Egyptian sculpture. Sometimes they disappear altogether and little grassy meadows, brilliant with wild flowers, take their place. At these points the mountains can be seen, mistily blue in the near distance, snow-capped on the horizon. And always there is the pervading atmosphere of wildness, of strength, of great, untrodden solitudes.

At first the channel is winding, slipping around great headlands, gliding through narrow stretches, swinging into broader reaches, giving enchanting vistas ahead of impressive banks, great forests, snow-capped mountains. The water is clear and sparkling, the current swift. The boat seems to have a strange method of progress. It appears to be swiftly drifting in shore, then, just when beaching seems inevitable, it turns and apparently as helplessly drifts to the other bank. But a strong hand and a keen eye are at the wheel. Piloting a Yukon boat is not an easy task. The channel changes constantly and the one at the wheel must almost listen to the voice of the waters for guidance as they ripple over bars, flow silently over the deep places, and fret over reefs and rocks.

The course lies through Lake Lebarge, a beautiful sheet of water hemmed in by hills, then through the tortuous, but picturesque Thirtymile River in which more boats were wrecked in the gold rush days than in the White Horse Rapids because of the swift current and the many submerged rocks; and then out into broader waters. Cassiar Bar is passed where may be said was the first real start of gold mining in the Yukon for placer mining was done here in the '80's. Various little settlements can be seen here and there on the banks as the boat steams onward, mere tiny clusters of log houses are they on the edge of the wilderness, for back of them the spruce forests be-

gin and stretch away beyond the vision. The stops at these primitive settlements are interesting. The steamer swings up to the bank. A gang plank is thrown ashore. Mail and supplies are carried off while the few inhabitants cluster about and eye the passengers along the rail or ask the news. Among them may be an Indian with a papoose on her back, emphasizing to the passengers their touch with the primeval. Or some prospector may leave the boat and with pack on back trudge off through the wilderness or put his belongings into a poling boat and start on his lonesome journey up some stream on a hopeful quest for gold. For it is said of the Alaskan prospector that he may be hatless and and shirtless and shoeless but never is he hopeless.

The individual, however, that awaits the boat with the most eagerness is the Yukon dog. At the first sound of the steamer's whistle he comes running, and so great is his ardor to be the first arrival, and so headlong his pace, that often he is unable to check himself and plunges over the banks into the water. But he shows no concern. His one eager, hungry desire is to get the scraps the cook may throw from the galley. Anxiously, apprehensively, he tears along the bank or splashes through the water, his face a picture of anxiety, his eyes, keen, alert. His expression is heartrending. It seems to say, "Is it possible you are going without giving me anything?" Under this pleading, distressed gaze the hardest hearted cook is apt to relent and before the boat steams away, something is tossed to the hungry horde whereat a fracas ensues of snaps and barks and growls ending in a rolling, frantic mass of animals not unlike, in the energy displayed, a football scrimmage.

Interesting features abound as the boat slips onward. Eagle's Nest Rock rears its hoary head with great cavities on its side that look like the entrance to mines. Tantalus Butte appears, a big headland that was given this name by early traders and explorers because owing to the windings of the river it had a tantalizing way of appearing and disappearing without apparently ever getting nearer. Coal has been found in this vicinity and is being mined to supply some of the boats and Dawson.

Wood is, however, the chief fuel of these boats and the operation of "wooding up" is one of the picturesque events of the trip. The boat runs up to the bank, a gang-plank is thrown off, and the wood which has been cut and stacked in neat piles on the shore is wheeled on in hand trucks. While the work is being done, the passengers stroll ashore if they so desire, and gather wild flowers, or wild berries which grow in great abundance all through Alaska. The smaller boats burn on an average a cord an hour, the larger boats, two cords.

Among the interesting features of this part of the river are the Five Finger and Rink Rapids. At the Five Finger Rapids the banks of the river rise sheer, a big rock in the middle disputes the way, and the steamer runs cautiously, but swiftly in the narrow channel left it. The Rink Rapids are a short distance beyond where the water foams rapidly down a rather steep grade. The experience is productive of pleasant thrills but no danger and then the voyage proceeds through even wilder, more beautiful scenery than that already passed.

Although all this stretch of water is popularly called the Yukon, the name is not correctly applied until the junction with the Pelly River is reached. This stream comes in from the north, and from here on the Yukon has many points of interest connected with its early history.

Down the Pelly in a canoe in 1842 floated Robert Campbell, a factor of the Hudson Bay Company, who had come overland from Montreal. He decided that the junction of these two streams was a good point for a trading post and he established here Fort Selkirk. A few years later, however, it was burned by the Indians. It was never rebuilt by the Hudson Bay Company, but years later when gold was being discovered throughout this section, one of the three traders, Harper, McQuesten and Mayo, whose names are almost synonymous with the development of the Yukon, established a trading post near the site of the old fort.

This settlement is now one of the most pretentious on this part of the river. Quite a number of houses are scattered along the bank and a schoolhouse and general store add to the importance of the place.

Past various little log settlements or perhaps a lonely cabin on the bank, the steamer glides and then a big dome-shaped mountain looms ahead with a strange looking scar on its side and Dawson is reached.

A change of boats is made here and a stop of several days is quite probable while waiting for the other steamer to arrive. This gives the traveler an opportunity to see the town and the surrounding country, a break in the river journey that is most enjoyable and interesting. There are comfortable hotels whose rates are not high, and autos can be hired for a trip to the creeks if one does not wish to walk.

The town is picturesque. Wild flowers bloom in its wide streets. Little log cabins reminiscent of the early days are seen. Some of the dance halls of '98 and '99 remain and bring to memory the tales of those wild times when showers of nuggets rained on dancers, when humanity gone mad through the sudden possession of gold plunged into a delirium of dissipation that startled the world. Sunset Dome, back of the town, offers a stiff climb for "hikers" and a fine view up and down the river and of a wilderness of mountain peaks to the east.

The trip to the creeks should not be missed. Mammoth dredges eat into the earth. Great hydraulic streams wash away hillsides. By both methods man is still seeking the gleaming grains that have made this region one of the most noted gold-producing areas of the world. The process is vastly different from that of the days of '98 when pick and shovel, windlass and bucket, primitive steampipe or simple open fire gleaned their millions from these frozen gravels. Over these creeks in those days hung often a continuous curtain of smoke from the fires kept going to thaw the ground which is frozen the year round here a few feet below the surface. But today everything is modern and efficient, autos spin over good roads that have replaced the trial of the prospector and all that speaks of other days and other ways is a tumble down cabin here and there by the creek-side with moss growing on its sagging roof.

Back once more on the restful, quiet boat a panorama of enchanting scenery glides by. Fortymile is passed, a mining camp of importance in the early days, for the Fortymilers in Yukon history are akin to the Forty-niners in the annals of California. Then soon the boundary between Canada and Alaska is crossed and American waters reached. Eagle the first stop in Alaska proper, had at one time a promising future. The first United States District Court in Alaska was established here, a road was mapped and partially surveyed to the Pacific Coast at Valdez, and Eagle in those days felt it had a right to scream loudly. But gold was discovered at Fairbanks, the court was moved thither, the highway remained chiefly on the map, and Eagle had to content itself with what is still today, the usual Yukon settlement of log houses, stores and a few other buildings.

Circle City, the next stop, also had its dream of growth and prosperity. Gold was found on nearby creeks and as the city that immediately sprang into life thought itself on the Arctic Circle, it took the name. But this, like some of its other claims, proved a matter of hasty judgment. The Arctic Circle is some eighty miles farther down the river. The gold discovered was not in the paying quantities hoped for and so the settlement did not become the great city it had visioned.

A change in the river is noticeable here. It broadens until in places the shores become mere dim lines. Trees, roots, branches and logs float in it. Channels are everywhere and islands are numerous. Indeed the waters take on the appearance of a flood or an inland sea, for here at Circle began the Yukon Flats which extend for some two hundred and fifty miles and in which the river loses the aspect it has hitherto worn and rolls, a great, muddy waste of waters, ten miles broad at times.

The next stop is Fort Yukon and the first building the traveler is apt to notice is a large, neat log structure with shining windows, snowy curtains and blooming plants. This is the hospital of the mission established here by the Protestant Episcopal Church and other of the mission buildings are grouped nearby.

The town though of the same primitive appearance as the others passed, is one of the most important on the upper Yukon. It was one of the earliest of the Hudson Bay posts being established a few years before Fort Selkirk. It was, too, one of the most pretentious, the log trading post being said to have had glazed windows, plastered walls and other comforts hitherto unknown to the wilderness. Near the present settlement is the old Hudson Bay cemetery in which are the oldest known graves of white people on this part of the Yukon.

The town also achieves distinction from being on the Arctic Circle and the objective point of the "sunners" as those who come to see the midnight sun are called. And they come in increasing numbers yearly. The trip in itself is delightful, and the sight of the sun sinking over the stretch of waters almost to the horizon, remaining there seemingly stationary for a few moments as if undecided whether to go to bed or to go to work again, and, having decided for the daily grind, proceeding along the horizon for a space and then slowly ascending, adds a unique feature to a trip already out of the common.

At Rampart quite some distance beyond Fort Yukon the high cut banks appear again, welcome with their greenery and impressive lines after the waste of waters. Rampart also has distinction for here lived for a time Rex Beach, chronicler of Alaskan life. Across from the little settlement is one of Uncle Sam's experimental farms where wheat, oats, barley and other crops suitable for Arctic climates are being evolved.

The most interesting stop of the middle river is Tanana for here boats are again changed for the last lap of the journey. The town lies along the bank of the river which here is broad and swift and on the far horizon can be seen misty blue mountains. Clean, neat log and frame houses and stores, the yellow, red-roofed buildings of Fort Gibbon at one end of the town and the bright quarters of the Protestant Episcopal Mission at the other end give the place an attractive appearance.

The Tanana River joins the Yukon here and those bound for Fairbanks proceed up this stream to this metropolis of the interior, "the golden heart of Alaska" as it is called. From Fairbanks, the coast can be quickly reached by auto stage through magnificent scenery by those who wish to get back to the States more rapidly than by the Yukon route.

But the traveler on the Yukon glides on down the river, past Ruby, the latest mining town to achieve fame; past the mouth of the Koyukuk, an important stream coming in from the North and easily recognizable by a high bluff that is quite a landmark and on which is a cross for a Roman Catholic archbishop murdered in the vicinity; past Nualto, the scene of an Indian massacre in the early days, and on by settlements of varying importance to the mouth.

The scenery of this part of the river is pleasantly restful. It has little of the rugged beauty of the stretches farther north but it has the charm of broader waters and gentler shore lines. At times the banks rise in steep bluffs but the general tendency is to soften outlines. Wooded islands add picturesqueness here and there.

The historical associations from Tanama down are chiefly Russian as those of the upper river are mostly English.

In the early days it was not known that the river of the north frequented by the Hudson Bay traders and the mighty stream on which the Russians had established their trading posts was the same. The Hudson Bay people thought the Yukon emptied into the Arctic Ocean, the present Colville River being supposed to be a continuation of the Yukon. The Russians called their stream the Kwikpak and believed it unnavigable a short distance beyond Tanana. It was not until the traders of the two companies met at the gatherings of the Indians at Tanana, for this was a great meeting place of the natives in the early days for the purpose

of barter, that the two streams were found to be the same.

The records of the upper Yukon show but one destructive act of the Indians, the burning of Fort Selkirk, and then little or no injury was done to human life. But the lower river has several tales of massacre. At Nulato was enacted one of these tragedies. The settlement was practically wiped out, and Lieutenant Barnard of the English navy who was there at the time searching for news of Sir John Franklin's party was one of the victims. He was buried there and his grave, marked with a simple cross, can still be seen.

Another grave of note is also at Nualto, that of Robert Kennicott, the naturalist. He was in charge of the scientific corps of the expedition sent by the Western Union Telegraph Company to find a route by way of Alaska and Siberia to Europe when the failure to lay the Atlantic cable seemed to make the finding of some overland way necessary. He died from the exposures and hardships.

As the mouth of the river is approached, the country grows increasingly flat and desolate. Occasionally in the distance hills can be seen, but these also gradually disappear and the country loses all distinctive features. Low mud banks and bleaching driftwood add to the dreary effect. Only the width and sweep of the waters is impressive for it is no longer a river but a sea.

The Yukon has many mouths. The low lying land that causes these numerous channels has been built up from the vast volume of silt and mud the stream brings down. Without doubt as the years pass, this land will continue to be built farther and farther out into Bering Sea.

From the mouth of the river a short run is made to St. Michael's, today' version of an early Russian settlement. It is on an island in Bering Sea and consists of a little cluster of houses, stores and what is called by courtesy a hotel. Here the steamer is taken via Nome for Seattle and soon one is again in the bustle of modern life which seems all the more complex and noisy after these days of communion with the primeval on this great stream of the North.

Second Hand

By Charlie Jeffries

"WOO OO OO EE! Woo oo oop ee ee!" came the notes, clear and carrying; and again through the river bottom they rang, "Woo oo pee ee, pig, pig, pig." By the effortless way that the young herdsman called, one might know that he had called swine before, many times before. And by the prompt way that the animals came tearing out of the thicket to him, one might know that this particular herd had answered his call many times before.

The last squealing pig in, the herdsman counted them, made a mental note of the ones that were present, as well as those that were absent, threw them a few ears of corn, then prowled on down the bottom.

Similar scenes often took place there in the bottom; for Jim Anderson was one that looked after his hogs, kept them rounded up and out of danger, kept them on a good range, doctored them when sick or crippled. Jim thought a great deal of his hogs. He never needlessly hurt them; never used a dog to nip them on the hind legs when driving them; nor cut their ears cruelly deep when marking them. And they, in return, put unlimited confidence in him. In any kind of weather, as far as they could hear him, they would come at his call.

If you have been enticed into reading this far, turn back a few pages to where Jim first acquired the nucleus of a herd —an old sow and seven pigs. Gradually, he picked up others, a runty shoat here, a fine gilt there, Berkshires, Poland-Chinas, Razorbacks, any kind. And the way he, without an ear of corn, carried them through the long dry summer months was an epic. He pulled weeds for them at noon and before breakfast; he toted watermelon rinds from the store, and, later on, he fed them slop from the rail-road construction camp. True, they never knew the satisfaction of a full feed, and squealed with hunger whenever Jim came near them, and though they grew lean and weak, he managed to keep them alive till the crops were gathered; then he turned them on the open range. After a few weeks running in the corn fields and potato patches, he tolled them to the river bottom. Here they found such feeding ground as they had never known. The rains had washed acorns and pecans in piles; out of the sloughs, sprang many succulent Autumn weeds, while, in the rich, alluvial loam, earth worms, as big around as a lead pencil, were to be had for the rooting.

And Jim saw to it that they got the best that the land afforded. If down the river a little way, the mast was better, or the ground softer for rooting, he led them to it. He gave them copperas and charcoal to keep them healthy. He poured crude oil on their sleeping places to keep them clean. They thrived.

And they went wild. It was surprising how quickly they went wild. One night in the bottom was sufficient to make them skittish. From that, their lapse into hog-barbarism was fast. They grew watchful and suspicious of sounds. A stranger could not approach them. They grew swift and active. They learned to give the quick death-stroke that only the wild hog can give.

But their return to the primal was not complete. As the pictures of pen-life and the ways of pen-life faded from their memories, they drew closer to Jim. They were always glad to see him. He had but to appear among them, when from the tiniest pig to the roughest boar, they would come and lie down to be scratched. They would follow him anywhere, and that without the medium of an ear of corn. With only an occasional "Woo pee," he could have lead them to the end of the world.

As they grew and fattened, the rivermen took notice of them. Many a hunter stopped to admire the great, strapping barrows, as they, half hidden in a trash pile, rummaged for the soured acorns. In particular, Lem Higgins, a trapper, who lived in a house-boat, did this. From admiring the hogs, it was but a step to wishing they were his, and from wishing they were his to wondering how he could make them his. In the past, he had often made other men's hogs his own, but it was something he never attempted unless the opportunities were exceptionally favorable; for, of all thievery, hog stealing requires the most cunning work. So he planned and waited.

A certain deep slough made out from the river a short distance, then turned and ran parallel with the main stream. The range on this strip of cut-off land was very fine. Overcup acorns, by the barrel, lay in the drifts. Many a time had Jim longingly wandered over this untouched range. But he, as well as the other stockmen, was afraid of it. A sudden rise in the river would throw the water through the slough and effectually trap any animal caught on the strip.

Nobody knew this better than Lem Higgins. He reasoned that if Jim's hogs should be swept away, he could rescue a number in his small boat, load them on his house-boat, then cut loose and drop down stream to safety. Accordingly, he dinned into Jim's ears the excellence of the acorns on the cut-off and poohooed at the danger of an overflow. Jim shook his head. Higgins was tenacious. "You can bridge the slough," he suggested. "Get you a spool of barbwire, twist it into cables, and make you a suspension bridge. There are all kinds of trees on the bank that you can use as posts, and there are poles handy that you can make a floor out of; you can build it in a day."

The plan certainly did look feasible to Jim—and the acorns along the river bank were very fine. The bridge was built. Jim lead his herd across it and back several times to test it. It proved as practical as the finest steel structure in the state. And in the untouched acorns of the cut-off he left his hogs.

Now, Jim did not live in the bottom, and when his herd was doing fairly well, he only went down every day or so to look at them. One morning, a neighbor came to his house and told him the river was up. Jim stuffed a few ears of corn in his pocket and started for the bottom. He struck the river some distance above where his hogs were feeding. The stream was nearly bank-full and rising rapidly. He hastened down to the big slough and found the water pouring through it a miniature river itself. He crossed on a swinging vine, and went on in search of his hogs. When he found them, he hurried them down to the bridge. Here he was abruptly stopped. The bridge was destroyed. Some fiend had cut the cables and what remained of the work churned and bobbed in the roaring current, hopelessly beyond repair.

Who had played him so dastardly a trick, Jim had no idea. But one thing he did know, his hogs were trapped. He knew that he could not hem them in a bend of the slough and force them to swim across, for the simple reason that they were not afraid of him. The only plan that he could think of was to lead them down the river seven miles to the wagon bridge. Of this, he was not very sanguine; for, not counting the distance, the way was extremely rough and muddy. However, he called the herd and started.

They followed like a pack of dogs, playing around his feet, and cutting capers of joy. After a mile or two, the undergrowth, at times, became so dense that Jim was forced to almost crawl. Boggy, and treacherous little sloughs had to be crossed. Enormous, fallen trees had to be gone around. Often he had to take his knife and cut his way through to open ground. From winding and scrambling and doubling in the thickets, they had a season of bogging and sticking in the waxy gumbo, and progress was very slow. The hogs tired easily. The herd that had started out a close packed, energetic bunch, gradually strung back and became silent. Jim called incessantly. At the sloughs, he was forced

5

to stop and coax and help the small ones over. He was tired himself, and muddy and cold. He trudged on calling, calling, calling. He called in his most persuasive note. He called till he was hoarse. The herd became more sluggish. The strong lean ones kept up fairly well, but the fat ones, grunting and panting, waddled far behind, and still behind them, trailed the little pigs, too tired to make a noise. Jim, at intervals, stopped and bunched them and gave them a few grains of corn. After eating, they would lie down. It was difficult to start them again. Worn as the hogs were, and the overflow, Jim knew not how near, if he ever gained the bridge, he knew it would be next to a miracle.

The worst part of the way, Green Brier Rough, lay just ahead. This was a thicket of thorns and briers, so dense that the cattle and wild animals even never tried to go through it. The only possible way around this barrier, was by following the margin of the river, the few feet of steep bank between the water and the top. Jim climbed down to investigate. He found it worse than he expected. Instead of being boggy and affording foothold, the banks were shelving, difficult enough for a man, and as for hogs, Jim knew the way was all but impossible.

Jim did not know what to do. He sat down on a drift log and pulled off little pieces of bark and threw them in the water. He looked up the stream and down. Not a thing suggestive of a way out did he see. He looked wistfully at the oposite bank that, in great, towering hills, came down almost to the water's edge. He looked back at the seething, boiling flood that steadily climbed the bank.

Well, if his hogs were doomed to drown, he preferred that it should be by a quick plunge in the roaring river than to be caught by the slow, creeping over-flow. So, scraping the mud from his shoes, he called the herd. They did not come. He called again. They came to the bank and stopped and looked around uncertainly. As he continued to call, and the plaintive notes rang through the bottom, the action of the animals became more unusual. They sniffed the air. They held their heads high, as if trying to see.

They turned their heads sidewise, listening intently. Jim wondered why they did not come down. True, he was nearly hidden by the drift, but that ought not to bother them. He called louder, as an elocutionist would say, he put expression in it. From the towering heights on the other side and through the wild-wood, the quavering wail reverberated and rang. Then it was a great, rough Razorback, with tusks like a mammoth, broke ranks. Half walking, half sliding, he went down to the water and plunged in. The entire herd followed him. To Jim's utter astonishment, instead of swimming down toward him, they held their course straight out in the stream. Jim called frantically. It did no good. The louder he called, the more anxious they seemed to get away. Jim wondered if they, having sensed their danger, were trying to escape by swimming across, or if they, like their Biblical progenators, were possessed with the devil. Jim called his last time, then stopped to listen to the sound as it rang and rang. He made the discovery. It was the echo of his voice, the hogs were following. Because of his peculiar acoustic situation, they had been deceived as to his location, and faithful to the last, they, as they thought, had braved the water to reach him.

When the last little squealer had climbed the bank in safety, Jim, ever a rewarder of faithfulness, pulled off his belt and, using it as a sling, hurled after them three good ears of corn.

The Dinner Guest

By Anne Esty

SAVE him if ye can, Lord! Save him if ye can!" silently Professor Gallup reiterates this prayer as he stands in College Chapel on a warm, June day. Whether by audible or inaudible petition, this kindly, big-hearted, old man always aproaches the deity as a confidential adviser who has investigated and knows the justice of the cause he pleads.

Chip, chip, chip. A stone-mason is cutting an initial letter in the slab, set in the wall to the right of the pulpit, where already chiseled into the stone are the names of twenty sons of the college, fallen in battle. The morning light, streaming through the high, round-arched windows, brightens the buff-colored walls and glistens on the classic, white columns of the colonial hall. The gray benches are pushed away where hurrying boys left them. Only the professor, his collie dog, "Amo," the white-clad mason, and his dull assistant are gathered for the ceremony. It is quiet in the great room, except for the twitter of birds in the maples that push their green branches almost through the open half of the windows, and the steady chip, chip, chip as the mallet drives the edged tool. To stop his ears against this sound the professor repeats his ritual.

It is six months since Nick was reported "missing in action." During all that time the flickering optimism of the old teacher has striven against the darkness of facts. Now the fingers of the stone-cutter seem itching to carve the irrevocable as his heavy-faced boy hands him the delicate tool and he forms the "N" in "Nickolas Swenson."

"Stand back a little, Purfessa. Ef one o' them chips gits in yer eye, it's some chore to git it out." The stone-mason grins down correctively from the top of the step-ladder.

Professor Gallup walks away and seats himself by the side wall of the chapel. His vision is safe enough but he must have a care lest any of the stone enter his heart. Yet, at that very moment, Nick's voice has spoken to him through the unshaven lips of the mason. "Some chore," the rough slang rings in his ears as the boy used to say it. That's just the way of it, Nick lives and speaks in every minute of the day!

Chip, chip, chip from the chisel, and again the battling words of the prayer in the old man's heart are hurled defiantly against the sound. "Save him if ye can, Lord! Save him if ye can!" The very form of the appeal acts as a charm against the noise of the tool, recalling the day five years ago, when the professor rose before the faculty-meeting to plead for Nick. "Save him if ye can!" he had thundered at those human judges, "His father's got a cancer and fourteen children. The boy'll make a good second-rate minister. Save him if ye can!" His sharp tongue made impress on those academic hearts of stone. Nick, saved from deserved dismissal from college, was hunted out that winter evening, in his cold room in "North Dorm," where the half-starved, country boy nursed his only asset, an aspiring faith in himself, and at the same time turned over in his mind a bit of resentment against his savior's rating of his future, ministerial career.

Soothing the boy's pride, as he would stroke the up-standing bristles of Amo's neck, Professor Gallup led Nick home like a rescued cur from the pound. During the next four years he lived in the Gallups' childless home. Before supper was over that first night, he laughed with the bubbling joy of a child whose stomach is full; and, after all, little Nick with his downy chin and his out-shooting arms and legs was only a child for all his manly dreams. He smiled over his allotment of tasks in the simple household, laughed at the difficulties of college studies tackled with the flabby arm of a "poor fit." But in the end he succeeded. "All because Professor Gallup helped me," said Nick. "All because the boy had the stuff in him," was his old friend's rebuttal.

He was always known as "Nick Gallup." Few of his classmates would recognize the "Nickolas Swenson" of the stonemason's pattern as their red-headed Nick Gallup who broke the swimming record junior year.

The mason pauses in his work to squint his eyes and blow the stone-dust from the half-completed name, then turns to engage the professor in conversation, the duties of host justly falling to him on this occasion.

"I most ferget he weren't your boy, everybody calling him 'Gallup.' It's a lively kind o' name, too, sorta spereted to cut in stone." Chuckling, the stone-cutter reaches down for a sharpened chisel from the slow hand of his helper, then continues, "Last time I seen him, when I was working up to his fraternity-house, I says to him, 'Mr. Gallup,' I says, 'what's your pa purfessa of?' and he says, quick as anything, he says, 'Why, he's purfessa o' human kindness!'"

There again! The voice of Nick speaks from the very stone. The professor closes his eyes and leans his white head against the wall. It is no simple matter to bury his dead, Nick's resurrection is perpetual within him, revisualizing the merry boy and his vigorous ways as he slammed in and out of the home he so quickly accepted as his right, twisting the rugs about in the hall and filling the prim house with evidences of youthful energies. Never since their own little son died, years before, had the even growth of the Gallups' lives burst into the bloom of joy. The boy had grown to be theirs as truly as if he had been born in their house, instead of in that lonely, Vermont parsonage where disease and childbirth raced the dispirited parents of his body to their graves.

After he was graduated from college, Nick had enlisted and gone overseas. A few scribbled letters had found their way home and then silence.

A wave of loneliness breaks over the professor and he gropes for that which can save him from self-pity. The living still call. He remembers repentantly that he did not ask his wife to come to the chapel with him that morning. He had dreaded her talk; she would slip her hand in his and tell him again that their boy, if he had lived, would be just Nick's age. Things said that should be silent are harder on the ears than the chip of stone. The little wife knew where he was going, and in the resentment in her eyes, as he left her without urging her to accompany him, he had read where her morning would be spent. Pique always drove her to the child's grave, to weed and water in the sun until she came home wheezing with asthma increased by renewed sorrow and stooping in the heat There has been too much of that since Nick's going lightened the housework. Springing to his feet, the professor hurries his long strides across the hall to an office where there is a telephone. Amo, startled from sleep, follows cringingly, realizing by animal telepathy his master's shameful intention to deceive his wife.

"Yes, dear," by good luck he catches her before she leaves the house, "if it is perfectly convenient, I will bring a gentleman home to dinner." The white-haired hypocrite hangs up the receiver and returns to the bench by the chapel wall, smiling to think how Nick would have enjoyed his naughtiness. The little wife won't bend under the hot, cemetery sun. Company! How often has he felt the electric change wrought of that mighty word in his frugal home—the parlor redusted, the dinner menu hastily amplified, and at the appointed hour the arriving guest, who until now has played such an insignificant part in the whole fracas, ushered into the little, old room where the sofa and chairs still wear those absurdly ruffled covers of faded chintz whose youthful brightness was synchronous with that of their plump owner's.

Between the windows, by the child's red rocking chair with its arm worn free of paint, Mrs. Gallup always stands, in her silk dress, her little round face—bless it—framed by her mother's lace collar and a wee dab of a cap perched between the scant, white memories of her own hair, curled over her forehead, and the big coil of gray, adopted hair, pinned on atop. Half the excited girl, dressed up to play party, and half the gracious hostess, defending the ease of her guest from suspicion of having caused a domestic occasion, she receives her visitor. But — the professor's thoughts pause — who will be guest today? Anyone will do for the little wife to fuss over—he will stop on his way home and take Lauerbach back to dinner. Poor, old Lauerbach with his hated, German blood and his everlasting longwindedness, he'll be glad to feed a good meal into his over-boarding-housed stomach. Today is Friday, salt-fish day! Thank Heaven, he telephoned! The dinner's addenda will cancel cod and his throat, dry from flying stone-dust, craves just those fresh fruits that he will gather from his deceit.

The stone-mason's work is done. The successful manservant of fate packs his tools, folds the step-ladder, and with his assistant at heel moves importantly away, brushing the flecks from his sleeve and throwing out "Good-bye, Purfessa!" as a last condecension from the artisan to the unemployed. As the door closes behind him, Professor Gallup pats Amo into quiescence and turns to silence forever the protesting prayer in his heart. Nick's laugh is stilled and he is sleeping for a moment on some old battle-field; but Nick who worked so steadily against odds, first in the hope of bettering himself and then with the desire of helping others, Nick's spirit isn't dead. A boy who has the stuff in him doesn't fail, and a boy who hasn't failed can't die. It is well with the child however deep they cut his name in stone and hope for the living only dims before brighter hopes for the dead.

The sound of the noon train drawing into the station has for years been the signal for the professor to leave off work and walk briskly home to dinner. Now, obedient to the noise of its arrival, he rises, whistles to Amo, and starts across the elm-arched campus.

The train has puffed away into silence by the time he reaches his home. He draws out the key-ring from his pocket, but the door is ceremoniously opened to him by the shiny-faced, Polish servant-maid, unfamiliar in stiff, white apron; and the professor awakes with a start from a dreamy consideration of keys. The Guest! Memory tears him as a bullet rips through the heart. Curse his constitutional forgetfulness! He had never given Lauerbach another thought. In order to moon over the memory of his dead, undisturbed in his own, mean, little corner, he has played a contemptible trick on the very one he should have comforted. Humbly he moves through his door to the confessional. The lie that flew so nimbly over the wire must be acknowledged to his wife. Through the hallway he walks, his eyes lowered to the polished floor and the geometrically placed rugs. At the parlor door he lifts them and stands, the dupe of his own duplicity, before his wife. There as he pictured her the little woman waits, her round face as pinkly expectant as the hollyhocks that peep through the open windows at her back.

"Annie. . . ," the professor begins, wishing with all his heart that Nick were here with his light touch on a heavy situation. It was really preposterous what the little woman would take from Nick, while her husband might expect nothing but dumb, incredulous indignation returned for his smallest sin.

"Annie. . . ," he begins again as he steps within the parlor door. The clang of the door-bell interrupts him and there is a welcome pause while the maid answers its call. Before he finds tongue to go on, Amo who is never allowed in the house, jumps over discipline and rushes through the open door, barking and thrusting the rugs about in clumsy excitement. Then the young maid, breathing heavily, enters the room. "Meesis," she calls, "master Neek, 'ee come back, all but 'ees arm!" Mrs. Gallup runs out into the hall with the funny, springing skip of a young lamb. Her husband follows to find her, with flushed face, rumpled collar, and upstanding cap, cry-ing and hugging a young man with red hair, whose lean, brown face is bending over hers. The laughing soldier pushes out his left arm above Mrs. Gallup's head and wrings the professor's hand.

"Nick, Nick!" They have to help the old man to a seat. He looks up at the soiled, khaki-clad figure with one empty coat sleeve tucked into a pocket. "Where ye been, boy?" he asks sternly, as if ques-tioning a naughty child.

"German hell-hole, hospital. It's a reel as long as one of old Lauerbach's ser-mons. I'll run it through after feed—haven't eaten since I left home!"

The older man rises with a vigorous grunt and plumps his great arm across the boy's square shoulders, above which he towers by several inches. "Come, boy, yer dinner's ready." Together the two follow the bustling, little woman to the dining-room's festal board.

The maimed soldier stands at attention behind his old place at the table, set ready for his use. A shyness like that that filled him at his first coming here in freshman year, makes him lower his eyes.

Rising odors of home-cooked roast beef are good in his nostrils, and into his con-sciousness floats his first complete real-ization of the devotion offered him by the loving, old couple.

"How did you know I was coming, sir?" he asks, "I didn't send any message. You must have thought I was dead all this time."

In the overwhelming joy of Nick's re-turn, the professor had lost thought of his deceit. Now it's out! He glances in fear at his wife. Thank goodness, she is occupied with the consummation of hos-pitalities and takes no notice of incon-sistencies that jump with her desires.

The old teacher swells out his chest in safe assurance, no need now when every-body is happy to feel squeamish about a little moral shiftiness. He beams benign-ly on Nick but, at the same time, fills his tone with a blast of finality that withers the budding questions on the young man's lips. "No need of a message, boy, I knew ye were coming," he thunders, and then, "Dead? Dead? How could ye be dead, when I was praying for ye, night and day?"

Captain Biggs

By Arthur Lawrence Bolton

Old Captain Biggs, of the Barque Malay,
Was fishing in Bolinas Bay,
An old arm chair in the stern of his skiff,
He seated there all pompous and stiff,
His colored lackey at the sculls,
Dipping indifferent, 'twixt breezes and lulls.
It happened that the Ida A
Slipping her moorings up the Bay,
Was dropping out on the out-going tide,
When the Captain's boat bumped into her side,
And Captain Biggs with his avoirdupois,
A graceful bow, and not any noise,
Went over the stern, to the fishes below,
And he's down there yet, for all I know.

Bebe Dortmore in Efficiency

By F. F. Smith

I HAD "gotten into the wrong pew." Instead of being the perfectly proper eighteen-year-old daughter of Major Ashley, I had broken all rules of propriety by going to Chinatown with Ted Pixley after solo practice, and getting lost.

Ted and I had known each other from childhood and, as I faced the family council at ten-thirty, after being rescued by our old cook, Jim Lee, they agreed that all childhood relationships and pranks should cease at 12. Ted said (under his breath) as he went out, looking at Aunt Nan, "Cat!"

I wanted a career and saw myself settled and centered in a wonderful room furnished with teakwood. My fad was at the bottom of all this trouble. Ted — special illustrator on one of the big dailies—had run into a wonderful bargain at Sing Fat's that morning. Davis had called me up as I was going out and Ted had made an appointment with me for nine o'clock.

"What a lark it will be, Ted," I whispered and hung up the 'phone. It was! We were going down Jackson Street and I was lost in wonder for I had never been there in the evening before, when Ted jumped in front of me just as a pistol shot rang out. "In, there, in there!" he shouted. "It's the highbinders! The Tongs are on the war-path."

I was in, and I was in darkness, but where was Ted? I stumbled down some steps and saw a wee twinkling light in the distance before me. I made for it and got to a landing only to see three narrow passages going off into the darkness. Out from the right one forms were coming toward me. I gave one look and fled down the left. Fear? I did not know the meaning of the word, but I had a very queer sensation in my knees.

Soon I went down another five steps and saw an outer opening to the left. I could see the stars. I crept slowly on, then up a few steps and on again. I thought I heard my name called behind me, but I kept on going. I reached the opening and was making a quick run for freedom when a strong arm pulled me into a room. Turning, I faced a dozen or more Chinese, all talking at once to me. It sounded like the wailing of a lost soul and I backed up against the wall.

"How dare you?" I demanded of the man who had pulled me into the room. It was of no use to scream. My brain worked like lightning. I was just going to proclaim the fact that I was the daughter of Major Ashley, U. S. A., when a happy thought struck me. The man on my right was peering into my face when, quick as thought, I pulled out of my bosom a good-sized flag of the Stars and Stripes. (It was a fancy of mine to wear it.) Folding it around my shoulders, I held up one corner in front of me. Every Chinaman stood up, and I took command.

"Attention!" I called. "Every man pass by me out of this room. Woe to the one who puts a finger on this flag. Open that door!" and quick as a flash they did. "March, every man of you! Right, left; right, left," and just as the last man passed me another form came from somewhere, from an inner room. It was Jim Lee, our cook. His face was a study, of course, and I could have hugged him.

"These men all right, Miss Bebe," he was telling me, at the same time carrying on a conversation with the disappearing crowd of Chinese.

"Take me home, Jim!" I commanded. "Here, come this way. There's an opening."

"No, that no opening, that go down very far."

"But the stairs, Jim?"

"Oh, that just where old stairs was long 'go. We go this way," and he led me out the same way I had come in. We reached the wee light at the turn when, out of breath, bringing a policeman, came Ted.

"Hurry, Bebe. The folks are on edge, they are up in arms."

"Oh, Ted, what made you tell them?" I wailed. "I'm in for it now. It means a lecture from Dad, and Aunt Nan won't let up for weeks. But then, there's mother dear — she'll understand. Of course, the boys will tease, but I won't mind, for I am standing at the threshold of my career."

Mother met us first. She said in her kind, gentle voice:

"C. S. stands for many things, dear, and one is Common Sense."

Just then Doris brought a telegram from Dad. He had been called South, but then, Aunt Nan — writer of free verse—and the boys had to be faced. I made a face at Leslie as I passed him. "Remember you cut school today," I whispered and he wilted. John was secretly too glad to see me; so Aunt Nan, in the state of a roaring lion, was the only serious one to settle. She clamored, the minute I entered the room, "Bebe Dortmore, there is only one thing I would advise your mother to have you schooled in, and that is——" It was coming, I knew, and I saw my career vanishing like mist before the sun. Ted looked daggers. I would be sent away somewhere to more schools! Only mother knew I was taking the course of lessons in "How to Discover and Express Your Gift." Tomorrow was the third lesson and my turn to give a paper.

"You do not know the meaning of the word 'efficiency,'" she continued. "You should become acquainted with it, assimilate and possess it. It has made me what I am, and——" It was right here that Ted walked out, as I said before, whispering, "Cat!" Aunt Nan was still talking but I went out to see Ted off. "She's a dear, Ted, after all," and, waving him a good-night, I slipped by the library door up to my room.

"Phew! what a narrow escape!" I said

to Polly who, hearing me come in, started to mutter quickly. Telling Betty not to mind, I was glad to be alone to think things over. The "lark" had not amounted to much, the scolding was forgotten, but the fact that I had been able to live up to my new name—the one given to me in the first lesson of this wonderful course—made my pulse beat and, reaching for The American Dictionary, I felt ready for anything.

"Efficiency—C—D—E—Ee—Ef—here it is," and so studying I fell asleep.

The morning was glorious. "Good morning, Polly! Polly want breakfast?" I called, jumping out of bed.

"Efficiency, efficiency!" shrieked Polly, then went off into "Ha, ha! Polly's the bird!"

"Yes, Polly, I must become acquainted with and possess it"—and I hurried down to breakfast. The dining-room with its oval windows looked out on San Francisco Bay and a huge transport was making the Golden Gate, while the ferryboats were going in different directions. All the world was alive and active. The boys had gone an hour ago to Mare Island. Doris said mother was taking coffee in her room.

"And where's Aunt Nan?" I whispered.

"Look!" and Doris pointed to a dark object at that point of the garden just over the cliffs. "Writing!"

"All right, Doris. I'll have coffee with mother." So I bounded up the stairs.

"You're the dearest mother in the world," I said at the end of the third kiss.

"And Prue," — she always called me Prue when we were alone — "you will prove efficiency in your life. I know you will!" and, patting my hand, she said, "John has decided to bo gack to Harvard now that the war is over, and Leslie is going with him. Dad and I go to the Islands at the end of the year."

"And I, mother, I will meanwhile be looking for 'efficiency!'"

Two o'clock found me at the Montgomery. I said to the elevator boy, "Fourth floor, please." At the second we stopped and took in a young man in uniform. I saw he was a First Lieutenant, but got no farther. "Fourth floor," called the boy and, he of the uniform leading the way out, turned the passage and preceded me into Room 63. As I took my seat in class I felt the psychological moment of my career had come. There were twelve of us and we were all named. I was Harmony. Then there were Charity, Joy, Wisdom, Prosperity, Love and the rest. I was curious. Of course the new-comer would receive a name after the first concentration was over. Our teacher (I sometimes thought his sex a mistake. He was so gentle and I had been used to comparing every man with Dad and the boys), had said from the first, "I am Inspiration," and of course it was from this inspiration we had received our names. When, after a five-minute period of concentration, he had turned to me and said, "I name you Harmony." I certainly was surprised, it seemed so foreign to my nature. Dad called me 'Little Cyclone!' I quickly ran over the names in my $m_i n_d$ as I looked into the different faces. Charity was whispering to Prosperity; Wisdom sat with closed eyes; Peace was looking peeved at an open window. Behind her two chairs were still vacant, and I couldn't remember their occupants' names, but Inspiration was beginning. He always took a drink and then smelled the flowers which he insisted on having before him—he said they were like angels and he liked their fragrance. "Now, Joy," he was saying, "will you go to the door, please? and you, Love, sit here at my right-hand, I like to have you here. And this dear one (meaning the new-comer), must have a name before we take up the class work for today." Punctuality, out of breath, having arrived with Truth, the seats were full. I just then discovered there were thirteen of us and whispered to Victory about it. Victory slapped back, "That's only a false belief, let go of it," and, turning, beamed on the new-comer. She was forty and single.

"Now, children, we will concentrate," said Inspiration and after another drink he sank down into the only comfortable chair in the room. The rest of us were in straight-backed ones—he had told us they were better for the spine. His must

have been portable and elastic for he fitted perfectly into the rolling back of his rocker. Then there was a deep silence, broken only by the faint swishing of the rockers on Inspiration's chair. I sensed a sneeze coming and, opening my eyes to look for my handkerchief, felt the gaze of the brown eyes of the new-comer on me. Yes, there was just a wee bit of mischief in them and something in me, outside of the Harmony part, responded.

"Young man, I have named you. You are Efficiency," and Inspiration heaved a heavy sigh as though he longed to be what the name implied. Then followed a heated discussion as to its meaning. Prosperity said it meant "Character; full of energy." Wisdom was not quite certain, but said her mother-in-law was always called efficient, as she could always produce the desired results in anything she started. Ted, the Dearest, told her so. A quick tap from Inspiration brought us to order and the class was ready for the afternoon's special work.

"Harmony, we will have your paper read." I started, as though from a dream. I glanced at Joy, a bud of eighteen. Her dimples came and went as she nodded, "Go on." Love was slightly interested and Charity pointed to the clock. In spite of all I could do, I had to meet the brown eyes opposite me and in their depths I read the definition which I had found in the dictionary, of "efficiency." "Efficiency has the power to produce the result intended," I remembered, blushing, and hastily I found my paper and read:

Harmony, I am she who wins you and, having won you, loses you within myself.

The brown eyes twinkled, I know they did.

I am she who, running before you, hide from you. So, searching, you find me.

"Leave that to me!" flashed the eyes of Efficiency as I met his look.

It is I who, reaching and teaching, hold you while Love awakens you.

I looked at Joy for courage to go on. Both dimples were showing.

I am Truth's offspring, Wisdom's scout, Peace's victory. I am——

I could go no farther. Efficiency had won. "The power to produce the result intended" had worked. I was in the throes of love's awakening and he knew it.

After class I hurried to meet Ted. I had promised to help him select it—it was to be a cluster, not a solitaire. She preferred it, he had discovered. After an endless time, and no Ted, I hurried home. John met me with a telegram from Ted. It read: "Just leaving for South on some special work. Remembered date. Ted."

Dad's deep tones came from the library. He was talking to mother. Leslie was leaning over the stairway, beckoning like a naval ensign: "He's in there, Bebe, with Aunt Nan and she's reading her latest to him—Child Lovers—," he whispered, pointing down to the living-room.

"Who, Leslie?"

"Oh, some son of an old friend of Dad's.

Met him on the way home. He's great, Bebe!" he went on, following me into my room.

Later. I decided to wear my new gown which I had christened Harmony. It was soft and sheeny, like a bride's rose, and I felt in full atune when I entered the living-room.

"This is our daughter," Dad said, leading a form away from Aunt Nan.

"Efficiency!" I gasped, and, in the explanations which followed, my secret studying for a career was out.

At the close of the next lesson, after Inspiration had given out the new work, I heard Efficiency say to him:

"I have found my gift and am going to work it out with Joy and Harmony."

He did. Joy was my bridesmaid and Efficiency proved "the power to produce the result intended" with Harmony.

The Olympics

By Victor Buchanan

When rains have ceased and drooping clouds from out the sky have
    vanished,
And heavy-hanging mists at last have rolled away,
When from the freshened earth and air the gloom and smoke are
    banished,
To west the fair Olympics greet the coming day.

The lofty peaks snow-covered rise in grandeur rugged and cold,
And jut like turreted ramparts high into the upper blue.
Silent and stern outposts are they on the edge of a Kingdom, old,
But firm and fast in cloud and gloom, changeless and ever true.

However thick the clouds around may shroud them from all sight,
The falling snow doth gather and mantle their summits gray,
Till comes the time, as ever it comes, when the darkness and the night
Shall break and reveal their beauty in the shining light of day.

Why a War May Be Precipitated in Six Years

By Frank Harris

WARS are inevitable; our interest centers on whether they are proximate, or remote. Nations like individuals, with selfish aims, can only attain these by force. The League of Nations attempts to yoke equals and unequals together. With monarchies and republics in the same league, the odds are in favor of the former, as under a monarchical form a more continuous foreign policy is possible.

Surprise is the basic element in strategy, and nations will not be slow to use the league as a cloak, even as they used Christianity for centuries, to cover the secret aspirations of imperial policies.

The strength and weakness of a democracy is shown in war. The Draft and Espionage Act, are the sinister facts of the war. We must be prepared to wage war as a democracy. In the United States there is a constant effort to supplant government by law, for a government by functionaries; hence, the censor and all his ilk. The censor deceived none but ourselves, for as long as Germany could approximate our forces within 200,000 men the personnel and details were insignificant; they knew to a tooth-brush what was required to train, equip, and set in motion an army of one million men. Our indifference to all military affairs is a direct result of this censorship.

In this day, inventions change the tactics of war with great rapidity. To profit by the experiences of the late war it will be necessary to wage war within the next decade. The scuttling of the German Fleet in Scapa Flow, frees the German mind from this encumbrance, and compels them to adopt new military tactics. The surprises of the next war will be perfected in peace.

The failure of the Peace Conference to openly award to Russia a free seaway through the Dardenelles; the giving away of Shantung, these acts of ingratitude merely indicate the quicksand on which rests the present League of Nations.

The lesson of the last war, and the Paris Peace Conferences; to prepare for the next. Americans are asked to join in a league honeycombed with secret treaties and arrangements, under the flimsy pretext that it is a step in the brotherhood of nations. The highest ideals of Christianity will never materialize through such political channels.

The Peace Conference leaves the world with a new line-up. Great Britain retains all of her world-wide holdings. France occupies a precarious situation. The French people are very thrifty, and in a country where thrift rules in all classes, the status quo remains undisturbed — the peasants remain peasants, and the aristocracy are not always going up or down. They have defaced their churches by painting "Liberty, Fraternity, and Equality" on them, but outside of these signs, the condition of the peasantry remains the same.

The French are adepts at international flattery, and the United States is peculiarly susceptible to their wiles. We export to them wheat and steel products of all kinds, and in return we get a lace handkerchief and a bottle of perfumery.

The weakness of France is the dispersion of energies on the African possessions. The Colonies of France will one day ruin her. The French love the soil of France, they have no desire to emigrate. They should give away their navy and colonies and concentrate all their energies to make something out of France. They are exploiters and not colonizers. Necessity will demand a high order of brains on the French General Staff; we should look to France for military instruction.

Germany is the greatest nation of one strain in Europe. They think alike, and this is a tremendous force. They have the advantage of living next to Russia, they will exploit this country and build up a great trade. In the war, the losing of their African colonies was a great benefit to them. They only lost one colonial town of any value, and that was Kiau Chau. The Germans have brains and organizing ability—it is useless to predict the limits of their future.

Germany needed a defeat,, and their real history will date from November 11th, 1918. The tremendous influence of Frederick the Great had grown to be a yoke on the people. Russia is a new country—in fact is now being born. The weak point about Russia is the Capitol at Petrograd. The Capitol belongs in Moscow. The great coming City of Russia is Odessa. Batum should be a great port.

Russia's great national aspiration is for a free seaway through the Dardenelles. The Dardenelles will cause another war. Russia is entitled to a railway from Merv to Chahbar Bay, this railway to be a strip of land one-half mile in width, with a lease of one hundred square miles of land on Chahbar Bay. Railway and port should not be fortified. Russia and England should leave Persia. Persia should be a French sphere of influence.

China is a country in a trance. Their only hope of amounting to anything is to become a bi-lingual people. Every educated Chinaman should speak Chinese and English, all business to be transacted in English. China is a country without patriots, or public opinion. It is impossible for every small Chinese town to have a newspaper, as Chinese ideographs require too much time to set up in the printing press; and they have not ideo-

graphs to express modern ideas; hence no public opinion. The future of China is safe, for by the time they wake up the world will be more democratic than it is today.

Japan is a country with an intense National consciousness, a characteristic of island people. The extraordinary activity of Russia explorers in the North Pacific Ocean, coupled with Chinese apathy, was almost the undoing of Japan.

They can thank Admiral Perry for winding up the alarm clock that woke them up. When Russia took the Ussuri Region from China it was a great blow to Japan. We may sympathize with Japan's aspirations to control all of the country between the South, or right bank of the Amur River, and the Gulf of Liau-Tung, and as far east as the 120th Parallel of Longitude. This area may, with reason be construed a sphere of influence for Japan.

Russia is entitled to access to the sea, and should be given a railroad from Irkutsk to Urga—from Urga to Kalgan: Kalgan to a point near Taku. Ten square miles of land could be sold to the Russians for a railway terminal on the Gulf of Pechili. Japan has no rights on the Shantung Peninsula, but they make a good argument to secure concessions elsewhere.

Japan knows how to play the war game. They flatter every nation; but, they never give out any figures regarding their military strength. No American knows the real strength of the Japanese Army and Navy.

Secrecy and surprise, are the basic elements of strategy, and the Japanese know this great cardinal principle of warfare. Germany, Russia, Japan, are three countries seeking readjustments of territory. In all conflicts between the white nations, Japan's only interest is to be on the winning side.

In the tradition of the celestial ancestry of the Emperor, the Japanese have a great Central fact on which to build a strong military organization. This tradition is now at its maximum power. Association with white races will gradually weaken it. The sagacity of Japan in modeling their Navy after England, and their Army after Germany, show tha.t they have good ideas. What plans they have for foreign conquest, are as secret as their military establishment.

Do they want to own Manchuria? Do they want to own Alaska? Do they want to own the Philippines? Do they want to own the Hawaiian Islands? Do they want to own Guam? We cannot answer these questions; but we can be prepared.

We may expect another war by about 1925. This peace made two powerful mal-contents, Germany and Russia. Both are practically shut off from the sea. Germany will furnish the brains and Russia the manpower. There is not a great deal of danger of Russia and Germany overwhelming the Allies, although it is quite possible that they will have the power to compel the Allies to grant them access to all the seas.

One of the many reasons that may compel war by 1925 is invention. Nations have an experience in the present methods of warfare; now, if war is postponed thirty years, invention will render half of these methods obsolete. The German leaders will seek to take advantage of their present experience, for time runs against them. Another reason is the strong hold of Socialism on Russia and

Germany; they regard the Allies as Imperial democracies. The League of Nations is considered by Germany and Russia to be merely a League of the Allies, hence we may be reasonably sure of another war about 1925.

Our enemies count on a great re-action from this war, they expect us to sink back in peaceful lethargy. They know that all reconstruction plans deal solely with peace. In thinking thus, they alas! are not far astray—thus we contribute to the causes of the next war.

The League of Nations will probably be a much greater power for peace after the next war. This League will familiarize men with the idea. The revolution in Russia coming unexpectedly destroyed all pre-war plans. Germany and Russia will combine to overcome or neutralize, the commercial supremacy of Great Britain and France in Europe and Asia. They cannot win; but it is possible that they will in a very few years' time hold a balance of power sufficient to compel the Allies, to admit them on terms of equality, as joint authors and guarantors of a new constitution for a League of Nations. However, we may be reasonably sure that it will take another war to change the present covenant.

San Francisco

By Charles Horace Meiers

A saline breeze sails through the Golden Gate,
  And, as a challenge calls forth its reply,
  So does this wind encounter civic eye
And heart determined on a loftier state.
This sturdy city does not whine nor prate
  Amid the grievous tests which come to try
  Her spirit that, unfaltering, rises high,
Surmounting all grim obstacles of Fate.

With vision peering forward and above
  The point and level reached each current day
  And pressing onward in virility,
Upheld and succored by the force of love,—
  Thus, resolute, resourceful, yet half gay,
  Lives San Francisco, Sweetheart of the Sea!

Speedomania

By Frederic H. Sidney

T was in the year 3015 that the terrible epidemic of Speedomania broke out; the result of which was that every human being in the world, excepting fourteen perished. Two of those who escaped were in the United States, but the others were scattered in different parts of the earth.

The terrible disease of Speedomania was caused by the excessive speed the people were obliged to make in order to keep up with the customs of the times. For many generations the working classes had been working under the speeding system in order that they might produce more wealth for the masters. The children of the workers studied under the same system so that too much time would not be spent on their education, as their services were needed in the various industries, which had multiplied so fast that there was a dearth of workers. The saddest part of it all was that labor organizations had ceased to exist, and the result was pitifully small wages and the "speeding system."

The master classes had to resort to the speeding system in order to enable them to keep up with the demand on their time in attending the thousands of various enjoyments that had been devised for their pleasure.

All vehicles of transportation had been constructed along the lines of excessive speed. Devices were in use that enabled people to obtain their food from the air. There were two grades of machinery in use for generating nourishment. The master classes had their laboratories installed with the machinery of the most delicate and most expensive kind; this enabled them to obtain the very finest nourishment. On the other hand the machinery which the workers had in their kitchens was of the cheaper sort and their nourishment was much coarser and less nourishing than that of the masters. The devices in use for generating nourishment were controlled by a large and powerful corporation, which employed many low-paid workers. This concern was protected by the most rigid patent law the world has ever known.

After so many generations of excessive speed the human race became weakened, and was unable to throw off the epidemic of Speedomania when it attacked them. From the first this terrible disease baffled all scientists and physicians. People were attacked with it without any warning whatever. If they happened to be walking along the street when attacked by it, they would start and run, and not stop until they had dropped dead from exhaustion. It was an utter impossibility to stop a person who had run amuck with Speedomania. They ran with the speed of the wind, knocking over anyone who attempted to obstruct their passage. It was ridiculous at the same time, pitiful, to see some sedate and dignified member of the master class, bedecked in jewels and finery, rushing madly through a crowded street, knocking people right and left and finally dropping dead in his tracks. The saddest sight of all was when a poor, haggard, half-starved worker became attacked, the tense drawn expression of the face, and the agony that appeared on it was something never to be forgotten.

Men in charge of machines of transportation, when attacked with this disease would speed their crafts beyond all reason and safety, and the result was that the conveyance would be wrecked and everybody riding in it would be killed. Children were attacked with the disease at their studies and at their play. So swift and terrible was this plague that practically the whole world was depopulated within thirty days from the time the epidemic began. Why fourteen people escaped will always remain a mystery. It was probably a dispensation of Providence in order that the world might again become inhabited. One of the strangest things of it all was, that the bodies of those who died did not decompose; they simply shriveled like a mummy. This was probably due to the food they ate.

CHAPTER TWO.

The only two human beings in the United States who managed to escape the malady, were Jack Smith, a radio telegrapher, and Miss Daisy Butterfly a member of the master class, and a member of Boston's most exclusive society. After the ravages of the epidemic had passed, Jack wandered about the streets of Boston, and everywhere he saw the mummyized bodies of his friends and acquaintances. "Oh, if I could only find someone alive to keep me company," he thought. He tried to get into communication with other places by using the radio; but he was unsuccessful, the whole world was silent. "I'm afraid I shall go mad with loneliness," he said to himself. It was in the springtime and the flowers were in bloom; but they, too, seemed sad and lonely for the lack of human companionship to appreciate their beauty. Whenever Jack felt hungry he walked into some one of the laboratories that were equipped with machinery for generating the finest grade of nourishment; turned a few valves and his food was ready for him. He wore a new suit of clothes every day; all he had to do was to walk into a clothing shop and select the best there was, and wear it. "This is as it should be," he said. "If the workers had their rights, the benefits of the wealth they produced, they could have eaten the finest food, worn the best of clothes, and enjoyed all the comforts in the world." Jack made his headquarters at one of the finest hotels in the city. This hostelry was equipped with every known device to make its guests comfortable. After Jack saw he was, in all probability, the only person alive in the city, he kept away

from the locality where the workers had lived. "What's the use," he thought. "I lived there all my life; and this is my first opportunity to enjoy real luxury and I might as well make the best of it while I can." Jack often wished there were a little less luxury and a little more company. He spent a great deal of time studying in the libraries and art museums; and was fast becoming an art critic. He hoped eventually, to take up painting, for if he painted a picture he would hang it in the great art museum, there was no one to prevent it. Then he could class himself as one of the great American Masters.

One thing in Jack's favor was that in those days all generative power for operating machinery was derived from the air. This machinery was so simple that he mastered its theory within a very short time. Consequently he could enter a power station and light the city when it became dark. He also learned to operate the machines of transportation then in use, consequently he was able to travel and see the world. It was his intention to take a trip around the world in a large airship, and see if he could find any survivors of the plague, whom he could induce to come to Boston with him and form a co-operative commonwealth. This colony if formed, might result in the world again becoming populated. For some reason he found it hard work to tear himself away from Boston. New England was then a very pleasant place to live in, owing to the waters of the Atlantic and Pacific oceans intermingling through the Panama Canal, the climate had altered, and there was no such thing as snow and cold weather.

Miss Daisy Butterfly, the other person who had escaped the plague, had wandered through the streets of Boston for over a month without meeting Jack. In her despair and loneliness she had thoroughly explored the section where the working classes lived, in hopes of finding some survivor of the epidemic. All of her "set" she knew had perished. In visiting the quarters of the working classes Daisy learned how these people had lived, and she shuddered at the thoughts of it. She felt guilty because she had not helped

these people when she had an opportunity. Of course she had done charity and
settlement work when it happened to be
a fad among her associates. "It cannot
be that these people of the same flesh
and blood as myself live in these miserable squalid quarters from choice," she
exclaimed. "Oh, if I had only helped
them I would not have this to think of
now."

One morning Daisy happened to be
walking along Boylston street, just as
Jack Smith stepped out of one of the
"swell" clothing shops; he had been se-
lecting a new wardrobe for the day. At
first, Daisy was frightened, but Jack had
such a manly face, that she soon recovered herself, and said: "How do you do?"
Jack raised his hat and answered her
salutation. Daisy put out her hand and
Jack shook hands with her. Then it
seemed to both of them as if they had
known each other always. Daisy at that
moment realized that she was alone in
the world, and she seemed loath to drop
his hand, for fear that she might lose
him. This man she thought was no doubt
destined by fate to be her protector. Jack
led Daisy into the Public Gardens close
by and they sat down on one of the
benches. It was a beautiful day and the
tulips with their wonderful masses of
color were in bloom. For a few moments
neither of them spoke, then Jack told
Daisy who he was and gave her a brief
history of his life. At the conclusion of
his story he said: "You need not tell me
who you are, Daisy, for I well know. I
have seen your picture in the society
columns of the press many times."

Daisy smiled at him and said: "We two,
no doubt are alone in this great, big
world, we must live for each other."
Then as though each of them knew what
was passing the other's mind, they rose
from their seat and walked hand in hand
to Trinity Church, where Daisy's family
had worshipped for generations. They
entered the church and walked to the
altar, there they both knelt and prayed.
Rising to their feet Jack opened the book
and they read the marriage service aloud
together. After this Jack recorded the
marriage on the Church records, in order
that future generations might know that

he and Daisy were married there. They
both decided to make their home at
Daisy's old home on Commonwealth avenue.

Jack loaded the bodies of Daisy's parents and the servants in an automobile
and carried them to the vaults where
they were cremated. Daisy felt very sad
when the bodies of her parents were
placed in the furnace. She gave thanks
to heaven that she was not alone, there
seemed to be some hope now that Jack
was with her.

CHAPTER THREE.

In talking over their future plans,
Jack and Daisy decided to follow Jack's
original idea of making a trip around the
world in an airship in hopes of finding
a sufficient number of survivors who
would consent to come to Boston with
them and assist in forming a Co-operative
Commonwealth.

They planned their route as follows:
over the Southern States, into Mexico,
from Laredo, Texas, then swing around
through El Paso, Texas, into Arizona,
New Mexico, California, and skirt the Pacific Coast to Alaska, and visit the North
Pole. From the Pole they were to head
across the Pacific, to Asia, Australia,
South America, Europe, from Europe
they would cross the Atlantic Ocean to
Newfoundland, then sail westward over
Canada, entering the western and eastern
sections of the country on their way to
Boston.

Jack had familiarized himself with the
various types of airships and was able to
handle them perfectly. All of the large
airships were equipped with every device necessary for long journeys. There
were food generators, also generators
for obtaining power to operate the ship,
sleeping compartments, powerful telescopes, radio apparatus, baths, and incin-
erators for the disposal of sanitary
waste. By using the telescope they could
discover any persons who happened to be
on the earth as they flew over; it was a
simple matter to swoop down upon them
and invite them aboard. Jack also intended to use the radio and attempt to
get into communication with any possible survivor. As American had become

the universal language there was no trouble to be experienced in making anyone in any part of the world understand them.

CHAPTER FOUR.

Jack selected the finest airship to be found in the city, and on the first day of October, 3015, Daisy's 21st birthday, they started on their trip around the world. They were to fly from Boston to New York the first day stopping at Providence and Newport on the way, resting in New York over night, and after looking around New York in order to view the result of the epidemic there, they intended to head southward sweeping the country with the powerful telescope as they flew along.

"This, Jack," said Daisy as the ship rose in the air, "is to be our wedding tour."

Jack did not allow the ship to make more than a mile a minute speed. "Because," he said. "We do not wish to become victims of Speedomania." Forty minutes from the time the ship rose in the air on Boston Common they landed in Roger Williams' Park in Providence, R. I. There was not a sign of life in the city; "this don't look very encouraging does it?" asked Jack. "Let's fly over to Newport, the famous watering place of the master classes."

Newport, like Providence, was dead. They entered one of the great palaces there, the summer home of the world's greatest financier, and here they found a ball room full of mummified bodies of some of the most prominent people of the country. They no doubt had been attacked with Speedomania while dancing the tango. Many of Daisy's former friends and associates were in the group. Poor Daisy was unnerved at the sight. "Let's get away from here Jack," she cried.

The great ship rose like a bird, then Jack circled around the city, and stopped the engines, and floated in midair a little while in order that they might get a good view of the splendid palaces for which Newport was famous.

"Those beautiful structures will no doubt be crumbling ruins before the world again becomes populated," said Jack, sadly, as he headed the ship towards New York. They reached there just as the sun, a great red ball of fire, was dipping over the edge of the world on the Jersey side. Jack headed the ship for the Waldorf, where they were to make their headquarters. On the roof of this magnificent hotel was one of the finest equipped hangars in the world. As soon as the ship was stored, Jack and Daisy, ran down to the great marble swimming pool, and took a plunge. "Say, but it's great to be rich," exclaimed Jack. "I'm the richest man in the United States today, and at the same time no doubt the only man. There never was any reason why my people shouldn't have enjoyed these luxuries. The world was theirs, if they only had known it. We outnumbered the masters, ten to one; but on account of blind and implicit obedience to the will of the ruling classes, we kept going continually backward instead of forward."

"Let us hope the next generation will be wiser, Jack," said Daisy. "Now we had better go to the blue and gold dining room for refreshments."

This room was one of the most magnificent affairs of its kind. "I never even dreamed of such luxury," exclaimed Jack. The laboratory was equipped with the finest and most delicate machinery known for generating nourishment, and Jack ate the finest dinner he had ever sat down to that night.

After dinner Daisy, who knew the Waldorf as well as she did her own home, took Jack to the galleries to see the paintings of some of the famous American masters, who in those days were the greatest artists in the world. "To think," exclaimed Jack indignantly, "that the workers were not allowed the pleasure of gazing at these wonderful works of art."

"We were afraid it might make them dissatisfied and rebellious," replied Daisy timidly. Perhaps we had better retire in order that we may make an early start, as we wish to look around the city before starting south."

"Your advice is good," answered Jack. "I can't help feeling provoked when I think of how the workers allowed themselves to be deprived of their rights."

6

"I don't blame you a bit," answered
Daisy. "I'm just beginning to see things
the way you do."

"Good," cried Jack, and he took her in
his arms and kissed her.

Immediately after breakfast next morning Jack and Daisy started to look around
the city. The ravages of the plague in
New York, the fastest city in the world,
was beyond all description. "This is
worse than I dreamed it might be; for
heavens' sake let us get away from here
as soon as we can," cried Jack. Consequently they hurried back to the Waldorf,
boarded the ship, and started on their
journey southward. They were to follow
the coast as far south as the Virginia
Capes, then fly inland for a while. Daisy
rode with Jack in the pilot house, and
she soon learned how to operate the huge
machine. From time to time Jack called
various cities on the radio, in hopes of
getting into communication with some
survivor; he was very much startled
while passing over the State of Georgia,
to receive an answer to his call. "Great
guns, Daisy," he cried, "somebody has
answered me," and he kissed her joyfully.

Then he started to find out who it was
answered his call. "Who are you?" he
asked.

"Joaquin Vila," came the reply.

"Where are you?"

"In the central radio office at Monterey, Mexico. I am the only person
alive in the whole of Mexico, and until
now I thought the whole world. Who
are you, and where are you now?"

"My wife and I are in an airship, heading south."

"I wish you would come here. I feel too
sick and discouraged to attempt to venture out of the city alone. The thoughts
of being alone in this great, big silent
world appall me."

"We are headed for Monterey now and
should reach you by daylight tomorrow,"
answered Jack.

"I'll be here waiting for you."

"Good-bye till tomorrow then."

"Good-bye and Godspeed your journey
here."

The airship came in sight of Monterey
shortly after daybreak; and with the aid
of the telescope Daisy discovered Vila on
the top of the Radio building waiting for
them. There were tears of joy in Vila's
eyes as he clasped both their hands.

"How I longed for human companionship," he said. "I did not try to get out
of here because it seemed to me that if
the effects of the plague were as bad elsewhere as they were in Monterey, and
from radio reports I received, such
seemed to be the case, I concluded I
might as well stay here as to go wandering around the earth alone. The history
of Mexico has been a sad one, the down
trodding and exploitation of her workers
from the time of the Spanish Conquest
up to the present, left our people in such
a physical state as to be unable to withstand the ravages of this great epidemic
that came upon us."

"I think it is the same story the world
over," replied Daisy. "But where there
is life, there's hope; there may be enough
of us left in the world to form the nucleus of a coming nation, one that will be
more prosperous and happier than the
one that has just perished."

Jack then explained their plan to Vila
who was more than glad to join them.
After this they all took refreshment, and
rested over night in the city, leaving
there early the next morning for the City
of Mexico and Vera Cruz. In a very short
time Vila learned to operate the ship,
this would enable them to fly night and
day, by each of them standing watches of
eight hours.

On the trip from Monterey to Mexico
City not a sign of life was to be seen;
the country was as silent as death. Vila
was no doubt the sole survivor of the
Astecs. They slept in the magnificent
president's palace, in the City of Mexico, and early next morning they flew
down to Vera Cruz, then swung around
towards the United States again, which
they intended to enter at El Paso, Texas.

CHAPTER FIVE.

This trip was one which they would always remember; it took them over magnificent mountains, and they often
stopped the ship in order to enjoy the
scenery. Jack let the ship down into
several canons and craters of extinct vol-
canoes in order that they might photo-

graph them. The trip from Vera Cruz to El Paso took twelve hours. It was very hot when they reached the city, and they decided to sleep in the air that night and look around the next day. The ship was lifted to a cool latitude, and the power shut off. It was as still, and comfortable aboard the ship as it would have been in any house down on the land; the moon and stars shone like so many precious stones.

"I wonder," said Jack, "if those far off worlds are inhabited; and if they, too, have had wars of nations, industrial wars and epidemics like 'Speedomania?'"

They tried with the powerful telescope to see if they could discover anything that resembled a human being on one of the planets; all they could see was huge mountains of rock.

"It is a mystery that will never be solved," declared Villa, and they all agreed with him; after this they retired for the night.

After breakfast next morning they looked over the city, but like every other place they had visited it was the same old story, everybody had perished. The ship was headed westward and their journey towards the Pacific Ocean began.

"We are now passing over what was once a vast desert of sand," said Jack, as the ship flew into New Mexico. "This desert was full of all sorts of deadly poisonous reptiles. Many men in search of gold perished with hunger and thirst here. It was on this desert that the fierce Apache Indians lived. From here they swooped down on the settlements of the white people like so many hawks; and after pillaging, burning and murdering, they would fly back to their desert hiding places. After the capture of their leader, Geronimo, their depreciations ceased. Through irrigation and the leak in the Colorado River, which formed the Great Salton Sea, this desert blossomed into a paradise of flowers and vegetation."

"I presume I read and studied about all these things at one time," said Daisy, "but our set were too busy with their social duties to think of practical things."

"This is the territory that the United States wrested from Mexico," said Villa.

"I hope," said Jack changing the subject; "that we can find a wife for Villa." Poor Villa who was a modest young man blushed to the roots of his hair.

"And I hope she will be real handsome and sweet-tempered," cried Daisy smiling.

"Let us hope so," answered Villa. "I'd much rather remain a bachelor than a henpecked husband."

"Oh, you horrid man," exclaimed Daisy.

CHAPTER 6.

The next stop they made was Los Angeles, California, and not finding any survivors there, they decided to fly over to Santa Monica Beach and spend a few days at the seashore. From there it was their intention to fly to San Diego, Mt. Lowe, and other places of interest. The ship had no sooner settled on the beach at Santa Monica, when they saw a young woman rushing towards them with outstretched arms and an expression of joy on her face.

"I am delighted to see some human beings alive," she cried, and she clasped Daisy in her arms and kissed her.

"A wife for Villa," said Jack to himself.

The young woman told her story in a very few words, it was the same experience they had all been through. Her name she told them was Rebecca Seigel, and she was twenty-three years old. After Daisy explained their plan to her, Rebecca said she was more than delighted to join them; there were no ties to keep her in California.

"Then you and Villa must be married at once," said Daisy.

"But this is so sudden," cried Rebecca, blushing prettily.

Villas' heart beat quickly as he waited for her answer, for Rebecca was very beautiful.

"It must be done," answered Daisy.

"Ish-ka-bibble," said Rebecca smiling sweetly. "If Villa is willing I am."

Villa, blushing to the roots of his hair, nodded his consent, and Jack performed the marriage in a nearby church, recording the marriage on the church records. After this they all went for a swim in the surf.

The next day they sailed over to Mt. Lowe and looked through the powerful telescopes at the observatory. After spending a few days sailing over Southern California, and the Mexican State of Lower California they started northward to San Francisco. On the way north the ship was zig-zagged from the coast over to the eastern boundary of the State, all the way, in order to cover as much territory and not miss any possible survivors.

"San Fráncisco," said Jack, "was at one time the center of the gold mining industry; this city has been destroyed several times by earthquake and fire. It was one of the wickedest places in the world. A large part of its yellow population lived underground. That part of the city was filled with opium dens and dives of all sorts. It was a dispensation of Providence that such a place was destroyed, the sad part of it is that the innocent suffered with the guilty."

"What a lot of ancient history you must have studied Jack," exclaimed Daisy.

A whole day was spent in San Francisco, but no survivors were located. Rebecca was no doubt California's only survivor.

"One of the world's greatest fiction writers was born in this city," said Villa, and his name was Jack also; he was elected the first socialist governor of California. For some reason or other Socialism did not cure California's industrial ills as rapidly as the people expected; and after one year of Socialism, they returned to the old party."

"Two thousand years ago," spoke Jack. "London's story 'The Red Plague,' predicted the depopulation of the world from a cause similar to Speedomania."

Their journey north from San Francisco took them through the "Valley of the Moon," where the famous writer spent his last days. In addition to sweeping the country with the telescope Jack tried to get into communication with various parts of the world by using the radio. No one answered his call; the whole world was as silent as death. The

first landing the party made after leaving San Francisco, was Rampart City, Alaska. As they came in sight of this city Daisy discovered a man trying to signal them, the ship was immediately lowered and soon they were shaking hands with a fine looking young man. He gave his name as Edward Black; he stated he was the only person alive in the whole State of Alaska as far as he knew, having sailed all over the State in his little flying boat he had been unable to find any sign of a single survivor.

After Jack explained their plan, Black said he was more than pleased to join them.

"I hope the next survivor we find will be a wife for Black," said Daisy.

"Thank you," replied Black with enthusiasm.

The night was spent at Rampart City, and early next morning the ship was headed for the North Pole.

The beautiful nights they spent riding through the Arctic regions were long to be remembered. The strangeness and silence of the Northland was different from that of any other land they had visited. The stars, the Northern Lights, and other phenomena made a lasting impression upon them. The ship was kept to the northerly course until one of the party who had been sweeping the country with the telescope exclaimed. "I see the shaft that marks the North Pole." The ship was immediately lowered as all were anxious to visit the spot that in years gone by so many brave men had suffered untold hardships to reach. On the granite shaft that marked the Pole was inscribed the name of the great explorer, Peary, who had been the first to reach the spot.

"When the brave Peary struggled to reach this place with sledge dogs," said Black, "this part of the world was a wilderness of snow and ice, instead of rolling green plains as today; but its inhabitants, like those of the rest of the world paid the penalty of their mad desire for speed, and perished with the great epidemic."

(To Be Continued.)

A Missionary?

By Charlotte Morgan

WAY back in the dark ages—oh! it must have been twenty years ago, when little Anne, she was little then, even quite small for her age so her parents said, which was "five years going on six," was being questioned along with the rest of the class by a most devout New England Sunday school teacher as to their personal plans for the future or, to quote the teacher, "just what would you like to be when you grow up."

If you have ever asked this question to a group of children, whether in a Sunday school class or out, you know the usual answers. From the boys—"A fireman—so's I can drive drate big horses," or "A policeman, then I kin scare everybody." Although it is a fact the majority of small boys think a street car conductor has the President of the United States job "skinned a mile," at least.

Little girls of five, or thereabouts, do not seem to have such decided opinions. Teaching school is the avowed future for many, while some who have seen mother sew, think dressmaking would be the higher goal. As you know, to be "a lady" holds a wonderful charm. However, when the all important question came to little Anne, it was plain to see she had had time, in years past, to properly weigh the matter of just what her life work should be. In fact she had gone so far as to consider two lines of endeavor. In a most serious tone she whispered confidentially to her teacher: "I want to be a missionary, or else I want to be a ballet dancer."

No doubt the teacher or Prophet and Precept was properly pleased with the missionary idea. She could feel that her untiring efforts with the little ones had not all been in vain. But horrors! Heaven forbid! "A ballet dancer." Where could the child have gotten such a notion.

Surely not in her Christian home where all was as it should be.

I pause to remark that notions will come and notions will go. There is always that blissful feeling of youth not knowing whither it listeth. Youth can say shocking things and can do thrilling things, it is all embryo. Come to think of it though, why are some things good and some things bad? Is it youth or is it age that makes them so? At least we know youth does not devote hours to meditation. However, it is impossible to debate further on youth against age, as this is not to be a story of Eugenics, Prohibition, or Votes for Women, but of little Anne Boroughs, who made such a startling declaration to her Sunday School teacher, years ago.

Anne grew up in a well ordered home of New England tradition and lore where religion is a prerequisite, and social conventions are designed for matriculation purposes. To do or say anything bordering on originalty was not the thing at all. Very poor form, indeed. Besides ones relatives must be considered. If one did not care what one did oneself—one must think of ones relations, and govern oneself accordingly. To break a convention by thought or deed—an idle remark—anything bordering on the grotesque, positively could not be done in the best families. Profound seriousness was the keynote of deportment.

In spite of this very good environment and because of it, Anne had a rich inheritance of Mayflowers and Spring to help boost her over the old stone walls of convention. She actually grew up. Through all the years of early childhood and girlhood she was constantly startling her associates with remarks so foreign to their particular way of thinking that in time she acquired the reputation of being queer—not like other girls. Where she ever got those "notions" — no one could tell.

On a day when Mrs. Boroughs was entertaining the ladies of Trinity Church Guild, Anne had slipped on an Oriental at the top of the stairs, and came rolling down the long flight into the very lap of the assembled group. Her very forceful and convincing, "Oh, Damn," was proof positive that Anne was, indeed, queer. As a daughter of Mrs. Boroughs — "being queer" was about as strong as they could put it. Her fond parents were constantly on the alert for these queer outbursts which really were "quite humiliating at times, to be sure."

"But what can we do? She has always been that way it seems, from a little girl up," Mrs. Boroughs would often say. "Really though, with strangers, you know, it is most awkward and embarrassing. Why only the other day when we were coming up to Boston from Providence what did she do in the train before all those people but take off her hat and re-arrange her hair—she said, 'the pins were going through her head' — just imagine."

Mr. Boroughs could say nothing to these reports on daughter's behavior except, "Um— Um— So?"

The dead things of winter had given life to all nature's newborn things. The first "brown darlings" were bursting with song. The air was filled with that sweetness of odor and sound which make one glad just to be alive, to be a part of this new creation.

Something of this elixir must have taken possession of Paul Dearborn on this glorious spring morning, judging from the way he took the box-hedge which divided his home from Anne's. Two skips and a jump brought him face to face with Anne and Mrs. Boroughs, who were on the stone steps at the side of the house. With fingers pressed to their lips the two women warned him to be quiet—and look —pointing out on the lawn where a robin was turning its little head from one side to the other, listening — listening. The three on the steps were soon rewarded. They saw Mr. Robin Redbreast hop once to location—take the plunge—bring forth the coveted worm, and fly away to his family in a tree nearby.

"It is Spring and a Thousand Birds Sing," quoted Paul.

"Aren't the 'brown darlings' an inspiration," said Mrs. Boroughs, "and do look at that bed of tulips. How beautiful."

Anne suggested they sit down on the steps. Perhaps another robin would come for worms.

But Mrs. Boroughs immediately left the call of Spring to ask Anne if she had phoned Aunt Sally. Hardly waiting for a reply, Mrs. Boroughs solicitated Paul's views. Explaining to him Anne's refusal to go to Aunt Sally's "At Home."

Yes, he thought Anne should go whether she wanted to or not.

"But," cried Anne, "these At Homes are not in my line. I don't enjoy them, and what's more they don't enjoy me. All that sort of thing is waste of time. I have suggested they do some sewing for my youngsters at the Settlement House. They agree it is a noble work but that is as far as they go. They give money— yes—but not themselves. So you see we simply have nothing in common. No, Mumsie, I'm not to be among those present at Aunt Sally's."

Mrs. Boroughs cast her eyes heavenward and then looked at Paul in utter despair. He was soon to be a fully ordained clergyman so Mrs. Boroughs felt him to be a tower of strength. Just now she wanted him to say something to convince Anne that conventions were conventions. Paul caught Mrs. Boroughs' pleading look and turned smilingly to Anne—

"Diplomacy in life, you know, is quite as necessary as butter on bread—quite— One could not get along without it — roughly speaking. I will go so far as to say that selfishness is born of conceit, conceit is born of ego, and ego is the Old Adam and Eve—the original sin begetters."

Mrs. Boroughs' admiring gaze turned from Paul to Anne, "Now, my dear, can't you see what we all think about your— well, if I must say it,— stubbornness— Yes, that is the word. Why will you insist on doing and saying things only as it pleases you?"

"Well, Mumsie, do you expect a reasonable answer to that question? If you do, you are slated for a disappointment. Ha! Ha! you and Paul are rich enough in ideas to have them running around loose —as house pets. Furthermore, I think you two good scouts would enjoy this beautiful morning much better without me." Glancing at her watch, Anne rose to go into the house. At the door, she turned to say, laughingly, "I may be disagreeable, but I'm not dangerous, and that goes double for you, Paul. So long, everybody."

In her secret little heart Anne reasoned she was immensely fond of Paul. Her thoughts flew back to the days when they each claimed an apple tree as their domain. And then the day Paul fell from one of the topmost branches of his tree, breaking his arm. She remembered how she thought he had been killed. They had been such good playmates, and comrades always. Why would he insist now upon keeping his nose in those horrid theology books? As a clergyman she thought he should study people and their various needs. Then if his heart could not find enough reasonable words in the English language to express himself satisfactorily—why dig in to a book. But to be everlastingly over his books was too one-sided. He was a dreamer and not a doer. Now Anne felt she had correctly classified Paul.

Leaving the house by the front door, and taking a short cut out over the terraced lawn to the street below, Anne found herself walking briskly toward the car line. The five long blocks were soon covered. As she boarded the car, she reflected how even this act of hers was a source of great annoyance to Mumsie. Dad seldom criticized or questioned her, which certainly helped some — but then, Dad always thought whatever Mumsie did, or said, was above reproach. If Mumsie disapproved, Dad was sure to agree with her perfectly. How often she had heard her Father speak proudly of the Crowningshields—her Mother's name before she had married him. What blue blooded aristocrats they were. Blue, of course, meaning loyalty.

All this aroused Anne to her whole life's environment. What were the well known garden variety of Ninteenth Century Aristocrats—but snobs. Unless one was born in the inner circle, so to speak, unless their ancestors could be properly labeled and classified—well—it would be far easier for a camel to cover himself with a handkerchief—than it would be for a social climber to pull any threads— or is it ropes — which would ultimately make them one with these exclusive bodies of humans.

Anne was so absorbed with her thoughts that she was hardly aware she had finally reached the North End Settlement House. Most of her days were spent here; telling stories to the youngsters, directing their games, giving them their glass of milk at the specified hour, etc. The children were well cared for at the House during the long day the poor mothers toiled earning barely enough to keep soul and body together.

Along in the late Spring we find Anne very gay and hopeful. She had decided that 1917 was her lucky number. It meant she could leave the "blue bloods" at home and join the grand army of "red bloods" abroad. Red meaning, as you know, sacrifice. Can you imagine a girl who had every advantage of luxury and education —with all the good times associated with money, men, motors and music, actually wanting to leave home? I repeat, can you imagine it? Anne was queer—no doubt about it. She had notions. Leaving home now under the canopy of war work would not disgrace the whole outfit of one's relatives, she hoped.

Mr. and Mrs. Boroughs were properly shocked in just the proper way when Anne made bold to announce one morning over the grapefruit, her wild intention of going overseas.

"Yes, old dears, hoping for your kind permission—in the course of a few weeks I shall be tearing myself away."

A deluge of unadulterated grapefruit juice caught Mrs. Boroughs fairly in the eye, thus delaying an important remark. However, Mr. Boroughs seemed free to say that the spirit which prompted this action was splendid. Were she a son, he would indeed be proud.

"But, my dear child," he continued,

"this thought of yours is absurd. It's preposterous."

"Please don't let's argue Dad. It's war work. I've signed up. So that's an end to it."

Knowing how immovable Anne was once she had decided on a certain course, Mrs. Boroughs was finally able to ask if Anne had joined her classmates at Smiths, who were going as Canteeners. No. She was not.

"Well," demanded Mr. Boroughs, — "what is it—ambulance driver?"

"Ha! Ha! Wrong again. As you and Mother have never allowed me to forget the crushing blow my words, as a youngster proved to be—as much as it grieves me, I beg your kind indulgence for the little Ballet Dancer—or words to that effect," said Anne, with appropriate gestures.

Needless to say Mrs. Boroughs swooned—lost consciousness completely. While Mr. Boroughs, contrary to custom—wished himself "Damned."

Anne was neither heartless nor headless. She used every known means to restore peace and quiet. She only felt sorry that she could not have brought her parents up—differently. Why the prisms and prunes? If they chose to stir their coffee with a thermometer in order to be very sure the beverage was at the correct temperature—then she supposed life would continue for them as it had begun. Although, goodness knows, the tidal waves of "queer notions" to Anne's credit or discredit, whichever the case may be, should have loosened them up a little.

Two months later the little entertainer went overseas with the jolliest bunch of soldiers and soldierettes that our Uncle Sam ever knew. "Quiet Talks on Power" and "How to Win the War Tho' Married," were subjects in the discard. "Who's Who in Bradstreet," the latest quotations from Wall Street held no interest for anyone on ship board.

The first few days out, Anne could seem to think of nothing but her wonderful freedom. She could now actually feel the pulse of the world. Why, though, did it take this awful war of sorrow, sickness, privation, and death to liberate me, just little me, thought Anne. The world

needs a waking up to humans—giving our hands and hearts to their needs. Oh, I'm so glad to be free of the Smart Set, and their constant quest of pleasure. These soldiers do not care whether my grandfather was a Crowningshield or a window pane—they accept me at my own value, and vice-versa. How glorious to feel we are on a common ground. This is a la bonne heure, indeed.

* * * *

The Y Hut, just back of the front lines was filled to capacity that night. The boom—boom—boom—from Jerry's instruments of war played a steady grinding accompaniment to everything. It might have been a Bach Fugue that was disturbing Jerry's internal economy. However, what it might have been, and what it was, cast no shadow of gloom or depression over the crowd in the Hut. The merry song and patter of the little Entertainer was the only thing that mattered. Her pianologues were ripping. The way she could play Yankee Doodle with one hand and Dixie with the other, all at the same time called for encore after encore. And when she sang "Annie Laurie" and "I Love You, California" the boys went wild in their cheering. There was something besides technique and correct phrasing in that music—something that went home—something that registered in the heart of everyone who heard.

The entertainment over for the evening the boys rushed up to shake hands. One khaki-clad fellow, tall and straight as a young pine, seemed to be holding the hand of the little Entertainer against all comers. Those close by heard a startled little cry, and then — "Why, Paul Dearborn, this is a surprise. When did you come over?"

"Oh, haven't been here long, just came across to help put on the finishing touches, you know. Left my clericals on the other side— Came as a regular guy. And believe me, Anne, I've learned a few things a'ready."

"Nuff said, — 'You Needa Biscuit' — come over this way and have some hot chocolate, or would you rather have coffee," said Anne as she linked her arm in Paul's and led him to the refreshment counter.

"Listen Anne," continued Paul, "why didn't you dance this evening?"

"Ha! Then you did not like my sketch—eh, what?"

"Indeed, I did," Paul hastened to reply, "it sure was the real thing. You were wonderful, I could hardly believe that you were you. But you know, I understood from the folks at home that your stunt over here was dancing."

At this Anne was convulsed with laughter. Finally the large brown eyes, sparkling roguishly, turned to the intent gaze of Paul's luminous blue eyes.

"Oh, isn't it too funny? Isn't it perfectly killing—to think I have so far corrupted the morals of Mother and Dad, and all the folks at home?"

"I'd hardly say that," broke in Paul.

"Well, you see, Mr. Preacher-man, I'll have to confess I discovered long ago, merely by accident, of course—that there were only three ways of dancing—graceful — ungraceful — and disgraceful. Not being able to qualify under any of these heads—solo dancing for me has been a lost art."

"Then you don't dance here at all," said Paul in great astonishment.

"No, no. And I simply told the folks that as a joke, don't you see? They would have been just as much upset over my coming here labeled as an entertainer, as a missionary. So I thought they were not too old to receive a regular jolt—and gave it to them. 'Ballet Dancer' Oh! ch! oh! that's good."

"Anne, you are splendid. Glad to hear such good news. Could go on talking all night, but duty calls, so must go. See you later. Good-bye."

"Good-bye, Paul."

The momentous happenings of the first weeks of November, 1918, the attending rush of stupendous events, brought Anne and Paul another surprise. They met in Paris.

Some of the American boys in Paris were calling it Old Home Week.

Some were already counting the beans they were to have when they reached old Bean Town. Said beans consisting chiefly of porterhouse steak with a side of ham and eggs. Eats—regular eats, and then some was the English for parle

vous. The Yanks could be seen marching in the center of the streets serpentine fashion, chanting:

"No more chow—no more shoots,
No more rows—no more coots,
No more mud—no more duds,
Rub de dub—dub—dub."

Paris was alive again, the cafes were ablaze with lights and music. In one of the smaller street cafes where there was soft music and no dancing — at a small table near the wall, Anne Boroughs and Paul Dearborn could be seen holding hands in a scandalous fashion. By looking carefully you could see there was something mutual about it. Neither of them seemed conscious of these digitory members.

"Look here, Anne," Paul was saying, "the signing of the armistice means peace, peace means home, and home — means everything that's best. Isn't that the truth? But, why so downhearted—surrounded with all this cheer? What's on your mind?"

"Oh, I have been thinking," roused Anne, "ha! — it's a fatiguing process sometimes. Yes, the terrible bloodshed is over, but won't the world still be at war with itself—as personalities, I mean?"

"Fiddlesticks — time enough later to think of that. Haven't seen you in a month of Sundays, and here you are talking deep stuff. Ah, I have it, you've got another notion brewing as of old, eh? Out with it. Fess up to an old pal, for I've got something serious on my own mind."

"I think I can tell you something of the way I feel. You see I have been so absolutely happy in my work here. I have known hardships. I have realized, at least to some extent, what this awful war has done, I have really found myself. At home I never could understand just why I was not happy or satisfied. But I know now. I feel transformed. Nothing can ever happen to make me really unhappy again."

"Oh, I say," interrupted Paul, "aren't you getting in pretty deep—'never to be unhappy again'—wow—that's putting it pretty strong."

"Well, there are never going to be any

more boundaries for me. At last I'm going to be a missionary. Not the 'holier than thou' sort—you know. There will be no creed or sect, understand. I shall just go on continuing to loose myself in others. Really it is a most illuminating experience."

"Registering a hundred per cent. Is that the big idea?"

"Yes, if you want to put it that way. I'm going to start an international, individual peace—propaganda. Behold the chairman of the I. I. P. P. Committee."

"Sounds mighty fine, Anne, and you speak as an authority on this peace business. A personal peace—brotherly love, and a working knowledge of right living should crystallize our energies."

"Ah, now you can see why I shall never be really unhappy again. If the folks at home have not been through enough fire to melt them and mold their lives differently hereafter—well then our boys—and girls going home from here are the logical missionaries."

"Now you're talking. I agree with you. And now let's close that argument for a while. I, too, have had something on my mind the past few weeks. Correctly speaking, the matter has not been troubling my mind as much as my heart. The truth is I have had this same heart trouble ever since you wore pig-tails and I wore short pants. Anne, dear, do you know I have always thought of you as my future wife."

"Oh, Paul," said Anne, blushing beautifully.

"I have grown up loving you, and shall grow old loving just you. Anne, dear, will you be my wife?"

Oblivious to the crowd which now filled the cafe, the two sat there at the table looking so intently at each other one might have thought most anything from shell shock to an apparition.

Anne, even though she stared wide-eyed at Paul, was not greatly surprised at this declaration. It all seemed so natural. As if they had always talked of love and marriage. When in truth, this was Anne's very first proposal.

"Paul, you aren't a preachie-preacher any more, are you? That was the only thing—the only thing—"

"Then you do love me, sweetheart?"

"Yes," said Anne nodding her head seriously.

There was another long feasting of the eyes when Paul wanted to hold more than her hands. His desire, in this crowded cafe, to feel his arms about her could only be appeased by a firmer grasp of the pretty hands, he already held.

Presently Anne's sweet face revealed a new light. Another notion was born. "Oh, Paul, dear, I can—er—ah—we can now have a—large—committee."

"A large committee, now? I guess I don't quite understand. What notion is it now, dearest?"

"Oh, you know—," said Anne, as she reached over the table to whisper in Paul's ear, and then aloud, she added, "mostly boys."

Red Begle of the Seventh

By Paul Annixter

DAD EVANS told me this tale. He was an old cavalryman, Dad was, born with a saddle between his thighs, if troop reports were to be believed — a soldier by temperament and every inch a man. Old Dad was like a weathered troop horse, he withered like the rose when severed from the service. He had been in the troop thirty years when I met him, but he was so miserable after he got back to San Anton' that Colonel Bradshaw took him back in spite of his dimmed eyes and chalky joints.

Memories of rebellion and bolo-massacres were rampart in Dad's old mind. He was a little bow-legged cavalryman — tough as a hickory limb and about the same color, with more than a dozen Indian fights marked on his discharge papers. Besides that he was one of the old guard who had left their horses in the States in '98 and pushed up the sand-soaked hills to Santiago, the once coveted.

There was one scene which Old Dad's eyes had looked upon when they were not dim—a scene and a story which he does not tell except at the Canteen Bar of an evening when his month's pay flowed with his words.

Then he would tell us about Rain-in-the-Face, the ugliest of the Sioux, and craftiest of red men, and about the deserter from the ranks of Uncle Sam's horsemen who was chained to him. He would tell us how Indians fought, how devilish was the fury of their squaws, how terrible their numbers. All the troopers would forget their glasses in their hands when Dad Evans told of how the field looked when he helped bury the dead of Custer's band way out in Montana that hot June day.

It has been committed to memory by school children what kind of a fellow was that Michigan man whom the Sioux called Yellow Hair. He was a soldier, first and last, not an indulgent officer, but one who feared nothing living or dead. It was Custer who declared:

"Give me my old regiment and I will wipe out the whole Sioux nation."

Custer was tingling with the true soldier spirit when he uttered those words. He was confident, experienced — a campaigner born. He did not think then that his picked regiment of horsemen would ever be called the "Unlucky Seventh." But all this is too well known. Here is the story of Red Begle, deserter, once in "I" troop of Custer's command—the story which Dad Evans told. It is a true story, for Dad Evans saw it enacted.

Begle was a bad man—a mixture of the lawless West and the old bad East. His worst enemies were whiskey and himself. His bunk was found deserted one morning at reveille call and his troop was sent out to hunt him up. The boys found him in a cave, to which they were led by an Indian scout. Begle was helplessly obfuscated, probably through the medium of unmellowed corn-juice. The Indian scout shuffled about the cave feeling and smelling things. There were some puzzling circumstances about. Someone had been in the cave with Begle, but the identity of this party was an opaque mystery. Nothing but a can of bear's grease was found. The Mandan scout grunted.

Now it was well known that Sioux squaws made their braids shiny with bear's grease. Also Red Begle was a black sheep and a discard, one who would not draw the color line. One of the troopers laid a wager that Kate Poison Water had taken Begle for her paramour. The boys were not long in finding the truth of the trooper's deduction.

When Begle awoke from his stupor he found himself chained to Rain-in-the-Face of the sleepy eyes, sub-chief of the Sioux. He had dropped too low to feel the ignominy of his position, but the hard-boiled ejaculations he used would have put an army mule to flight

Kate Poison Water was a sort of De Stael among the Sioux. She was a serpent in cunning, a tigress in strength and agility—a Sioux squaw in general devilty. Between her and Rain-in-the-Face there was a standing pact.

Custer was in a land ridden with redskins. He had no near reserve. It was not a time for court-martials. So Red Begle ate and slept, but did not become chummy with the rising young war chief. The two were together until that momentous day when Reno took a third of the regiment and branched off to the south. Rain-in-the-Face was taken from Reno, while Begle rejoined his old troop in Custer's division. It is needless to say in whose command Dad Evans was, for had he not been with Reno he would not have sipped canteen beer or told tales, or climbed the Cuban hills two years later under Mauser fire.

That night the guard in charge of the Sioux prisoner was found neatly and quietly murdered. It was done so quietly in fact that the sentry walking fifty yards away, heard no sound and saw nothing. There was wanton devilishness in the cutting-up. When Dad told us the details—we turned away shuddering.

"Only a squaw does the trick," Evans explained. Immediately we thought of Kate Poison Water because of the manner of the deed. Meanwhile that day of history dawned.

Custer's command was four miles from Reno's camp. Every trooper felt that there were hordes of redmen in the surrounding foothills. But not a white guessed their real number. The Indian scouts were puzzled by cross-trails. They hugged the vanguard and could not be pushed ahead. The troops fell quiet, not a jest was exchanged that morning.

The sun rose hot and high and still no hostile sign was made. No steady or rapid fire could be heard from any direction. It was nearly noon before Reno's division formed skirmish lines and circled back. Number four in each set stayed back with the horses, as ragged volleys began to pour down upon them from the rocks and woody places. Few of the fours lived when the sun's rays were slanting that afternoon. Camp was struck at sundown. No bacon sputtered in the mess tins that night, and the weary soldiers rolled themselves in their blankets without a smoke. The Red Cross men did not sleep.

No one believed the courier who rode into the camp before midnight, with the word that Custer and all his band had been slain that day by the Sioux and that their bodies lay scattered in the moonlight four miles away.

Before daybreak Reno's men were in the saddle. The silence in front was deathly and ominous. The weird crooning monotone of the Sioux death-song was not heard this day, nor were any cross-trails encountered. The turf simply bore evidence of a massed flight. As they neared the great hollow between the hills the scouts began hugging the forward fours. The silence was frightening, and there was an odor in the air which they alone distinguished.

The body of a trooper, gashed, perforated and dismembered, was strewn across the line of march. Hard and unsmiling were the faces of Reno's men now. Signals from high points brought back no answer from Custer's corps. The words of the courier were beginning to be believed. Great and awful thoughts crawled into the trooper's minds. Where was Yellow Hair, the intrepid, the invincible? Where were the friends of yesterday?

They stopped oftener now to cover up the red stains upon the earth. The men's faces had become white and the air they breathed more ghastly.

Ahead of them rose a hill. The pitiless heat shimmered upon its summit; flies buzzed about the sweating horses. Great black birds made circling shadows beyond the rise ahead.

The men tried not to breathe in the tainted air, but still they pushed onward. Horror and fascination gripped them. Countless red devils might have been ambushed in the surrounding hills, yet the veriest coward would have gone forward that day, such is the pull of morbid curiosity in men. The vanguard reached the summit and looked down.

For a moment all that could be heard was the droning of myriads of flies. Then to the ears of those behind was borne the murmur of curses, deep and terrible.

From every bush and rock arrows had whizzed down upon that plain. From behind every rock and tree a crouching Sioux had glared down through the smoke. Every able-bodied buck of the Sioux nation had ridden down those slopes yesterday.

And when the bravest had left no horse or horseman standing, young bucks had trampled the white faces into the earth and mutilated the prone bodies. And after their voices were hoarse and their demon desires were satiated, hordes of hideous mumbling squaws, more inhuman than any in venomous hate, had stripped the suits from every man and plied their knives in hellish ecstasy.

Meanwhile the braves had wrapped their dead in blankets and tied them in the branches of the larger trees. Not until the sunset land was growing dim did the redmen face toward it and disappear. They were very happy.

Reno's cavalrymen looked down. Great black birds rose and hovered over the plain. The sky was dotted with them. Dad will never forget that day.

Not a vestige of individuality remained with the dead upon the field. There was not a scalp—not a form left intact—save two. It was as if the fiend himself in a black mood had directed the carnage.

In the center of the plain on a slight rise they found the prone body that had not been mutilated. The broad yellow stripes of a cavalry officer was upon the trousers. An officer's blouse covered the face. The Sioux warriors had crossed the sleeves as a sign that the body should not be touched. The blouse was lifted and the men stared down at the lean fighting face of their commanding officer. The cheek was pressed down, and the long, light brown curls clustered about it. Not a hair was touched, not a weapon taken.

The Sioux braves feared the living Yellow Hair. They revered him dead, because of his prowess. It was a moment of delicate mystery. Thus it was that his own men found Custer, the hero of a dozen campaigns. Not long afterward a certain small town in Michigan was shrouded in crepe and a whole nation mourned.

The other scalp saved was that of a private.

"Don't touch him!" The troopers heard this warning as they came near. It was a squaw's voice. She was wounded, dying. She had raised her body on one hand and was fighting off Reno's cavalrymen, her crazed eyes snapping with anger. Below her was another body with sleeves crossed. It was all that remained of Red Begle, deserter, and the dying squaw, Kate Poison Water, was fighting for it with her last strength.

These two, the commander, and the deserter, scorned by all, were all that the Sioux squaws had left untouched.

It came out later that it was Kate Poison Water who slew the guard and released Rain-in-the-Face, so that the sub-chief might have Red Begle spared in the projected attack. None but the Great Spirit, however, could have saved Red Begle that day.

Yes, the Sioux were a happy nation when they retreated that day. Their craft was not forgotten and the trails diverged. One was two miles wide. What squadron of cavalry could follow such a trail.

Most of the band were ultimately caught, including Sitting Bull, the head chief. Rain-in-the-Face, the fire eater, lived to glower in the faces of distinguished Eastern audiences years later.

And old Dad Evans, who helped bury the dead among feasting vultures that hot June day, lived to the good old age of ninety, sipping canteen beer and telling his tales until the end.

Lonesome Time

By Farnsworth Wright

THE sun poised like a glowing cannon ball on top of the ridge, and slowly began to sink as the last of the airplanes lighted gently, like a bird, on the plain. Allen, whose machine had been the first to land, looked on and admired the light build of the planes and the easy grace of the landings. These were fighting craft, the wasps of the sky, the smallest and the fleetest of the squadron. They had been engaged that afternoon in mimic warfare—rearing like horses, looping, rolling, tumbling, two miles above the ground, to keep in trim for the reality of actual combat.

Allen was in love with the graceful little biplanes in which he had been playing war behind the fighting line for the last two weeks. Measuring only thirteen feet from tip to tip of the wings, built lightly, fitted with sturdy liberty engines, they responded instantly to their pilot's touch, and were a welcome change from the large observation and bombing planes to which he was accustomed.

A swarm of mechanics and helpers ran the biplanes into the airdrome and commenced to overhaul them, while gunsmiths speedily dismounted the machine guns and began to clean them and make them ready for the next flight. The aviator that had just landed came over to Allen, and opened his cigarette case. Allen declined the proffered smoke, and the lieutenant passed on to the farther end of the shed, where a group of aviators were talking and laughing, and playing with a frolicsome spaniel that belonged to the squadron.

Allen did not join them, but sat alone, resting his chin on his hands. He was busy with his thoughts, and did not want his mood disturbed. The glowing disk of the sun disappeared, and the low crest of the ridge was sharply silhouetted against the western sky, with its little grove of shell torn trees standing out in relief like a wharf jutting into the water. Beyond that ridge was the Atlantic Ocean, and home. Allen heard only the laughter of his brother officers, the barking of the spaniel, and the distant irregular shouting of cannon. The sounds did not register on his consciousness. He heard them, but he did not notice them, for he was absorbed in his musings.

Allen did not need to feast his eyes on the little snapshot that he carried always with him, for the picture was graven on his memory. He saw Helen plainly in his mind's eyes, her long yellow hair cascading over her shoulders in bewitching disarray, her blue eyes dancing with light, her face radiant with sunshine. He pictured her countenance as he liked it best, brimming with love, and he lived over in happy retrospect the blissful vacation they had spent together, less than a year before. They had canoed and tramped much, and the acid test of spending a month almost constantly in each other's company had only made him love her even more devotedly than before. He had studied her moods, her expression, her every gesture, longing, doubting, carefully noting each litle sign that perhaps she returned the love that filled his being.

It was at this same lonesome hour of the day, the restful period just after sunset, that he had found the courage to speak what was on his mind. Tonight there would be another big round moon, like the one that had made a long flashing lane across the lake to them that evening, as they drifted on in dreamy silence in the canoe, forgetting place, forgetting time, forgetting everything except that they loved each other.

Now he was a lieutenant in the aviation corps, fighting in France against his country's enemies. She was immensely proud of her big soldier boy, but he knew that she watched every mail in dread, lest it bring news that would break her heart. She had smiled bravely when she bade him good-bye at the railroad station, but the trembling of her lips showed the effort she was making to keep back her tears. She knew how eager he was to go, after he received his commission, and she was ready to make the sacrifice, if need be, for her country's good, but she dreaded to part from him lest he might never return.

To his mind, death was only an incident, a necessary risk, but not one to be weighed too gravely. But now he suddenly realized what it would mean to her. Most of the light and sweetness of life had gone when he went to France, for she loved him deeply.

He pictured her face at news of his death, and tried to realize the sickening catch at her heart, the growing sense of bereavement, the aching pain, the sleepless nights, the scalding tears, the void in her life that would never be entirely filled. The unutterable sadness of it so depressed him that he took out her picture, which he always kept nearest his heart, and gazed long into the laughing eyes of the photograph.

His mood was interrupted by an outcry. Warning had come of the approach of hostile airplanes. Allen rushed to his machine, thrilled with the realization that he was at last to experience actual combat in the sky. Several black dots showed high up in the east, and he knew that these were his antagonists.

Twenty American planes skimmed over the ground and began to climb, not in spirals, but directly upwards, to reach the great height at which their foes were flying. Allen had made this climb many times during the past two weeks, to engage in mock battle, but never so eagerly as now, when he flew to meet the thrilling reality. Up, up, straight into the sky he shot. He paid no attention to the three large bombing planes that were approaching him for his game was high up in the sky above him.

Leading his comrades by a hundred yards, he plunged into a group of ten German planes, opened on one with his machine gun, and passed through to attack a lone German airplane that was flying a great distance above the rest.

Up, still up, he climbed, straight at the German aviator, who suddenly dived at him. They trained their machine guns on each other simultaneously, and the shots glanced from Allen's engine as the German machine dipped beneath him. He turned, endeavoring to get his enemy in front of him, but the German skilfully maneuvered to keep Allen from opening fire. They flew around each other in circles, looking for an opening, and again the German raked Allen with his machine gun. Despite his slower airplane, he was more skilfull than the American.

Allen dived repeatedly, trying to come up on the German from beneath, but he only exposed himself to attack, so he circled again to keep the German from facing him. Suddenly he depressed his right wing-tip, and began to roll over. The German, seeing his adversary apparently collapsing, turned and poured a hail of bullets into the American plane. They did not take effect, but Allen's dangerous ruse brought his foe in front of him. As his plane righted, he shot upwards, like a hawk standing on its tail, and opened fire.

The German convulsively threw up his arms, for he was mortally hit. With a look of terrible agony on his face, he tore open his uniform and thrust his hand deep into his breast. He withdrew some small pasteboard object and pressed it passionately, to his lips. His plane fell earthwards, and Allen looped upwards just in time to avoid a collision.

The other enemy air scouts had been driven off, and the returning planes of Allen's comrades were visible in the east. Beneath him the darkness was beginning to flow over the landscape, pouring over every ridge and low-lying hill, streaming out from the highland and filling the chinks and hollows. The airdrome was dimly visible directly underneath him, in the pool of darkness that was rising steadily higher.

He began to descend, for his work was

done. Unaided, he had won his first air fight and shot down his foe from the sky, while his companions had merely driven their enemies away.

As his biplane gracefully sped over the field and came to a stop, his captain threw aside military restraint and hailed him joyously.

"It is Freihofen," he shouted, "the best of the German aces, who has brought down more than sixty planes. You will be recommended for this, Lieutenant Allen, and the French will undoubtedly give you the Legion of Honor also, for most of Freihofen's victims were French. I want to thank you and give you my heartiest congratulations. Freihofen has been the terror of the French and English airmen."

Allen saluted, and strode silently over to the fallen airplane. The mechanicians were at work disentangling Freihofen's body. The machine had been smashed to bits by its drop of more than two miles, but the body showed few traces of its fearful fall.

The hands were still pressed tightly to the dead man's lips. Allen gently straightened the rigid fingers, one by one, and took from their grasp a small oval portrait. The fading twilight disclosed the laughing features of a beautiful German girl.

Allen received the congratulations and handclasps of his fellow officers in silence. He went at once to his quarters, a fire in his brain, and in his heart a fever. The girl of the portrait, to whom Freihofen's thoughts had flown in the moment of his death agony, might cry her eyes out, but Freihofen would never come back to her. How many tens of thousands of girls in the warring countries must wait in vain for their soldiers? Allen sat on his cot a long time, meditating. His face was wet with tears,

California

From sub-tropic shores to Alpine snows,
How varied is thy scene. Clear cut against
Thy ever sunny skies rise peak on peak,
Pleasant valleys at their feet, fat with
Fruited trees, or golden grain.
The gigantic sequoia high on mountainside
O'erlooks the valley where the palm
.   rustles
Its leaves in air laden with sweet scent
Of blossoming trees, the apricot, plum
And cherry. Of fruit, grain, timber
And precious ore out of thy bounteous
Store, thou sendest to many lands.
From deep forest-clad hills of the north
To glistening sands of fair San Diego,

How beauteous is thy far-flung shore!
Off thy coast lie the isles of enchantment,
Bold mountain peaks thrust from ocean depths.
Beautiful San Clemente and Catalina.
Cabrillo, who found the sea path to thy shore,   .
Brave Portola, the first pathmaker
Of thy inland trails, Junipero Serra,
And the other godly padres who
Thy missions founded. These, the makers
Of thy romantic history, and other
Great names pass before us. Oh, sunset,
How inspiring is thy present land, how
Glorious thy futures for reaching dreams.

The War of 1920

By Charles Hancock Forster

I TRIED my best to sleep in the same bed as Hindenburg in the Hotel de l'Europe in Lille, but the Frenchman who occupied the chamber did not appreciate my eagerness and I could not persuade him to change rooms with me. The valet de chambre, when I told him of my disappointment, informed me that the Kaiser had slept in room four, but the unromantic Frenchman who had the room refused to give it up. I was one of a very few Americans in Lille at the time, and I thought that my purely American desire to have a unique, souvenir-like experience should receive some appreciation.

My mission in Lille, however, was an altogether serious one. For six months I had directed the work of The Department of General Relief of The American Red Cross in the Haute Vienne, and while there I made the acquaintance of some of the leading manufacturers of the Lille district. Lille is the industrial capital of France and the chief city in a department upon which the future of the nation depends. Before the war this department produced one-sixteenth of all the agricultural products of France and paid one-fourteenth of the taxes. In pre-war days, the traveler, who entered the Lille region, after having journeyed in other parts of France, had a sense of entering a new but familiar world. It reminded the Englishman of Lancashire and the American of the industrial portions of New England. They found there an Anglo-Saxon atmosphere that was not typical of France, according to their conception of things French. It was a land of big business and large factories, of clean cities and towns and well-kept fields. Of course one missed the color and romance that the tourist seeks. Paris has its industries, but they are hidden behind pleasure and brilliance, behind the music, the cafes and the boulevards. One remembers Normandy and Brittany for their backward, little towns and their quaintly costumed people. So, in all France, outside this busy Northern region, with its factories and canals, one recalls the winding rivers, the peaceful landscapes, and the little villages, with their ancient churches and perhaps, a few miles away, a ruined feudal castle. We think, too, of the fascinating, little restaurants, and the summer evenings in the cafe-gardens on the river banks where we rested in the spirit of leisure that seemed to pervade the very atmosphere.

I never really understood the efficiency and the far-sightedness of Germany's war plans until I sat with a group of business men in a crowded cafe in the center of Lille shortly after the Armistice. Only a few weeks before, Prussian officers had reserved it for their own exclusive use and had left a good many bullet holes in the plate-glass mirrors that surrounded the room to remind us that they had been there once. British veterans, who had lived in the line for months, heroes of Vimy, La Bassee, Armentieres and Bethune, sat with French civilians at the tables. The scene was full of animation and the Frenchmen were busily engaged discussing the problems of reconstruction. I learned, from what I saw and heard, that, after all is said and done, Germany had done a good job and gained a subtle victory.

A book that I found on the desk of the German commandant at Lomme, an industrial suburb of Lille, happened to introduce the subject of German philosophy to our little group. The commandant had evidently made a hurried departure, leaving the book open on his desk, and all his files and papers intact.

The book was written in 1917 by an author named Heinrich Mann, and I was glad that it suggested a subject that I considered quite timely under the circumstances. I usually avoided German philosophy while in France, because I knew that it had been discussed threadbare, and I knew also, that it was entirely unnecessary to quote Prussian authors to prove that the Germans were barbarians. Surrounding us at that moment was every evidence of ruthlessness.

The discussion followed familiar lines. In the years preceding the war Germany believed that she was surrounded by decadent nations, and the underlying motive of the war had its origin in this belief. The Germans despised the nations with whom they fought and regarded them as weaklings. They did not move forward, as they tried to make us believe, as missionaries of their "kultur," to force it down the necks of decadent peoples as one would give medicine to a dying child. They aimed to crush these nations, already weak, by a long and devasting war. By such a war they considered it possible to undermine the physique and morale of their enemies to such a degree, that, after the war, they would be compelled to fall behind in the competitions of peace. We all agreed, that, even in suffering a military defeat, Germany had, at the same time, gained a great and subtle victory. To prevent Germany from reaping any benefit from such a victory a war must be carried on for the next five years, not with deadly weapons, but with energies that will revitalize and reconstruct the nations that surround Germany.

A few days after this discussion I dined with a cultured, French family. They remained in Lille during the period of German occupation, and were confined to two rooms of their handsome residence, the remainder of which was occupied by German officers. They assured me that these officers had acted the part of gentlemen, although they certainly lacked tact when they explained to members of the family the subtle and efficient war aims of Germany. "All we in-

tend to leave you," they said, "are the heavens above and your eyes to weep." "Even if you win," said a middle-aged officer, "we will leave you so that you cannot recover for half a century." Those who have not seen and studied conditions at first-hand cannot realize how Germany has carried out these aims with a subtle completeness, a completeness that is developing all over Europe as the days go by.

We were all of one mind in Lille, that Germany was still at war, with weapons far more dangerous and subtle than Big Berthas, Submarines, and poison gases. She knew that these material weapons might fail, but she knew also, that she could create weapons of another kind, living weapons, that of themselves, without the need of an army to use them, could completely subdue the most powerful enemy. In the fever and flush of the struggle, backed by rich and powerful allies, France did not realize that the germs of deadly diseases lay dormant within her body, kept under until the fever had spent itself in victory. Germany knew the power of these germs, she knew it when she made peace with Russia, and when she later surrendered to the Allies. It was the time to let the fever subside, and to give the dangerous germs free play. She gave up her weapons because they had completed their part of the task and the soil was prepared to let subtle and unseen forces finish the victory. She waited until she had racked the body of her neighboring enemies so that they no longer had the power to resist. Germany's latest and most powerful piece of strategy, we may later learn to our sorrow, was to surrender.

She had this aim in mind when she destroyed completely the industrial heart of France. I arranged to visit all the large industries in the Lille district and I chose first a textile plant in Roubaix. It was the best preserved factory in the region. The proprietor, who accompanied me around the factory remained during the German occupation and he bribed the German officers in charge with large sums of money and thus prevented the wholesale destruction and dismantling of his property. In one room about ten machines had been destroyed, but the remainder of the factory had merely been dismantled of certain parts that would be difficult to replace. After examining the extent of the damage we went over facts and figures in order to get a correct idea of the possibility of resuming the industrial life in the devastated areas.

This plant in Roubaix was about ten per cent destroyed and all the others were from 60 to 100 per cent. The owner of the Roubaix factory, after carefully going over the figures decided, that under the best possible conditions, he could not resume operations for at least nine months and that then he could only employ twenty-five per cent of the former working staff. Nearly all the factories I later visited were totally dismantled, with many of the buildings destroyed, so that they could not resume operations on a pre-war scale for at least five years, and to be more conservative I would say twenty-five years.

A few days later I sat in the office of one of the leading textile manufacturers in the department, a public-spirited man, and the mayor of the town in which his factories were the biggest asset. I had just finished an examination of these factories. They were entirely dismantled and many of the buildings destroyed. The Germans had compelled the inhabitants of the town to load the machinery, by the running of which they gained a livelihood, on cars for transportation into Germany. There wasn't a wheel left in this plant that had taken half a century to develop. My guide, a man of sixty-five years, had been exiled for nine months to Russia because he protested against the wholesale destruction of machinery. The cost of the reconstruction of the plant would be at least one hundred and fifty per cent higher than pre-war prices. The town, too, was in ruins, and the mayor fully realized the problem of re-establishing the former population of workers. Even if the factories could resume operations the working force would have no suitable abodes and the food conditions were such, that a return of the former residents in large numbers would breed a famine. The helpful and constructive elements of a modern, civilized community would be absent for a long time, and dangerous discontent would surely develop in a people whose nerves had already been unstrung by many privations. I was amazed at the mayor's optimism when he told me that he hoped to get things something like normal in a year.

The countryside, around these industrial centers, was an abomination of desolation, and reminded me very much of the logged-off burned-over wastes of the West. I rode all day through stretches of awful, uninhabited monotony that was once the scene of a peaceful rural life. The black crows were the only living creatures to be seen as they flitted back and forth out of the debris and the shell-torn earth into the clear, winter air. As far as one could see, on each side of the road, was the choas of shell craters and trenches, barbed-wire, ammunition dumps, villages of dugouts, remnants of camouflage and all the sordid debris of modern war. So one could pass on, through piles of rubbish, where once, villages stood, on and on through stretches of desolation, in the midst of a silence that reminded one of death and that made one think of what some day may be the end of all our boasted civilization. I often sat alone in the midst of the ruins to think things through, but the desolation developed emotions that made practical thinking almost impossible. One might as well imagine oneself sitting alone in the midst of the world after the Judgment Day, planning to start in again.

The reconstruction of the country should follow the natural lines of development. It would be a serious error to attempt to start the industrial life before the rural life of the department. Of course, under the circumstances, both can be developed together, but to establish industrial communities surrounded by unproductive desolation would breed the worst forms of discontent. This industrial population would mostly be made up of returned refugees, who have been the greatest sufferers of the war, and who have idealized, during their forced exile in the interior, the days when they would establish themselves in their native places. While in exile they developed a serious dislike for the people of central and southern France. They are sure to be severely disappointed when they return North. They will make extravagant demands. They think France owes them much and when they fail to receive what they expect they will grow bitter. They will be compelled to live in the midst of devastation and ruin for a good many years to come and the result, if the situation is not properly handled, will menace the future unity of the French people.

A divisional spirit had already taken alarming proportions before I left Lille last January, and I also saw warnings of it in the interior of France as far back as last August. I was sitting in a quaint, little restaurant in Roubaix with a retired manufacturers who belongs to one of the most conservative groups in France. He told me what I afterwards found to be true all over the North among the best and most conservative people. He had no sympathy with the French Government and its officials. He regarded them as we regard paid politicians of old-fashioned type. He expressed almost a hatred for the South and the Interior, and I was surprised when he said that the people of Lille and the departments of Nord and Pas de Calais advocated a separation from the rest of France and the organization of a new republic including themselves, Belgium, Luxembourg, Alsace and Lorraine, with Lille as the capital. A few days later I was being entertained in the home of a prominent merchant in La Madeline, and he showed me an unsigned pamphlet, with a yellow cover, which had been distributed by thousands throughout the North. It advocated separation from the central government. It exaggerated the difference between the North and the South of France. It attempted to show how poverty had always been prevalent in the interior and the South because the people were indolent but it claimed, at the same time, that they spent their time in politics and in working against the interests of the North. It branded them

as unpatriotic. The people who agreed with the claims of the pamphlet were not radical socialists but the aggressive leaders of the industrial North.

I had a splendid opportunity to observe, while directing the work of relief for The American Red Cross in the Haute Vienne, that the people of the North were not without good grounds for this criticism and dissatisfaction. Much of the South and the interior is backward and dirty and the majority are radical, negative Socialists. About a year before the armistice they advocated peace at any price and were never really in full sympathy with the war. In Limoges, at the beginning of the war, the government had a good deal of trouble with the people. I, myself, witnessed a scene in front of the Hotel de Ville, one Sunday afternoon, when hundreds of people listened to a declaiming Socialist who spoke under the patronage of the municipal authorities. He would have been arrested for sedition had he said the same things in the United States. He raised the crowd to such a pitch of fury, that when a patriotic officer shouted his objections, the crowd stoned him and chased him until he took refuge in a nearby hospital.

I also found a strong prejudice against the North on the part of the municipal authorities which they unconsciously revealed in their attitude toward the refugees who were exiles in their midst. In many instances they exploited the refugees and I knew more than one official who made a good deal of money by getting contracts for government work and then using cheap refugee labor. What was done for the relief of the refugees on the part of France was by the central government, through the prefectures of various departments. I always went first to the prefect with my plans, and after we had discussed them, I would lay the matter before the mayor who was a member of the Chamber of Deputies and a radical Socialist. He at times objected to my plans to exclusively work for the refugee population and wanted me to include all the local poor. I explained to him that that was the function of the local authorities and that the American Red Cross concerned itself solely with refugees who were stricken by the war. They resented this attitude of the Red Cross to such an extent that they at times hindered our work and I frequently had to work through the better classes over the heads of the municipal authorities. These officials were merely politicians, interested in votes, and the refugees had no voting power. It was really unpopular to sympathize too freely with the refugees.

The people among whom the refugees were compelled to live were distinctly an inferior class, often dirty and ill-bred, and their lack of sympathy and understanding for their war-stricken compatriots was at times so cruel that I had to enterfere. On one occasion the mayor of a large commune denounced the refugees and called them "Boche" which is the gravest kind of insult in France. He denounced them in my presence as immoral and lazy. Upon investigation I found the mayor and the people of his commune to be a very inferior type, and the mayor, himself, had attempted to exploit the refugees by offering them one franc and twenty-five centimes for a day's work when he received four francs for the work they did each day. The fact was that the refugees were a vigorous people and their blonde type strongly contrasted with the dark Spanish type around them. Then, too, had the accent of the North and some of them spoke Flemish. They were industrious, thrifty, and scrupulously clean, even in the dirty, unsanitary surroundings that prevailed.

The attitude of many parts of the South toward the devastated North was revealed one day when I called a few business men of the interior into my office to discuss the problem of the return of the refugees. They got away from the subject in trying to explain to me that the North would never again be the industrial center of France, and they told me of a movement to start the industries in the interior, which, they claimed, was better situated than the North and had more natural resources. They believed that other parts of France should take advantage of the opportunity and build up industrial life before the North got

started and for that reason they hoped that the refugee industrial workers would remain in the interior. I told them that I regarded their attitude good business but selfish and lacking patriotism.

There are many other factors more well-known than this one that are subtle weapons in aiding Germany to gain a victory over France. She knew that the government of France was not popular in the North, and she also knew that it was filled with graft, corruption and office-seeking politicians. She knew that the people of the North cared little for politics and regarded the government as controlled by the South against the interests of the North. She knew that a broken and discouraged North would not only mean the destruction for a long time of the industrial life of France, but would also breed serious internal dissension. Knowing these things she carried on the biggest and most destructive part of her fighting in the richest industrial sections of France and destroyed them in a manner far surpassing the reaches of imagination.

On the second floor of The Prefecture at Lille, in what was a large, assembly hall, are the offices that represent the machinery organized by the government to carry on the work of reconstruction in the department of Nord. The prejudice of the people of Lille against these offices was very strong so I visited them to find out whether it had any real foundation. The functions of many of the offices were duplicated and there was a great host of paid men who were, without a doubt, receiving the rewards of faithfulness to partisan politics. I had seen similar sights in America. I came away rather pessimistic regarding the early resumption of agricultural life. The work was for big men and I found very few and I sympathized with the attitude of the real, business men of Lille. The officials in The Prefecture had plans, complex and innumerable, but they did not seem to get anywhere. They could tell how many houses had been destroyed, and how many chickens, cows, goats and horses had been taken by the Germans, but they did not seem to realize that making surveys and gathering statistics failed to satisfy an impatient people who asked for real things to work with and live by. One had to go the rounds of official red tape, sent from one bureau to another until one landed finally at the starting point to be sent the rounds again.

The following instance will explain the appalling situation. Lying in Versailles were literally thousands of new auto-trucks belonging to the French army. Every day the engines were turned over to keep them in condition. The regions around Lille were solely in need of supplies and the people were suffering. The American Red Cross and the Hoover Commission had the supplies in Paris, but could not get transportation and when they asked for the use of these un-used trucks they were refused, or at least told that red-tape stood in the way and the people went without the supplies. This same situation had to be endured by the people of Lille who wished to re-sume normal conditions and could not because of the lack of transportation.

There are other evils connected with the transportation problem that are sub-tly aiding Germany. When I went into the devasted zones I expected to find a great scarcity of food but was surprised to find that the quality and variety was far superior to other parts of France. The shop windows were filled with appe-tizing dainties, candies, pastry of every sort, butter, eggs, cheese, sugar and even white bread. Just after I returned to Paris I could not buy many of these arti-cles at any price. I found that the big-gest part of the produce came from Bel-gium. Of course the prices were high. These vast devasted areas bordered on Belgium, where most of the land was un-harmed and in a fine state of cultivation, largely because the Germans demanded that the farmers of Belgium, during the period of occupation, produce the maxi-mum from the farms. Belgium, therefore, is ready to get rich by supplying her stricken neighbors. I found a hatred for Belgium growing like a prairie fire, fanned, I am certain, by the winds of Ger-man propaganda.

Germany knows that France cannot stand alone and that she needs allied the sympathy and the help of the Allies. She knew the power of American aid. She therefore took advantage of the fact that Americans were homesick in a strange land and started a plague of criticism that spread everywhere through our forces in France. I remember well when the tendency to criticize began and it grew to alarming proportions about the time of the signing of the armistice and the opening of peace negotiations. Men and women whom I had known in July to be broad in their sympathies and to have an intelligent appreciation for the courage and sacrifice of the French people, were in November denouncing France and all things French in the most irrational manner. I cannot just now tell all that I would otherwise wish to make public because I think it would be an in-jury to the cause of reconstruction to do so, but the result of this plague of criti-cism was a very serious one, but I must jump to another phase of my subject. French people of culture and education often tried to assure me that the danger of revolution after the cessation of hos-tilities was not a mere fancy. They pointed out the signs to me and I could not escape noticing a dangerous class-consciousness developing everywhere. On one occasion I discussed the labor unrest with a man who employed a very large working force. He deplored the work of the French government in caring for the refugees. Each refugee was given an al-location. A parent, including the father, when he was unemployed, received one franc and a half a day, and each child received a franc. This amount was later raised. When the family was large they would have an income, without labor, of more than the father could earn before the war. One can easily see the evil ef-fect of this system and can sympathize with the point-of-view of the manufac-turer. I found that the large employers of labor did not seem to realize that labor can never return to its former standards. They did not take into ac-count the high prices and the changed conditions. When the thousands of com-mon soldiers return to work they will make demands, and if not satisfied, they will very likely force their demands by revolution. They, the majority of them, have suffered much and have risked their lives for France, and they are property-less. The danger lies in the fact that the life of a soldier at the front creates a disregard for property rights. All the rights of private property are practically relinquished and soldiers can enter and use it as they like. Anything that falls into their hands is theirs to use and this has a serious effect upon the minds of the men. The result is a form of war psychology — which is already working ruin in Russia and in other parts of Europe and it will do the same in France if the hopes of Germany are realized and if the many conditions are not quickly improved.

We must remain the ally of France in the new war now upon us. Germany has not been defeated yet, and she knows it and she understands how to fan the flames that are beginning to spread over the face of Europe. The French know, also, that, if things go forward again in the old way, she will fall behind in the supposed legitimate competitions of peace, when the better situated nations, forgetting the comradeship in the war for liberty, will selfishly build their own lives upon the weakness of others. France realizes that the goods of her enemies will come in a flood across her borders if she cannot manufacture, herself. This flood, of course, may not appear to come directly at first, but people soon forget, and in a few years Germany will trade with her enemies. **German goods are already being sold in the devastated zones. I saw them in shop windows in Lille.** If we fail to prepare for the day that is upon us, and if we forsake our weaker allies, all their sacrifices and all our sacrifices, will be in vain.

In the Realm of Bookland

Under the title, "The Command is Forward," Sergeant Alexander Woollcott, in times of peace dramatic critic of the New York Times, has compiled in book form a series of articles, written by himself and published in Stars and Stripes, the journal conducted under official approval by the enlisted men of the American Expeditionary Force.

The articles, which are disconnected, deal with the operations of the American Army in France from the anxious early days of June, 1918, to the final triumphant climax in November of that year.

While not constituting a continuous narrative, the successive articles, written by a soldier for soldiers and civilians alike, gives perhaps the most graphic account not only of the actual operations of the A. E. F. but of the actual conditions under which our troops carried the world war to victory.

Not only the dangers, hardships and self denial of our men, but many of the softer aspects of the campaign are dwelt upon eloquently in the volume. The spirits of companionship, of earnest effort, of patience under suffering, of amusement and downright fun are set forth by the side of the darker phases of a particularly cruel war.

Special attention is devoted to the operations of St. Mihiel and the Meuse-Argonne theatre. But more space is allotted to the essentially human side, not only of our lads themselves, but of those with whom they came in contact on and near the front.

The book is admirably illustrated with sketches by Private LeRoy Baldridge, A. E. F.   The Century Co., $1.75.

"A Woman Named Smith" is another charming volume by Marie Conway Oemler, authoress of "Slippy McGee." It is a love story of what may be termed the new Old South, the South of the present day retaining much of the savor of the old, old South, particularly in its traditions. The scene is laid in South Carolina and the characters, at least most of them, are easily recognized by those born and raised in the South. Mrs. Oemler is particularly happy in her interpretations of the mental attitude of the old Southerners, even when breathing the twentieth century atmosphere. Zest is imparted at the outset by the announcement that the heroine herself is not Southern herself but a woman from Boston, of English parentage, grafted by marriage upon a pedigreed Southern family. It is a story that attracts at once and retains its grasp until the end. The Century Co., $1.60.

———

Georges Duhamel, with his "Civilization," of the Goncourt fiction prize for 1918, has produced, from the turmoil, suffering and bitterness of war, another work masterpiece, well named "The Heart's Domain," which is so sweet, human and appealing that one wonders how so dreadful an environment as war could have so delightful, soothing a product. One sentence, taken at random, is an example of the spirit that animates the book:

"A tuft of violets is worth a great deal for its perfume and beauty, it can bring joy or consolation to a great many hearts. But it has only the slightest commercial value; estimated in terms of building lumber or freestone it signifies nothing, or virtually nothing."

A philosophic work, beautifully written, "The Heart's Domain" is eminently entertaining, instructive and soothing.

The Century Co., $1.50.

———

In "Sorcery," Francis Charles MacDonald has woven a tale of magic in our own day, in our own island possession of Hawaii, where, according to the story, sorcery yet survives, as it does in some of the West Indian islands and even in some isolated sections of the Southern States of the Union, under the name of voodooism. "Sorcery" has its scene laid in Honolulu and its action is limited to the events of a single day, in which are concentrated the mental and physical inheritances from generations of Hawaiian ancestors. Magic, incantations and other strange, weird phenomena are exhibited at a mixed gathering of up-to-date Americans, people of the world, and some with strains of Hawaiian blood in their veins. The story is interesting, albeit uncanny. It sheds peculiar light upon the natures of our new wards of the islands.

The Century Co., $1.50.

NOVEMBER, 1919

Overland
Monthly

PRICE 15 CENTS

THIS ISSUE CONTAINS

AIRS

Opportunity's One Knock

When *Opportunity* knocks, will we hear her?

Or will our ears be so deafened with debts and our minds so filled with money worries that we do not hear her happy message?

W. S. S. and Thrift Stamps help Opportunity knock loudly—one knock enough.

W. S. S.—
Everybody's Opportunity

Savings' Division
War Loan Organization
Treasury Department

Vol. LXXIV

No. 5

Overland Monthly

AN ILLUSTRATED MAGAZINE OF THE WEST

CONTENTS FOR NOVEMBER, 1919

NOTICE.—Contributions to the Overland Monthly should be typewritten, accompanied by full return postage, and with the author's name and address plainly written in upper corner of first page. Manuscripts should never be rolled.

The Publisher of the Overland Monthly will not be responsible for the preservation or mail miscarriage of unsolicited contributions and photographs.

Issued Monthly. $1.50 per year in advance. Fifteen cents per copy. Back numbers 3 months or over 25c; six months or over 50c; nine months or over 75c; 1 year or over $1.00. Postage: To Canada, 3 cents; Foreign, 5 cents.

Copyrighted, 1919, by the Overland Monthly Company.

Entered at the San Francisco, Cal., Post-office as second-class matter.

Published by the OVERLAND MONTHLY COMPANY, San Francisco, California.

259 MINNA STREET.

The Greatest Novel Ever Written—by the
Most Popular Author in All the World

Harold Bell Wright

Vibrant with the local color of the mystic,
enchanted Ozarks—The Shepherd of the Hills
country. Brian Kent, Auntie Sue, Judy and
Betty Jo are more than creations—they are
actual, human realities.

Illustrations by J. Allen St. John

THE RE=CREATION OF BRIAN KENT

First Printing—Forty Carloads—750,000 Copies

THE RE-CREATION OF BRIAN KENT carries a message that will strengthen human
faith to happiness: "The foundation principles of life—honesty, courage, fidelity, morality,
etc.—are eternal facts. Life must and will go on. You can neither stop it nor turn it
back." In the author's inimitable, fascinating style this message is like a heaven-sent blessing that will cheer and give courage to millions of weary, storm-tossed souls that have all but
gone down in these recent years of world chaos. "The Re-Creation of Brian Kent" is a
delightful Ozark story of life and love, sweet and appealing with pathos, rich in philosophy,
masterful in character analysis, charming in description and intensely dramatic, not with
physical combat, but with skillful visualization of the clash and conflicts of the invisible forces
of life.

Full Cloth, 12mo., $1.50

Other Novels by Harold Bell Wright—Over Eight Million Sold
That Printer of Udell's—The Shepherd of the Hills—The Calling of Dan Matthews—The
Winning of Barbara Worth—Their Yesterdays—The Eyes of the World—When a Man's a Man

Harold Bell Wright's Books Are Sold Everywhere

Mr. Wright's Allegory of Life
"A literary gem that will live" The Uncrowned King 16mo., Cloth
60 Cents

**Our Big Catalog of
Books of All Publishers FREE** We catalog and sell by mail, at a big saving to you,
over 25,000 books of other publishers. We supply
the largest number of public, private and school libraries and individuals with all their books.
Our service is quick and satisfying. Write for catalog today. A post card will bring it.

THE BOOK SUPPLY COMPANY, Publishers and Booksellers
E. W. REYNOLDS, President   231-233 West Monroe Street, CHICAGO

OVERLAND  MONTHLY

Founded 1868

BRET HARTE

| VOL. LXXVI | San Francisco, November, 1919 | No. 5 |

Announcement

THIS new department of Oriental affairs, which from now on will become a part of The Overland Monthly, is the outcome of a conviction. Many of the most thoughtful people on the Pacific Coast earnestly believe that here, where East meets West, we should take the lead in developing a sympathetic, intelligent and constructive understanding between the Occident and the Orient. They are deeply convinced that the peace of the future will depend upon such an understanding, and that this coast is the strategic geographical point from which should go forth a sound leadership in these matters. Only by such leadership can the next great world war be prevented, a war that will very likely come within this generation. In order to do a small part for the constructive peace that is now the earnest hope of all far-seeing men and women, The Overland Monthly ventures upon the task of starting this department on Oriental affairs, and in doing so frankly asks the co-operation and support of the thoughtful people of the West.

We cannot make this first issue a sample of the strength that we hope will characterize the department, because we did not feel that we should delay the opening of it until the men who have consented to write prepared their material. In the next issue we hope to publish the names of the editorial staff, which will include some of the leading and most thoughtful men and women in California, as well as the names of writers who will faithfully represent China and Japan. We will always welcome letters from our readers, and will publish as many as we feel will fit into the aim and purpose of the department.

Japan has every reason to believe that she is the scapegoat nation of the world. She is not only a nation circled by oceans, but she is surrounded and isolated by a world that, to all appearances, regards her with suspicion and seeks to despise her. In the heart of every nation lives the Prussian and the Prince of Peace, fighting each other to gain control, and the surest way to assist the Prussian to gain control in the life of any nation is for other bigger nations to get that nation with her back against the wall, and to aggravate and taunt her until she is desperate. We are arousing the Prussian in Japan, and to do so will mean the death of that courageous little nation that has risen to power in the face of tremendous difficulties. She is overstepping now, or at least the Prussian element within her borders is overstepping. We are responsible for arousing it. The encroachments of the Powers in the Far East are also responsible. It is our duty to Japan and the world's peace to recognize her worth, her courage and her right to live, and to so deal with her without passion and prejudice, that we may strengthen the better elements that we know are a part of her national life, that they may arise in their strength and reveal the true Japan to the eyes of the world.

"It was Germany's rights in Shantung and not Chinese that we conceded by the treaty to Japan. But with a condition which never occurred in any of these other cases, a condition which was not insisted upon at the cession of Port Ar-

thur—upon a condition that no other nation in doing similar things in' China
has ever yielded to—Japan is under solemn promise to forego all sovereign
rights in the province of Shantung, and
to retain only what private corporations
have elsewhere in China, the right of con-
cessionaires with regard to the operation of the railway and exploitation of
the mines. Scores of foreign corporations have that right in other parts of ·
China."

"What I want to call to your attention
is that the treaty of peace does not take
Shantung from China, it takes it from
Germany. There are seventy-eight years
of the ninety-nine of that lease still to
run. And not only do we not take it from
China, but Japan agrees, in an agreement
which is formally recorded, which is acknowledged by the Japanese government,
to return all the sovereign rights which
Germany enjoyed in Shantung without
qualification to China, and to retain nothing except what foreign corporations
have throughout China, the right to run
a railroad and to exploit those mines.

"There is not a great commercial and
industrial nation in Europe that does not
enjoy privileges of that sort in China,
and some of them enjoy them at the expense of the sovereignty of China, and
Japan has promised to release everything
that savors of sovereignty and return it
to China itself. She will have no right
to put armed men anywhere into that
portion of China; she will have no right
to interfere with the civil adminstration
of that portion of China; she will have
no rights but economic and commercial
rights."—President Wilson.

"The question is often asked as to when
Japan will return Kiao-Chow to China.

I would point out on the reply that for
the restitution of Kiao-Chow, detailed arrangement should be worked out before-
hand in common accord between the Japanese and Chinese governments, and that
the length of time required for such arrangement depends largely, upon the attitude of China."—Premier Hara of
Japan.

"We are prepared to restore full territorial rights in Kiao Chow to China inside of six months. We are anxious to
settle the whole question. We ask nothing better than a return of territory in
accordance · with the treaty of 1915. It
is necessary, however, that China enter
into negotiations with us which hitherto
she has declined to do."—A Member of
Japanese Peace Delegation, quoted by
International News Service.

"The reason why China refuses to sign
the peace treaty is because the Shantung settlement has caused us serious
disappointment. The reason why the
peace conference is unjust in making the
decision and why China's claims are all
refused is because of Japanese influence.
If Japan is capable of exercising such influence at the world peace conference,
at which the eyes of the world are fixed,
it can easily be imagined what her power
will be if China tried to negotiate for a
settlement direct with Japan. We are
confident that it is not the free wish of
the government to open direct negotiations with Japan, for the Japanese are a
crafty race. It is impossible to take too
careful precautions against the plots of
our traitors who are willing to lend
themselves to Japanese. It is to be hoped
that our government will refuse to listen
to the cunning arguments of the traitors."
—Sin Wan Pao, Shanghai, China.

The Flingers of Shantung

By Charles Hancock Foster

THERE are men in our country who are flinging Shantung around in a most dangerous fashion. As soon as the text of the Peace Treaty arrived in Washington, certain legislators, who were totally unfitted for the task, began to examine its contents, but as a matter of fact they were looking for something to fling around, and when they thought they had found what they were seeking, they commenced to fling, wildly and in all directions, giving no thought to the things of infinite value to the world that they might smash. It seemed, indeed, that their chief purpose was to smash.

How many Americans ever heard of Shantung before this year! The men who are talking about this portion of China are wise enough to know that they can make any statement they please without fear of contradiction. In the first place they are safeguarded by our prejudice toward the Japanese, and in the second place, they know that the average American has neither the time nor the inclination to get back into history of diplomacy in the Orient to learn the real facts in the case. Shantung is, there-fore, a very expedient subject for poli-ticians, and the present loving regard ex-pressed by these gentlemen for China must surely be more sinister than sen-timental.

I have no desire, in this editorial, to appear pro-Japanese, and this new de-partment on Oriental relationships in-tends to tell facts without coloring them, without sentiment, believing that such an attitude is the only one that will en-sure the peace of the world and the in-telligent understanding without which such a peace is not possible. This atti-tude is well stated in a letter I have just received from Dr. David P. Barrows of the University of California. The people of California are beginning to admire and consider of great value the utterances of Dr. Barrows since his return from the Far East, and I am glad to be able to use the following extract from his letter to express the purpose and attitude of this department with regard to Oriental affairs:

"Your plan," wrote Dr. Barrows, "to conduct through The Overland Monthly a department on Oriental affairs is interesting and important. It is very necessary that these affairs be discussed for our own enlightenment and for their influence upon Japanese policy. I have come to the conclusion that there is nothing else to be done but tell the Japanese frankly that we think that their procedure on the Continent of Asia is disastrous to our friendship and menacing to the prospects of an international understanding and comity in the Far East. I do not want to be associated with any movement to conceal the facts or to minimize the seriousness of the situation there, but I would be glad to associate myself with your department if it is what I believe you and the editors of The Overland Monthly will make it."

It is my purpose, in this editorial, to state Japan's side of the case, not as it is put by Japan, but as it is seen by many thoughtful Americans who try to regard the situation without bias or sentiment. I feel very confident that every observing man must recognize that Japan is confronted by a very grave issue—the gravest issue that any nation can face—whether she shall live or die! This is not an overstatement of the case. I can do no better here than quote from my esteemed friend, Mr. K. K. Kawakami. Mr. Kawakami lives in America and is the leading Japanese writer and publicist in the United States. His books and writings are regarded as fair and frank statements of the case for Japan, praising his country when he feels she should be praised and condemning her when he feels she deserves condemnation. Writing of Japan's greatest problem, Mr. Kawakami says:

"The teeming millions of Nippon, confined within her own narrow precincts, and forbidden, by the mandates of Western powers, to emigrate to any of the territories occupied or controlled by them, must perforce find a field of activity within their own sphere. With this in view Japan is eager to convert herself into a great industrial and commercial country. If she fails in this endeavor, she knows that her progress must cease from congestion, stagnation, and inan-

ition. To understand this point of view it is necessary to know something of the population question with which Japan has been grappling.

"During the past half century Japan's population has been increasing at the rate of 400,000 a year. Where there were 33,000,000 Japanese fifty years ago, there are today about 53,000,000. As the total area of Japan proper is about 148,756 square miles, the density of population is about 356 per square mile. If we leave out of consideration Hokkaido, the northern island, the density increases to 451 per square mile.

"We have seen that during the past five decades Japan's population has increased by 20,000,000. As against this increase, Japan has sent out but 2,900,000 emigrants to various countries as follows: Hokkaido (northern island of Japan proper), 2,000,000; Formosa (southern island of Japan), 100,000; Korea, 300,000; Manchuria, 309,981; Hawaii, 96,749; continental United States, 101,000; China, South America and other countries combined, 40,000.

"It may be safely said that all European countries at one stage or another of their national development have alleviated the congestion of population at home by encouraging emigration. But Japan, one of the most crowded countries in the world, is compelled to solve the same question without sending emigrants to any of those countries which offer the greatest opportunities to men with modest means. True, some European countries are even more densely populated than Japan, but these countries, in addition to the advantages of unrestricted emigration, have each acquired extensive colonies, which either afford room for a large population, or store abundant natural resources to be utilized for the advancement of industries at home. On the other hand, Japan has no colonial land to speak of. Such territories as Korea or Formosa cannot be regarded as colonies, for they are already thickly populated—having 187 inhabitants to the square mile.

"Under these circumstances Japan must seek relief from the distressing congestion of population in methods other than emigration or colonial expansion. Her only way out lies in her industrial and commercial expansion. That is why she is anxious to build up industry at home and extend commerce abroad. But in order to become a foremost industrial nation Japan must have iron and coal, two essentials of modern industry. Unfortunately, Japan's home territory has little of either in store. The volume of iron ores produced at home is but a fraction of what Japan actually consumes. Of coal she has a considerable output, but none that is available for coking purposes. Without coke the steel industry is impossible. China is the country to which Japan must logically and naturally look for the supply of iron ores and coking coal. That is why Japan is anxious to secure mining concessions in China, before China's mines and collieries, unutilzed by herself, will be all mortgaged to other nations—nations which have already secured vast colonies in different parts of the world, and which have plenty of raw materials and a large quantity of mineral supplies in their own territories."

Chinese and American Divorces

I shall always remember Ah Toy, our cook, as he sat around the campfire at Donner Lake. Everyone in camp loved Toy, and by the way he fed us I think he returned the affection.

When I think of Ah Toy I am compelled to think of other camp cooks—Swedes, Irish, German and even American, who kept up a constant grouch and gave every person in camp the indigestion But we cannot get even a grouch for a cook nowadays. Only one can be found when demands are out for fifty.

In the early days of America we had negroes for house-servants. It seems that only people of another race can fit themselves to this kind of work, and the Chinaman fits in more, perhaps, than anyone else on earth. When he gets settled in a household he becomes an essential and a respected unit in the home, and he creates an atmosphere of comfort that is not only a practical but a spiritual value as well. I know some of the readers will think, at this point, that I must have had a rotten dinner and am longing for the old Chinese cook, but I confidently believe that if we imported two hundred thousand Chinamen to work in our households and restricted them to that work alone and allowed them to live here just for a period of five years, that there would be a hundred or two thousand less divorces, as well as larger families in the United States. It would help to make home spell H-O-M-E in America. It would help China also, for if we kept up the scheme we would keep streaming back to China a host· of Chinese who have learned American ideals and habits in the American Home. It would be a mutual benefit all around. Will our readers kindly start a many-sided discussion of this subject?

The attitude taken toward the Orient by many Americans, the kind who flippantly talk about the dishonesty of the yellow race, and who declaim on the street cars about Shantung, is expressed in the following incident:

A Japanese gentleman, whose influence upon the world's affairs, is recognized over three continents, and whose education, culture and refinement would at once reveal themselves to a person who had like traits of character, while riding in a day coach on one of our railroads here in California, unconsciously allowed his suitcase to protrude a little into the aisle. A well-dressed American boarded the train at a small station, and when he saw the protruding suitcase he turned to the Japanese gentleman and said:

"Say, John! Don't hog the whole aisle! Pull in your bag; some ladies want to get by!" The speaker regarded himself as belonging to a superior race!

Japan and Shantung Question

APAN, facing, as she does, this great problem of national preservation, has had reason to be provoked at the attitude taken toward her by China during the past two decades. There have been elements in Japanese life that have angered China. The trouble with both countries, in their relationships, has been the old one of unprincipled politics overruling the better elements in the nation's life. The best elements in both countries have coveted the unity of the Orient. The Peking government has unfortunately represented the worst side of the life of China. It has regarded all the acts of Japan with suspicion. European powers have played upon this spirit of suspicion and hatred toward Japan to work their own selfish ends in China. The fact of the matter is that China regarded with suspicion and hatred the Occidental powers as well as Japan, but she found such a wholesale hatred very unprofitable. She therefore swallowed her hatred for the Occident, and in a spirit of humility she gave up parts of her territory to them.

No more perfect illustration can be found of this spirit of humility than the attitude of the Chinese government when she gave up Shantung to Germany. When two German missionaries were killed by Chinese in Shantung, Germany started military maneuvers that ended in the taking of Shantung by Germany, China agreeing to the same in a treaty that leased the peninsula for a term of years. In the words of this treaty the government of China regarded the act as an appropriate and concrete piece of evidence, as well as a grateful recognition, of the friendship that existed between China and Germany! It was the outcome of a reciprocal and friendly desire to develop and further the economic interests of the two countries. It was also, according to the treaty, the recognition of a social obligation! It was regarded as a move to strengthen the military preparedness of the Chinese Empire. The truth of the whole matter we all now know. It was a scheme to strengthen Prussian militarism for the great war.

In view of China's attitude toward Germany, when the latter took Shantung, and in view of the fact that Japan ousted the Prussians from Shantung, it seems to me very strange that China and the rest of us should make such a noise over the present situation.

In a recent number of "The Nation" a writer named Snow, speaking in favor of China, says that "China properly insists upon the right to choose among all the states of the world, without regard to their location, those whom it regards as states of good will, and to select those whom it may properly admit to its honor and confidence and to lodgment within its own domains, in order that they may help it in helping itself during the trying period of its transition from an Oriental to an Occidental economic status."

He further goes on to say that: "Germany's privileges, under the treaty, though essentially economic, were also social and of a strictly personal and highly confidential character. The spheres of influence were granted by China to Germany and to the other states as personal and social privileges, in order that both might receive benefits. All social privileges are based on friendship and a desire to help one's friends and one's self, and are by their nature non-transferable. The relations of close friendship on which such privileges are based do not rise from 'propinquity.' A neighbor is not necessarily a friend; certainly not always one whom one would choose as a trusted associate in developing one's own property, or to whom one would give the privilege of a continuous lodgment on one's homestead. On the contrary, a neighbor who is untrustworthy is by his neighborhood doubly disqualified from being admitted into such a confidential social relationship, and neighborhood in such case is only disadvantageous. The only 'special relations' which any state can properly put forward as entitling it to a sphere of influence within the body-politic of another state, are the 'special relations' of friendship, mutual confidence and mutual aid, which grow up between states and persons of good will toward each other; and the only 'special interests' are those which each state and each person has in advancing the welfare of all other states and all other persons."

Mr. Snow's serious emphasis upon the friendship, the goodwill, and the loving interest of the European powers toward China, when they grabbed her territory, is almost a caricature! Whether China has good reasons for her attitude toward Japan I will not now discuss, but any fair-minded American must admit that this attitude has been, and is now, a grave menace to Japan.

Perhaps the best way to understand the position of Japan is to carry out an analogy. Let us suppose that our population is over-crowded, that the world has shut its doors against us, and that we are hated on every side. Let us suppose that the very existence of our nation is imperilled, just as is the national existence of Japan. Let us suppose, further, that Mexico holds the same attitude toward us as China does toward Japan. She shuts us out of all privileges and at the same time gives over parts of her territory that are adjacent to our borders to powers that are dangerous to us, allowing them to build forts and establish naval bases. I leave the reader to draw his own conclusions from this, and I think the analogy is not a bit overdrawn.

We have always regarded the inefficient government of Mexico as a menace. We know that this government might at any time negotiate with our enemies. Japan has far more reason to be suspicious of China than we have to fear Mexico. The spirit of the Peking government has not represented the real China. This government has at times acted unscrupulously, regarding bribes above patriotism, with a seeming willingness to sell out its country for a mess of pottage. It has grovelled in the dust at the feet of Occidental powers. Through this attitude Japan has found her liberty of action threatened by constant European encroachments in the Far East, and if her foreign policy deserves criticism we must remember that she has been driven to take it by the attitude of China

and by her many unfortunate experiences with European powers. She is now being shouted down, and the imaginations of politicians and press propaganda are drawing pictures of her that are unfair and untrue, and the anathemas of the world are falling upon her head because she is doing what other nations have been doing and are still doing. If we demand that Japan act in a certain manner toward China we should make the same demand of every other nation. Only by the creation of a new policy, a policy that will be applied to all alike, can we find a way out of the present difficult situation.

That Japan could easily make a case for herself before a court of nations can be illustrated by the events that followed her war with China. After this war, China agreed to cede to Japan the Liaotung peninsula, whereupon Russia, Germany and France protested. They took such a threatening attitude that Japan complied. All the world knew at the time that the action of the three powers was not impelled by a motive of friendliness for China. Shortly after Japan complied, China gave the same territory to Russia. Japan fought. Any self-respecting nation would have done the same. Later, Germany came along, using the death of two missioneries as a pretext, and took Shantung. Viewing these developments with concern, Japan asserted her right to a place in the Far East. She asks no greater things than other powers demand. It is true she has over-stepped. It is true she has acted with cruelty in many instances, but other nations have acted with cruelty and have over-stepped, and when we talk of curbing Japan's imperialistic policy in the Far East, we should demand that the policies of other powers be also curbed, including the power of American capital. We should recognize Japan's problems. We should treat her justly and honorably, giving her every opportunity of development that is her right. We should act toward her as we would that others nations should act toward us, for only by so doing can we bring about that great peace for which we all earnestly hope.

China Needs the Assistance of the United States

By Sun Ching Siao

AMONG the world nations, China has been the least understood and the most criticized. Many who hold that the Chinese people, although civilized and clever as they are, are a people with commercial genius but no political ability. They sometimes class the Chinese people with the Jews, who have made a wonderful commercial success in the world but can not have a government of their own. This is, of course, only the idea of those who have a very little or almost no knowledge about Chinese history, except merely being confronted by the recent struggle since the establishment of the Republic, which are but the results of political reaction and confliction in interest, just as that which happened in France after the Great Revolution, or the Civil War in the United States.

A delusion of this kind will certainly do not a little harm to the future of China, especially during the present transitory stage. Some audacious and unscrupulous foreigners, after taking this idea into their heads, even unhesitatingly advocate the international control of Chinese affairs, such as the foreign control of finance, the internationalization of railways, etc.

That the Chinese people possess the same political ability as every other great nation in the world, is a matter of no question at all if one knows the history of China. Not to mention remote events, but the overthrow of the Manchu dynasty with its misrule and inefficiency, and the establishment of the Republic, the first nation to introduce the democratic form of government on Asiatic soil, are the best evidences of the self-consciousness of the Chinese people, who are not indifferent in the political affairs and are really able to realize the highest political ideal.

As we possess the best and also an enormous amount of natural resources in the world, and at the same time a race of people intelligent and energetic, we ought to make remarkable progress in our favorable situation and contribute much for the welfare of the world. Politically we may spread the Confucian principle of universal peace and realize the world of the league of nations on grounds of justice and righteousness. Industrially we may adapt our immense force of labor to develop the enormous untouched resources to supply the world with material means for improvement of world civilization. We fail now to do so and in great part remain in an unprogressive state and make exceedingly slow headway, you may say, and that it is due to inability of the Chinese people to govern themselves and make progress. Nay, this will never be the case.

We have not had a chance to assert ourselves freely. We are constantly under the shackles and bonds of foreign powers. The most important thing I shall mention is the very heaviest of burdens, the indemnity imposed upon China by foreign powers in 1901, amounting to 450,000,000 taels, distributed over forty years, and customs revenues are entirely used for its payment; and taxes on necessities are resorted to to pay the interest and the loss incurred in the lowering of the price of silver. There is scarcely any revenue left that can be used for national development. The financial condition is badly impaired and the country is generally impoverished. It is really a death blow to China's progress.

Another thing standing in the way of our industrial development is the tariff rate which is fixed by a convention of foreign powers at 5 per cent ad valorem, regardless of the kind and character of commodities. The keen competition of foreign manufacturers causes them to dump their surplus but inferior goods on our markets.

There is no chance for our people to start new industries, and the old hand-labor industries can not meet the keen competition of foreign machine industries without suffering huge losses. The imports exceed the exports by millions in value, and the balance of trade has constantly been unfavorable to us. This is one of the main reasons for the industrial backwardness and poverty of China.

As to the present political condition in China, it is still worse. A greater majority of the people want to build a real constitutional and democratic form of government on a firm and stable basis. But foreign powers in China gave their helping hands to Yuan-Shi-Kai to assist the monarchial movement which caused the civil war in 1917. Later on, our neighboring power helped the militarists to dissolve the Parliament and contributed money and munitions to the military leader, to wage war against the southern constitutionalists, who made all efforts to put the constitutions in force. This power has been playing all sorts of intrigue and deception, favoring a detrimental policy in China and causing the latter to remain in petty warfare and disorder.

That China, at present, wants help is not a question of doubt, but it is a necessity. The Chinese people can help themselves in internal affairs and have the ability to build a stable and strong government, but the world must give her longer time for this accomplishment. The help which China needs is a guardianship from outside aggressions and all sorts of interferences and unreasonable demands. If she were left alone, free from foreign aggression and interference she certainly would make a remarkable progress and would be the great democratic and independent nation on the western coast of the Pacific, just as the United States is on the east.

Look around the globe and you will find no country so well qualified to the guardianship as the United States of America. The United States is the only country in the world which stands for justice and humanity. It is she who sent millions of her sons to Europe to fight and to have thousands of them killed for no national aggrandizement or territorial acquisition, but for liberty and justice. With regard to her relation to China, the United States has always been most friendly toward China, beginning in 1844, when Caleb Cushing, the American minister, delivered the letter from President Tyler to the Chinese Emperor, Tao-Kuang; after the Chino-Japanese war, when China seemed on the point of being partitioned; and in the years 1894-1898, a period of "scramble for concessions," when all important seaports were seized by European powers and the country was divided into "spheres of influence." But these dangerous crises were tided over by the open-door policy of John Hay, the Secretary of State of the United States, in securing written pledges to preserve the political independence and territorial integrity of China from all powers. These are really great services performed by the United States for China. In the "Boxer" trouble of 1900 the United States reinforced the principle of "open door" and also succeeded in protecting the country from being dismembered at a time when foreign soldiers had already occupied the most important points in North China. It was the United States who advised other nations to ask indemnities of not more than $300,000,000, though, unfortunately, it did not succeed. But in after years she generously gave back to China, from her share of the indemnity, which amounted to $100,000,000, a sum now used to educate Chinese students in her institutions.

Mutual good will has always existed between the two nations. We are always grateful and indebted to her actions on our behalf and we always look to her as our natural guide, and follow her advice without hesitation. Our entrance into the great war was strongly opposed by Japan, but as soon as the United States gave the advice our government declared war with Germany at once, in spite of the Japanese opposition. In the unjust disposition of Shantung by the "Big Three," we appealed to no other country but the Republic of the United States, because on one hand since the adoption of the "open door" policy by Secretary Hay, the United States seemed to have assumed the responsibility to preserve the integrity of China, and on the other hand the people of China are just like an individual, always recalling to mind first, the best friend in time of misfortune. During the European war, the United States has distinguished herself to lead the world to justice and liberty. She contributed a large share in the victory over Germany and restoring peace to the world. Her supremacy is recognized by the whole world. She has the ideals, the power, and the position to stand for the right against wrong and justice against force. The United States can help China to overcome all kinds of difficulties. The United States has been the benefactor of the Armenians, the helper to the Polish, and a sympathetic supporter of the Irish. She has helped China many times in the past, and there is no reason why she will not lend a helping hand in the future.

The rise of a new power in the Pacific Ocean with militaristic authority imperialistic in policy is certainly a menace to the Unted States, especially to her possessions, the Philippines and Hawaii, and the States on the Pacific Coast. If China were to be left without any help out of her difficulties, be annexed by other powers, they utilizing the vast resources and man power, a militaristic government would undoubtedly be a great danger to the future peace of Pacific waters. To help China to build a strong democratic government would mean a check to imperialism and militarism. China a republic and her people liberal and peace-loving, the existence of an independent China is in reality a common good to the world. With her vast territory and an immense population possessing the highest intelligence and energy of the race, China will surely become one of the greatest powers in the world. When the two sister republics on both sides of the Pacific work hand in hand they will undoubtedly dictate to the world in the promotion of peace, humanity and justice.

(We are indebted to "The Far Eastern Republic" for the above article.)

Heart of Gold   By Helen Frazee-Bower

Two Roses bloomed by a garden wall,
　Where summer Zephyrs played,
The one was crimson, fair and tall;
The other piuk and oh, so small,
It hardly seemed a Rose at all!—
　So bashful and afraid.

And could it be these different two
　Bore yet a kindred name?
The stately flower, of flaming hue,
With petals spread to drink the dew,
And the tiny bud, so pink and new,—
　How could they be the same?

The heart of every Rose is gold,
Whate'er its petals hide:
Pink, crimson, white—the buds unfold
A Heart of Gold inside!

Then let me bloom by Life's Garden Wall,
　As the dreams of Life unfold:
And if the blossoms be but small
And frail,—I shall not mind at all,
If only the petals, as they fall,
　Reveal a Heart of Gold.

Does America Menace the Advance of Democracy in Japan?

By K. K. Kawakami

(Mr. Kawakami is a resident of San Francisco, and is, perhaps, the leading writer on Japanese affairs in the United States. His books and articles have attracted world-wide attention. I do not hesitate to say that Mr. Kawakami will become one of the greatest factors in preserving intelligent and friendly relationships between the Occident and the Orient. We are indebted to him, and to the Macmillan Company, for the following article, which is taken from his book, just out, "Japan and World Peace." The title is our own, and we feel that it should suggest to many people, whose attitude toward Japan is biased and unjust, as well as ignorant and discourteous, what might be the effect upon the life of Japan if such an attitude became persistent, continuous and increasingly aggravating.)

PROFESSOR ISOWO ABE, the greatest authority on social problems in Japan, writes concerning the spread of Socialism in Japan as follows:

"Socialistic ideas have been widely diffused throughout the empire in the past five years, and scholars and statesmen are, in increasing numbers, devoting themselves to its study, while a great many students are interested in the subject. It would be a great mistake to judge the influence of Socialism from the yet small number of professed Socialists only. The Socialistic spirit is afloat everywhere. To what, then, is the fact attributable, that the political movement of the Socialists is yet very insignificant in influence? Certainly to the narrow limitation in suffrage, by virtue of which a large number of Socialists have no qualification to participate in the elections. Once the scope of suffrage is enlarged, their activities will be brilliant. It is for this reason that they are now crying for the adoption of suffrage."

After all has been said about the unsatisfactory condition of politics in Japan, it is fair to admit that democracy does not grow over night like Topsy. We, who know how long it took England to reach her present stage of political freedom, must not be impatient with the apparently slow progress of democratic ideals in Japan. Considering the short period in which Japan has transformed her political system, we cannot but admire the courage and the singleness of purpose with which her leaders have devoted their energies to the difficult task of rehabilitation. What has already been done is remarkable and promises greater achievement for the days to come.

Few nations have turned to outside influences with a more sensitive front as have the Japanese. The efforts they made upon the opening of their country to adapt themselves to the ideas and customs of the advanced peoples of the West were almost pathetic in their steadfastness of purpose. The supreme end to which those prodigious efforts were bent was, of course, the elevation of their country to the plane of the Western nations, which assumed an air of authority over them. The laws were codified in accordance with the modern principles of jurisprudence; their time-honored social usages and customs were modified so as to bring them more or less into harmony with Western ideas; foreign dress became the official dress, both for men and women, in the imperial court and in the various departments of the government; the use of English was encouraged throughout the country; even Christianity, which had long been under the ban of the government, began to receive official recognition, if not encouragement. All this was not without its comical aspect, but no one will deny to the Japanese well-deserved credit for their determination to attain equality with the civilized nations of the West. Through all its apparently flippancy the outstanding quality of the Japanese reveals itself, and that is their extreme sensitiveness to external forces, and their ability to adjust themselves to new conditions of life which they deem beneficial or inevitable. If this quality is turned to good use, as it has been in the past, Japan's political ideals and her governmental system, will, in due season, receive a salutary evolution.

Japan's continuous struggle for existence against formidable and powerful neighbors has been an important factor in retarding the progress of democracy in that country. When she opened her doors to foreigners she was at once confronted by aggressive powers threatening her integrity and independence. Naturally the first task she was compelled to undertake was the organization of a centralized government, which seemed, under the circumstances, best suited to secure national security. The war with China of 1895 was, from the Japanese point of view, entirely a war of self-preservation. China, then regarded as a sleeping giant, infinitely more powerful than Japan, had been determined to annex Korea, whose independence was deemed essential to the existence of Japan. The war ended in Japan's victory, and China accepted Japanese demands, which were by no means exhorbitant. Then Germany, France and Russia combined their influence to deprive the Japanese of the fruits of their victory. This again impelled them to fortify their position in a military sense to cope with powers that had no scruples in trespassing upon the rights of Japan. Japan's fear of the West became even more intense when, only three years after the Chinese war, those very powers which had compelled her to surrender what she had rightfully secured from China, began to slice China into large sections for themselves. Russia, in particular proved so audacious as to appropriate for herself the very territory that she had, in the name of the peace of the Far East,

advised Japan to surrender. Not satisfied with the absorption of Manchuria, Russia cast covetous eyes toward the peninsula of Korea. Had Korea been annexed by the aggressive military power of Russia the fate of Japan would have been sealed. In combatting Russia in the arena of Manchuria, Japan was inspired by no other motives than those of self-preservation.

Few nations have had such a tremendous existence as Japan has had in the past half century. She has been pulled by external forces to a height for which she was not internally prepared. What wonder that she has been going forward with makeshifts improvised as necessity dictates? Such circumstances are not conducive to the growth of democracy.

To the Liberals of Japan, these critical times are a period of suspense, of doubt, of apprehension. They entertain sincere doubt as to the nature of the new age which is to dawn upon the ruins of the war. How will the tremendous armament which the war called into existence be retrenched? How will the powers dispose of the gigantic fleets of warships which they have built and are building? Will they agree to put their dreadnaughts and their guns upon the scrap heap? And, again, what will become of the magnificent fleets of merchant vessels which the nations have built for the transportation of troops and war supplies? Will they become a formidable factor in the international rivalry for commercial supremacy?—a rivalry which, no one can be sure, will not develop into an armed conflict, as has too often happened in the past. These are the questions which the Japanese advocates of liberalism are constantly asking. What they are particularly concerned with at present is the possible attitude of the powers toward China after the conclusion of peace.

In such a mental state of apprehension and doubt prevailing among the Japanese, the Imperialists of Japan will undoubtedly find a receptive ground to sew the seeds of militarism. Whether the cause of democracy in Japan will be promoted after the war, therefore, must, to no small extent, depend upon the attitude of the powers toward the Orient.

If, after the war, the Western powers continue to deal with the Orient as they have in the past been accustomed to deal, the cry of "preparedneess" will continue to be the dominant note, in the opinion of the leading men of Japan. Not long ago an Occidental writer declared that the "only Chinese question that exists is, what the Powers of Europe will decide to do with China." If such continues to be the attitude of the Powers, its effect upon Japanese internal politics cannot but be unfortunate. For it will furnish the military party a convenient pretext not only to keep a large army and navy, but for them to foster imperalistic ideas as against the progress of liberalism and democracy.

A Chinaman's Impressions of Japan

By S. C. Kiang Kang-Hu

(Mr. Kiang Kang-Hu, who is now with the University of California, was formerly a professor in the Peking Government University. We are indebted to him, and to the new journal of The Chinese National Welfare Society of America—"THE FAR EASTERN REPUBLIC"—for this article, which, we believe, represents the attitude of the true China toward Japan. We believe that in both countries this spirit will ultimately prevail, bringing about the unity and the co-operation of the great peoples of the Orient, a unity upon which the great peace of the future will depend.)

WHAT is the first impression of a Chinese when he visits Japan," I was asked by an American friend. To answer the question I am forced to say that the impression varies with different individuals, with the time of the visit, and with the various parts of Japan visited. All I can do in the way of giving a definite answer is to indicate what my impressions were when I first landed at Nagasaki some years ago.

After a sea voyage of thirty-six hours from Shanghai I reached Japan, landing with a preconceived notion of Japan as a foreign land, thick with modern European ideas and customs. Judge my surprise, then, to find here instead an old Chinese colony, a reincarnation of the life described in the Confucian classics and Chinese ancient history, and which exists today nowhere but in Japan!

When I read the Chinese classics and histories before the T'ang dynasty, I found, as I suppose all Chinese students do, that many of the things there described are now impracticable. Some are even unintelligible to us. In the Book of Rites we find such expressions as "Before entering a house, shoes must be removed"; "To speak to a superior, one must first kneel down and then proceed toward him"; "Never sit with the legs crossed"; "Man and woman, if not husband and wife, even though relatives, are not allowed to sit at the same dinner table;" "Every night a dutiful son must ask his parents toward which direction the bed should be set," etc. All these and many others are, of course, impracticable under present conditions of life in China, and I have wondered why they were ever practiced.

In the ancient histories, too, we read many stories that seem queer to us now. For instance, Lu chi of the Three Kingdoms period, when a child, received a gift of oranges, and he kept them in his sleeve to take home to his parents. Kuang ning, of the same period, sat respectfully even when alone. The seat on which his knees touched formed two hollows. Hsieh An, of the Ch'in dynasty, climbed mountains and broke the front teeth of his shoes. There is also the story in Meng tzu about the shoe thief, and one in Chuang-tzu about a famous scholar whose doorway was blocked with the shoes of his visitors!

All these old proverbs and customs are brought back to us and made clear by a visit to Japan, for the ancient customs, the food, clothing and dwellings that have been gradually and entirely lost in China since the T'ang dynasty are still preserved in Japan. In Japan we discover that the word for dinner table, "hsi," was not originally meant for dinner table at all, but for "mat," which in Japanese is "tatami." The word for skirt, "shang," is in Japanese "hakama," which means a dress common to both sexes; while the word for shoe, "lu" or "chi," is in Japanese "geda," which has two rows of teeth, one in front and the other in back, of the sole, and the shoes must be removed when entering a house. The sleeves of the ancient Chinese dress were large, like those of the modern Japanese kimono, and could hold things much as do pockets. The expression "to sit," " tso," was used as though it had the same meaning as "to kneel," since there were no chairs or stools, and the respectful way of sitting was to kneel on the mat. When chairs and stools were invented, at the end of the Chin dynasty, the Chinese failed to originate a new word for "high seat" to indicate the change. The Japanese used the Chinese character "kwei," which means "to hang," to indicate "high seat" or a seat on a chair or stool, as distinguished from the old custom of sitting on a mat. This odd use of the character "to hang" is indeed rather queer and even laughable.

Not only are these ancient customs and words preserved by the Japanese, but even the ancient Chinese pronunciations, not preserved by the Chinese themselves. Many Chinese characters which, in ancient times, began with the same initials are now written with different ones, and many which were rhymed in ancient poetry are now different in the finals. These can still be traced, however, in the Japanese pronunciation. All of the fifth tones which ended with the consonant sounds "K," "P," "T," are now dropped from the Chinese language except in the Cantonese dialect, but they are still preserved and distinctly pronounced in Japanese. It seems probable that the preservation of these old pronunciations in the Japanese, while great changes were undergone in the Chinese, is due to the adoption of the "kana" or Japanese alphabets. It is remarkable, however, to see also many preservations in Japanese of the old written forms and meanings of Chinese characters.

My first impression of Japan, then, was that everything was Chinese—the old Chinese—except only those customs from the West that appeared on the surface. Not only that, but what is commonly known to the world, and conceded even by the Japanese, is that the philosophy of Wang yang ming is the keynote to the success of modern Japan; the test of the Mikado's edict which becomes the Bible of the Japanese state religion is based on the Confucian teachings; while Japanese literature and art are legitimate off-springs from the Chinese. If from the spirit, thought, tradition and superstitions of the Japanese as a whole we take away all that is Chinese, there will be little left except a few recent importations from the Occident.

The reason that Japan is, or was, so largely Chinese in character is explained by the same conditions that cause us to find in America, for example, many things English in character. The new Japanese race, the conquerors of the aboriginal Ainos, is approximately 40 per cent Chinese, 40 per cent Korean, and 20 per cent Malay. And as Korea is 90 per cent Chinese, it is, of course, obvious that the Japanese are more than 7 per cent Chinese in blood. The Chinese Taoist expedition to Japan, comprising 5,000 boys and girls under the command of Hsu Fu, in the Ch'in dynasty, is one of the few historical illustrations showing the origin of the new Japanese people.

When I first visited Japan I felt as though I was entering the T'ao yuan— the country described by the great poet T'ao Ch'ien, who told of an ideal life away from the world—of the inhabitants whose ancestors took refuge in a mountain cave in the Ch'in dynasty about the same time when Hsu Fu colonizeed the Three Divine Islands.

In spite of all these historical proofs, blood identifications and sympathetic feelings, Japan is now, however, very different from China. Her interests are now diametrically opposed to those of China. Since the centuries she has been separated from the main continent, and so developed into the disposition and type of an island nation of the European

—chiefly Hun—type, though small and new, has gained such a hold upon the Japanese people that it will never be loosened except by bitter lesson or an unusual change in the attitude of the people. It is a difficult task to lead a straying son back to his father's bosom while he is still enjoying his "run-away-from-home" life.

I can not but deeply regret the attitude and policy of Japanese statesmen, especially the militarists, toward China. It is a grave mistake and a great wrong to Japan as well as to China. Japan will be crowned with world success if she but accepts and treats China as a member of the same family. She will be at peace when she learns how to treat the Chinese as neighbors and friends, but if she persists in regarding the Chinese as enemies and subjects, Japan will surely perish sooner or later.

While I am grieved over the present antagonism and hostility existing between these two, the only independent Eastern nations, I reflect more and more on my first impression of Japan and the warm welcome and good friendship there. Tokyo was once the home of 20,000 Chi-

nese students, and Peking Imperial University had more than twenty Japanese professors, many of them heads of departments. Japanese scholars were received in every province of China, both in the government and private schools. They taught zealously to repay the instructions and civilizations their ancestors received from China. Chinese students and the people of China as a whole respected and loved them. What a change now!

Those Chinese who hate and attack the Japanese most bitterly are the very ones who for years studied in Japan! No Chinese may make friends with a Japanese without incurring the criticism of his own people. Who is responsible for this? Have the Japanese statesmen, especially the militarists, so much improved the relationship between China and Japan over those that existed twenty years ago? They have, instead, succeeded in incurring the ill-will and hatred of 400,000,000 people, and the jealousy and suspicion of the whole world. Along with this they have acquired a few pitiful possessions which are poisonous for her to digest.

An American's Impression of Japan

By W. D. Wheelwright

(Mr. W. D. Wheelwright is an Oregon business man, who knows Japan and who recently visited that country. We are indebted to him and to the "Oregon Voter" for the following interesting article.)

ARRIVING at Yokohama on the 11th day of December in a hailstorm, we shortly found clear skies there, and in Tokio — sixteen miles distant — a city of 3,000,000 people, which is now planning to follow the example of New York, London and other modern cities and to develop suddenly, by the annexation of contiguous small communities, into one of 9,000,000 inhabitants, thus making it the largest city in the world. It has now many of the aspects of the great modern municipalities of Europe and America, but still

has its own distinctive Oriental atmosphere, which, however, is disappearing somewhat as the progressive people adopt Western methods. One characteristic, at least, it has in the possession of which it might well be envied by some of our most highly civilized communities, which distinguishes it as "the safest city in the world," as is shown by the fact that the young women of the Y. W. C. A. go about its streets, in rickshaws, in trams or on their feet, alone and unattended, at all hours of the day or night in that vast city, made up of aliens, with every assurance of perfect safety because in all their errands of love and mercy they have never suffered insult or injury in a single instance.

In all Japan there was no sign of anything like race suicide; the late Theodore Roosevelt would have used his favorite ejaculation at every corner, as he contemplated the hordes of happy children, tended by their parents with the most assiduous care and with manifestations of parental love that are at times positively affecting. And, here at the start, we have one of the most serious problems that confront the Japanese people, an alert, vigorous and unusually prolific race, inhabiting a group of islands that have an area of 161,000 square miles, only a very small proportion of which consists of arable land, numbering (in 1900) some 50,000,000 people, whose chief occupation was put down in the encyclopedia as agriculture; with the gates of most modern civilized countries and their dependencies closed against their emigrants, let me ask you "what are they to do?" The extent and seriousness of their struggle for existence become apparent when you compare Japan with our own garden State of Minnesota, whose area of 83,000 square miles is called on to support only a little over 2,000,000 people —some twenty-five to the square mile, as against 308 to the same space in Japan, where only 15 per cent of the soil is arable, or over 2,000 people to the square mile of fertile land! This difficulty is met, as far as possible, by the transformation of the Japanese people from an agricultural nation into one of manufactures, who import a large proportion of their food supplies and pay for them by the products of their factories. Great Britain had done this before the fateful days of 1914—almost to her endless sorrow; Germany, more far-seeing, while developing her manufactures, made strenuous efforts to bring the volume of her food products up to the point of self-support, and but for the hard and arid soil of Prussia would have succeeded in so doing. She came very near it as it was, and the kaiser announced in 1907, or thereabouts, that she had accomplished it. This war has demonstrated the importance to each nation of having the capacity to support itself, at least in case of emergency; Japan considers it essential to her safey (and who shall say, with the fate of the League of Nations hanging in the balance, that she is wrong?) that she should have control of territory from which she can garner a harvest sufficient to feed her people without aid from any outside power.

One such opportunity she found in Korea, which was annexed by Japan about ten years ago (as the result of negotiation and not by conquest) to the great material benefit of Korea and of its people. The construction of railroads, the modernization of the old cities by the erection of imposing buildings, the making of streets and sewers, the organization of suitable police forces, the introduction of gas, electric lights, tram cars and proper sanitation and the establishment of banks in which the Koreans are depositing their money freely instead of burying it in the ground, are giving the natives advantages that they never had before and never would have had under their own rule. But it is equally true, as it was inevitable, that there was, and is, some discontent among the native population. Such dissatisfaction was till recently confined almost entirely to a small portion of the people who are not absolutely indifferent to the personnel of the government under which they live, but this proportion has been increased by the activities of agitators who are at all times opposed to all government, whether just or unjust, stimulated by certain indiscreet utterances in high places which have seemed to advocate the rights of men and all peoples to govern themselves, whether they are fit to do so or not, without curtailment of their power to misgovern themselves so as to bring calamity to their neighbors.

Unquestionably there has been undue severity in the suppression of disorders in Korea. The Japanese adminstrator in Korea has admitted the fact and has denounced the harsh measures adopted by some of his subordinates, and has declared that punishment shall be inflicted upon the guilty ones, some of whom already are under arrest. The Nichi-Nichi;

a partisan Japanese newspaper, in an editorial says:

"The disturbances have now spread all over the peninsula—a condition without precedent since Korea passed under Japanese sway, and we cannot refrain from saying that although the present disturbances may be pacified by arms, it is impossible to expect that the spiritual upheaval of the Koreans, due to the new current of thought running all over the world, will be so easily set to rest.

"The immediate cause of the disturbances lies in the misconception on the part of the Koreans of the principle of self-determination of peoples. Unscrupulous agitators duped the Koreans into believing that President Wilson had already recognized Korea as a republic, and, believing blindly in the truth of this report they organized demonstrations. This was the beginning of the present riots in Korea, equally unfortunate for them and for us."

The Diving Girl

By Charles Horace Meiers

Nymph-like upon the plank she stands,
Then smoothly glides, with outstretched hands,
Into the arms of Neptune, there
To shed the burden of her care.

And I aver that Neptune is
In luck to hold such sphere as his;
For she possesses many charms,
And must be welcome in his arms.

But, were I Neptune, I should be
So sad when she was gone from me
That I would overrun the beach,
In hope my absent love to reach.

Neptune might hold her fast some day,
So that she could not get away,
In mad desire to keep such grace
Forever in his fond embrace.

But, though he pressed her body cold,
All Neptune's power could not hold
That charm which sinks not in the sea—
The spirit, which from death is free!

Breaking It Gently

By Ray St. Vrain

"YOU tell her, Bill," said Longlegs. "Why me any mor'n you?"

"You tell her, McGeehan," said One Eye.

"Tell her yourself," McGeehan flung back. "I guess I'm as human as the next one."

And so it went on down the line of the dozen or more miners of Charlietown, everyone only too willing for the other fellow to do the telling, until the last man was reached — Nugget Casey, the youngest, biggest, strongest, most diffident of the bunch.

"It's up to you, Nug," grinned one of the boys. "If your lips can't say it to Missus Charlie, your eyes can. Them sky-blue blinks of yourn was made to break just this kind of news—and break it gently."

Nugget Casey's sky-blue eyes, under the sudden frown, looked a shade darker. "I reckon we'll play this here thing square. Anyone of us'd rather die than tell Missus Charlie. So none of us is going to lay down the law about the other fellow telling her. We'll draw straws. The shortest is the unlucky man."

It was over in a minute, and Fate picked Nugget Casey himself. Immediately the others began condoling with him, But he silenced them peremptorily. "Noth- to it, fellows. Why, maybe it'll be pie. All according to the sort Missus Charlie is."

There was no stage running between Charlietown and Buffalo Creek, two tnou- sand feet down the mountain, the nearest railroad station, but Nugget Casey, after tinkering half a day with his 1912 flivver, had coaxed it to run. The boys waved him an encouraging goodbye as the old boat laboriously and squeakingly sailed away, reminding him—half a dozen voices at once—that he had drawn the shortest straw, and that he ought to be man enough to tell her before she reached Charlietown. "Don't let's have no scene," begged Longlegs. "It's up to you, Nug, to provide her a dignified advent." Nug just raised a saucy cloud of dust.

It was coasting all the way down to Buffalo Creek—easy going for the 1912 rattler. The train was an hour late and then only one passenger alighted — a woman, young, pretty, modishly attired, carrying a smart alligator suitcase — Missus Charlie, of course. Nugget Casey felt the sudden blood up at his hairline. A dazzling smile irradiated the atmos- phere and an eager voice said:

"I'm sure you're here to take me up to Charlietown—but where's Charlie?"

Nugget said something—he didn't know exactly what. He had read of multiple personalities. As he spoke he had the notion that maybe the curious breed of psychologists were right, after all, and that a secondary personality had laid Nugget Casey low for the moment and was jumping right up on the job and as- suming the prerogative with a capital P.

"Charlie's gone to the Hogback to see Joe Smith, a sick friend of his," said Mr. Secondary Personality. "Maybe Joe's croaking—and maybe Charlie won't be back till night. Charlie's crazy good- hearted; brother's keeper business and all that. He's mighty sorry he can't be here. I'm Charlie's shackmate and bunkie." And out went the rehearsed fingers.

Missus Charlie grasped them heartily —with a second edition of that world- transforming smile. "You're Francis Xavier Casey, nicknamed Nugget, aren't you? Well, there's nobody I'd rather be looking at right now than Nugget Casey —except Charlie—"

"I reckon, yes," agreed Nugget solemnly. Then he took up the alligator and led the way to the flivver. "A rheumatic old 1912, Missus Charlie," he apologized. "She squeaks and jerks and lunges and rattles and balks. But it's some walk up to Charlietown—and we can imagine we're riding anyway." He explained there was more room in the back seat but fewer jolts in the front, if she didn't mind sitting by him—which she didn't at all. So he put her things in the "tony"—that's what he called it—then helped her in, cranked heroically; the old engine responding, and they started gayly off. Immediately Missus Charlie began chatting in the friendliest way, lauding the boat on the strenuous manner in which it attacked the hill, admiring the scenery, thanking whoever it was that had named Charlietown for her own Charlie—and, by the way—Charlie was well, wasn't he?—and fat?—and brown? —and longing for Missus Charlie?

"You know it's six long months since he left me to come away up here to timberline," she said with the shake in her voice that Nugget had been dreading, "and we'd been married only a little while then. Maybe you don't know what that means—but surely you can realize I'm wild to see him and—"

"I knew it!" exclaimed Nugget at a sudden shot-like sound, applying the reluctant old emergency brake and leaping out. "That left-hand hind tire's blowed out just as I foresaw."

"How interesting!" laughed Missus Charlie.

She alighted and insisted on helping him jack up the car. He had never had such enthusiastic — if bungling — assistance; and he would have been sorry the operation wasn't to last all day if she hadn't begun talking of Charlie again. She asked him a lot of questions that turned him faint, but he bent over the exploded tire doggedly, at last reminding her a bit testily that mending blowouts wasn't any picnic and talking was simply out of the question. After that Missus Charlie just looked on—sympathetically.

The old 1912 pulled up the mean grade corkingly after that, and when they reached the level plateau that led to Charlietown, Nugget gave her gas and they tore in spectacularly, scattering Longlegs, McGeehan, One Eye and the rest, who were picturesquely on hand to greet the first white lady that had ever invaded Charlietown.

The boys all stood in a ring-around-a-rosy circle, doffed their headgears and almost bowed to the ground, their faces no redder than before.

"Welcome to Charlietown, Missus Charlie," tremulously began One Eye. "We're sorry—"

"Sorry?" boomed Nugget Casey, catapulting toward him from his seat beside Missus Charlie. "What have we got to be sorry for? Just because we ain't got a brass band here to meet our honored visitor—and so on? Come, One Eye, use your brains—Missus Charlie's not looking for New York attractions at timberline."

The boys flashed puzzled glances at one another. What was all this apocryphal gassing of Nugget Casey's about? Hadn't he told her about Charlie? Of course not—look at that smile on her pretty face. Well, then—

But Nugget was asking Missus Charlie to wait right where she was for a couple of minutes; then he signed to the others to follow him behind One Eye's shack. Then he turned on them fiercely, exploding in pent whispers:

"Now, don't nobody say a word. None of you could have done any different. I've got a hundred on my clothes that I'll give to the first one that'll go out there and tell her the truth about Charlie. Look at that face on her. Was there ever another such face created by God Almighty? How could I tell her—looking into them eyes, stalled by that smile? Well, then. Now, I'm not forgetting I drew the shortest straw; I'm going to tell her—but not yet. We're going to let her get unpacked first—let her sit down in a rocking chair—and take a look at these glorious mountains—and get to calling us by our names—then, when the sun dips over Schoolgirl hill, I'll take her two little hands in mine and tell her about Charlie."

There was mysterious whisperings pro and con, while One Eye used his solitary peeper' round the corner of the shack to see that Missus Charlie kept her seat and did not wander towards them. But suddenly Longlegs startled everybody with a belated piece of aptness:

"You say, Nugget, you want the lady to set down in a rocking chair and so forth. Fine. But where? Not in Charlie's shack, surely?"

"Lord, no," gasped Nugget—as the others groaned.

Longlegs smiled—he liked the role of damper. "Ain't no lady's house to take her to—Charlietown's a stage town, as all of us know. Can't take her to my shack, or yours, or anybody else's. Charlietown's out of the world; but decency's decency. I reckon you'll agree a lady's sometimes a white elephant. You want to wait till sunset to tell Missus Charlie about Charlie—well, she can't set in the fliv till then, can she? She wants to wash up; mebbe she desires a siesta—certainly she'll want that rocking chair you mentioned so eloquent. And how about a meal of victuals? Now, since Black Violetta's left us high and dry and the mess house is no more, there ain't a decent cook in the place—"

"Shut up, will you?" growled Nugget Casey. "Where'd you get so many words? Listen, boys; I've got an inspiration. There's that elegant little shack poor Jimsie lived in before he moved out to the City of the Dead. It's empty, but why can't we move the best all of us have into the place and fix up a regular home for Missus Charlie? She—"

"Jest for her to set in till sunset — while you're screwing up your nerve?" cut in Longlegs incredulously.

"'Till sunset? All night, you mean," corrected Nugget. "That's only humanity —imagine her over at Charlie's tonight! What d'ye say, boys? Can't we fix her up an Exclusive Ladies' Hotel as an emergency measure?"

Certainly they could; and they proceeded to prove it. So Missus Charlie, perched up in the old 1912, saw diverting doings—a bed brought from this shack, a table from that, a strip of rag carpet from another; chairs, lamps, a kitchen stove, dishes, pots and pans; a sofa covered with a Navajo blanket, a Bible—

carried solemnly and sowewhat ostentatiously by One Eye, and other stuff— stacks of it. In half an hour everything was ready, so fast did those boys work; and Nugget Casey, whom a post-impressionist would have painted just then as one world-embracing grin, garnished with illusory bits of a human face, came up to the car to escort Missus Charlie to the shack of poor Jimsie, who had taken up quarters in the City of the Dead, incidentally the sole inhabitant of that sinister town, as the one wooden slab up on Schoolgirl hill testified.

"It's all fixed," Nugget said bloomingly. "You'll find it chock full of all the comforts of home."

Missus Charlie was pardonably puzzled. "Mighty nice of you, Mr. Francis Xavier Casey, nicknamed Nugget. But what's the matter with Charlie's house—the one you and he occupied?" Nugget hesitated. "Where is it?" she persisted.

"There—" pointing to one on the edge of the cluster standing slightly apart, curtains covering the two niggardly windows, the door inhospitably closed—and locked, one would have wagered.

"But why have you taken all this trouble? Take me to Charlie's; he'll expect to find me there when he comes back—won't he?" Nugget still hesitated. "There must be something the matter with—maybe you fear it's not in condition to receive me. Nonsense! I'll get to work and clean it; I know how men hate housework—they're busy at other things. You, Mr. Nugget, may help me—"

"It's—it's not that, exactly," stammered Nugget. "It's the—the mountain rats—"

"Mountain rats? Horrors!"

"Exactly — horrors and no mistake — twice as fierce as ordinary rats, three times as hungry, five times as big!"

That settled it. Missus Charlie accompanied Nugget Casey to the Exclusive Ladies' Hotel without further objections. On the way he cheerfully promised to get after the mountain rats with a shotgun in the morning. "That'll scatter 'em, I reckon," he said. "They hate shotguns. Meanwhile let's forget 'em."

The Exclusive Ladies' Hotel was a sight—also a sort of mystic maze. The two rooms of poor Jimsie's shack were literally piled with junk—the only word. Four tables, fifteen chairs, three wash-tubs, two Pharaoh's horses and a tragically incomplete St. Cecilia—these were random items picked from the medley of household wreckage that the Charlietown boys in their mad enthusiasm had stuffed, packed, jammed into Jimsie's.

"Beautiful!" cried Missus Charlie with that God's-angel smile of hers. "I could live here forever and be happy—"

"Wait one small little minute," put in Damper Longlegs triumphantly. "We ain't forgotten nothing but the unforgettables. Where's the eats?"

All looked at one another, then at Nugget Casey, who blushed like a windy sunset. "It ain't that we ain't got the eats," he gravely delivered, "it's just that we're chipmunk-brained fools. Scat, boys, to your various mansions and scrape your cupboards. Missus Charlie's human, which means prone to hunger." And Nugget was the first one out of the house, the rest whooping it after.

But Damper Longlegs was on the job throwing wet blankets. "Ain't this mirth unseemly, as the poet remarks?" he inquired of Nugget on the run. "What about poor Charlie? Won't she hold it agin us after everything's out?"

"Crossing bridges," sniffled Nugget. "Besides, ain't this a tonic treatment—giving her something to fall back on when I tell her about Charlie? Wring your blankets, Longlegs—hang 'em out to dry."

In five minutes just about all the presentable eatables in Charlietown had been transported to the Exclusive Ladies' Hotel—from flour and frying compounds to canned chile con carne and potted cheese. The delectable conglomeration inspired Missus Charlie with a brilliant thought, designed to ravish hungry timberliners:

"Boys, what do you say? Charlie insists I'm almost as good a cook as his dead mother. Do you think a square meal would taste civilized again? Also how many of you don't like pie and hot biscuit? Now, if that stove will only draw—"

Draw? That little old-fashioned box cooker? Longlegs himself—blanketless

for once—would vouch for it—it'd draw like a March wind through the Narrows on Moonshine Gulch—and he'd prove it by making the fire himself.

The little stove lived up to his encomiums—it drew like a tornado. Missus Charlie, happy as a child, put a big barber-like apron over her finery and proceeded to cook the finest dinner Charlietown could remember—shaming Black Violetta's best efforts in the mess house's palmiest days. Nugget Casey saw to the souring of the canned milk on the champion cooker, and they had—O, luxury!—sour-milk-and-soda biscuit; and big, deep apple pies made from canned apples that tasted like the orchard itself; and too many other palate-tickelers for one to tell about.

Then they sat down to the feast, and, of course, Missus Charlie, flushed and beautiful, had to say with a heart-breaking sigh:

"Oh, if Charlie were only here—!"

Then a silence fell on the board, and those of the Charlietowners who could look through the window at Charlie's shack did so. Nugget Casey almost grew pale, and the biscuit going down his throat met something coming up. Longlegs, the wet blanketer, seemed on the point of unfurling his specialty, but a fierce glare from Casey's sky-blue eyes changed his mind. Missus Charlie, fearing that her frequent reference to Charlie's absence smacked of ingratitude to these boys who were doing the honors for him so gloriously, suddenly determined to let him rest for a while, so she plunged into the smallest and gayest sort of chatter, astonishing and charming Charlie's friends, lifting the oppression that had begun to hang like a cloud over Nugget Casey, and playing havoc with Longleg's blankets.

So the meal went off to a fizzling finale. One Eye produced the pop from some movie serial secret panel in his shack, and after a dozen healths to Missus Charlie, and a dozen sneaking looks through the window at Charlie's lonesome shack, all but Nugget Casey backed off and made a flourishy getaway. By tacit agreement they had decided that now was Nugget's time to vindicate his drawing of the smallest straw and "tell" Missus Charlie.

Nugget, unmistakably nervous, suggested that he wash the dishes. Missus Charlie would not hear to this. She had a counter proposal—suppose they take a walk? Fine. Nugget loved walking.

They had a good long walk. He showed her everything in Charlietown—the several shafts, the shaft house, the mill, the electric plant, the big slag dump—

"And why isn't anybody working?" she asked, puzzled.

"Sunday, ma'am—didn't you know?"

She had forgotten all about it—wasn't that jolly? And where was the Hogback —was that its name?—the place where Charlie was tending his sick friend? And Nugget Casey told her with a staggering mass of details and great splashes of local color, talking half an hour about the Hogback so she couldn't ask any questions about Joe Smith, who was croaking. But she asked many anyway. And then he shook her very soul with grisly tales of poor Joe's suffering. It would be a merciful death. "I reckon poor old Joe—"

But she gave a little cry that switched the current. They had been absent-mindedly ascending Schoolgirl hill, and suddenly Missus Charlie spied a field of columbines, a lavender glory, impinging on a belated snowdrift.

"Oh, how beautiful!"

Immediately Nugget gathered her an armful, and then he told her of the delicate bluebells, the flaming artist's brush, the sand-lilies that came later in the summer, and thus he put in another half hour of Charlie-less chat, at the end of which Missus Charlie, forgetting her late resolve, said heartfully:

"Charlie has written me so much about these wonderful timberline flowers!"

And then Nugget, desperate, seized her hands, gazed deep into her eyes, told her—almost. Almost! His lips trembled, his great, powerful hands pressing hers, murdered them; then he fell into a furious inarticulateness — chaos — let out a hair-raising "Damnation!" broke from her and ran wildly up over the snowy apex of Schoolgirl hill, out of her startled sight, away—leaving the columbines scattered

on the ground, some of the queenliest of the blooms crushed by his ruthless boot. And Missus Charlie, after coming to, wondered where the Hogback was and how she could get there.

An hour later, at sunset, Nugget Casey, flushed, smiling strangely, his eyes gleaming with a hard brilliance, sought Missus Charlie at the Exclusive Ladies' Hotel, took her two hands again and began leading her outside.

"Where?" she asked, struck by the change in him.

"To—Charlie's."

"Charlie's!" she screamed. "He's at the shack-"

"Waiting for you."

She would have broken into a run, but Nugget still held one of her hands tightly. Charlie's door was closed; she hazily wondered why. The Hogback was miles away—he had footed it home; he was tired; lying down, maybe; but that wasn't like Charlie; Charlie would have crawled to meet her—

"He's tired to death?" she queried. "Lying down?"

"Yes," said Nugget Casey in curiously hushed tones, "lying down."

And that's the way they found Charlie when his shackmate and bunkie opened the door—lying down, dead. Not only dead was Charlie, but laid out, and looking so lifelike in his strong and beautiful youth you knew without being told that he had been stricken without warning.

But Nugget Casey told Missus Charlie anyway—in choked, husky tones:

"It was his heart—last night—we was foot-racing, him and I, like fools—fools because Charlie knew his heart was weak —the high altitude had almost got him before. We're doing a hundred-yard dash—Charlie's in the lead—snap! goes his heart all of a sudden—and then Charlie sags—falls—never to get up again. The boys and me, we who loved Charlie, we was cowards and we hated to tell you, clampin' widowhood down on you then and there. I drew the shortest straw and it was up to me to do the telling— but Lord help me, ain't I the biggest coward of the bunch?"

Missus Charlie, paler than the pale man on the cot, just kept her wide eyes fastened on Charlie's peacefully closed ones—trembling like the one stunted aspen on Schoolgirl hill—paying not the least attention to Nugget Casey, who, in tones always huskier, told her his stark little story again—again—again. And then, when at last she drew a long, fluttering breath and glanced Casey's way and saw him taking a surreptitious swallow from a bottle already half empty—when he crowned his cruel silence with this unforgivable act, there in Charlie's presence, she rushed to the door, before falling on the dead man's breast, flung it open and then in uncontrollable rage ordered his shackmate and bunkie to leave. And the shackmate and bunkie, paling suddenly to Charlie's own whiteness, took his bottle, hung his head, held his tongue—left.

Outside was one of the gray lichened rocks that strewed Charlietown. With an oath Nugget Casey broke the neck of the bottle on it, releasing unmistakably alcoholic fumes that reached certain noses over behind One Eye's shack and made them sniff.

"Whew! Yum! Yum!" breathed One Eye. "After a year's swearing off Casey's at that old bottle again, standing there with unabridged hell on his face. And did he tell Missus Charlie with a breath like that? Boys, expostulations is in order. Come."

Nugget Casey saw them with bloodshot eyes.

"Wheel about, the crowd of you," he warned them hoarsely. "I'll murder the first man that invades my sacred right of solitude."

"Let's let him get over it," suggested McGeehan warily.

"Poor Missus Charlie," lamented Longlegs.

Aye, poor Missus Charlie! What was she doing? Weeping her heart out, a crushed little heap on the floor? Or lying tearless, prone, frozen over Charlie's big chest, her erstwhile refuge? Nugget Casey, sagged down beside the perfumed rock, wondered dully; but as the hours went by the dullness of his wonder changed to the acuteness of anxiety. No sound came from Charlie's shack, no light from the windows. The moon swung up over the hills, over the City of the Dead, where Jimsie was mayor and everything else. Midnight came—then the first of the small hours. Was Missus Charlie dead, then, dead as Charlie himself? Nugget Casey went to the door and listened. Jimsie's city was no more silent.

"Say, Missus Charlie, let a human in to say something to you," Casey said—almost. But he didn't. Instead he stood motionless and grim as a totem pole, thinking; then with a whoop—down in his soul—he went to the Exclusive Ladies' Hotel and got One Eye's Bible, rushed up on Schoolgirl hill and tore from the ground another load of the pale columbines; then, thus fortified, he returned to Charlie's and knocked on the door—stubbornly, half a dozen times.

Missus Charlie, who wasn't dead after all, at last came to the door and presented a white, stony little face with dead, staring eyes that began blazing the moment she saw that the awful, unspeakable, drunken—

"No," said Nugget Casey sweetly, "I'm sober as St. Peter." And he poked the Bible at her — and the columbines. "There's lots of Holy Scripture here in this book—and you remember how you raved over these flowers this afternoon."

The door had been closing slowly, inch by inch, the blazing eyes—

"Wait a minute, Missus Charlie — for God's sake," wailed Nugget Casey. I had to get sort of semi-drunk—is semi the word?—before I could tell you. Charlie and I was brothers. Who named this place Charlietown but me? I don't like autobiographies—and specially self-praising ones which are half-scandalous. But this is a crucial moment. Who got the fellows—a finer breed than they look—to work this old mine that fools thought was played-out on shares for Charlie, but me, rounding 'em up, whipping 'em into line, keeping 'em here at Charlietown on golden promises—who done all this, but me, I say, but me? And now who but me'll make 'em stay on here to work the mine for Missus Charlie, who'll live here in Charlie's house after Charlie is pals with Jimsie in the Silent City—"

"I'll not live here! I'll not bury Charlie

here! I'll not—I'll not—"

But she burst into life-saving tears—and Nugget Casey edged in.

"Now," he said, "we'll light the lamp and sit by Charlie—and we'll thank God we're able to do it. And the Bible's in reserve—if you need it; and these flowers—God's work too. Excuse me if I bring in God too much—it's that sort of time. Charlie loved Charlietown better'n anybody but you— Lord! ain't I got a match? There — comforting, that flare, ain't it? Where's the lamp? Sure, here— Thank God for the party that invented lamps— Yes, Charlietown was Charlie's pride. You'll put him up there in the City by Jimsie, won't you, Missus Charlie—and then stay and plant flowers on his grave—?"

Missus Charlie was crying harder than ever. "Oh, N—Nugget, oh, N—Nugget—"

"Come," said Nugget, taking her hand and leading her to Charlie, "we'll set by him now. The parson-undertaker — he's one and the same—will be here tomorrow. If he could have come today you'd have been told about Charlie decently—but he had a funeral on down in Moonshine Gulch. Old Bill Meskimen's—Bill died of old age. Charlie ever write you about him? Hundred and one in the shade. Longest whiskers you ever saw —and the tobacco that old duffer could smoke! Say, Missus Charlie, that old Bill Meskimen. . . . " And so Nugget Casey rambled on, trying desperately to soften the blow.

The next day the parson-undertaker came with the casket and a few funeral trappings—such as could be carried in his ancient flivver; and after a brief service they took Missus Charlie's Charlie up to the City of the Dead, there to be chums again with Jimsie. And Missus Charlie stayed on to plant some simple wild flowers on the grave—and on Jimsie's, too; and then she stayed longer to tend them and watch them grow, just as Nugget had prophesied; so she became the patron saint of Charlietown, dreaming of her Charlie at night and doing for the Charlietowners by day.

And when at last the boys struck it rich, and a miracle ore deposit came into view deep down in the diggings, and Charlietown boomed, and men flocked there in crowds and a real town sprang up overnight Missus Charlie still stayed on. How could she find it in her heart to leave that slimly-populated City of the Dead—and Nugget Casey?

One Sunday afternoon in the tranquil autumn of the next year they went up to Charlie's grave and talked it over—with each other and with Charlie, too. And Charlie seemed to say it was all right. So shortly thereafter the parson-undertaker came up to Charlietown on a more cheerful errand than his last. This time it was a marriage that brought him.

At the Sign of the Palm

By Ethel Kirk Grayson

HERE was no wind stirring, or any other sound to break the quiet, and yet, deep within that velvet hush, there seemed to be lingering the burden of some ill-omened, sinister mood, frought only with disaster. Stafford remained motionless; he felt that he had scarcely breathed for many minutes now, though a cold dew was standing upon his forehead, and the loud beating of his heart was distinctly audible. He wondered whether that uncanny restling would come again—and, if it should, would he have time to snatch his revolver from the table on the far side of the room? It challenged him mockingly in the lamplight. He hated to turn around, even to procure it, for the walls of nipa palm were treacherous at best, and he had mental visions of some savage Moro lying craftily in wait, or a poisoned dagger finding dexterous goal from behind the interlacing creepers. The shutters had been flung wide open, for the window was thickly screened with vines. And, as he waited cautiously, there came once more that shivering in the great heart-shaped leaves.

The young soldier sprang from his chair and seized the weapon. Now there were stealthy footsteps, a dull, muffled sound, as of a prone weight falling, and then an incoherent cry. He fired impetuously. Footsteps in mad retreat—and, after an interval, a pitiful moan.

"Good Heavens!" he exclaimed, "can I have really shot him? No, I heard the noise first. Hi, there, Candido, bring another light and help me. I'll be hanged if it isn't the fellow I cured of fever last August!"

Down among the matted shrubbery, crushing the gaudy canna blossoms and the pale yellow trumpets of ylang-ylang, a lithe young figure lay still as death.

As the lamp revealed the face, its coppery hue appeared suddenly ghastly, while a stream of crimson trickled slowly from one arm.

"Nasty cut with an assegai," commented Stafford, "but only a flesh wound. Ye Gods! What a glorious spear he carries himself."

Candido was grinning broadly. "From up mountain," he supplied.

"But how in the deuce," began his master, and then wisely decided to refrain from further observations until the injured man was resting comfortably upon a wicker couch in the sitting room, deftly and securely bandaged.

"I heard people running away, Candido," he explained to his servant in Spanish, "so I fancy this chap must have been trying to make his escape. My shot probably scared them off. Get a little brandy, and when he's feeling right again you must try your various lingoes on him and find out the cause of the rumpus."

In the period of waiting he surveyed with interest the handsome creature before him. He could not have been more than nineteen, with a marvelously perfect physique, and Malayan characteristics blended with the more vital energy of the primitive hillsman.

"It's the same fellow, all right," Stafford soliloquised.

"Very good man, Senor," Candido was eagerly remarking to him later. "He say Moro come quick—very much Moro —tonight, maybe—make big raid. His people fight Moro and he run quick to tell the Senor. Medicine is so good— one year ago—on the Agusan river."

"Whew," whistled the soldier softly. His was a lonely station, a native house on the outskirts of Liong, though he might still have time to gather his men together and resist the onslaught. Only

—"This man was followed," he said abruptly.

"Yes, Senor. Three Moro follow for two day to make stop. He always ahead. Catch up and stab him—then get scare and go off in boat. But much men come tonight—very much."

"Grateful sort of beggar this fellow must me," ruminated the other. He did not betray any great surprise in the intelligence that he had just received, for that would have been contrary to Dick Stafford's custom. Seldom, indeed, did his blue eyes lose a dreamy, tentative expression, or his freshly colored face its boyish, leisurely smile. To be sure, he had a natural antipathy towards inexplicable noises 'mid the blackness and mystery of a tropic night. For the terror "that walketh at noon-day" he had ever a laugh and a word of greeting.

Perhaps it was his debonair fashion of meeting with danger that rendered him so great a favorite of Fortune, and sent him so frequently, a venturous free-lance, into the very heart of evil. Of a certainty, it could only have been his enthusiastic bravery which saved the day for Liong that eventful Thursday. The scanty train of his followers was mustered in a twinkling, and the discomfited Moros were beaten back with their dead and wounded, with scarce time to recover their equilibrium.

Most splendid happening of all, Dick received a summons to Manila and promotion. And promotion spelt itself in two ways to the young American officer at that time. Most impressively it blazoned forth in gilded characters the name of Phyllis Oaks. He had not seen that charming maiden since the news of her father's death had reached him—Dr. Marmaduke Oaks, the distinguished English scientist, but he knew that she was still a resident of their delightful old bungalow on the Castile Road. Tom Prescott would be there, too, her half-brother. Filled with the elation of the lover who realizes his claims are on the eve of fulfillment, Stafford threaded his way gaily through a narrow street of Filipino houses and then, following the intricate maze of a garden studded with palm trees and beds of flaming foliage,

he came upon the rambling brown house. His most ardent wish was immediately granted.

"Phyl!" he cried.

A white-clad girl at once arose from her chair on the piazza and came quickly forward.

"You dear thing!" she exclaimed. "I can never tell how glad I am to see you, and how it relieves me to have you here. But have you thought of any possible solution?"

"Solution!" he echoed vaguely.

"How stupid of me! Of course you've just come to town and would scarcely have heard as yet. I'm so terribly flustered myself that I keep imagining it must be on everybodys tongues. I do want to congratulate you on your success, too, but just for the moment I can't talk of that either. Hasn't anyone told you?"

"Told me what?" he repeated blankly as ever.

"There! I see you're completely in the dark, so sit right down and I'll tell you all about it."

He obeyed her pretty, imperious gesture, noting with the keen eye of affection the slightly pale face—"an hour's defect of the rose"—and an ever deepening anxiety in her brown eyes.

"After father died, Tom and I went to stay with the Hungerfords for a while. That was six weeks ago, and we have only been home three days, though we have run in occasionally to see that everything was going all right. The servants have all been with us a year and more, and we have never had any special reason to be dissatisfied with any one of them. At the end of the first week of our absence the boy who had charge of the sweeping and dusting died after several days' illness, presumably of a low fever. Ten days later one of the table boys followed him. The rest of the servants, blindly superstitious at best, left the house and refused to come back until our return. And this morning I have been told of the illness of a third person. I am nearly distracted."

"What about the water?" he asked briefly.

"We only drink the imported variety.

Tom had an investigation immediately, and nothing whatever was discovered."

"A low fever, you say?"

"Yes; following a general feeling of inertia. In every case the patient was apparently ill for three or four days."

"And you are living here now?"

"Oh, certainly. Esme Hungerford is staying with us."

"You must not remain any longer. I shall see that you go back to her home tonight. Meanwhile let us go for a drive and try to clear our bewildered senses."

A driver was summoned, and a few minutes later they were rolling smoothly over the roads in a trim little carriage. The open country invited them. Away they went, past spacious residences and alluring parks, over ancient Spanish bridges and through natural avenues of acacia and plantain. Now the native huts smiled at them from embowering thickets of bananas, and countless little children ran across their path, shouting and laughing. Several women passed them, huge cigars in their mouths, flat baskets heaped with fruit upon their heads. Around a crumbling stone church came a young girl wearing a red robe, poising a brown water jar. A group of men chatted amiably of the cock fight on the following Sunday. Then they were alone amid the dark, cool green of the forest, ever sloping to the azure line of sea.

Let us stop somewhere and buy a cocoanut," said the girl suddenly, "it is all the lunch I care about today."

"What is Tom doing with himself now?"

"Still dabbling in paint," she answered with a little laugh. "I admire his energy, and I only wish there was a larger market for Oriental watercolors. I was frightfully indignant yesterday—" She paused, a flush mounting to her cheeks.

"What happened?"

"Professor Delmar came over from the Bureau of Science. He said—oh, I can't just tell you—but he almost insinuated poor old Tom had something to do with this frightful business. Do you remember the terms of the will?"

"No. I don't believe I heard anything at all about it."

"You scarcely would, I suppose, but Dad stipulated that the house should be mine unless I married. In that case it would become Tom's. Tom's usual down-upon-his-luck attitude would just give certain people the chance to say horrid things if they wanted to, even to go so far as to say he was anxious to hurry me into marriage. Did you ever hear anything so preposterous?"

"It's an outrage," returned the man tersely. "I have no hesitation at all in saying so, knowing Tom Prescott as I do."

"Thank you," said Phyllis gratefully "I knew I could depend on you, Dick."

He pressed her hand in silence.

"I haven't heard your version of that gallant defence down in Mindanao," she said presently, "perhaps if you will tell me about it I shall be enabled to forget other things."

He complied with the request willingly enough and added a few amusing details concerning the native who had brought the warning.

"It has been impossible to shake him, Phyl. He has become a sort of private bodyguard for me, and my head boy is quite jealous of him."

"Is he with you here?"

"Oh, yes—and creating a real sensation. He is not even semi-civilized, you see."

The carriage turned up the winding palm-bordered way. At the piazza steps they were met by Esme Hungerford and Tom Prescott, plainly in a state of tense agitation.

"Phyllis!" exclaimed the former at once. "Juan, the cook, died half an hour ago. How do you do, Lieutenant? Have you ever ran up against a more inexplicable mystery? Heavens! The place seems to be bewitched."

"Don't you think these two girls should leave immediately? asked Prescott.

"I certainly do. Get right into the carriage and go back to the Hungerfords, and don't return until we send for you. No need to worry, Phyl, dear; Tom and I will take every precaution. I want to look around a bit, and then we'll go over to the hotel for the night. Good bye, both of you."

When the girls had taken their some what reluctant departure, he addressed Tom briefly. "The servants are all leaving, needleess to say?"

"Oh, yes, indeed; they are attending to Juan now, poor fellow; and in half an hour there will be absolutely no one in the house. Shall we dine at the Army and Navy Club? I haven't any appetite, but I suppose the form must be gone through with. I'm about all in, Stafford."

Dick looked his sympathy. "Cheer up, old fellow," he said kindly, "we'll get to the root of it, all right. By the way, what caused your step-father's death?"

Prescott looked blank for an instant. "By Jove!" he exclaimed, "you're the first person who ever asked that question. The doctor said it was a general breakup, although now that I come to think of it, I believe he evinced the very same symptoms of illness that these Filipinos have done. Isn't it astounding, Dick?"

"It surely is," mused the other. "How did he usually occupy his time, Tom?"

"Oh, just in the same old way. Always pottering among his flowers and butterflies and that kind of thing. He was engaged in some very important research work at the time of his death, I believe, and was bitterly disappointed that he would not be enabled to finish it. Poor old Dad! He was a princely chap."

A long silence followed. When dinner was at length over, Stafford expressed a desire to re-visit the bungalow. "I should like to go in alone if you don't mind, Tom," he said, "and you can wait for me in the garden."

"Don't mind if I do; I will confess that I am beginning to think of the house as a hideous nightmare. I'll stay within hearing, of course."

Stafford at once made his way to the room which had been formerly occupied by Dr. Oaks. It was in perfect order and there was nothing about it to suggest the unusual. Baffled, he stood staring at the different articles of furniture for a moment or two, and then he turned and passed swiftly towards his study. The latter was a delightful room, large and airy, with windows that opened from floor to ceiling upon a veranda lavishly adorned with flowers. The floor was bare and polished; there were bamboo chairs and numerous bookcases, a table with papers methodically arranged, and a huge begonia growing in a brass cauldron—a quivering mass of diminutive pale pink blossoms, like fairies dancing. There were glass specimen-cases of pressed plants and butterflies, and a small cabinet containing various glass retorts and chemicals. The veranda beyond was shaded by a magnificent vine of purple bourgainvillia, and its long boxes were rife with jasmine, cannas and lilies. While Stafford stood intently watching, a small gray object scuttled over the ceiling above his head, the harmless variety of lizard to be seen in almost any Filipino house.

He was about to leave, and then something prompted him to turn once more. From a further, darker corner, an exquisite miracle bloomed upon the silence. It was a rare orchid, planted in a large porcelain box, though it had twined itself closely around the latticed windows, and spread afar its aerial roots. For one moment he stood in mute admiration. Its blossoms were like tiny birds of pure apple green, vividly splashed with crimson. They hovered amid the twilight of the room as if in sheer ecstacy.

When he entered the garden again he found Dr. Delmar talking with Prescott. He was a small, wiry man, one who gave the impression of being ever on the alert.

"A bad business, Stafford," he said by way of greeting. "What have you to say about it?"

"I am utterly at a loss. By the way, did not nearly six weeks elapse between Dr. Oaks' death and that of the first servant?"

"Yes— exactly."

"And was the study very much occupied during that interval, Prescott?"

"Not to any extent," returned the young man wearily, "but the week before the first boy died he was in there a very great deal, sweeping and cleaning up and putting things to rights generally."

"And after his death his work was done by another boy, I suppose?"

"Yes—and by the very fellow who was next taken ill. By George! I see what you mean. All of these chaps have been busied in that room a considerable part of their time (there was really a lot of straightening to attend to), and it has been they who suffered. The other servants were immune."

"Therefore," concluded Delmar briefly, "the mystery must certainly exist within the late professor's study. So much to work on."

"It strikes me as being very slender data," interposed the lieutenant, "a botanical atmosphere is an innocent one, as a rule."

"Oh, not always. You forget the possibility of poisonous insects, or—"

"The medical men discussed that phase," put in Tom Prescott, "and were unanimous in saying that death could not be traceable in either of the three instances to any such cause."

"Hum-hum," mused Dr. Delmar. "Well, then, that theory is disposed of. Now for a second one—"

He had many of them at his command, it appeared, but they were frustrated without exception. The three men repaired to the hotel and continued the discussion until a late hour. Morning found them, if possible, in a greater state of bewilderment than ever.

About 10 o'clock Stafford had a short telephone conversation with Phyllis, as he felt a disinclination to see her until he had something definite to say regarding the events that had just transpired. Then he walked in the direction of the Oaks' bungalow. As he quitted the grounds of the hotel, however, his glance fell upon the young tribesman dreaming away the hours under an hibiscus hedge.

"Come, my boy," he called tersely, "I don't believe it would be a half bad idea to take you with me."

The fellow was at his side in a moment, his dark face aglow with happiness. As they proceeded on their way Lieutenant Stafford told him, in a queer Anglo-Spanish, something of the mystery that engrossed him. The servant listened eagerly, but it was difficult to ascertain with what degree of comprehension. When they arrived at the house he followed his master into the study like an obedient dog, and then began an indolent

survey of the room. Pausing near the orchids, he inhaled a breath of their odor and gave vent to an unintelligible exclamation.

"What is it?" demanded the lieutenant sharply.

The native made a rapid gesture. "This thing, Senor—it not smell so in my country—it not good."

Like a flash the soldier was beside him. "What! It is poisonous?"

The other shook his head, vastly puzzled. "No, no, Senor. Him very nice flower; very good smell. In other place, yes. No good here."

"What the deuce are you driving at? Do you mean that a man should not keep a plant like that in the house?"

"Senor not understand — plant good — plant not the same." While the soldier looked on perplexedly he touched it with an awe-inspiring finger. "Must make bad inside. Other plant not same."

Steps sounded behind them and Stafford turned quickly to confront Prescott and Delmar. "Tell him to go on," said the professor at once, "I believe we have found our clue."

The native, divining the import of the words, severed a flower with his curious, tall sword. It fell on the table beneath and lay there in its pale green glory like the humming bird it resembled, with the blood-red gash upon it like a wound. Pointing with his weapon to the inner heart of the blossom, they noted a peculiar brownish tinge, spreading slowly upwards from the calyx.

"Is it some deadly variety?" asked Prescott.

"No," returned Professor Delmar, "it is a moth orchid of the genus Phalaenopsis. It is exceedingly hard to cultivate, and Dr. Oaks was quite justly proud of it. Usually the odor is sweet and powerful. This wild fellow at once detected something strange about it, though, and because of that, and the peculiar hue it is now assuming, I am led to believe that it has been treated with chemicals, possibly by Dr. Oaks, and with some experimental purpose in view.

"Awful chump I've been," said Tom Prescott suddenly and in a very contrite voice. "I distinctly remember Dad telling me, possibly a year ago, that he was possessed of a strong desire to know what effect certain drugs would have upon certain plants."

They looked at each other in surprise and trepidation.

"The effeect has been more far-reaching than he could ever have dreamed it would be," said Delmar at last. "He has possibly instilled poison through this brilliantly-colored pouch — the labellum, we call it—by means of a camel's-hair brush. The result has been to produce a peculiarly noxious gas, whose odor has been disguised both by the heavy scent of the orchid itself and all these other flowers. It has proved fatal to the persons who were in contact with it so very frequently, and was, I fear, the real cause of our poor friend's death, though he evidently never suspected it. May I suggest that the plant be cut down immediately and enclosed in glass, Mr. Prescott? It will afford great interest to my colleagues at the Bureau—with the aid of rubber gloves and glass masks—he added significantly.

When they were leaving the apartment he held out his hand to Prescott. "I want to apologize; I will confess that I had— had entertained doubts—"

"As I should probably have done in your position, sir," returned the young man frankly. "I beg of you not to refer to it again."

"And, Dick," Phyllis Oaks said very softly when they were alone together that evening, "we will never let that splendid young barbarian go away from us. It takes a true son of nature to interpret her secrets, doesn't it? Oh, how invaluable he has been to both of us!"

His arm encircling her and his lips brushing her hair, they gazed out into the velvet tropic darkness to where, beneath a flowering tree, the young tribesman lay peacefully strumming upon some crudely devised instrument. Its jangling music came to them plaintively, while he, all unconscious, was dreaming of the stars above his mountain village and the pleasant, murmuring voices of his own people.

The Long Road

By Elsie Jewett Webster

There's a long road winding down,
A fair road, a fragrant road,
Where plumed Eucalyptus trees brush a copper sky.
There's a soft wind sweeping down,
A kind wind, a kissing wind,
Whispering to the branches that bow as I pass by.

There's a sweet song drifting down,
A low song, a lulling song,
From birds who call a greeting to the silver evening star.
There's a great flame shining down,
A red flame, a rosy flame,
Burning all the little waves out upon the bar.

There's a long road winding down,
A cool road, a calling road,
The hills are slipping past me as on the road I wend.
There's a long road winding down,
A fair road, a fragrant road,
I go a singing on it for you are at the end.

When the Gates Were Open

By Grace Atherton Dennen

(Moving Picture Rights Reserved.)

TRUXTON arrived in Guanajuato at eleven P. M., by the Mexican Central and went at once to the hotel to sleep off the effects. He found the hotel surprisingly crowded. Two years ago when he had passed through the town, he had been offered the whole second floor for his one night's stay. But tonight he was told, with many apologies and in English of the most broken, that a bed at the end of the hall, with a screen in front of it, was the utmost that could be done for him.

"But why?" he questioned, incredulous. "What's the excitement?"

There was only one answer from proprietor to bell boy, "la fiesta!"

Truxton was too sleepy to argue. After a day on the Mexican Central, bed anywhere was an open door to paradise. He tumbled in.

The next morning when Truxton emerged from behind the screen, refreshed and fit, he began to learn the true meaning of those words, "la fiesta!" The square outside was brilliant with the national colors and thronged with Mexicans in their really wonderful holiday best. A generous sprinkling of tourists in more sober attire gave a background. The doors of the shops about the square were open, but not for business, oh, no! Papa and mamacita with half a dozen of their progeny, stood in these front doors, absorbed completely in the pageant of color and movement outside. All attempts to do business with any of them failed —his business being to ascertain their attitude of mind toward the possible establishing of an ice and cold storage plant. Today there was only one attitude of mind in all Guanajuato — "la fiesta!"

Plainly there was nothing to do but enjoy himself. Truxton was wonderfully whole-hearted in whatever he undertook. In a few moments he had become one of the throng in the square, a prince among revelers, squeezing out of each hour as it passed its last drop of pleasure.

This was at ten o'clock. At twelve he was heading a procession down the principal streets in an effective spiral learned at his university. At two o'clock he was self-appointed yell-leader for a thousand or more people gathered to witness the games and races. He guided their ragged but enthusiastic cheering through the pauses left by the Mexican band. At three o'clock he found himself in need of liquid refreshment and visited a booth by the grandstand.

"This is a great day!" he remarked to a young fellow at the bar beside him. For some reason their arms were about each others shoulders, there seemed to be a newly discovered but extraordinary bond of sympathy between them, they were as brothers.

The young man smiled radiantly, with many white teeth. "Today? Yes, but manana—tomorrow—ah, manana!"

Truxton looked at him earnestly. Was there more to come?

"Why tomorrow?"

"Tomorrow they open las compuertas— ah—muy fino!—the gates!"

"The gates?"

"Si, senor, las compuertas."

Truxton turned to the man at the bar. "What does he think he means?"

"Dam gates," said the bar-tender. "Dam's just above the town. Once a year when the dam gets full the gates have to be opened. Water runs down the hillside wending its way, riffling

2

through gulleys out into the fields. That's what they'll do tomorrow."

"Muy fino!" murmured the Mexican fervently.

"But where's the excitement in that?" persisted Truxton. "Just opening some gates—"

The bar-keeper's face lighted too, he leaned over the bar and spoke eagerly.

"Ef 'twas just opening gates, they wouldn't be no excitement. It's the way them gates has got to be opened."

"Don't they open by machinery?"

"Mos' generally. They're out o' order now. Tomorrow they's going to be opened by hand."

"By hand? But—"

"Two men has got to climb up there and open 'em, one fer each gate."

"But—" Truxton's eyes bulged a little, "they'll get themselves killed, of course."

"One chance in ten to get away with it. They use two prisoners out of the jail; one's a bandit, he'd hang anyway. The other stole a horse. If they come out alive they'll go free. It'll be a great sight."

"I believe you," agreed Truxton. He was busy visualizing the scene. The crowd of staring people, the swollen waters heaped up behind the dam—two little figures crawling out onto the concrete, the signal given, the overwhelming rush of water, two dark heads bobbing in the sudden current.

"Prisoners used to do it every year," the bar-keeper was saying. "Then a guy come along and fixed up machinery."

Truxton made his way into the outer air and joined the merrymakers again.

"Some little town, Guanajualo," he murmured to himself.

At four o'clock he saw HER. From the first moment his eyes rested upon her dark loveliness he spelt her in capitals. She was in a carriage with another and older woman—mamacita, of course—and a small, dark man, young enough to fill Truxton's soul with fierce dislike. The games were just ended and the spectators, on foot or in carriages, were crowding through the narrow entrance gates. The congestion was great enough to hold her carriage with its three occupants mo-

tionless beside him for several moments. Her eyes, eager and interested, met his. Truxton with the healthy young scorn of twenty-four had always bitterly ridiculed love at first sight. But in that moment's look into her eyes he had uttered a dozen passionate, pleading words, read a very shy response in drooping lids and yielding form, and was standing with her all in white beside him, in the old cathedral church of Guanajuato.

A forward movement of the crowd brought him back to reality. He knew that he must have been staring at her rudely, for the man beside her was returning the stare. Her cheeks were flushed, but about the corners of her mouth two dimples showed themselves. Then her carriage rolled forward and she was lost to him. For a moment he still stared, thinking he must have dreamed that lovely face, then he took to his heels and ran after her as fast as he could.

At that place there was an abrupt turn in the road. The congestion of teams, people and automobiles reached a dangerous point. Truxton who kept his eyes fastened on the open barouche with its matched grays, saw them rear suddenly as an automobile back-fired, then plunged forward. The wheel of the barouche locked with that of a wagon in front. There was a crash, the carriage tipped dangerously. Women screamed, men called out, vehicles and people pressed back as far as possible in a widening circle. Truxton saw his opportunity, he leaped forward, seized the grays, forced them back on their haunches until the wheels unlocked. By that time half a dozen men had sprung to his assistance. He let them take control of the situation and leaned back against the wheel of the barouche breathing hard. The flower face, rather pale now, was close to him. The mother, half fainting, was occupying the full attention of the dark little man. It was a golden moment.

He murmured quickly, "Forgive me for staring so rudely at the flower of Guanajuato."

Again the rush of lovely color, again the dimples—then a voice low and musical, he had to lean forward to catch the words.

"One forgives a brave man anything."

"I am so happy if my slight services—"

"Slight— You who have saved our lives! What reward could be enough?"

"Reward!" He had a sudden daring impulse.

"If you feel that way—there is a reward—"

"And what?"

"A dance with you at the ball this evening."

Mamacita, reviving, raised her head, the golden moment was slipping fast.

"One dance," he pleaded. He was goaded by a desperate fear of losing her. The barouche must not bear her out of his sight without some assurance of a future meeting.

The dark eyes met his, half-frightened, half fascinated. She leaned toward him, his ear caught, or thought it caught two mumured words, "The eighth." Joy filled him with a rush.

"I will be there!" he exclaimed.

Then mamacita claimed him and he listened to a flood of thanks and protestations and met the stare of the little dark man, not at all softened by recent happenings. At last the excitement subsided, vehicles and people took up their slow advance, and Truxton was left in the middle of the road.

The music was uttering all sorts of yearning and inexpressible things when Truxton made his way into the Casino at nine o'clock that evening. He stood in the door a moment watching the picture before him with eager curiosity. Masked figures in every kind of brilliant costume drifted past him, blown along by the music, like gaily colored leaves driven by the wind. Streamers of red, green, and yellow bunting hung from the walls and rafters. The ball was at its height, for he had delayed his coming until late. For him the interest centered in the eighth dance.

The time since he saw her and won her half-frightened promise had passed like a dream.

Her face went with him everywhere, her voice rang softly in his ears. Many times before in his active, wholesome young life, Truxton had thrilled at the look in a girl's eyes or a tone of her voice, but never in this way. It seemed to him that nothing had really been worth while before he saw her that afternoon. He lived in the thought of seeing her again. He meant to pour all the intensity of his wooing into those few moments with her, like rich wine into a great, golden cup, which he would drain to the last drop. After that—there was still tomorrow.

His eager glance found her at once, she was glowing like a crimson rose in a red, satin dress and mask. He watched her for a few moments with mingled delight and despair, delight at the sight of her young grace and charm, fierce jealously at the man who danced with her, his arm around her waist; of her smile as she looked up at him. The next dance was the eighth. Had she seen him? Should he wait for her to give him some sign? Would she remember?

Truxton usually took one way with any knotty problem—he cut the knot at once. So the music had scarcely died away when he was at her side.

"This is our dance," he said briefly.

"My mother," she murmured; "we must speak to her."

He drew her hand firmly through his arm. "We will—afterward," he said.

The dance was all that he had dreamed. He drew her close to him with a joy too deep for any words, and they floated down the stream of the music to some inexpressible happiness which seemed waiting just beyond. Never a doubt assailed his mind that his feelings were shared, to some degree at least, by her. Suddenly he stopped and led her toward the balcony just outside.

"I don't want to hear the end of the music," he said.

She followed him without question. The balcony overlooked the square, it was flooded with moonlight, a soft breeze caressed their faces. Truxton's heart was throbbing eagerly, no presentiment of coming evil chilled him. They sat down on a bench and the moonlight touched their faces with radiance. They slipped into the silence of a measureless content, his eyes spoke to her and hers answered and neither was aware of what their looks revealed.

"How do you happen to speak English so well?" he demanded, abruptly.

"I went two years to school in San Francisco."

"How long ago?"

"It was a year in June that I came home."

"Then—I must have been there at the same time— I never knew it."

"How should you?"

"Something should have told me."

She looked down at her clasped hands. He was aware of the swift color and the dimples. He lost himself in contemplation of them.

After a while— "When shall I see you again?" he asked.

She looked up at him with an adorable smile. He knew it for quite a different sort from the one she had given to her recent partner. "There is tomorrow," she murmured.

"That's just what I've been telling myself," he stammered eagerly. "There's tomorrow. What do they do tomorrow?"

"Oh, that is the great day, that is when the gates are opened."

"Oh, yes, I heard something— Tell me about it."

"Years ago," she began, with the eagerness of one who tells an absorbing tale. Truxton listened dreamily, watching the play of the moonlight across her face, the shine of her eyes, the quick changes of emotion expressed in her charming features. Soon, however, he became aware that he was hearing an intensely dramatic story, he roused himself to listen more closely.

"For five years now the gates have been opened by machinery, but tomorrow it is different. The machinery is out of order, it works no more, so once again the prisoners must open the gates. They have already been chosen."

"That's great stuff." What time do they pull it off?"

"Just at noon."

"We'll be there, you and I—together. What?"

Her answer was lost in the hoarse scream of a crow overhead, but it could not have been discouraging for Truxton caught her hand and drew her close to him. The harsh cry of the crow sounded again and it was like derisive laughter. He looked up to see where it came from. When he turned his eyes back to her she was rising to her feet in agitation. The little dark man stood in the window watching them.

"I must go in now— I must," she said.

He had just time to catch her hand, recklessly in his and press it tight. "Tomorrow," he whispered.

There was a slight vibrating quiver in the hand he held, and she was gone.

After that things began to happen swiftly.

Not wishing to dance again, Truxton walked over to the railing, lit a cigarette and stood looking down at the square below. Many Mexicans were dancing in the square — the picturesque, native dances. They made a changing play of light and color. One couple especially caught his attention, there was a grace and abandon in their movements like the spirit of youth. They swung and pirouetted, weaving in and out among the other dancers, brushing them close, circling them, but never losing their own rhythm. There was a subtle meaning in every movement. He watched them fascinated, there was something of her grace in the girl's figure; the strong clasp of the man's arm about her, the protecting tenderness of his broad shoulders bending over her seemed the outward expression of the passion that burned in his own veins. Youth and love — those two below him were Youth and Love weaving their idyl into the dance, his heart quickened in response.

At that moment he noticed a policeman, followed by two angry, gesticulating men, working their way among the dancers toward the two of his choice. He leaned out over the railing in sudden anxiety. Danger was threatening the two. They seemed quite unconscious of it, moving on in perfect rhythm. At that moment the girl was lifting a small, flushed face to the man, he bent close to hear what she said. Was it Truxton's fancy or did the man cast a quick, anxious glance around? Yes, they were edging toward the Casino. But already they were too late. Truxton saw that the men had separated and were approaching them from different angles. They were running into the jaws of the trap.

Then Truxton obeyed a quick, restless impulse. He leaped over the balcony into the square. He found himself close beside the two. His unexpected arrival had caught their attention, in fact everybody in the square was watching him. He called to the two in low tones, "Look out, you are surrounded!"

They caught the warning, whether or not they understood the English. With a quick movement they separated and darted into the crowd. But their pursuers were quicker. Truxton witnessed their capture and the angry excitement increasing about them. With an uneasy feeling that he had been very foolish he turned back toward the Casino. Then he discovered that the Casino arch had hidden a fourth policeman who was now heading directly for him.

"You come along wid me!" he shouted in good Irish-American. "You're one of the gang!"

Truxton protested vigorously but vainly. The hand of the law was upon his shoulders.

"You give them thieves the tip to get away. I seen you do it.".

There was nothing to be answered to this. Truxton's conviction of folly deepened into something like fear. He was in a wild bit of country, a long way from the American flag which was not popular there at any time. If these people he had tried to befriend were really thieves—

They were. Encircled by a threatening ring of angry people, he saw rings, pins and trinkets taken from hidden places in the clothes of both of them. Then he himself was searched roughly. Then discovery of two or three uncut turquoises and a lady's watch (his mother's) seemed to prove his complicity. Then his common sense deserted him all at once, he struck out right and left in a mad attempt to get away. He was quickly overpowered and beaten into semi-consciousness.

An hour or so later he awoke to find himself staring through the barred window of an adobe jail on the outskirts of Guanajuato. Truxton was astounded at the swiftness and the completeness of the disaster. An hour ago he was a free man, on the verge of a big business success, the favorite of fortune, madly in love and with more than a slight hope of winning a response to his cyclonic love making. Now he stood here in the cell of a Mexican jail, convicted of being one of a gang of thieves. Who would believe or how could he explain the absurd and romantic impulse which had made him leap over the railing to warn two criminals against capture? It would be almost better for him to offer no explanation.

Keenest torture of all, she would hear of this, if she had not already heard. For his last dim consciousness had been of the shouts of maskers running out from the Casino to see what was happening. She would believe the worst of him, she would think that his rescue of her in the afternoon, his bold request to dance with her at the ball, those wonderful moments on the balcony were all so many clumsy attempts to get close enough to her to rob her of some trinket. He turned sick at the thought. Nothing in all his life had ever caused him such pain. He took his throbbing head between his hands and groaned aloud.

His groan was echoed fervently from a corner of the cell. He looked hastily around, he had thought himself alone. The knowledge of alien eyes upon him brought him back to self control. He walked over to the corner and peered into the shadows. A Mexican was crouched there squatting on his haunches like a dog, and mumbling to himself. He looked up as Truxton bent over him and his face was full of misery.

"What's wrong?" demanded Truxton, "sick or only drunk?"

"No, senor, but tomorrow—las compuertas—"

"The gates?"

"Si, Senor, they open!"

"And you won't be there to see? Neither shall I. We'll be having a different kind of celebration."

"No, senor—I—I open las compuertas."

"What! You're one of the men to open the gates?"

"Si!"

"Which one are you—the bandit or the horse thief?"

"I take one horse—one leetle horse—it was all one meestake."

"Why didn't you take an automobile? Then you'd have been all right."

The man's reply was another groan, hollow, hopeless.

"You don't care for the gate opening job, eh?"

"Senor, it ees death!"

"O come, there's a chance, at least."

But the man sat back upon his haunches and resumed his grumbling. Truxton gathered that he was repeating his prayers. He stared down at him for several moments. His face grew keen, alert, the blood pounded at his temples. He was remembering certain words of her's. "One forgives a brave man anything." This was what she had said.

He sat down in the shadow by the mumbling figure and laid a hand on his shoulder.

"I want to talk to you," he declared briskly.

* * * * * *

The gates of the dam were to be opened at noon. By quarter of twelve the high ground on either side was crowded with people making holiday. A long procession came winding through the town, headed by two priests who chanted a dirge. They were followed by the prisoners and after them trailed half of Guanajuato. The bandit walked with head high, exchanging greetings here and there and flashing his teeth at the women. Execrations, mingled with murmurs of reluctant admiration, followed his progress. The other walked with head down, muffled in the long coat which both wore. He glanced neither to right nor left but shuffled along miserably.

"He is a coword, that one!" exclaimed the crowd. "He is brave to steal horses but he is afraid to open the gates."

The people on the hills caught sight of the procession and uttered a mighty roar. The chanting of the priests was drowned in it, the hills rocked. Fearful expectation gripped every one, a mad thirst for excitement, as when the bull is led into the arena. The procession wound its way through the valley and up to the great dam. There it stopped and from the cathedral tower a bell began to toll. A hush fell upon the people. A great, dramatic moment was at hand. The hush became intense, the thousands on the hillside seemed scarcely to breathe, but for an occasional choked cry or exclamation.

A pistol shot shattered the silence. It was the signal. The two prisoners threw aside their coats and leaped on to the wall of the dam. They wore black swimming tights and their figures were clearly outlined against the sky. The bandit stood with head lifted and waved his hand in gay bravado. But a murmur of surprise went up from the crowd which grew in volume and intensity—the second man, who was he? Not the horse thief, they all knew him. Most of them had never seen this man before, but there were some who knew and the murmur swelled into a shout, "The American! The American!"

On the hill a girl, sitting heavy eyed and listless among the merrymakers, heard it and started wildly to her feet. She saw the second figure, tall and alert, she stretched out trembling hands toward him and echoed the cry: "The American!"

As if he had heard her voice above them all, Truxton turned his head and looked directly at her. The girl clasped her hands in uncontrollable agitation, heedless of her mother's reproaches and the curious looks of those about her.

Now the men stood at either side of the great gates, waiting. There was a second pistol shot, the great gates stirred and began slowly to open with a groan of iron hinges. There was a great shout of warning, then a mighty exultant roar as the pent-up waters of the lake hurled themselves through the narrow opening out into the country beyond. The mad swirl of the oncoming flood raced far up into the hills and sent many of the onlookers fleeing for their lives. Masses of debris were broken out and carried along with it, boulders, young trees and in their midst, now on the surface, now beneath, two black, bobbing specks which were two men fighting hard for life.

The crowd was on its feet now, surging back and forth, shouting incoherently, mad with excitement. On the hill a white-faced girl broke away from her companions and ran blindly toward the bank of the gulley, calling and stumbling in her hurry.

Truxton was caught in the first great rush of water and hurled a hundred feet before he could fight his way to the surface. Mere instinct made him grasp the trunk of a small tree as it whirled by him and the same instinct forced him to cling to it with a grip which could not be loosened. The roar of the water was thunder in his ears, bewildering and deafening him. The weight of it on his chest was an acute agony. He was suffocating, strangling, he felt that he was being hurled to his death, but underneath it all was a sort of fierce exultation. This was no ordinary death, no mere snuffing out of exhausted powers, but a thrilling struggle against a tremendous opponent, whose titanic strength awed even while it crushed him. And beneath the agony and the awe was the face of the girl and her hands stretched out to him. Then pain and awe faded away, only the face persisted.

It never left him, it was the first thing he saw when he struggled up again' out of the darkness a few days later in his bed in the hospital. Truxton looking into it, knew it for reality and understood that he was the favorite of fortune still. She was still at her old tricks with him, bestowing upon him at once the two greatest gifts in her keeping, life and love.

An Abalone Shell

By Belle Willey Gue

It has kept the brown of the rugged rock
    Where it clung within the deep,
It has borne the brunt of many a shock
    Where strange beings dart and creep.

The unrivaled red of the sunset's glow
    And an opalescent sheen,
With the magic light that the calm nights know,
    In its brave, bright heart are seen.

It has caught the green of the grass that grows
    On the ground beneath the sea,
It has found the strength of the wind that blows
    Where the waves are wild and free.

There's the milky gray of the sea-bird's wing—
    Like a soft cloud in the sky—
Shining 'round the shell like a living thing—
    Like a shadow floating by.

The Tattooed Leg

By John Chilton

TWO scenes seemed to live themselves over and over in his mind as he lay outstretched on the narrow hospital bed — one his good-bye to Bess, and somehow he seemed to be taking the kisses he had not quite dared to take, Bess was always so standoffish. He saw her face and figure quite clearly against a black background. Bess· was distractingly pretty, but always she faded away and he saw himself lying on a roughly improvised table in a freight shed struggling with a keen-eyed, thin-lipped man who pressed a wet towel over his face—and everything was blotted out; yet, even as life faded he heard a voice say:

"It is the chance I have prayed for and I shall take it—he can only die!"

Then one morning he woke up. He was lying in a small room where everything was white and clean and smelled strongly of antiseptics, and a strange woman, a nurse in white cap and apron, was sitting by an open window rolling bandages. He tried to roll over and found he could not move. The woman looked up:

"Oh, you're all right again," she said, laying down her work and rising.

"I want to get up," he said shakily in a voice faraway and quite unlike his own.

"You must be patient and get strong first."

The nurse placed her cool, firm hand lightly on his head and smiled. "Just a little while and you will be quite well. I am glad to see you conscious."

"Tell me—"

"Drink this."

And then he slept, this time dreamlessly and like a child, and awakened refreshed and clear-headed, and life· began again.

Then came long, happy days of convalescence, and the great day of days when he sat up for the first time. He felt strong with renewed life and vigor as he threw his limbs over the edge of the bed and laughed up at his nurse for her assisting arm·

"You can bet I'm not sorry to get out of that plaster and on my pins again."

"You've been a wonderfully fortunate young man, and that girl who has been haunting the hospital is waiting down stairs ·to tell you so," answered the nurse.

Just then he glanced down at his legs protruding from the bed covers.

"Gee! What's the matter with my legs? What's that blue mark? Who's been tattooing me? Good Lord! Why, that isn't my leg—what is it?"

He glared wildly up into the serene face above him.

"You lost your leg in the wreck, and Dr. Amsden, the great surgeon, has successfully grafted on another. It is the most wonderful piece of work that was ever done, and—"

"Whose leg have I got?" he asked faintly, his face whitening.

"There, there, brace up — be brave, you haven't anything to worry about now; it's all over and you are going to be as good as new."

Then he weakened and fell back on the pillow sick with the horror of the thing and not daring to ask further, his still weakened mind unable to grasp what had happened while he cried over and over childishly:

"I want by leg—Give me my leg!" until nurse was obliged to give him a quieting powder and put him back to bed.

It took several days of care before he could reconcile himself to a certain nervous horror that seemed to pervade his being whenever he thought of what had happéned to him and then Bess came and he talked it all over with her. She was a girl among a thousand, with a wealth of good common sense, and whatever she thought in her heart she loved him enough to dissemble and encourage him, and so he came out from the fear and horror and gradually grew strong until the time came when he left the hospital and took up his old life, with only a slight limp to remind his friends of his accident.

Then came his marriage to Bess, and in his new happiness he almost forgot the strange blue marks that had so puzzled him at first, and yet sometimes, when rubbing himself down after a bath, he would pause and endeavor to decipher the meaning of the crosses and circles and the long, straight mark between.

Then a strange thing happened to him which he did not tell Bess for very shame. He was walking down a side street in a not very respectable part of the town, making a short-cut to the ferry, when he passed a low corner groggery, a sinister sort of place with a half door of faded, dirty green lattice, when, without volition on his part he found himself pushing through the lattice in an endeavor to enter. Horrified, he turned with visible effort and almost ran down the street. If anyone had seen him—a prominent member of the Y. M. C. A.! A few days afterward he found himself following a common, bedraggled, painted creature down an alley, and only turned back by the greatest effort.

After several like experiences he went to a specialist for treatment. He was so ashamed of it all that it affected his manner at home, and Bess noticed it and questioned him. Finding him reticent, she resented it, and a coolness came between them. The medicine the doctor gave him did no special good. Perhaps it might have been that he controlled his inclinations a bit more easily for a while, but the effect wore away and it was all worse than ever. He began to be obsessed by a craving for strong drink, and found himself inventing excuses for going out at night at late hours. Then Bess and he quarreled out-

right. She cried, and told him she never would have believed a man could change so, and then he broke down and told her all, and with her usual common sense she went right to the root of the matter and wondered why they hadn't thought of it before. It was the strange leg beyond the shadow of a doubt. The man from whom it had been taken was a bad man, and the influence had grown and the blood, the vicious blood, had simply poisoned her dear, true-hearted, honest husband, and if not treated properly would ruin him mentally and physically. The first thing to do was to go to the best blood specialist they could find and be thoroughly cleansed, and if that were not efficacious, then they, as a last resort, could have the leg amputated again. But, after all, would that be a cure? Wasn't the whole system of the man so permeated that nothing save a seven-years' course of treatment could help him. Poor things! They worried and fretted until Bess had gotten him ready, and they set out to discover a certain Dr. Everett, who was of great repute.

The learned man was delighted with the case, but, being in consultation with a very great and celebrated detective over a criminal case of much importance, could only make an appointment with them for the following morning, and so it came about that as they wandered through a small park on their way to the ferry they met with an adventure that changed everything for them.

Bess was carrying one of those fancy gold meshed bags so much affected by young women, one of her wedding gifts of which she was very fond, when a small, mean-looking man jostled her and she felt it suddenly jerked from her hand. She turned with a cry and saw him running around a corner — gave chase, followed by her husband, who went blindly, only sensing the fact that something had happened. Bess was an athletic young woman, and at first gained on the thief, but he got among the crowd of people on the streeet and eluded her. She stopped as a crowd gathered, and a policeman came hurrying up for explanation, and half crying over her loss, gave a description of the man who had robbed her, as well as a close description of the contents of the bag.

They took a short-cut through a by-street, and walking slowly along close together, hand in hand, as each sought to comfort the other, they saw a crowd gathered about a fallen man. As they passed, Bess looked.

"There he is!" she cried, dashing through and catching hold of the fallen man: "Oh, aren't you ashamed of your-self to steal my bag! If you are hurt, it serves you right."

Everyone looked at Bess, and her husband tried to draw her away.

"No, I will not come till I have given him in charge. Why doesn't a policeman come?"

"The man's hurt, Miss," said a rough-looking bystander. "He was hit by an automobile as he was running across the street, an' I guess he's pretty bad for he hasn't spoke a word since. We're wait-ing for an ambulance—here it comes!"

They took a car to the hospital and ar-riving there found that the man was seriously injured, also that Bess' bag had been found in his pocket. They would not give it up at first, but on her prov-ing the property finally said they would risk it, after taking the address and ask-ing innumerable questions.

As they were leaving, a nurse came hurrying after them.

"Good morning," she said, "perhaps you don't remember me, but I used to help watch when you were here. How's your leg?"

Bess recalled the woman, though her husband did not.

"That poor man that was run down by a motor," she explained," is con-scious. He cannot live, and I promised to bring you. He wants to see you."

"Wants to see me," cried Bess;" I don't want to see him. He stole my pretty bag, and I never want to see him again. Of course I'm sorry he's not going to get well—" then as a sense of what it really meant came over her, she said, shame-facedly: "Oh, I didn't really mean to be so thoughtless; come, let us go to him at once and see if there is anything we can do."

Her husband smiled a little sadly. He was so filled with his own trouble that he had little thought for anything else just then, but the nurse electrified him into the present.

"He is the man that—the man, you know, whose leg they took—he didn't die—"

"What? Good God! Come—take me to him at once—let us hurry!

The man lay white and sunken among the pillows. His eyes gleamed strangely from his pinched face.

"I'm glad she got you," he said faintly. "I guess I'm all in this time, all right: It's all the fault of that damned cork leg—it played out on me just when I needed it most. Well—you know me, don't you? I know you—I've followed you long enough to get your points down pretty fine—an' I've had my fun with you all right—you ain't such a bad sub-ject when it comes to hypnotisin', an' I'd got you if it hadn't been for her—" he laughed, a rattling, mirthless, cackling laugh that chilled his hearers. "Say, you nurse, how long have I got? There's a lot to tell—"

"You mustn't excite yourself, try and keep calm," said the nurse, moistening his lips with a bit of cotton after dipping it in liquid, "there, is that better?"

He did not answer her, but kept his fading eyes fixed on his visitors by turns.

"I don't know what I'm tellng you for—I guess because of her, she always looked good to me, an' she sure always was lookin' out for you—or I'd have got my leg back long ago—" he mumbled a bit to himself, and then his voice came clearer. "It's a long story, an' I ain't got time for it all, so I'll cut it short an' say as my pal was run out of Colorado a couple o' years ago an' by fate as he was footin' it over the hills he stumbled on the richest lead as he ever saw. The gold stuck out in regular chunks. He covered it up after takin' the bearings of it so's he could locate if he wanted to come back, but when we got together he thought it'd be safer to send me, an' so he give me a paper with a plan o' the location on it, an' for safety he tattooed the same on my leg. If I lost the paper or had it swiped from me I could follow my leg, see?" The voice trailed off and the eager listeners feared the end had come.

"Oh, give him something, quick," cried Bess; "you don't know what this means; it is more than life to my husband; do, do something—"

As if in answer to her pleading the dying man opened his closing eyes and began speaking again:

"I was on my way out to Colorado when I got caught in that wreck and that damned doctor, thinking I was dead—oh, he knew I wasn't, all right—all he wanted was his damned experiment, I'd like to live long enough to get him—Well, you got my leg all right, though I s'pose it wasn't your fault. It put me back, and I've had the devil's luck ever since with one thing after another, an' I haven't got out to that gold mine—an' now I never shall, so's I'm goin' to give you the chance. It's for her, for her," his eyes rested on Bess with a sort of dog-like devotion that seemed somehow to dignify the meanness of the poor creature.

"It's to pay you for takin' that bag. I didn't go for to steal it—I was takin' it for luck—an' I meant all the time to give you part of the mine when I got it, I did, so help me—"

They hung breathless on his broken words, not daring to question, but the man who listened felt the load of horror lifted from his soul and knew himself free from the hideous bond.

"The circles are the big boulders at the north edge of the town—listen close —I'm goin' now—the straight line runs north one mile on the county road—the crosses—oh, God!—thirty feet—west.."

"The town?" cried Bess breathlessly.

There was only a hideous gurgle as he tried to answer, and then his jaw dropped as his last breath sighed forth.

Virginia Dancing

By Adeline Fordham

I watched a child in the moonlight
    dancing,
  Unconscious as willows swayed by the
    breeze
Of her childish body's fluent grace,
  Or of art that impels as the moon the
    seas.

She was all that is evanescent—
  Clouds that gather, and float, and pass;
Wings that fly and flutter and droop,
  And the rippling sweep of hillside grass.

She was all that is everlasting—
  The springing spirit that yearns and
    strives;
The rose of art from a bud unfolding
  To immortal beauty in mortal lives.

The Hermit of Redwood Gulch

By Mrs. F. F. Smith

ERE, Fang,—here you—it's time to start. Let's see: beans, flour, bacon, tea, coffee— Here, sir, what are you after, darting under that box? Dog-biscuit? Oh, I see we should add dog-biscuit to the list. All right. The sun is tipping Lonesome Pine, on Bordie Hill, so its close on to six. I say, Fang, what are you barking at?" continued the voice as Fang, barking furiously, ran from a group of rocks, at the corner of the house, where trickling water continually oozed out of the ground. One more spasm brought Bill out croaking. "Oh, Fang, you would make a splendid secretary. It's loaf sugar for Bill. I wonder if the scientific world knows that bullfrogs eat sugar. Here, sir, take the path!"

So talking, they started for the town of Saratoga to lay in the monthly supply of groceries.

Redwood Gulch was unique — deep in the heart of the Santa Cruz mountains, it had all the signs of civilization; isolated, yet still it showed the human touch. Civilization had built stone bridges over Stevens Creek, the new State Highway was finishing into Big Basin, and men were building cozy cabins under the stately redwoods. Up on the hill overlooking the Gulch, in the midst of an old apple orchard, stood a deserted house—its silence told no tales and Clark Edison asked no questions when he rented it, in nineteen fourteen. The country around was magnificent. The people, few in number, were civil. They had nicknamed him the "Gentleman Hermit," and kept their distance.

Down the beaten path they went, Fang leading between the old knarled apple tree, where apples with wrinkled skins were strewn all around, out to the mountain road, where their climb began. Up,

up they went, with ferns of a dozen varieties mixed with wild blackberries on either side, while overhead the limbs of the silver-barked maple and the red madrone interlocked. To the right and left pine, redwood, and the sturdy oak, covered the mountains. Stevens Creek watered their roots and the speckled trout hid under the boulders.

The distance covered to Congress Springs, it took no time to reach Saratoga. Saratoga with its junction of three roads was alive and bustling, and a curt "Good morning" to Snider, the groceryman, attracted his attention. He nodded and, taking the list from Edison's hand, kept on explaining to the deaf paper carrier, the fact that his son had left the day before for France. Fang spied a tailless cat and both ran out between Snider's legs. Edison shook with laughter as Snider landed in the Loganberry box, while barks and hisses came from the rear.

"Here, Fang, Fang! this will never do! I say, Snider, it's too bad"—as Snider picked himself up and brushed off the juice of the berries. "You, Fang, no more mischief, and keep your nose to my heels."

Fifteen minutes later Edison and Fang entered the postoffice and got the usual roll of papers from New York, also today the letter which came semi-annually was added. Then they entered the bank where the check was drawn and made out to Snider. Fang rested at Edison's feet as he slowly wrote out the slip of green paper and tore the last slip out of the book.

"Now, Fang, we'll go home over the hills up by the Fathers' Villa, past the Sellinger ranch and then cut through by the woodmen's cabin."

Just ahead of them, chug-chugging up

the grade in their roadster, were Bettie Hanson, daughter of the present owner of the Sellinger ranch and her college chum, Dorothea Vane. Dorothea had just returned from the Base Hospital work. She was a Western bud and had been studying art in France when the war broke out, and quickly offered her services for Red Cross work. As they made the grade and the long stretch of road ahead was shaded, Dorothea told Bettie how she got the long scar on her right arm. "It was a day like this, dear, and I was dressing the wound of a young American officer when something happened — one long, quick roar, then screams, smoke and horror. The young officer made a great effort to catch me, and then came a blank. What followed I do not know, but when I recovered, I was well on my way to Paris with my arm in a sling. The young officer was nowhere around and I was invalided home. I long to go back to my boys, Bettie, over there—they need me."

"Yes, Dorothea, but you are just in time to help me here. Tomorrow is the "drive" and all this mountain district is under my charge and you know it better than I. We will have a glorious drive." So talking, they reached the ranch home.

Dorothea and Bettie had met at Radcliffe and, five years later, Bettie's father had come West and bought the Sellinger ranch. What a picture they made as they sat there on the velvety lawn with Sue Sen serving lunch. Tall pink and white hollyhocks surrounded them, while deep purple mountains formed the background. Santa Clara Valley stretched out before them, and Mount Hamilton with its Lick Observatory showed in the distance.

"Look, dear," said Bettie, "to your right and here to the left, and up there near the summit. Those moving objects are Old Glory. You will see tomorrow the patriotism of our mountain folk — there is wealth here as well as generous hearts."

Dorothea's eyes were sparkling and she stood at attention as in the clear atmosphere she could see Old Glory waving from the different ranches.

"How well I know, Bettie, for from childhood I have tramped these mountains. We'll take the Highway at Congress Springs, then up past Booker's school to the King ranch, then on down the old county road, to Stevens Creek up to Bordie's, coming home by Soda Rock. Glorious! glorious! all for our boys!"

It was three o'clock when Edison and Fang passed the Sellinger ranch and cut across country past Meringoe's and came out on a ridge overlooking Redwood Gulch. Slowly they wended their way over pine needles and scented scrub and just as Old Sol dipped his golden rays into Stevens Creek back of Bordie's they entered Cathedral Hollow. What a sense of peace was here! Great, tall trees, formed a perfect dome—there to the right were mossy steps leading up to an altar formed by a redwood stump. Over against the left bank of the path a beautiful mountain stream had formed and filled a baptismal font. Sitting on the mossy steps leading to the altar Edison watched Fang as he lapped the cool mountain water from the font. Strange thoughts filled his mind; old memories stirred his emotions and a deep longing for love surged through him. Fang, starting to unearth a squirrel, seemed to sense this, for he came and put his cold nose into Edison's hands.

"Yes, Fang, I hear you and—oh, my God, Fang!"—and Clark Edison put his arms around his collie and sobbed and sobbed.

The next morning, breakfast over, the three—Edison, Fang and Bill—were contented. Edison had read and re-read the roll of papers, but the letter lay unopened on the log table, which held his pipe. It would be like all the rest he had received—six lines telling him Ted was well and doing fine at West Point. Just then the distant bells of the woodmen's wagon toiling up the mountain near was broken by the rumble of wheels and a loud voice yelling, "Whoa! Hey, there!" and a fat, round face came in view, up the beaten path between the knarled apple trees.

"Right to your left, young man," said Edison, as the youth started to walk into the main door with a sack of potatoes on his back. "Storehouse to the rear? Great day," said he, puffing under his load. "Great day, and I passed Miss Bettie an hour ago, going up the State Highway. Don't know them? Well, I do—I've had a case on Miss Dorothea ever since I picked her first primer outa the creek when we went to Booker's. Here, call your dog off. He's likely to chew mine up," and it did look like it for Fang had a scrubby little mongrel up in one of the old knarled apple trees.

"Fang, sir, charge!" and Fang immediately turned and flew around the house and into a thicket. Ten minutes later he returned with a flock of beautiful hens, one of Edison's hobbies. The lad was driving away as this happened and, giving a low whistle, he said: "Hermit? Yes, Gentleman Hermit; some sport, too."

Bettie and Dorothea meanwhile were resting under the hilly shadows at Dutch Flat while their horses sipped the water from Stevens Creek. "What a glorious day, Bettie, and oh, the results are wonderful. Tomorrow I will be on my way back to my boys over there." So saying Dorothea read aloud a letter received by the morning mail, telling her to report for duty at headquarters.

"And just think, Bettie, my work will be only three miles from the Base Hospital where I was dressing the hand of the young American officer when one of those German's 'hellers' fell. We'll go on now to Bordie's—stopping at Cypress Lodge, Laurel Court and Alderwood House. We'll get to Bordie's about noon."

Noon found them at the front gate of Bordie's where the keeper told them the family was gone. However, there was the usual invitation to rest and enjoy the milk, or taste the old wine on the cool porches of the ranch house. The long cool kitchen was just back of them and while Bettie, sitting on a three-legged stool, was writing a letter to the family, Dorothea was plying the keeper with questions.

"That cut, ma'am? Yes, just over the hill yonder. Take the trail close by Lonesome Pine"—pointing east—"coming out on the old county road just below the Gentleman Hermit's."

Bettie here broke in: "Gentleman Hermit! Who's that?"

"I don't know," laughed Long Jim. "Just Gentleman Hermit."

"Well, we'll find out," and nodding good-bye, they started on. It took only a few moments to reach Lonesome Pine, standing on the top of a high hill, those grand landmarks. Just over a smaller hill the Deserted House came into view. "Oh," said Dorothea, "I know, that is the old Sylvester place, noted for its apples in days gone by, but no one has lived there for years."

Dismounting, they took the beaten path through the trees, and both girls simultaneously bit into one of the apples with wrinkled skins — then there were cries of "bitter" mingled with peals of laughter. Screams filled the air, but failed to arouse anyone, so joyously they ran on.

"Here is the door, Bettie. I believe it will be fearfully dirty inside."

"Yes, dear, let's knock." Very gently —no response. Another tap with the same result, then Bettie raised her hand and, giving a heavy knock, sent the door open with a bang. Both girls crossed the threshold into a long living room. "Fearfully dirty" was still in both minds, but here was beauty, refinement, with exquisite color, including every shade of green. The walls were in burlap. The hand of the artist had continued where the dozens of ferns and plants ended. A long, low bookcase filled with green, leather books, green candelsticks and green cushions, scattered over the spotless waxed floor, held the girls charmed. On a raised platform by the north window stood an easel holding an unused canvas. Through the low half-opened windows they could see the wide veranda furnished with tables and rush chairs. "Gentleman Hermit," whispered Dorothea. "This beats anything I ever saw."

"Let's go," softly whispered Bettie.

"Ladies, you honor me," said a deep, stern voice, and both girls turned to face a form standing in the shadow of the easel.

Dorothea started to speak but a flood of memories engrossed her. Those eyes

—whom did he look like? Bettie came forward, explaining and handed him a small American flag. They had covered the whole district for this drive and his place was the last one—they could not pass him by. Edison invited them to be seated and Bettie continued: "We have a wonderful day." Dorothea's tongue was silent, but her brain was active as she painted a mental picture of Edison —tall, six feet; broad-shouldered; hair beautifully white; face youthful; hazel eyes (those eyes — where had she seen them?) peculiarly dressed in grey corduroy. "Looks just like an artist," she thought, when she caught these words: "My son is at West Point. He—" Just at this moment Fang came in through the low window and both girls exclaimed "What a beautiful dog!" and Bettie in a moment was down on her knees with Fang. Edison continued: "I am with you heart and soul," and, putting his hand in his pocket, took out his check book. Then he became silent. Fang and Bettie were still on the floor, and Bettie was telling him: "There is not a collie like yours in all No Man's Land." Fang was enjoying the situation when, to his surprise, Bettie pushed him away.

"Yes, dear," Dorothea's quick, firm voice said. "Look!"   •

Edison's head was in his hands and his whole body trembling. At his feet lay a check book open. Dorothea's womanly instinct had understood as she saw the book of empty stubs and she motioned Bettie to steal away. They reached the path when Fang, full of fun, barked. Edison rose quickly and, taking him by the collar, called to Dorothea: "Here, take Fang! This is my gift to the boys over there. If he serves Uncle Sam as faithfully as he has served me he will come back with a medal." He spoke quickly, firmly, not a tremor in his voice. With a loving pat on Fang's head he said: "Obedience, sir, to your mistress!" and, turning, entered the house and closed the door.

Sunset over Redwood Gulch found Edison looking for his pipe. It had fallen behind the log table and in reaching for it his hand touched the unopened letter from New York. He had not noticed be-fore that this one was much thicker than the others had been and, as he open-ed it, a folded snapshot in sepia dropped in his lap. The next fifteen minutes Clark Edison looked into the eyes of his son, Ted, a young officer of West Point. Then he read the letter telling of his going over there—one of the first to go— also how he had learned of his, Edison's, great sacrifice for him that he might go to West Point to carry out his mother's wishes for her boy. He ended: "And I am coming back, Dad, to you and Fang. It was a fancy of mine to send him to you—his pedigree is O. K. and his stock did service in the Civil War." Bill's croaking brought Edison back to earth and, taking a cube of sugar, he fed him as the afterglow flooded the gulch.

Meanwhile Fang was traveling at the rate of forty miles an hour in a baggage car, while Dorothea in a Pullman of the Lark, which they had managed to catch at San Jose, kept a porter busy answering questions: "Was Fang fed? Did he have water?" "Yes, ma'am, I done as you told me—I done it all."

"Well, here's a dollar. Be sure he's warm and has attention."

"No Vanderbilt dog gets more," muttered Washington James as, going out, he bumped into the brakeman.

Four weeks later Dorothea—over there —delivered Fang to an orderly and told him to take him to General Pershing's Headquarters — "For," said she, "Fang, the sooner we report for duty the quicker we win."

Clark Edison, with brush and palette in hand, had the same determination, as he tramped over the pine needles in the redwoods of California. He soon found a ready market in San Francisco for his work and, at the Red Cross headquarters each month they received a greenback from "C. E., for the boys over there," in a long narrow envelope.

* * * *

November 25, 1918, three years later, a tall figure dressed in the uniform of an American officer, with a dainty little woman following, left the office of a certain judge in Santa Clara county. Folding a paper, he put it into his hip pocket. "All right, Dorothea, now we'll go to Dad.

Here, Fang — Here, in, sir! — Eighteen miles, did you say, dear?"

"Yes, go straight ahead, then due west over through those foothills," and Dorothea cuddled down under the warm robe— "I do hope the creeks are not up," she said. We have to cross nine times before we reach Soda Rock. Sit down, Fang! Let me fix your medal. You insist in wearing it over your left ear." So the three—Ted, Dorothea and Fang—sped over the road to Redwood Gulch. The last creek crossed, they soon left Stevens Creek and, turning up the old county road, they went chug-chugging up the steep grade. "Right ahead, there!" exclaimed Dorothea, and Ted craned his neck to catch the first glimpse, but Fang gave one leap and was going down that beaten path between the knarled apple trees like a streak of lightning, the apples with their wrinkled skins flying in all directions. Dorothea followed and Ted brought up the rear, calling: "Oh, Dad! I say, Dad!" He gave three bounds toward the door but Fang, barking his head off for every joy, made them look back. Yes, there they were coming down the beaten path under the apple trees, Fang leaping and leading, Edison patting and wondering. What a home-coming! what exchanges of events followed around the open fire. How Ted made Edison tell over again the promise to the young mother to raise her boy to be a perfect soldier at all costs. Then in turn Ted's eyes would shine as he told Dad and Dorothea how his company was one of the first to go over, how they met the Huns and how, on that night after San Quentin was taken, he still lay out there in a shell-hole when he felt the cold nose of Fang against his neck. Then a warm gentle hand put something to his mouth, while strong arms lifted and carried him to safety. How Fang got his medal—for warning a company of twenty-five by his furious barking of the approach of snipers. "Then, Dad, there were the weeks following—for the wound (the one under my knee) refused to heal. Then it was Dorothea who dressed and nursed me. Yes, Dad, we were married in the first week of our furlough and Fang, being honorably discharged after the pistol shot in his hind leg, was best man. Then the journey home — as we were laboring through a high sea, Dad, we got the glorious news of victory. How the whole ship celebrated through the night—great!

Then came the Thanksgiving breakfast, when Ted took the folded paper out of his breast pocket and gave Edison a deed to the old Deserted House. Out there, at the end of the beaten path, between the knarled trees was a tall, new pole and a merry voice was calling them as Dorothea raised the Stars and Stripes over Redwood Gulch.

"We'll keep it in the family, Ted, old boy!" said Edison, "and, I say, Fang, come here, sir, let those squirrels alone—they're not Huns!"

Free

By Nelson Antrim Crawford

I miss your golden-glowing hair,
I miss your rain-soft eyes,
I miss your step upon the stair,
Where now but silence lies.

Yet hair and eyes and footsteps' song
Are little things to me—
I see a white road and a long:
At last my soul is free.

The Last to Desert

By Viola Ransom Wood

IT was a few minutes of closing time at the Palace of Fine Arts, when the door-man called to the chief of the guards, who was passing through the main gallery on his round of closing-hour inspection.

"Here's your letter, Reynolds," he said. "When you write, tell him we miss him, but we're all glad to hear he likes it up there in British Columbia, and is doing so well with the wheat-raising.

"All right, I will, Mart," said the other, taking the letter. Then after a moment's thoughtful look at the envelope, he asked, "What do you think of it?"

"Goes to show you never can tell," returned the door-man, in the same thoughtful strain.

"Rather makes one believe the saying that there's good somewhere in the worst of us, doesn't it?"

"It does. . . . Makes one think, too, that it isn't always wrong for a man to go counter to his sworn duty. . . . That Foursands seemed anything but a justifiable reason for such an act of leniency that day, though."

"He certainly did, that! I thought Greg was making himself responsible for a thoroughly 'weak sister,' and they're worse to handle than the hardened criminal. I thought he'd live to be sorry he didn't let us send for the patrol wagon. The boy would have drawn a few more years. As it is——" He left the sentence unfinished, which was characteristic of him.

"As it is," the door-man completed it for him after a moment, "according to this," and he nodded toward the letter in the other's hand, "he got into it over there with the Canadians."

"Yes, and accounted for a machine-gun crew before he went west with a cross of war——"

"He'd earned," interpolated the door-man significantly.

"Instead of——"

"Yes," the door-man nodded, and they both finished the thought without giving it voice. Then he went on, "It goes to show, that the Almighty comes very near to knowing His business when He gives mothers and sisters that unfaltering brand of fidelity. You know, prison statistics show that they are always the last to desert a convict."

"So I've heard. . . . Yes, I'm glad Greg had courage enough to insist upon acting wrong, according to our codes."

"So am I, Reynolds—after reading that letter. Though, that day, I was inclined to be—well, disappointed in him! But I can see by what he says in there, it has all worked out for the best. And since she has received this justification of her faithfulness, he feels he has his reward, too, for having closed the door on this kind of work, for all future time."

"I think he'll be happier doing the sort of work he's doing, now," remarked the chief of the guards.

"I think so, too."

"Yes," observed the chief, as he started on his way again, "all in all, life gives us some queer examples to think about, when we think we know all there is to be known about right and wrong."

He had not taken many steps before the door-man stopped him to add to the message he wished sent to their former fellow employee there at the Gallery.

"Tell him for me, Reynolds," he said with a meaning laugh, "that the 'Duck Baby' is gone, but the pedestal is still outside in the old place—if he ever decides to come back and do that impersonation."

The chief laughed. "We did have a lot of sport at his expense those days before

he found out who she was! . . . All right,
Martin, I'll tell him."

* * * *

The girl had intrigued Gregory Thompson's curiosity several days before he
spoke of her to anyone.

Every noon, when he was returning
from the little cafe just outside of the
Presidio, where he ate luncheon, he
would discover her seated in the same
place, by the Lagoon in front of the
Palace of Fine Arts. Always her back
was turned toward the colonnaded pathway, and she never paid the slightest attention to any of the passersby—but, sat
there, looking straight across the Lagoon
toward the rotunda—and although there
was always an open book or magazine
on her lap, Gregory never actually saw
her reading, or giving any further interest in that art.

The very fact that her attitude never
varied day after day, awakened his interest. She was like a living model
among the many pedestaled figures along
the colonnade—for this was in the early
days after the close of the great Exposition, and the marbles and bronzes which
beautified the walks between the Palace
of Fine Arts and the Lagoon were still in
place.

Then came the noon when he caught
the first glimpse of her profile—a fact
which caused his curiosity to be put into
speculative speech.

"Funny thing, just now," he said, when
he met his "chief" after he was back on
duty in the right wing of the building.
"There's a girl out there on the colonnade, that has me guessing. I'm sure
that I ought to know her — but I can't
place her to save me. She's been sitting
there on that bench near the 'Duck
Baby,' every day here lately, when I come
back from lunch. I never see her in
here, though, and she's gone at five. She
just sits there, looking across the lake
toward the rotunda, and doesn't pay the
slightest attention to anyone walking by
on the path—that I can see. Have you
noticed her, Reynolds?"

"No, I can't say that I have, Greg. Is
she out there now?"

"Was when I came in a few minutes
ago. And I caught a glimpse of her profile for the first time. That's what has
me guessing. I've certainly seen her
some place!"

"Perhaps she was a regular visitor
here, during the Fair," suggested Reynolds.

"No, I thought of that, too. I'm sure it
isn't that. Seems to be farther back. I
know that much—yes, I can't seem to
place her."

That tantalizing glimpse he had of her
profile served to whet his interest in her,
and having once spoken on the subject,
he continued to mention her from time
to time, to the other Gallery attaches.
None of them, however, could tell him
more than he already knew about her,
and none of them remembered having
seen her before. Then as days passed,
and his curiosity concerning her continued to keep him talking on the subject, the matter developed into a sort of
standing joke among his associates.
They every one began scanning that portion of the colonnade with lively interest
during the noon, and early afternoon
hours, and every time, it seemed, that
he met one of them in his patrol of the
building, he heard some story, or suggestion, or explanation concerning her.

The "chief" happened along the colonnade one afternoon and saw her making
practical use of her handkerchief.
Straightway he hunted for Thompson, to
tell him, he had discovered her identity.
She was none other than the model who
had posed for Troccoli's "Girl With a
Handkerchief."

And because she was always dressed
in black, they began to speak of her as
"Greg's Girl in Black," and the first
thing he would hear when he came in
after luncheon, would be, "Well, how's
your friend 'In Black,' today?"

Since it was the first subject they had
discovered on which Thompson could be
twitted, they kept it alive. He was ever
setting some jestful traps for one or the
other of them—and retaliation is sweet!

Gregory Thompson was a man who
looked a youth in spite of thirty-odd
years, and had a smile that maturity had
robbed of none of its boyish fascination.
He often remarked, he liked to smile, he
liked to laugh,—and those who were his

daily associates there at the Art Gallery believed it, because he practiced what he professed. To him, perhaps, more than to anyone else, was due the credit for the cheerful atmosphere which seemed to radiate throughout the Palace of Fine Arts. And there were times, when this cheeriness reached a point where the very pictures doubtlessly grinned beneath their inscrutable layers of paint after he had passed blithely through their midst, that my-but-life-is-a-joyous-old-game expression beaming on his face. He boasted, too, on occasion, that the only things he had found in life at which he couldn't laugh or smile, were the two months he had worked as a prison guard at San Quentin,—and the sight of birds shut up in cages. He claimed the sight of one, and the thought of the other, gave him a heartache. Said he had had to give up the work at the end of the second month, or else there would have been a wholesale jail delivery,—and that he'd never knowingly enter a house where there was a pet canary.

As the Girl continued to come day after day, and take up her station there in the same place on the colonnade, ignoring the very existence of any other person in that neighborhood, Thompson's friends' activities in his behalf increased. Their suggestions of ways and means by which he might make her acquaintance, or at least meet her face to face, multiplied in numbers and gained in absurdity.

His "chief" suggested they all club together and purchase a huge magnifying glass, and present it to Thompson, that he might go about his "detecting" of her identity in a befitting "Hawkshavian" manner.

The catalogue lady advised the overhauling of one of the pageant gondolas, which were left over from Fair-days. She said, she felt certain that Gregory would make a deep and lasting impression, should he dress to the role of gondolier and come gliding around the rotunda, singing some heart-rendering melancholic serenade. And, the youth who had charge of the guarding of the numismatic exhibit, offered his aid here. He said he could play the banjo, and would gladly go along as accompanist—even though the gondola did leak! If the darn thing sank — to use his words! — they could wade out. The lake was only three feet deep, any way!

Martin, the door-man, quite climaxed these, when he gave it as his opinion, that none of these schemes would be nearly as effective, as would Thompson's posing as the "Duck Baby." He went on to explain amid much laughter—as they were all walking toward the Fillmore gate, after closing hour—that if "Greg's Girl in Black" detected the remarkable difference in the sizes of the figure on the pedestal, all he would have to do, would be to quietly assure her that this sudden growth was due entirely to the wonderful salubriousness of the California climate — which could make even metal grow!

Not since the Palace of Fine Arts was opened to the public, had this efficient protective corps, whose duty it was to guard an exhibit valued into millions, secured more keen enjoyment than they got out of Thompson's "mystery."

Then came the day when, unprompted, he decided to give mental telepathy a trial. He walked slowly along the colonnade, his mind concentrating on this single thought: "Look at me, now! Look at me, now!" And behold, the effort bore results!

Not, by that, that he had influenced her mind. Oh, no! But by some angle of thought refraction, his mental influence became focused about eight feet too high. A fat, fuzzy caterpillar, mooning on an overhanging acacia bough, was irresistibly impelled to look that way. Turning its head a bit too far off the swaying leaf, it fell headlong through space.

Plump! Onto the open magazine it landed. Almost simultaneous with its arrival at that destination, there was a horrified shriek, a fling, a series of jumpings up and down in one place, more shrieks of lesser volume, some few more jumps, shudders, and hurtling around the bench—and the Girl and Thompson stood facing each other in the center of the gravelled walk, and the caterpillar was riding tempestously on a magazine raft out in the Lagoon.

The suddenness of it all, left Thompson speechless for a moment. He stood gasping in astonishment. Even his smile was temporarily dazed out of working order.

"Why, what's the—what was it?" he finally managed to ask.

"O-oh! A nasty — o-oh! — fuzzy bug — o-oh!" was the shuddering answer.

His "oh," of enlightenment, ended in a laugh, which in turn was suddenly suppressed, when he caught the look of recognition in her eyes — a recognition coupled unmistakably with hostility!

"How do you do," he said, rather inanely, seeing that they had already gone beyond the point of formal first-greetings.

"How do you do," she echoed, coolly ungracious.

"I've met you somewhere, before — haven't I?" he went on, still somewhat lacking in conversational poise.

"Yes," she acknowledged, and that look of hostility was in her eyes again.

"I thought so," he said. Then his smile broke through the daze, and all but eradicated the tiny wrinkle, this inexplicable look of hostility of hers had etched between his eyes. "I knew I knew you," he went on brightly, "but—I can't quite place you, yet."

He paused to give her a chance to explain, and smiled at her in easy friendliness.

When she failed to respond to both hint and good-humor, he amplified, "I knew that I had seen you. There has been a familiarity about you, that I've been noticing every day, the past two weeks out here."

Her reply astounded him.

"So you've been following me out here," she exclaimed. Then her voice broke. She seemed about to cry. "I'd read they did such things—but I didn't dream they'd have me followed!"

"Following you!" Gregory ejaculated by way of quick, emphatic denial. "Good Lord, no!"

"You just said so!"

"I didn't! I said I'd been noticing—"

"The same thing!" she cut in, shortly.

"It isn't the same thing! I said, I'd

been noticing you — when I passed by here, after eating my lunch—like now," he explained insistently. "That's what I meant. Good Lord, I'm no masher! I work here in the Art Gallery!"

She started to say something, stopped, and then after giving him a quick, unbending glance, made this noncommittal reply, "So, that's it!"

He couldn't tell if there was relief of mind in the words or not, but when she volunteered no more information in the short silence that followed, the buoyant humor of him kept him from following the subject further. If she didn't want to "come through," regarding past meetings, well, there were other topics for conversation. In fact, he knew of one at that moment. And, when he broached it. his eyes were dancing with fun.

"Shall I rescue the poor castaway — that is," he tried to finish soberly, "do you want me to get your magazine for you, before it gets soaked through?"

He thought he saw a faint suggestion of a smile at the corners of her mouth, when she answered.

"No," she said, "Let the miserable thing have it for a boat, as long as it'll keep afloat."

Then because of the smile-suggestion he thought he'd detected, Thompson permitted his good-humor full play. He laughed in his most delightfully wholesome fashion.

They—or rather he!—talked a minute or so about the weather, the flowers, and then, consulting his watch, he wanted to know if she had been inside the Gallery yet that day.

She shook her head.

"You ought to," he told her. "We've just installed some new Dixon's — the 'Cowboy Artist,' you know. If you're coming in now, I'll show you where they are. I'd like to hear what you think of them. I like them immensely myself."

All this was pure strategy. He wanted to induce her to accompany him indoors. He wanted greatly to learn, if he could, who she was and where they had met. And, too, he wanted to show his brother officers that he had attained the hitherto unattained, without resorting to any of the dozens of absurd schemes they had formulated!

She looked toward the bench and gave an involuntary shudder. Evidently the possibility of having another fuzzy "bug" drop down on her was not a pleasing thing to contemplate.

"Oh, all right, if you care to waste your time on me," she accepted most ungraciously, and in a decidedly unenthusiastic manner.

Gregory Thompson's geniality, however, was not to be so easily squelched. The mere acquiescence made him beam. Just watch Martin and Reynolds, now!

If he had entered the brown holland-draped doorway, leading Edwin Abbey's "Eleanor" back to do further panance in the Gallery, he couldn't have shot a more triumphant look at Martin, as they passed. Martin, the author of the absurdest scheme of them all!

When they advanced into the main gallery, Thompson's attentiveness increased—for a reason! He asked in his most courteous fashion, if she wouldn't like to look at the new arrangement of the sculpture and the Frank Brangwyn murals, before going to see the Dixon's. And, without waiting for her to reply, he plunged into an explanation of the motifs of the eight mammoth murals, calling her attention as to the manner in which they treated the four elements, both in regards to pre-civilized and modern times. Then without pause, he pointed out Karl Bitters' "Signing of the Louisiana Purchase Treaty," remarking, "That's quite interesting. Have you ever read the inscription?"

She shook her head. "No. I've only been in here once before. That was right after the opening of the Exposition."

"That so. . . . Then this'll interest you. The one standing on the left," he went on to explain, as they walked toward the work in question, "is Munroe, I believe, and the one seated is Livingston, and that is Marbois standing on the right." When they stopped in front of it he added, "The old-style lettering will probably confuse you at first, but you'll soon get the hang of it. People in those days seemed to spend a lot of time in the effort to keep folks from finding out just what it was they were writing about!"

As she read the inscription, he looked about hopefully for some of his friends. All this lingering in the main gallery was for this purpose: He wanted the "chief" or some of the other guards to come in and see them! But when she had finished the reading, and none had showed up, he had to content himself with casting another triumphant glance at Martin, there by the door, and lead the way into the right wing of the building.

The Dixon's called out an exclamation of delighted approval from the Girl, and Gregory smiled in satisfaction. He'd had a sort of a "hunch," he told himself, that these cowboys and out-of-door scenes would appeal to her. Why? Whoever heard of a plausible explanation of a hunch?

And as he watched her wondering over and over, "Who?" and "Where?" she looked long and intently at the "Prairie," and as she looked, she seemed to drop that manner of guarded antagonism toward him, and become naturally at ease in his presence.

"I used to go up on a hilltop and watch the men herding the cattle out on the plains like that," she remarked presently, and Thompson caught the note of home-sickness in her voice.

"It's true to life, then," he returned tentatively, seeking to draw her out, and still not check the thaw in her manner by too pronounced an interest in her remark.

"Oh, yes," she replied with a sudden eagerness, it seemed, to speak. "All of those men are real! Take that group over there," pointing toward the one called "Home Pastures." "Those couldn't be more like actual people. See that one in his vest and shirt-sleeves! That one's overalls! And, that one's crushed-top Stetson—and their spurs, and riatas, and all! Why, it couldn't be more like them. I'd call it 'Starting to Town,' if I had the naming of it. When we lived on the ranch, that's just the way the boys would look when they started off to Los Banos on a 'time.' That was the hardest part of coming to the city to live. The giving up of the ranch and—"

She glanced at Gregory, catching him

unawares, with alert interest predominat-ing his expression. She didn't finish what she was going to say, and once more her manner toward him became that of guarded ill will.

He tried to bridge the chasm that seem-ed to widen suddenly between them, but he could instinctively sense she wasn't listening with comprehending ears to his gossip about Maynard Dixon's visit to the Palace of Fine Arts the early part of that week. He felt that her brain was busy with thoughts having to do with those former days, which he couldn't place, any more than he could recall any reason for her continued evidences of animosity toward him. The whole mys-tery was becoming decidely more a puz-zle.

So, he sought to win her interest in another way. Tried to appeal to her aesthetic sense—once more relying upon a "hunch."

"There's a beautiful autumn scene over in the Holland section, that I'd like for you to see," he told her. "It has a clear-ness and richness about it that makes me think of the woods down in Maine. Makes me homesick for the times when I used to go down into the wood-lot beyond our lower pasture to gather nuts, wade in the brook—and do all of the things a boy likes to remember having done at some time or other in his life."

Without any show of enthusiasm she accompanied him toward this new bait he was endeavoring to dangle temptingly be-fore her eyes. And, as they walked along through the various galleries, he was commenting on, and repeating little amusing or interesting bits of gossip anent this or that painting, or artist. But before they reached the Holland section, a familiar scene on one of the gallery walls, arrested her attention, and she paused to look at it.

"That must be Mt. Tamalpais," she said, calling his attention to it, also.

It was. It was that little canvas by Carel Dake, Jr.

"It's the old mountain, all right;" Gregory affirmed. "Looks as though it might have been painted from some where around San Quentin, too," he ad-ded.

She caught her breath with such au-dible sharpness, it brought his gaze quickly to her face — and with recogni-tion!

"Miss Foursands!" he exclaimed. "Now, I know you."

"Yes, I'm June Foursands. Number—748's sister! I didn't suppose it would take you this long to remember! I didn't think you fellows ever forget even that much!" Her voice as she said this was not so bitter, as it was that of a pride-broken person who feels the gall of shame.

* * * *

After the closing hour, Thompson walked out toward the Fillmore Gate with Reynolds. He was smiling notice-ably less than usual, and the chief in-quired with exaggerated solicitude if his "case" had progressed to that "serious stage, already."

Of course all of Thompson's fellow offi-cers there at the Gallery knew that his "Girl in Black" had spent little time in his company that afternoon. That when she left, he had accompanied her to the door, and had shaken hands with her, and said, "I'll look for you on the colonnade tomorrow, about one, now." Martin had eagerly supplied them with this informa-tion.

Gregory didn't answer the "chief's" sally with the usual easy repartee. In-stead he observed seriously, "It certainly beats all, Reynolds, the way some wo-men—mothers and sisters, especially! — will stick to a man through everything!"

Reynolds replied to this with a ques-tioning glance.

Thompson continued earnestly, "You know I've been trying to remember where I'd seen her? Well, I found out. And ever since I've been provoked at wo-men generally. The weaker the man, the harder they'll stick. The oftener he falls, the more convinced they are that each time is the last—and he'll pick himself up—all man!"

He paused a little, and again Reynolds looked at him in questioning curiosity.

"You know," he went on presently, "be-fore I came here to work, I had a job as a guard across the bay. That's where I'd seen her."

Reynolds whistled softly. "So she's done her bit?"

"No!" his companion contradicted with rather unnecessary sharpness, so Reynolds thought. "It's her brother. She used to come over to see him visiting days. And, he's poor clay, Reynolds. Weak-fibered. The sort that has difficulty in keeping their fingers off of things lying around loose and handy."

"A klepto, eh?"

"Yes. And," he added, frowning in the direction of the now-jewelless tower, "he's due out again, soon."

"What was it he tried to pick up and carry off that got him in San Quentin? Usually those chaps just pilfer——"

"Embezzlement," answered Thompson, when the chief left the sentence suspended in air. "His old man had got him out of several little things," he went on to explain, "but this was his first—and only, she thinks!—big job. He was working as a sort of assistant bookkeeper in a bank there in Los Banos. He'd been taking small sums for four or five months and getting away with it. This time, he tried to hike off with a grip load. The fool didn't have sense enough to keep going, or take to cover. He stopped off in Oakland, and tried to dazzle Broadway! They caught him with most of the goods on him, for he wasn't enough of a sport to know how to spend much money on a gay time, and he'd only been there two nights when they found him. . . . The shock of the thing practically killed his mother and old man. They didn't die right on the minute, but she told me today, they never got over it. The mother died first, and about three weeks ago, the father crossed over. . . . The old man tried hard to square things for the boy. He had the coin to do it with, all right, and had done it before—but this time he couldn't work fast enough. Jack was in the hands of the law before he knew it. After that money couldn't stop it. It might have under ordinary circumstances—but the boy picked out the wrong time. A lot of officials down there had just been raked over some campaign coals, and were smarting still. They felt they must make an example of some wrong-doer right away, to show, how

strictly attending to business they were! So, young Foursands' case, being the first one of any prominence to come up, elected him the shining example. I don't mean by that that he wasn't guilty. Everybody knows that he did it. Even she doesn't deny that. . . . They gave him a light sentence considering — five years! But I surmise he would have been soaked the limit, if the old man hadn't managed some way to sprinkle some coin in the pathway of justice."

"And you say he's due to come out soon?"

"Yes — good behavior, you know, has shortened it some. . . . He's not a deep-dyed criminal. So long as he's under discipline, he's all right. . . . This pick-up stuff is queer business. A sort of a twist in the brain of persons who are otherwise as normal as you or I. They'll go along for weeks, months, maybe years, without doing a thing. Then suddenly their fingers will stick to something that belongs to someone else."

"Yes, it's a queer thing," agreed Reynolds. "It's an irresistible impulse — one that they can't control, it seems. They're rather to be pitied, I think."

"Pitied and watched," returned Gregory, shoving his hands deeper into his coat pockets. "And that watching job," he concluded with a frown "is one she is setting for herself, and pinning all of her chances of future happiness onto."

"A difficult job, I should say — for a girl," observed Reynolds. "Is there no man in the family to help her?"

Gregory shook his head. "They're the whole family. . . . And, it is a man's size job." Presently he continued the subject. "She told me the old man sold the ranch after her mother died, and they moved up here, so as to be near enough to visit Jack at every possible opportunity. In order to keep busy and not think too much—she feels the disgrace, let me tell you!—she's been teaching a night school here. But when the old man got sick, she gave up the job, and she didn't go back to it again. He left her all of his business to look after, and she's been getting things into shape, so as to leave this country when her brother gets out. She says, they'll go to Canada. To give

Jack a fresh start in a new place, among strangers, and where his regeneration can be brought about without any of the handicaps he'd have to live under here."

They had reached the Service Building, and Reynolds had to leave him to go inside to turn in the day's report. As he turned to go up the steps the last thing he heard Thompson say, was something about the "confidence" that some women had was "certainly beyond human comprehension."

* * * *

Gregory met and talked with June every day of the week that followed the renewal of their acquaintance. He now knew he had always felt attracted to her, even in such a romance-stunting place as that in which they had formerly met. And, to see her out here in the open, among the greening, flowering things along the colonnade, or meet her unexpectedly upon his patrol of the galleries —for she now came in almost daily to look with hungry eyes at the Dixon's ranch-life scenes—intensified this bond.

There was nothing striking, either in her appearance or her personality, but there was a wholesome goodness about her that caused those who knew her to feel there was no limit to the trust that might be imposed in her. She was very quiet of manner—talked little, and laughed less. But the few times that Gregory's illimitable good-humor did get her to smiling in return, he noticed that in its appealing charm there was a striking resemblance to Chase's "Woman in White Buttoning Gloves." And after he had seen this resemblance, he never passed through the Chase room, without flashing that lady a special smile.

He would have liked to have spoken to June of her brother with the same degree of frankness he had used in confiding to Reynolds, but he couldn't bring himself to do it after she had told him why it was she had been sitting out there on the colonnade, day after day, looking across the lagoon. She had, she said, been looking at one of those massive urns, which top some of the basal columns of the rotunda.

"I've been playing a sort of a game," she said, anent this the second day they met there by the "Duck Baby." "It hasn't been exactly a pleasant one, though. . . . Each day I've been putting something into that urn, across there. Thoughts of things that I've wanted to do, and vaguely planned to do in the future. And, at the same time, in my heart, I've been trying to entrench the thoughts of the new plans I must carry out, and learn to love to do—for Jack's and mother's sake. I promised mother, I'd look after him when she was gone. Especially when he was free—but handicapped in his freedom by this — this stigma. He has never been strong of will since he had that fall off of Pintol, when he was about twelve years old. But he is easily influenced. My influence for — goodness and strength, must help him and keep him headed straight from now on. I must see that he doesn't fall among evil associates—since his power of resistance isn't strong — by himself! And, in a new place, among strangers, with the lesson against this easy yielding he has had at such a cost!—with my love and faith and desire to help, to cheer and to encourage him—perhaps in time will bring about a complete regeneration. That is what my future must mean to me, Mr. Thompson. Don't think by that," she added quickly, "that I'm complaining. That I don't believe I won't get any of the good things out of life for myself — for I know that I shall. . . . But," she concluded, after a moment, looking a bit wistful at the urn, "you know and I know that we all have our dreams—and we are each of us selfish enough to want to live the things of our own planning. Isn't that right?"

What could he say in face of this complete unselfishness, this faith in the boy's ultimate regeneration? He felt that to speak his candid opinion would be like telling a little child there was no such person as Santa Claus.

So, as the days passed, he merely listened while she went on picturing the dreams that were to be brought to materialization in British Columbia. This was to be their future home, she told him. They would get a ranch up there.

"It needed only those pictures," she said as to this, "to bring me to this decision. They have awakened in me the longing for ranch life once more. British Columbia, they say, is the coming country in that. Tomorrow when I go over to see Jack, I'll tell him, and see if he doesn't think that that's where we ought to go."

That next day, when he didn't see her, brought Gregory the realization of how much she had come to mean to him, and as he made the systematic patrol of the galleries, and mechanically noted that picture after picture, and statue after statue was in its accustomed place, he was formulating some plans and dreams of plans for future, also.

The day following this, when he came back from a scarcely tasted luncheon in the little cafe outside the Presidio, he found her waiting for him, there on the colonnade beside Berge's "Muse Finding the Head of Orpheus." She was both nervous and excited, and as she talked she couldn't keep her hands still, but twirled the cord of her hand-bag round and round, and then round and round the other way, to unwind it.

Jack, she said, would be free tomorrow. She was going across after him in the morning. They'd probably leave right away for the North. She had been packing all morning. Would finish up this afternoon. Had come out here, only to say good-bye.

Right there Thompson's plans and dreams of plans of the day and the night before, and of every hour of this day, came forth into words.

"It can't be good-bye between us, June. I love you."

"Oh, I'm so sorry you've said that! I wish you hadn't said it."

"But I love you, June. . . . Won't you marry me?"

"Oh, you must forgive me, Mr. Thompson. I wish I'd never come out here now! If you love me, I'm—I'll have to hurt you. I hate to hurt you! But I can't—don't you see what you ask is impossible?" There were tears in her eyes.

"Why? Don't you love me, June, dear? Can't you—don't you think you could ever?"

"Oh, I'm sorry!" Then quickly she ex-

plained, "Love and marriage — for me — are over there in that urn. . . . And, she added, seeing he was about to protest this, "there's another reason. Even if I loved you, I couldn't marry you—because of Jack. You would be a constant source of reminder to him of — across there! That first day I saw you here, I almost hated you, because I had seen you when you were — guarding him with a gun! Since then, though, I've come to look upon you as a—a friend. I told Jack about you yesterday. He said you were all right. That you had always treated him 'white.' Had treated them all that way. Some of them don't — poor boy! Poor chaps!"

"But, June, I love you," Gregory insisted simply. "And no one can be sorrier than I am, that I ever worked across there. My heart aches to think of them. Don't blame me for that mistake, dear."

"I'm not blaming you—but Jack must be my first consideration in the future."

"But he would be my consideration, too. And, dear, I've hated to say it—but I think it'll take more than your hand— it'll take a man's—to keep him—going straight."

But she wouldn't believe or be warned, and was stubborn in her resolve to sacrifice self to duty, and their parting there on the colonnade was a painful thing for them both.

"I'll live for your letters, June," he told her, holding tightly to her hand. "Now, if the time ever comes when you need help—just send for me, dear. I'll do anything, and go any place you say— for I love you, and always will."

"I'll remember," she told him, and as she withdrew her hand from his clasp, she said, as she had acknowledged before, "Jack must always come first—but what I think of you, is something that isn't possible to leave — across in that urn. That goes with me."

"And, yet it can't be 'yes,' June?"

"Don't—please. It's useless to say it again. . . . Good-bye."

* * * *

Mid-afternoon of the next day, Gregory came face to face with June in the Sargent room. He had been thinking of her so steadily that he scarcely accredited his eyes at first—thinking his heart-hunger for her had conjured an hallucination. Then when he was sure that she was real, he gathered her into his arms, and kissed her until the "Study in Nude" must have considerately turned her back wholly toward them, and "Joseph Jefferson" closed his eyes, giving an Rip Van Winkle impersonation solely in the interests of romance.

"Girl, girl! I thought you were gone! I thought I had lost you. Oh, my dear, I can't believe my eyes—yet!"

She extricated herself from his embrace, but left her hands in his while she explained her presence.

"Jack—poor kid!—wanted to see what was left of the Exposition. So we didn't leave this morning. We're going on the nine o'clock train out of Oakland tonight." And, as she talked, her glad love-filled eyes looked into eyes that were almost worshipful in their happiness.

"Where is he—Jack?" Gregory asked, looking beyond her, searchingly.

"He's over in the other wing—in the Hungarian section. He was interested in those futurists and cubists, and all that. It's the first time he's ever seen anything of the kind. I told him I'd come over here, and look you up, while he was finishing them, and bring you back with me." She then concluded in a voice a trifle throaty from nervous uncertainty, "He remembers you, and wants to see you—to thank you for your kindness—and——"

"No kindness," he broke in, understanding her feelings, and endeavoring to aid her by appearing matter-of-fact. "I'm glad he wanted to see what is left over of the Big Time. More than glad since it brought you here again. June; dear, dear June," he added, in a voice that was far from matter-of-fact, "I don't see how I'm ever going to let you say goodbye, now!"

When he was surely going to take her into his arms again, she stopped him quickly.

"Don't, Gregory—please! It's no use—even thinking of it, is of no use! What has to be, just has to be—regardless! I must think of Jack——"

"Let me think of him with you. Let

me, June. I want to teach you to smile and laugh, and find the smiling and the laughing things in life. And I want to help you to teach the boy the way to them, too."

"No, no! It couldn't be. He'd always see in you the reminder of the days that couldn't be laughed at."

"That hurts, June!"

"I'm so, so sorry—but, it's true."

After a moment of sheer downcast, hope again came to him.

"But maybe he wouldn't feel that way, dear," he suggested. Then he explained the basis of this hope. "He wanted to see me! If he had felt so—so awful toward me — he couldn't have wanted that! . . . Perhaps he understands how I loathe the thought of those two months. Oh, you don't know how I have loathed them and myself for gritting my teeth and keeping on rubbing my very soul the wrong way, day after day, for two months! I want to forget it, as much as he will want to forget it. . . . Just say the word, June, dear. Just say it, and I'll quit my job here, now, and go to Canada with you tonight. Just say it, dear."

"Oh, that is madness, Gregory—sheer madness! Let's go to Jack before I become as mad as you are! Come!" And without giving him further chance to plead his cause, she led the way out of the little Sargent room, into and through other galleries where people were roaming about, neither pausing or speaking until they reached the "Chamber of Horrors," as the guards always referred to a certain room in the Hungarian section, and found Jack seated on one of the central benches, evidently nervously waiting their coming.

The meeting of the two men was awkward, made so by Gregory's desire to demonstrate his friendly attitude toward the brother of the girl he loved, and still not be effusive; and, because Jack hadn't as yet gotten back the feeling of equality with other men. And, the weather, which is usually considered a safe topic for inane conversation, almost brought Thompson to the commission of an embarrassing faux pas. It had been on his tongue's tip to say, "It's nice out, isn't it?" when the double construction possible to that observation, sent the blood coursing to his face, and his tongue tripped stammeringly over the revised version of the sentence, "It's nice—on the colonnade today, isn't it?"

Just when the conversation was showing alarming signs of becoming afflicted with locomotor ataxy, the "chief" came hurrying in, and called Thompson a few pace to one side.

"Say, the dickens is to pay in the next gallery," he said, his voice low, but still not so low but what he was saying being plainly audible to the other two persons in that narrow room. "Somebody's bunched off with one of those little Nagy's. In the last quarter of an hour, too, for I was through there not more than that long ago."

"What!" exclaimed Thompson, astonished, and not absolutely believing his ears. Never before had there been a theft of a picture in the whole gallery. Never even during the thronged Exposition days.

"That little thing called 'Fairyland'," Reynolds went on to confirm. "It's small, but it's worth a bunch of money. Have you noticed any suspicious—"

He didn't complete the question, for his glance took in "Greg's Girl in Black"— and her companion. He knew her story, and there was no mistaking the pallor on the young man's face—prison complexion. The kleptomaniac.

Involuntarily Thompson's eyes followed his "chief's" and his heart seemed to be weighted beyond beating for a moment. Then he looked at June, to find her eyes, also fixed with a sort of soul-hurt despair on her brother's face. In the next few seconds, the silence in that little gallery was pregnant, tense.

The quick perspiration of fear gathered on the boy's brow. He reached nervous fingers into a pocket for his handkerchief to wipe away the tell-tale moisture.

There was a clatter of something falling to the floor and a white plaster of paris object rolled in under the bench. Reynolds retrieved it, and turning it over and over, examined it a second or so before speaking.

"What's this, now?" he asked, frowning puzzled. It had an oddly familiar appearance. He then looked again at young Foursands and saw, what the other two there had also seen with heavy hearts— that the boy's eyes were now pools of guilty fear.

June crouched down upon the seat, and covered her face with her hands to shut out the sight she felt was to come. Seeing her in this hurt, despairing attitude, filled Gregory with a sudden fury against the one who had caused it. But before he could say or do anything under sway of the sudden passion, Reynolds stepped closer to Foursands and commanded sharply to be told where this small white object came from.

"It's just a little souvenir I picked up down there where they're smashing the Jewel Tower," the boy tried to lie, but his tongue would not be glib.

An exclamation from the "chief" put an end to the futile explanation any way. He now recognized the bit of plaster of paris.

"Why, this is the toe off that Boccioni, 'Muscles in Quick Action'," he said, directing the remark to Thompson particularly. "You know we noticed it was pegged on—was loose."

Thompson nodded, growing more and more sick of heart. He, too, anticipated what was coming.

Reynolds grasped Foursands' arm. "Isn't that where you got this?" he demanded. "Isn't it? Now, don't try to lie to me," he finished sternly.

Jack cringed.

"I didn't think it amounted to anything," he sought to excuse weakly. "I just took it for a souvenir. Honest—"

Reynolds cut him short. "That'll do! I guess we'll have to see if you've picked up any more souvenirs!"

When from under the young man's coat he brought to light the missing "Fairyland," Thompson sat down heavily beside June, and put his arm about her in sympathy, and protective possession.

"That settles it, dear," he said with finality. "The fight's going to be mine now. From this on the responsibility is going to be mine, too."

"Can you—do you think you can get him out—save him?" she asked through tears. "The very thought of his going back across there—kills me!"

"I know—I know too well about that! I'll do my best to prevent it * * * If they'll let me," he said after a moment of wild ideas, "and I give my word to take

him out of the country—shall we three leave for Canada tonight, June?"

And, since the last part of the story was told first, you know what her answer was.

A "Two-Reel" Romance By Ruth Young

Her tent was pitched just down the trail,
  A little ways from mine,
Like a saucy white-winged bird it perched
  Beneath a mountain pine;
And in the early hours of dawn
  Up through the whispering trees,
Her merry songs were wafted
  On a mischievous morning breeze.

She did not wish for company,
  Save of the sparkling brook;
Or birds and bees and flowers,
  Or a glist'ning trout on hook;
And I tried by best to see her
  Tho' my woodsman's art was naught
When the biggest catch of the season
  Refused, point-blank, to be caught.

So my heart was very heavy,
  All things jingled out of tune,
As I wandered at the water's edge
  One perfect afternoon;
On coming from a sheltered cove,
  On a rock out in mid-stream,
I saw a man and yelled "hello!"
  He turned—and then I heard a scream.

Surprised, I saw the angler fall;
  I leaped into the tide,
To find 'twas not a man—but her;
  I splashed out to her side.
At first she seemed quite angry,
  Disheveled, too, and wet,
But when I carried her to shore
  She seemed quite glad we met.

My life! but she was pretty,
  Tho' attired just like a man,
With great gray eyes and curly hair
  And a healthy coat of tan;
And while she dried her garments
  By sitting in the sun,
We reached the same conclusion—
  Our "fishing luck" had but begun.

At sunset, as we strolled toward camp,
  When she had fished for trout,
I told her as I held her—reel
  I'd rather fish her out.

Doc Weed's Daughter

By Milton Barth

FORTY years had passed since the San Andreas hills first felt the miner's pick. The diggings had been rich and every stream and gulch in Calaveras county, which bordered on the Mother Lode, had given richly of her treasure. Ten miles to the southeast, Angels Camp, labored in her deep bowled mines for the gold which was planted too deep for the pick and shovel of the forty-niner. The Southern mines had proved exceedingly rich and the Sierras were famous for their yellow metal.

In the waiting room of the old brick Metropolitan Hotel sat two men, one a grizzled tramp-like fellow, a miner, in his younger days. His beard was long and gray; his eyebrows were large, white and bushy. Beside him, near the stove, sat a young man who might have been twenty-five or more. His hair was black and shiny and slickly parted in the middle. He puffed vigorously at a cigar of quality.

The old man spit a volley of tobacco juice at the stove (and missed it). "Say," he said, addressing the young man. "I heerd you askin' the proprietor about mines. Know anything about them?"

"Not much?" answered the youth.

"Well, I'm going to tell you about sluice-minin' or rather sluice-stealing. Ever heard of Doc Weedy?"

"No," drawled the youth. "Who was he?"

"Doc Weedy!" drawled the miner. "Well, he was some doctor; best we ever had in these parts. I come here in '49 and pitched my tent, or shanty rather, just a block down the grade from here. Things was rich, here, then. All we had to do was to shovel up the gold; it lay all around; any kid could pick it up. We spent lots too; everybody had lots of money. By and by, in a couple of years, things was pretty well torn up on the surface and gold got scarce. Out near Calveritas there was still pretty good sluicin'.

"Weedy was a good doc, all right, and I ought to know; he pulled a bullet out o' my left arm. Mike Sims put it in with his old Colt. I was a damn fool to let him do it, but they puts Sims in the graveyard soon after and I ain't sayin' just how he came to cash in. I've seen men hang to a tree for tellin' too much.

"Well, I knew old Doc Weedy pretty well. Doc's wife died in Tennessee and he came West with little Myrtle the next Spring. She was only ten years old, the only gal in camp and the boys went crazy about her.

"In a few years she had reached sixteen—sweet as honey and pretty as a picture. She acted as housekeeper for the old doc. He want much on dressin' up, though this little gal used to make a gentleman out o' him. He had long white, terbacher-slopped whiskers which always reminded me o' pine trees and darn poor ones at that. She used to wear her sleeves rolled up to the elbows showing her pretty arms. She always wore a flower. She was the only rose I ever seen here in them days. There want any roses planted here then.

"Doc Weedy poured red-hot mercury into the fellows' wounds and—killed all the germs—they didn't know about these pesky germs then. Then, he would heal the burn. He could heal a burn every time—leave that to doc.

"Doc took quite a fancy to me. I was a young fellow of about twenty-a-a-oh, about your age. Doc called me to him one day and said: 'John Patrick, I like you! You know arithmetic and literature; you spell pretty good; come to my house as often as you like and teach my Myrtle. I trust you. Keep the other geeks away;

they aren't around here for any good. I want her to learn writing and arithmetic; you teach her.'

" 'I'll do it fer you,' I said, taking his bony hand in mine. 'Fer you, doc, I would do anything. (A word for him and two for myself—I loved that gal.)

"There was lots o' sluice-robbin' about that time and the sheriff, who lived next door to the doc, was hard after the thieves.

"On stormy nights the sluice-boxes at Calveritas would be robbed. The robbers always escaped.

"Doc Weedy attended many calls from far and near. His services were in great demand. On rainy nights, his calls came often. The sheriff didn't suspect his good and trusted neighbor 'till one night when the Doc galloped out o' the stable during a terrific cloudburst. The sheriff heard the doc splash by.

"He ran to his barn and sprang upon a horse which was saddled and ready for action. He mounted and started in pursuit, keeping at a respectful distance.

Yes, the doc went toward Calveritas. In a bunch o' brush the doc left his horse and, sack in hand, went after the gold.

"Pretty soon he returned and started toward his horse. As he mounted a shot rang out and a streak o' fire pierced the black night. You can bet your stars who was hit. Doc Weedy never came home—alive.

"As he lay there soaked in water and blood, he muttered a few words. The sheriff kneeled in the pouring rain beside him.

" 'Don't tell the kiddie,' he gasped. Then he checked in.

"The truth was a terrible shock to the whole diggin's.

"I had promised old doc to look after the gal if anything ever happened to him."

"And did you?" asked the youth.

"Drop into my parlor, kid, and you will see. We've been married some thirty years and remember—she knows all the readin' writin' and arithmetic that's good fer her.' "

A Snapshot of the Sierras

By Willis Hudspeth

Far down a canyon curves a caravan
  Of covered wagons on a lonesome trail
  That leads from California's fruitful vale
And marks the progress of the merchantman.
The sluggish mules of six and seven span,
  Beneath their burden of the box and bale,
  Crawl through the reddish dust-cloud like a snail,
  Or prehistorical crustacean.

The countless pinnacles above impress
  Us as the teeth uneven of a saw;
As old as Tyre, a redwood's loftiness
  Defies the prestige of botanic law,
And while we peer and wonder, doubt and guess,
  Our scholarship is swallowed up in awe.

The Old Field School

By Frank M. Vancil

Here, 'mid Nature's wild and rugged
  scenes,
With no inviting prospects to adorn,
The latent spark of genius brightened
  forth—
The greatest lives in history were born.

BACKWARD, far backward, in the dim vista of bygone years, there is no dearer or more revered spot in memory than that embodied in our early school days. To most of those of advanced years, these scenes were enacted amid the primeval shades of the old Field School House.

Generally, this pioneer landmark was conveniently located upon some country thoroughfare within a grove of natural forest trees; and, if possible, in proximity to a spring of water. The school district, of which this rural temple of learning was the nucleus, included an irregular area of many square miles in extent, and embraced an isolated population of from 40 to 60 children of school age.

The present system of free schools was unknown in those days. All terms of school were organized and conducted on the subscription plan; that is, the patrons subscribed to an article of agreement with the teacher for a certain number of pupils at a stated rate of tuition per scholar, and paid therefor out of their own pockets at the close of the term. Board for the teacher was generally included, whereby it became necessary for him to "board round," visiting each patron with a frequency proportionate to the number of pupils sent by him to school.

The school building, erected by the volunteer labor of the citizens of the district, was generally made of logs or of hand-made brick on the ground, and seldom exceeded in size, 25 by 30 feet. A large open fire-place occupied one or both the ends of the structure, the fuel for which was contributed by the parents of the pupils, corresponding in quantity to the number of children sent by each to school. The chopping and bringing in of the sticks were alike done by teacher and pupils.

The furnishings of the room were wholly the handiwork of the amateur mechanics of the neighborhood, and consisted of two or three stout wall tables, some three feet wide and ten feet long, used for writing, and upon which were placed· the divers lunch baskets and buckets, and a motley array of wearing apparel, not convenient to hang upon the wooden pegs that ornamented all the vacant spaces between the one door and the four little windows of the building.

The seats for the pupils were rough benches of various heights and lengths, made from slabs, flat side up; and were placed parallel to the sides of the room, the inner and lower ones for the smaller pupils, leaving a central rectangle, at the end of which was the ink-bespatterd desk of the teacher. There· was not, as a rule, a semblance of a blackboard or wall map; and the only decorations, aside from the gauzy network of the geometrical spider in the corners of the ceilings and the paper wads adhering thereto, were the hieroglyphics of keel and charcoal, left by spectacular urchins on the wall.

School was called by loud rappings of the teacher upon the window sash, while the entrance of the mixed throng of knowledge-seekers into the room was characterized by an indiscriminate rush for the more desirable seats. It was strictly a case of "first come, first serve"; and everywhere there might be observed animated bevies of both sexes in promiscuous and hilarious enjoyment. Nothing but the most flagrant violations of decorum was noticed by the teacher, and the hickory rod was the panacea for all severe offenses. Pupils attended school at pleasure, and seldom did the instructor rebuke the social communications and sly mischieviousness of the students. Willful misdemeanors and serious disturbances were common, and the severest chastisements were promptly inflicted. There were no school officers to whom to appeal for assistance in subduing the unruly, and the teacher was truly "monarch of all he surveyed," and governed and controlled the infant republic or abdicated the premises. The contest for supremacy between the teacher and the combined forces of disorderly boys was often spirited and sometimes tragical.

The three R's — "Readin', 'Ritin' and 'Rithmetic," were the chief studies, to which might be added that of spelling. Geography, grammar and history were considered advanced studies, of no practical importance, and were pursued only by an occasional student of mature years. Outside of spelling and reading, there were no regular classes, owing to the great disparity of text books. Nearly every publication extant was represented by the pupils in reading, from the backless Testament to the last year's almanac. Most every one brought a copy of Webster's Blue-back Speller, which was also used for a reader in the more elementary grades. The copies of arithmetics most in evidence were those of Deboe, Pike and Ray. Slates were exclusively used, and many ciphered out the intricate problems with bits of soapstone or keel for pencils, gathered from the banks of neighboring streams.

There was a time especially set apart for writing. The copy book was a home product, made from blue, fools-cap paper, and the pens were fashioned from goose quills, under the skillful hands of the teacher. Copies were set, suitable to the various capacities of the pupils, and ranged in character all the way from the initiatory step of "pot-hooks" to that of "Many men of many minds," etc. The writing class sat before the ponderous tables facing the wall, and the only time of the day's session of school in which there was an approximation of quietness in the room was the half-hour devoted to writing, broken only by the musical squeak of a score of goose-quill pens.

The study of spelling was made very prominent, and the recitations were always oral. The classes lined up in a long row, and the words of the lesson were pronounced to each pupil in turn. When a word was mispelled, the pupil below, who spelt it correctly, took his place above the one who missed it; and the pupil who stood at the head of the class at the close of the recitation, was given a "head mark," and took his place next day at the foot of the class. The pupil obtaining the greatest number of "head-marks," during the term of school was given a premium at the close.

There were "spelling matches" at night, which was a season of unbridled fun and frolic. Two captains were designated who "chose up," and the house was divided, when the battle raged for supremacy. The most exciting time came when both sides stood up and "spelled down," each contestant sitting down when missing a word. This contest was frequently extended, as there were many good spellers; and it often happened that some diminutive pupil, generally a little girl, would hold a half dozen stalwart opponents in check, and oftentimes come off victorious.

It goes without saying that the arithmaticians as well as the spellers of the Old Field School days were far more proficient than those of the present. Now, spelling and reading are well nigh lost arts, as is evidenced by the inefficiency of a majority of graduates of our high schools and colleges. Pupils are rushed from arithmetic into algebra with a very superficial knowledge of practical mathematics. Orthoepy and syllabication are touched with scrupulous care, and articulation and modulation in reading are smothered in the arduous effort to get "the tho't."

The difficulty is not so much in the incompetency of teachers of the present, nor in the inferiority of text books, but in the limited time of instruction given, incident to the derogatory expansion of the common school course of study. There have been too many frills, furbelows and fads attached, instituted chiefly by designing speculators, forcing a too rapid, and hence inadequate study of the fundamental principals. It is a serious fact that in the rush and cram of graduation, the vital elements of education are too often ignored, and boys and girls go out into the world with their gaudy diplomas sadly deficient in useful and practical education.

The recreative sports and amusements of the old country schools were many and varied in character. The boys mostly engaged in what was termed, "Town Ball," "Bull Pen," "Cat," "Dare Base," "Marbles," and "Mumble Peg"; while the girls played, "Puss Wants a Corner,"

"Jump the Rope," "Ante-over," "Ring-round-rosy," and a great many other quiet games.

Jumping, foot-racing, wrestling, and "Black-man," were also favorite pastime of the boys, and skating and snow-balling in winter were highly enjoyed by all. Attending all these were innumerable little joyous pleasures of youthful associations that have passed with the age of long ago. The grape-vine swing is ruined now, and bright-eyed boys and girls no longer as of yore troop the woods in nutting parties; search for wild strawberries in the meadows, or ramble beside an ice-fetted brook in early spring time looking for the early "Johnny-jump-ups." The cherished, halcyon scenes come back to us, but only upon the silent, mystic wings of memory.

The Desert Land

By Alice l'Anson

I am going far from the mad turmoil
To a sun-baked ranch on the desert soil,
From long years spent mid the city's noise
To the simple life and the primal joys,
To the wide blue sky and the warm brown sand
And the silent deeps of the Desert Land.

There is room to breathe, there is room to grow,
But not where the tides of traffic flow
'Round the money marts and the human hives
Where men are chained to their sordid lives—
Souls that will never understand
The dreamy lure of the Desert Land.

When I leave the doubts and the pallid fears
That have stalked my soul thro' the grinding years
For the mystery of the realm I love,
With its mountain peaks and the stars above,
I shall feel the peace that the world has bann'd—
I shall find it there in the Desert Land.

I am going back to the heart of things,
Where the desert wren in the cactus sings;
Away from the weary, jostling throng,
In the merciless maelstrom all day long—
For I hear the call of the Desert Land—
Oh, I feel God's there and will understand!

4

The Silver Sea

By M. Barth

THE Mendocino coast boldly faced the approaching storm. The frowning bluffs and rugged pinnacles of barren rock stood proudly guarding the mainland. The blue sea usually peaceful, pounded hard this bit of jagged coastline.

A mile to the south of the prosperous lumbering town of Fort Bragg, the Noyo river empties into the Pacific. The tide ascends the river for a distance of three or four miles. On either side of the cove which forms the river outlet, rocky bluffs arise and tower mightily over the entrance of the Noyo. At times the river water is entirely shut away from the ocean by the sand which the waves pound into a bar at its mouth.

The Storm King had piled a high bar across the entrance and had effectually bound in the river.

Several huts, the homes of hardy fishermen, squatted on the river's edge under the towering cliff near a dilapidated saw mill long since abandoned.

The wind shrieked and tore hard at the weathered shakes which covered the cabins. In the cabin which stands nearest the sea sat an old man. He was talking to a girl at his side.

"Your father," said he, "was drowned on such a day as this. Yes, yes, I remember well. I seen him go down for I was with him until the last. I tried to hold him as I clung to the rudder of the upturned dory but I was too weak and he was not himself that day, and he went down."

The old man lifted the calico curtain that Dollie had placed before the window.

"Look," he said pointing at the sea. "We'll not fish for some days; the salmon will go uncaught. I am old; I must not take chances in such a sea. If I would go what would become of you, dear."

Dropping the curtain, he bent over and kissed her rosy cheeks.

"There," he said, "the storm may blow over but we have each other."

"I am glad God gave me you, Uncle, and we have much to be thankful for. Hand me my shawl, Uncle, dear. I must go and walk on the cliff. In a storm like this I love to face the wind and tempest. I love to watch the waves break high and splash against the barren rock. Out there, I feel so little and God seems so great; I can almost hear his voice. And I know that Daddy is safe in a better place. It makes me so happy and yet so sad."

Dollie poured the black coffee into a thick white cup and set it on the rough-hewn log table to cool a bit. When it had cooled sufficiently, the old man drank it, smacking his lips when he had finished.

"Here is your wrap, and come back by noon little girl," he said.

Dollie threw the shawl over her pretty yellow locks and kissing the old man good-bye she shut the cabin door. She ran eagerly forward toward the wind-swept bar.

Large heaps of moss and kelp were lying on the beach. Seaweed of every variety was piled on the sand. Dollie slipped her hands in the pockets of her big coat for the wind was cold. Soon she ascended the winding path up the cliff which leads toward the blow-hole. As was her custom during a storm, she walked to the end of the promontory which juts like a huge finger out into the sea. The mighty waves crashed and thundered as they ascended the blow-hole and shot skyward.

The sea was rough; so rough that the Phyllis Dollar had left her anchorage in

Noyo Cove and now stood bobbing like a cork on the storm swept sea. Two other lumber schooners from Fort Bragg had cut their anchor-lines and were putting to sea only half loaded to avoid being crushed by the awful pounding of the tempest. Some damage had already been done by the mad waves. Large logs from some ill-fated raft tumbled and pitched in the breaking surf. Harder and harder blew the wind; higher and higher rose the milky waves.

For an hour she stood gazing, her blue knitted shawl streaming in the wind. Here and there a strand of yellow hair peeped through the blue yarn. Redder became the roses on her cheeks. Larger and whiter grew the white-caps until they became a mass of snow-white water. The sun found its way through the break in the clouds and the ocean glittered like a large diamond.

"The silver sea!" she exclaimed. "The silver sea! How beautiful! How beautiful!"

She shaded her eyes with her hand. What was that she saw? Something clinging to a spar—could it be a body? The spray rose like white fog over the cliff and wet her cheeks. Through the mist a rainbow smiled.

"There is hope—the rainbow," she sighed.

Again she looked for the spar but the object on it had disappeared.

The black clouds rushed against the sun; it grew dark. She could hardly stand against the wind so terrific had become the gale. She waved her arm at the ships and uttered a fervent prayer for their safety. Well, she knew, that morning might find them piled upon the heartless rocks and their crews drowned.

With her blessing bestowed, she turned homeward.

An awful night passed, such as the Mendocino coast, rough as it is, seldom experiences. The wind came in blasts, the rain poured. It seemed as if nothing could live in such a sea. The lamp in Tony's cabin was still burning when the light of day again looked forth upon the world.

On stormy nights, the lamp always lighted Tony's cabin window and his hut,

crude though it was, was always open to the unfortunate.

The morning sun hid behind the black clouds; the wind had considerably abated.

When breakfast was over Dollie washed and dried the dishes. Then she hurried to the beach.

Wreckage was scattered every where. The Storm King had done his work; logs and lumber were lying about or tossing on the breakers.

As Dollie Hardy skirted the Noyo beach, her keen eye caught a glimpse of a life preserver floating in the receding tide. She read the inscription, "Queen of Dawson." A few yards away, half concealed from view near a large rock, lay the body of a man. Still and lifeless he lay upon the wet sand.

She ran forward; her little fingers clenched his coat. With a determined effort she dragged him back to the dry sand. An ugly gash crossed his forehead; his lips were purple. Two gray eyes stared vacantly from a bleached face; black rings half circled his eyes. His chin was square; his hair was red. His square shoulders were built upon a big framed body.

Dollie quickly unbuttoned his wet shirt. She placed her ear to his huge breast; his heart was still. She unbuttoned his shoes and threw her shawl over his bare feet. She turned him upon his face and tried to lift him by the waist to let the water out of his lungs but he was too heavy. Running toward the cabin, she called the old man.

"Uncle!" she cried, "a man, a man is drowned—come!"

Uncle Tony reached for the whisky flask, his friend in time of need, and hobbling out followed the girl to the beach.

For two hours they worked his arms and forced his huge bellow-like lungs into action. At last his eyelids quivered—moved. Life was in him and Dollie rejoiced.

The old man placed the whisky flask to Carlton Darrow's lips. The reviving man choked.

Again the sun emerged from behind the clouds and the sea shone as silver.

The young man closed his eyes and lay silent, breathing heavily.

When he awakened he found himself lying in a strange hut with rough furniture and crude implements about. Best of all he gazed into the face of a beautiful girl, with yellow locks, who smiled down at him from two pretty blue eyes.

A week of Dollie's nursing brought him back to health and vigor. He admired her simplicity and honesty. The women he knew had been mostly worldly, they did not say what they meant—what they really thought—but were smothered in conventions which induced hypocrisy and lying. She was unstained, untainted by such teachings and it did not take Carlton long to realize that she loved him. He was in return charmed and delighted with her straight-forward ways.

Uncle Tony told Carlton of Dollie's father, of the wreck, and of her mother. Carlton related the ship wreck, its cause and the terror and horror of it all.

In a week Carlton was walking around and Dolly insisted on his accompanying her in her rowboat, the Tango. Up the Noyo they trolled as far as the company's tunnel some four miles upstream. For a week they boated, or tramped the redwood forests together. Dolly knew where the dewberries were thickest; where the thimble berries strayed along the river bank, where the huckleberries and the wild blackberries grew. She showed him these places but it was too early in the season for them to bear fruit.

Best of all, they gathered wild flowers together, and if you were ever in love you will understand. Many a baby-blue-eye and posy they gathered.

"Here, see this one," he would say when he found a pretty wild rose or posy. She would take it and kiss it; then pin it on his coat.

Several times he unconsciously placed his arm about her but she did not resent it—she had not learned to pretend to hate the things she loved.

A fortnight had passed. The old man spoke to Carlson saying:

"Stick around a-while, me son, and maybe you can get a job at the Fort Bragg mills or maybe help me a bit with the fishing."

Life had been very interesting on the Noyo and Carlton decided to stay. He applied at the mills but no suitable position was open.

One evening he met a surveyor in a hotel at Fort Bragg.

"Come along with me," said the chunky, red-faced surveyor. I'm surveying a bridge in the redwoods over a gorge. Meet me at the station at seven when the logging train pulls out tomorrow morning."

"I'm with you," replied Carlton. He was aching for a chance like this. "It might lead to something better," he mused.

The next morning he stepped aboard the logging train and was pulled and jerked up the Sherwood-Greenwater road.

Carlton drove stakes, made computations, hatcheted the underbrush and thoroughly enjoyed the day. The blue sky overhead, the rugged redwoods standing like giants, the sage, the oak and the pine all had a song for him and it was a song of gladness.

He spent his Sundays on the Noyo with Dolly and Uncle Tony.

He dressed well and made friends easily. Soon he found himself the objective of several of the town girls. Strong, broad-shouldered and healthy, he was regarded by the Fort Bragg lasses as a prize to be sought after and many a redwood belle pinned on extra finery and put an extra puff of powder on her nose.

Phillis Dorsey, the banker's only daughter, learning that Carlton was a young man of good family and that his father had mining interests in Alaska smiled artfully on him and cast her net in his direction. He was asked to visit at her stately mansion and he went often for many were the invitations he received. She was twenty-three summers old and had remained single because the local boys didn't suit her. At least that is the way she explained it.

Carlton stayed with his job and prospered. He loved the wild free life.

Mr. Dorsey, perseiving that Phillis had taken a mortgage on the young man's affections offered him a place in the bank. Mr. Dorsey insisted and Carlton finally accepted.

Soon the engagement of Phillis was whispered around and although only a rumor it spread like wild-fire. It even extended to the little hut on the Noyo and Dolly's eyes were filled with tears. Many a day and night her little fists rubbed her wet blue eyes and she sobbed like her heart would break.

Carlton called less frequently at the hut. He found Miss Phillis exceedingly charming and felt that she would grace any man's home, yet, with all her polish, she lacked something; he did not feel the same toward her as he had toward Dolly. Mr. Dorsey lavished many presents upon him and the Dorsey twelve-cylinder car was always at his disposal. He could plainly see that the Dorseys expected him to join the family tree. A blind man could see that and Carlton was not blind.

In a shady path bordering Pudding Creek one Sunday afternoon, Phillis and Carlton were strolling beneath the redwoods north of the county bridge. Phillis spied a stately redwood. She made her way to a log beneath it and sat down. Carlton sat down beside her. She nestled close.

"Do you know what the girls are saying, Carlton?" she began.

"Why, —a—no," he stammered, though in his heart he suspected.

Her head now rested upon his shoulder.

"They say we're engaged—say you'll have me, Carlton," she urged, "and let's have it over with."

He choked: "I, I—love—you very much."

"It's a go then, isn't it, Carlton, dear," she said embracing him.

"Yu—y-e-s," he stuttered. He tried to put his arms around her but it was an awkard attempt.

"Kiss me, honey," she cooed.

Carlton did as he was bade. A lump caught in his throat. He did not mind kissing her or making love to her but the idea of marrying her stunned him. A picture of Dolly stood before his eyes. He left like a sneak, her betrayer. Mechanically he arose and they walked to the Dorsey home. Phillis beamed with happiness. She was too intoxicated with

victory to notice his awkwardness.

"Now kiss me," she said as they reached the gate. "Kiss me and come back tonight. I am so happy. I can't tell you how happy you have made me."

Carlton involuntarily obeyed her command. Some of the Fort Bragg belles lingered at a respectful distance to see it through and the engagement report was confirmed.

Thursday evening he picked up the Fort Bragg Chronicle. On the front page in broad faced type he read:

ENGAGEMENT OF CARLTON DARROW TO PHILLIS DORSEY

He threw the paper on the floor and crushed it with his heel. He was angry.

"Damn!" he cried.

He felt like fainting; he caught hold of a chair and held himself on his feet. Before him fluttered a vision of a girl with yellow locks and tender blue eyes; the picture of Dolly. Madly, he rushed out of the hotel. He arrived at the fisherman's hut all out of breath. Heavily, he knocked upon the door. Dolly opened it. Tears stood in her swollen eyes. He caught her in his strong arms and kissed her.

"Don't touch me! Go 'way!" she cried. "Go to your rich man's daughter! Go to Phillis!"

"Don't you love me?"

"Yes, but you don't love me."

"But I'm going to marry you," he said, taking her in his arms.

"Really—will you?" she asked pathetically.

"The sooner the better," he answered.

"And give up that rich girl?"

"Yes."

"Forever?"

"Yes."

The stars beamed in the heavens and the river reflected her smile.

The next morning at seven a knock awakened him.

"Yes, sir," Carlton replied, opening the door a few inches. He took the telegram.

"Any charges?"

"No."

"All right."

Nervously he ripped open the yellow envelope. It read:

"Nome, Alaska, Sept. 10, 1910.—Carlton Darrow, Fort Bragg, Calif.: Struck it rich in your old prospect hole—runs 150 to 200 to the ton.—Dad Darrow."

Hastily he dressed. Eight o'clock found him at the fisherman's hut. He had a kiss for Dolly ready on his lips. He lead her out on the sand. Together they walked to the rock where she had found him cast up by the sea. He encircled her waist with his arm and held her close.

"When shall the wedding be?" he asked.

"Today," she answered. "Are you sure you don't love the rich girl? I am only a poor girl."

"You are rich," he smiled. "I am rich."

He planted a kiss on her ruby lips; her cheeks bloomed like roses red; her yellow hair floated in the breeze.

He handed her the telegram. "Read this," he said.

She read the writing on the yellow paper.

"Carlton," she breathed, "I'm so happy."

The sun pierced the black clouds and smiled upon a shimmering ocean.

"Look," she said, pointing at the white capped waves, "the silver sea."

Just "Pat"

By Henry Walker Noyes

Whin Paddy is but Paddy,
    Sure all th' wor-rld is gay;
But whin he's Misther Mulligan
    Th' divil-an-all's to pay.
Wid Nora, too, or Mickey,
    Or anny wan ye know,
Whin they put on their dignity
    Jist take yer hat an' go.

Sure Pat is iver laughin'
    An' full av wit an' fun—
But whin th' kids see Mulligan
    They quit th' play an' run.
O, Pat is always welcome
    As th' flowers av bloomin' May.
Whin Mulligan goes callin', sure
    Th' folks is all away.

Forget th' thriflin' worries,
    Ye know they'll nivver last—
Eat, drink an' love—be merry,
    Th' wor-rld is movin' fast.
An' as ye must move wid it,
    Why not—whilst on th' way—
Be wan an' all like Paddy,
    Wid smiles f'r ivry day?

O, Paddy knows he's Paddy,
    Jist wan wee bit av life,
An' finds himsilf continted
    Wid home an' kids an' wife.
But pompous Pathrick Mulligan,
    So dignified an' cool,
He's jist wan big disthurbance
    In a ver-ry little pool.

Speedomania

By Frederic H. Sidney

(Continued from Last Month)

CHAPTER SEVEN.

FTER leaving the Pole the ship was headed towards Siberia.

"What a sad history Siberia has," said Rebecca. "For centuries my ancestors suffered persecution at the hands of the despots that ruled that unhappy country. The cruelties practiced upon the poor Russian peasants and Jews were beyond all reason. Today we see the result of the world suffering for its sins. To my mind the epidemic was nothing more than a punishment meted out to the world for its wickedness."

Not a sign of a survivor being seen while passing over Siberia, the ship was headed over the mountains into Tibet. The country that only within a hundred years had opened her gates to strangers. Even in these days many strange customs were observed by the people of this land of mystery.

"I wonder if we will find any survivors here?" asked Jack as the ship was lowering to land near a huge Buddist monastery.

In exploring the monastery they found where the monks had died at their praying wheels, which were equipped with electric motors.

"Just as I thought," exclaimed Villa. "these people prayed too fast."

The great Buddist University was visited, and a number of valuable manuscripts secured, but apparently no one in the country had escaped the epidemic.

After leaving Tibet they flew over the mountains into India and China. They visited many temples and places of interest in both these countries, but found no signs of life.

"I presume," said Black, "the people of these countries married so young that they hadn't the stamina to withstand the ravages of Speedomania. I'm in hopes we will find some survivors in Japan, the Japanese were a sturdy race and there is a possibility some of them escaped."

The ship was then headed towards Tokyo; and as they approached the city, Jack noticed a woman on the veranda of a house watching them. The ship was lowered and she rushed to meet them, but true to the Oriental custom, she did not offer to kiss Daisy or Rebecca.

"Isn't she a beautiful woman," thought Black.

The young woman told them her name was Wistiria, and that the plague had carried off the Japanese very rapidly.

When Daisy told her of their mission she readily fell in with the plan and consented to join them; she blushed very prettily when told she must marry Black immediately, and finally she murmured her consent. The result was the wedding was solemnized in Tokyo's largest cathedral. The marriage was recorded, then the other members of the party threw cherry blossoms at the bride and groom.

There were now three families aboard the ship, and they all agreed that if three more families could be secured they could return to Boston with a splendid nucleus for the formation of a co-operative commonwealth. The area of the Japanese Empire not being very great, the airship covered it in a short space of time, but Wistiria was the only survivor of the plague.

CHAPTER EIGHT.

The party visits the East Indies, Australia and the Cannibal Islands.

"Now," said Jack, "we'll sail over the open sea to Siam, Java and the islands that compose what was once known as the 'East Indies.' The islands were at one time the home of a very savage race, and the forests were full of wild beasts, huge snakes and all sorts of creeping things. After the country came into possession of the Dutch, the people were civilized, then exploited; and I presume through the effects of Speedomania the people of these islands cease to exist. The scene of one of Kipling's famous short stories, 'The Ourang-Outang' took place on one of these islands.'

"Do you believe in the Darwinian theory, Jack?" asked Black.

"I certainly do," replied Jack. "I can look back through the ages and see myself jumping from tree to tree—Daisy and me." Then Jack looked at her and smiled.

"Yes, Jack," she smilingly replied. "We did nothing but play all through the long sun-shiny day." At this retort the entire party laughed heartily.

Siam and the islands in that part of the world were thoroughly explored, but the effects of the plague had been such that none of the inhabitants of that section had escaped.

"Now that we are in this locality, why not make a pilgrimage to Mecca?" asked Villa.

"Oh, do," they all cried. Consequently the ship was headed for Arabia. They completely circled Arabia before visiting Mecca.

"It's wonderful when we think of the millions of people that made this pilgrimage. How fiercely the fires of religious enthusiasm must have burned in the breasts of those devotees who put out their eyes with red hot stones after gazing upon Mecca—it's terrible to think of it."

"Now that I've seen, I don't think much of it," said Villa.

"Let's take a sail over Persia," suggested Wistiria.

"Persia it is then," said Jack, and the ship was headed in that direction.

"I have always been anxious to visit Persia," said Rebecca. "I wanted to see the famous Ghetto, where for fifteen hundred years the Jews were imprisoned. How I love the story of the beautiful

Queen Esther, who risked her life to save the Chosen People."

Some very beautiful specimens of Persian rugs were secured, but not a sign of a single survivor was seen in the whole Persian Empire.

"Now," said Daisy, "we must sail over to Jerusalem."

"That will be grand," they. all cried.

"I've always wanted to see the site of Solomon's Temple," said Jack, who was a member of the Masonic fraternity. "If I had my way, every man would have been a member of the Masonic order. It would have made them better men and better Christians. Next to the Christian church the Masonic fraternity is the greatest institution that ever existed. Its creed is as broad as humanity itself. I hope to revive the Masonic organization, make you men Masons, and the ladies members of the Eastern Star, I am a member of both organizations. We are now traveling towards Jerusalem, the city where Solomon built his great temple and where Free Masonry was born; from there we must journey to Bethlehem, the birthplace of the Savior; the Star in the East guided the shepherds to the manger where the Christ Child lay. The order of the Eastern Star takes this beautiful event for the basis of their organization. I hope we can journey from Jerusalem to Bethlehem by night and possibly this same star may be our guide."

"I'll tell you, Jack," said Black, "why not convene a lodge of Masons in Jerusalem, initiate us three men into the mysteries of the craft, then at Bethlehem institute a Chapter of the Eastern Star, and as both male and females are eligible to membership in that organization, we can all become members."

"Good," cried Jack, "I'll be more than glad to do that.

"The Temple of Solomon," he continued, "stood where the Mosque of Omar now stands in Jerusalem."

Immediately upon their arrival in the "Holy City" the men entered the Mosque of Omar. Jack convened a lodge of Free Masons, and three degrees were conferred upon Villa and Black. Then an election of officers was held and Jack was elected Grand Master of Masons of the World; Villa was chosen Grand Senior Warden, and Black Grand Junior Warden. The three fraternal brothers then joined their ladies and they searched the city for survivors, but none were to be found. After this they visited the tomb of Christ.

Rebecca wept as she said, "And at last the Jews accepted the Savior just one year before the great epidemic came; and in all probability I am the only survivor of the Jewish race." Then she laid her head on Villa's shoulder and cried it out.

After the stars came out that night the ship rose in the air, and as Jack headed the ship towards Bethlehem a brilliant star appeared just ahead of the ship.

"The Star of the East," they all cried at once. Jack fixed the course of the ship on this star and, strange to say, the ship landed near the birthplace of the Savior of men, which was marked by a huge inscribed granite shaft.

At the foot of this shaft they all knelt and prayed. Then a lodge of the Eastern Star was instituted and Daisy was elected Grand Matron, and Jack the Grand Patron.

Although a diligent search was made, the indications were such that everyone must have perished.

"Now," said Black, "let's make a bee line for Australia."

"Agreed," answered Jack as he headed the nose of the ship in that direction.

The ship was lowered at Melbourne and they spent several days looking around this beautiful city. There, the same as everywhere they had visited, Speedomania had reaped a complete harvest. From Melbourne they covered the whole of the island, making numerous landings, but no survivors were found. After completing their search of Australia the ship was headed for Solomon Islands, up to the twenty-fifth century the home of a fierce cannibal race.

"Through education," said Jack, "the cannibals learned to abstain from eating human flesh; they also learned to wear clothes, use tobacco and drink rum. Rum and tobacco were the greatest curses the world ever knew, and when prohibition became a law all over the world, then the manufacture of these stimulants was stopped and the people were unable to obtain them. In my opinion, if the human race had not been so weakened by the use of rum and tobacco for centuries they would have been more physically able to stand the effects of Speedomania, and we would have found more survivors in the different parts of the world that we have visited."

"It is just as I expected," exclaimed Jack, after they had completed their search of these islands without finding any survivors.

CHAPTER NINE.

"We'll try South America next," said Jack, as he headed the ship towards Cape Horn. Stops were made at New Zealand, Tasmania and numerous other islands, but not a sign of life was to be seen. As they neared the Cape they began discussing the history of the twentieth century South Pole expeditions, when such brave men as Shackleton and Scott sacrificed their lives for science.

"Think of the contrast between then and today," said Black. "Today we find the lives of the world's population sacrificed to satisfy a mad desire for speed; and a false conception of efficiency."

"That's the whole thing in a nut shell, Black," cried Villa enthusiastially; then Rebecca smiled at him as she squeezed his hand.

"Let's swing towards the Pole, Jack, look that territory over, then head back to Cape Horn," suggested Black.

"Good idea," answered Jack as he headed for the South Pole. The South Pole region, like the North Pole had been transformed from a land of ice and snow to one of grassy plains and mountains. A sharp lookout was kept for possible survivors of the epidemic all the way to the pole, but none were to be seen. The ship landed at the pole, and they inspected the granite shaft that marked the pole.

"The sufferings and hardships of the explorers who tried to reach this spot were even worse than those of the North Pole explorers," said Wistiria.

"Yes," replied Jack. "In addition to the intense cold, snow and ice, there were the terrible fogs to contend with, which have since disappeared."

"Well, Jack," Villa said. "Let's head for Cape Horn and the Land of The Guacho."

"All aboard for South America," cried Jack, and the huge ship sailed into the air as gracefully as a bird and headed for Cape Horn. As they neared the Cape they began discussing the early history of South America, particularly the part they were now about to visit.

"The natives of this locality were exploited unmercifully for so many generations; I very much doubt if any of them possessed sufficient vitality to withstand the epidemic," said Villa sadly.

"I have read," replied Black of how in early days the Indians of this locality were very cruel and often murdered whole crews of ship-wrecked sailors."

They were also accused of cannibalism," replied Daisy.

The ship sailed over the Cape and the Straits of Magellan into Argentine, and they did not notice any signs of life until they came to Buenos Aires; when Wistiria who had been looking through the telescope exclaimed: "I see a child walking down there, and he is looking upward; now he is holding out his little arms to us."

This announcement caused great excitement and the ship was lowered. The child came running towards them and Daisy grasped him in her arms. The poor, lonely little fellow broke down and sobbed. After a while he told his story, everybody in that section had perished. He told them how he had wandered about for days looking for some one to keep him company. Whenever he became hungry he entered a kitchen, started the machinery and generated nourishment for himself. At night he laid down wherever he happened to be and cried himself to sleep.

"A great fear and loneliness always came over me when night came on," he said.

"You poor little fellow," cried Daisy. "We'll adopt him Jack." This Jack was glad to do, and the others in the party acquiesced. The child was more than delighted to go with them. He was such a

bright little fellow they all fell in love with him. The ship rose in the air and the journey through South America was continued. They zig-zagged from coast to coast in order to cover the whole territory. They did not land but kept up a sharp lookout for possible survivors. From Para, they followed the Amazon River to its source. The trip through the valley was interesting but unproductive of results. They soared over the highest peaks of the Andes, then followed the coast around to the Caribean Sea.

"Little Miguel is South America's only survivor," said Jack, as he smiled at the child. From South America they headed for the open sea, the West Indies, and the African continent being their goal.

CHAPTER TEN.

The airship party spent several days in the West Indies, then flew across the Gulf of Mexico to the Florida Coast, but in neither of these places did they find any one who had escaped the epidemic.

"Now across the open sea for the Cape Of Good Hope," cried Jack. "We are going a rather round about way, but we have plenty of time and everybody is happy, consequently we need not worry."

They stopped at hundreds of islands on their trip across the ocean, but like other places they had visited the human race had passed out with the great epidemic of Speedomania. They arrived in Cape Town in due time and spent several days there, visiting places of interest, including the diamond mines; they saw evidences of how the effects of the plague had been terrible on the mine workers; and thousands of them had died at their work in the pits.

"At one time," said Jack the native African was black as pitch, but through education, so it is claimed, their skins bleached, and they are as white skinned as any of us."

"And through exploitation they're as dead as the rest of the world," exclaimed Black. "I doubt if we find a single survivor in the whole of Africa."

Leaving Cape Town the airship party headed for Rhodesia, as they all wished to visit the seat of the Great African Empire that was founded by the famous Ce-

cil Rhodes, the man who made his fortune in the gold and diamond mines in
Africa back in the twentieth century.
After this, they journeyed northward zig-
zagging from coast to coast, the same as
they did in South America. The party decided to spend a day in the Lake Nyanza
Region in order to view the wonderful
falls of that place, the greatest falls in
the world, greater than even those of
Niagara. These falls at one time generated power for the whole of Africa.

"Now," said Jack. "We'll head for the
Great Desert of Sahara." Although a
strict watch was kept, no signs of survivors were seen on the trip from the
lakes to the Great Desert, which through
irrigation had been made into a beautiful
spot, it was in reality "The Garden of
the Gods."

"Just think," said Villa. "How salt
water was piped from the sea to this
desert, then condensed in order to fresh-
en it, and afterwards used to irrigate the
desert with, and from a wilderness of
sand it was transformed into a beautiful
garden of shrubs and flowers."

"It's simply shows what has been accomplished through efficiency," replied
Black. "But alas efficiency was overdone.
Efficiency developed into Speedomania
and today we view the results. In the
twentieth century the Germans were the
most efficient nation on earth; and what
happened? They started what turned out
to be the most terrible war in the history
of the world. They were not to blame,
they just had to test their efficiency. For
my part I believe moderation in everything is the best policy.

"You're right, Black." They all cried
in unison.

They sailed over the "Desert" from
east to west, and from north to south;
and they all agreed it was a beautiful
country, but sad to say, not one of the
"Desert" dwellers survived the plague.

After traversing the "Desert" the ship
was headed to the Mediterranean Sea, on
their way they covered the whole of what
was once known as the Barbary States,
whose people resisted the advances of
civilization until within a hundred years;
notwithstanding this they also perished
with the great plague of Speedomania.

Previous to their becoming civilized, they
had travelled a terrible pace.

CHAPTER ELEVEN.

The ship crossed the Mediterranean
and headed for the City of Lisbon in Portugal. While flying over the city, they
noticed some one waving at them from
the upper story of a dwelling house. The
ship was immediately lowered, and they
found a young married couple, who stated
they were the only survivors of the
plague in the whole of Portugal. They
were both glad to join the party, they
said their names were Vierra, the husband's given name was John, and that of
his wife was Isabel. This made the
fourth family aboard the ship, all were
happy and contented, and apparently
well mated. It seemed as though "soul
mate affinities" had been made possible
through the great catastrophe that had
recently taken place.

"If we continue to agree as well as the
years go by, as we do now," said Jack,
"we may possibly transmit this spirit of
contentment to our posterity; and in
time the world will be populated with a
happier and saner race than the one that
has just passed out. Who knows but that
this epidemic may have been a dispensation of Providence to bring about the sur-
vival of the fittest."

"Let us hope it may prove the case,"
answered Villa.

After leaving Portugal they sailed over
Spain and into France, Paris, being their
first stop, and up to this time they had
observed no signs of life as they sailed
over the country. They spent a day looking around Paris, and in this city Daisy
recognized many of the mummified bodies of her former friends who happened
to be in Paris when the epidemic broke
out.

"I hardly expected to find any one in
Paris who survived the plague," said
Black; "for here it was necessary to live
at a very fast pace to keep up with everything."

Vienna was their next stopping place,
and here the same as in Paris, Daisy saw
the bodies of a great many of her former
friends.

"Let's get away from here as soon as

we can," she cried.

"All right," replied Jack. "But where will we head for next?"

"Why not make a circuit of the battle-fields of the great war of the twentieth century, and then look over the rest of Europe?" asked Vierra. "Good," cried the rest. "Let's do it."

CHAPTER TWELVE.

The big ship rose in the air and headed for Belgium, where they intended to begin their circuit of the theatre of the Great War.

They crossed the Belgian border at the point where the Belgians so gallantly defended their forts against the vastly superior German Army; then shaped their course through Belgium, into France, back into Austria, Poland and Russia. The whole country that had once been the scene of the world's greatest battles was as silent as though it had been invaded and devastated by a modern "Attalia"; no one had escaped the plague.

Very little was said during the time the ship was making the circuit of the battlefields, all were apparently in deep thought.

Wistiria was the first to speak after the circuit had been completed. "It seems sad that the people of the twentieth century after advancing to a high degree of civilization and efficiency should engage in such a terrible and barbarous war. The history of that war is the most terrible thing in print today. The effect of the engines and munitions of war used in those days were far worse than being attacked with Speedomania. The bloodshed, carnage, and putrefying flesh, with the diseases that accompanied those conditions are something too terrifying for my thoughts."

"It was far better that the world perish with Speedomania, if Providence so decreed it should perish; than with such a war as took place here in the twentieth century," replied Black.

"Amen," replied Jack, and the subject was dropped.

"Now let's sail over into Italy," said Black.

"Agreed," cried the rest.

Rome was their first stopping place in Italy.

"This city," said Jack, "was at one time the seat of government of the whole world; and for many years it was the capital of the religious world as well. After the people of the world adopted a universal system of religion then there was no need of maintaining a large religious establishment, and the Vatican was turned into an art museum."

They traversed Italy from the top to the heel of the boot, visited every large city, and inspected hundreds of beautiful cathedrals and art museums; but not a single survivor did they find in the whole country.

"I am afraid," said Vierra, "that myself and wife are the only two survivors of the Latin race."

After leaving Italy they flew over the Alps into Switzerland.

"This was once a land of glaciers," spoke Villa. "But now instead of fields of ice, we see green grass and flowers."

"I have read," said Isabel, "that the government of Switzerland was the most progressive and most humane in existence; but after the money powers obtained control; it became as corrupt as the other governments and the workers were unmercifully exploited, and, of course the Swiss contracted Speedomania, and perished with the rest of humanity."

"I doubt," said Daisy, "if we find any survivors in Switzerland." And in this she was right.

"I expect," said Jack, "that we will find some survivors in Germany. The Teutons were a hardy race and some of them may have escaped. Although they began living very fast in the Twentieth century, and the great war they carried on at that time must have taken a great deal out of the race. It was during the war that the Germans demonstrated the feasibility of government control of public utilities, food supplies and other public commodities. This prevented what might have been a burden on the people by having to pay excessively high prices for the necessities of life. Where Germany made her mistake was by not continuing the system. The capitalistic element, of course, objected because they wished to

return to the profit system in order to enrich themselves during the period of reconstruction, which lasted fifty years."

They did find someone very much alive
in Berlin. She was a handsome German
girl who was delighted to look upon
some live human beings. She wept like
a child in Daisy's arms.

"My name is Gretchen," she said. She
proved a very agreeable person.

"I hope we can find Gretchen a husband," said Daisy, for she's liable to be
an old maid if she has to wait till little
Miguel grows up."

Gretchen nearly laughed herself into
hysterics at these remarks. They found
a husband for Gretchen in Petrograd,
Russia. He was a giant, but as gentle as
he was large. His name Ivan Burwen,
and Jack joined the two together in the
great Cathedral in Petrograd, the church
famous because the rulers of Russia had
worshiped there for centuries. The airship party being in a festive mood, revived an ancient custom and pelted the
bridal couple with old shoes and confetti.

After making a complete circle of Russia and not finding any survivors, the
ship headed for the Scandanavian countries. While flying over the northern
part of Sweden they spied a woman wandering along the roadside. They lowered
the ship, and the young woman, apparently occupied with her thoughts, had not
noticed it. She was startled at first, but
after seeing so many friendly faces she
ran toward them.

Her name was Lena Nelson, she told
them, and that every soul in Sweden excepting herself had perished with the
plague. Tiring of the loneliness in Stock-
holm, she decided to walk over into Russia in hopes of finding some survivors.
When they invited her to join them, she
was delighted to do so, and she stepped
aboard the airship, and once more the
big craft rose in the air and pointed "her"
nose towards Norway.

"Now we must find a husband for
Lena," said Gretchen.

"I shall never marry," replied Lena
sadly. "My affianced perished with the
plague the day before our wedding was
to have taken place."

"If we run across a nice young man,

you must marry him in order to follow
out the plan we are trying to bring about,"
said Daisy.

"Well," replied Lena more cheerfully,
"if he were real nice I might consider it."

At this they all laughed heartily. They
sailed over both Norway and Denmark,
then swung north to Iceland, but in
neither of these places did they find any
sign of life. Two days were spent resting
in Iceland and then the ship was headed
direct towards England. A landing was
made in London, near the famous Tower
of London. After exploring the city for
possible survivors, of which there were
none, they spent their time visiting the
wonderful palaces and places of historical
interest in the city. After leaving London
they journeyed through the Shakespeare
country, and the party had an enjoyable
time discussing the works of that famous
author. They sailed all over England,
Wales and Ireland without seeing a single
sign of human being.

It was in the highlands of Scotland
that they found a husband for Lena. He
was a giant Highlander, and, seated on a
lonely crag in the mountains, he was singing "Jessie's Dream." How beautiful his
mellow tones floated upward to the ship,
which was slowly lowering. Never did
those phrases, "Hear ye no the Mac-
gregor, the grandest o' them all," and
"The Campbells are Kimin'," fall on more
appreciative ears. Suddenly he looked up
and saw the airship. He sprang to his
feet and stretched out his arms to them.

"A husband for Lena," they cried, and
the ship began to lower more rapidly. In
a few moments they were shaking hands
with Scotland's only survivor.

The young Scot's name was Angus Mc-
Kay, and apparently he fell in love with
Lena at first sight, for he said if Lena
was willing, he would marry her at once
and go to America with them. Lena
blushingly consented, and Jack immediately performed the ceremony. Then
with great rejoicing the ship was headed
for the open sea and America.

CHAPTER THIRTEEN

"We'll now head for Newfoundland,
cross Canada to the Pacific Coast, then
zigzag east to Boston, looking over that
part of the United States that we missed

when we started on our trip from Boston two months ago."

The trip across the ocean to Newfoundland occupied about twenty-four hours, the sentiment of the entire party was to make the trip at slow speed in order that the rest of the day and the night should be spent over the water. To those who had never crossed the ocean, it proved a novel and interesting experience. While crossing the banks of Newfoundland, shortly after sunrise next morning, the little Guacho, who was looking through the telescope noticed a long, dark object on the water. He thought it some sort of a marine vine, and called Jack's attention to it. Jack looked at it through the glass and he immediately saw it was a huge sea serpent, and that the creature was alive. When the others heard about the serpent they all insisted in having the ship lowered so they could get a good look at it and try to photograph it. The ship was lowered far enough for them to view the creature. This serpent was a hundred feet long, its body was covered with huge scales, it possessed a pair of large, wicked-looking eyes, set widely apart and well to the top of its head, which was as large as an ordinary water pail, and when the creature opened its mouth they saw it was full of sharp, sabre-like teeth.

"The existence of sea serpents has generally been denied," said Jack. "Some scientists have always maintained that these creatures exist but very seldom some to the surface, and here at last is the proof. I hope we can secure a good picture in order to place it among the archives of the scientific laboratory at Harvard, and place an enlargement of it in the Art Museum in Boston. After we photograph it, perhaps we had better shoot and kill it for, as the world again becomes populated, such creatures as these might do a great deal of harm. Who knows but it might some day take a notion to invade the land; and what consternation it would cause if such a creature should ascend the Charles river, land somewhere up in the 'Back Bay' and be seen crawling down Commonwealth avenue?"

With these words, Jack snapped the shutter of the camera, which had been exposed for over a minute. He then reached for the radio gun. Up to this time the serpent hadn't paid any attention to the airship. Then suddenly, without any warning whatever, the creature sprang out of the water and threw itself at the airship, with its mouth, full of horrible looking teeth, wide open. The women screamed with fright, but Jack, cool and calm, took a quick aim and sent a bullet from the radio rifle into one of the creature's eyes, and it dropped back into the water, dead, and immediately sank from sight.

"For goodness sake, Jack, let's get away from here before its mate comes up at us," cried Daisy.

Jack started the ship, and within a short time they came in sight of the city of St. Johns, Newfoundland, and here the ship was lowered and the party started to walk around the city, when, much to their surprise, a woman stepped out of a house and confronted them.

"Who, in the name of goodness, are you?" she asked.

"We," replied Jack, "are the neculeus of the world's co-operative community," and he introduced each of them separately and told her their stories, and invited her to join them.

"I shall be delighted to do so," she replied. "Up to now," she said, "I actually thought I was the only person alive in the whole world."

She told them her name was Lucy Thayer, forty-three years of age, and that she had taught school in that city for twenty years.

"Perhaps we may be able to find a husband for Lucy before we reach Boston," said Lena.

"Young woman," answered Lucy rather severely, "I do not wish to marry. I remained single all these years from choice. In my day I have had many flattering offers of marriage. My mission was to teach. Some day I hoped to be president of a college."

"Perhaps, when we reach Boston, you may be able to realize that ambition," replied Jack.

Lucy thanked him for his kind thoughts.

"Now," said Jack, "all aboard, and we will head for Hudson Bay, and from there west to the Pacific. The ship rose upwards and headed for the mainland and then north towards the bay.

They made the bay inside of twelve hours. Although a close watch was kept all the way, no signs of any survivors were seen.

"Hudson Bay," exclaimed Jack as they came in sight of that sheet of water. "At one time The Hudson Bay Company controlled the fur markets of the world and dictated the policies by which Canada was ruled. It was one of the most autocratic concerns that ever existed, but with the passing of animal life, the changing of the climate, which made the wearing of furs unnecessary, this concern went out of existence."

After spending a day and a night around the Hudson Bay country, the airship started for the Pacific Coast, shifting their route in such a way as to cover the whole country as they went along, they were three days crossing the country. After making a two-days' stay in Vancouver, B. C., they decided to head into the United States, land at Seattle, then make their way across country to Boston, covering the part of the country as they went along that had not been covered when the ship left Boston nearly two months previous.

A day was spent looking around Seattle; then the ship zigzagged slowly eastward to the Rockies, where a stay of several days was made. The scenery in the mountains was so grand and beautiful they hated to leave.

"We'll 'cross-lots' to Chicago and stay there two weeks," said Jack.

"Good," cried the others.

Chicago in those days was the most wonderful city in the world and well worth a two-weeks' stay.

They enjoyed themselves immensely in Chicago; there were many wonderful things to see, beautiful art galleries to visit, and they enjoyed sailing over the Great Lakes in some of those marvelous floating palaces that they found deserted at the docks, and some were found where they had stopped in mid-lake or ran ashore and wrecked when the terrible epidemic struck the Great Lakes section. They did not find a single survivor in Chicago or around the Great Lakes.

"We must tear ourselves away from here and start on the last lap of our journey," cried Jack one morning.

"All right," they answered.

Jack started the engines, the ship rose upward and again the big flier began her zigzag journey eastward in hopes of finding some more survivors before reaching Boston. No signs of life were to be seen anywhere and it was concluded they were the only people in the world that had survived the terrible epidemic of "Speedomania."

The entire party took up residences on Commonwealth avenue, Boston. A co-operative form of government was established. Jack was elected Governor, and Rebecca Villa was chosen Lieutenant Governor. Every member of the colony was entitled to a seat in the legislature and there were some lively and interesting sessions at the State House. One of the first acts of the legislature was the consolidation of Harvard, Radcliffe and Simmons Colleges with Boston University, with headquarters at the latter institution because it was centrally located and near Boston's wonderful library. Miss Lucy Thayer was elected President of the Consolidated Universities. Every member of the colony enrolled as a University student, and in time received a degree. The first class day of the University was a jolly affair. It was held on Boston Common, and Villa delivered the Ivy oration.

The colony prospered and increased in numbers from additions of the various families. In the course of three thousand years the world again became populated, and on account of eugenic marriages, saner and better living, the new generations proved to be a sturdy and happier race than the one that passed out with the great epidemic of "Speedomania."

FINIS

Ambrose Bierce

By R. F. Dibble

OMEWHERE, probably on the tawny, cactus-covered sands of Mexico, the bones of Ambrose Bierce are blanching under the torrid rays of the sun, while the ominous vulture flaps lazily along glimmering dully beneath the coppery moon as the gaunt, gray wolf, "whose howl's his watch," glides silently, intent on some murderous design, and the skulking coyote yelps his plaintive cry upon the slumbrous, nocturnal air. Or, if by chance some uncouth though kindly hand afforded his body the final service of pickaxe and spade, even so, but little consolation would result therefrom to his friends, . for of Bierce, as of Moses, it can be said that "no man knoweth of his sepulchre unto this day." From the time of the battle of Torreon in 1914, when Bierce was on the staff of Villa, his fate has been clouded in mystery, and since he had then already exceeded the limit of days which the Psalmist set for man's mortal pilgrimage, there can be but little question that he has passed into the uncharted regions of the everlasting silence. If his immortality might put on mortality for a brief space of time so that he could return from that undiscovered country, it is probable that he would assure his friends that nothing in his life became him more than the mysterious manner in which he left it; for mystery in a thousand diverse shapes meant more than anything else to him while he lived. So, possibly, Hawthorne, too, might say that fate was very gracious in permitting him to glide softly from the gentle embrace of dreams into that spirit world which was always so much more real to him than mere sensuous existence.

And to Ambrose Bierce, as to Hawthorne, the life of the senses meant comparatively little. His imagination was forever roving through the boundless, untrammeled stretches of an unearthly, super-sensuous country—

"A wild weird clime that lieth, sublime,
Out of Space, out of Time."

His critical writings were indeed pungent and pitiless; he preferred to open wounds rather than to cauterize them; he was an iconoclast, not a constructive reformer; his searing satire, aimed at a multitude of hostile contemporaries, at the fidelity of woman, at church and State, and in general at what he believed to be the many sins of modern society, never admitted of let or hindrance. But because of their very nature, those portions of his writings which were concerned distinctively with social matters of his day are bound to have less and less appeal, and whatever his final rank may be, after the tribulations of several decades have winnowed out all that was strictly ephemeral in his works, he is quite certain to be remembered primarily as an artist who dealt with the uncanny forces that lie outside of life rather than with life itself. He will live, if he lives at all, not as one who had some moral message, some doctrinaire preachment, for his generation, but rather as one who, largely unconcerned with theories of amelioration of any kind whatever, beguiled his life's day by constructing a world almost wholly out of his own fantastic imagination.

Since this world is to a large extent singularly his own, it is fitting that its composition, even though in some degree shapeless and indeterminate, should be subjected to as definite an analysing process as is possible. Right here is where inveterate lovers of literary influences and of the general heritage of the past as it affects our modern writers may have their fling, and dally with such matters to their hearts' desires. With commendable accuracy they may point out that Gothic Romance, initiated in England more than a century and a half ago by Horace Walpole in his crudely supernatural and bloody "Castle of Otranto," which innocently fathered a host of bawling English, Continental and American children during the next few decades, is the literary pigeon-hole in which the works of Ambrose Bierce may be filed for the benefit of gaping college classes forced to endure the pangs of despised required courses in the history of literature. And these critics would be perfectly right in so doing; as right, that is, as are physicists who explain the rainbow to their own satisfaction by affirming that it is merely the result of the refraction of rays of light passing through drops of water. But, though the product of explicable scientific laws, the rainbow is still essentially as much a thing of baffling, poetic splendor as it was when first it leaped across the clouds that covered the vaporous, inchoate mass we now call earth; and the writings of Bierce, indubitably the product of a definite tendency in literature, would still hold the mind in a fascinating grip even if their literary parentage were unknown.

There is, to be sure, some reason for thinking that in Poe and Hawthorne the art of Gothic Romance reached its highest possibilities and that little or nothing of novelty in method or subject matter remains. Certainly the number of present-day pseudo-scientific romanticists, almost all of whom have knelt before the throne of Poe, have given us practically nothing more than countless variations of themes first introduced by him; the great advance in scientific knowledge since Poe's time has surely been accompanied by no similar increase in artistic ability to utilize this new material for fiction. Nor have Hawthorne's tales of the Puritanic conscience working usually amid direful situations been surpassed, and probably not equalled; though it is quite certain that only a very bold person would claim that the morality of the world has advanced, since Hawthorne's time, equally with scientific discovery. But it is just here that Ambrose Bierce must be reck-

oned with as one who accomplished something that Hawthorne and Poe each did in part, though seldom or never wholly: he took the omnipresent but rarely appalling supernaturalism of Hawthorne, combined with it the almost purely physical horrors of Poe, and thus produced what is virtually a new type of fiction—a type which others have occasionally used, but which perhaps no one previously has made specifically his own. In his best stories he created a world whose beings are absolutely dominated by unreasoning, aboriginal, cosmic fear.

This fear, which constitutes the warp and woof of Bierce's most significant tales, grips the reader almost, if not quite, as powerfully as do Poe's ghastly creations, but it springs from as unearthly sources as do the milder terrors of Hawthorne. At times it manifests itself in at least partially tangible form, but it is most effective when strictly impalpable. It is the fear that twisted the hearts of our most primitive progenitors when first they realized that there were phenomenal forces far more to be shunned and fled from than the ponderous foot of the mammoth or the scimitar-like claws of the cave-lion. It is the fear that left their bodies unscathed, but clutched their minds with paralyzing force. It leaped upon them infinitely swifter than their arboreal enemies. They may have scorned the arrow that flieth by day, but of the terror by night they were woefully afraid. Brute strength and cunning availed them nothing, for it was not a part of the sensuous world. It is the fear and trembling that came upon Eliphaz, the Temanite, in the visions of the night when deep sleep falls upon men, and made all his bones to shake; for a spirit passed before his face. It is the penalty which all mankind must pay for being elevated above the brute world into a sphere where intellectual and emotional processes usurp the place of mere thews and sinews of physical strength. It is a part of the primal curse which, according to the fable, fell upon man because he inquisitively tasted the fruit of the tree of knowledge. Neither adamantine barriers of imponderable granite or marble, nor any "unswept stone be-

Form 5

smeared with sluttish time" can fortify man against it, for it is the fear of the unseen.

The art of Bierce may be seen at its best in the two volumes entitled "Can Such Things Be?" and "In the Midst of Life (Tales of Soldiers and Civilians", the latter book having been "denied existence by the chief publishing houses in the country"—a significant commentary on the financial wisdom our publishers show in catering to our deeply ingrained, Anglo-Saxon antipathy to literature or other work done for art's sake only, and our immaculately chaste delight in witnessing the triumphant victory of vapidly orthodox virtues over the sinister forces of iniquity. The works of Bierce, like those of Poe and Whitman, have been read far more sedulously in Europe than in America—another testimonial to the wiser charity of peoples who care less for esoteric morality than they care for eclectic art. It needs no connoisseur of literature to see, in these two books, plenteous traces of ideas garnered from many modern writers. Thus in "A Psychological Shipwreck" the theme is prescience granted in a dream; in "The Realm of the Unreal" it is hypnotism; "One Summer Night," a story less than four pages long, captivates by reason of the horror aroused by premature burial, grave-robbing and murder; and reincarnation is the motif of several tales. Bierce apparently followed De Maupassant, though independently as to subject matter, in the employment of deliberately unconventional beginnings, extremely bizarre situations and smashing climaxes. Thus, "A Jug of Sirup" opens with the laconic statement, "This narrative begins with the death of the hero;" "An Occurrence at Owl Creek Bridge" details, with a minuteness worthy of Henry James, the introspections of a criminal on the scaffold during the short interval between the adjusting of the noose and the springing of the trap; in "Chickamauga" a child, deaf and mute, wanders through a battlefield splotched with decaying corpses; in "One of the Missing" a soldier, imprisoned by fallen timbers, finds himself staring into the muzzle of his own cocked rifle, and, unable to release himself,

finally dies because of the hypnotic fear inspired by the "menacing stare of the gun barrel," which actually is empty and harmless; in "The Man and the Snake" a man is literally frightened to death by the "unspeakable malignant" eyes of a snake which, as the closing sentence pithily states, was "a stuffed snake; its eyes were two shoe buttons." In "The Boarded Window" a man, alone at night with his supposedly dead wife, suddenly hears a panther trying to drag away the body, but it fails, and the terse ending sentence suggests why, for "between the teeth was a fragment of the animal's ear." Best of all, perhaps, is that superb tour de force in staggering situation, "The Eyes of the Panther," in which prenatal influence, as well as "the menace of those awful eyes," plays a ghastly part. Moreover, the drab realism of Flaubert, and perhaps of the Russian school, is to be seen in such a sentence as this, taken from "Chickamauga": "The greater part of the forehead was torn away, and from the jagged hole the brain protruded, overflowing the temple, a frothy mass of gray, crowned with clusters of crimson bubbles—the work of a shell." There are crudities in these tales, even in the best of them: Bierce is too fond of the emotion mechanically stirred by the exclamation point, he often strives for shocks at the expense of even remote plausibility; he takes a ghoulish delight in dishing up carrion banquets for his readers; he piles horror on horror, after the manner of those Elizabethan masters of diablerie, Tourneur, Webster, and Ford; but at his best he has an austere reserve and a power of creating an atmosphere of all-enveloping ill unsurpassed, probably, by any writer who has specialized in these two particular literary devices. Furthermore, his stories are commonly interspersed with bursts of humor which, grimly sardonic as it is, still furnishes the emotional relief that the exponents of Gothic art have quite generally failed to give.

It is, however, in those tales which portray the workings of wholly immaterial powers of darkness and evil that Bierce is most original and thrilling, tales in which the usual theme is the return

of menacing wraiths for venegeance denied them in the flesh. In these stories
there is practically no use made of sensuous terrors that palsy the senses only;
rather, the motivation springs from the
infinitely more dreadful horror that arises
from the presence of "supernatural malevolences," which far excel the pigmy
forces of mere material fright. Bierce
is, of course, compelled to use physical
metaphors in describing these "invisible
existences"—for he regards them as such,
and far more powerful than are matter
and energy. He portrays a universe
shadowed by "one primeval mystery of
darkness, without form or void," in which
there is "a portentous conspiracy of night
and solitude." In "A Watcher By the
Dead" and "The Suitable Surroundings,"
death comes solely from fear of these
"supernatural malevolences." In "The
Damned Thing," "The Moonlit Road,"
"Stanley Fleming's Hallucination," "The
Secret of Macarger's Gulch," and in "The
Death of Halpin Frayser," however, the
"accursed beings" work their will by
temporarily using physical force. "The
Death of Halpin Frayser" is perhaps the
best of all Bierce's stories in creating an
impression of the incarnate verisimili-
tude of those "invisible existences that
swarm" about the earth. The following
poem, taken from this story, is possibly
as powerful a piece of unalloyed mor-
bidity as poetic pen ever produced:

"Enthralled by some mysterious spell, I
    stood
In the lit gloom of an enchanted wood.
  The cypress there and myrtle twined
    their boughs,
Significant, in baleful brotherhood.

"The brooding willow whispered to the
    yew;
Beneath, the deadly night shade and the
    rue,
  With immortelles self-woven into
    strange
Funereal shapes, and horrid nettles
    grew.

"No song of bird nor any drone of bees,
Nor light leaf lifted by the wholesome
    breeze:

The air was stagnant all, and Silence
    was
A living thing that breathed among the
    trees.

"Conspiring spirits whispered in the
    gloom,
Half-heard, the stilly secrets of the tomb.
  With blood the trees were all adrip;
    the leaves
Shone in the witch-light with a ruddy
    bloom.

"I cried aloud!—the spell, unbroken still,
Rested upon my spirit and my will.
  Unsouled, unhearted, hopeless and
    forlorn,
I strove with monstrous presages of ill!"

The world of Ambrose Bierce, as pictured in a score or so of his best tales,
is a phantasmagorical world, teeming
with terrific hallucinations and illusory
shades; a world where all familiar things
seem to have been swallowed up in some
prodigious cataclysm. It is born of an
imagination that cared nothing for conventional traditions of right and wrong,
but only for pure, disinterested art; an
imagination that was totally untouched
by any fervor for pragmatic or ethical
codes. This world is never subject to
principles of cause and effect; it tran-
scends all the properties of physics and
chemistry; it cannot be mapped by the
aid of compass and surveying instruments. It can be compacted within a
single brain, yet it stretches immeasur-
ably beyond the confines of the known
universe. Only one form of government
it knows—the autocracy of forever enthroned Fear, who rules with diabolical
pitilessness. No ray of light, save the
"darkness visible" that comes from fitful
gleams of baleful lightning, ever penetrate the vast funereal gloom that en-
compasses all its domain; murky night,
sable as crape, enshrouds all its labrin-
thine mazes. Its sere, blasted wolds and
bleak plains seem to have suffered a
blight more drear and deadly than that
wrought by a plague of locusts. It is
peopled only by gibbering imps, frantic
fiends, sheeted apparitions, ogreish gob-
lins, pallid spectres and wan ghosts, who

protrude their idiotically grinning countenances on every side, hoarsely croak forth in hiccoughing gasps and rasping screeches lugubrious mutterings of imminent destruction, utter derisive, mocking jeers, and shoot basilisk glances as death-dealing as Medusa's snaky tresses: till finally, after this babbling hubbub has risen to a veritable pandemonium of doleful shrieks, these frenzied demons, wearying of malicious leers and ferocious gnashings of rage, change their riotous tones to subdued howls of anger, wail and moan their sorrow in mournful ululating dirges, and at last conclude their maniacal concert with a tumultuous surge of delirious convulsive cachinnations. Clanking skeletons, which have .wrenched away from hideous gibbets or come from corrupt charnel-houses reeking with miasmatic vapors distilled from noisome pollutions, thrust forth gruesome, clammy fingers; stark corpses, hearsed in dank cerements of death or just risen from coffins immured in the pestilential putrefactions of the tomb, stalk along their dismal way, mumbling in hollow, sepulchral tones presages of impending doom, and stare blankly around with blear eyes that pour rheum down ashen, cadaverous cheeks. The very air murmurs portents of disaster, and all things seem crushed beneath a sweeping anathema. It is an infernal world, filled with heinous beings and damned with everlasting desolation.

In the Realm of Bookland

"Souvenirs," by Stanley Preston Kimmel.

About the size and color of an Autumn leaf is the tiny volume of verses by Stanley Preston Kimmel, brought out by the "Publishers of Little Books," San Francisco.

These "Souvenirs" were written while doing service at the front by Mr. Kimmel, who was on duty for eight months in the Norton-Hargess unit of the French Red Cross before this country went into the great war. Mr. Kimmel, who is only twenty-four years old, shows great promise, not so much in his verse construction (which is faulty at times), but in the obvious fact that he is a poet at heart, with, needless to say, the usual capacity for suffering rather than for enjoyment, for, through most of his writings, the minor note is predominant.

In looking over the small but comprehensive collection of experiences as ambulance driver in France, the following is worthy of note:

"BLUE RAIN."

Rain in the forest and evening,
　Blue rain and things which are green,
And squares where a shadow lingers—
　Where Death stalks about, unseen.
The echoing roar of cannons,
　The click of the horses' hoofs,
Rattling camions passing
　The shell-shattered walls and roofs.
The post de secours, the hillsides,
　Skeleton towers of Verdun,
The fading line of the troopers
　Passing along through the gloom.
Rain in the forest and evening,
　Blue rain and things which are green,
And squares where a shadow lingers,
　Where Death stalks about, unseen.

"Left Overs," "Blue Steel," "Morning Near Mort Homme," "The Dead," are all realistic and terrible, and "Rue de l'Hotel de Ville," which follows below, is as vivid as some of Victor Hugo's prose descriptions:

Like an old, hump-backed woman
With heavy feet you pass,

Carrying huge lamps upon your aged
   shoulders;
Creeping, crawling, staggering,
On to the river,
Your shoes are worn and your clothes
   smell of centuries.
You are a mother of criminals and saints,
Your breath comes in jerks,
And is like the foul air of a damp cellar;
Your hair is musty with cobwebs,
Yet you have defied Time;
Still, Time is a poor, weak thing!

"October" has a light and delicate touch
to it, and "The Dancer" has a sprightly
rhythm.

Mr. Kimmel has just returned from a
trip through Japan and China, and is now
at his studio, 1133 B. Filbert street, this
city. Possibly some Oriental sketches
may evolve from his pen upon this recent
experience.

"Souvenirs" by Stanley Preston Kimmel, 50c.

———

"The World of Wonderful Realty," by
E. Temple Thurston.

All through E. Temple Thurston's new
book, "The World of Wonderful Reality,"
runs the comforting philosophy that happiness does not spring from material
things, but rather from an imaginative
love of beauty and truth and ideality.
And still, in the end, the youthful and
enthusiastic exponent of this belief discovers the "feet of clay" in his idol.

John Grey, the hero, is a dreamer and
poet, poor in worldly goods, as poets are,
while the girl he loves, Jill Dealtry, is
swayed between love of John and what
she considers duty to her parents, who
have arranged a marriage between their
daughter and a friend of Mr. Dealtry's—
a Mr. Skipworth.

After each meeting with her lover, Jill's
soul is lulled into a sort of somnolence,
until association again with her material-
minded parents wakes her to the fact
that poverty, even with the adored one,
is a condition which she is not idealistic
enough to endure.

It ends, unhappily, with the death of
Mr. Skipworth, who leaves all his riches
to Jill, but even after Jill has sent for
John and told him the happy news of
her sudden wealth (which makes their
union feasible to her, and her parents),
John sees plainly, at last, that Jill could
not have loved him for himself alone,
and gives her up.

It is a bookful of whimsical nonsense,
that yet has many a truth in it—a book
that touches lightly but effectively on
several vital questions—the lack of sympathy in the church, the utter futility of
imprisonment for debt, the absorbing de-
side for physical comfort of the ordinary
human, the gradual squelching of the
soul, which modern life is bringing about.
And through it all, John Grey's poetical
and childlike faith in the ultimate triumph of love, his understanding of nature, his pretty, fantastic fairy tales of
birds, which speak more of the Gaelic in
John than the Saxon.

"The World of Wonderful Reality," by
E. Temple Thurston, D. Appleton & Co.,
New York, Publishers, $1.75.

DECEMBER, 1919

Overland Monthly

Vol. LXXIV

No. 6

Overland Monthly

AN ILLUSTRATED MAGAZINE OF THE WEST

CONTENTS FOR DECEMBER, 1919

NOTICE.—Contributions to the Overland Monthly should be typewritten, accompanied by full return postage, and with the author's name and address plainly written in upper corner of first page. Manuscripts should never be rolled.

The Publisher of the Overland Monthly will not be responsible for the preservation or mail miscarriage of unsolicited contributions and photographs.

Issued Monthly. $1.50 per year in advance. Fifteen cents per copy. Back numbers 3 months or over 25c; six months or over 50c; nine months or over 75c; 1 year or over $1.00. Postage: To Canada, 3 cents; Foreign, 5 cents.

Copyrighted, 1919, by the Overland Monthly Company.

Entered at the San Francisco, Cal., Post-office as second-class matter.

Published by the OVERLAND MONTHLY COMPANY, San Francisco, California.

259 MINNA STREET.

The Right to Live

Little Americans have just as much right to health and happiness as the children of France, Belgium, or any other country in the world, and yet Tuberculosis killed 12,000 American children last year, and crippled many more.

FIGHT TUBERCULOSIS
USE RED CROSS CHRISTMAS SEALS

"NYMPH"

Photograph by Dorothea Lange

"STUDY OF A HEAD"

Photograph by Dorothea Lange

"PORTRAIT OF A YOUNG GIRL"

Photograph by Dorothea Lange

"SYMPATHY"

Photograph by Dorothea Lange

OVERLAND  MONTHLY

Founded 1868

BRET HARTE

| VOL. LXXIV | San Francisco, December, 1919 | No. 6 |

"GRADATIONS"

Photograph by Dorothea Lange

The Art of Dorothea Lange

By Carmen Ballen

I N THESE days, when photography is taking its place as one of the recognized arts, and the camera has shown itself as pliant in the hand of the artist as the palette of pigments, it is not without application to mention the art of Dorothea Lange, as one refers to the individual expressions of the mas-ters of the brush.

There is that in Dorothea Lange which places her among the starry-eyed aspir-ants to Olympus, and at once removes her portraits from the deplorable per-version of the many so-called ultra mod-ern schools. She has the finer sense, the more exquisite affinity with beauty, and her ideals are of a greater oneness with the Divine Harmony. She is, as was the

"STUDY IN SILVER"

Photograph by Dorothea Lange

"IN THE GARDEN"

Photograph by Dorothea Lange

"*REVERIE*"   *Photograph by Dorothea Lange*

knight of King Arthur, a crusader against the false, a seeker for the sublime and beautiful truth of things in her work with the camera, of which she says:

"A likeness, yes; but conveying the spirit of the person—always!"

The spirit is ever lovely in its perfect translation, although a human likeness may not be, so you perceive the difficult goal she has set herself and is achieving with breathless rapidity. It is not so much the quality of her objective that has set this young aspirant apart from her fellows, it is her power to realize it—the all but impossible reconciliation of the greatest good—pictured in its fleeting revelations—with the unlovely human masks people go about constructing for themselves each day! And this is done not through any combination of lenses or chemical exactness, according to Miss Lange, but with sympathy and understanding—the meeting of each individual in his own life interests. She has the gift of seeking out the finest in

her subject, of bringing it happily to view, and this talent and other subtleties, combined with a rare sensitiveness to light, on whose radiant wings the image is conveyed to the lenses, go into the making of Dorothea Lange's portraits.

"All education is self-education. Everything comes from within," says Miss Lange when asked to explain her method, "It is just finding one's personal equation for beauty."

To the writer, the balancing of personal peculiarities necessary in reaching one' equation is a far more difficult thing than mastering the esoteries of photography, and, indeed, it seems that nothing is impossible to one who has done so. Miss Lange, however, is firm in her belief that the personal equation can be met by anyone if he so wills. Unlike many in the possession of a singular knowledge, she is generous with her encouragement to others, and is of the opinion that there should be more schools of photography. It is a field compara-

"STUDY IN TONES"　　　*Photograph by Dorothea Lange*

"AT HOME"　　　*Photograph by Dorothea Lange*

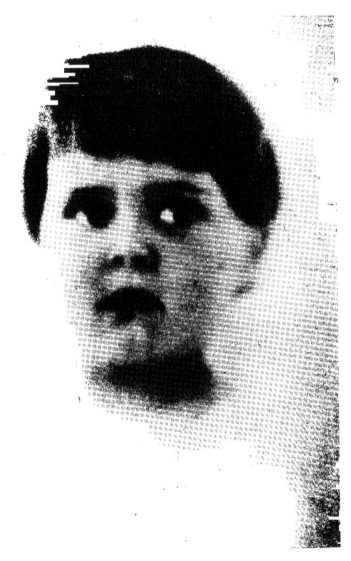

"CHILDHOOD"   *Photograph by Dorothea Lange*

"STEPHANIE SCHEHATOWITCH"
Photograph by Dorothea Lange

tively undeveloped, she says, and a profession to which women are especially adapted. Her boundless vitality and enthusiasm are not confined to her own work. About her she has gathered a coterie of those destined to wear the laurel. In the burnished surface of the old samovar on her hearthstone there are reflected faces—young, eager, hopeful faces—of the weavers of dreams and fantasies. Her tea hour is seldom a lonely one.

Still, with more the restfulness of peace than a surcease from turmoil, is the studio of Dorothea Lange in the Hill Tolerton Print Rooms on Sutter street. No sound of traffic penetrates here, and only the drip of the fountain makes infinitesmal silvery clashes on the quiet hour. No sound nor sight of the busy street, with the clear light of Heaven limning down, unobstructed, into the open courtyard and across the paved portico. Secluded by the protection of the exhibition rooms in the front, there is in this place of mellowed pillars, flowers and sunlight, a repose all but unbelievable in the heart of a teeming city. It is here that people, young and beautiful, or old and beautiful (for in the artist's eyes there is reflected only the beautiful), come to sit for portrait photographs. It is here they feel world-worries slipping from them like false coverings to reveal the innate sweetenss and purity of spirit, and, lo, they find that spirit pictured there on paper when Miss Lange has done with them.

A Fountain in The Studio

Occident and Orient

An Open Forum for the Discussion of Western and Eastern Affairs

Conducted by Charles Hancock Forster and Gladys Bowman Forster

NEW Japan has already acquired the Mechanical instruments, the political, economic and industrial methods, and the science, education, ideas and ideals of occidental civilization. New China is rapidly following in the footsteps of Japan. Both are increasingly self-conscious and insistent on courteous treatment and observance of treaties. They are asking, with growing earnestness, for recognition on a basis of equality with nations of the West.

The great world problem of the twentieth century is undoubtedly the problem of the contact of the East and the West. Whether it shall bring us weal or woe depends largely on the United States. Shall our Oriental policy be based on race pride, disdain and selfishness? Shall it be entirely devoid of sympathy? And shall we rely on brute force for carrying it through. Or shall we give justice, courtesy and a square deal, refusing to be stamped by ignorance, ill founded suspicion and falsehood? Shall we "prepare" to maintain by our military might a policy of arrogant disregard of their needs and feelings, or shall we remove dangers of conflict by a policy of friendly consideration and genuine helpfulness?"

Here in California the ends of the earth meet. Ancient civilization, awakening from its long sleep, and the new civilization of the West, have at last met face to face. The future holds just one of two things in the relationship between these two civilizations: The passion of conflict or the intelligence of co-operation. The first will mean a great war between the races that will involve the en-

tire world, the second—the unity of the Occident and the Orient and the development of a universal civilization founded upon peaceful co-operation and aiming to preserve what is best in all human life.

To realize such a purpose this department is dedicated, and we invite the co-operation of all who are interested in developing a friendly and intelligent understanding between the East and the West. We believe that California is the strategic geographical position from which should go forth a sound and not an unsound leadership in these matters, and it is fitting that one of California's oldest magazines should include a department on Oriental affairs—taking up the task of helping to create such a leadership.

China and Japan must some day come to realize that friendship and co-operation will enrich both nations. Corrupt elements are doing much of late to divide the Orient, and behind these elements is the power of Occidental greed

Japan is China's best customer. In the year 1918 China's export trade amounted to 485,883,031 taels. Of this amount Japan took 163,394,092 taels. Thus over one-fourth of all China's export trade went to Japan.

Japan needs a vast amount of raw materials that China is able to supply. It is very plain that the Orient can develop only by a united spirit and the realization by China and Japan of each others needs. Suspicion and hatred between these two great peoples will destroy them and hurt the world.

The Occident should change its attitude to the Orient and should bring to a standstill those selfish and dangerous elements that aim to create a bad spirit between China and Japan. We should allow to a united Orient a free hand to develop, by its great surplus of human energy, the vast, untouched resources of far-eastern Asia.

There are elements in Occidental nations that call for close scrutiny—a scrutiny that aims to penetrate behind the scenes in order to discover the hidden and sinister forces that are the source of the unholy influences that menace the peace and security of the human race. These influences, whatever they may be, take advantage of every oppor-

tunity to set the teeth of the Orient against Japan, because they imagine that a united Orient, led by Japan, would take a great many dollars out of the coffers of Occidental traders.

The eagerness of Japan to get a foothold in China and the Far East, providing she does it legitimately, should be regarded as natural and right. No unfair means should be used to injure her in her just conquests. The more she puts her energies to work to develop the Far East the better it will be for the entire world, and for the development of China. The best men in China know this. The peace of the world can never be realized without a united Orient.

The Awakening of Asia

By H. M. Hyndman

(Editor's note: The following excerpts are quoted from "The Awakening of Asia," written by the noted English author, H. M. Hyndman, whose opinions on the Orient are highly regarded the world over.)

NOT long ago, European nations were discussing and deciding among themselves how much more of sleepy Asia they should appropriate, for the benefit, do doubt, of the peoples brought under this foreign rule. But now our sense of conscious superiority is being shaken, and when we find the inscrutable Asiatic learning to meet us successfully with our own weapons, we draw back a little. We even begin to see that he may have good grounds for regarding his white rivals as the barbarians that, in some respects, we are.

"Yet the white man still holds control over nearly half of Asia and its vast population. Asia comprises, including its islands, less than 1,000,000,000 of the human race. England, France, Russia, Holland and the United States are all deeply concerned in the future of this mass of

people, in view of the scope of territory and population they control. All will be greatly affected by the general political, economic and social movement of Japan, China and India. In a word, the position of Great Britain is foremost, and of the other Powers in their degree, is now being steadily undermined. The determined effort to secure Asia for the Asiatics, once begun as earnestly in action as it is now being seriously considered in thought, might spread with a rapidity which would paralyze all attempts at reconquest, if, indeed, such attempts could ever be effectively made.

"Asia, in short, is already far from being the Asia which was fair game for adventurous European experiments. New conditions must be dealt with by a new policy.

"And who shall say that the frank

abandonment of the fallacious polity of Imperialism will not greatly benefit the countries which boldly enter upon this honorable course? The possession of India has been a curse to England, alike in her domestic and foreign affairs. Democracy at home has greatly suffered from the maintenance of despotism abroad. The two can never be harmonized, nor kept simultaneously in being, without danger to the popular cause. The fear of what might happen to the English in India has frequently perverted the action of British policy. In economics also the tribute from Hindustan, which must be paid, no matter at what price, in saleable commodities, has done mischief to the producers of Great Britain as to the riots of India.

"So with France and her Asiatic possessions. What have the French peasants and bourgeoisie to gain, from any point of view, by retaining provinces that must be defended at the cost of their blood and treasure, and must introduce a dangerous military sentiment into the management of their affairs?

"Happily the same views as to the madness of modern warfare which are now being forced upon the rest of the world are also making way with Asiatic statesmen. They, too, see that friendly co-operation for common advantage might be far more advantageous to all than rivalry for power or competition for gain. Freedom of nationalities, equality of rights, respect for treaties and conventions, international arrangements for securing permanent peace are as important for Asia as for any other continent. But the responsibility for adopting them, should the Japanese democratic party prevail, and India and China press their demands without violence, rests entirely with Europe. The Asiatic nations are so far threatening no legitimate European interest: they ask only that the principles for which the Allies justly claim they fought Germany should be applied in the most populous regions of the world.

"But it is useless to disguise from ourselves that this concession would involve of itself a complete revolution in the East. For such policy honestly applied would mean:

"1. The emancipation of India from foreign rule by peaceful agreements with its numerous peoples.

"2. The cessation of attempts to force foreign capitalism and foreign trade upon Asiatic countries.

"3. The recognition that Japanese and Chinese are entitled, in countries and colonies inhabited or controlled by Europeans, to rights equal with those of Europeans in China and Japan.

"4. The granting of similar rights to Indians on the same basis.

"5. The acceptance by Europeans of the principle of 'Asia for the Asiatics' as a rightful claim.

"But no student and no statesman would contend that such a wide policy of justice can be suddenly realized. Yet if in the near future public opinion in Europe and America were to endorse such a program, and the nations interested would take the first steps towards its realization, much of the antagonism which is already manifesting itself in Asia might be removed. Past injuries cannot now be remedied. The most to hope for is that, in the Asiatic mind, they may be held to balance those eastern attacks upon the West which belong to a past more remote.

"We are turning over a new page in the history of the human race. What will be written upon it will depend on the men and women of the rising generation. If, in international relations, the old race and color prejudices are maintained, if trade and commerce, interest and profit, continue to be the principal objects of our statesmanship, then troubles may easily ensue beside which event the world war may take second place. On the other hand, should wider views and nobler aspirations animate both branches of civilized mankind, then indeed a magnificent vista of common achievement will open out before our immediate descendents."

How We Can Help China

By Professor Payson J. Treat

THE widespread discussion of the Shantung affair in this country has again demonstrated that the American people as a whole are deeply interested in the welfare of China and are ready to help the great republic of Asia if some concrete method can be pointed out. In spite of the almost universal condemnation of the award to Japan of the German lease and interests in Shantung it required only a little thought to convince many Americans that an amendment of the treaty would be of little help to China, and would certainly jeopardize the well-being of all the world through a delay in ratification. And further consideration would show that the Shantung situation was only a result of more fundamental condition. The cause, not the effect, must be remedied before constructive measures can be applied.

China certainly needs understanding, sympathy and help. She has received too much of the second in proportion to the first and third. The American government has maintained a consistent policy of friendship for China, and, in spite of local agitations, the feelings of the American people have been as well disposed. Government and people have realized that something was wrong in China, but the diagnosis of the ailment has differed from decade to decade. Fifty years ago the fault was ascribed to Chinese conservatism and the Confucian teachings, which prevented China from following the lead of Japan in studying and mastering the secrets of Western progress. Later the blame was laid to the ignorant and reactionary Manchu dynasty, which, it was alleged, prevented the more enlightened Chinese from entering the paths of modern achievement.

After the Chino—Japanese war the trouble was generally ascribed to the selfish interference of the European powers, notably Russia, Great Britain, France and Germay. And since 1905, Japan has been held responsible for the present ills of China.

A survey of the past fifty years leads one to conclude that the fundamental difficulty has been with the Chinese themselves, and not with the other factors which have aggravated rather than occasioned the difficulties. Thus, when the Manchu dynasty was swept aside in 1911-1912 and the friends of China believed that a new era had dawned, it was soon found that with few exceptions all the old abuses continued. Too much was expected of the Revolution. The substitution of a President for an Emperor cannot make over the culture of a people in a day, or perhaps even in a generation. And so when, during the Great War, the pressure of the European powers was removed, the Peking Government was unable to profit through this respite. China should have emerged from the Great War rich and strong. Instead she has been torn by civil strife, and two governments are functioning within the bounds of the Flowery Republic at the present time. Nor can Japan be held accountable for the present unhappy situation. Her policy has been based upon Chinese conditions, it has not produced them.

The Chinese people possess a great asset in the admiration and real affection which they awaken in almost every foreigner who dwells for any length of time among them. Yet many of these well-wishers have been brought to a despondent state because of the developments during the past seven years. Many of them have tried to remove one of the troublesome factors by a campaign of criticism and denunciation of the Japanese. But others have sought to remedy the fundamental difficulties by advocating some form of foreign supervision which would insure an honest and efficient administration at Peking, believing that when this has been gained a general improvement throughout the country will follow. Many schemes of this kind have been proposed and in most cases they have emanated from sincere friends of the Chinese people.

China needs many things before she can make proper use of her splendid resources in man-power and natural endowment. She needs a sound currency system, a well-organized and humane industrial system, a small but efficient army, a modern system of courts and codes, a well-trained body of police, and certain changes in her social institutions.

But the most important thing that China needs is an adequate system of universal education. The present plight of China is due to this defect more than to any other one thing. Down until 1905 the educational system was one which had functioned for centuries. It was one of private instruction and governmental supervision through the great competitive examinations. So long as the old curriculum was in use it might truly be said that China faced backward, to the ideas and models of the Confucian classes. Except for the few who had studied in Western schools, (almost entirely mission schools,) there were practically no Chinese who had any conception of modern life and what it demanded. The official classes were recruited from men who possessed scarcely any qualifications for service in the twentieth century. In Japan the change from the old to the new order was presaged in the Emperor's oath of 1868, and the system of general education was commenced in 1872, so that "there should not be found one family in the whole empire, nor one member of a family, ignor-

ant and illiterate." This early recognition of the importance of universal education accounts, more than any one thing, for the rise of Japan as a great power. By 1889, when the constitution was promulgated, Japan had a very considerable body of trained leaders who had been educated in the national schools and universities, as well as those who had studied abroad. But the new national system was only authorized in China in 1905, and the succession of civil disturbances since 1911 has sadly hampered its development. Thus, in 1919, there are still relatively few Chinese who have had an adequate modern training, and most of the older officials are men who were educated according to the old system. Adequate leadership cannot exist in China until more of the young men have attained that maturity of experience which makes for sound judgment. And a republican form of government cannot function satisfactorily until the nation possesses a considerable body of educated and thoughtful citizens. These essentials were realized during the reform days of the Manchu period. The nine year "program of preparation" adopted in 1908 called for such educational measures that in 1917 five per cent. of the people should be literate. The three year program, hurriedly revised just before the successful revolution, sacrificed the educational features of the old scheme in order to hasten the preparation for parliamentary government. One of the most promising signs in China today is the recognition by the liberal leaders that more time must be allowed for preparing the people for popular government. Education, widely diffused, but taking time for its introduction, must be the foundation stone of the new edifice.

We must recognize this fundamental need of China. We must not expect too much of the republic until its citizens are able to contribute much. Then, if they fail, we have some reason for disappointment. Each year sees more and more young men prepared and ready to accept the responsibilities of government, and more of the old officials dis-placed. Each year sees more and more young men and women able and ready to serve the state and to hold to a strict accountability the men whom they choose to represent them. And Ameri-cans, who know that their own national achievements and the very stability of their institutions have been founded upon general education, should be ready and willing to help the Chinese. Our gov-ernment made the most profitable in-vestment ever known when it returned some $10,000,000 of the Boxer Indemnity and suggested that China use it for the education of her students in this coun-try. The Rockefeller Foundation is rendering an invaluable service not only to China but to the world in its support of medical education. American mission-ary organizations have rendered magni-ficent service through their schools and colleges, for girls as well as for boys. And the students and alumni of some American colleges have raised funds to support in whole or in part some of the best schools in China. Yale College, in Changsha, has spread abroad the reputa-tion of the New England university in the Central Flowery Republic. Ameri-can young men and women can find in the schools of China a great field for constructive service. Generous Ameri-cans who like to have a stake in every good enterprise can enjoy large divi-dends of satisfaction through support-ing educational enterprises in China. And many of us at home can contribute to the desired end. At the present time it is estimated that about 4,000 Chinese young men and women are studying in our schools and colleges. Our educa-tional institutions offer them every fac-ility, but they need more than the train-ing of the class-room or laboratory. They should have opportunities to know Amer-icans and to study American social and political institutions. There are many ways in which Americans can help China by helping the Chinese students make the most of their opportunities while they are residents among us.

Americans will soon have an oppor-tunity to help China in a more immed-iate, though less fundamental, way than has just been considered. Next to the internal problems of China are those arising from foreign control and inter-ference. Many of the old treaties gave foreigners exceptional privileges in China notably, extraterritorial jurisdiction and control of the Chinese tariff. And in more recent years came the foreign lease holders and economic concessions. Up to about 1885, Great Britain led in demanding commercial concessions which, under her "open door" policy, were enjoyed by all the treaty powers. France seems to have introduced the idea of special con-cessions in 1885, and the other European powers followed her lead. At the out-break of the Russo-Japanese war, in 1904, Russia held the leasehold of Port Arthur and enjoyed a monopoly of econ-omic opportunity in all Manchuria and Mongolia; Great Britain held two lease-holds and her nations had railway and mining rights—it has often been forgot-ten that the only bit of territory within the Eighteen Provinces to pass into for-eign ownership is the little tract of Old Kowloon acquired by Great Britain in 1860, to complete the defences of Hong Kong, acquired in 1842; France had a leasehold and important railway and mining rights; and Germany had Kiao-chow Bay and a monopoly of develop-ment rights in Shantung province. Since 1904 Japan has ousted Russia from South Manchuria and Germany from Shantung, and she has shown an ability to play the old game of "grab" even more successfully than her European teachers. In the past the United States could only look on at these proceedings. She had to accept the leaseholds and spheres of interest created in 1898 as facts, although John Hay acted on the advice of W. W. Rockhill and won the formal acceptance by the powers of the originally British doctrine of the "open door." When Russia set out to acquire all of Manchuria the United States pro-tested, and she protested again during the Japanese demands upon China in

1915. But there was no machinery for a ,united protest of the powers interested in protecting China. This needed machinery is provided by the League of Nations, and after the United States enters the League she will be able as never before to move in defense of China. The much discussed Article X guarantees the territorial integrity of China—and of all the other members of the League. The day will then have passed when Russian or Japanese expansionists can hope for the possession of Manchuria, Mongolia, Shantung or Fukien. Article XI provides: "It is also declared to be the friendly right of each Member of the League to bring to the attention of the Assembly or of the Council any circumstance whatever affecting international relations which threatens to disturb international peace or the good understanding between nations upon which peace depends." Under this clause China can bring up the question of all the treaty limitations upon her sovereignty, and of all the concessions extorted in the past which hamper her economic development. It may be taken for granted that the United States will support her, and that Great Britain and her dominions will join with us. France may be counted upon to stand with the great Western democracies, and any liberal government which may· be stabilized in Russia will do the same. And as for Japan, even though 'some of the chauvinists may take the short-sighted view, there is every reason to believe that no Japanese cabinet would refuse to fall in line with a proposal to remove ALL foreign interference from China. Every farsighter Japanese realizes that international rivalries in China can only end in strife. They realize also that when every door is open Japan, because of her propinquity and her cultural background, can compete, without any special advantages, with all the other powers. President Wilson, in one of his San Francisco addresses, looked forward to this day. "Sitting around our council board in Paris," he said, "I put this question: 'May I expect that this will be the beginning of the retrocession to China of the exceptional rights which other governments have enjoyed there?' And the responsible representatives of the other great governments said, 'Yes, you may expect it.'"

So the day is near at hand when Americans can offer great constructive aid to China. The consortium will substitute international financial aid and supervision for national competition. The League of Nations will guarantee the integrity of China and furnish a method for removing the political and economic disadvantages under which she suffers. But none of these agencies can furnish any permanent solution of China's present weakness. That solution must come from within China, and all forward - looking people the world over should try to help China help herself.

SPECIAL NOTICE:

Letters and manuscripts dealing with matters that fit into the aim of the department will be gladly received. Also photographs of the Far East. Every manuscript and photograph received will be given careful attention. Stamped, addressed envelope must be enclosed for the return of unavailable matter.

Address:

Editor Overland Monthly,

259, Minna St., San Francisco, Cal.

Smiting the Rock

By Charles Jeffries

HE clang of tank building, the rattle of rotaries, the blast of countless furnaces rose in one deafening roar—the roar of the Sour Lake oilfields in the boom days.

On an upturned keg, with a tow sack for a cushion, a young man sat running a drilling rig. Round and round the rotary whirled. With his hand on the brake and his mind on some girl in Houston, the man sensed the downward pull of the drill. Mechanically a few inches at a time he let it slip deeper in the earth. Mechanically he noted the hum of the machinery. Mechanically he shouted to the fireman:

"Shoot the juice to her, Shorty; let's toot 'em up."

"You'll have to give me something to shoot with, Billy boy."

"What! The water out again?"

"There may be enough here to boil a pot of cabbage."

"This place certainly has one appropriate name—Sour Lake—lake, lake; and a man can't get enough water to drink; and what few drops you do get, some durn thief is eternally trying to steal. Stop the engine a minute; I've been aiming all day to examine that water hole."

Arising, he and the fireman walked over to the reservoir, a pit in the ground, resembling a large grave. It contained about a foot of water, and Bill, the driller, picking up a stick, began probing and sloshing around in it. He found something imbedded in the bank, under the water, and tried to fish it out, but failed. He climbed down in the pit, caught hold of the object and slowly drew it to the top. It was a one-inch pipe, and as the free end came to the surface, it gave a sucking sound. Climbing out of the pit and pointing to a crew of men a hundred yards away, Bill said:

"They're the ones. They have been stealing water around here a month," and taking three feet at a step, he was gone. A minute later he was heard saying words to the grafters that chorded well with the general tones of the surrounding oil field.

From another direction came another man. Carefully picking his way across the mud and slush of Shoestring on half submerged plank and pipe he came up to where the well was being put down. He was an old man, and by his first sentence you might know him to be the owner of the well.

"How is the work progressing, Mr. Jackson?" he asked the driller.

"None too well, Mr. Curry; the water supply is poor, and I am hindered other ways."

By the old man's second sentence you might know that he had had a good case of the oil fever and was now entering the very first stage of convelescence.

"What kind of a well do you think it will be?" he asked.

"Honestly, I don't think it will every pay for the drilling."

"There are producing wells all around," almost pleaded Curry, waving his hand toward the forest of derricks that crowded in on every side.

"That's it. There are too many of them, and they are too close to you. Oil doesn't grow, and these other fellows have about bled your little one-sixteenth of an acre dry. They are still doing all they can to retard work on this well."

That night Bill went to the pool-hall. In a cloud of smoke and a bedlam of racket he boisterously played pool for an hour. During a lull in the game a man who had watched Bill for some time brushed by, and, turning, as if surprised, exclaimed:

"Hello, there, Bill; that you? Come take one."

Bill was dry and hadn't had "one" in some time and, though not a particular friend to the man, he complied. They stood with a foot on the rail and talked oil till the bartender worked around to them, then they ordered and drank the best the house afforded, and the man proposed a game of pool. Bill felt that there was design in all this as the man owned wells near the Curry holding and had lately done several underhand tricks. To learn what the fellow was after, Bill played with him.

Acquaintance ripened rapidly in the oil field, especially when stimulated by good Milwaukee beer. By the end of the first game the man was showing the cloven foot; by the time three balls were pocketed in the second game he was saying:

"If you could find some way to stop work on that well, I could tell you where a man named Bill Jackson could win some mighty nice money in a poker game."

To make sure he had caught the man's meaning, Bill evaded. "I don't see how I could stop now; we are nearly down to cap-rock, and the well is due to come in tomorrow."

"Pshaw; that's nothing; what's the matter with using this scarcity of water as an excuse? or better yet, grinding there on the rock with a dull bit? Old Curry knows about as much about drilling as a sow, and while you are holding your hand in his pocket during the day, every night you can walk over to my office and win your five bucks. How does it hit you, son?"

Bill went quite close to the man, pulled down an eye-lid, and asked:

"Do you see anything green in my eye?"

"What?"

"I said, do you see anything green in my eye?"

"You'd better keep your red snout out of my face if you don't want it mashed."

"Mash it! Mash it! you slippery, low-life scoundrel; why don't you mash it? If you don't aim to mash it, listen here— if you ever come to me again with your sneaking, dirty schemes, I'll kick your rotten carcass clear out of Texas, you hear me?"

Next morning a well-crew, working near Curry's, could be seen tinkering with their gas-escape. Finally they tore it up completely so that the gas, instead of blowing harmlessly out at the top of the derrick, came out near the ground, endangering everybody around. Bill kept his eye on them some time, and when the wind whipped the gas toward him, he, none too politely, asked:

"What are you all trying to do?"

"Who's running this business?" answered one of the men.

Bill said no more for the time, and the man fastened an ell on the well so that it shot gas in Bill's direction. Bill, as best he could, by taking advantage of the wind, continued work. But it was impossible to avoid the gas entirely, and soon he began to feel it in his eyes. A few minutes later one of his men, walking off for a breath of fresh air, suddenly became very weak. He staggered a step, reached toward a post for support, then tumbled over in the slush. In a second his comrades had picked him up and were carrying him out of the gas. He had not inhaled a strong dose of the poison and regained consciousness quickly enough. Leaving him to the care of the other men, Bill, without a word of explanation, walked over to the gas well. and, being experienced in oil-field affairs, he picked up a wrench on the way and slipped it in his hip pocket.

The gas well crew had been working all day for just this. Each one of them had five dollars in his pocket as advanced blood-money, with a promise of more if Bill should be laid up with a broken arm or a cracked head; and it was with joy in their hearts that they heard Bill say to their foreman:

"I want to know what you mean, anyhow?"

"I mean to wipe up the earth with you if you come over here messin' with me. Anything else fresh on your mind, haay?"

Action was quick in those days. As soon as Bill set foot on the derrick floor, the gasmen began maneuvering for his back. One of them, after gaining that vantage point, picked up a pair of heavy chain-tongs and advanced toward him like a cat. Bill was wiser than his years. He did not look around, and appeared to be utterly unconscious of the fellow's movement. But, with the eye of a hawk, he watched the fellow's shadow, noted his every move, and when the fellow swung back the unwieldy bludgeon, Bill, with all the spring that his young frame possesed, whirled and struck. The fellow dropped to the floor and the gasmen were one fighter short.

Bill's crew were as covetous of glory as Henry V. Seeing the turn of affairs, they came on the run. Followed as clean-cut an oilfield fight as was every joined with monkey wrenches and pieces of pipe. It did not last long. The man who had been recently gased regained his strength and, coming on the scene with a good, stout club and a hunger for hide, turned the tide of battle, and the derrick floor, like the deck of some captured frigate, remained to Bill's crew. Like true victors, they sent a few be-fitting epithets after the retreating foe, kicked the objectionable ell around and went back to work.

In spite of the hindering efforts of hostile neighbors, they at last reached the cap-rock. The day was too near spent to try to bring in the well, and Bill, setting a double guard over the works, knocked off for the day.

The next day Bill put on a good, sharp bit and started the rotary to running. The rock proved soft, the machinery ran smoothly, and any moment they expected to punch through into the oil sand.

Whether the well came in with the strength of a volcano, blowing the whole string of piping, derricks and all sky-ward, or whether it came in quietly, like water seeping into a posthole, it stood the men in hand to be on the lookout. Keenly on the alert they watched all the morning, but nothing developed. They hurried back after dinner and worked steadily all evening. Six o'clock found them still on the rock. This was disappointing, to say the least. Bill had drilled several wells in the field and had never before found the rock so thick. However, it cut readily, and Bill felt sure he could work through it the following

day. But he didn't; nor did he the next nor the next. At the end of a week they had nothing to show for their labor but a lot of dull bits.

As if the machinations of the rival companies were not enough, here was nature leagued against them. The air of confidence, that sets so well on a driller, forsook Bill. He couldn't but think that the oil thieves were playing him some trick. Still there was the indisputable tapeline—for rock work they were going down satisfactorily enough. Poor old man Curry's visits to the well became shorter and farther between. And when he did come around he seemed not to appreciate so keenly as formerly the "click," "clack," of the rival company's pumps.

One day the expected happened. The drill slipped a little and began eating downward with a speed that showed it was through the rock. Expecting at least a small blow-out, everyone hurriedly left the well. No blow-out came, and the men cautiously inched their way back and examined the slush-water that boiled up outside the pipe. Not a single gas bubble did they find—not a drop of live oil.

"Pinched," commented Shorty, the fireman. "The thieves beat you to it, Mr. Curry."

"Worse than that," disagreed Bill. "That rock was thick; it completely filled Mr. Curry's part of the oil stratum, and now we are through it and into earth that never contained a drop of oil. Well, we are done; all our work and all Mr. Curry's money and all the scheming of those rascals went for nothing—stop the engine, Shorty."

"Isn't it possible that we might go a little deeper and strike it?" pleaded the old man.

Bill smiled in pity. "Might as well be digging on top of Pike's Peak with a stove shovel. No; the best thing you can do is to have this piping pulled out before it sticks; you will be that much to the good."

And walking over to the well he, after the way of men, shook the projecting pipe. And while he stood there he noticed that the water was coming up on the outside in a stronger flow than usual and much clearer. This was doubly remarkable, since the pumps were stopped.

"What have we got here?" said Bill.

The others gathered around, and Bill, using a cut-off tomato can, dipped up some of the new water and tasted it—drank it.

"How does it taste?" asked Shorty.

"Don't bother me," said Bill, reaching for more. This is the first drink of water I have had since I hit Sour Lake."

Then he arose and congratulated Curry on his good fortune. Curry did not exactly understand, and Bill enlightened him.

"Good gracious, I'd rather have that water well than the Lucus gusher. This town is starving for good water. They'll pay you your own price for it. The oilmen who have been giving you dirt will get down on their knees for a little. They will lay the pipe lines to your well. All you'll have to do is to collect the jits. Dad, you're a rich man. You will have to reinforce your pockets with buckskin and wear leather suspenders."

Her Heart

By Henry Walker Noyes

I spied Dan Cupid yestere'en
   While resting 'tween the dances;
He sat enshrined two palms between,
   A furbishing his lances.
A little tear was in his eye,
   His curved bow unstrung—
"How now, my sweet, what luck?" quoth I;
   "I prithee, find thy tongue."

He cast a broken lance aside
   And shook his curly head—
" 'Tis useless, quite," he sadly sighed,
   "And all the rest are sped.
She led me on from dart to dart,"
   (He sobbed in quav'ring treble,
"And when at last I hit her heart
   My point broke—on a pebble."

WESTERN TANAGER

Bird Voices of the Foothills

By P. M. Silloway

Illustrated by Bettina Bruckman

THE foothills buttress the great Rockies, extending their giant tentacles far beyond the bluish skyline and gripping our interest with a hold invisible yet tangible. The wooded ridges loom near us with ravines leading into parks of wild beauty, a wilderness of Nature's expansive handiwork, variegated with streams that lure the troutfisher abroad; precipices where rocks hang bare and threatening, and shoulders of coniferous woods that rise in suggestive dominance. The spell of the foothills is on us, drawing us over the basal benches and prairies and into the succession of rocky canyons, around the precipitous cliffs and up the slopes clad with a wealth of evergreen woodlands redolent with the odors of pine and balsam, of fir and spruce and hemlock. It is not the forest alone that invites our fancy today, however, for in the sunlighted margins and openings we hear voices that manifest animation and activity designed for appreciative ears and eyes, and hence we pause now and then to listen to the varied bird voices of the foothills.

Living at ease in the radiating coulees and canyons, the magpie is among the first to announce its presence by its harsh calls. To the settled rancher and horticulturist the voice of the magpie has little charm, for an acquaintance with this inquisitive, loquacious inhabitant of the foothill thickets has dispelled the illusion that distance gave as the tenderfoot met with this bird of the West. The magpie is a large, handsome fellow, at any rate, garbed in showy black with white markings, and he has a liking for human associations, making himself freely at home around the ranch premises if unmolested. What the crow is to the Eastern farmer, the magpie is all that and even more to the rancher of the foothills, for the latter bird is much more familiar and ubiquitous. The magpie's vocabulary is quite extensive, and at times his tones seem almost human as he chatters his reproof of intrusion of his domestic affairs, though in general the utterances of the magpie are merely harsh gutturals and croakings.

While the magpie sits scolding us at a safe distance, another bird-voice comes to us with a far different message from a nearby tree-top—the singing of the familiar robin. High in the sunlight he utters his recitals, always a lyric of spring. There are but few feet in a verse of robin music, and that verse is oft repeated. Pausing to listen to this energetic voice, we note the loud, hurried expressions of emotion, marked by a nervousness that makes us fancy that our musician is losing breath. At times in the performance, however, the robin's songs are uttered in a high, squeaky falsetto tone, and again, robin sings in a low, subdued voice, as if in poetic, persuasive mood, for perhaps his fair charmer is within hearing and he would whisper his flatteries for her ear alone.

A voice of unusual power and charm in the bird music of the foothills is that of the Western tanager. This songster frequents the coniferous trees of larger size, where its bright yellow attire, ornamented with black wings and crimson head, seems in strange contrast to the dark evergreen of its forest home. The singing of the tanager is very much like that of the robin, and the listener must discriminate very closely to distinguish the difference. The tanager's productions are more nervous, more energetic and more sharply uttered, lacking something of the fullness of the robin's voice. This splendid gem of the coniferous woodlands is not sparing of its music, and it chooses open stations for its recitals, a-perch in the full sunlight in the top of a tree in the wood's margin.

Most of the songsters become silent early in summer, but not so with the lazuli bunting. Its song is a pleasing little roundelay of chatter, uttered with persistency of repetition and energy of enunciation. This performer is a sprightly little fellow, one of our handsomest residents of the foothills, wearing a coat of indigo blue, with orange-tinted breast and light under-parts. He also loves the sunshine, and on a topmost spray of tree or tall bush he voices his expressions of content. At times the lazuli bunting flutters upward in an ecstacy of spirit, chattering in a jumble of his regular notes, and then dropping downward as the song dies away after the outgushing overflow—all this performance for the benefit of his demurely attired spouse nestling her pale blue eggs in a cozy nook in the bush.

The black-headed grosbeak has a voice of fullness and beauty, offering a rich contribution to Nature's chorus of bird music in the foothills. The productions of the blackheaded grosbeak, like those of the Western tanager, are also much like those of the robin, more like a medley of the robin and the oriole. This grosbeak chooses the associations of the deciduous trees rather than the conifers,

MAGPIE

WESTERN TOWHEE

preferably the dwarf trees in low situations, where dwell the vireos and their
associates. This songster is also fairly
generous in its musical offerings, singing best in late spring and much in
early summer, its rich, mellow utterances charming the listener frequently
in early July. The male is one of the
bird beauties of the foothills, having the
head and upper parts deep black, the
lower back marked with cinnamon, like
the under parts, besides various showy
patches of white and yellow. Mr. Grosbeak is a model husband for he is noted
for his unusual attention to home duties.
It is he that sits at home brooding the
eggs, while Mrs. Grosbeak can visit about
the neighborhood with other grosbeak
mesdames, attend club meetings and be
a thorough suffragette without a word of
remonstrance from her better-half. When
the youngsters are ready to leave the
parental walls, it is the male that takes
them in charge and instructs them at first
in the ways of gaining an honest grosbeak living. Well, if the male furnishes
the music, we see no reason why he

should not have his own way in caring
for the main household duties and taking
charge of the education of the children;
at any rate, his mate seems to offer no
objection.

The song sparrow has a voice of persistent and energetic song. It is a hardy
little creature, one of the earliest to participate in the vernal season of bird
music. The early spring is the high tide
of song sparrow music, but thenceforth
throughout most of the summer it utters
its tuneful roundelays. The males generally sing at any season they are present—spring, summer and fall, and at any
time one of them is likely to be heard
in subdued, abbreviated recital. The
song sparrow has a varied repertoire in
its musical performances. The singing
of any particular song sparrow sounds
much the same to ordinary listeners, but
with a slight degree of discrimination
the hearer can perceive that a number
of different songs make up a day's program of this familiar virtuoso. The same
song may be repeated an indefinite number of times, but at length the performer
will vary the arrangement of the notes
so strikingly that the result will be a
different song, again repeated ad libitum.
From time to time each song sparrow
shows himself to be a master of several
songs, each combination of notes being
so unlike the others that it will pass for
a different song. Generally the performance begins with several distinct
whistles of equal value, then follows a
series of hurried, blending notes ending
with a cadenza of force and spirit.

A bird-voice of the foothills not to be
ignored is that of the catbird, for everywhere along the bases of the Rockies
this gifted songster makes its home and
enlivens the hours with its splendid
music. In the bush it nests until late
in summer, and as it thus prolongs its
domestic duties it carries the spirit of
songs far beyond the season common to
most of our bird musicians. Sitting in
a secluded nook in the shrubbery, the
catbird gives expression to its impulses
in voice loud and vibrant in early spring,
or in tones low and sympathetic in late
summer. The opening hours of the day
are generally used by the catbird in its

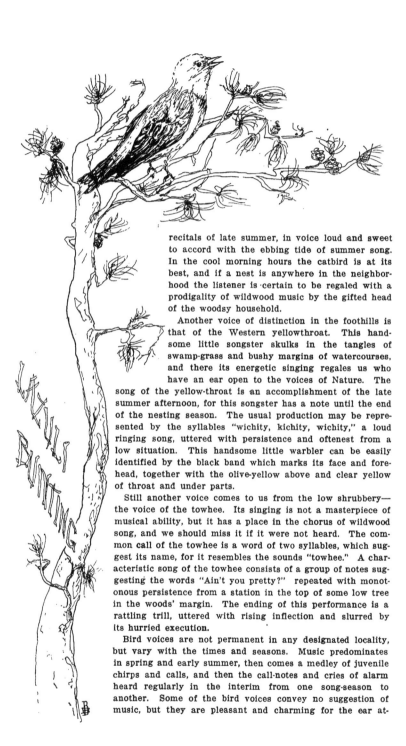

recitals of late summer, in voice loud and sweet to accord with the ebbing tide of summer song. In the cool morning hours the catbird is at its best, and if a nest is anywhere in the neighborhood the listener is ·certain to be regaled with a prodigality of wildwood music by the gifted head of the woodsy household.

Another voice of distinction in the foothills is that of the Western yellowthroat. This handsome little songster skulks in the tangles of swamp-grass and bushy margins of watercourses, and there its energetic singing regales us who have an ear open to the voices of Nature. The song of the yellow-throat is an accomplishment of the late summer afternoon, for this songster has a note until the end of the nesting season. The usual production may be represented by the syllables "wichity, kichity, wichity," a loud ringing song, uttered with persistence and oftenest from a low situation. This handsome little warbler can be easily identified by the black band which marks its face and forehead, together with the olive-yellow above and clear yellow of throat and under parts.

Still another voice comes to us from the low shrubbery— the voice of the towhee. Its singing is not a masterpiece of musical ability, but it has a place in the chorus of wildwood song, and we should miss it if it were not heard. The common call of the towhee is a word of two syllables, which suggest its name, for it resembles the sounds "towhee." A characteristic song of the towhee consists of a group of notes suggesting the words "Ain't you pretty?" repeated with monotonous persistence from a station in the top of some low tree in the woods' margin. The ending of this performance is a rattling trill, uttered with rising inflection and slurred by its hurried execution.

Bird voices are not permanent in any designated locality, but vary with the times and seasons. Music predominates in spring and early summer, then comes a medley of juvenile chirps and calls, and then the call-notes and cries of alarm heard regularly in the interim from one song-season to another. Some of the bird voices convey no suggestion of music, but they are pleasant and charming for the ear attuned in harmony with nature. Among the evergreens of the rock ledges we can hear the grasshopper - like chirps of the kinglets, and in the lower open woods the chickadee has an occasional word to say. The nuthatches utter their queer nasal calls, and the woodpeckers raise their voices in sharp cries of alarm. Occasionally one of the larger hawks screams sharply overhead, and the harsh call of a mountain jay attracts our attention along the hillside. In all and thru all, however, it is Nature's voice through the calls and songs we hear.

Marooned

By Arthur Lawrence Bolton

(Letterman Hospital)

The salt fog drifts through the Golden Gate
    And brings the scent of The Sea,
The Sea Birds call with strident cry,
    And their cry is a call to me,
Yet here I wait from dawn till late
    For a ship to bear me away,
To bear me out with the Setting Sun,
    To lasting Tranquillity.

I am one of the men from Belleau Wood,
    Brough here from Over-Sea,
I once had claim to a hero's fame,
    Which was all that was left of me,
But now forgot, in this lovely spot
    By the edge of The Western Sea,
I wait for the Ship with silver sails,
    That clears for Eternity.

Crucifixion

By Stanley Preston Kimmel

EDITOR'S NOTE—The following is the first installment of the diary kept by Stanley Preston Kimmel at the front while driving an ambulance in the Norton-Hargess unit of the French Red Cross. Mr. Kimmel paid his own way to France several months before America went into the war, to enlist in the Red Cross, and served for nearly a year. He is at present a resident of San Francisco.

This compilation of notes from his diary will run for the next four months in the Overland Monthly.

 O-DAY it is very calm. We are silently plowing along. Our steamer is a good one, considering everything, with a brave little Frenchman as captain, who never leaves the bridge for a minute. All is ready for an emergency in case there should be one.

The cabins are suffocating, and most of us sleep on the upper deck. Each day there is service at three in the afternoon. Some very good advice is given, which will not long be remembered, concerning our ways of life, etc., on the other side.

I have found a friend in an ex-secretary of Rodin, and she has promised an entree for me when we arrive in Paris, or some time before we leave for the front. Rodin is sick at his home near Meudon, so she says, and remains very quiet.

The people in the steerage have a merry time every day singing and dancing. The other passengers do not move about so much. It is queer. The fact that educated people think beyond the moment is likely the explanation. Here, in the midst of a great danger, they are happy and free from worry, while those who are about me seem unable to hide their thoughts and anxieties.

The poor humans below are going back to their own country to help or fight with their brothers and sisters. Is this the reason they are happy? I wonder.

When night comes, K—— and myself go to the bow. As a rule no one sleeps there except us. The passengers walk a great deal on the decks if they cannot rest, and their nervousness keeps everyone awake.

It is weird. The darkness takes everything from sight until the object suddenly looms up like a monster when one comes too near. We are always falling over each other or tripping on the chairs, etc., about the decks. In such an atmosphere as this one forgets he is alive. The voices are heard but they have a hollow sound. The steamer glides through the night with an uncanny swishing noise. It is packed with human flesh and defies everything.

We have passed three steamers on their way to America. America—

*   *   *   *   *   *

We ran into a storm yesterday. The sea is still very rough and foggy. The fogs are a great help now and lessen the danger.

It is a peculiar thing, no one is sick. There is too much excitement for anyone to think of that.

Last night, after we had gone to bed in the deck chairs (the bow was too wet), people came running over to the starboard side of the steamer. A great black blot passed us. Part of a convoy of English battleships, we were told. A hideous thing like an apparition. What is it for? It is for the destruction or subjugation of you, no matter who you may be, if you should dare defy it. The flag which it flies does not matter. It is the thing itself that matters.

I look from the drawing room window. What do I see? The gunners are pacing around the gun turrets. Yes, they are doing that for my protection, but why? It is because there are other gunners and gun turrets. Have these men a personal grudge against one another? What are they doing, wasting their time in this affair when they could be helping themselves or benefiting mankind in some profitable way? Ask Jean why he is fighting. Will he answer you? Perhaps.

We are told our first sight of Germans will be at Bordeaux, but they are prisoners.

Our steamer has taken a different route than the one we were following a few days ago. This will delay us in getting into port.

It is time for gun practice. Now and then a barrel is thrown into the water and used as a target by the gunners. The passengers all run for the boats, thinking something is wrong. They are on edge all the time. At the least provocation they are up and out in a second.

*   *   *   *   *   *   *

This is a wonderful day, but it is also very dangerous for us. The life boats are just above the water, ready for immediate use. A notice has been posted. It is typical of the others we have had from time to time. Here is the warning:

"The commander kindly advises the passengers on the account of submarines, starting from tonight, not to undress for to go to bed, and to have their life belts ready at hand so as to be ready to join the boat assigned to them at the first signal."

I will be glad when we are off this watery grave. It is hard to think of the sea as a blue desert; nevertheless I shall be a little sorry, after all, to leave it.

One of the boys on board suddenly went insane. He has been watched for the last few days. His actions about the steamer have been very queer. We are not allowed to have a light of any kind on the decks at night. He strolled about the first night in the danger zone with a cigar, which had a light on the end like a torch. They have locked him in one of the cabins below. I suppose he will be deported.

*   *   *   *   *   *   *

Bay of Biscay!

We have just passed what is left of a steamer. The sea is full of boards and all kinds of floating debris. No human beings have been seen, and there is not much chance of their having survived. The Germans shell the life boats if they happen to contain any soldiers. Nothing like doing a good job of it!

We are compelled to keep our life belts on until we reach the mouth of the river Girond, which takes us up to Bordeaux. We expect to arrive there about 2 a. m. tomorrow. It will be too late for the day train to Paris, so we will remain over night and go up the next day. I am getting accustomed to being in my clothes two or three days at a time, and do not mind it so much.

*   *   *   *   *   *   *

We just had another alarm. Everyone ran out onto the deck. I can see nothing from the windows. If I could, what good would it do? The ship will be sunk just the same, and there will be plenty of time to get off when the alarm to abandon the vessel is given. The ship is taking a zig-zag course through the water.

A gentleman next to me is seemingly unconcerned. He looked up from his paper and said: "Fine time to be writing a letter," but he continued reading as though nothing was going on. We are alone in the room.

*   *   *   *   *   *   *

Evidently it is over. They will come back into the room now and bring their scared faces with them.

What could really happen to any of us? It is amusing after all. If our steamer should go down it would mean very little. I am sure it would be a blessing to many who, perhaps, fear it. The water would run into our eyes and ears, it would rush into our nostrils, but only for a moment. A vain effort, a cry, and then—nothing. I find myself wishing the thing would happen. I am sick of the sights on the water and this is trivial to what will come later. I suppose, though, if the steamer did go down I would fight for life like the others. If I were saved, and there is not a doubt about it, the whole thing would still be in front of me.

The deck steward has just told me we must wait at the mouth of the river for full tide. We will not reach Bordeaux until 6 p. m. tomorrow evening.

It is little wonder these people are so frightened. The sea is very calm and clear. We can see miles away to the horizon. I imagine it would be a pretty picture through a periscope.

* * * * * * *

We are anchored off the coast of France until noon, when we go up the river to Bordeaux. This is a bright, sunny morning, and the coast is lined with villages, which we see very plainly. The quaint, red-tiled roofs bob up here and there among the green hills. It is all so very peaceful and quiet. We can rest now for we are safe.

There are many small fishing boats in various colors near us. Most of them are red or green. A few yellow and half a dozen blues are among them. What a sight it is! They fill the bay with color and make a wonderful picture.

In the distance can be seen the top mast of a steamer, which was sunk at the beginning of the war. They have never raised it, and, I understand, do not intend to do so. It is a monument and serves its purpose.

There are also captive balloons all along the coast, and an aeroplane passes now and then, coming in or going out on patrol duty.

I have not had more than thirty hours' sleep all week, and have not been able to change my clothes the last three days. The general relaxation will be good for all.

* * * * * * *

We are in Paris. Our quarters are in an old chateau, which was the home of an American dentist at one time. It was from here, and in the carriage of the American, that the Princess Eugenia escaped to the English Channel and then to England.

Coming from Bordeaux we were told that all cafes, etc., in Paris close at 9:30

STANLEY PRESTON KIMMEL

o'clock, and that it would be impossible to get anything to eat after we arrived there. However, we were able to get into the kitchen of an English restaurant, and the owner gave us a light lunch, for which we paid two dollars and fifty cents apiece. The Englishman explained that it would be necessary to charge us "hush money" for the whole establishment, which we had to pay. The two waiters and the cook came to the table and each received his share. A fine reception (?).

It does not take long to get onto the Frenchman's idea, either. We soon found that we were being short-changed, or charged exorbitant prices.

The streets are very dark, but they are filled with women and girls. The Allies are also well represented along the boulevards. As far as morals are concerned, I haven't as yet discovered any. It seems to be a wide-open shop, where you buy what you please.

How do these panderers evade service in the army? We are wondering if France is really bleeding. The English show up at this trade also. In fact, I think we have been accosted by more English than French. Very few Americans speak French, and that probably accounts for it to some extent. The Frenchman has a very cordial way. If one does not understand him, he takes the privilege of escorting the person to the place of amusement.

I am sick of the thing already. The men at the front giving their lives so that this may go on. They are all slacking as much as possible. Outside of their personal safety I don't think they care anything about the war.

Coming from Bordeaux we saw some of the prison camps. The prisoners seem to be treated very well. They all stopped working when we passed and made use of all the English they knew in calling to us. About the only expression we could understand was, "Hello, how are you?" They said it in a sneering way. It is plain they hate us.

* * * * * * *

We have been on duty for three nights. The wounded are arriving by the train loads. They always manage to have them brought in after dark so that the public will not see or hear the men while they are being unloaded and rushed to the hospitals. It is a dreadful sight The men moan and groan continually. Sometimes they cry out, and occasionally one will go insane. What is all this suffering for? If I go through the war, how can I enjoy the fruits of so much misery? It is better to be a part of it and die. If a man brings this upon himself it is bad enough, but he has had nothing to do with it. How can those who are to blame expect absolution?

Look at the man lying so still on the cot. His blood-soaked leg looks like a shriveled rag. The flesh is there—a chunk of raw meat. He is so weak he cannot move. I am told it is not his leg which gives him so much pain, but the left shoulder, which has been partly shot away. The blanket is over the wound and I did not see it.

How is it possible to be in such a condition and live? What would the men who have been able to profit by this war think if they were bending over this man?—or, let me ask, what would he think?

Each generation sees this same pitiful condition, and yet we continue. Must it go on for ever and ever?

There is only one way to stop it and that is to put an end to the factions which are established in its favor.

* * * * * * *

There are certain days when it is impossible to bathe. It is also impossible to obtain sweets except at specified intervals. The war bread is very poor. It is sold in one-yard rolls. Everything eatable is at a fabulous price, so that a good dinner costs one a fortune.

The surroundings seem to be well fortified, and I think the French people do not fear the Germans getting into Paris. There is an aeroplane patrol constantly. We have not had a raid for about four months, and as it has been very clear the last few nights, we expect one at any time.

It is impossible to remain here unless one is connected with the war. There is no sight-seeing. Everything is closed. We must carry a pass or be liable to arrest.

The condition of the people in Paris is something awful. There are many refugees without food or fuel. It is necessary to have a card for almost everything, and as the prices are very high, it is impossible for the poor people to get what they really need in order to live.

Their homes are still in "no man's land," and many have lost all they ever possessed. Those who were lucky enough to be in the rear managed to take some things with them in the first retreat of the battle of the Marne, but it is not much, and as a whole, they are helpless.

I cannot see how they expect to get through the coming winter months. If something is not done for them I am afraid there will be some serious riots. It is the poor people who bear the world's burdens whether in peace or war. Why should they?

If this war does not answer that question, then it has been fought in vain. If suffering and pleasure are not equalized we have not taken one step in civilization, and think what we have lost!

* * * * * * *

It rains incessantly. We have been very busy again and had little sleep this week. The Germans have attempted an air raid every evening during the last five, and I suppose it will be the same thing again tonight. They do only a small amount of destruction as far as I am able to find out, and as yet no one has been killed. It is believed they are trying it out, and that a grand fleet of machines may appear any evening. They usually come just at dark. A machine goes rushing about the Paris streets blowing a siren. Everyone finds cover as soon as possible and remains in the "caves" until the "all clear" signal is blown.

On the walls of the houses are posted large figures, stating how many people the cave will hold. During the raid the lights are turned out all over the city, and it remains in complete darkness until the thing is over.

From all accounts everyone here (Neuilly Hospital) thinks it an uncalled for move to take over the hospital as the army has done. It has been kept up by private funds and provisions, and, they think, should remain so. These people have been instrumental in making it a success, and now, of course, those originally in charge will be put out.

We worked all yesterday afternoon, as there was evidently a big battle raging along the front somewhere near Verdun. When there is a general rush, the trains arrive at all hours of the day and night. It is so close in the cars, and the men are very uncomfortable. Everything smells of medicine. We work at the receiving station, where the men are numbered and divided among the hospitals before being sent to their destinations.

We all hope the section will leave for the front in a week or so at least. The men are becoming restless here.

* * * * * * *

Our orders have been received for the front and everyone will be glad to get away. No one knows the exact date we are to leave. The rains have come on again and it is very gloomy in Paris. The winter is setting in and I don't know how the poor people will stand it. They have nothing. The suffering which one sees over here is terrible. It will be a blessing when the thing is finished. We have a sign in the office which reads:

"Don't waste one minute. In that time six men are killed at the front."

Six men a minute! What a terrible truth!

It will be something to be on the front and be in the fight instead of remaining here in comfort and ease, such as it is.

We cannot grumble in Paris when conditions at the front are so bad, and those who are in the States have a great deal to be thankful for if they only knew it.

The section will be attached to a French regiment and will likely be in the Verdun sector most or all of the time during the first three months. We will then be on repose for ten days.

Three months! It sounds like an eternity. If we live through the first three months it will be three more and ad infinitum.

When will it ever end? Heaven only knows. If it is not over soon we will have to tear up the map. I don't know but what it would be a good plan anyway.

Everyone here seems to be watching the United States. I hope the Americans will uphold the ideals with which they entered the war and come in strong so that the end may be in sight soon.

The British are looming up here and there on the front and many think they would like to end the war before America has had much to do with it. All honor to Great Britain if she does. I don't think the Americans have any fear of that, at least not the ones who are here.

The sirens are sounding in the streets. An air raid is on.

When the German machines pass the first air posts an alarm is sounded. When they are nearing Paris there is a second alarm. If they get to the outside walls, a third alarm is given and everyone must go into the caves

I have never seen an American excited over one of these air raids, but the French people sometimes go crazy. They push, scream, yell and jump about like demons. I suppose it is because they have been under the strain so long.

The Germans are evidently trying to wear down the morale of the civilian population in this way, and, if possible, break the support which they give to the men at the front. It can never be done. The French are firm.

*   *   *   *   *   *   *

The lights went out and the concierge came in with a candle, begging me to go to the cellar with the rest of the occupants. By the time I reached the cave it was pretty well filled, not only with people from the house, but also with those who were passing along the streets and who had to find shelter. It is certainly a cosmopolitan crowd. I am the only American.

(I have taken a small room in the Latin quarter in order to get away from the chateau and drill grounds when permission is given. We are not on duty now and are simply "standing by" awaiting more orders. This gives us many free hours. We only have to report twice a day and do some guard duty now and then.)

The cave in this establishment is very large. There are three or four rooms. One woman was hysterical. She had three small children who cried all the time. There was an old man who protested continually against air raids. He would shout and throw his hands in the air, clenching his fists and daring the Germans to "come down." Some of the younger women smiled at the poor old man.

A group of girls came in, followed by two soldiers. They made so much noise talking and laughing that everyone remained silent for a few minutes watching them.

The soldiers and one of the girls went into another room. In a short time one of the men returned. We could hear the couple very plainly as there was no door between the rooms. It was evident from the voices, etc., what was going on. No one seemed to bother about it or be jealous. The girls in the group giggled every time certain sounds came from the room, and the old man continued to blaspheme.

The "all clear" signal was heard and the forms filed out of the cave.

It was necessary for the soldier and the group of girls to wait for the absent couple.

The concierge has informed me that I owe a laundry bill, but, of course, I did not understand, and will not until I get a check. The French are the same. They never understand when it is convenient not to do so. The fact is they had the honor of teaching us the trick.

B—— has just come in. He was in a cave near here during the raid. He tells me one of the bombs dropped near the station where we were on duty last week. No one was killed, but several were injured. Some women, who were trying to get to one of the caves near by. They were working on the tramway.

Why does a nation stoop to such things? What is the ultimate gain of a victory won in this manner? Suppose the Germans win the war; do they think civilization will forget such things? I hope not!

I understand we are to have service tomorrow. We know what that means. We will be on the front in a few days. It is the same old routine. Service, inspection, and another section is off to the front.

I am glad. The strain is over. But what about these who will not come back? Will I be one of them? Will B——? Of course there is not any gloom about the thing. We are not the only ones who are going out. There are others who have been on the front for a long time, while we have been enjoying the comforts here in Paris. No, we are not gloomy. We will go out tonight and have a good time. It is early and the boulevards will be filled with people. The night is very clear and the stars are out. We will find Charlotte and Helene and take them for a ride in the bois and then to the Folies Bergere.

Yes, we will have a grand time tonight. Tomorrow we leave for the front.

(To be Continued.)

Land by the Western Sea

By Daisie L. Smith

O, this beautiful land by the Western
  sea
Has a witching charm · and a lure for
  me
 Wherever I may roam;
This land of mountains, and streams, and
  lakes,
Where the meadowlark his sweet song
  wakes, •
 And the robin builds his home;
Where the roses blow, and the sunset's
  glow
 Has a touch of beauty divine;
Where the fir-trees, grand, like beacons
  stand
 Beside the stately pine.

O, this beautiful land by the Western
  sea,
With its air so pure and its life so
  free,
 There is no land like this;
Its mystic haze, where the sunset's rays
 The purple hilltops kiss;
Its mines of gold that the mountains
  hold;
 Its wealth of orchards rare;
Its fields of grain; its sun and rain,
 With roses everywhere.

The Voice of Fear

By Evelyn Lowry

JOHN LA RUE drove steadily up the twisted, winding road. The mountain highway seemed to extend on and on and get nowhere as it threaded the tangled forest.

The whir of his motor under the strain of climbing at fair speed up this steep, rugged mountain defied the weird stillness of the wild surroundings. The sound bounded onward. till its life was spent then echoed back from the distant caverns.

A jack-rabbit rambled across the path in front of him scurrying for dear life to avoid an impact with the front wheel. Further on as he rounded a sharp turn a coyote, shaggy-haired and vicious looking skulked along the road-side and disappeared below the grade. In the dimness of the gathering dusk that sight seemed significant. For some reason it made La Rue shudder. He felt an overwhelming sense of fear that made him feel thankful that he was in his car rambling along at a good clip instead of traversing that lonely road on foot.

But in the rear seat of his machine was the express company's box which contained a package which might cause him far more reason for fear than any wild animal of the night who ranged the forest in search of prey. He knew not what skulking figure in human form might step from the shadows around any turn and under the cold steel impress of a rifle or revolver compel him to throw up his hands or claim his life.

And he was alone. Misery loves company even among the bravest. And La Rue, though brave, would just as soon have had the guard, who was to accompany him on the latter part of his journey, with him now instead of picking him up as had been pre-arranged at the Woodward place, an hour's drive hence.

He had tried to make it there before dark but his luck and the elements had been against him and he had failed. Now with the voice of fear ringing in his ears, taunting him, urging him to his full capacity onward, the dusk of doom seemed spread o'er the passing landscape and his thoughts were wild and vague.

It had been a little over two years since he had put into operation his auto stage line running on schedule between the city in the valley and the isolated mountain villages. During that time he had driven in all kinds of weather, in all hours of night, and with all types of passengers over the same road. And he had come to truly know the road, every inch of it. He knew where the grades were steepest, the turns sharpest. The bridges were so clearly marked in his mind that he could almost drive over them blindfolded.

He had a Government contract which called for the daily delivery of the United States Mail during the six months of the year that the mountain Post Office did business. He also carried all the express which passed between the railroad station in the valley and the terminus in the mountains.

It was that express box and a certain important package which it contained that worried him now. Money it was. Hundreds of dollars. But he had carried it before dozens of times and the trips had always been uneventful. It was sent regularly every approaching pay-day by a liquor firm to their store in the mountains. It was used to cash the several hundred checks of the employees of a near-by saw-mill.

Sometimes a trusted member of the firm would come himself in his own machine and bring it. Then, again it would be sent by express. It was never generally known which way it would go consequently the carrier was never in much danger of being molested. But this time it was different. For the past three days the company had delayed sending the money up owing to an anonymous warning which had been received. Because of that a guard had been dispatched to ride a short distance behind on a motorcycle during the later and most perilous part of the journey.

It was after he had crossed a rickety board bridge, which spanned one of the numerous gluches that wend their way between the towering hills, that he found his front tire to be flat.

Though he felt sure no other traveler would be apt to pass him on that desolate highway at this hour, it wasn't so very wise to take a chance. It might invite an unpleasant collision and anyway there was not room for another vehicle to pass.

Just about this time he came to a delapidated road which some unfortunate home-steader had made to reach his now deserted claim.

He drove up only a few feet and found a level spot. But even at this short distance the trees and shrubbery hid him from the main road. He had his headlights dimmed as was necessary for mountain traveling. As they shone full on a large boulder a few feet away they reflected back a weird, somber light that was confusing.

With the aid of his pocket searchlight he busied himself with the transfering of his tires. His mind concentrated on his work, he had for the time being forgotten about the precious express package he was carrying. While stooping over to remove the jack from under his machine he was suddenly conscious of someone standing near him.

Slowly it dawned upon him that he was trapped. The stranger fingered nervously the trigger of his Winchester rifle. La Rue could see in the dimness that his face was obscured by a bandanna handkerchief. He was tall and wirey and moved about with cat-like agility.

"Well, where's the money?" he snarled. "Hand it over or you're a dead man."

La Rue threw up his hands and did it

quickly, too. He knew his chances to get away from there alive depended upon it. He still made no move to get the box but stood staring at the bandit's hidden face.

"What are you waiting for?" the bandit grumbled, giving La Rue a vigorous punch with his gun.

But La Rue believed his bold affront to be mostly sham; that under that guise he was bluffing and really a coward at heart. So he took a risky chance at bluffing, too. He started for the box but moved slowly and aimlessly while he bartered for time. He knew the guard would start out to hunt for him when he failed to appear at his place of appointment. He was by now long overdue. He regretted that he had driven off on the side-road. He cast a wary glance behind him to see if he could tell how far he was from the main road.

But the stranger seemed to divine his thoughts.

"You're expecting reinforcements?" he hissed. "I counted on that. That's why you're up here. It was my fault that your tire went flat. But that's all right; I've got no grudge against you. Just hand over the money and give me a chance to beat it and you can go safely on your way."

But La Rue thought less of his life and more of uprightedness and honor than to let that box go too easily. To hand it over without a struggle would be nothing less than cowardice. And La Rue prided himself on being no coward.

He had never had any trouble with that still small voice men call Conscience. It had always been a good friend to him, because he had stood ever loyal to its high exactions. And he didn't intend to be a traitor now.

So strolling around to the other side of the machine he took his time about lifting the cumbersome box out from under the back seat and depositing it on the ground.

"That's heavy for one man to lift," he complained, sitting it down rather suddenly.

After some fumbling he remarked that he was unable to see without the aid of his search-light. La Rue pointed to where it was under the car and the bandit after deliberating decided to let him use it.

His tone had become a little milder and more human. This led La Rue to venture the remark that the bandit must find these mountains rather dismal and terrifying to ramble over in the middle of the night on foot, even if you did have a gun and nerve to use it.

"There's nothing to be afraid of if you keep your wits about you," the bandit replied simply.

La Rue replied with a shrug of his shoulders that he did not envy the bandit his job; to him it would not be worth the effort.

"That's just your way of looking at life," he replied. "It's not my way," he went on grimly.

The bandit regarded him in silence for a few moments, then went on in an even voice in which there was a tone of triumph:

"I know who you are when I see you. I even know your name. I lived here in these parts myself one time. You don't know me, though. That doesn't matter, either. What concerns me now is that money. Hurry up! I say, and open that box!"

La Rue did finally pry the lid off and was groping among its contents with his mind working rapidly to form some plan to yet out-wit his opponent, when the bandit became nervously alert. He took a few steps forward and pointed his gun directly in La Rue's face.

In an instant La Rue grasped what the trouble was. The bandit's keen ears had sensed trouble. In the distance the faint purr of a motor could be heard. Sometimes it was muffled—almost soundless. Then again loud and distinct as the sound would come from the outer side of the mountain.

"Turn off your lights," the bandit commanded sharply. "Now if you make one move I'll shoot."

The sound came nearer and nearer— a noisy rattle through the still night. La Rue almost knew that it was the guard on his motorcycle, heavily armed and alert and watching; so he decided to stake his life on one last bold act.

He still held in his hand his search-light. With remarkable quickness he flashed it in the bandit's face, temporarily blinding him, then grappled for his gun. At the same time he called to the guard, who was not now many yards away. But the bandit, prepared for an emergency, drew a revolver from his pocket and fired. La Rue sank unconscious to the ground.

Meanwhile the guard, with a dire premonition that all was not well, had, as La Rue believed he would do, set out to meet the stage. He traveled slowly; as silently as possible so as to hear La Rue coming, for he did not wish to risk having a collision around a curve.

He thought it possible that La Rue might, when he found he was compelled to travel in the night, shut off his lights and make his way in the dark. Otherwise any hostile bandit could watch his approach from a great distance because of the reflection the lights would cast, even if much dimmed, up and down the mountain side as he wended his way.

It was mostly with the fear that La Rue had met with some accident due to hazardous driving without lights rather than that any highwaymen had molested him that he set out to find the tracings of a clue. He hoped to find that, at the worst, La Rue's machine had only broken down or that some other minor trouble had befallen him. He reasoned that even had the stage been robbed it would have been allowed to proceed on its way long before this.

He traveled on and on and still no sign of the stage nor its driver. It was as he was climbing up a steep grade that he fancied he saw a flash of light in front of him. But he was not sure. He was still more uncertain as to whether it was followed by a muffled shot, which seemed to ring out in the still night air or whether it was just a clear-cut echo of his own noisy motor.

He stopped shortly and listened but nothing but the monotonous gurgling of the near-by brook could be heard. He was not wholly convinced that it was an illusion, but there was nothing else to do but to make his way onward.

Arriving at the next postoffice, some little distance down the road, he knocked on the door till he aroused the sleeping occupants. After making inquiries he learned that La Rue had left there some hours before.

Knowing that he had never arrived at the next station, which was some miles beyond the Woodward place, the guard realized that there was something wrong. Yet, to make doubly sure that he had not missed La Rue along the road, for he could have taken some short-cut, he went into the telephone, and after some difficulty and much waiting, a droll, sleepy voice answered from the other end of the line:

"No; there's been no mail stage up this way tonight," came the careless reply. The other postmaster further stated that he guessed La Rue had broken down, as usual; or maybe he was in the ditch this time. But he wanted it to be known that he wasn't going to stay awake and wait for him like he used to; that sort of thing belonged to the past. If the mail came, all right. He would get up and sort it. If it didn't, he wasn't going to lose any sleep over it.

Deciding not to enlighten his irate friend, the guard thanked him and hung up the receiver.

Realizing that time was very valuable, and knowing the uselessness of going again over the road at night in search of La Rue, he decided to notify the express company in the valley so that they might have searchers out up that way soon after daylight.

This he accomplished with little trouble. He then racked his mind for the next move to make. Without any definite idea of going anywhere he set out again up the road.

After going some distance he thought of a ranger's cabin which was located on a hill a short distance from where he thought he heard the shot as he came over the road before. But in order to reach it on his motorcycle he would have to travel miles around as the road forked leading to it below the postoffice from which he had just come.

After some deliberation he decided to walk across. He was taking a chance on there being someone there to serve as a companion. Yet in the summer months this cabin was hardly ever entirely vacant, for it was a central location, a sort of district headquarters at which there was usually one or more rangers stopping at all times.

He reasoned that they might be able to enlighten him, give him some clue, or at any rate be ready to go with him in the morning to aid in the search.

Securely locking his motorcycle, he left it behind a large pine tree near the road and started out to walk. After some maneuvering he finally struck the trail, which he knew led across the canyon to the cabin.

He hadn't gone far when he heard a rustling noise and the cracking of twigs in front of him. He stopped abruptly and listened. It could have been one of many things had not the noise been so strange and unusual It was a heavy step not unlike cattle or perhaps the ranger's horses. Yet it moved with much more agility and swiftness than either of these. Whatever it was it seemed to be running pell-mell into the distance. In the darkness, human footsteps have no special sound. But the guard's inner judgment seemed to tell him that was what he was hearing.

But in ignorance of all that was transpiring so near at hand, he went on to the cabin. When he got there he found it locked, but could feel a notice pasted on the door. Striking a match he read it and found it to be a notice for all rangers to report to the Forest Supervisor on the following day.

With his own pass-key he entered and was making preparations to spend the night there when he heard another key turning in the self-locking door. A moment later both he and the stranger evidently received the surprise of their lives.

"Well, Jim Smith," the guard greeted. "I didn't expect to see you here tonight. The last time I heard of you, you were in Klondike."

"I was," the stranger replied briefly, "but tonight I'm here. Look here, Joe Taylor, you see this gun. That means you're to do as I say," he said boldly.

"And what do you say?" the guard asked, straightening up.

"To keep mum my identity here. No one knows I'm in this part of the country, and if you hadn't of been where you had no business, here in this cabin tonight, you'd of been none the wiser either."

Joe Thayer, with folded arms, stared the stranger square in the face. He assumed a rather hypnotic attitude which compelled attention.

"Jim Smith, I can almost guess what your mission here is tonight. I think I've caught you red-handed. You was always a worthless, good-for-nothing when you worked here as a fellow ranger. I don't know what right I would have to defend you."

"Well, if you don't," Jim Smith hissed, "you'll never live to tell the tale, for I've killed one man already since sundown for impertinence, and many a one in the last few years."

"This revolver game is one two can play very easily," the guard replied. Though I lack your grim experience, I am an expert at it myself."

And when Joe Thayer left the cabin at day-break, Jim Smith was securely bound hand and foot to the post of the cumberous home-made wooden bedstead.

It was some hours before La Rue came to his sense. When he did it was some minutes before he realized where he was. Then he began to grope through his dazed mind for the reason. He tried to rise but his strength failed him. The express box was by his side. He reached out and found that the money was still there. It was too heavy to lift and it was only after much effort that he was able to get it out of the box. He put it down by his side and for the first time realized that he was lying in a pool of blood.

Again he heard the low, trembling voice of fear—the fear of death. The dawn broke like a beacon light in the East. In that dawn he seemed to see a symbol to guide him in the world to come. And gazing there through hazy eyes he felt the tides of oblivion surging o'er him.

It was just as the sun was rising that the guard, having gone over for his motorcycle, proceeded along up the road. He came to the by-road and, noticing that a machine had recently gone up that way decided he would follow in that direction.

He soon came upon the deserted auto stage and the contents scattered about. Around on the other side he stumbled onto La Rue. At first he passed him up as dead and began to search for the mute evidence which told so plainly the story.

Stooping down for a closer examination he found in La Rue still signs of life. He lost no time in rushing him down to the hospital, three miles down the road, which was owned and operated by the lumber company.

La Rue's recovery was doubtful at first. Then he began to improve, slowly, steadily, surely.

A few days later Joe Thayer came to see him. It took La Rue some time to get through his muddled brain the truth of the story.

"It's no use," La Rue at last remarked, "when you have that indefinable hunch so strong, like I did, that you're going to be held up, you can't side-track it. You can't get away from it. I suppose if you were wise you'd obey those promptings and avoid disaster, such as narrowly befell me. A fellow never can tell, though, when it's not his own imagination running wild. How can he tell when he does sense the coming events ahead of him? Oh, well, such as that'll come only once in a life-time, I guess."

The guard thought so, too, and a long silence fell between them.

The Army Cat

By Thomas Marshall Spaulding

HE 700th Infantry landed yesterday. Seventeen of its members have won decorations. The regiment brought home five dogs."

An item something like this might be read in the morning paper on almost any day in the spring or summer of 1919. Always dogs; sometimes other livestock in addition, as lion cubs, bears, goats or cats, but not often. This is natural enough. No doubt the dog makes the better field soldier, but for garrison duty there is much to be said in favor of the cat. In the old army, before the war, the cat had his place, and he will surely come into his own again as the army settles down once more to a sedentary life.

It was my fortune once to spend two years at a post which, I am convinced, was the earthly paradise of cats. And I am proud to remember that it was Abraham Lincoln, my own Maltese tomcat, who was the unquestioned leader of feline society there. This was Abraham's second military station. At his first, where he originally came to live with me, he was only a small and fluffy kitten, and, although already showing signs of future greatness, he could not yet aspire to supremacy. Unquestionably the most eminent cat at that time and place was one Jimmy, the property of a devoted captain of engineers, who might daily be observed descending to put his automobile engine in order, a bag of tools in one hand and Jimmy in the other. This captain's absence from a tea party one afternoon was explained by his wife by the fact that he had taken Jimmy up to town to see the Christmas decorations in the shop windows.

His first change of station, as I have said, brought Abraham to a terrestrial paradise. No census of cats was ever taken, but their name was legion. There was Billy, the burly tabby animal at the hospital, without question the leading citizen next to A. Lincoln himself. Then there was Thomas, whom Abraham nightly sought to destroy. Thomas had the advantage in weight, but he was getting on in years while Abraham had the dash and spirit of the young soldier; in short, his morale was superior. What caused the feud between them could never be surmised, unless it was that each was irritated by their resemblance; careless people often mistook one for the other. Yet Abraham was on the friendliest terms with his other double — the commissary cat.

Those I have mentioned were cats of distinct individuality and ownership. In and around the stable gathered a community of plebeian cats, the pensioners of the "stable boss." It was an inspiring sight—his return from his barrack mess-hall, basket of food in hand. At his whistle every door, window and chink in the stable poured forth cats. How many boarded there regularly I do not know, and probably the boss himself could have given only a rough estimate. I never counted more than thirteen assembled at any one time, but all authorities agree that there must have been some absentees on that occasion.

Blessed is the nation that has no history. The history of this post, from the cat point of view, records only one event —the great licensing ordinance. Licenses had for years been required for all dogs. One day this edict was extended to include cats. Not that cats were to be compelled to wear collars and muzzles—no, they were merely to be registered at the guardhouse, and their descriptions noted so that when a cat passed by the sergeant of the guard could refer to the book and determine whether or not the animal had a legalized existence. It was an anxious time for proprietors. The Hospital Corps detachment resolved to take no chances, but got an identification tag for Billy at once, with name, organization and company number stamped on it. Billy was not the only tabby on the post, and mistakes might happen.

But the most perturbed man of all on the day the order was issued was the sergeant of the guard. He had received no detailed instructions and had to devise the registry system for himself. After long and anxious reflection he ruled a ledger in five columns, headed respectively, "Name," "Owner," "Breed," "Color," and "Weight," and was ready for business. But now a difficulty arose. Owners were unable to state the breeds of their cats; did not know the names of any breeds of cats; in fact, were not aware that cats had any breeds. Here the sergeant, ever helpful, pointed to the first entry in the ledger, where Abraham Lincoln's description was set forth. The hint was sufficient. Every respectable cat on the post was recorded as of Maltese breed; color, yellow; tabby, black or spotted, as the case might be.

So, almost ten per cent of the post cats were licensed, and thus authorized to continue to reside among us. The rest were outlaws. But in spite of conspicuous activity on the part of the soldier charged with the enforcement of the law, the population did not visibly diminish. The mystery was cleared up when this man, in a burst of confidence, explained: "I wouldn't drown any cat; you know it's bad luck; I just carry 'em down toward the dock and let 'em loose. It gives me a job catchin' 'em again."

Years have passed since we left that post, and a great war has come and gone. Abraham has grown old and—no, he was gray to begin with. But I am sure, from the wistful look in his eye, that his mind sometimes goes back regretfully to those happy days in the Garden of Eden.

The Bridge of Love

By Belle Willey Gue

The tender light that is in lovers' eyes,
The shadow of the palm tree on the lawn,.
The misty fog that comes in majestically
From mighty ocean's dim and shrouded depths.
To sweep across the helpless, shrinking land
And blot the brightness of the shining sun;
The grass that makes the meadows of the sea
And covers with its long and silken strands
The rocks that rest upon the ocean's floor;
The gentle moonlight on the breaking wave,
Are all a part of our humanity;
But that through which we see beyond the eyes
And look into the soul that sheds the light,
The faith that leads us past all blinding doubt
And sets our feet upon a sure, safe road,
The keen discernment that enables us
To gaze through narrow meshes in the veil
That hides infinity from those who creep
With heavy tread along the lowly earth,
These come from the divine to make us know
Our world is bounded by a greater one,
And that between the two there is a bridge
That ev'ryone may cross—the bridge of love.

Swift Justice

By Lucian M. Lewis

H, that river!" said Father Bagley, as we sat listening to the thunder of its swollen waters roaring down the valley, leaping and striking like a thing of life at high-water marks along the rip-rapped banks.

The heavy rainstorm had subsided, giving way to a night of stars, and the good Father and I sat in the moonlit patio.

"Do you know," he continued, " I never see a river that it does not remind me of God's eternal justice! For, like a river, His justice sometimes moves with apparent slowness and deliberation—but always surely. Then, again, it may come with the roar and rush of a mountain torrent. I have seen this latter sort of justice hurl itself on the heels of a man with incredible rapidity, with a swiftness so appalling that it literally swept the unsuspecting victim off his feet."

Father Bagley tilted back his big arm-chair and his splendid ' old face stood out in the moonlit shadows like a rare cameo. It was a face softened and subdued by witnessing the sorrow and suffering of more than a generation of humanity, yet one that could become as hard and unyielding as granite before flagrant sin or injustice. It was the face of a man whose soul had been tested by fire and had come out victorious.

I knew by his vibrant tones that a story was forthcoming, so I tilted back my chair and waited.

For a number of years Father Bagley and I had been next door neighbors. I had grown to love him for his universal charity, his simplicity and nobility of character, and for his sweet, Christ-like life, given unselfishly in the cause of his Master. And in those years there had sprung up between us one of those rare, enduring friendships of old age and youth —a friendship cemented the stronger by the two score years that separated us.

And so it was my good fortune to sit with him on moonlit evenings and listen to his tales of the past. For the good Father was at that ripe time of life when one inevitably looks longingly backward. Not that he did not look hopefully toward the future, but rather that the past was so rich with interesting experiences.

"Yes," he said presently, "God's justice is sometimes swift and spectacular. One case especially I have in mind.

"It takes me back more than a score of years ago to an old ranch house in the upper valley. The house was of adobe and of ancient Spanish structure — a crumbling memorial to the days of the old Dons and their beneficent dominion. It had an old-fashioned flower garden outside the patio, and a graveled walk lined with pepper trees.

"In the front room of that house two men sat over a table, apparently in the midst of a heated discussion. One of them was a large man, slightly past middle age, and his loud tones and domineering manner showed him to be master of the situation.

"'Arabello,' he barked at his companion, bringing a big fist down upon the table, 'there's no use arguing the matter. It was all settled last week. I thought you understood that.'

"The little old, dark-skinned man before him winced and recoiled at those words. He was the picture of failure and misfortune, and over him sorrow brooded like a shadow.

"'But give us a little more time,' he pleaded. 'I took you up because I was in dire need of money.'

"The big man stood up and answered with decision: 'I can't possibly do it, Arabello. You've given your consent for a money consideration, and now, at the last minute, you are trying to hedge and leave me with an empty matrimonial bag to hold. This is no time to thresh the thing over, with the priest expected at any minute.'

" 'But the girl,' wheedled the old man. 'She—'

" 'Never mind the girl!' the other interrupted, striding across the room and wheeling back upon him. 'I've put the entire matter up to her—and she's agreed to marry me. If she's willing, you oughtn't have any kick coming. Besides, Angela is not your daughter.'

"He gave an undue emphasis to those final words as though to convey the impression of some sinister discovery. The shaft evidently went home, for the old man's jaw dropped and his shoulders sagged.

" 'Oh, you see,' the big man continued, watching the other intently, 'I know all about Angela. I'm not making this matrimonial jump blindfolded. Her father was a scapegoat adventurer who faked a marriage with Angela's mother, then skipped the country. But that makes no difference to me—I'm not marrying her ancestors.'

"The old man shook himself together with an effort. 'Mr. Widner,' he said timidly, hesitatingly, 'you know, I suppose, about Angela and — er — young Serranno?'

" 'Serranno?' Widner echoed with a cynical laugh. 'Yes, I knew that there was some sort of a foolish love affair between them. But what does it amount to? Love is all right, I guess, in a way—but it won't buy the baby a new pair of shoes. Why, that fellow is as poor as a kangaroo sagerat.'

" 'But—'

" 'Now, Arabello,' the big man again interrupted, 'just think what this means to Angela! I'm not the sort to throw bouquets at myself, but I must say that there are any number of girls in this valley who'd jump at the chance to sit at the head of my table. A life estate in the Widner rancho is not to be laughed at by anyone, much less by a little country girl like Angela!'

"He strode over to the window, snapped open his watch and looked out up the road. 'I wonder why that darned priest don't come!' he growled.

" "He whirled upon the old man: 'Remember, Arabello, you are not to make a scene before that priest. I'm to be spokesman of this party. Where's Angela, anyway?'.

"The old man got up resignedly, opened an inner door and called in Spanish. Then a little old woman, with face wrinkled and brown as an autumn leaf, appeared on the threshold. With her was a girl.

"The girl was young and of a Spanish beauty. She was all in white with a wreath of red rose blossoms in her hair. She walked with head up, her pretty red lips pressed tightly together. But when she looked at the man before her, all the light and joy and girlhood died in her face.

" 'Why, Angela!' Widner cried, stepping forward and taking both her hands in his, 'you never looked so pretty as you do at this minute.'

"He bowed low, kissing the girl's hand as he did so.

"She smiled faintly and made a little formal courtesy and looked quickly away, her great black eyes brimming with tears.

" 'Ah, the Father comes!' whimpered the old woman. ·

"Up the narrow, graveled walk, darkened by great spreading pepper trees on either side, walked a man clad in ministerial dress. He was talking to a tall, raw-boned man who walked beside him.

"The priest stepped upon the threshold of the open door and greeted the little party, then turned to the tall man standing in the doorway:

" 'This is my good friend, the sheriff,' he announced. 'I have brought him along to witness the ceremony.'

"While Widner and Arabello shook hands with the sheriff, the priest walked over to the open window and stood looking out, his head bowed, his hands folded behind him.

"It was an early April morning, bright with sun. The valley was pink and white with blossoms, and the soft air entered through the open door and windows laden with the sweet breath of budding trees.

The hillsides were golden with flaming wild poppies, while beyond were blue-purpled peaks of mountain ranges. And as the priest stood at the window looking far out up the valley and to the hills and mountains beyond, he seemed lost in reverie, his eyes gazing into space as though fixed on some vision of the spirit.

"For several minutes he stood thus, then turned to Widner, who was plainly growing impatient at the unusual delay.

"'Mr. Widner,' he began, 'I have come to this house at your request to perform a marriage ceremony. But before we proceed, I have a few questions concerning yourself.'

"Widner looked up quickly, his keen eyes narrowing.

"'Certainly,' he replied, 'go right ahead. But you must know that I have lived in this valley for two years and am owner of Widner Rancho. If you wish any further testimonials, I can refer you to my banker.'

"One could see from the man's irritation that he wished to discourage further questions. But the priest was inexorable.

"'You misunderstood me, Mr. Widner. I didn't mean financial responsibility. I'm satisfied as to that. But you must know that there are some things that bank accounts and lands can't buy—an unimpeachable character, for instance.'

"Widner was standing now. His face reddened and darkened, his fingers were gripped to the back of the chair.

"'Sir!' he spoke—and his voice rasped —'in deference to this girl, I asked you here to perform this marriage ceremony. But I didn't bargain, as a preliminary, to be put through a public confessional. I deny the right of you or any man to sit in judgment on my character. If Angela and her people are willing, what business is it of yours, anyway?'

"The priest stood looking at the man before him, then took up the question:

"'What business is it of mine? Listen: I have known this girl from babyhood. In fact, it was I who christened her. Just eighteen years ago this very month her mother brought her to me in all the innocence and sweetness of childhood; and a few years later, when I stood beside the deathbed of that broken-hearted mother, her last whispered words were a prayer that I look after her orphaned child. Is it not, then, my busines to know something of the man's character who asks Angela's hand in marriage? Is not that my business, sir?'

"It was a tense moment. Save for Widner's heavy breathing and the droning of insects among the blossoms, there was scarcely a sound. The priest and Widner stood facing, the former cool and self-possessed, the other angry and threatening. The sheriff leaned against the wall; while Arabello, his wife and Angela sat with bated breaths, vaguely sensing the imminence of something unforeseen.

"The priest broke the silence. 'As you all know, the law requires that I shall read the marriage certificate before performing the ceremony.'

"He turned to Widner: 'Mr. Widner, will you kindly produce the marriage certificate?'

"Widner's clouded face brightened, and he reached into an inner pocket and pulled out the certificate bearing a notary's seal that attested its validity.

"'Here it is, sir, all legal and regular,' he said.

"The priest took the proffered document, unfolded it and began to slowly read it as if in deliberation.

"When he had finished he folded the paper and put it in his pocket. Then he turned to Widner.

"'Yes, Mr. Widner, it seems regular and legal, as you say. But I observe that you state in that certificate that you are single and have never been married. Is that statement correct?'

"For a full minute the man did not move, but stood studying the priest's face like one who feels the presence of a danger that he cannot locate.

"'What do you mean?' he said.

"'I mean,' replied the priest, 'to ask you if that statement is true.'

"'Certainly it is true,' Widner answered uneasily. 'Why not?'

"'Widner,' the priest cried—and his voice broke in like a pistol shot—'did you ever live in Milldale, New Jersey?'

"The effect was startling. Widner fell back as if struck. His face whitened and

4

was sprayed with moisture, his knees seemed incapable of sustaining him.

" 'Milldale!' he gasped—and the words seemed to sear his lips—'Milldale!'

"But the man's nerves were of steel and in a moment he had himself in hand. His big shoulders squared, his color returned, his fighting jaws tightened. He peered intently at the priest as though by sheer force of will he would read the other's mind.

" 'No,' he answered with decision. 'I never heard of such a place. Why do you ask?'

" 'Never heard of it?' the priest replied, his eyes on Widner. 'Never heard of Milldale? Perhaps there is some mistake. But you asked why I put that question. I'll tell you. A month or more ago, when I first observed that you were going with Angela, something prompted me to find out more about you. Perhaps my solicitude for my little friend's welfare moved me to unusual caution. Just how I got my information is not material; however, if you insist, the sheriff will enlighten you.'

"He paused and looked steadily at Widner.

"Again that strange, deathly pallor overspread the man's face and a look of terror came into his eyes. All the fight and bravado seemed to have oozed out of him.

" 'We found,' continued the priest in the same even voice, 'that there lived a man in Milldale whose description tallied strangely with your own; that a little over two years ago he deserted a wife and babe and fled to parts unknown; and lastly, that the officers of the law were anxiously searching for that man to take him back on a charge of wife-desertion.'

"Again the priest paused and stood looking at Widner, then continued:

" 'I might add that the sheriff wished to take you back a week ago, when we discovered your identity, but I interceded and had you brought before God's judgment bar instead of man's.'

"Widner sank into his chair and covered his face with his hands. He looked like an animal on which the trap has closed.

" 'What proof have you?' he demanded at last in a hoarse voice.

" 'What proof?' answered the priest. 'Why, sir, you stand self-convicted. But as I told you, if you insist, the sheriff stands ready to furnish ample proof.'

"He nodded to that officer.

" 'Yes, spoke up the sheriff, 'we have the proof all right. Let us begin by calling you by your real name. Yes, Mr. John Winters, of Milldale, New Jersey, we've got the goods on you.'

"The accused man gasped, he seemed momentarily to lose the power of speech. Instinctively he held his hands over his face as though to ward off an impending blow.

"Angela, who, pale and trembling, had sat glued to her chair throughout the trying ordeal, now arose and took a step toward the cowering man. 'Is it true?' she asked, with a look of mingled pity and scorn.

"The priest motioned the girl to her seat, and continued:

" 'Mr. Winters (Ishall call you by your real name), I think that your main difficulty has been that you have lacked vision—spiritual vision, I mean. In your rather successful life, you have failed to grasp the significance of the eternal law that an evil deed is like a boomerang, which, sooner or later, flies back and cracks the offender over the head. If you don't believe that my statement is true, then ask the inmates of our penal institutions and see if they won't agree with me."

"Then the priest's voice suddenly became subdued, almost as if in prayer. 'But God has been merciful to us all today. He has saved you from the infamous crime of bigamy, and He has spared this girl and her people the shame and humiliation of becoming innocent parties thereto. As He has been merciful, even we, the sheriff and I, His humble servants, will show you mercy. But there is this one stipulation: You must go back to that deserted wife and babe, throw yourself at your wife's feet and when she has forgiven you, be true to her all the days of your life. You have broken to pieces a loving woman's life. Go back and put those broken pieces together as best you can.'

"The condemned man looked up, a ray of hope in his hunted eyes.

" 'Do you think she would take me back?' he asked huskily.

" 'Will she take you back?' the priest answered quickly. 'Yes,' and he pulled from an inner pocket a letter, unfolded it and gave it to the man.

" 'Read that, then ask God and that good woman to forgive you. Oh, what a wonderful thing is woman's love!'

"While the accused man sat with bowed head reading the letter, again there was a deathly stillness in the room. The priest stood with folded arms, waiting, watching while a human soul was being brought to bay by the relentless hounds of an awakened conscience.

"And then, in the clear April air, there floated through the open window from far down the valley the faint sound of the old Mission bells chimed by the hand of a passing tourist. As the last vague sound died away, Winters arose unsteadily and took the priest's hand.

" 'I—am—going—back—to—my — wife,' he said brokenly.

"The priest laid a hand upon the man's broad shoulder, and the look he gave him was one of pity and love:

" 'My son,' he said, 'I knew you would go back. In fact, I was so sure of it that I wired your wife this very morning that you were coming. Now, go—and God bless you!'

"When the last sound of the man's retreating footsteps on the graveled walk was heard, the priest turned around with a smile.

" 'Cheer up, Angela! this is no funeral. I came here to perform a marriage ceremony, and I don't propose to go away empty handed.'

" 'Sheriff!' he called, stepping to the door, 'where are you?'

"Immediately thereafter the sheriff, who had followed Winters from the room, stepped upon the threshold. There was a jingle of spurs as the graceful figure of a black-haired youth loomed in the doorway beside him. He wore a broad sombrero tilted a little to one side, a new suit of dark corduroy, with pantaloons tucked in high-heeled boots elaborately stitched.

"At sight of this youth, Angela's white face turned as red as the rose-wreath in her shining black hair.

" 'Madre de Dios!' she gasped in wonder and joy, and flew straight to the arms that awaited her."

Father Bagley sat silent for a moment. The moon sailed out from behind a palm and its soft light shone full upon his face. His head dropped upon his breast, his eyes half closed, a smile was on his lips and his long white hair shone like a halo.

I tiptoed softly out, leaving the good Father alone in the moonlight with his dreams.

Land of Promise

By Neville Colfax

CHAPTER I.

FROM his point of vantage, astride his wiry buckskin, "Red" Greggins grinned sarcastically and lit his newly rolled cigarette with a flourish.

"I ain't agoin' to argue with yuh, stranger. Yuh can either take it or leave it. I'm just a tellin' yuh for yore own good. If there's anything the old man hates it's a squatter. He's done run about a dozen of 'em ragged already an' he won't make any exception of yuh. Take a tip from th' wise and pull yore freight."

A twitch of the rein whirled the little buckskin like a top and set him tearing out across the flat, up the twisting trail of the bluff and over the skyline into the greasewood of the upper plateau.

The squatter watched the progress of horse and rider with moody eyes and knitted brow. He gazed for a long time at the spot where they disappeared. Then he turned and made his way down to the neatly-kept shanty nestling among the cottonwoods that bordered the noisy, boulder-filled creek. It was a beautiful spot, this quarter-section he determined to make his home. The total acreage was contained in a long, fairly narrow valley protected on the north, east and west by abrupt, age-scarred bluffs, and opening on the south into the rolling, fertile bottom-lands of the Little Missouri. Winging carelessly along the grassy valley, the creek, fed by the eternal springs of the upper plateau, gave a year-'round supply of clear, cold water, and the drooping, whispering cottonwoods that thickly fringed its banks furnished firewood in plenty. Truly it seemed a bit of Eden, and John Merrill told himself bitterly that it would be hard—hard—to give up. He took off his wide-brimmed sombrero and twirled it idly in his hand. The clear, crisp sunshine was warm on his head, and the wild, sweet winds of the open spaces fanned his sun-browned features. High above him at the edge of the bluffs a quail whistled clearly. He gulped suddenly, and with bowed head stepped through the cool, inviting doorway.

Before the wide, deep fireplace with its row of carefully scoured pots was a huge bear rug, and from the middle of it a warm-eyed Airedale rose with patent pleasure to greet the man. John Merrill slouched down on a bench and fell to idly caressing the dog's head. After a long silence he spoke.

"Old pal, it's come at last. The thing I've been hopin' and prayin' against for the last six months showed up today. They're goin' to run us out of this little home that's been a heaven to us ever since we first saw it. All our workin' and plannin' and happiness is goin' to be smashed and we'll be turned out of what is our own by every right under the sun. And just because they're fifty to one. They don't fight fair, old pal."

The dog whined softly and licked the man's hand.

Hanging from a wooden peg in the wall was a worn holster and cartridge belt. Protruding from the holster the black butt of a gun showed ominously. The man reached out and drew it onto his knee, where he turned it over and over noting its well oiled, worn surface.

"Another old friend," he muttered slowly, "an' one that never failed or went back on me. Damn 'em, they ought to know better than to tempt me this way. I wonder if they'd push me this hard if they knew who I am. Lord, how I'd like to meander into their hangout and teach 'em some manners. But I can't, pup—I

can't. I promised mammy when I left
I'd lay off the gun fightin', an' I couldn't
break a promise to our kind old mammy,
could I, pup?"

He returned the gun to the holster and
stood up, stretching his arms and flex-
ing his muscles. His jaw was set and
his eyes bright with anticipation.

"But we'll fight 'em, pup—fight 'em
hard and square and straight an' with
nothing else but these two fists. I got
the law and the right on my side and I'll
win in spite of hell and high water."

With this satisfying conclusion arrived
at, he began preparations for the evening
meal. The sun was dropping low down
to the western horizon, and before long
the shadows would reach the cabin. The
dog sat before the fire gravely contem-
plating the mystery of the flames, his
nose twitching the while at the delectable odor of the frying venison. When
the coffee pot began to simmer, Merrill
sat down to his meal. He ate slowly, his
brain busy with various plans by which
he might avert the impending disaster.
He saw clearly that diplomacy, if it
might be used, would serve his case to
a more satisfactory end than physical
resistance of any kind. Also he was not
in the least possessed with enough colossal egotism to imagine he would have
any chance whatever against such superior numbers should the issue come to
one of force. And before he could decide on any action, it was necessary that
he have a definite understanding with
"Old Man Bartlett" as to the course the
latter intended to pursue if opposed in
his acclaimed plan of 'running the squatter ragged.' Merrill determined to ride
over that evening to the headquarters of
the Bartlett ranch and have a talk with
the owner. It was the only course left
open to him.

A half hour later he rode away from
the cabin and took the trail up the bluffs
into the maze of greasewood beyond.
The trail would have been indistinct to
an unpracticed eye, but Merrill was
plains-born and raised, and he followed
it without difficulty. His horse swung
away the shuffling half-trot, half-canter
peculiar to the horse of the range, which
is tiring on neither horse or rider, yet

eats up the miles in a most surprising
manner. Far out to the west the sky
was rioting in the flaming color of the
sunset and all the country around him
was filmed with a faint bluish haze, the
witching forerunner of the coming darkness. Merrill rode in a comfortable
slouch, the tip of his cigarette glowing
in the twilight. Three miles were thus
traversed, the only sounds being those
of the horse and the soft squeak of the
saddle leather. Suddenly the silence was
broken by the clamor of a coyote on a
near-by ridge. Merrill caught sight of
the slinking form against the skyline
and pulled his horse back on its haunches.
Jerking his rifle from its scabbard under
his thigh, he slid to the ground, judged
his sights as best he could in the fading
light, and pulled. The report sounded
flat and sharp and the coyote disappeared. Merrill led his horse up to the
spot where his quarry vanished. He
found the animal there in a heap, the
last spark of life just leaving its twitching body.

"Pretty lucky, Monty," he told his horse,
"but it's one more rug for the shanty—
maybe."

He fastened the limp animal behind
the saddle and was just about to mount
again when his eye caught a flicker of
white in a little shrub beside him. Curiously he picked it up then swore in soft
amaze. It was a woman's handkerchief
—a dainty square of sheerest linen. As
he held it up for closer observation in
the velvety dusk he caught but the faintest breath of perfume. It reminded him
of the old rose garden he had known in
the far-off days of his childhood.

"Don't it beat all hell, Monty? Who'd
uh though to find this out here?"

He sniffed it again, then, moved by a
sudden impulse, folded it very carefully
and deposited it in the breast-pocket of
his shirt.

As he mounted he grinned a bit apolo-
getically.

"Guess we never get too old to be foolish, Monty horse, but that perfume kinda
reminds me of the fairy princess I used
to dream of when I was a kid." His
voice was wistful when he finished.

He rode off in silence, living over the

years with thoughts such as he had known little of for months back. Sunk in this reverie, the remaining distance of his destination was covered swiftly and without further incident. On a rise above the Bartlett ranch he drew rein. The windows of the ranch house and those of the riders' bunkhouse showed in oblongs of cheery light. Someone, a Mexican vacquero probably, was strumming gently on a guitar and singing in soft, mellow notes a native love song. From the big corral a horse neighed lustily. Monty answered before Merrill could stop him. The singing ceased rather suddenly in the middle of a line. Merrill heard the murmur of voices. He urged Monty off the ridge and rode straight towards the lights of the ranch house.

As he drew up in front of the long, deep veranda, two figures detached themselves from the surrounding darkness and sauntered carelessly up to him. As they crossed the path of light from the open door, Merrill recognized one as the red-headed rider who had given him the warning that afternoon.

The squatter lost no time on preliminaries but came straight to the point.

"Is 'Old Man Bartlett' in?"

Greggins swore sharply.

"Damned if it ain't the squatter. Yuh ain't goin' to try and get around the 'old man,' are yuh? Yore wastin' yore breath if yuh do He ain't got time to fool with no squatter. 'Sides he's kinda grumpy tonight an' might'—'

Merrill slid off his horse.

"I asked to see 'Old Man Bartlett,'" he interrupted quietly. "Where is he?"

"Right here." The voice was heavy and resonant and came from a dark corner of the veranda.

The squatter made his way past several lounging-chairs to where a huge, black bulk lounged indolently in a canvas hammock.

The face of the man was indistinct, but Merrill could sense an atmosphere of force and power about him.

"Have a chair," rumbled the big voice. Merrill drew one up and seated himself.

"Smoke?"

The squatter accepted the proffered cigar with a word of thanks. A great hope was beginning to mount. He felt sure he was going to succeed in his plea. There was no doubt any longer in his mind as to the big-heartedness and fairness of this man before him. Which goes to prove that John Merrill's judgment of human nature was not infallible.

Big Tom Bartlett was big-hearted — along certain lines. No man ever wanted for food and a bed around the Crooked L ranch. The wages he paid his riders were the highest in the country and the accommodations for them kept pace with the wages. He had been known to slaughter more than one head of cattle during the long, cold winters to simplify the food question of some wandering band of Indians. In fact, his pocket was always open to the needy. But Tom Bartlett had fought for every yard of range he controlled. His father and two elder brothers had died in the earlier range wars and paid with their blood for the grazing land now claimed by the Crooked L. For that one reason a squatter was to Tom Bartlett as a red rag to a bull. He treated them all alike and without the least partiality. A warning to move was given first. If not complied with, the resisting squatter would be confronted one fine morning by a lusty and very business-like bunch of cowpunchers who calmly loaded the squatter and all his household effects, living and otherwise, into the huge round-up wagon and remove the entire outfit to the nearest railroad station. Here he was left with the polite suggestion that he keep on traveling.

But to all this Merrill was blissfully ignorant, and with his cigar burning evenly and his feet cocked up on the veranda rail, he drew a deep breath and began.

"Mr. Bartlett, I was informed this afternoon by one of your riders that if I didn't leave my quarter-section on my own accord I'd be thrown off forcibly, and this 'thrown off' proposition would be under your direct supervision. Is that straight?"

"Exactly right, stranger. Either you move off or get thrown off. It's six-to-one and half-a-dozen to the other. The choice is strictly up to you. You can suit your-self."

"Even though you know that the law and right is on my side?"

"Law be damned," suddenly exploded the big man. "Law—law—I'm tired of hearing the word. That's the same stall every one of you fellows put up. Let me tell you something, friend. Out here on the range, law don't amount to a plugged nickel. Tell me this. Was it law that drove the Indians off these ranges? Was it law that fought year in and year out against every conceivable kind of an ob-stacle to get these herds of cattle to-gether that are now the basis of food for hundreds and thousands of people? No, it wasn't law, except, perhaps, the law of the guns—guns wielded by men like myself—some of them who died in the fighting. But we won out, and what we won—we keep!"

Merrill had been a cowman himself in the Panhandle and acknowledged the truth of the older man's words. But he felt his own need of the homestead was more than equal to that of Bartlett's and he determined on a fuller explanation of his own claims.

"I understand your point of view bet-ter than you may imagine, Mr. Bartlett," said Merrill reflectively. "Perhaps you'll understand mine if you'll let me explain a bit."

"Humph," grunted Bartlett. "Fire away. I'm warning you it will be wasted breath."

"Perhaps," nodded the squatter pa-tiently. "We'll see."

Merrill sat quietly for a time collect-ing his thoughts and framing them for utterance in a manner most calculated to create an impression. Somehow he was not as sure of himself as he had been immediately after the first gener-ous greeting he received. In truth, he felt somewhat puzzled. The man in the hammock seemed an enigma—so gener-ous in some ways, so hostile in others. Merrill ran his hand slowly through his hair. The night air was soft and cool and full of the incense of the wide spaces. The stars were white and leap-ing and low-hung. In the door of the bunkhouse the Mexican was crooning

again over his guitar. Unconsciously he lowered his voice as he began to plead his case.

"When I left my old mammy, about four months ago, down in Brazos county in the Panhandle, the doctor told me that another year of Texas climate would put her in her grave. If I got her up into Wyoming or Montana she'd be well again in no time. She's been a mighty good mammy to me, an' I'm tryin' to be a good son to her. When I was younger I reckon I was pretty wild at times an' put a good many gray hairs in her head. But I've changed now an' I'm makin' it up. I'm all she has left, an' I'd be a hell of a man if I failed her in this pinch. So I came up here an' squatted on that section along McCloud creek. I've got the house all ready for her, and she's due about the middle of next month. I'd like powerful well, Mr. Bartlett, to have it waitin' when she gets here." Merrill drew a big breath as he finished.

The big man in the hammock was silent. Merrill could see the point of his cigar moving about in the dark as he chewed on it reflectively. He cleared his voice noisily before he answered.

"I'm sorry, stranger," he said almost gently, "but you can't stay on this place as a squatter. If you did, others would come and I couldn't in justice let you stay without keeping the rest. I'm sorry about your mother, and have an idea of how you feel. But I have my daughter and myself to look after, and if I ever let the squatters start coming, I'm done for."

Merrill stood stiffly. It was well for Bartlett that he could not see the bitter hardness that crept into the squatter's face. The latter stalked slowly to the stair before he spoke. Then he turned.

"Ever hear of 'Curley' Merrill in these parts, Bartlett?" he demanded tersely.

His query startled the big man to the extent that he stumbled rather awk-wardly to his feet.

"'Curley' Merrill, the gunfighter? I've heard of him several times. Why?"

"Nothin,'" jerked out the squatter; "only I'm him."

With that he swung astride his horse and loped swiftly away into the darkness.

CHAPTER II.

The first light of dawn broke in a gray blanket over John Merrill's cabin, for the misty fog wraiths of the night, spawned of the stretches of the Little Missouri, had crept up the valley of Mc-Cloud creek and hung in feathery, dripping silence among the drowsing cottonwoods. A fox squirrel dropped with a soft, furry thump upon one corner of the cabin roof, then, intoxicated with the joy of perfect life and the beckoning vistas of a new-born day, dashed madly along the ridgepole and flung himself recklessly through a ten-foot leap to another drooping branch.

The muffled scamper of tiny feet woke the squatter and set the dog sniffing at the doorsill. Merrill stirred uneasily and sat up. He glanced through the open window at the gray, moist silence without and began to dress. A thorough dousing in the cold waters of the creek cleared the sleep from his brain and put him in accord with the world. He began to whistle softly through his teeth. When fully dressed he reached out for the heavy belt and gun hanging close to his bunk. He hung it loosely about his waist and by means of a strip of buckskin fastened the holster firmly to his thigh. He flipped the gun dexterously from the holster once or twice and was satisfied.

Over his second cup of coffee he caught the first echoes of a galloping horse. The hoof beats grew rapidly and the squatter reached the door in time to see the horse jerked back on his haunches and a figure slid to the ground. It was 'Red' Greggins, foreman of the Crooked L. The horse was flecked with the sweat of hard riding. The rider advanced with quick, nervous steps. Merrill leaned carelessly in the doorway.

"Why all the hurry this mornin' pardner?" he drawled indolently.

Greggins never answered until he was looking straight into the squatter's eyes.

"Plenty uh reason," he gritted grimly. "Yuh seen anythin' uh the old man's daughter since yesterday mornin'?"

Merrill's direct, steel gray glance never wavered. He shook his head slowly.

"No. Why?"

" 'Cause she left the ranch about 10 o'clock yesterday an' ain't been seen since, an' her hoss ain't showed up, either."

"I see. No accident then."

"Nope, not uh chance. She's range bred — she knows hosses. Somebody's run off with her, sure'n blazes."

The squatter smiled slightly.

"You think I done it?" he questioned.

Greggins was caught off his guard. His eyes fell in a moment of confusion. He shook his head rather sheepishly as he looked up.

"Nope, not exactly, but the old man's darn near bughouse an' he's not overlookin' any bets. He's got every rider on th' ranch combin' th' range for a trace of her."

"Well, if you do, I can set your mind at rest on that score," said Merrill. "I never had the honor of seein' the young lady. Fact is, I never knew he had a daughter 'till he told me so last night. I'm sure sorry if any harm's been done her."

"I dunno." Greggins' face was very sober. "It looks bad for sure. She wouldn't stay away like this if somebody wasn't holdin' her. She never done it before."

"Anybody roamin' this range that might pull a trick like that?" queried the squatter thoughtfully.

Greggins nodded.

"That's what I'm afeared uh. About three weeks ago th' old man fired one uh his men—some kind of uh dago breed —'cause he didn't like th' way th' spig acted towards Jean. He had a nasty way uh watchin' her an' it got th' old man sore. Th' spig did a heap uh ravin' in some crazy lingo when he got his walkin' papers—somethin' about gettin' even. I thought it was funny then, but I'm kinda scared now. It looks bad."

Merrill nodded his sympathy.

"I'll keep my eyes open, pardner. If I run across anythin' I'll let you know."

"That's white uh yuh, stranger," acknowledged Greggins as he caught the bridle rein of his horse and swung astride. "If yuh do anythin' that's much help to the old man he might—mind, now,

I'm just a-sayin' might—talk business with yuh. It'll pay yuh to keep on th' lookout anyway."

Again the buckskin raced away across the flat and up the bluff into the greasewood, and again the squatter watched his progress with knitted brow. But his thoughts were of a different nature this time. They were of a dainty bit of lace and linen he had picked up the night before far out in the sagebrush wastes. He drew it from his shirt pocket and examined it with new interest in the light of day. Once more, as he unfolded it, a faint perfume kissed his nostrils with sweetness. He handled it very gently. Suddenly with a sharp exclamation he bent closer. In one carner, traced in tiny black letters, were the initials "J. L. B."

At once his eyes glowed with the light of inspiration. He turned with quick decision and called cheerfully to his dog.

"Come on, pup; let's get started; there's a good job ahead of us."

He saddled his horse and brought him to the door. A blanket was rolled inside a slicker and tied behind his saddle. At the horn he tied a little food and his canteen. His last act before leaving was to fill his belt with fat, yellow cartridges. Then he mounted and cantered off to the foot of the bluffs. At the edge of the greasewood he headed his horse straight to the spot where he had killed the coyote the night before and incidentally found the handkherchief with its bewitching perfume and the initials "J. L. B."

"J. L. B.—Jean Bartlett," muttered Merrill thoughtfully, "I wonder what her middle name is." The name had a pleasing sound to him and he said it over several times to himself. Then he smiled a little ruefully.

"Monty, old horse, let's ramble along. Somewhere out in this country there's a little lady that may be needin' us bad, so shuffle along, old hardshell—shuffle along."

A twitch at the reins lifted the horse into a long, gliding gallop, and the meditating look on Merrill's face faded to one of grim determination.

When Merrill reached his destination he had no need to dismount. The trail lay plain before him. Two horses had passed—running. They were traveling due south—toward the open valley of the Little Missouri. The squatter rode with his eyes to the ground, steering his horse to left or right as required by a pressure of either knee. The trail wound in and out through sage brush clumps and jagged lava outcroppings. Now and then it would dip into a little arroyo or gulch, but the main trend never left the crest of the plateau. Finally the brush began to thin out, and quite suddenly Merrill found the plateau dropping down in long shale slides to the valley of the Little Missouri.

When he reached the main floor of the valley and found the trail leading over the rolling prairie towards the river's edge, some of the wrinkles of trouble left his forehead.

"Just as I hoped, Monty horse," he confided. "He must of traveled all night. He wouldn't try to cross this open country in the day time 'cause somebody would sure see him with the girl and investigate. He must of laid up in some gulch on the plateau and started travelin' right after dark. Bet we didn't miss him more than a few minutes last night. We won't miss him this time, though, old-timer. He's got a pretty good start, but he can't travel as fast as we can. The girl will hold him back all she can."

At the edge of the river the trail turned to the west and followed the course of the river.

"Lookin' for a ford," muttered Merrill. "Hope he chooses a good one or it'll be all off with both of them."

For ten miles he rode with the roily brown water glittering beside him. Then abruptly, beyond a group of cottonwoods, it dipped to the water's edge and disappeared. The squatter reined in and eyed the mocking waters anxiously. Then he nodded grimly.

"He knows his business. It's a ford, alright."

A touch of the spur sent Monty into the water, which almost came to the stirrups. Very carefully, with a caution bred of long experience, he felt his way along, placing each hoof firmly and snatching little sips as he progressed. In a few moments he was safely over and out on the trail that left the river bank immediately and headed for the faraway blue outlines of some distant buttes.

"Good old chap," muttered his rider, patting his neck affectionately.

Merrill rode steadily until the sun was straight overhead. Then he halted and unsaddled in a hollow where the bunch grass grew rank.

"Go to it, Monty horse. You got an hour to fill up on grass before we travel again."

Monty understood for he only wasted time enough to indulge in a good roll before setting busily to work on the luxurious feed. Merrill lounged beside his saddle, chewing a piece of jerky. Later he smoked and spent twenty minutes flat on his back watching bits of fleecy clouds float lazily by. But he was impatient for the trail and with difficulty restrained from starting before the hour was up. Finally he rose and whistled. Monty, from the opposite side of the hollow, lifted his head and whickered in reply. Another whistle brought him swiftly to his master, where he held his head conveniently low for the bridle.

As Merrill swung into the saddle again he marked the position of the sun with anxious eyes. Then he measured the distance to the buttes and mentally computed his chances of reaching them before nightfall.

"By hard ridin' we'll just about make it," he muttered. Then he leaned over until his mouth was close to the horse's ear.

"We got to make those buttes before night, Monty—it'll mean hard traveling, old-timer. Do we make it?"

The horse turned his head and muzzled his nose against his rider's boot. He was willing.

Monty ran easily, head held low and far to the front. Merrill could feel the deep, regular breathing of his mount and the swelling, gliding muscles that writhed like snakes beneath the glossy, black skin. Mile after mile drifted backward under the magic of the pounding hoofs. As the sun dropped down to the horizon

and the buttes loomed closer and closer with never slackening on the part of the horse, Merrill thrilled with pride.

"If we're in time, boy, it's you that's done it," he told the horse as he pulled him down to a halt where the first little foothill hovered under the protection of knarled, gray buttes. Merrill swung to the ground and dropped on one knee to examine the trail more closely. Behind him the horse stood, his black satiny coat streaked with foam, his legs spread wide to give his tortured lungs more room. Merrill stood up and cradled the big black head in his arms.

"Monty horse — we're in time," he gulped. "The track ain't more than an hour old. We'll get 'em before dark. An' you done it, you big fire-eater."

Up the hill they went, the man bending low over the crushed grass stems that marked the trail he followed. Behind him came the horse, breathing easier now and stepping deftly as a cat. The trail led them through a narrow gap and around a sharp corner of butte. Quite suddenly, as they turned the corner, they came upon the objects of their pursuit. But under what circumstances! Out across a wide flat the girl was running, her hair in wild disorder over her shoulders and her clothing ripped half from her back. Close behind her, his hand just reaching for her half-bare shoulder, leaped the man. His hand closed upon her and jerked her backward. Only once she screamed—wildly, despairingly.

It galvanized Merrill into action. One leap put him in the saddle. He leaned far up over the horse's back.

"Just once more, Monty horse," he pleaded. "Run, boy—for God's sake— run!"

Monty heard and understood. Like a great, black thunderbolt he swept out across that last quarter mile. Merrill rode as a part of his horse and he counted the yards as he flashed down on the last stretch of his rescue.

The girl's assailant heard the tattoo of hoofs and looked around. For a few precious seconds he seemed dazed and at a loss of what to do, then he ran for a scrubby pinion, under which was piled a heap of camping equipment. A rifle butt protruded from the pile. Merrill knew it was a race for the gun. He had two hundred yards to go—the other but fifty. He drew his own gun and leaned lower over Monty's neck. The black mane whipped into his face and he thrilled at the magnificent speed of his horse. The girl, half sitting and with wide, fear-clouded eyes, watched them flash by, a lean, hard-eyed man astride a huge, black horse streaked with foam and froth and tearing like a mad thing. The running man looked back, then spurted with all his strength to cover the last ten yards. He jerked the gun to him and whirled, bringing it to his shoulder with the same movement. Then Merrill began to shoot. He saw his quarry stagger at his first shot and the rifle slip from his hand, but he remained on his feet, swaying, while the squatter emptied his gun. The last shot was fired as close as twenty yards, and Merrill almost saw it go home. The dark, evil face before him suddenly sagged into a look of stupid wonderment. Too late Merrill tried to pull Monty aside, but the horse was not to be denied. He crashed into the slowly toppling form, hauling it to the ground and crushing it sickenly with his thudding hoofs. The trail of vengeance had ended.

CHAPTER III.

The Crooked L ranch was shrouded in an atmosphere of desolation. Everyone moved and spoke in an attitude of solemnity and hushed reverence lest they disturb the big, broken-hearted man who sat huddled upon the veranda. For hours he had remained in the same position, —leonine head sunk upon his chest —his big, work-hardened hands folded and listless. After hours of hoping against hope he accepted the apparent inevitable. His riders had combed the range from end to end and returned empty-handed, only to be sent forth again and again on their fruitless search by the frantic father. Now, after an absence of two days and nights, Big Tom Bartlett shrunk down into his chair and gave his daughter up for lost. The others about the ranch had given up long ago.

It was with a crushed, deadened spirit that Bartlett accepted a final realization of his loss. And the Crooked L mourned with the father.

* * * * * * *

Merrill stopped just below the crest of the ridge and turned in his saddle to face the girl.

"As you know, Miss Bartlett," he said soberly, "the ranch lies just over this ridge. I'll leave you to make the rest of the way alone."

He lifted his hat and wheeled Monty off the path, waiting for her to pass. But she did not move. Instead she looked at him rather queerly and spoke with great determination.

"I'm not going to that house, Mr. Merrill, unless you go with me. I can't understand why you should have such a silly idea of wishing to leave unseen after all you have done for me. My father will be the most grateful man in the world, and will never be able to thank you enough. And he won't rest until he has seen you personally and shaken hands with you."

Her directness confused Merrill.

"But I don't want any thanks. I only done what any other man would have done. And besides, Monty should get the credit, not me."

His excuse was very lame and he knew it. A flood of red crept over his tanned face.

"That does not make our debt of gratitude any the less to you. What any other man might have done is nothing. The fact remains that you did it and that is what matters to myself and my father. You must come with me." She leaned over and laid her hand on his sleeve. "Please, Mr. Merrill," there was a little catch in her voice. "Don't keep me from my daddy any longer."

Merrill saw the glint of tears in her frank gray eyes and mentally cursed himself savagely as a fool and a brute. He answered her by taking the trail and leading the way over the ridge to the house of desolation below.

The sound of hoofs penetrated dimly through the sorrow that blanketed the senses of Big Tom Bartlett. He lifted a face that had grown old in a night. A lithe, auburn-haired figure stood before his unbelieving eyes. She was smiling through a flood of unshed tears

"Daddy," she whispered, and crept into his sheltering outstretched arms.

Merrill observed the meeting from the step and felt that he was intruding, so he slipped quietly away to the bunkhouse, where he borrowed the makings from an open-mouthed Mexican and settled down on a rickety chair for a smoke. They found him there a little later.

For a moment Bartlett said nothing, but his big paw crushed Merrill's hand like a vise. Straight into each others eyes they looked — two strong men, searching the windows of the mind and soul for the hall-mark therein. And they saw and were satisfied.

"Anything I have is yours," said Bartlett simply. "I'll be proud to have you for a neighbor, my boy. You've picked the best spot on my range for a home— but it's yours, and more, too, if you want it."

Merrill shook his head smilingly.

"I have plenty, Mr. Bartlett. Enough to make my mammy well and happy. That little valley on the McCloud will make an ideal little home for us. And now I reckon I'll be gettin' along. I left my pup to take care of the shanty while I was away. He must be pretty hungry by this time."

He whistled for Monty and swung into the saddle. Father and daughter stood side by side watching him. A great gratitude was in their faces. Swiftly the girl slipped up to the horse's head. She put her cheek against his velvety muzzle.

"Big, wonderful Monty, you brought your master to me before, will you bring him again?"

The horse whickered gently and rubbed his nose against her shoulder.

Her eyes were luminous as she lifted them bravely to Merrill's gaze.

"Monty is willing; are you?"

(The End)

Flowers of Death

By May Thomas Milain

Flowers of death, you cover my love
　With pillow of violets at her head,
　And blanket of roses over her spread.
Does she know, in her dark, of you above,
　And rejoice in your beauty, though she be dead?

Radiant lilies within her hand,
　The cold of the grave with her you share—
Will she carry you into a brighter land?
Will she 'wake, and smile, and understand
　That I who loved her placed you there?

The Last of the Old-Timers

By Hazel F. Walsh

A FEW months ago, a man who was a very close friend to my grandfather in the early days in San Francisco, and who has been living for the past forty-one years in Guatemala, returned to San Francisco.

To me, he seemed to have walked straight out of our old family photograph album. He is very tall and very thin, bony in fact, and has a very large Adam's apple. His hair is pure white, and thick, with no intimation of a bald spot, and he wears a white mustache, and a white goatee. His small, deep-set, but very bright brown eyes, and his large nose with a hump on it, give him the appearance of an eagle. He was originally a Southerner, and forty-one years of speaking the Spanish language have given him a remarkable accent.

I happened to be the only member of my family in San Francisco at the time, and the duties of hospitality fell to me.

We started out at eight o'clock in the morning, "to see the old town," as he put it. He wanted first to go to Rincon Hill. He said Rincon Hill was the first district he had known when he came to San Francisco a young fellow, and that he is like an old jack-rabbit of the foothills; drive him out in the morning, but he is sure to to come back to his old haunts in the evening.

I do not know, myself, what Rincon Hill used to be, but now it certainly is not an inspiring neighborhood. It is the least reclaimed of any of the burned sections of the city. Portions of stone stairways lead to nothing. Remains of brick chimneys stick up in empty lots. Here and there a queer-shaped, black, leafless tree tells where once upon a time there was a garden. What few houses have been built are wooden flats of the cheapest kind.

"So this is Rincon Hill!" my friend kept repeating to himself; "so this is Rincon Hill!"

"Well, well!" he said, finally, turning to me; "the day of Rincon Hill was past before I left San Francisco, but who would have thought that it ever would come to this!"

From Rincon Hill, we walked along Brannan Street. My friend wanted to go to Saint Rose's Church. He told me that he was married in Saint Rose's Church, and two years later his wife was buried from it. When he asked me if the church had been rebuilt since the fire, I took a chance and said, 'yes. I was ashamed to admit that I did not know. At Third Street, I caught a glimpse of two brick spires, and breathed with relief.

"So they have a brick church now!" said my friend. "Yes, I recollect now, they were talking of building a brick church about the time I left."

The church has been rebuilt with the bricks which went through the fire, and to me it had a bruised and scarred appearance; but my friend did not seem to notice. We sat in the church for about half an hour. It seemed to me to be rather barren. The roof is very high. Only half the floor space is taken up with pews, the back portion being absolutely bare. A few of the windows are stained glass, but by far the greater number are plain glass.

On leaving the church, my friend stopped in the vestibule and read the list of parish pew-holders. The list is comprised of two names. Then he read the church's honor-roll of enlisted men. "Not a name that I know," he said.

At the corner of Fourth and Brannan Streets, he turned and stood for some time gazing back at the church. He still carried his hat in his hand, and as he stood there, absorbed in thought, he looked like a lonely eagle. He glanced around the neighborhood. There are no dwelling houses. The opposite side of the street is occupied by a lumber-yard, and near the corner, a dingy little restaurant. He turned unexpectedly, and surprised me watching him. He smiled down at me kindly. "I reckon I am about the last of the old-timers," he said.

He wanted next to go to Telegraph Hill. I was trying to decide which street car would take us nearest, but he suggested that we walk, and then we could see all the down-town buildings on our way.

We walked up Fourth Street, down Market Street, and up Montgomery. My friend walked out near the curbing, so as to get the best possible view of the buildings on both sides of the street. Of each building, he asked me if it had been burned, if the new building had been erected on the old foundations, who was the architect, who was the owner, how much did the erection cost, what was the rent, how many stories was it, and was there still water in the basement.

All I was able to answer was that they still have to pump water out of the basements. I was beginning to realize, with somewhat of astonishment, how many things I do not know about San Francisco.

At first, on my being unable to say how high a building was, my friend essayed to count the stories from where he stood, but owing to the glare of the sun, the noise and bustle of traffic, and so on, results were not satisfactory, and he desisted.

"That fire must have been a corker!" he repeated, several times. His tone was indulgent, as though it was just like San Francisco, if it must have a fire, to have a corker!

We traversed every inch of Telegraph Hill. My friend had his cane to assist him over the ups and downs, and I clambered after, as best I could. Children stopped playing to stare at us, and the women, leaning out of windows, and standing in open doorways, broke off their everlasting chattering long enough to stare at us.

On one crooked side-street, we met a very especially dirty baby. I think even according to the standards of Telegraph Hill, it would be considered a dirty baby. It was all alone. I have no idea how old it might have been. Its hair was clipped close like a boy, and it wore earrings. What served it for apparel was equally contradictory as an indiction as to what its sex might be.

My friend bent way down in an endeavor to get on a level with the child. "What are you doing out here?" he asked.

The baby looked up at him with round, uncomprehending eyes. It probably did not understand a word of English.

My friend clapped his hands twice, close to the child's face. "Why don't you go home?" he asked.

The baby backed away, and looked ready to cry.

"Wait now, until I see," said my friend; "wait now until I see, if perhaps I might not have a dime about me!" He placed a ten-cent piece in the baby's hand.

The child looked at the money intently, and then up at us. There seemed to be a gleam of understanding in its eyes.

"Is that good for sweets, eh?" asked my friend.

Very deliberately, the child closed its fingers on the money, and turned from us and truddled down the street on its little bow legs.

"He knows what that is, right enough, the little rogue!" said my friend.

At the top of the hill, my friend stood and took a survey of the city. "The old town certainly has seen changes," he said; "many changes!"

From Telegraph Hill, we rode to the Fine Arts Palace in the Exposition Grounds. From my experiences in the down-town district, I had expected a multitude of questions at the Fair Grounds, but I escaped quite easily. He was greatly interested, of course; but it is Rincon Hill, and Brannan Street, and Montgomery Street that he loves.

Going back to town from the Fine Arts Palace, we rode on the little cable hill car. Just as the car was mounting the first steep hill, my friend decided he felt a draught. He rose, and with his cane, proceeded to close the ventilators. The car gave a sudden jolt, and my friend lurched against a woman, treading on her toes, and dislocating her hat. Holding his cane and his hat in one hand, and clinging precariously to a strap with the other, he apologized, explaining that his sea-legs are not as good now as when he was a young fellow. From her expression, one would not say that the woman was altogether pleased.

When the car reached the top of the hill, all the ventilators had not yet been closed. The people who had ridden up with us left the car, and others who were going down hill got on, while I sat and waited. The closing of the ventilators was rather a difficult task. They probably had been open, just as they were, all summer. Finally, my friend brought the last, and most refractory, one to with a sharp impact, and turned to the somewhat indignant conductor. "There now, my lad, I fixed them as they should be," he said.

We had lunch down-town, and my friend delivered, to a very apparently bored waitress, a discourse on the cultivation of coffee, which as to clearness and detail, might well put Burton Holmes to shame.

We spent the afternoon at Golden Gate Park, and I do believe that on that one afternoon I saw more of Golden Gate Park than I had ever seen on all the occasions I have been there before, put together.

At half past six, we were down-town again, having dinner. I had walked so much, and looked at so many different objects, and had done so much talking since eight o'clock that morning, that my head was fairly swimming. My companion sat opposite me at the table, as fresh as a daisy.

During the course of the meal, it was borne in on my dazed mind that he was suggesting that we go to the theatre. I could hardly believe it, but I thought if a man old enough to be my grandfather

could stand it, I would not cry quits. I was strengthened in my heroic attitude by the reflection that it would be impossible to obtain seats at that late hour.

The long line of people in front of the box office was a very hopeful sight to me. My friend led me to one side, where a policeman was standing, and told the policeman that he would leave the young lady there while he bought tickets. The policeman saluted, and indicated that he would keep an eye on the young lady.

My friend walked directly to the ticket office, and reaching his long arm beyond the people who were nearest the window, rapped on the marble edge with his cane, and ordered two seats. Without a murmur, the man inside the window handed out two tickets.

Our seats in the theatre were three-quarters way back. During the intermission, the doors in back were opened. My friend shifted in his seat, and I watched him nervously. He climbed out to the aisle. "Close the doors, or we will all be frosted," he said in loud, clear tones.

Instantly the buzz of conversation in the down-stairs portion of the house ceased, and all heads were turned toward where my friend stood in the aisle, in the majesty of his white goatee and his gold-headed cane. For a minute people seemed to think he was a part of the performance.

"Close them," he repeated, utterly oblivious of the staring eyes.

By then it was time for the next number, and the doors were closed.

After the theatre we had supper. Looking about him, my friend decided that the women of San Francisco today are not as pretty as when he was a young fellow. He recalled by name all the pretty ones he had known. He told me what an especially pretty girl the aunt for whom I am named was, and added that I do not in the least resemble her.

It was two-fifteen A. M., when I reached home, and my welcome bed.

Ambushed by Fortune

By Francis Lee Rogers

THIS is the tale that I gathered from Shotgun Joe when he was working in gum boots alongside of me in a wet gravel mine. We stood in a foot of water, and water dripped down upon us, and the shovel handles were slippery, and the work hard, and the loose roof above us dangerous. Notwithstanding these features, Joe whistled and sang continually, for he lived in memories of a radiant past and saw a sunrise glow upon the mists of the future and cared nothing about the passing present. Though today he had little money, a year ago he had had less; but in the between time—well, here is his adventure as he related it:

On the afternoon before Christmas a year ago he had set forth toward Sonora, wearing his best suit, which was ragged, indeed, and with a single fifty-cent piece in his pockets, to celebrate Christmas Eve as best circumstances allowed. For several months he had had no luck at prospecting, which is the usual condition of a prospector, and few of them worry about that. So he was not downhearted, that quality not entering into the make-up of a genuine prospector; and he was glad in his heart for no reason at all, except that the Christmas gladness was in the atmosphere. Perhaps there was another reason, though, for soon he came in sight of a white cottage with green shutters, and there was a pleasing young woman by the open gate, and a handsome shepherd dog beside her. As Joe neared, the dog ran out and greeted him with delighted yelps, and the girl smiled at him, and Joe smiled back; but he did not stop, but called out some excuse about having to be in town to meet someone. But his real reason was that he thought that his clothes were not good enough for him to want to talk with her now, and for the first time this day he felt discontented.

He rounded the curve of the road, still imagining her smile and the red geranium in her hair, and how neat she looked in her blue dress; and he thought that she would be his choice of all womankind if he were in position to choose. While thinking thus he noticed a piece of quartz lying beside the road, and, as was his invariable custom, picked it up and scrutinized it with trained eye. It had an iron vein, and crystals, and the stain of blue slate—good indications. In the bank above it he saw another piece of quartz and examined that. Then he saw an odd-shaped lump projecting and took a rock and knocked it out and examined it, and when he first felt the weight of it he suspected the truth. It was the three-hundred dollar nugget, of whose finding local people still relate; and it is to this day in the collection of Jeweler Haiden, polished and glowing—a thing of beauty.

But its real nature was all hidden then, and Joe scraatched it in several places with his knife before he was sure that the lump was all gold. Then he proceeded to town, calm outwardly, but much exalted inwardly. Had not the impression of Meena been fresh in his mind, doubtless he would have called about him a party of friends when he arrived and made a glorious celebration and departed home as ragged as he had come, and maybe fifty cents poorer. But this time he was very crafty with himself and made a strictly private matter of selling the nugget. Jeweler Haiden paid him cash, full value, or very near it, for he was too honest to cheat even if he could have done, which he couldn't, for Joe knew gold too well. But he had to pay him part of the price in silver dollars, and a double handful of these looked so impressive in bulk that it gave Joe an inspiration. He went out to buy a new suit and other things, and at each place asked for his change in dollars and put them into a small valise, which he had purchased, until it contained over two hundred of the big coins.

It was now dark and he started back. When he reached Meena's house his courage almost failed him. He paused by the gate quite a while, then finally went up to the door and knocked. And when the door was opened and Meena stood before him he felt strangely diffident.

"My goodness, Joe, is this you?" she exclaimed; "Come in! Grandmother," she said, turning around, "do look at Joe in his new suit!"

The old woman in the chair by the stove mumbled with toothless cordiality and motioned him to a seat, and put another stick of manzanita on the fire. Joe sat down by the glowing fire, and he had to explain everything, and they talked for a long while.

"Grandmother, it's time for you to go to bed," said Meena at length. And the old woman bade them goodnight and left them alone.

Now, thought Joe, is the decisive moment.

"Meena," he said slowly, "Christmas is a good day to get married on."

Meena blushed a little and looked into Joe's genial eyes, but made no reply. Joe reflectively picked up the valise, opened it and poured its contents upon the rug, where they made a massive, shining heap.

"Meena, that's enough for a start. Let's get married tomorrow evening. What do you say?"

She contemplated. She liked Joe. Life she had found often lonesome.

"All right," she answered, smiling.

Joe laughed with relief that it should be so quick and simple as this, and a great happiness came upon him. He took Meena into his arms and kissed her Then they sat and talked, heedless of time, after the manner of lovers, until it was very late. And it took them a long time to say goodnight then.

The next night—Christmas night—was a wonderful, clear night, and the wedding was at Meena's home and came off splendidly. Friends of the couple sat about two great tables, and there was jest and merriment and a supply of native wine without limit. Joe felt very happy, for Meena was truly his now. The happier he felt, the more he drank, and the more he drank the happier he felt.

But soon a disturbing thought crept into his mind. His best friend, Sam, was missing from the feast; Sam, with whom he had taken so many prospecting trips and shared luck with so often. He lived only half a mile distant—on Table Mountain—and Joe decided to walk over and get him. Without a word to anyone he slipped out of the yard and out into the road, and, as nearly as he could judge in his elevated but confused state of consciousness, was soon upon the short-cut path to Sam's dwelling.

The moon, too, was full, and it seemed to Joe, as he strode lightly over the lava, that he was treading on moonlight and breathing it, and was himself a part of the glamorous illusion of the wondrous night. Joyously he moved and swiftly, until the light from a cabin was before him. He knocked, and the door was opened, but a stranger and not Sam greeted him. Then he knew that he must have branched from the right trail. The stranger, after treating Joe to a glass of wine, gave him directions for the right path. He did not grasp the directions with clearness, but did not like to ask again, so thanked him and boldly set out once more.

His vague memory of the remainder of that night is of toilsome travel over rocks, through brush; after the moon had set he still stumbled on, up slopes and down, and when dawn came he laid himself down under a tree and slept. When he awoke the sun was high. The first thing that his eyes rested upon was a piece of quartz float, and, according to his invariable custom, he scrutinized it carefully and found it excellent. He saw another piece nearby and picked it up and saw upon it a streak of gold. At this you may be sure that Joe became wide awake and sober, for he saw that chance had led him to a rare spot, and there was no sign of any mining having been done hereabouts.

Homeward he traveled and related his experience to Meena, who, after some tears, forgave him. But he did not tell even her about the quartz he had found until he had filed and recorded a claim upon the ground. Then he set to work mining. The rest is commonplace. He took out $90,000, and he and Meena went to San Francisco to spend it, and the details of getting rid of this sum would doubtless be interesting, but Joe did not tell me of them, but only of the climax, which was that one day they found that it was all gone.

So they went back to the mountains, and Meena put on gingham and Joe put on overalls and went to work to earn another grubstake. It was shortly after this time that I met him. A year later I heard that he had made another big strike in his mine and had bought the finest ranch in Tuolumne county.

There are three morals to this story—first, that Christmas is some people's lucky day; second, that in a gold country it is well to cultivate the invariable custom of scutinizing all quartz rock; third, that if you waste one fortune, it is well to treat the next one you get with more wisdom.

A Vision

By Manuella Dawson

A vision comes before me—
  Drifts before the printed page,
Half blurs out the wall that holds me—
  Just a rolling plain and sage.
A free and boundless prairie,
  At the setting of the sun;
A cool breeze gently blowing
  And a homeward race to run.

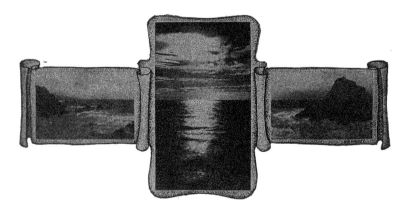

Pepe, El Tonto

By Homer Thomas

PEPE, El Tonto, was a dreamer; one of those simple creatures that are forever gazing into the future, hopefully, trustfully, serenely sure of the goodness of Mother Earth. Always did this child of the Great Desert seem to be communing with the Star Spirit. There was no denying he was different from the other vaqueros of the ranchos of Arizona, for, unlike them, he was quiet, reserved, and, indeed, often appeared timorous. Never did Pepe tell any soul of his hopes and dreams, for to him they were too sacred for the wild jests and amusements of the cowboys.

For you must believe that Pepe dreamed and hoped for wonderful things. For to him there was no invitation in the square-faced bottles that enchained the souls of many luckless vaqueros; for Pepe there were no thoughts of wild passions and the lurid lives that led to utter abasement to the poor people of the border-lands. Rather to this man, who yet had the heart of a child, and whom all called El Tonto (The Fool), came hopes of owning a rancho far out in God's own clean desert lands. He knew of a place where a well gushed in the midst of the fairest oasis of cottonwoods and river-willows, of living there, where his nature could absorb the wondrous beauties of the desert and the mysteries of the sunny sky that smiled above him. These thoughts came to him, for "The Fool" loved the works of God, passionately and understandingly.

So Pepe, the poor vaquero on Sam Barnett's rancho in Arizona, lived the life of the dreamer, apart from his fellow men, and, as is the brutal nature of mankind, because he was not as they were, they laughed at Pepe, and all men called him Pepe, El Tonto.

In all the wide world but one understood this dreamer of dreams. And the understanding came from the depths of a heart of love—for the black-eyed Paquita, daughter of the mayor-domo of the Great Bar Circle Ranch, had given her love to the poor vaquero who dreamed.

But love could not overcome the material obstacle and obstinancy of the father of Paquita. Never, had he sworn, would his jewel of a daughter marry a poor, ignorant vaquero, who only stared and dreamed foolish things. Carambal—by all the saints! Never would Paquita marry any but one who possessed wealth and position!

So Pepe and Paquita loved, but were denied the rights of love; and only dreams of the rancho at the oasis of cottonwoods and river-willows, with Paquita reigning as queen in his faithful heart, had Pepe, El Tonto.

Pepe had no chance to rise to the desired wealth and position, for the vaqueros did not have large wages for their long days and nights of dreary work. So how could man gain wealth? But the world was good—perhaps the saints that protected all true lovers would lead him to Paquita—so thought Pepe.

One bright day of midsummer, when all the desert dozed in dreamy meditation and, even the great, gray buzzards sailed slowly from the languor of the season, Pepe was riding out in the broken lava-studded hills of El Oro Perdido. The way was new to Pepe. Never had he seen that part of the desert, but he remembered that campfire legends told of fabulous stores of gold in hidden creek-beds. Only the old padres had seen the gold, and they had never told any of the curious where the lodes were, for gold always breeds trouble and the padres loved peace. Thus, this part of the desert was known as the Hills of the Lost Gold.

Pepe rode slowly and carefully down a ragged trail of flinty lava into a little box-like valley. Wonderingly he gazed around him.

Gone were the dancing lights of desert heat; gone were the dry clumps of choya spines and gray desert grass, for in this valley a spring had given life to a luxuriant growth of verdant beauty. River-willow edged the banks of the little silvery, tinkling stream; the beautiful sego lily even had found root in this garden spot. Green, sweet-smelling grass bedded the floor of the valley.

All this the beauty-loving soul of Pepe, the dreamer, absorbed in one long rapturous look of adoration. Heaven could be no fairer to Pepe.

He was thirsty, and, flinging himself down full length, he lowered his face to the cool water. Near the basin, where the water gleamed and flickered in the bright sun of an Arizona day, drew his eager face, and then Pepe, the dreamer, called by all men El Tonto, stiffened and stared into the water.

A yellow, dully-glistening substance lay thickly on the bottom and sloping sides of the water basin. All along the banks and shelves of sand of the stream gleamed that yellow, dull substance. The heart of Pepe was pounding furiously, his head swam dizzily with the emotion of joy.

Gold! Gold it was, ready for Pepe to scoop out in handsfull.

To Pepe, the dreamer, who dreamed of a rancho in the desert, where the cottonwoods and river-willows made a tiny paradise, came this gift of the saints. Surely the saints of faithful lovers had taken pity on this poor vaquero.

Pepe gathered the heavy yellow substance. Yes, it was gold, for which men will buy and sell lives and souls.

Pepe soon had his pockets and saddlebags crammed with the great discovery. He even filled his felt sombrero and carried it in the crook of his arm. The father of Paquita would demand much wealth for his jewel of a daughter. And poor Pepe, who had loved in vain for so

long, did not desire to take chances.

He turned his horse from the little box-like valley, where the spring had given life to the bloom in the desert, and began the long ride to the rancho of his patron—Sam Barnett.

As the dreamer of dreams, who had never been able to believe that his dreams would come true, rode along, he talked happily to his horse.

"Ah, caballito mio, we are to go to Paquita first of all. Paquito will be happy for this news, for he whom she loves has found gold! Now can I be forever happy. Si, si, senor. Paquita and the rancho where the cottonwoods and river-willows grow are now mine." So Pepe, the dreamer, still dreamed of the black-eyed nina, who alone understood and loved him. His heart would no longer be heavy with despair, for the saints that protect lovers had aided him. Poor Pepe, who had never had enough of the world's goods to live and love as became his nature, was now suddenly loaded with wealth.

Pepe rode directly to the Bar Circle Ranch, where he would tell Paquita of his fortune. He would also ask the mayor-domo for the hand of Paquita; si, senor, that very day would he ask. He did not doubt that the father of Paquita would be glad to have such a wealthy son-in-law. The father of Paquita had never seen half the wealth that Pepe now carried in his felt sombrero.

When Pepe came to the scattered group of gray barns and corrals that was the heart of the Bar Circle Ranch, he turned to the adobe house of Paquita's father.

Luck was smiling brightly for Pepe that day. The father of Paquita was lounging in the shade of the house as Pepe rode up. The mayor-domo stood up to watch this visitor of his. An angry and malicious gleam shot from his small jet-black eyes. He was a man of much importance, and Pepe was but a poor vaquero; pues, senor, should he not show his disdain of this foolish youth? Of a surety he should!

But one glance at the face of Pepe and he stopped and waited for Pepe to dismount.

Pepe, El Tonto, seemed strangely excited, and over his lean, fine face a smile of joy supreme played that changed his entire aspect.

The father of Paquita wondered. Never had Pepe looked so happy. Little could the mayor-domo realize the visions of Pepe, who was now so near to realizing the utter ecstacy of dreams come true.

Pepe flung himself from his horse and faced the man who had scorned his love for Paquita.

"Senor," he cried in ringing tones, "behold Pepe, El Tonto, who is now a rich man. Pepe has found gold; si, si, seguro que si, senor, heavy yellow gold.

"Many times have you told me that Paquita would never marry anyone who did not possess wealth. I ask for the hand of Paquita. Senor, you do not believe Pepe? Mira, take but one look and stare not so at Pepe!"

The father of Paquita was staring at this wildly gesticulating vaquero, who never before had spoken so to him.

Pepe was now very close to the mayor-domo. He stood swaying from the force of his emotion, and he was eagerly digging his trembling fingers into his old felt sombrero.

The mayor-domo watched. Pepe withdrew his fingers from the sombrero and showed the bewildered watcher a hand filled with a dully-gleaming, heavy substance. Pepe's gold!

Pepe looked triumphantly at the staring father of his beloved.

"See!" he said, "gold! yellow gold! And I, El Tonto, have found it! Quick— your answer! Do you give me your daughter?"

Over the face of the mayor-domo a shock of surprise leaped. He started forward and stared; stared at the heavy, yellow substance.

As he gazed, a queer look came into his eyes, and an ugly, malicious smile twisted his lips.

"Pepe," he said slowly, "never will you marry Paquita. Well have men called you El Tonto, the Fool, for you have carried home nothing but El Oro Volador— Fool's Gold!"

Pepe, the dreamer of dreams, called by all men El Tonto, is an old, gray man. He still rides the range as a vaquero for Sam Barnett.

Pepe has never married.

Perhaps he still has dreams; nobody knows and nobody cares; but Pepe, let it be understood, can now tell the difference between the yellow, heavy gold, for which men buy and sell lives and souls, and El Oro Volador, or Fool's Gold.

An Honest Agreement

(Editor's Note.—The following article (by an official in Washington who wishes to appear anonymously) while arguing neither for nor against the League of Nations Treaty, attacks this interesting subject from a different angle than that which has been already interpreted by the usual advocate or opponent.)

AMONG the many criticisms directed at the proposed covenant for a league of nations, one of those most commonly repeated is that, while intended to compel peace, it will in fact compel war; it comes not to bring peace upon earth, but a sword. Worse than that, from our American point of view, it will force the participation of the United States in wars over questions with which this country has no concern and in whose settlement it has no interest. Few objections to the proposed covenant appeal so forcibly to the average man as the one that "our boys will have to police Europe." It may be that this attitude is justifiable; fifty thousand Americans have died in battle on European soil within the last two years, and perhaps we may fairly say that this is enough. Or it may be that this is nothing but selfishness masquerading as patriotism, as it often does; it is a poor sort of country, as it is a poor sort of man, that will not sometimes sacrifice a little ease and comfort for the good of others. But whether it be right or wrong, no one can doubt that this feeling is widespread. If this one objection can be removed, if men can be satisfied that their fear of such a result is unfounded, one of the greatest obstacles to agreement on the covenant will be destroyed.

On first thought this appears a hard thing to do. The plain language of the covenant seems to make it obligatory for the member nations to resort to extreme measures, even war, for the maintenance of the status quo, and so, in a sense, it does. But it will not do, with this as with any other legal instrument or statute, to accept first impressions as finally correct; we must go deeper—follow out all that is necessarily and inevitably implied, though not directly expressed—and perhaps the matter will assume a very different aspect. So it is in the present case. Among the first to bring this to public notice was a lawyer and statesman of no less standing than Mr. Taft, who discussed the questions fully in one of his editorials. His arguments have frequently been repeated on the floor of Congress, and, so far as I am aware, have never been directly answered. Indeed, direct refutation is nothing short of impossible.

Briefly, the argument may be stated thus: It is true that under the terms of the covenant the governing body of the league may decide upon drastic action— perhaps commercial and economic boycott, perhaps war—but so far as the United States is concerned, that decision is a nullity unless and until enforced by appropriate legislation by Congress. Congress alone can declare war, and if it decides against war, the state of peace must continue, unless the President, in disregard of his oath of office, begins military operations, and so commits us, against our will, beyond the possibility of withdrawal. This will be possible to the same extent that it is possible now, and no more. The boycott, too, cannot exist without Congressional action, except as the voluntary act of individuals, as it may at the present time. All this is undeniable.

I have said that direct refutation of this argument is impossible. Can it be attacked indirectly? Granting every word of it to be true, is there anything about it which should make us reluctant to be influenced by it? Let us put into words the action that is recommended to us. "We will sign the covenant as it stands, pledging the faith of the nation to maintain the territorial integrity of states, their existing boundaries, and all the rest. We may do this without hesitation, for when any of these things is threatened, we will use our own best judgment as to whether we shall keep our word or not." This does not read well. It would sound better if more vaguely phrased. But does it not express precisely the idea that many have in mind?

I do not mean here to argue either for or against the ratification of the covenant, but only to plead that such action as we may take shall be with clear understanding of what it means. First, putting aside the appeals to petty prejudice and to silly sentimentalism which constitute a considerable part of the case as presented by partisans of both sides, let us examine what remains as carefully and as thoughtfully as we should any important matter in our business or personal experience. With thorough understanding of what the covenant means, some of us will favor it and some oppose, but the disagreement will be an intelligent one, and we shall get what the majority of us really want, instead of something very different from what we want or think we are getting. Eminent as are some of those who advance the arguments which have just been stated, it is difficult to believe that they have thought the thing through to the end.

We have had a great deal to say during the past few years of the sanctity of treaties and the iniquity of violating them. It is easy to remember occasions, not long remote, when our national conduct did not betray a blind devotion to the principle that a treaty is under all circumstances inviolable, but probably never before has it been seriously suggested that we enter into an international agreement with the deliberate intention, formed in advance, of keeping only so much of it as we may choose.

Such a policy, if once fully accepted, will greatly facilitate the ratification of treaties, since no Senator need hesitate a moment in giving an affirmative vote. The negotiation of treaties, to be sure, whatever his personal opinions may be, might be somewhat more difficult.

Not many years ago we entered into a treaty with the republic of Panama for the acquisition of the Canal Zone. Part of the consideration agreed upon consisted in an annual cash payment by the United States to Panama. There was a good deal of opposition to this treaty, as most of us recall, but it finally ratified. Perhaps some of this opposition could have been overcome, and some ill-feeling averted, if it had been more clearly pointed out that the payments to Panama could not be made except upon appropriation by Congress, which it could, of course, deny at any time. In reality, then, the treaty only required that we should pay such sums as we might see fit, and the fear that perhaps we were being over-charged could have been shown to be absurd.

Is the case of the Panama treaty essentially different from that before us now? I have no intention either of forcing an analogy or of being flippant over a serious matter. It may be that it is at times excusable to repudiate a promise; perhaps sometimes it would be morally wrong not to do so; perhaps to repudiate a contract extorted by force is morally as well as legally justifiable; but for an individual or a nation voluntarily to enter into an agreement or contract or treaty which it does not intend to keep, can be nothing but dishonest and dishonorable. Those of us who wish the United States to assume the duties and to gain the privileges which membership in the proposed league of nations will bring, must urge the ratification of the covenant; those who are unwilling that the United States should assume those duties should oppose. On this point the issue is not one of expediency, but of common honesty. Let us make an honest agreement or none.

Make no agreement with Britain

In the Depths

By Farnsworth Wright

DAN CARLSON looked down at the oily waters of Puget Sound and wondered what strange creatures lived in its slimy depths, and whether they were not really happier, after all, than he. A whirlwind racked his brain, for he faced involuntary separation from his job, and, being young, he was not used to it. For three days he had been a reporter on one of the city dailies—his first job, and he had failed on three assignments, so the city editor told him that he lacked aptitude and could not be used as a reporter. The boy pleaded for one more chance.

"I'll give you another chance," the city editor finally promised him, "if you go down to the waterfront and find a deep-sea diver named Angus McLeod and get his story of his fight with a devilfish three weeks ago. Look up the story in the files. Myers should have been able to interview him, for he has been marine reporter for years and ought to know everybody on the waterfront. But Myers hasn't been able to find him, and I can't tell you where you can locate him except that he ought to be somewhere on the waterfront. McLeod's story would have been a corker three weeks ago, but we can still use it."

Myers, the marine reporter, had learned only by chance of the diver's thrilling struggle with a giant octopus, and his rescue after he had lost consciousness, for McLeod was little known on the waterfront. The newspaper account of the battle under the waves was for the most part drawn by Myers from his imagination, for he had been unable to find and interview the dour Scot who was the hero of it.

Dan set out at once in search of McLeod, and he found that the old Scotch diver had moved from his lodgings sev-eral days before he was sent out on the job which so nearly cost him his life. Nobody seemed to know where he was living.

"He's about your height and pretty well tanned," the man in the salvage company's office described him to Dan. "He's got a grayish-reddish beard and he don't wear a mustache. He's an oldish fellow, a little bit deaf from being under the water so much, and he's got red hair and blue eyes."

On this meagre information Dan made the rounds of the waterfront saloons, but failed to find the man he was seeking. He did not want to go back to his city editor and report failure, so he stood on the wharf and speculated on the things that live under the water, and on his own drowning career.

The mystery of the ocean depths had always fired his imagination, but now it depressed him. He compared himself to the diver. The world was an enormous octopus, twisting its arms about his neck to drag him down. The breaking of the diver's air-tube was the fell stroke of chance, which had caused him to fail on his assignments and now prevented him from finding McLeod. Dan's star of hope, which had lit up his sky for an instant when he had been given this last chance to make good was sinking fast behind vast clouds of gloom. Hardly a ray now lighted the muddy depths of his despondency.

Looking up from his gloomy musings he noticed a roughly-dressed, ragged man, unshaven, dirty and hatless, leaning against a pile. His torn shirt was open at the throat. A queer moaning gurgle came from his half-opened mouth. He reeled as if he were drunk.

Dan feared the old fellow would fall into the bay, so he seized him quickly from behind, by the arms, just below the shoulders. The man shrank from his grasp with a moaning cry, and would have fallen from the dock had Dan not pulled him quickly back from the edge.

The stranger twisted around to face the youth, and he struck Dan's hands away as he did so. He gazed for an instant full into Dan's eyes with the fright of a hunted animal showing on his face. Then his gaze roved, and a puzzled, intent expression came over his face, as if he were vainly trying to recall something to his memory. He ran his fingers through his long, coarse hair and stared into Dan's eyes again. Dan noticed that the man's eyes were blue.

"You almost fell into the water," laughed Dan, reassuringly. "I guess you're sick, but at first I thought you were drunk when I saw you hanging to that post and reeling."

"Drunk," asked the stranger. The intent, puzzled expression came over his face again and he rubbed his fingertips over his stubby, reddish-gray beard.

"Drunk?" he repeated, and his bewildered look became pitiful in its intensity and suffering.

"Oh, no! I mean I thought so at first—the way you staggered! Of course you're not drunk. But you did nearly fall into the water," Dan went on, hastening to change the subject. "You don't want to make fish-food of yourself, and be washed out into the sound where the devilfish can twist his snaky tentacles around your neck and little fishes come and swim through the holes in your skull, where your eyes are now."

"Fishes?" the man asked. "Oh, ay, there are millions of 'em, lad, millions of 'em! I've seen whole armies of 'em come and look at me while I worked, and one big fish came and looked in the little window to see what made the bubbles come up. But he swam away quick when I tried to grab him."

Dan was still deep in his gloom and took in the import of the old man's strange words only vaguely as in a dream. He looked up wonderingly.

"There are strange things down there in the depths," he said slowly.

"In the depths," moaned the old man.

"Oh, ay, in the depths!" His eyes opened big and he stared at Dan as at some dreadful specter.

A flash of comprehension came to the youth as he pondered the stranger's peculiar utterance about the fish armies and the big fish that looked into the little window; and Dan suddenly noticed that the stranger's close-cut beard was reddish and that he did not possess a mustache. But his hair was not red—it was snow-white!

Dan's heart jumped and the star of hope suddenly flooded his firmament with light again. The clouds of gloom were dissipated as if by the fresh wind which was springing up from the sound. Dan's thoughts were no longer vague and wandering.

"Is your name Angus McLeod?" he asked his odd acquaintance.

"Ay," answered the diver, his eyes intently searching Dan's face.

"Carlson's my name—Dan Carlson," Dan introduced himself, his eyes sparkling. "Come over and have a glass of beer with me."

McLeod did not answer, neither did he clasp Dan's outstretched hand.

"Come on," urged Dan, and he took the diver by the arm.

McLeod struck the boy's hand away as if in terror, but he followed him to the saloon. They were soon seated at a table and the bartender brought some beer.

"Now," demanded Dan eagerly, "tell me all about it."

"All about what?" asked McLeod.

"Why, about your fight with the devilfish up near Anacortes, of course."

"Oh, ay, the devilfish!"

The diver's eyes wandered; he looked terrified, and he passed his hands several times through his hair, then rubbed his stubby beard with his fingertips.

"Set 'em up again," called Dan to the bartender, for McLeod had drained his glass at a gulp.

"You were exploring an old wreck, weren't you?" he went on. "How long had the wreck been there?"

"Ay, a wreck it was. Several years old. It wasn't so awful deep, but I stayed too long."

McLeod ran his fingers through his hair again and horror was written in scarehead letters on his face.

"Come, come; you're all right now." Dan tried to calm him. "Drink your beer. Now go on. How deep was it?"

"Not too deep, for the sunlight was shimmering and shivering over the bones o' the ship, according as the waves was rippling and curling on top o' the water. It wasn't too deep, and there was a lot o' little fishes kept looking, and then they'd scamper away all of a sudden when they was frighted, like a lot o' minnows. But down in the ship it was dark and there was strange creatures there."

The diver shuddered and beads of sweat stood out on his furrowed forehead.

"Drink some more beer," Dan urged.

The former intense bewilderment again furrowed McLeod's face as if something he was seeking kept hiding just beyond reach of his memory. He drank the beer and wiped the foam from his lips and chin on his sleeve.

"How did the octopus get hold of you? Tell me all about your fight with it. Nobody knows anything about it except what you told them through your diver's telephone while you were slicing the beast's arms off," Dan explained.

"Got hold on me? Oh, ay, it got hold on me all right," answered McLeod. "It must have got me from behind, because I didn't see it till it was around my neck. Long arms, like snakes, and it gets hold on me with two of 'em at once. First thing I knows about it, it draws me to one side, and I try to get away, but my feet are weighted and I can't move fast enough. But I'm just as cool as a clam. 'Never lose your head now or you'll never see Seattle again,' I says to myself. But it's hard to saw through those slippery, tough arms with my knife, though they look so soft and easy when the thing's captured and lying on shore, dead. But I've lost my knife," he moaned. "I tell you it's gone, and I can't pick it up."

The intent, bewildered look had again given place to horror.

"Come, come," Dan soothed him, "what ails you? Here, let me pour you some

more beer. You say you had a knife?"

"I tell you I dropped it," exclaimed the diver with growing excitement. "Pick it up! Quick, I tell you!"

Pressing one knee against the table as if he were still struggling in the tight grip of the eight-armed monster, the diver gave a sudden push, upsetting the beer onto Dan, and sending his own chair backward onto the floor. He struggled to his feet with a frightened oath. As Dan sprang to help him, the diver seized his arms, pinning them to his sides and stared hard into his face, panting and shrieked—

"Where's that knife? I dropped it, I tell you!"

Dan struggled to free himself, but the diver with wild, livid, staring eyeballs, held him fast. The sweat poured from the old man's face. Dan was thoroughly frightened and was about to call loudly for help when McLeod relaxed his hold and sank to the floor, moaning as if in agony.

Dan lifted him up and helped him to a chair. McLeod was as weak as a kitten. He stared helplessly around the room, while the sweat ran down his face in tiny rivulets. Boisterous laughter from the barroom explained why nobody had heard the struggle.

"Come, now," urged Dan. "You had a knife, you tell me, and you lost it. How did the air-hose break?"

"I cut it," McLeod answered, very slowly. "I didn't mean to, but the beast drew me towards him, and kept shooting a black, inky stuff at me, so by and by I couldn't see him for the dark clouds of it in the water. I sawed through three of its ugly hands, and I'll get away all right, only it's got me by the arm, and I've cut into the air-tube over my head, and I've dropped my knife and I can't pick it up.

"Where is that knife, lad?" he whined. "There's no time to lose, for I've got no air, I tell you! They're pulling on the ropes up there, can't you feel 'em? Give me that knife! I've got to cut loose, I tell you! They're trying to pull me up, and the air-tube's cut, and I can't breathe, and I've got to cut away! Don't you hear me?"

He covered his face with his hands, moaning piteously.

"It's no use! It's no use!" he whimpered. "I've lost the knife."

His unkempt, coarse white hair was wet with perspiration. Understanding began to dawn on Dan.

"Come, now," Dan said at last. "Nobody's going to hurt you. You're all right now. Tell me, how did you get to the surface?"

McLeod took his hands from his face and stared at Dan blankly.

"How did they get you up? How did you get to the top?" Dan repeated.

"Get to the top?" the diver moaned. "I didn't."

He covered his face again with his hands.

Dan felt a strange sinking of the stomach as he looked at the moaning creature before him, who was still fighting hopelessly on in his mind, with blank horror always at the end of his tale. For the diver's mind had given way under the strain of the desperate struggle under the waves and recorded no memories beyond that terrific combat, nor gave any glimmer of hope as to the outcome.

Dan had his story. And that same day tender hands took McLeod into their care and ministered to his overwrought nerves and anguished brain.

Spanish Broom

By Jessie Harrier

A hymn to the glorious golden broom
   That grows in my garden-side;
It fills and gladdens my narrow room
   With color and perfume and pride.

Gathering sunshine through golden springs,
   Showering it back through the rain;
You are no idle emblem of kings—
   Planta-genista of Spain!

You are the flower of my happy heart
   That forgets old care and pain,
And, singing, takes of your sun its part—
   Oh, golden Broom of Spain!

"Eulalie"

California's First Woman Poet

By Boutwell Dunlap

Eulalie; Photograph taken before 1854.

FORGOTTEN and unknown by historians of California letters, "Eulalie," pseudonym of Mary Eulalie (Fee) Shannon, seems to have been a California woman author, first to have had a volume of her poems published. At the request of Librarian Joseph Rowell of the University of California, I make a bibliographical note of this priority for permanent preservation in the Overland Monthly. If her verse had little merit, its existence is at least a literary curiosity.

In looking over last spring some of my historical notes and collections, made some years ago upon the mining section of the Sierras in the '50s, I found a reference to the Placer Herald of March 18, 1854, containing the statement John Shannon, Jr., had on January 31, 1854, at New Richmond, Ohio, married Mary E. Fee, "who had contributed many graceful poems to Western periodicals over the nom de plume of 'Eulalie,'" and that Shannon planned to return to California. A citation to the Auburn Whig of December 30, 1854, noted her brief obituary, with nothing on her antecedents. A Placer county history without detail barely speaks of her poetry, but not her book.

There is no mention of her in the literary histories of California, by the official literary historian of the State, nor in other histories of California literature nor Pacific coast anthologies. Librarians, booksellers and collectors of Californiana told me they had never heard of her residence in California. The California State Library, which has not listed her in its printed names of California authors, referred me to "Literary Women of California Who Have Passed Away," an article in the Sacramento Wednesday Press of March 11, 1903. This was written by Winfield J. Davis, the Sacramento historian and native of the county of "Eulalie's" residence in California. It contains a repetition of her obituary from the Auburn Whig, and the assertion "of her there is very little available."

A hurried and incomplete examination of Eastern publications reveals she was not unknown and forgotten in the East.

William Cushing's "Initials and Pseu-
donyms" has the following: "Shannon,
Mrs. Mary Eulalie (Fee), 1824-55 [sic].
Eulalie. An American poet, of Auburn,
Cal." Joseph Sabin's "Dictionary of
Books Relating to America From Its Discovery to the Present Time" lists her
volume of poems under her married ame
and gives her pseudonym.
  I used antiquarian methods in searching old files and following clues, and
located, after much correspondence, her
nephew, Dr. Frank Fee, a physician of
Cincinnati, Ohio, to whom I am indebted
for data on her early life.
  Mary Eulalie Fee was born in Flem-
ingsburg, Kentucky, February 9, 1824,
daughter of William Robert Fee, a native of Scott county, Kentucky, born in
the pioneer days of 1793. She was thus
one of the first few women poets of
Southern birth, although I do not find
her in Lucian Lamar Knight's valuable
biographical dictionary of Southern literary people in the "Library of Southern Literature." Her mother, Elizabeth Dutten
Carver, born at Castleton, Rutland county,
Vermont, in 1795, was the seventh generation from John Carver, first Governor of
Plymouth. The mother and her parents
crossed the Alleghenies in covered
wagons and settled at Marietta, Ohio, in
1812, where, at seventeen, she became a
school teacher, and is said to have been
a "great student of history, Shakespeare
and the Bible."
  Miss Fee was educated by the best
private tutors in Cincinnati. Among her
intimates there were Tosso, perhaps the
greatest violinist of the Middle West of
the period; Alice and Phoebe Cary, and
Henry Warrels, a great guitarist. Her
home was at "Dove Cottage," built by her
father at New Richmond, Ohio.
  Her husband, John Shannon, Jr., a California editor of the early '50s, was afterward one of the publishers of the Calaveras Chronicle. He established the Vi-
salia Delta, a Democratic paper, in an
intensely Southern settlement. As the
result of a bitter newspaper controversy
with William Gouverneur Morris—whose
name suggests a connection with a talented family—editor of a Republican
publication of that locality, he was shot

to death by Morris in 1860 in a violent
rencounter. Shannon returned to the
East in 1853 and married Miss Fee on
January 31' 1854, going immediately to
California, where I have a record of her
residence as early as April 10, 1854.
  Her volume of poems, "Buds, Blossoms
and Leaves," a well-printed book of vii,
194 pages, 4⅜x7 inches, has this title
page: "Buds, Blossoms and Leaves:‖
Poems,‖ By Eulalie.‖· Cincinnati.‖
Moore, Wilstach & Keys.‖ MDCCCLIV."
If there were no other evidence, its preface, dated June, 1854, indicates she was
a resident of California when the book
left the press.
  None of the poems show a California
influence, and all were probably written
before her departure. One is entitled
"To Frank—In California." "Lines" was
"suggested by the death of James D.
Turner, who died in Nevada City, California, August 4th, 1851," according to a
note. "The Desert Burial" resulted from
the receipt of a letter on the death on
the desert of an immigrant to California.
The poems must have had a considerable circulation in this State, because to
this day they are often found there in
second-hand book shops.
  Depending upon the definition of the
term, it may be declared she was hardly
a California poet. She calls herself "a
Californian" in her correspondence with
Eastern newspapers.
  From a scrapbook of her newspaper
writings, I find she contributed a series.
"Travel Scenes," written for the Daily
Times of Cincinnati, after her arrival in
California, beginning in April, 1854, and
extending to December, 1854, the last
date a few weeks before her death. In
this scrapbook there are nine columns
by her, "Leaves From the Diary of a
Californian," cut from the Dollar Times.
There is also a story, "Frank Waterford,
a Tale of the Mines," written for the
Placer Democrat, published at Auburn
by her husband. Following is a three-
column story, "A Lost Waif, Mining, in
California," dated Auburn, October, 1854,
written for the Dollar Times. All this
is among the first California story
writing.
  In this scrapbook there is an announce-

ment from the Daily Democratic State Journal, once published in Sacramento by the father of Joseph D. Redding, of a lecture by her on "Home," delivered at McNulty's Music Hall.

Her California home was at The Junction House, in the Sierras, a stage station two miles from Auburn, where branched in the '50s the stage line from Sacramento to Dutch Flat and Yankee Jim's, one of the largest and liveliest mining camps in California. The retiring and idealistic poet, I learn from a pioneer, was the object of pride, love and interest by hundreds of young mining adventurers who daily passed the station, and her fame became wide in the mines.

Dying in December, 1854, her obituary in the Auburn Whig says, "she was generally known in this State as 'Eulalie.'" Her tombstone in an abandoned cemetery in Auburn had nothing inscribed on it but the word, "Eulalie." Ambrose Bierce makes this graveyard one of the scenes of his story, "The Realm of the Unreal," and says the delapidated burial ground was "a dishonor to the living, a calumny on the dead, a blasphemy against God." It was removed a few years ago, and it seems no one knows what became of "Eulalie's" remains.

The earliest book of poems published in California in the collection of the California State Library is "Idealina and Other Poems," by E. J. C. Kewen, printed in San Francisco in 1853. Colonel Kewen was a Mississippian, Attorney-General of California, 1849-50; editor, orator, State legislator and financial agent and aide of Walker in Nicaragua.

William Henry Rhodes, later a Californian, had published in New York in 1846 a book of poems entitled "Indian Gallows and Other Poems." Probably there were other books of verse published in the East at an early date by those who were to become Californians. Rhodes was the San Francisco lawyer who as "Caxton" wrote the great short story, "The Case of Summerfield." He was a South Carolinian by birth. His widow published in 1875 his stories and poems under the title, "Caxton's Book," which contained sketches by Daniel O'Connell and General W. H. L. Barnes.

Thus, California, never provincial, either in the log cabin or the metropolis, was a finished civilization set down over night in the early '50s. Its world-wide lure was due to high class publicity, never equalled on any frontier, such as that of "Eulalie," who was able to write home in a compelling way.

Given

By Jo Hartman

Beloved, a lotus flower from out my heart
I gave to you that unforgotten night,
And set my pagan candle for your eyes—
Whose flame can image nothing save
Delight!

And to your burning lips I gave—my own,
All cool with pain of too exquisite bliss;
I flung the hoarded star-dust of my dream
Along your path; and now I give you
—this!

A Cookery Queen

By Farnsworth Wright

T IME was when Standish MacNab was a tireless explorer among Chicago's eating houses. Memories of San Francisco drove him from one to another in search of something to remind him of the sea-girt city of the Golden West. For San Francisco is the best fed city on the continent, while Chicago, for its size, is the poorest fed.

On food, Standish spent careful thought and most of the income from his law practice. The greater part of what he ate he termed "grub." As for the rest, the service was slow, or the table cloths dirty, or the waiters surly; anyway, he found it hard to imagine himself in the Techau Tavern or Tait-Zinkand's. His gastronomic ramblings carried him into every cafe on Michigan boulevard, from the palatial Blackstone, where the waiters take themselves very seriously, to the Russian Tea Room and other pleasant sample establishments where one can enjoy the dainty portions served to him, if his appetite is not too big. In Marshall Field's tea room he sat among ladies who wore earrings and sealskin coats and stuck out their little fingers when they ate; he dined in cafes where heavy-jowled gourmands with bald heads and fat necks drank the juice from their oyster shells and gnawed the last speck of meat from their broiled lobsters; he also ate where hungry shop-girls counted out pennies for their meals, for his quest took him to the tops of skyscrapers and down into basement cafeterias. He nibbled at egg "fo young" in the Mandarin Inn and King Joy Lo's in search of something as tasty as the chop suey and bird's nest hoong chop blooey of Chinatown-by-the-Golden-Gate, but Chicago's almond-eyed waiters soon saw him no more. He manipulated spaghetti in Italian restaurants over saloons, and mourned the days before the earthquake (this word has disappeared from California lexicons) when for two-bits in the Fior d'Italia on the Barbary Coast he could eat a meal that shamed anything Chicago could offer for a dollar. He tried goulash in four or five Little Hungary restaurants, swallowed chicken and lamb a la Greek at Protopapa's, and wandered far from the "loop" to taste Venetian chicken at the Bismarck Garden. Time was when the young Chicago lawyer changed his eating-place thrice daily, but that was before he met Sadie.

Sadie was without doubt the most divine waitress that ever slung hash in a restaurant. She wasn't a raving beauty, yet despite that she had wonderful blue eyes like the sky seen from the top of Mt. McKinley; her smile was a stunner; her little pug nose was fascinating, and as for grace, she made all other waitresses look like Zeppelins and dreadnaughts cruising among the tables.

Standish stuffed a slice of bread into his ample mouth and stared in astonishment at finding such a sylph in a hashery. She was of that buxom type of women whose age cannot be judged from their looks. She might be twenty-three, or she might be over forty. Standish surmised that the lower limit was about correct.

His search for an eating-house was ended, and attacking forty-cent table d'hotes became henceforth his favorite pastime. The food was not better than otherwhere; in fact, an unprejudiced judge might have pronounced it a great deal worse. But Standish would not have rolled the College Inn, Kunz-Remmler's and the Boston Oyster House into one and taken the choicest viands from each in exchange for a daily seat in the Quality Lunchroom, after he first met Sadie waiting on the tables there.

"Whatcha going to eat?" she smacked. "Just a minute — hm! — now let me see — nice restaurant you have here, huh?"

"Want our businessmen's lunch?" she questioned. "It costs forty cents, but it's real good."

She took his order, stuck her pencil into her hair—light brown, flavored with golden—and walked away, leaving Standish with his head in a whirl. He never had been in love before, at least not seriously, but this time the little winged boy had twanged an arrow with terrific force through his chest. Henceforth he thought and dreamed and lived for Sadie.

Yet he dared not make love at once. She had not yet learned to reciprocate his affection, and besides, she might think he was flirting, and lose respect for him. So for the present he must be satisfied to leave a quarter for her on his plate, and get better acquainted later on.

Every day Standish ate in the Quality Lunchroom, except when urgent business called him elsewhere. He opened his thoughts to Sadie, told her his business, confided in her that he was making nearly $200 a month from his law practice, and would soon be able to get married.

But she never allowed him to talk of what lay uppermost in his thoughts. She would often sit opposite him and chat while he ate, after he had learned to come in during the slack hours, but she always found something to occupy her and take her away from him whenever he began talking about his heart.

Sometimes it seemed to him that the cashier, a man about the same age as Standish, was narrowly eyeing his tete-a-tetes with Sadie, and he attributed it to jealousy. It worried him, too, for he feared lest the young man, with his handsome face and gracile mustache, might already have the key to Sadie's heart. So he determined to bring matters to a head and declare his love.

Fifteen cents for breakfast and a quarter each noon and evening. This was the unvarying amount of his daily tips. Sixty-five cents a day. Sadie did not lack spending money. Three dollars and ninety cents a week. She bought new hats, and sometimes forsook the movies for the Follies. Sixteen dollars a month. She could pay her entire confectionery bill with the lawyer's tips. Forty-eight dollars in three months. But here Sadie's pin money suddenly ceased, as it now becomes my heavy duty to relate.

At half-past three one afternoon Standish entered the lunchroom. Experience had taught him that the restaurant business was slackest at that hour. Luck seemed to be with him, for the other girls were out (gone to lunch, probably), and there was not another soul in the place besides Sadie and the good-looking, but jealous cashier.

Standish ordered eggs and coffee, and Sadie sat down opposite him to gather an earful of talk.

"Sadie," Standish began, "Sadie, what's the use of going on like this? You weren't meant to work in a restaurant. I want you to be my wife, and we can get a cozy flat up on the north side, and I'll buy a flivver, and—"

"Stop it," Sadie interrupted, rising. "Not another word about love. Not a word."

"But Sadie, don't you care for me?" Standish pleaded.

The cashier frowningly left his desk and strode toward them.

"I like you well enough, Mr. MacNab, but I can't marry you. Because—"

She burst out laughing, and sank weakly into a chair.

"Frank," she gasped, when her mirth had somewhat subsided, "Mr. MacNab has asked me to marry him. Can you beat it?"

A sudden suspicion flashed into Standish's brain as he saw the angry face and threatening fists of the cashier.

"You aren't — already — married?" he gasped.

"You said it," she affirmed. "You can't blame me for laughing, Mr. MacNab, although I know it isn't a bit funny to you. I kind of thought you were in love with me, but—can't you see how funny it is?"

"I am deeply mortified," Standish confessed. "I apologize most humbly to you, and to your husband."

"My husband!" Sadie exclaimed.

"Yes. Isn't he your husband?"

The cashier shook with silent laughter, and Standish gravely surveyed him from the points of his patent leathers to the tips of his neatly curled mustache.

"My husband," said Sadie, "is the chef who owns the lunchroom. Frank is my youngest son."

Time was when Standish MacNab forgot San Francisco and her cafes de luxe, and was content to eat forty-cent dinners in a lunchroom under the elevated. But that time is also past, and a ceaseless hunger drives him from cafe to cafe, for the fire of hope burns bright in the breast of youth, and he still dreams that some day he may find a real San Francisco restaurant in Chicago.

To a Virtuous Woman

By Arthur Powell

It is I, Manigoldo the Rogue, who confess
    To you, Lady, the sins of my youth.
Your reproach may be just; yet, that zephyr-wooed tress—
    Seeks it not to escape your drear truth?

There was Palla the pale with her smouldering eyes,
    And her hair a cascade of dull gold;
You have heard the soft snow as it falls, how it sighs;
    So breathed she, so fell she, of old.

Then came Gilda, her mouth a red poppy aflame;
    Her little delirious laugh
Set the moonlight atremble. And Glory and Shame
    Reeled together, to thirst and to quaff.

Lithe Eve with her panther-like, gliding advance
    Was lured by the love-song of Life;
And Beryl, high sacrifice couched in her glance,
    Bravely bared her white breast to the knife.

You love growing flow'rs, and you gather their blooms
    To languish and fade, and to die;
Each day a new garland new beauty assumes . . . .
    Well, that's my sin, too—so did I!

Plant a Tree!

By Eleanore Farrand Ross

WITH the crushed berries of the Toyon tree underfoot, and the spicy breath of redwood branches in our nostrils, we are taken in spirit to the Christmas woods—not to the bare, snowy Eastern woods, nor to the gleaming, frosted firs of the Sierra forests, but to our own dear woods in the Coast Range mountains! We see again the blue mists disappear from the hillsides, the rising sun fleck with gold each shining leaf and spire, the shadowy canyons lighten up with the radiance of day. We watch the wind shake the dew from the glowing pink-blossomed incense bush—we lean down and gather fern-like sprays from the vancouveria vine, and press the sweet-smelling yerba buena to our faces.

Christmas, to most of the world, means the resting time of Nature—its introspective and force-gathering period before the resurrection of Spring. But in these California woods, Mother Nature never takes a holiday—there is always some green thing bursting with life and music.

And then we look up the long canyons of the city streets, and sigh, and wonder why, in a city so blessed with sunshine and fresh winds and cooling fogs, there are no trees to soothe and charm the weary eyes, no shining greenery to break the monotony of gray stone walls and staring windows! "But San Francisco is rather a damp city anyway, and trees mean more dampness," I hear someone exclaim. I have as authority that trees bring warmth and shelter no less a person than the California naturalist, Virginia Ballen: "Stand on a bleak, bare hillside in a cold wind," she said to me, once, when we were discussing the subject and the mistaken idea connected with it; "and realize how you long and look for a tree, even a small, scrubby one, to cower under!"

Small, graceful trees, like the maple or native walnut, would not only bring charm to the cobbled city streets, but warmth also! There are numerous trees which we could plant to advantage in San Francisco, and which, I am sure, would flourish and give a natural touch of beauty which the city sadly needs. Why, just the sight of something green rests tired nerves and eyes! Often the sight of the flower vendors' carts in the ceaseless roar and clatter of the city's voice, strikes a sudden chord of music to tortured ears! Notice how the block of Maple trees along Powell street are growing strong and putting forth the best that is in them, and how an occasional eucalyptus with its bluish-green drapery, standing out against the blue sky, relieves the sombre hues of our "good, gray city." If our lives do not warrant us a (usually) hideous statue, or memorial hall, or monument, we can at least plant a tree to flourish adown the years, and gladden the passerby with its loveliness, after we ourselves are not even a memory!

TREES.

I think that I shall never see
A poem lovely as a tree;
A tree whose hungry mouth is pressed
Against the earth's sweet flowing breast;
A tree that looks at God all day,
And lifts her leafy arms to pray;
A tree that may in Summer wear
A nest of robins in her hair;
Upon whose bosom snow has lain,
Who intimately lives with rain;
Poems are made by fools like me,
But only God can make a tree.

—Joyce Kilmer.

In the Realm of Bookland

"The Shadow of Rosalie, Byrnes," by Grace Sartwell Mason.

Rather old is the plot in the story dealing as it does, with twin sisters, who are the living image of each other; both young and beautiful, one sweet and virtuous, the other the reverse. The story opens with the hurried marriage between Rosalie Byrnes, (a concert singer, whose real name is Leona Maddern,) and Gerald Cromwell, a young lieutenant in the American army, just on the eve of Gerald's leaving for France. Then follows Gerald's letter to his family, the consternation of his sister Eleanor, who keeps the news from the invalid mother, and the plotting between Eleanor and her fiancee, to annul the marriage.

"The Shadow" (which is really the unsavory reputation of Leontine Maddern, Rosalie's sister,) looms large from then on, and the supposed murder by Leontine, of an old time lover, the escape from his house, without being seen, her sister's horror, and her promise to get Leontine's bag and furs which have been left in the library of the lover's house; Rosalie's visit to the deserted home on Long Island, the miraculous meeting with her returned husband, invalided home from France, and their ultimate reconciliation with Gerald's family and wonderful happiness, is all thrillingly told.

"The Shadow of Rosalie Byrnes," D. Appleton & Co., Publishers, New York. $1.60 net.

"After Thirty." A novel by Julian Street, author of "American Adventures;" "Abroad At Home;" etc., is an amusing chronicle of a New York coffee merchant's philandering. Shelly Wickett, having reached the age of thirty, feels that life is becoming too slow for him and sets out in quest of adventure with the fair sex. His path is not a smooth one, but Molly—Mrs. Wickett—forgives and forgets, (if ever a woman can forget,) the various escapades of her husband.

The opening romance is staged upon the coast of Maine at one of the sea resorts. Wickett, mistaking one girl for another with whom he had spent his first days at Seaview Inn, proceeds to give her a ducking in revenge for one received days before. But when the girl comes up "like a disheveled mermaid, blowing, dripping, angry," Wickett sees his mistake. "And she had a right to be angry, for she had never seen Wickett before." But when she heard the story of the other girl and the other ducking, and because he was so ashamed, and his apologies so pathetic, and most of all because he was good-looking, she forgave him. That was Molly. And from that time on there was only one girl for Shelly Wickett.

Their first baby was called Shelly and their second, Molly. During the winter they lived in a New York apartment but spent the summer at their country home. Life became a round of every-day duties and the "Strong Rapids of Romance" which engulfed their earlier years became a calm "River of Affection" upon which they floated placidly. When one day Wickett dreamed of the rapids left behind him and longed for adventure. Molly was "settled." She did not stimulate him as she once did. As they floated serenely along in their canoe of seeming contentment, "Wickett's eyes began to rove a little and for the first time since the beginning of the voyage he noticed that a handkerchief was being fluttered at him, as in flirtatious signal from the shore." And Shelly Wickett began his philandering.

All the way from "Mrs. Railey" to "The Recovery" he philanders, but with a deep consciousness that Molly must know all about it—or most all—and forgive him.

The characters are well brought out and there is humor and wit in the handling of the embarrassing situations in which Wickett finds himself at times. The varied philosophy and observations with which the author cloaks each affair du coeur give "After Thirty" a charming individuality. The story is an entertaining and well balanced narrative of what might occur in the life of any Mr. and Mrs. Wickett and if the wife was as sensible and unselfish as Molly there could only be one outcome, and that the author has truly and delightfully portrayed.

"After Thirty," The Century Company.

BOOK NOTES FROM THE CENTURY COMPANY

Ever since the appearance of a novel by a nine-year-old worldly child, there has been no peace for the musty, cobwebbed attics and dust-covered ancient trunks of this land. And judging from the treasures that are being salvaged daily from the depths of these antiquated chests, it seems that nearly every member of the past generation started out upon the road of life as an author and most of them failed to "arrive" because there was no James Barrie, in those days, to encourage and act as agents for these small tempermental artists. Among the most recent discoveries of early unpublished manuscripts is Jeremy Lane, who was one of the exceptions. Taking no one's advice, he continued his literary endeavors and made good. He is the author of "Yellow Men Sleep," recently published by The Century Co. Referring to his collection of worn and almost illegible manuscripts, he says, "I was writing short stories and plays all the while, from my fifth year, but nothing happened until I tried novelettes and a novel."

Another recent visitor, whose early work passed unnoticed and unappreciated to an untimely resting place, is Edith Ballinger Price, author of "Blue Magic" (The Century Co.). Mrs. Price found during her last attic hunt, a book of sketches which she executed at the age of eight to illustrate a poem, or a story, or it might have been a novel—she is not sure now just which it was—that she was plotting at that time. One of these sketches is of a very stirring scene involving a handsome (?) soldier. The caption of this picture was : "He was groping in the tobacco jar as I entered, and looked up shuddering like an aspen leaf!"

One does not, as a rule, think of an officer of the U. S. Navy as being a great inventor. To the general public, an officer of the navy is an officer of the navy and nothing more, or less. However, Rear-Admiral Bradley A. Fiske, author of "From Midshipman to Rear-Admiral," just published by The Century Co., is an inventor of the first rank. Few outside of the circle of his most intimate professional associates realize how many successful and important inventions Admiral Fiske has to his credit. Since the day of his childhood upon which he asked his father what an inventor was, he has invented a sleeve button, a typewriter "which did not work very well," a mechanical pencil (from which he received a royalty of $1,000 that emboldened him to marry), an electric log, a magazine rifle, a range-finder, an improved stock ticker, a further development of his range-finder, an automatic machine gun (the patent of which he allowed to lapse and the principle of which it is stated is now the basis of the Browning gun), a stadimeter, an electric motor that was developed into the electric ammunition-hoist, a method of pointing a gun at sea, a telescopic sight for a ship's guns, a practical application of electricity to moving turrets, a helm-indicator, steering telegraph, engine telegraph, speed and direction indicator, position-finder, signaling apparatus sounding machine, an electric wireless scheme, a turbine-driven torpedo, naval telescope and mount, combined range-finder and turret, and a horizometer.

(Editor's Note: Mr. Dunlap, author of "Eulalie," which appears in this issue, begs to state that the year of publication of "Caxton's Book" was 1876, instead of 1875, and his birth place was North Carolina, instead of South Carolina, as published in the above article. These errors are due to certain books of reference, which Mr. Dunlap first consulted.)

Lightning Source UK Ltd.
Milton Keynes UK
UKHW011246310119
336488UK00006B/312/P